4 R's Complete Series

Roped
Rescued
Risked
Romanced

by Julie Castle

Warning: Not intended for persons under the age of 18. May contain coarse language and mature content that may disturb some readers. Reader discretion advised.

Cover Art Design by: Rowan Prose Publishing

Photo Credit: Adobe Images

First Printing

ISBN: 978-1-961967-29-8

Rowan Prose Publishing, LLC

www.RowanProsePublishing.com

Published in the United States of America

"The interaction between them makes for hot reading. You can feel the sizzle these two make."

-Fallen Angel Reviews

"Keep ice water near. This is one read that will make you sweat."

-Coffee Time Romance

FOOL'S GOLD

Julie Castle

Chapter One

"You're going to do what?"

Sarah Maxwell gazed at her cousin's mutinous expression, willing her to understand. "Rafe's reputation has been in shreds since I left. I need, deep in my soul, to set things right. Please try to understand, Pipi. I must go back."

"Back into the lion's den." Pipi shook her head. "Listen to me, cousin. You'll be going on a fool's errand. You don't think the man will take you back with open arms after you deserted him on your wedding night six months ago, do you?"

"Rafe's housekeeper is going on a long-deserved vacation. I'm all set to fill in for her at the ranch."

"So, she's the one who's been feeding you all these gloom and doom stories about him." Pipi scowled. "It could be a setup, you know."

"No, Rafe's not that devious." Sarah added sadly, "He can't even tell a decent white lie. That's how I found out he doesn't love me. He only married me because of my family connections." The memory of finding the plans for his dude ranch and learning why made her crumble. If only he'd have asked, she'd have told him she'd walked away from her trust fund and her controlling grandfather long ago. She'd never believed in love at first sight, but she'd fallen fast and hard for the cowboy when he'd rescued her from a blizzard while she'd been shooting her Wolf Pack Zero story. She'd been so in the zone she hadn't even noticed they were both about to get stranded in the snow. He'd been out checking the perimeter of his ranch on his horse when he'd come to her rescue. He'd swept her up and saved her just like an old-time cowboy, and that had been that. A whirlwind courtship followed by a quick wedding.

Now, she had to be strong for both of them.

Pipi shook her head. "You, a housekeeper? I can't picture it."

Sarah shrugged. "How hard can it be? You mop a few floors and open a few cans. I should have enough spare time to finish the series of endangered species photos I was doing. It's the best work I've ever done, and my editor said it could lead to some prestigious work."

"That's just an excuse, Sarah, and you know it. You aren't responsible for ruining the cowboy any more than your mother was responsible for ruining your father. That was all our grumpy old grandfather's imagination. You can't fix the past by doing this."

"That's not why." Sarah noted Pipi's expression of disbelief and sighed. "Maybe that's part of it, but the plain truth is, I love the hardheaded, stubborn cowboy, and I won't see his life ruined."

"Somebody's sure in an all-fired hurry, boss."

Rafe leaned forward in his rocker. His fatigue after a long dusty day on the range melted as he watched the silver Jeep Cherokee kick up a plume of dust in its wake. It sped toward them down the long driveway. "It's the wife."

"Wife." Zeke Taylor, his ranch foreman, made the word sound like a curse. "I can't believe she has the guts to show her face around here after hightailing it on your wedding night."

Rafe noted the sour expression on Zeke's wizened face, but ignored it. This wasn't up for debate. "I want you to spread the word. She's to be treated with respect."

"I don't get it. The woman runs roughshod over you, and you'll lay out the red carpet for her."

"Don't worry about it, Zeke." Rafe smiled, adding confidently, "I've got everything under control this time."

"What you plan to do, sweet talk her into sticking around?" Zeke scowled and spat on the ground.

Rafe shook his head, his jaw tightening. "No, it'll take more than sweet talk to bind a saddle-shy filly like Sarah to my side. Don't worry. I've got her figured out, and I'll have her tied to my side before she knows it."

Zeke slowly got up from the creaky rocker, slapping his battered Stetson against his leg. "I hope you know what you're doing, boy."

"So do I." Rafe watched Zeke stomp toward the bunk house.

He had to make this work. His future depended on it because he just plain didn't see one without her.

The Jeep came to a halt amid a cloud of dust. The inevitability of the moment hit him hard. He never doubted Sarah would return one day, and when she did, he would be in control. But first, he planned to extract a little payback before they settled down to domestic bliss.

She got out of the Jeep, and he swallowed the lump in his throat. Dying embers of the sun caught the golden highlights in her long, red hair, turning it to molten fire. Her sigh carried to him on the cool evening breeze, and it did something to him. His heart was racing. He took a deep breath to calm down. Her scent of strawberries and butterscotch, with just a hint of something uniquely feminine, made him hungry. He could almost taste her. If he played his cards right, he would.

As she walked toward him, he was struck anew by the confident way she moved. It attracted him in the first place six months ago when she'd come to the area to shoot a series on the Grand Teton wildlife. It was a damned fool thing to do in the dead of winter, or maybe incredibly courageous, which she was. Dealing with her was going to be a challenge. And oh, how he loved challenges. The first moment they'd met, he'd known he had to have her, and he almost did. Until she ran off screaming on their wedding night. Six months later, he still wasn't sure what had spooked her, but he knew to put blinders on to treat a spooked filly. Instead, he put up a blinder via a small white lie. Sure, it was true there'd been unmerciful gossip, but he could take it. And yes, his expansion loan had been turned down, but there were ways to keep from selling up.

He figured her sense of honor would make her come back to right a wrong, and he intended to capitalize on her integrity. He studied her as he would any opponent. There was strength in the proud angle of her chin and a keen intelligence in her sparkling green eyes.

Rafe sat motionlessly in the shadows of the porch and watched her stride falter as she neared the steps. He almost felt her instinctive desire to turn tail and run as she gazed up at him. His fist tightened on the chair arm, awaiting her decision.

She took the first porch step, and Rafe leaned back, letting out an imperceptible sigh.

He tilted his head back, snagging her gaze as she drew near. "It's mighty nice of you to come a' calling, wife. To what do I owe the pleasure of your company?"

She frowned, her chin rising defiantly. "I can see you're not surprised to see me. Rose must have filled you in on our conversation."

"That's right." He kept a tight rein on his reaction as he watched the play of emotions across her expressive face, yearning for what might have been intrigue, but mostly of pain. He wanted to kick himself for having hurt her, even though he still didn't know what he'd done, why she'd run. That was the first thing he'd have to fix. "So, you want to sign on as my housekeeper. Have you got any references?"

"It's no joking matter, Rafe." She scowled at him. "To put it bluntly, I've come to save your reputation. Now, do you want my help or not?"

He slowly got to his feet, feeling her simmering resentment. But he felt something else, as well—the unrequited passion that hung between them. He walked past her, smirking at her sharp indrawn breath as he brushed by her and opened the door.

"Why don't we take this inside, wife? There's no need to give the hands more food for gossip."

She nodded and briskly walked through, Rafe at her heels.

"Let's go into the study," he directed.

He followed her. The door clicked shut behind him with a soft finality.

Her shoulders tensed before she turned to face him, her expression enigmatic.

He hastened to relieve her mind. "Don't worry. There aren't going to be any tearful recriminations. I'm willing to let bygones be bygones."

She wrinkled her nose. "That's very generous of you. As you know, I've heard about your alleged problems. I've come to offer you a deal."

"Do tell." He straightened and sauntered toward her.

She backed away, coming to rest against his desk.

Rafe caught a whiff of her scent again. Strawberries and butterscotch. His mouth watered, and his senses went into overload.

She drew a shaky breath. The pulse flickered at the base of her throat, and he recalled how she dabbed herself with perfume there. He was ever so tempted to nuzzle that sweet spot. Brought him right back to the moment they'd met when he saved her from a blizzard. She was close to being buried in an avalanche, but she was so focused on the wolves she was taking pictures of, she'd been oblivious to the danger. He'd dismounted, scaring off the wolves, when she spun to scold him. Their eyes met, and he'd been well and truly smitten. Lone wolf confirmed bachelor. Her pure spunk, her love of life had intrigued him. They'd both holed up in a line cabin until the storm passed, and by then, they were mated and soon married.

She gulped. "Yes, I've heard you've been having some problems since we split."

"You mean since you tore out of here on our wedding night like your tail was on fire?" He closed the gap between them, put his hands on her waist, and lifted her onto the desk.

She gasped, and he smiled, pleased by her response. Oh yes, she wanted him just as much as he wanted her. He couldn't help focusing on her slightly parted lips. It brought back memories of when he'd tasted that intriguing line.

She shimmied back on the desk surface and smoothed her skirt. "Stop that! I didn't come here to be manhandled. As I said, I'm prepared to help you under certain conditions..."

"What's in it for you?"

She hesitated, biting her lip. "My editor has been clamoring for the series I started shooting. I could finish it in addition to my housekeeping duties."

"Hmm..." He slid his index finger along her smooth calf, drawing an outraged glower from her.

She shook her hair back over her shoulder. What would it look like spread out on his pillow? That he'd never found out was one of his many regrets. He intended to rectify the error soon.

"So, we both win. That's generous of you, wife. Just what did you have in mind?"

"As I said, I've returned to save your reputation. I'll fill in for Rose for the next two weeks, and people will assume we've gotten back together. The talk will die down. I'll finish my series, and then I can quietly slip out of town."

He frowned at her eager tone. Could she dismiss him that easily? "Just like that, huh?"

She quickly added, "Of course, there can't be any intimacy between us."

He shook his head. "I wouldn't be too sure about that. We have a natural attraction, just like a couple of magnets."

"You don't love me." She glared at him. "This attraction you mention is meaningless. What we had was just physical on your part. Sooner or later, it'll go away."

He frowned as his suspicions were confirmed. "So, that's why you left. Because I didn't give you the words."

"Among other things. Important things..." She sighed, her tone growing wistful. "We won't work, Rafe. I thought a sudden break would be less painful."

Sensing her vulnerability, he closed in for the kill. "Because you love me."

She shrugged, looking away. "Don't worry about it. I'll get over it."

He trapped her chin with his callused fingers, holding her still while he studied her face. She looked as panicked as a deer caught in a car's headlights, telling him she regretted her decision to return. He could see it in her startled gaze, but he couldn't let her get away again. He didn't think he could take it if she did.

"It's actions that count for me. The words are meaningless. And your actions hurt me a lot."

She closed her eyes. "I wanted to do the right thing, but it was a mistake to come here. Sorry."

He muttered a curse. Damn, he'd pushed her too far. He dropped his hands to his side. "It wasn't a mistake. I do need your help, but under certain conditions."

She opened her eyes, her expression brightening. "Such as?"

He held up one finger. "First, if you're going to give me back my reputation, it's got to look real."

She nodded. "Of course, within reason."

He eyed her sourly. "Word spread when you ran off screaming on our wedding night. People started speculating on what kind of kinky things I might have tried on you. A few even wondered whether I was over-endowed. Some tried to find out."

Her mouth kicked up in a startled grin as if she'd thought of other men trying to sneak peeks at him in the restroom. She bit her lip, but a giggle escaped. "After six months, I'm sure the talk has died down."

"Not in a small town like Shelbyville, especially with you coming back. The telephone lines are probably buzzing."

"I never thought of that." She let out a shocked grunt.

He nodded. "I did. As I said, it needs to look real."

Her eyes narrowed. "How real?"

"Here's the deal. You move in with me for the rest of the summer. By then, the talk will have settled. That should also give you plenty of time to complete your series." He tilted his head, studying her reaction.

"Three months is a lot longer than I was counting on." She scooted even further back on the desk. "I can't spend the rest of the summer here. I do have a life of my own, you know." She pouted as if resigned. "I guess this isn't going to work..."

"Ever hear of a little thing called grand theft auto?" he asked dryly.

Her head shot up, and she gazed at him warily. "What do you mean?"

He smiled. "You stole my truck when you ran off."

"That old rattle trap wasn't worth a grand." She scowled. "The thing is held together with bailing wire and string. I just borrowed it to get to the airport. And besides, you got it back, didn't you? I saw it parked in the yard."

He shrugged. "That's not how the sheriff saw it when I reported it missing that night."

Her jaw dropped. "You called the cops on me? I can't believe you would do such a dastardly thing."

"I wasn't exactly in a sweet, understanding mood." A nerve ticked in his jaw as he gazed at her. "That night, I would have done anything to retrieve you."

She frowned at him, her chin rising with defiance. "It's good there's been some cooling off time in the interim."

"You're darned right. It's good. Otherwise, I might be tempted to turn you over my knee."

She snorted. "Mr. Halliday, sexist remarks like that aren't going to win my good will."

He shrugged. "That's what you get for picking an unenlightened rancher like me for a husband. Now, shall I call the sheriff, or are you staying?"

She bit her lip. "You wouldn't call him."

"Try me."

"You win, but you don't play fair, cowboy." She glared at him.

He turned and started to walk away. "I don't play at all."

"So, when do you want to begin this great deception?"

He turned back, a few steps away from the door. "There's no time like the present."

She raised an eyebrow. "How can I convince people we're a real couple?"

He smiled triumphantly. "For starters, you're going to be a perfect ranch wife. Or, at least, as perfect as you can be with your limited abilities. You're also going to act like I'm the hottest thing in pants."

"That's a stretch." She ignored his disapproving glower and hopped off the desk.

"That brings me to item number two," he said. "You owe me a wedding night. I intend to collect."

She poked his chest with her index finger. "No way. There is absolutely no way I'm going to sleep with you!"

Rafe smiled at her like a cat with a bowl of cream. "Sure, you are, sweet Sarah. You want me as much as I want you. You won't be able to resist the temptation."

Chapter Two

"Where do you think you're going?"

Sarah stopped in her tracks halfway to the study door and turned toward Rafe. She noted the challenge in his dark eyes and how a muscle twitched in his tight jaw. Even if she wanted to escape, there was no way he would let her. It was a good thing she had no intention of doing so. "I'm going out to the car to get my things."

Rafe took a step toward her. "I'll help you."

She turned away, avoiding his penetrating gaze. "No thanks, there isn't that much to carry."

The thud of his boots on the wood floor as he followed her was in sync with her heartbeat. He didn't even trust her not to run away again. The knowledge she'd caused him so much pain appalled her.

She grabbed her duffel bag out of the passenger side of the Jeep and glanced toward the house. Rafe was leaning against a post in the shadows, watching her. He probably thought she was going to flee. She could see it in his eyes. And he had good reason to doubt her word. He conjured up the image of a coiled lariat, prepared to reach out and snag her. She hesitated for a moment, suddenly unsure of her ability to handle him.

He pushed away from the porch railing as she walked up the steps.

"So, I see. I'll show you to our room."

He picked up on her quickly indrawn breath because his focus became her.

"Our room?" she asked, eyes narrowed. He didn't think she would capitulate that easily, did he? She might be in love, but she wasn't stupid.

Rafe frowned. "What did you expect? We can't make people believe we're a couple if we sleep in separate rooms, can we?"

She studied his implacable expression for a moment. His line of reasoning was correct, even if it did irk her. "No, I suppose not. But I'm not sleeping with you. I told you that before. Remember?"

A smile played about the edges of his hard mouth. "I know what you said, and if you'll think back, you'll recall I said you won't be able to resist the temptation."

"Your ego is about to take a beating. You, sir, are very resistible. You don't have to show me the way to the bedroom. I remember where it is." Sarah strode past him, totally embarrassed by what she'd blurted out. Good heavens, she'd have to be careful around him. Reminding him of their wedding night was a dumb move.

She opened the door to the master bedroom, feeling caught in a time warp. This was where it had all gone wrong six months ago. Rafe had carried her into this room on their wedding night. He'd left her alone to get ready as he went in search of champagne. On the bed, she'd found an envelope addressed to her. It explained that Rafe had married her for her business connections. She didn't know who had tipped him off, but in the end, it didn't really matter.

Rafe had wanted to convert part of the ranch into a country inn, and Sarah was the granddaughter of Samuel Maxwell, who owned a worldwide consortium of hotels and inns. It was a match made in Heaven.

Then, she'd noticed a rolled-up blueprint on the dresser, and unrolled it to find the conversion drawings. She'd gone to confront Rafe, and overheard him telling Zeke his plan to add a dude ranch would move forward. In that cold moment of realization, her dream world had shattered.

So, she'd run off into the night, just as Rafe had said. She'd run as far and as fast as she could go, using her credit cards to buy an airplane ticket. She even fell so low as to allow her grandfather's lawyers to brush off Rafe's inquiries. She was told Grandfather said he was disappointed she'd taken up with a common rancher, but it was understandable, considering the stock she'd come from.

Sarah sucked in a deep breath and entered the room. No use dwelling on the past. This was a different place and time. She was determined to set things right and walk away, even if it did break her heart. It was better than love with strings attached.

Rafe strode into the bedroom behind her. "I cleared out a few drawers for you."

Sarah laid her bag on the bed and pulled out a bunch of wadded-up garments. She glanced at Rafe. His face was a gambler's one, closed and calculating. Not wanting to delve too deeply into his emotions, Sarah turned away and went to the closet.

"Thanks, but I probably won't need all the space."

The bed creaked as he sat. She could feel his gaze on her as she shook out a green dress and hung it up. She walked back to her bag, only inches from Rafe, and hesitated with her hand on a stack of frothy undergarments, unwilling to share such intimate things with him.

She glanced at him. There was a softness in his brown eyes and a slightly dazed expression on his handsome face. The sensual awareness sizzling between them took her breath away.

Suddenly, he frowned and got to his feet. "I've got some paperwork to do. I'll be back in half an hour."

She could only gape at him when he strode from the room as if the devil himself were on his heels.

She finished putting her few things away. It didn't take long. In her line of work as a nature photographer, she had to be able to move quickly.

Rafe strode down the hall and made his way to the study. His hand shook as he shut the door behind him.

Oh God, how he ached to throw her on the bed and ease his frustrations inside her beautiful body. And she'd like it, too. He knew she would. He stalked over to the desk and slumped in his chair. To have her here, smell her perfume, and brush up against her was more than he could handle.

He jerked open the bottom desk drawer and pulled out the bottle of whiskey he had stashed inside. Reaching for a glass, he poured out two fingers of the amber liquid. He brought the glass to his lips, swirling the liquor around and inhaling its intoxicating aroma.

Gazing into its honeyed depths, he saw the fiery flash of her green witchy eyes and the pouty curve of her mouth. Would her lips still have the potent kick of the alcohol? He groaned at the tempting thought and closed his eyes. Shifting his hips, he tried to loosen the hold his jeans had on his burgeoning erection.

Scowling, he slammed down the glass, splashing his hand with whiskey. Damn it, he wouldn't turn into a lovesick fool over her again. Last time, she'd nearly cost him his sanity. Picking up the bottle of whiskey, he stuffed it back into the desk drawer. He wouldn't let the little witch in the bedroom weaken him, either.

He wiped his hand on his jeans, stretching his legs out in front of him. His gaze fell on the paper lying on the desktop. He picked up the document and scowled at it again, although he knew the words by heart. That skunk, Nevell Blackthorn, had been a burr in his side since they were kids. And now the polecat was trying to force him to sell the ranch. Rafe crumpled the offer from the realtor. He'd see Blackthorn in hell before he'd fork over the deed to the Double-H to him.

He threw the paper in the trash and leaned back to think of a more exciting subject. Sweet Sarah, with her witchy eyes, soft sexy body, and fiery hair. Would she be just as hot? He smiled because he would do his best to find out.

Sarah gathered her sleep wear and went into the bathroom to change. She wasn't willing to risk Rafe walking in on her.

When she came out, Rafe sat on the bed, pulling off his boots. He did a double-take when he saw her. "What in the heck are you wearing?"

Sarah smiled and glanced at her red long johns. "My pajamas." She made her way around him and got into bed.

"It looks like an old union suit that's seen better days." He frowned at her obstinate smile. "In case you haven't noticed, it gets hot here in the summertime. You're going to roast in that thing."

She decided he looked as disappointed as a child denied a piece of candy.

"Tough, it's what I feel like wearing to bed." She watched him unbutton his shirt, pulling the tails free of his jeans. When he unsnapped his fly, she cleared her throat. "Aren't you going to go into the bathroom to change?"

"Nope."

The wicked twinkle in his eyes made her grit her teeth. He was aware of his effect on her nerves, and was enjoying it. The rat! She laid down and turned her back to him, determined to hide how rattled she was. As the covers flipped back, she cautiously glanced over her shoulder.

He stood there, naked as the day he was born. Good heavens, he was magnificent.

"Slide over, princess. I'm ready for bed."

"Naked?" she squeaked and sat up.

His nude body was everything her imagination had conjured up in spades.

"That's right. Nothing is what I want to wear. Any objections?"

"Suit yourself. Makes no difference to me."

She clung to her side of the bed, feeling it sag as he climbed in. He took up too much room, making her feel small and vulnerable. She watched his muscles ripple as he reached across her to turn out the light. As his chest brushed against her breasts, she gasped.

He smiled down at her, a gunfighter's smile, relaxed and sure of victory.

She shrank away from the contact, laying her head back onto the pillow.

"What, no goodnight kiss?" he asked.

She glared at him. There was a need in his eye that didn't correspond with his mocking tone. "Dream on, buddy."

It was going to be a long night.

The bed moved as she murmured in her sleep and rolled over. Something shook her shoulder, but she ignored it. A swat to her bottom forced her to sit up.

Rafe was dressed, and there was a strained look on his face.

"What did you do that for?" she sputtered.

"It's time to start your new life as Mrs. Raphael Halliday, wife. Rise and shine."

Sarah yawned. "What time is it?"

"Four-thirty. Mrs. Murphy starts breakfast right about now. If you plan to take over her duties, you'd better get a move on, Sarah. You do know how to cook, don't you?"

She frowned.

The crease between his mouth and cheek deepened as he smiled in response.

"Don't worry. You won't starve."

He grinned. "It's not me I'm worried about. It's the hands. They're used to Rose's lovely home cooking. I don't want them to up and quit after they get a taste of yours. Good hands are hard to find."

She yawned. Maybe being a housekeeper wouldn't be the snap she'd expected. "So cold cereal and toast aren't what they're used to?"

"Afraid not, sugar. The hands want a hot, hearty breakfast, and they want it in an hour." His brown eyes twinkled. "Think you can handle it, wifey?"

"Stop calling me that," she grumped back at him. "You stink, Halliday, you know that?" His answering smile made her grit her teeth. "Get out of here so I can get dressed."

She scowled as he swaggered to the door. His cocky attitude made her blood boil!

He'd been right. Sleeping in the long johns had been a bad idea. She'd roasted all night. But roasting wasn't half as bad as lying next to Rafe and not reaching over to hold him. She had spent weeks fantasizing about what sleeping with him would be like. Now, she couldn't let herself touch him when she had the chance. If she did, she had a feeling she'd be trapped.

And would that be so bad? a little voice in her head echoed.

Rafe stopped in the doorway and stated, "Time's a wasting. You won't have time to primp and preen in front of the mirror this morning."

She threw her pillow at him. It bounced off his head.

He grinned, picked it up, and lobbed it back at her. "If you wanted to play, you should have done it while I was still in bed. Although, you're about as sexy as old Zeke, dressed in that union suit."

She glanced down at her red long johns as the door closed. They were warm and serviceable and about as sexy as warm mush. That was why she'd chosen them. She'd used them to fend him off like garlic with a vampire.

Awhile later, Sarah hastily scraped the burned bits off a stack of frazzled toast when there was a noise from behind her. She went to hide the evidence and then gave it up as a lost cause. How could you hide a disaster as big as the Titanic?

She glanced over her shoulder, blowing a sweaty tendril of hair away from her damp face.

Rafe stood in the middle of the kitchen, hands on his hips, eyebrows raised, as he surveyed the mess.

She resisted the urge to throw a piece of burned toast at him and reminded herself it had been her idea to save his reputation.

"Well, what did you expect? I didn't say how well I could cook. Especially not for twelve hungry hands at five in the morning, for Pete's sake."

A smile found its way to the edges of his mouth. "I didn't know it was possible to burn the oatmeal." He investigated a large pot on the range that was sending up whiffs of smoke, then focused on her. "It is oatmeal, isn't it?"

Her ire increased at his amused tone. "Yes, it's oatmeal. This is starting to look like a rotten deal from my end of things, Halliday. I'm not so sure I'm housekeeper material."

The smile left his face. "You'd better try, Sarah. You were going to be a perfect ranch wife, remember? Did you at least make coffee?"

She scowled at his overly patient tone. "Of course, I'm not that big of a screw-up."

He nodded. "I'll carry the urn into the dining hall. You grab some bowls. We'll have to make do with burned oatmeal this morning. Lunch can be cold sandwiches and lemonade, but by supper time, you'd better have figured out how to cook."

"Or else what?" she asked as they walked into the dining hall.

He smiled at her surly tone. "Or else you will be sitting across from a passel of ornery, starving cowboys."

She cringed at the picture he'd laid out for her. " I figured I'd take my meals in the kitchen."

"Well, then you figured wrong. We eat together like one big happy family."

He returned to the kitchen and made one last trip to the dining hall with the platter of scorched toast.

Sarah sighed as she viewed the yucky mess. At least she'd made enough to feed an army, which was what she was feeding, judging from the sounds of a dozen pairs of boots coming toward them down the hallway.

Rafe reached out to take her hand, drawing her to his side when she would sooner have backed out of the room. "Remember," he said softly, "you promised to make this look real."

She looked at his rugged face uneasily, and wondered how she could have thought a tough hombre like him needed rescuing. Quickly, she turned her attention from his enigmatic expression to the ranch hands filing into the room.

"Well, I'll be, will you look at that god-awful spread."

She glanced at the speaker, a young cowboy barely out of his teens.

"Watch your language, Travis. There's a lady present," Rafe stated in an authoritative voice. "I'd like you all to meet my wife. You will all mind your manners in front of her, understood?"

She understood he was chastising the cowboy while staking his claim publicly. She turned to scowl at him. "Why don't you just slap a brand on my behind and get it over with?"

Rafe raised an imperious eyebrow at her. "Now, honey, is that any way for a sweet young wife like you to talk? The boys won't know that you're kidding."

She heard the challenge in his voice and knew he had her trapped. If she went against him now, she would break their bargain. She'd set herself a chore and intended to see it through for her own peace of mind.

"Don't worry about it." She turned and smiled at the men. "Come on in and try to enjoy the food."

The group filed past her. There were plenty of "thank you, ma'am's" and curious glances shot her way. It was apparent she had been the subject of gossip the night before. If she remembered right, Zeke couldn't keep a secret to save his soul.

The cowboys were a mixed bunch of sizes and ages, but they all had one common denominator. They were deeply tanned and looked tough as nails. One tall, blond, older cowboy stood apart from the rest. Zeke gave her a probing glance as he passed by.

Sarah smiled and held her hand out.

He scowled at her and brushed past without speaking.

Surprised by his sullen expression, she hastily withdrew her hand. It was plain to see he wasn't happy to see her.

"Go ahead and get started. There's more food in the kitchen if we run out."

Sarah was loading the dishwasher after breakfast when the screen door slammed as the last of the workers left the dining hall. At least she didn't have to worry about doing all these dishes by hand. Now all she had to do was find a cookbook and figure out what she could make for supper. Whatever she chose, it would have to be enormous because they ate like horses.

After pouring herself a cup of coffee, she sat on a porch chair and sighed. It was going to be a difficult summer, and it had just begun. She wasn't sure she was up to the task of cooking for this mob, let alone defending her heart from Rafe's assault. The man had only married her for her family name. It was still a bitter pill to swallow.

He'd deny it to his last breath if she confronted him about it, she was sure of that. Rafe might desire her for other reasons, but marrying into the Maxwell Family didn't harm a man who had plans to turn his large working ranch into a dude ranch on the side. What he didn't know was that she'd walked away from her heritage years ago because there were too many strings attached. Just like there were too many strings attached to their marriage. There was no way she could be all Rafe expected her to be.

No doubt, the extra income would come in handy, she thought as she glanced around the slightly shabby surroundings. Zeke's exasperated voice broke into her reverie.

"I still think you're a damned fool, Rafe. Sleep with her if you've got to, but then get her the hell out of here before she screws you up again."

"Don't worry about it, old friend. I know what I'm doing this time around. But sleeping with her does sound like an excellent idea. Maybe then, I'll be able to think straight around the little witch."

Sarah got out of the chair and tiptoed into the kitchen. Her hands shook as she set her coffee mug on the counter. So, he was going to get her out of his system. How? By using her until she was wrung dry?

It served to increase her resolve to remain immune to his charms.

The doorbell rang. She swung open the door to find a petite brunette with a girl in tow. "Can I help you?"

The lady pulled back the screen door and grinned. "I'm not surprised you don't remember me. We only met once at the Ramseys' barbecue. You and Rafe only had eyes for each other that night."

Sarah's cheeks heated remembering. It had been the star-filled night when Rafe had proposed. It seemed like ages had passed since then, but it had only been a few weeks ago.

The lady grinned and held out her hand. "I'm Lisa Halliday, Rafe's sister-in-law. And this is my daughter, Mandy."

Sarah couldn't help smiling back. Lisa's cheeriness was infectious. "Hi there. Come on inside. I don't know what brought you here, Lisa, but you're a lifesaver."

Lisa's eyes opened wide in alarm. "Why, is there something wrong?"

"No, nothing like that," Sarah hastily reassured her, "but do you know how to cook?"

Lisa's nose wrinkled as she grinned. "Sure do. I heard that Rose is on vacation. I stopped by to see if Rafe needed a hand."

Sarah sighed in relief. "Thank goodness. I've taken over the cooking, and it's a disaster. Would you be willing to give me a few cooking lessons?"

Lisa grinned. "No problem. When do you want them?"

Sarah bit her lip. "Now. I need to learn by supper time."

"Well, in that case, we'd better get busy." She turned to look at Mandy. "Go play, honey. And stay out of trouble."

"Okay." The girl dashed outside.

"I wish I had her energy." Sarah smiled at Mandy's exuberance.

Lisa laughed. "Me, too. She went on a sleepover last night, and I bet she did more giggling than sleeping. She ought to be exhausted. Instead, she's ready for more."

Sarah smiled. "Would you like some coffee?"

"I'd love some."

Sarah led the way. "Come on into the kitchen. I'll pour you a cup." She filled two mugs with coffee and carried them to the dinette.

Lisa took the cup Sarah offered and smiled. "Rafe is sure a fast worker. He told me he'd get you back, but I hadn't thought it would be this soon."

Sarah was taken aback by the statement. "He did, huh? I'm beginning to think Rafe and Rose were in cahoots." Maybe Pipi was right, and this was a sensual trap.

Lisa smiled. "No doubt. Rafe usually manages to get what he wants, but what do you mean about them being in cahoots?"

Sarah looked away from the woman's curious gaze. "Rose has been writing telling me how much trouble Rafe's had since I left. She said he might have to sell the ranch. So, I came back to make things right."

Lisa glanced at her probingly. "For good."

Sarah thought back on her promise to make it look natural. "Of course." The lie came out smoothly from her lips, too easily for comfort. Did a part of her wish it was true?

"I'm sorry for prying. It's just that I'd hate to see Rafe hurt again." Lisa reached out to pat Sarah's hand. "Don't be embarrassed. Passion is a natural thing in a marriage. So, you two started a bit rocky. It's how you end up that matters."

Sarah muttered, "Passion's one thing, but what about love?"

Lisa shrugged. "Why, I thought Rafe would pine away after you left. Then he turned so ornery, most of us just stayed out of his way."

Had Rafe pined for her? It seemed too much to hope for now. "I didn't know he missed me that much."

No, he just missed my help in opening the dude ranch.

Lisa put a hand over her mouth. "Oh, me and my big mouth. I hope I didn't upset you by bringing up the past. No offense, I hope."

Sarah smiled in what she hoped was a reassuring manner. "I suppose it was hard for Rafe. His expansion plans hinged on me."

Lisa shook her head. "I wouldn't say that. Don't worry, if he wanted to expand, he'd do it with or without you. It's been a challenging year for ranchers, but Rafe is too good a manager to fold. He was pretty resistant to Gabe's suggestion that he take in tourists. After all, Rafe is a dyed-in-the-wool traditionalist. But Gabe and I explained we could throw a lot of business his way through our travel agency.

"He's got this big empty house going to waste, so why not make extra income to take him over the lean times? Heck, it would help grow our business, too. In the end, he was coming around to our way of thinking. Now that his home life is normal, he can concentrate on the changes."

Sarah stared at Lisa. "Let me get this straight. It was Gabe's idea that Rafe turns part of the Double-H into a dude ranch. When did he first suggest this?"

"Oh, about a year ago. As I said, Rafe initially didn't take to the idea much, but he's a smart guy. Eventually, he saw the light. He was drawing up the plans when you met. I'm sure he must have told you about them."

Sarah thought about the night she'd found the plans and nearly groaned. Could she possibly have been wrong about Rafe's motive for marrying her? If so, somebody had deliberately set her running. But who?

Lisa brightened. "So, Rafe tells us that you're a nature photographer. Well, you'll have no end of beautiful nature to shoot around here. Your skills could come in handy with the guests. You could offer a course on nature photography. That is, if you wouldn't mind helping."

Sarah smiled wistfully. "No, I wouldn't mind. A photographer could spend a lifetime here and never miss new subjects."

Lisa grinned. "And you'll get to do just that."

Sarah kept her smile, but pain pinged deep inside. The lady didn't know this was just a sham. By the end of the summer, she'd be gone, and Rafe wanted it that way.

At least he hadn't tried to talk her into staying. He wanted her back to satisfy his sexual itch. At least, that's what he'd told Zeke.

"You know, I'm so glad that you came back. Rafe may seem tough, but he needs a wife to soften those hard edges."

Sarah cringed at Lisa's confident words. "I suppose so."

"Now, how about I teach you Chicken and Dumplings 101?"

Chapter Three

Sarah sighed as she looked at her reflection in the bathroom mirror. Three days of stress had taken its toll. Dark circles underscored her eyes, weary from the restless nights she'd spent lying next to Rafe. She glanced at the prickly heat covering her chest and couldn't resist giving it another scratch, even though it only worsened the itch. She shuddered as she contemplated getting into the hot, irritating long johns again. Still, she couldn't bring herself to back down from her original position. It would make her look weak, and weakness was a luxury she couldn't afford in her battle of wills with Rafe.

Even though she loved him, he didn't love her back. That was no basis for intimacy. She needed the words even though he seemed incapable of saying them.

He never missed an opportunity to brush against her in the house or cuddle her in bed. Each time, he pushed the barrier of her resistance a little farther.

A tap on the door caused her to spin toward it while covering herself. When it didn't open, she slumped against the counter. Relief washed over her. "Yes?"

"Hurry up." Rafe's voice was impatient. "Are you going to stay in there all night?"

Sarah gritted her teeth. He'd been as grumpy as a wounded bear lately. "I'll be out in a minute."

After cooking and cleaning the first two days, she was exhausted. Thanks to Lisa's coaching, she'd fallen in sync with the routine of ranch life by day three. The worst part of her day had to be acting like a loving couple in front of the men. Only the strain she saw on Rafe's face made it all worthwhile. At least it let her know he was suffering, too. She pulled on the long johns and opened the door.

Rafe leaned against the jam. His sensual mouth curved into a rueful smile at the sight of her. "You know, wife, that union suit is getting ripe. Maybe you should throw it into the wash tomorrow."

Sarah snorted and moved past him. "If I find a little time, I might do that." She walked to the bed, pulled back the covers, and got in. Leaving the blankets down, she rolled onto her side, not wanting to see Rafe's nudity.

The other side of the bed sank as he got in. He flipped the covers over the two of them, and her body temperature immediately elevated. It was going to be another unbearable night. She squirmed, stifling a moan when the wool rubbed against her irritated skin. Then she scratched her shoulder.

"Does that abomination have fleas, too?"

She shot a dirty look his way. "Of course not."

He was leaning up on his elbow, watching her. "Then why are you scratching like my old hound dog, Luke?"

She inched away from him, irritated by his mocking tone. "Drop it. It's none of your business."

His dark eyes narrowed with suspicion as his free hand went to the top button on her long johns. As he started to unbutton it, she jerked away. The last thing she wanted was for him to see her painful rash, the penalty she'd paid for being stubborn.

"Don't worry about it, okay."

His gaze grew concerned. "No, it's not okay. You're burning up, blast it."

Why did he care? Sarah remembered Zeke's comment that she had ruined Rafe and wondered again exactly what toll her leaving had taken on him. He seemed to be functioning well, as far as she could see. Rafe reached for the button again, and she shrank back.

He whispered dangerously, "Don't even think of moving away. I'm a lot stronger than you are. I'll hold you down if I have to."

She froze. He didn't make idle threats.

He carefully pulled the garment away from her skin, a look of pure outrage on his face. As his index finger smoothed lightly over her irritated skin, she sighed with bliss and closed her eyes.

Until his harsh voice broke into the silence. "Go put on something light, and I'll get the calamine lotion."

She knew it was the sensible thing to do, yet she balked at the idea. Seeing his exasperated glower, she realized he'd strip the clothes right off her if she hesitated much longer.

She got out of bed, walked to the dresser, and got a blue satin slip out of the drawer. He wouldn't be able to see through it, and it would feel wonderfully cool against her skin.

Rafe's gaze followed her to the bathroom door. She hurriedly closed it behind her, blocking his view.

She climbed out of the long johns and slid the slip over her shoulders. She gasped when she studied her reflection in the mirror. The garment clung to her breasts, highlighting the peaks. She stepped back, and it swung around her hips, the movement a bit enticing.

This was a terrible idea, but it was too late to change without looking stupid.

Opening the door slowly, she peeked around it, looking for him. He was nowhere in sight.

Wonderful. She could make it to the bed without him noticing her skimpy attire. She shut the bathroom door behind her and made a beeline for the bed. When she was halfway there, the bedroom door opened.

Rafe stood in the doorway, clad in a pair of briefs that gleamed in the shadows. He stepped forward, a bottle of pink liquid in hand. His briefs were the same pink shade as the result of a laundry mishap. The fact that he wore them with nary a comment had softened her heart toward him.

She stood motionless, alarmed by his heated gaze, feeling bare to the touch as he stepped nearer.

He opened the bottle and poured the cooling liquid into his hand. He set the bottle on the dresser and rubbed his large, callused hands together, evenly distributing the solution.

Sarah was mesmerized. His hands were so strong, and she'd dreamed of having them touch her. As he stepped into her space, she sucked in a deep breath, drawing in his masculine scent of leather and sandalwood.

His hands rested on her shoulders. The instant he laid them on her, she shuddered, her treacherous body responding to a call as old as time. His hooded gaze locked onto hers as he smoothed his palms along her oversensitive shoulders. His sensual smile ignited a fire that made her nerve endings supercharged.

His index fingers flicked at her spaghetti straps. The fabric skittered off her shoulders, leaving them bare.

She was rooted to the spot.

The slip dropped down to dangle from her upper arms, allowing him a generous glimpse of her cleavage.

His breathing became ragged. His hands slid lower, gliding over the tops of her breasts.

She gasped as a pulling deep inside her ached. It was hot, elemental passion, and all her instincts for self-preservation fought against it. She couldn't fall under his spell again and lose herself.

She stepped back, breaking the contact and the sensual spell between them.

He let out a deep breath, his nostrils flaring, his mouth curving into a rueful smile. He slowly assessed her shell-shocked expression. "That should make you sleep a little better, wife."

"I doubt it." She still trembled from the force of her desire.

Regret and loss were evident in his eyes when she stepped away. He wanted her, but could he ever love her? As he watched her walk toward the bed, his steady gaze told that he may have lost the battle, but he was still going to try to win the war.

He needed to sleep with her to get her out of his system. He'd said as much to Zeke. This little setback wouldn't stop his march on her defenses.

She glanced at him warily after she climbed into bed.

He smiled when he caught her lingering gaze on him. With slow, deliberate motions, he slid off his briefs.

He climbed into bed next to her, his upper body raised on an elbow. "Honey, if you want me, all you have to do is ask."

She recalled his boast that she'd have to ask for it, and frowned. "Forget it, big boy. There isn't going to be that kind of contact between us."

"Honey, if I'd wanted to, all I had to do was continue spreading lotion all over your delectable body," his dark eyes flared, "and you'd be under me, screaming my name."

She cocked an eyebrow at his vivid description. "You think so, huh?"

"Yeah, I think so. I'm progressive. You can get on top if you want."

"Oh, shut up." She turned her back on him, the big overconfident lug. She vowed to do everything she could to keep from succumbing to his sexual magnetism. To give in to the fire between them would be to lose herself.

Rafe had never given her words of love. She doubted he even thought in such terms. He wanted her, plain and simple, but it wasn't enough.

Sarah awoke before the alarm went off. She was used to getting up at four-thirty now. She shifted in bed and realized Rafe was sleeping against her, spoon-fashion, his hand clinging softly to her breast. The growing bulge at her rear told her he had a morning erection.

A fleeting thought of giving in to her desires ran through her mind. Why shouldn't she make love with him once, to see what she was missing? She shook off her sleepy lethargy and stifled the idea. She softly placed her hand over his, so as not to wake him, and began to lift it from her breast. His hot palm tightened around her.

"What? No good morning kisses?"

She turned to look over her shoulder at him. Stubble shadowed his jaw. Instead of making him look dissolute, it heightened his masculine appeal. His sleepy bedroom eyes and soft smile wordlessly invited her to stay put. She pulled away, but only pushed herself more firmly into his palm.

He fingered her nipple, instantly making it hard and sensitive.

She inhaled hard at his seductive, predatory gaze. "You said you wouldn't take me unless I asked you to."

He smiled and continued to circle the budding nipple with a callused finger. "But I didn't say I wouldn't encourage you."

She kicked him. Her heel made soft but determined contact with his leg.

He yelped and let go.

She slid out of bed and spun around to glare at him. "That's what you get for trying to manhandle me. From now on, keep your hands to yourself."

He doubled over with laughter.

She glared down at him, incensed by his reaction.

He straightened, tears of mirth beading the corners of his eyes. "Wife, you kick like our old lame mule, Clyde. You've got more spunk than I figured you for, but it will take a heap more to keep me away. You might say, I can't help myself when it comes to you."

His dark, heated gaze drank in the sight of her as she gathered her clothes from the dresser and headed into the bathroom. She felt like a lamb watched by a timber wolf.

Once dressed, Sarah was flipping pancakes when Lisa's daughter Mandy walked into the room. "I want some juice, Aunt Sarah."

Sarah smiled at the little girl's cute lisp. She'd agreed to keep her for the weekend so Lisa and Gabe could escape for a short holiday.

During the past week, while Sarah had learned to cook, she and Lisa had become fast friends. She'd even taken to little Mandy, although she hadn't been around children much. In the end, Sarah knew walking away from Rafe and Lisa would prove difficult.

She put down the spatula she was using to flip pancakes and turned to smile. "I'll get you some, honey. How'd you like to go on a nature hike today?"

Mandy grinned. "Oh, boy."

Sarah gazed at the sparkling dark eyes that looked like Rafe's. If she and Rafe stayed together, they might have a child that looked like this. The thought was both compelling and scary. Could she open herself up to that kind of risk?

Rafe walked into the kitchen and smiled. "Something smells good."

Mandy piped up, "Aunt Sarah is making pancakes, my favorite."

Rafe picked her up and twirled her around, making Mandy giggle. "Hey there, munchkin. How's my favorite girl?"

Sarah leaned back and watched the affection between them. He would make an excellent father.

"I'm good. Aunt Sarah is going to take me on a nature hike today."

"That's great, munchkin." He set the girl down. "We'll have to thank Sarah for being so nice." He walked over and planted a quick hot kiss on Sarah's surprised mouth.

She blinked at him when he pulled away. "What was that for?"

"Do I have to have a reason? Let's say it's for learning how to cook. I'm impressed, extremely impressed. You fit into my life beautifully, wife." He reached out to snag a slice of crisp bacon from the warm platter.

She slapped his hand while she gazed at him, stunned and warmed by the compliment. "Save some for the hands."

"A fella can't live on love alone," he joked.

She gaped at his mention of love, and Zeke entered the room. It was probably all part of the public show.

Feeling flustered, she turned to fix a plate for Mandy. "Let's fix you a picnic tray to eat in front of the TV."

"Oh, goodie," Mandy said.

Rafe poured himself a mug of coffee from the big, steaming pot on the table. It smelled wonderful. Mrs. Murphy was due back from vacation in two days, but Rafe considered extending her break longer. He enjoyed having Sarah take care of him.

Reaching for the sugar bowl, he stirred in two teaspoons and took a sip. He gagged and glared at her. "Good Lord, Sarah, are you trying to kill me?"

Several of the men made choking sounds, too.

"What's the problem?" she asked in a bewildered tone.

He grimaced. "This coffee's saltier than Hades!"

She frowned. "It can't be."

He picked up his cup and passed it to her.

What was she trying to do, get back at him for their cuddle this morning? Somehow this childish trick didn't seem like her style, although a week ago, he might have thought differently.

"Try it." He watched her taste it. Her eyes widened with surprise.

"Oh, good grief! I must have mixed up the salt and sugar canisters." Sarah stood and started to gather the mugs. "I'm so sorry. I'll get some fresh cups."

He couldn't help chuckling. So much for her cooking attempts. They were hit and miss, but he sure admired her dedication to learning something new. He had to admit, he wouldn't have learned something from her world of photography as quickly.

Tab Whittacker, a tall blond older cowboy, grinned. "Hey, Rafe, maybe your wife is dosing you with saltpeter. That's one way to keep a good man down."

This brought a series of laughs from the hands.

Rafe frowned at the lingering glance Tab gave Sarah as she rushed from the room.

Oh, hell. He was getting jealous.

Tab was a good hand, and he knew enough not to poach. Rafe smiled, going along with the ribbing. He watched Sarah blush as she entered the room and thought back to the evening before. He'd almost had her last night. It was a tantalizing taste of what was to come.

She put a fresh bowl of sugar on the table and walked around, distributing the cups.

Zeke grudgingly took the cup she offered him. Zeke, who was as close to Rafe as a father, still didn't trust her. He hoped the two would mend their rift because Rafe was counting on her realizing that this was where she belonged by summer's end.

Rafe's hand lingered on hers for a moment. Her pulse raced. "So, are the boys, right? Are you trying to slip saltpeter into me?"

Anger flared momentarily in her eyes, but then she smiled back at him. "It wouldn't hurt."

The men at the table responded with laughter.

She sat at the table with complete aplomb, unfazed by the sexual double entendre.

Yes, sweet Sarah was more than he'd bargained for.

After Sarah finished the breakfast dishes, she went to the bedroom for her camera. Mandy watched her as she walked back into the kitchen with it.

"What are you going to do with that?"

While loading the Nikon with thirty-five-millimeter film, Sarah smiled at the little girl's curiosity. It was nice to experience old familiar things through a child's bright, curious eyes. "I'm going to take a few pictures of ranch life."

"Why?" There was more than a hint of interest in Mandy's voice.

Sarah noted the girl's lingering glance at the inner workings of the expensive camera. "I'm a nature photographer, honey. It's what I do for a living."

Mandy tilted her head and leaned forward to get a closer look. "I never heard of that."

Sarah held the camera still so she could get a good look. "I'll give you a few photography lessons if you'd like."

Mandy grinned, clapping her hands. "Yes, yes, please."

Sarah grabbed the sack lunch she'd packed and followed Mandy out the door. They strolled toward the corral, where some commotion was going on.

"Let's see what's happening."

In addition to her Endangered Species Shoot, she'd decided on a Western Life series featuring Rafe's ranch and men. It would give her something productive to do and keep her mind off Rafe.

"Are we asking Zeke to saddle us some horses to take us on our picnic and hike?" Mandy asked.

Sarah winced at the thought. She'd been afraid of horses since childhood. "No, I don't think so. I'm not comfortable around horses."

"Why?" She gazed up at her inquisitively.

"I had a bad experience on a horse once. So, if you don't mind, I'd rather walk."

Sarah thought back to her grandfather's insistence she take riding lessons because it was expected of a young lady, and shuddered. She'd been terrified of the hulking beasts and, as a result, had a bad fall, breaking a leg. Thankfully, after that, he hadn't pressed the issue.

Feeling someone's scrutiny, she looked up and caught Zeke listening. Tab and Travis gazed at her intently from their perches on the fence. She didn't like the hands spying on her, but she supposed she was a novelty to the men. The younger guys turned away at her notice, but Zeke scowled at her.

"That's okay. I like to walk, too." Mandy ran ahead, stopping to clamber up the side of the corral.

Sarah took in the flurry of activity as they drew near. Men hung around the railing, cheering, and watching what was happening in the center.

A wild black horse jumped off the ground and turned in a half circle. It took her half a second to realize Rafe was astride the animal. She winced at the jarring leaps that shook his body. The horse could kill him. The horrible thought held her frozen while the horse leaped to the left and pitched to the right.

Rafe flew off the furious animal, landing on his behind in the sand.

He laughed, got to his feet, and walked over to the horse that threw him. He crooned softly to the wild-eyed animal. Sweet sounds came from his mouth as he put a hand on the horse's shoulder and stroked his palm down its quivering side. It calmed, ears coming forward.

Who would've thought such sweetness could come from the man's throat?

She scowled. She couldn't be jealous of a stupid animal, could she?

She had to turn away from the sight, unsettled by Rafe's carefree attitude. She'd been terrified, and he'd acted like he was having the time of his life.

She angrily picked up the camera from its strap and snapped several shots. Tab climbed on the back of a fresh horse, and she got several great photos of his handsome face. This would sell. The sunlight glinted off his blond hair and muscular, tanned body.

She smiled, loosening up now that she was in her element, and moved on to the other busy men. Turning a little farther to the right, she brought Rafe's scowling face into focus. He strode toward her at a furious pace. Sarah snapped off a final shot. It would be a keepsake to put this fiasco in proper focus after she left.

He stopped a few paces before her, a frown furrowing his brow. "I thought you specialized in nature photography?"

She was surprised by his angry reaction and embarrassed by the attention it drew. The men nearby stopped what they were doing and looked their way. She let the camera dangle from its strap and leaned against the wooden corral. There was no way she would let him get to her this time.

"There are horses in the shots."

He crossed his dusty arms over his chest and scowled. "There are also cowboys, and you're in their way. Knock it off."

She cocked an eyebrow at his imperious tone. Could the man be jealous?

She decided to egg him on to see if it was true. "Maybe I should do a beefcake catalog. 'Men of the West.'"

He put his foot on the bottom rung of the corral and leaned toward her. His expression became more determined, but his voice grew softer. "I said no. Go take pictures of prairie dogs or something."

His worn jeans conformed to the shape of his well-muscled body. He was a walking advertisement for hot, cowboy love. All she had to do was say the word, and she could have him.

Tempted, she sighed and turned her back to him. "Fine. I don't have to put up with your foul temper. Come on, Mandy, let's go out onto the south pasture for our picnic."

Rafe *was* jealous. But what did it mean? Was he beginning to care for her?

She grinned as she heard his parting words because they sounded as confused as she felt.

"Damned fool woman."

Sarah took a shot of a hawk swooping majestically overhead while Mandy picked wildflowers nearby.

Suddenly, the pristine silence was shattered by the thunder of hooves. She looked to the left. A speeding black horse barreled down on them, followed by several other dark, dusty shapes.

Sarah shouted, "Get behind the tree, Mandy!"

Mandy's high-pitched scream echoed, and she ducked behind a big oak tree.

Sarah froze momentarily, then climbed onto the tree's first branch for safety.

Rafe came into view from the other direction on Umbriago. He leaned, and his horse veered in front of the wild horses, changing their path just in time.

Rafe muttered what could have been a curse or a prayer as his horse stopped short, and he turned in the saddle to look at her.

Sweat ran down his face, and his breathing was hard. A nerve pulsed tightly in his jaw as he sidled his horse up next to her. He plucked her out of the tree and pulled her effortlessly onto the saddle in front of him. As he held her close, she was enveloped by the scent of cologne, sweat, and horse.

He was the most reassuring thing she'd ever smelled in her life. She slumped against him, his heartbeat thundering in his hard, muscular chest. As she lay trembling against him, it began to slow. She was too stunned to even worry about being astride a horse.

Hiss voice shook. "My God, woman. The stampede could have killed you."

Sarah mumbled against his chest. "I know. Thank you for saving me."

Mandy raced toward them, tears running down her face.

Rafe turned the horse, so it faced her. "Are you okay?"

"Yes, Aunt Sarah saved me."

"I guess that's one more thing to thank you for, wife," Rafe husked.

Tab rode up, followed by several other hands.

Rafe sighed. "Mandy, go back to the house with Tab."

Tab bent to scoop up the girl after giving Sarah a thorough once-over. "Everything okay here, boss?"

Rafe said tightly, "No harm done. They're both just a little shaken up."

"I can't think how that latch came loose, Rafe. Sorry about that," Tab added apologetically.

"It's not your fault. Somebody must have bumped it."

Rafe turned to look at Sarah as Tab rode away. "I've got a question for you. Why didn't you get out of the way sooner?"

Sarah clung to the bouncing saddle and closed her eyes. "I'm scared of horses. I froze."

"Of all the damned fool things," Rafe replied sourly. "Tomorrow, I'll get you used to them."

She gritted her teeth. Riding a horse wasn't part of the deal. "I won't get on a horse."

He chuckled, drawing her up close against him. "In case you haven't noticed, you're on a horse now."

She scowled at his mocking tone and overly friendly hands, but didn't dare pull away from his embrace for fear of falling.

Rafe abruptly reined up the horse. Sarah gasped as he swung her off the saddle. Before she could let out the panicked scream caught in her throat, she was standing. She slumped to the ground.

He slid out of the saddle and picked her up. He brushed the gravel off the seat of her jeans. "Are you sure you're okay?"

She pulled away, embarrassed by her weakness. "I'm fine."

His eyes narrowed as he looked her over. "No, you're not." He scooped her up and carried her back to the house, going inside and placing her on the sofa. Grabbing an Afghan off a chair, he carefully covered her with it, tucking it around her.

She scowled at him. "Rafe, I'm not some fragile doll you have to coddle. I'm perfectly fine."

"I say you're not fine." Rafe frowned. "Besides, if I want to coddle you, I will coddle you. Now you sit back and relax, and I'll brew you a cup of the tea you like. Then I'll go up and check on Mandy."

Flustered, she sat up. "Oh, my gosh, Mandy. I'd better go check on her."

He gently pushed her back. "I'll take care of it. You sit tight."

Rafe carried a tray into the living room fifteen minutes later. "Mandy's fine. She was more worried about you than anything else. She's down for her afternoon nap, so you should have some quiet time."

He set the tray on the coffee table and handed Sarah a cup of the fragrant tea she enjoyed. *How out of place this big cowboy looked pouring tea, and how endearing,* she thought fondly.

"Those horses that stampeded? Were they the ones you were breaking?"

"Yeah. I'm still trying to figure out how they got out of the paddock. In all the commotion, someone forgot to ensure the gate latched, and something must have spooked the horses," he added regretfully. "I'm awful sorry for putting you in danger, Sarah."

She reached out to touch his arm, feeling his contrition. "It wasn't your fault, Rafe. Don't blame yourself."

"I don't see it that way. I'm your husband. I'm supposed to take care of you. To say nothing of Mandy."

"But we're not man and wife."

"We could be." Rafe gazed at her intently before exiting the room.

Chapter Four

Rafe wandered into the kitchen for a cool drink. He'd been going over his books, a job he didn't relish, and he was wiped out. He'd been having bad luck the last few months, ranging from broken equipment to torn fence lines that hurt his bottom line.

If his plan to open the ranch to tourists went through, he'd be sitting pretty. Everything hinged on an acceptance of an expansion loan from the bank. Things were looking up now that he had a more stable home life.

Sarah and Mandy were making sandwiches, their heads bent together as they worked, and Mandy giggled at something Sarah said. It made him smile.

"Hey, what are my two girls up to?"

Sarah's head shot up. "We're packing a picnic lunch." Her radiant smile lit up the room.

Mandy grinned and skipped up to him. "Aunt Sarah's teaching me how to use her camera. And we're going to take a picnic lunch with us."

Rafe sidled up to the table and grabbed one of the peanut butter cookies they had packed. He nibbled on it as he glanced at the top of Sarah's bent fiery head. She studiously ignored him. She'd been more watchful around him lately, and he wasn't sure why. It was as if she was waiting for something.

"It's nice of you to teach Mandy photography, Sarah. Maybe I can take a few lessons from you, too."

Mandy tugged on Rafe's sleeve, her cherubic face beaming. "Aunt Sarah is lots of fun. She's an excellent teacher, too."

"I'll just bet she is. I wonder what else she could teach me."

Sarah's eyes narrowed at the sexual undertone. She was still fighting the attraction between the two of them.

Rafe stood, watching Sarah put the sandwiches into the picnic basket. He studied her beautiful face. He didn't know her as well as he thought he did. "So, where are you ladies headed?"

Sarah picked up her camera from the counter and hung it around her neck. "The north pasture. There are some interesting rock formations and a nice big shade tree to have our lunch under."

She looked relieved to be on a safe subject.

Rafe narrowed his eyes. He liked having her on edge. It made her more aware of him. "That sounds fine."

Mandy tugged on his sleeve. "Hey, Uncle Rafe, why don't you come with us?"

He grinned at the horrified expression that washed across Sarah's expressive face. The tension had been building between them and was at the boiling point. He had to admit he hadn't been the easiest guy to live with of late. Being in a state of constant semi-arousal when she's around made him cranky. "Sorry, Mandy. I, for one, have to work on Sunday." Sarah's shoulders relaxed, and the predatory male in him made him add, "But I might join you for lunch."

Mandy grinned. "Promise?"

He laughed and picked her up. "Promise." He looked over at Sarah, standing by the back door, camera slung around her neck, picnic basket in hand. She smiled as she watched him nuzzle Mandy's neck. His heart melted at her poignant expression. "I'll see you both at noon."

Rafe rode his bay gelding over the ridge at quarter to twelve and found Sarah and Mandy lying on their bellies facing a prairie dog mound. He dismounted and tied the reins to a tree. He walked the rest of the way, not wanting to disturb their concentration.

Mandy held the camera, patiently aiming it at the burrow. "Is this right, Aunt Sarah? I don't want to mess it up."

"That's right, honey. And don't worry about messing anything up. Trying new things is good. Now I'm going to show you how to adjust the lens." She reached over and took Mandy's little hand, placing it on the mechanism. "See? You slide it like this to bring it into focus. Now look through the viewfinder and tell me when it gets clear."

"That's good right there," Mandy replied excitedly.

A prairie dog sat on its haunches and looked around.

Sarah and Mandy grew still.

Sarah whispered, "Okay, honey, now hold your breath and snap the shutter."

Mandy pressed her finger down on the shutter, and several shots whirred off rapidly. The alarmed prairie dog ducked back underground.

Mandy jumped up, grinning. "Thanks, Sarah, that was so much fun."

Sarah got to her hands and knees, giving him a beautiful view of her generously curved derriere encased in faded jeans. He locked in on the sight as a thirsty man would water.

She stood and pulled Mandy close for a hug. "You're welcome. I'm glad we could spend time together."

His heart stopped in his chest at the endearing sight.

He stepped forward and rasped, "Your lunch guest has arrived, ladies. Are you two ready to eat?"

Sarah spun toward him, her smile bright. "We were having a marvelous time, but now we're hungry." She reached down to pat Mandy's head. "Right?"

Mandy ran to get the basket. "That's right. Let's eat."

He spread out the blanket under the pinion tree. He sat, leaning back against the rough bark.

Mandy plopped on the left side of him, leaving the right for Sarah.

As Rafe delved into the picnic basket to help Sarah get the sandwiches and cool drinks, their hands bumped each other. He glanced at her questioningly. She didn't immediately pull away. Instead, she smiled. Rafe's breath caught in his throat. She was warming to him.

He unwrapped the ham and cheese sandwich she handed him and cleared his throat. "So, what have you two been up to?"

Sarah looked down while opening her can of juice. "We were taking some shots of the rock formations over there." She pointed to a jagged outcropping ten feet away. "Then we ran into the prairie dog burrow." She grinned conspiratorially at Mandy. "We had to sneak up on the little buggers."

Mandy giggled. "Yeah, Aunt Sarah showed me how to use her camera. Maybe when I grow up, I can be a photographer."

Sarah nodded and sipped her drink.

He felt himself falling into their upbeat mood. He smiled at Mandy's hopeful expression. "Munchkin, you can be anything you want to be."

He glanced fondly at the two of them and found himself wishing he could trap this day in a bottle. This was what it would be like when they were a real family. The thought only strengthened his determination not to let Sarah slip away again.

Mandy reached into her pocket and pulled out a handful of stones. She handed them to him with a smile. "See the rocks we collected?"

He turned the golden substance over in his hand.

Mandy leaned forward. "See how they shine, Uncle Rafe? I bet its real gold. We're going to be rich."

He looked into her eager eyes and smiled. "It's only fool's gold, honey. It shines bright, but it's worthless."

He glanced at Sarah. Her suddenly hollow expression left him no doubt she thought it was an apt description of their relationship. But it wasn't, blast it. She loved him, and he needed her. Couldn't she see how right they were together?

She blinked and looked away. He could have sworn there were tears in her eyes, but he knew she was happy with the status quo.

He quickly finished his lunch and got to his feet. Once he got her into bed, she'd understand something clearly at last. He counted on intimacy to cement their relationship. "Come back to the corral when you two finish up, I've got a surprise for you, Sarah."

Mandy grinned and jumped up. "Did Dazzle Air have her colt?"

He smiled at her curiosity. "You'll just have to wait and see." He walked over to Umbriago and climbed back into the saddle. "I'll see you both later."

Sadness overcame Sarah as she watched Rafe go, despite Mandy's excitement. His words about the shining rocks being pretty but worthless struck close to home. Their marriage might seem genuine to an outside observer, but they both knew it was fake. Still, it was the closest she would ever come to the real thing. She loved the hardheaded cowboy. Instead of hoping for more, she should hang on to what she had.

Mandy started tossing the remains of their meal into the hamper. "Come on, Aunt Sarah, don't you want to see what your surprise is?"

Sarah couldn't help smiling at her excited chatter. It didn't take much to make a five-year-old happy. If only adult life were that uncomplicated. "Okay, let's get going."

Mandy raced in front of her toward the ranch.

What could her mysterious surprise be? And why would Rafe want to give her a present, anyway? It was probably something to increase their mock closeness and impress the men, just like his soft words and husband-like pecks when others were around.

Sarah and Mandy walked up to the corral where Rafe was waiting for them. His dark eyes carried a soft but enigmatic expression. Even after all these days together, she still didn't have a handle on what he was thinking.

"So, what's the big surprise?"

He smiled and pointed to a speckled horse munching on hay. "I'm going to give you your first riding lesson."

Mandy giggled. "Uncle Rafe, that won't be any fun. Bay Rum is as sleepy as my old rocking horse."

He tipped back his head and laughed. "Well, honey, we want to start slow. Remember, Sarah isn't used to horses."

Sarah scowled at his mirthful expression and backed away. How dare he pull this on her! She'd made it plain that she wasn't getting on a horse. "We're not going to start at all."

Mandy looked up sharply. "But, Aunt Sarah, I thought you said it was good to try new things."

She looked into the child's bewildered gaze and got tongue-tied. How could she explain there were separate rules for adults and kids? "I did, but this is different."

The girl frowned. "How?"

Rafe's snug smile made Sarah want to kick him. He knew she was trapped, the rat.

"Come on, Sarah, you'll be safe as a baby in a cradle on old Bay Rum."

From Rafe's challenging grin to Mandy's questioning expression, Sarah knew she had lost. There was no way out. How could she refuse without destroying her credibility with Mandy?

She sidled up to Rafe while keeping a wary eye on the speckled horse. "I'll get you for this Halliday, if it's the last thing I do," she whispered.

He leaned close to her ear. "Now, is that any way for my sweet little wife to talk?"

She crossed her arms over her chest, pulling away from him. "Sweet little wife, my Aunt Fanny."

He smiled. "What was that honey?" he said loud enough for Mandy to hear.

Sarah gritted her teeth, well-aware little ears were listening. "How do I get started?"

He stepped behind her and put his hands on her waist. Sarah's skin burned from the contact, and she had to fight herself not to pull away. He nuzzled the nape of her neck with his warm lips, his breath stirring the tendrils. It tickled like hell, but she wouldn't give him the satisfaction of admitting it.

"First, you place your foot in the stirrup and your hand on the pommel. Then on the count of three, you're going to pull yourself up and swing your other leg over."

She shivered and pulled her head away from the distracting contact. "Are you sure this is a good idea?"

He tightened his grip on her waist. "Don't worry, honey, you're in good hands."

She snorted. She gave him a repressive glare over her shoulder. "Just keep your mind on the riding lesson, okay?"

He nodded, his smile widening. "Your wish is my command, wife. One, two—"

Sarah shrieked when he swung her up and plopped her behind hard on the saddle. "Hey, what about three?"

He shrugged. "Sorry, I got mixed up."

She glared down at the big, macho cowboy. "Sure, you did."

Mandy giggled and shot an embarrassed look Sarah's way.

Bay Rum shifted, and Sarah uttered a startled shriek, clutching the pommel as if it were a lifeline. Bay Rum blinked her eyes at the noise and then seemed to go into a daze.

Mandy laughed and pointed. "Look, Uncle Rafe, Bay Rum's falling asleep."

He patted the horse on the head, and he nuzzled Rafe's hand, making *wuffling* noises.

Rafe tipped back his hat and looked deep into Sarah's wide eyes. "You look right natural up there, wife."

She burned under the scrutiny while slowly realizing she wasn't going to fall off the horse, dead from fear as she first imagined. Still, this was all the riding lesson she would try. "I'm ready to get down now."

His eyes crinkled as he smiled. "We haven't even started yet. I'm going to lead Bay Rum around the corral so you can get the feel of the saddle."

She scowled. "I've already got the feel of the saddle. It's hard and too high off the ground."

He threw back his head and laughed, barely waking up the horse. "Come on, old girl, let's put her through her paces." He walked to the front of the horse and looked back. "Now, hold lightly onto the pommel and try to relax."

She held her breath when the horse started to move, but by the third time around the corral, she had loosened her grip and had become accustomed to the saddle rocking.

They stopped in front of Mandy, sitting on the rail.

Rafe stepped back and handed the reins to Sarah.

She took one hand off the pommel and took the leather straps reluctantly. She figured Rafe had stopped in front of Mandy on purpose. He thought she wouldn't want to look like a coward, and he was right.

"What now?" she asked churlishly.

"Now you get to take Bay Rum for a spin. Just remember not to tug on the reins. Nudge him gently, and he'll go where you want him to."

She stiffened her spine and gave the horse a little nudge with her knees. He took several slow steps. This wasn't so bad, she decided. She might even be able to handle this. Then she nudged him to the right, but he kept plodding straight ahead.

She spun her head and looked at Rafe leaning against the fence by Mandy. "How do I turn this thing?"

"Bay Rum is a little bit stubborn. Keep nudging him, and he'll get the idea."

"Come on, you fugitive from a glue factory." She pulled on the reins. The horse snorted and kept heading straight.

Sarah shot an embarrassed glance Mandy's way when she heard Rafe chuckle.

"If you turn like a nice horse, I'll give you a carrot," Sarah crooned.

The horse whinnied and turned, plodding back toward Rafe and Mandy. He came to a stop in front of them.

Rafe pushed away from the fence and took the reins from Sarah. He dropped them and placed a hot hand on her denim-covered thigh. When he looked into her eyes, there was a soft smile. "That's enough for today." He turned to look at Mandy. "Why don't you run off and play, honey."

"Okay, Uncle Rafe."

Mandy skipped away, leaving Sarah feeling vulnerable. Stuck on top of a horse with only Rafe nearby made her easy pickings. Was he getting Mandy out of the way so he could make advances? More importantly, did she want him to make advances? She glanced at him and was bemused by his tender smile.

"I'll give you lesson two tomorrow," he husked.

At his suggestive tone, alarm bells went off in Sarah's head, and she shook off the sensuous spell and looked away. "If I can find time out of my busy schedule."

"Mrs. Murphy is coming back from vacation tomorrow." His voice carried more than a hint of determination. "That way, you'll have time for other things."

She could imagine the other things he was thinking of as his heated gaze locked onto hers.

His strong hands went to her waist, tugging her unresisting body off the saddle toward him. He slowly slid her down the length of his muscular body, and she gasped as her breasts brushed against his lips. He placed a damp kiss on her cleavage.

She whimpered as her nipples formed tight buds. They dragged against his chest until she was standing on shaky legs. She closed her eyes as his lips claimed hers for a soft kiss.

Her breath came rapidly into her chest.

The sound of a car coming up the driveway brought her to her senses. She pulled away, blinking up into Rafe's heated gaze. A car door slammed, and she glanced over at it.

A tall, sandy-haired man got out of a sleek white Cadillac. He shrugged, rearranging his dark suit, and put a matching Stetson on his head.

Rafe looked furious at the interruption.

Who could the stranger be? And why didn't Rafe like him?

The man rapidly crossed the yard to where they stood. His cold, gray eyes roved over Sarah, still in Rafe's arms. Sarah bristled at the scrutiny. What business of his was it if she and her husband wanted to share a cuddle?

Rafe kept a snug arm around her waist. He didn't notice her questioning glance because his gaze locked on the stranger with utter contempt.

Sarah was shocked. Why was there such animosity between them?

"You're not welcome on the Double-H, Blackthorn." Rafe's voice was curt, his stance rigid.

Sarah started at the intensity in Rafe's voice. He was usually so controlled. This wasn't at all like him.

"This isn't a social call, Halliday. Besides, the way I see it, this land should be mine." Blackthorn's voice was cool and cultured as he took a step closer.

"I've heard that old song before," Rafe snarled. "I don't want to hear it again. Get back in your car and get out."

Blackthorn grinned, seeming to relish Rafe's animosity. He put his hands in his pockets and rocked back on his heels. "Your great-grandfather cheated my great-grandfather out of this claim, Halliday. Just because you don't like to hear the facts doesn't change them."

Rafe snorted. "That's your version, Blackthorn. You never had anything to back it up, and you still don't. Your great-grandfather lost that card game fair and square. It's not my fault he didn't have the guts to admit it to his family."

Blackthorn jerked his hands out of his pockets, clenching them into fists. He took a rigid step forward, his face contorting with rage. "Bull squat."

Rafe let go of Sarah and stepped toward the man. "Well, now that the pleasantries are over..."

Sarah had horrible visions of the OK Corral. "Rafe," she quickly interjected. "I need to talk to you."

He ignored her and took another step toward Blackthorn.

"*Now*," she added sharply.

It drew both men's attention. Rafe scowled at her, and Blackthorn looked intrigued.

She smiled at Blackthorn, hoping to defuse the situation.

Blackthorn seemed to relax. He smiled at Sarah, but his eyes were cold and calculating. "Aren't you going to introduce me to your lovely wife, Halliday?"

"I see you heard about her." Rafe crossed his arms in front of his chest and leaned back against the corral as he scowled at Blackthorn.

The man laughed. "Of course. The whole town is abuzz that the lady you scared off has come back for more."

Rafe's eyes narrowed while he tipped his head in Sarah's direction. "Nevell Blackthorn, meet my wife, Sarah Halliday."

Blackthorn doffed his hat. "Charmed. I hear you're one of the Maxwell family, a distinguished and wealthy clan. Quite a handy connection for a man who wants to open a dude ranch."

Sarah was put off by both his words and his smarmy gentility. She instinctively stepped closer to Rafe, linking her arm with his. "You seem to hear a great deal, Mr. Blackthorn, none of it any of your business. But yes, my maiden name was Maxwell."

Blackthorn watched the move with narrowed eyes. "So, are you going to bail hubby out of his financial difficulties?"

Sarah decided at once she didn't like this man any more than Rafe. "I'm sure my husband can take care of himself and any difficulties that might arise."

Blackthorn nodded and eyed at Rafe. "I came here to up my offer, Halliday."

Rafe put an arm around Sarah's shoulder and pulled her close. "No dice, Blackthorn. I'm not going to sell."

The man shrugged. "Very well, if that's the way you want it."

"It is."

Blackthorn glanced scathingly at Sarah, standing in the shelter of Rafe's arms. "Maybe you'll change your mind if your wife walks out again." The barb had been aimed at her, and she bristled at the intimation. Their relationship was none of this man's business.

"Don't count on it, Blackthorn. The ranch isn't up for sale no matter what the circumstances."

Blackthorn raised an eyebrow and smiled. "Is that right? The last time she walked out, you went off the deep end. I think I'll bide my time. You know what they say. Good things come to him who waits."

"I don't care what you do. Just get out."

Blackthorn smiled. "Nice meeting you, ma'am. I'm sure I'll see you at the Barclays Barbecue tonight. It's the high point of Shelbyville society, and I'm sure a city girl like you could use the distraction. You must not have very stimulating conversations around here. Most likely, you're bored to death in this rustic setting and will soon grow tired of it again."

Rafe tensed at the barb.

"I can see you don't know me very well. And like I said, what's between my husband and me is none of your business. Now, why don't you get in that big lumber wagon and get out of here."

"Very well. I'm sure we'll talk more another time."

She let out a sigh of relief when he drove away. She glanced at Rafe, but instead of concentrating on Blackthorn, he gazed at her with admiration.

"You're something. You keep on coming to my rescue, don't you?" He smiled warmly.

She was a bit embarrassed by his praise. "Well, somebody's got to. You handle everybody else's problems. It's high time someone looked after you."

He grinned. "And you've taken over that position?"

She shrugged. "Just consider it my wifely duty."

"There are a few other wifely duties I'd like to see you perform." Rafe winked.

Sarah frowned as the talk inevitably got down to sex again. The man never gave up. "What was all that business about the ranch belonging to Blackthorn?"

Rafe snorted. "He's been telling that story since we were kids. Blackthorn's great-grandfather used to own this spread, along with several others. He lost it to my great granddaddy in a poker game. It sticks in Blackthorn's craw, even though he still owns most of his family holdings. He usually isn't such a jackass about it, but something's been riling him lately."

She sighed. "I can see there's no love lost between you two."

He looked toward the dust cloud Blackthorn's car left with narrowed eyes. "You can say that again. Nevell's been dogging my heels since we were kids. The jerk rubs me the wrong way."

Rafe strode onto the Barclays' patio with Sarah at his side. He glanced at her usually animated face, now set in severe lines. Since their confrontation with Blackthorn in the driveway this afternoon, she'd been tense. He was still amazed at how she stood up to Blackthorn for him.

Jim and June Barclay were old friends and owners of the most extensive spread in the area. Their annual Barbecue was always well attended, and tonight was no exception.

Rafe guided Sarah through the crowd. He couldn't help wondering if she regretted her capitulation this afternoon. Well, he wanted much more than the burning kisses they'd shared. And from her enthusiastic reaction, deep down, so did she.

All through the day, he'd thought about the enigma that was his wife. All his preconceived notions about what made her tick had changed since she'd moved in. The way she always came to his rescue was terrific. It was rather novel having someone protect him, and he had to admit he liked the feeling.

"Hey there, Rafe, why don't you introduce us?" Jim Barclay, a tall man with silver hair, asked.

Rafe came out of his reverie. He nodded at Jim, then reached out to draw Sarah to his side. "Sarah, these are my neighbors, Jim and June Barclay."

Sarah reached for Jim's extended hand and shook it. "It's nice to meet you both. You have a lovely home here."

Jim grinned and patted Rafe on the shoulder. "I can see you've got yourself a sweet little filly, Rafe. You'll have to make sure no other stallions come sniffing around."

June nudged her husband in the ribs. "Pay no attention to Jim, Sarah. He suffers from hoof and mouth disease." She grinned and reached out to shake Sarah's hand. "Hello, Sarah. I'm glad to meet you finally. We'll have to get together for a cup of coffee sometime this week."

Rafe relaxed when Sarah grinned back at Jim and then shook June's hand. Sarah was a bit on edge from her showdown with Blackthorn, blast his hide. He'd been worried Jim's joking remark might set her off. He reached out to caress Sarah's shoulder, feeling the tension ebb away.

"That would be nice, wouldn't it, honey?"

Sarah smiled at June. "Yes, I'd like that." She turned back to Jim. "It was nice meeting you both."

June said, "Same here, honey. I'd better see to the refreshments. You two have a fun time now."

Jim said, "Rafe, I'll call you next week about your proposal. So far, it sounds good."

Rafe was relieved. It was the news he'd been waiting for. Now, he could move forward with his plans to convert part of the ranch into an inn. This would help create a more secure future for his family. "Great, I'll be waiting for your call." He turned and guided Sarah toward the bar. "What would you like to drink?"

Sarah shrugged. "I don't know. What are you having?"

"A beer."

"I'll have the same."

His eyebrows lifted. "You, a beer?"

She shrugged. "Maybe I don't have the high faulting tastes you assumed I'd have. I'm going to try to fit in with your crowd."

He grinned, happy that she was starting to relax. Her attempt to fit in with his neighbors was a good sign. "I appreciate it, darlin'. Two beers it is. I'll be right back."

Sarah looked around the crowd while Rafe went for the drinks, and saw Blackthorn. Wrinkling her nose, she turned her back on him. Then she spotted Lisa and Gabe.

Lisa walked up to her, trailed by Gabe, who bore a striking resemblance to Rafe, but was a little leaner. "Hi, Sarah. I see you beat us here."

Sarah smiled back. "We just got here. Rafe's up at the bar."

"I think I'll join him," Gabe said eagerly. "I'll bring you back a cold one, honey."

Lisa shooed him away. "Go on and have your man talk. Sarah and I will do some talking of our own."

Lisa led the way to one of the benches on the lawn. "Thanks a million for watching Mandy for me this past weekend. It gave Gabe and me a well-needed rest."

"Don't mention it. It was a pleasure to have her," Sarah hastened to reassure her. "I hope she wasn't too shaken by the stampede Saturday."

Lisa shook her head. "No, it doesn't seem to trouble her. She did tell me you saved her, though. I owe you a big one, Sarah."

Her cheeks heated at the praise. "All I did was tell her to get behind a tree. She would have figured that out on her own."

"But not as quickly. I can't figure out how the stampede happened," Lisa said softly. "As far as I know, it's never happened before."

She shrugged. "Who knows? Rafe figured that somebody forgot to latch a gate."

"Oh, look. Here come our two Western Romeos."

Sarah grinned at Lisa. "Western Romeos, huh?"

Lisa grinned back, unrepentant. "Sure, tonight's a perfect night for romance. The stars twinkle, music plays, and we have a night out with our hubbies. I don't know about you, but it gives me ideas."

Rafe and Gabe crossed the crowded dance floor. Rafe looked especially happy tonight, she thought wistfully. And why not? Like Lisa had just said, it was a special night.

Rafe handed her a beer. "Here you go, sweetheart."

Sarah smiled at him. He *was* her Western Romeo. "Thanks."

He looked startled by her change in attitude. He leaned down to brush a kiss across her lips.

"What's that for?"

His mouth curved into a smile. "Just for you being you."

Lisa got up. "Gabe and I are going to take a turn around the dance floor."

"Have fun," Sarah called out.

"Dance with me?" Rafe asked.

It wasn't an order, but a plea.

She smiled, instantly agreeing. "I'm not sure I know this dance."

He led her to the plank dance floor. "It's a country waltz. Just follow me."

She stepped into his strong arms and surrendered to the music. They twirled around the floor, and she gazed up at the stars wanting to press this night in her book of memories.

After the dance ended, Rafe led Sarah off the floor. "Hungry?"

"Not really."

"What do you want to do then?"

"It's such a beautiful night. Why don't we take a stroll?"

He linked his arm with hers. "Sounds good to me. But you're the beautiful one."

She was warmed by the compliment and the sincere way he'd said it. No matter what happened, she knew she didn't want to resist his advances any longer.

She gazed up at Rafe's profile as they walked. "What proposal was Jim talking about earlier?"

He leaned closer. "I might sell him a parcel of land from the Double-H."

She'd come back to keep him from losing the ranch. Why would he sell off a parcel? "Why?"

"It's a good business deal and nothing for you to worry about, sweetheart. I want to make some changes at the ranch, and I need an infusion of cash. Once the deal goes through, we'll be in decent shape."

This was serious. She hated to stand by and let him sell off part of his birthright. "I thought you were going to reapply for an expansion loan."

Rafe nodded grimly. "I did. It was a no-go. Blackthorn is on the board of directors at the bank. He persuaded the loan committee I was a poor credit risk."

"He must be pretty influential." Sarah scowled at the thought of Blackthorn meddling in Rafe's business.

He nodded. "You could say he's got his finger in just about every important pie in town."

She placed her hand on Rafe's arm, bringing them to a halt. "You can't sell off part of the ranch. It's your heritage."

He studied her intently. "The way the Maxwell Consortium is yours."

"Not quite. I've got some news for you, Rafe. I'm not the heiress you assumed. I walked away from my birthright years ago, but you don't need to do so."

She gazed at his sweet expression looking for any sign of disappointment.

"So, you're not put off by the fact that I have no ties to my grandfather's empire?"

He frowned at the question. "I didn't marry your grandfather. I married you."

His sincerity touched her, and she wanted to help. "I've got some money saved up. It's yours if you need it."

"I don't want your money, sweetheart."

"But..."

He cut off her protest with a kiss. Pulling back, he said softly, "It's too nice a night to argue. Just look at the blanket of stars and think about us."

She settled into the crook of his arm, and they strolled about the grounds.

When they neared the parking area, she gazed up at him and came to an instant decision. He was her Western Romeo, and she wanted him. She'd take whatever he had to offer. In time, he'd grow to return her love.

"Want to go back to the party, sweetheart?"

She knew what he wanted. She wanted it, too. "I want to be alone with you. Let's go home, cowboy."

His brilliant smile told her he got her meaning, and she'd made him an incredibly happy man.

Sarah slipped into the blue nightie and glanced at her reflection in the mirror. Her eyes were bright with excitement. Drawing a deep breath, she opened the bathroom door and went out to meet her destiny.

Rafe stood by his dresser, unbuttoning his blue cotton shirt. The color highlighted his tan skin and the fire in his eyes.

Her heart stopped in her throat when his gaze locked onto hers.

His shirt hung open, tempting her to reach out and touch his hot silky skin.

She froze. What if she didn't...please him?

Mesmerized, she watched the easy play of the muscles in his chest as he shrugged off his shirt. He reached down for his fly. The audible snap of the button undone made her flinch.

She looked deep into his scorching gaze. She wanted him with an unreasoning hunger she would no longer stifle. Her hands went to the hem of her slip, drawing it up and off her body. She carelessly tossed it onto the floor.

His sensual mouth arched in a grin, and he stepped toward her, rapidly closing the distance.

She breathed in his masculine scent, shaking with the hunger it stirred deep inside her.

He paused inches from her, his expression dazzled, his breathing ragged. "Want me?"

"Yes," she said with a breathy sigh. "More than you can know."

"Oh, I think I've got a pretty good idea." He glanced down at his too-tight jeans. "You've made an impression on me, too."

She followed his gaze to the ever-growing bulge. She sucked in a breath, shocked at how much he wanted her. "So I see."

Rafe scooped her up in his arms, turned, and carried her toward the bed. "You've had me tied up in knots, wife. Now we're going to do our best to unravel them." He leaned down to plant a passionate kiss on her lips.

She opened to him. Oh God, his taste was heavenly, and the rough texture of his tongue against hers was driving her wild. He slowly lowered himself onto her, pressing her heated body into the cool sheets.

She reached up, embracing his broad shoulders as she continued to kiss him. When his mouth lifted, she pulled him back down, scattering kisses across his face, trying to memorize every part of it. His strong hand cupped her breast, bringing the peak to aching tightness. She arched toward him, delighting in the sweet friction. He bent to tease the tight bud with his wet tongue, and she squirmed, gasping through her pleasure. Pressing herself tightly against him, she silently begged for more. Her legs thrashed restlessly against the cool sheets. With maddening slowness, Rafe's hand moved down, gently cupping her mound. His index finger insinuated itself between the folds.

"Open yourself, sweetheart," he husked. "Let me touch you."

She hesitated momentarily, looking into his heated gaze. He obviously wanted her with a fire that matched hers. She spread her legs, and his hand slid home while he bent to kiss her. She moaned into his mouth when his finger touched that exquisitely tender place. She felt his lips curve into a smile at her blatant reaction, but she didn't care. She cried out, burying her face in his muscular shoulder to stifle the sound. Her tongue flicked out, savoring the salty taste of him.

He laughed. "That's it, honey. Go wild for me."

She wrapped her fingers around his length, and he stopped laughing. He groaned and surged like hot, steely velvet into her hand. She reveled in his reaction.

He groaned again. "Oh, sweetheart, that feels like heaven, but if you don't stop, I will not be able to control myself." He pulled away and came down gently on top of her, making a place between her thighs.

She gripped his shoulders, her body humming with excitement. His shaft slid smoothly between her damp petals, and she cried out at the sudden aching discomfort.

He stilled, eyes widened with surprise. "This was your first time?"

Annoyed by his shocked tone, she glared at him, the wispy, sensual spell she was under evaporating. "Well, we never did consummate it last time."

He stared at her probingly. "But still, how old are you? Twenty-eight? And you mean to tell me, in all these years, you've never..."

She looked away. "Thanks a lot for pointing out what an anachronism I am." She pushed at his chest, trying to move him.

His stern face broke into a delighted grin, his hand absentmindedly caressing her thigh. "Oh no, sweetheart. You're not getting away from me now. Not ever!"

"But..."

He leaned in to nuzzle her neck while slipping his hand between their bodies to touch that tender spot.

She gasped at the sweet pleasure that rocked through her. Her eyes drifted shut as she concentrated on the sensation. When he took his hand away and moved gently inside her, she met his thrust, smiling at the feeling. This was going to be all right.

He surged into her, increasing the pressure, and she moaned, her hips springing to meet his.

"That's right, honey, let me pleasure you," Rafe murmured against her ear. "That's all I want to do."

She moved against him, her pleasure building.

He reached down, pulling her hips against him, and she screamed, coming apart. Rafe's muffled shout followed her over into the land of bliss.

Chapter Five

Sarah awoke to songbirds singing outside the bedroom window. She lifted her head off the pillow and looked around.

Judging from the sunlight streaming into the room, it had to be at least eight o'clock. Why hadn't Rafe woken her to fix breakfast? Then it dawned on her. Mrs. Murphy was home. She would not need to do all the wifely chores she'd grown used to. She'd started to enjoy taking care of her family.

Even so, Rafe could have roused her with a kiss. She would have welcomed a morning show of affection. He'd started a fire in her last night that would have joyously responded to a morning cuddle.

She sat up in bed, fluffing the pillows behind her. A twinge in her nether regions was a vivid reminder of their lovemaking last night. It had been the thrill of her life. Now, she felt used and abandoned.

Could she accept being shuttled off to one corner of his life? Was she to be the accommodating little wife at night and a polite stranger during the day?

What choice did she have? She loved Rafe. She knew that now with every fiber of her being.

Well, she couldn't hide in the shelter of their bed all day.

She got up, showered, and made her way to the kitchen. Vigorous lovemaking was a spur to the appetite.

She turned the corner and peered into the kitchen. Relief surged through her at the deserted room. She wasn't sure she'd have been able to hide her distress or engage in any awkward morning-after conversation should Rafe have been waiting.

She went to the cabinet, got a mug, and poured herself a cup of the coffee that smelled so good.

"There you are, my dear," a cheerful voice said. "I was wondering how long to hold your breakfast."

Sarah spun around to Rose Murphy, a tall, plump woman with sparkling blue eyes and salt-and-pepper hair. "Welcome back, Mrs. Murphy. Rafe said you'd be resuming your duties today."

Mrs. Murphy bustled into the room. "Now, you call me Rose, dearie. I don't hold with formality. You have a seat, and I'll fetch your breakfast. There's a good girl."

Sarah took a seat at the dinette, overwhelmed by all the motherly attention. She smiled when Rose set a plate of hot cakes and bacon in front of her. "Thanks, Rose, but there's no need to wait for me."

Rose flustered around her. "Now, now, I won't hear such talk. It's my job to take care of you. Eat heartily and enjoy it."

She wiped off the kitchen counter and started unloading the dishwasher.

Sarah felt like an idle bum, but she dug into the delicious-looking breakfast. Rose Murphy was an excellent cook. Sarah was sitting back, sipping her coffee, when Rose brought the pot and an extra mug to the table.

She poured a refill for Sarah and then sat across from her. "So, my dear, how are my two lovebirds getting along? I could see by the smile on Rafe's face he was happy as a calf in a field of daisies."

Sarah hesitated. How much should she reveal? "We're getting along all right, I guess. By my staying here, we're hoping to cut down on the gossip."

Rose clucked. "Bunch of busybodies, that's what the town folks are. Please don't give them a second thought. Did you sleep well?"

Sarah flushed at the question. She hadn't slept much because Rafe had woken her several times in the night for bouts of sweet lovemaking.

Rose chuckled. "Don't worry, my dear. Young married couples are supposed to have sleepless nights."

Sarah looked down into the steamy recesses of her mug to avoid Rose's merry gaze. "I suppose so," she mumbled. Did their night of passion show that much?

"I can see Rafe's a new man now that you're back where you belong."

Sarah glanced at Rose intently. "I was wondering. How much talking did Rafe have to do to get you to write asking me to come back?"

Rose stirred some sugar into her coffee, hesitating. "So, you caught onto that, did you."

Sarah grinned at Rose's guilty expression. "I could tell that I was expected. Don't worry. I'm not mad at you. Coming here was the best thing I could have done, if not the wisest."

Rose cocked her head. "Now, why would you say that?"

Sarah sighed. "I might be crazy in love with him, but I can't say the same thing for him."

Rose smiled. "Would a man that isn't crazy for you cook up this crazy scheme? For goodness's sake, he sent me on an all-expense paid trip to see my sister. Don't worry, some men take a while to come around."

Rose's enthusiasm bolstered Sarah. She pushed to her feet. "Well, I may as well get started on that series I want to finish. The daylight's burning."

Sarah returned to the bedroom and grabbed her purse off the bureau. She turned and eyed the rumpled bed. It was a vivid reminder of their night of love. She put down the bag and pulled up the sheets stiffly, trying to make order out of the chaos in the bed and her thoughts. She smoothed the bedspread across the top and then fluffed the pillows. Now nothing remained but her memories.

She picked up her purse and walked back down the hall to the kitchen, telling Rose, "I need to go to town to get some darkroom supplies. Is there anything you'd like me to pick up while I'm out?"

Rose waved her away. "No thanks, dearie. I've got everything I need. Make sure you drive carefully, and don't forget to put on your seatbelt. I'll see you later."

Sarah went out the door with a bemused smile. She wasn't used to such motherly cheerfulness. She hadn't had anyone to mother her since she was five.

The heat inside her Jeep was stifling. It had been closed since she'd arrived. She'd been too busy cooking and cleaning to think about going anywhere. She rolled down the windows. The breeze quickly cooled down the vehicle to a bearable temperature.

It felt good to get out of the pressure cooker she'd been living in the last couple of weeks. She popped a CD in the player and began to unwind. Things would simmer down now that she and Rafe had been intimate.

She slowly cruised down the main street. She pulled into a parking space when she spotted Daley's Camera Shop. Daley's had everything she needed. She filled her arms with items and went to the front counter to pay.

With an *"oof,"* she dumped the ample supplies on the counter.

The short, gray-haired man behind the counter smiled. "I see you're fixin' to take some pictures, young lady."

She smiled at the understatement, a seemingly typical western trait. "You might say that. I'm also going to need some developing fluid."

"I've got that in the back." He walked into the curtained area and returned with the toner. He smiled as he started to tally up her purchases. "I know most folks from around these parts. You must be new around here."

She sighed. She doubted she would get out of there until she satisfied the shopkeeper's curiosity. "I'm Sarah...Halliday. I'm staying at the Double-H."

The man reached across the counter to shake her hand. "Why, you must be Rafe's wife." He pumped her arm vigorously. "I'm mighty pleased to meet you, ma'am."

Sarah gingerly withdrew her hand from the firm handshake. "Same here. Are you Mr. Daley?"

He beamed, showing a gold-capped tooth. "That's me, Mike Daley, at your service. This is my store. It looks like the photography bug has bitten you."

She laughed. "That happened a long time ago, I'm afraid. I'm a professional photographer."

"You don't say. I've got a little granddaughter I'd like to get some pictures of."

She grinned. "I'd be glad to oblige sometime, but that's not my usual line. I'm a nature photographer. You know, scenery and animals."

Mike nodded. "That's quite a coincidence. I just developed some slides of scenery and animals. Except they were dead."

She recoiled from the thought. Who on earth would want to take pictures of dead animals? He was probably a hunter, showing off his kill. She tried to erase the repellent scene from her mind. She'd been around the wild long enough to understand the survival of the fittest. Every living thing was either predator or prey when you got to the basics. Still, she could never fathom the joy of killing a magnificent wild beast.

The door chimed.

Nevell Blackthorn walked up to the counter. "Do you have those slides ready for me yet, Mike?"

"They'll be ready in two shakes, Mr. Blackthorn. I've got to ring up this lady's purchase first."

Blackthorn glanced at Sarah's purchases and frowned. "It looks like you're buying enough supplies for a year."

Mike beamed while he reached for Sarah's credit card. "Yup, the little lady will be one of my best customers. It's good to have a professional photographer move into the area. This here's Mrs. Halliday, Rafe's wife."

"A photographer, you say? I didn't know that." Nevell doffed his hat. "Sarah and I have already been introduced, although it's a pleasant coincidence to run into her again." His eyes narrowed. "So, I take it you're planning on sticking around."

"That's Mrs. Halliday to you." She gritted her teeth, but added calmly, "What I do is none of your business. I thought Rafe and I made that clear yesterday." He was deliberately trying to upset her, the jerk, but she wasn't going to rise to the bait.

Blackthorn's thin lips compressed into a tight line. "You and Rafe planning on attending the Rancher's Association Meeting tonight?"

She shrugged. "Maybe." What business was it of his? She and Rafe hadn't even discussed it.

He sniffed. "I'd recommend it. You might find it instructive."

She noted Mr. Daley was lingering nearby to eavesdrop. No doubt, he'd repeat this acrimonious conversation all over town by nightfall. Maybe Blackthorn had planned it that way.

"It seems like you're pretty anxious we be there."

He shrugged and looked away. "It's my job to remind people of the meeting."

She didn't buy his nonchalant façade. Something amiss was in the wind, but she had no doubt Rafe could handle anything Blackthorn threw at him. "If it's that important, I'll try to get Rafe to go."

Blackthorn had a smug smile on his face. "Excellent. At least one of the Hallidays shows some intelligence."

She ignored the barb. She signed the charge slip and picked up the sack of supplies, feeling Blackthorn's gaze on her as she left the store.

As she drove home, she thought about his reason for wanting Rafe to attend the meeting. He was probably trying to cause some trouble, but Rafe could handle it.

She pulled up to the ranch house and killed the engine. As she opened the rear door of the Jeep to gather her purchases, a dark shape moved out of the shadows of the porch.

Startled, Sarah stared at it until it drew nearer.

Rafe, and there was a furious look in his eyes. What had him so upset?

He took the sack out of her hands and looked her up and down angrily. "Where in blue blazes were you?"

"I went to town to get supplies." She was startled by his raw anger. Then she spotted the truck keys in his hand. "What were you going to do? Track me down?"

He stepped closer. "I knew you didn't go far because Rose said you left two hours ago and didn't take a suitcase. I checked, and your clothes were still here."

She seethed in outrage. "You went through my things?"

He scowled. "Hell, yes, I went through your things. I have every right." He slid the keys into his hip pocket. "Remember, we have an agreement. You have to stay here for the whole summer. And I'm not going to let you run away."

Sarah snorted and yanked the bag out of his grip. She'd had enough of his high-handed attitude.

The bag ripped, spilling film canisters and darkroom supplies onto the ground. "Just look what you made me do." She bent down to gather up the supplies and glared at him.

He crouched next to her and helped.

They both stood, and she turned to walk to the house when Rafe's hand on her shoulder stopped her.

She looked up at him, annoyed. "Now what?"

His eyes narrowed, and he held out his open hand. "Give me your keys, Sarah."

Her mouth dropped open. "You can't be serious." The determined look in his brown eyes rocked her back on her heels.

A nerve pulsed in his jaw. "I'm dead serious, wife. I'm holding you to your part of the bargain."

Her heart twisted. Her word wasn't good enough.

She clenched the keys tightly, then tossed them at him. "Here they are, husband. I hope you choke on them."

She stomped off toward the ranch house, never looking back.

"So, what goes on at these meetings?" Sarah asked tightly.

Her interest encouraged Rafe, even though he knew she was madder than a wet hen right now. And she had cause because he'd acted like an ass. He'd panicked when he'd come home to find her gone. It was a replay of the night she'd run out on him.

"Any concerns or disputes between ranchers are worked out here. Also, if there are any problems with the local or federal government, they're brought up."

"What's on the agenda for the evening?" She glanced at him as they walked into the grange hall.

"I'm not sure. I've been too busy to go to many meetings lately." His eyes narrowed as he watched Blackthorn and Bob Wilson, the local US Game and Wildlife official, walk toward the platform.

Something must be up, he mused. It was unusual to see Bob at the meetings. He'd wondered what was on Blackthorn's mind since his visit the other day.

Nevell Blackthorn walked up to the podium. He glanced around the room, then his gaze settled on Rafe and Sarah. He smiled a self-satisfied smirk.

Rafe met Blackthorn's gaze and held it steady. He had never been able to beat Rafe in a fair fight, and he backed down now by looking away.

Rafe grew tense. He probably shouldn't have brought Sarah, but the opportunity to show her around town on his arm had been too tempting to resist.

He led her to a row of folding chairs and sat next to the Barclays.

"Hi there," June said.

"Hello," Sarah replied.

Blackthorn cleared his throat. "Settle down, people. I want to call this meeting to order." The room quieted. Blackthorn turned to the man seated on the platform. "Bob Wilson of the US Game and Wildlife service is here to address a grave concern that's recently come to my attention."

Bob Wilson, a short, dark-haired man, stood and walked to the podium. Rafe knew him as a fair guy, but a warden that went by the book. If there was a problem, he'd usually bring it up with the individual concerned rather than address them in a public forum. Just what was Blackthorn up to?

Suddenly, Rafe didn't want to know. Realizing Blackthorn was about to pull a fast one, Rafe grabbed Sarah's hand.

She turned to look at him. "What is it?"

He leaned toward her. "Come on, we're getting out of here."

She frowned and pulled her hand away. "But you're the one who insisted we come tonight."

"Well, now I want to leave."

She sat back in her seat. "Shh, the meetings already started."

Rafe grimaced. He gave Blackthorn a stern look as Wilson cleared his throat.

Wilson adjusted the microphone several inches lower and peered at the audience. "I'm here to talk about a problem I've discovered. The killing of wolves recently returned to the wild. Could I have the lights dimmed? I have some slides to show."

The lights lowered, and Rafe tensed as a picture of a dead wolf shone on the screen. He could hear Sarah's gasp of shock beside him and steadied himself for what was to come.

Wilson continued. "This first slide shows a female wolf, and the second shows her cub. Both were shot and killed, as can be seen. You can turn the lights back on now."

Rafe blinked as his eyes adjusted to the light. He'd recognized the land those slides were taken on, and it was the Double-H. This had to be Blackthorn's cowardly way to get Sarah to move away from him. She wouldn't hesitate to leave him if she thought he was involved.

He scowled at Blackthorn, who smiled at him. Damn, the sneaky bastard.

Wilson said, "Ladies and gentlemen, what you saw was a criminal act. You all know the maximum penalty for killing a wolf is two years in prison and a one hundred thousand dollar fine. I know some of you ranchers haven't been happy about the reintroduction of wolves in the area, but I thought you had come around to our way of thinking. I guess I was wrong."

Blackthorn stood and walked toward the podium. He shook his head sadly. "Where did you find the wolves?"

"They were found on the Double-H." Wilson looked at Rafe. "Well, Rafe, do you have anything to say for yourself?"

Rafe felt Sarah cringe beside him, and damned Blackthorn's smiling face to all the fires of hell. "What's the usual line? I plead the fifth."

"This isn't a joking matter, Rafe." Wilson frowned.

Rafe stood and pulled Sarah up beside him. This time she didn't resist. "Bob, we both know this isn't the place to talk about such matters, but I can make a pretty good guess at who persuaded you to do so. Since you did bring it up, I might as well give you and my neighbors my answer.

"It's no secret I opposed the reintroduction of wolves. All my neighbors know that, but I didn't kill the wolves in these pictures. That's not the way I operate." Rafe ignored the crowd's murmuring and focused on Wilson's frowning face. He didn't want to look at Blackthorn for fear that he'd give into the urge to go up there and kick the bastard's ass. He was in enough trouble with Sarah as it was.

Wilson nodded. "I admit this is an unusual procedure, but because the crime just became known and due to its severity, I thought this would be the quickest way to get things settled. Of course, an investigation will follow."

Sarah's hand struggled against his firm grasp. Her appalled reaction hurt him more than all the crap Blackthorn had thrown at him.

His fingers tightened, holding her still while he looked at Wilson. "Did you dig the slugs out of the wolves to see what kind of caliber shot them?"

Wilson said, "Not yet. But we will. Be at my office Monday morning."

Rafe tugged Sarah's hand, pulling her down the aisle with him. "I'll be there, but you damned well better have more proof than a couple of pictures."

"Get in the truck, Sarah. We're going home."

She glared at Rafe and yanked her wrist out of his grip, earning a scowl from him. She was so furious, she wanted to go back and demand what people would think of Rafe.

"I'm not ready to leave yet."

He leaned forward. "Get your ass in the truck before I throw you in."

He was just barbaric enough to carry out the threat.

She scowled at him and reluctantly complied. She turned to frown at him when he hopped into the driver's seat. Why didn't he go back and fight the allegations?

A tap on the driver's door made her spin toward the sound.

Nevell Blackthorn was standing there. He smiled when he saw her disgruntled expression.

Rafe rolled down his window. "What the hell do you want, Blackthorn? Haven't you caused me enough trouble for one day?"

"Me, cause you trouble?" Blackthorn said innocently. "What did I do?"

"You mean to tell me you weren't behind that little show?" Rafe snorted and started the engine.

"It was the US Game and Wildlife making the accusations." Blackthorn shrugged. "Not me."

Rafe smirked. "Yeah, right, and I believe in the Tooth Fairy, too. You must be plum stupid to come within striking distance of me right now."

Blackthorn smiled apologetically at Sarah. "You wouldn't want to upset the little woman any more than she already is." He inclined his head toward Sarah. "Evening, ma'am. It's a pity you had to see this."

Sarah glared at the two of them. They were like a couple of little boys squabbling over the same toy, and she wasn't going to play anymore.

"State your business and get out of here," Rafe said tightly.

"I've decided to be magnanimous and up my offer on the Double-H." Blackthorn grinned. "I figured you could use the money to pay your fine."

"Screw you, Blackthorn," Rafe growled. He put the truck in gear and swung out of his parking space. He looked out the side mirror as Blackthorn jumped out of the way.

Rafe's dry chuckle set her teeth on edge. How could he be laughing? The events of the evening were nothing to laugh about. She glared at him. He drove in silence down the dark streets. A nerve ticked in his tight jaw, and his mouth was rigid.

She was still sickened by the memory of those gruesome pictures. Who could have done it? There'd been no talk of wolves around the ranch, no reports of calves lost.

She interrupted the silence. "Well, what are you going to do about it?"

His glance was defiant, but there was something else there, as well. She almost thought it was fear. But what did he have to be afraid of anyway?

His gaze returned to the road. "Sarah, I don't have anything more to say on the subject tonight. I said it all at the meeting."

She was stung by his brusque words. "I know you didn't do it."

His hands tightened on the steering wheel as he drove toward the ranch. "Could've fooled me a minute ago."

"But the pictures." She knew in her heart Rafe was not responsible, but couldn't help recalling the horrifying slides.

Blackthorn was at Daley's Camera Shop to pick up some slides today. Were they the ones used tonight? The answer seemed obvious.

"From your point of view, pictures don't lie." Rafe's tone was bitter.

She recalled Blackthorn's mocking smirk up on the platform. Was he behind the shooting? "I wonder what Blackthorn's involvement is?" she said softly.

Rafe sighed. "Don't worry about it, Sarah. It's not your problem."

Chapter Six

Sarah buttoned up her white camp shirt and gave her sweptback hair a distracted glance in the mirror.

She'd decided something during the long, lonely night. Rafe didn't believe she trusted him, but that didn't matter in the end. If she could help prove him innocent, she would do it. Her observational skills were sharper than most. Maybe she could pick up on some clue in the backcountry of the Double-H that Bob Wilson's in his rush to judgment. If Rafe could go into the meeting Monday with conflicting evidence, it might make all the difference.

She walked out of the bedroom and down the hall to the kitchen. She had no intention of sharing her plans with Rafe. In his surly mood, he'd shoot them down for sure.

Rose was dishing up a plateful of breakfast sausages. She looked up as Sarah entered the room, a frown darkening her usually cheerful face.

"Good morning, Rose," Sarah said.

Rose put a serving fork on the platter and grimaced. "You wouldn't say it was a good morning if you'd seen the boss's face this morning."

Sarah sympathized. She'd gotten the cold shoulder from Rafe all night. "Rafe wasn't too cheerful this morning, huh?"

Rose rolled her eyes. "He was black as a thundercloud, and cross as a bear with a thorn in its paw. What in the heck did you do to him?"

Sarah sighed as she picked up the heavy coffee urn. They both headed toward the dining hall. "It wasn't me. It was Nevell Blackthorn. At the meeting last night, Rafe was accused of shooting some wolves on the Double-H. Good heavens, Rose, it's a federal offense. He could be looking at some substantial fines, not to mention jail time."

Rose set down the platter of sausages she was carrying and gasped. "Lord o' mercy, no wonder he's in such a mood this morning. But that's crazy, Rafe's not stupid enough to do something like that. Besides, we haven't had any losses from the wolves as far as I know."

Sarah placed the coffee urn by the head of the table and shrugged. "I don't believe it, either. Rafe's just not capable of doing such a cowardly thing."

Rose smiled. "I hope you told him that, dear. It would do him a world of good."

Sarah sighed and glanced away from Rose's sympathetic gaze. "I tried, but he didn't believe me. They showed some slides at the meeting last night, and I'm afraid my reaction made quite an impression on Rafe."

Rose smiled and patted Sarah's hand. "Still and all, dear, I'm sure you can patch it up. Talk to the man. He's your husband, after all. You should be able to tell him anything."

Sarah shook off the idea and looked directly at Rose. "My personal feelings aren't important right now. I have to prove Rafe didn't do it."

Rose gaped at her. "And just how are you going to come by such proof?"

Sarah leaned toward her and said conspiratorially, "Well, now. If a trained observer went to the spot and, say, got some evidence to the contrary, that would change things considerably, wouldn't it?"

Rose nodded and smiled brightly. "That it would." Then she rolled her eyes. "But the boss is in such an ornery mood, he'd never allow it."

Sarah shrugged and said nonchalantly, "He wouldn't have to know."

Rose smiled. "I like your style, young lady. You've got spunk, I'll say that for you." She glanced sharply to her left.

Sarah turned around and looked in that direction, but didn't see anything out of the ordinary. "What's the matter?"

Rose put her hand up to her chest. "I thought I saw somebody standing in the shadows. I was mistaken. It must be all this commotion shaking up my nerves."

Sarah patted her on the shoulder. "Don't worry. I've got everything under control. Now let's get the rest of the food on the table before the mob descends on us."

Rafe leaned back and sipped his coffee. "So, wife, I see you decided to join us this morning. What's on your agenda for today?"

Sarah stopped with her fork in mid-bite. She ought to be used to his surly visage by now, but it still managed to startle her. He couldn't know about her plans, could he? Unless he was the person Rose thought she saw in the shadows.

She tensed, knowing she had to choose her words carefully. "I thought I'd take some photographs."

He took another sip of coffee, then set down his mug. "Try to stay out of my men's way today. Okay?"

"Fine." She looked at her plate and went back to her meal.

Rafe was spoiling for a fight, but he wasn't going to get one from her. She had important business to take care of. And his wounded ego was the least of her concerns.

His chair scraped the floor as he stood, but she didn't glance his way. Moments later, his angry bootsteps headed to the door, then the bang of the screen door followed.

She finally glanced up to see inquisitive glances thrown her way by several of the men still at the table. Travis was goggle-eyed, Tab had an amused smile on his face, and Zeke looked downright surly.

Sarah shrugged and rose. "What can I say? He's not in a very good mood this morning."

The men looked back down at their food.

Sarah picked up her dishes and carried them into the kitchen. She walked to Rose, who was putting a stack of plates into the sink.

"Well, I'm off to investigate."

Rose wiped her hands on a dishtowel. "But how do you know where to go? The ranch is pretty big."

She was right, but what other choice did Sarah have? If luck was with her, she'd stumble across the right location.

"I recognized the topography from the slides last night. I figure if I head for that area, I'll run into what I'm looking for eventually."

Rose frowned and brushed a strand of hair behind her ear. "But that'll take you forever, dear. There has to be a better way to go about this."

Sarah shrugged and leaned back against the counter. "None I can think of. I really have no other choice than to go on my own. You know if Rafe finds out about it, he'll try to stop me. Don't worry. I'll be fine."

Rose smiled and put the dishtowel down. "I've got an idea. You wait right here, and I'll be back in a moment."

Sarah was surprised by the animation, but she didn't have time to stand around. "Rose, I need to get going."

Rose put her hands on her hips. "Have patience, child. A few minutes this way or that isn't going to make much difference, is it?"

"I suppose not." Sarah watched Rose go out the door, then busied herself by rinsing dishes and stacking them in the dishwasher.

She glanced impatiently at the clock, wishing Rose would hurry up. The door opened and Rose reentered the room, followed by a scowling Zeke.

Rose grinned and reached back to pull Zeke up beside her. "I found a guide for you, dear."

Sarah gritted her teeth. Zeke would just as soon let her get lost in the woods as guide her. "Him?"

Zeke snorted and glared between Sarah and Rose. "I told you it was a fool idea, woman. Me and Sarah don't cotton to each other."

Rose wheeled around to face him. "Now you hold on there, old man. Sarah is Rafe's wife, so you'd better keep a respectful tongue in your head. I don't want to hear any more sass from you. And take your hat off. Can't you see there are ladies present?"

Zeke snatched the battered old Stetson from his balding head. She couldn't help smiling at his sheepish expression as Rose railed at him. Evidently, they were old adversaries.

Rose finished chewing Zeke out and turned back to Sarah. "And as for you, missy, you aren't no better. Zeke knows this land like the back of his hand. If anybody can lead you to the spot, it's him. And we all want what's best for the boss, don't we?"

Sarah had to admit, Rose was right. She glanced at his sullen expression. "How about it, Zeke?"

He looked down and turned the hat around in his hands by the brim. "I'm game if you are. But I don't think Rafe's going to be too happy about it."

Sarah was relieved. Hopefully, they could check things out and be home before Rafe missed them. She smiled at Zeke. "I think you're right. Rafe's going to hate the idea. But don't worry about it, he won't fire you. Why, you're practically a family heirloom around here."

He cracked a tiny smile.

"Anyway, I'll take the heat when it comes down."

He looked up at her, and she thought she caught a grudging grain of respect in his eyes.

But then he frowned and resumed turning the hat again. "Rafe didn't tell me much about it, but my guess is that Blackthorn has something to do with this business."

Sarah nodded and stepped forward. "I saw him in town at Daley's Photo Shop yesterday. He was picking up some slides, probably the ones Wilson showed last night. Blackthorn was practically gloating when the news came down."

Zeke slapped his hat back on his head, while casting a wary eye Rose's way. "So where do we find this evidence that Rose was carrying on about?"

"The photographs were taken near a bluff that I'd say is on the east side of the ranch. The wolves were found by a lot of scrubby pines."

He frowned. "I bet the pictures were pretty gory, huh?"

She nodded, her stomach clenching in remembrance. "I'm afraid I reacted before thinking."

He scowled at her. "So that's why Rafe is so ornery today. I knew it would take a heap more than some false allegations to get his back up that bad."

She held his accusatory gaze. "Whether Rafe and I get along isn't important. What is important is clearing Rafe's name. Are you going to help me or not?"

He huffed out a breath. "I know the area you're talking about. It's pretty far out."

Shoot. This might screw up her plans to get back before Rafe noticed she was gone. Oh well, so what if he got mad. She couldn't let it stop her. "I was afraid of that."

Zeke cocked his head, watching her carefully. "We're going to have to ride. And I know how you feel about riding. Want to call it off?"

Ride. She hadn't even considered the possibility. But she couldn't back down now.

Zeke's doubtful expression said he clearly expected her to cry off.

"Not on your life. I'll get on a horse if it kills me. Besides, you're forgetting I had a riding lesson from Rafe."

He grinned and let out a snort. "Yeah, on Bay Rum. I'll tell you what. You can ride Bay Rum and I'll lead the way on Buttermilk. She's nice and slow so you'll be able to keep up. I'll go get them ready. Meet me in the stable in ten minutes."

"I'll be there," she told him with more confidence than she felt.

She went to the bedroom to fetch her camera and an extra roll of film from her case. She stopped by Rose in the kitchen on her way out. "Thanks a lot, Rose. I'll pay you back some day."

She grinned. "Helping the boss is payment enough. Now, you be careful and don't let Zeke bully you. You just stand up to the old coot."

Sarah laughed as she went out the door. "Will do."

She walked to the stable, keeping a wary eye out for Rafe, but didn't encounter anyone on her way. She entered the stable and spotted Zeke in the shadowy recesses of the building saddling Bay Rum.

"I didn't see any of the hands around, so the coast is clear."

Zeke cinched the saddle. "Everybody's too busy to pay any mind to us, anyway. Most of the hands are out mending fences today." He walked toward her and handed her the reins. "You need help mounting?"

She took the leather straps and glanced at Bay Rum. The horse looked as sleepy as ever. "Nah, I think I can manage." She put her foot in the stirrup and Bay Rum shifted. She glanced at Zeke in a panic. "Maybe you'd better stand by, just in case." She hopped and swung her leg around, but got stuck midway. "Help."

Zeke gave Sarah's hips a shove, depositing her crookedly on the saddle.

"That ought to do you," he grumbled. "Now, when we get started, just remember to keep a loose hold on the reins. Bay Rum will follow Buttermilk if you don't interfere."

"Thanks." She wiggled her bottom in the saddle, seeking a comfortable fit.

Zeke nimbly mount Buttermilk, belying his years. As soon as he started moving out of the stable, Bay Rum woke up and followed suit.

As they rode out of the building, they almost trampled Travis, who was hurrying toward the door.

Zeke pulled back on his reins. "Whoa, Buttermilk."

Bay Rum stopped abruptly, and Sarah lurched forward, catching herself by grabbing the pommel.

"Don't you have some work to do, boy?" Zeke yelled.

"The boss sent me to get some more wire," he squeaked, in a startled voice.

"Well get on with it then and stay out of our way. We've got business to do."

Sarah gave Travis a sympathetic smile as they rode by, trying to soothe his feelings. She rocked in the saddle as she and Zeke picked their way over the meadow. They passed a few hands on their way, but none of them asked what they were up to. She'd long ago left her fear behind and fell into a kind of peaceful daze that followed the rocking of the animal. A sleepless night was catching up with her.

Zeke reined up and turned to look at her. "Does this look like the right place?"

Sarah blinked and looked around. A sandstone bluff stood over a clearing edged by a stand of scrub pines. "Yes, I think this is it." She slowly dismounted, her muscles complained at the unusual activity.

He dismounted and walked over to her. He put a hand on her arm to steady her. "You, okay?"

After a moment, Sarah smiled at him. "Yes, I'm just not used to riding so long. Thanks for the hand, here and back in the stable."

He frowned and dropped his arm. "Don't mention it."

She was saddened at the break in connection. She wanted Zeke to like her, but she understood why he didn't. "You don't like me much, do you, Zeke?"

He took off his hat and slapped it against his leg, making dust fly. He fixed her with a hard glance. "I can't say as I do. You were pretty rough on Rafe. I can't forget it, just like that."

She sighed, but she knew she deserved the condemnation. He didn't realize she'd had to leave in order to guard her heart. "If I were you, I'd feel the same way." She shook off her melancholy and turned away. "Well, this isn't getting the job done. Let's take a look around."

He dropped the reins on the ground, and the horses bent to munch on the grass.

"What exactly are we looking for?" he asked.

Sarah glanced up at the bluff and snapped a photo. She could use it for comparison later.

"I'm not sure." She walked toward the open area. "I guess anything that looks out of order. You know this land. Maybe you can spot something that doesn't look right." She eyed some stacked rocks. "Those rocks were in the slides. The wolves were lying on the ground in front of them."

Zeke glanced up at the bluff and then at the rocks. "This would be a perfect place for an ambush. A feller could lay up on the cliff and have all the time in the world to take pot shots at any wolves that happened by."

She shivered. "Do you think that's what happened?"

She shook off the ominous thought and turned back to the rocks. A dried pool of blood had stained the sand. There were several chipped stones littering the ground. As she bent to pick up a fragment of rock, the sound of a horse cantering their way thundered.

Rafe astride Umbriago.

Zeke turned. "Uh oh. The jig is up."

She grinned at his sour expression. She knew they were both in hot water. "Yup, Zeke, I'd say the sheet is just about to hit the fan."

He gave a dry snort of laughter, and walked toward his horse. "Like you said, I'm going to let you take the heat."

"Chicken."

Rafe stopped next to Zeke's mount. He fixed them both with a steely glare. "What in the name of heaven do you two think you're doing?"

"I just came along to keep her out of trouble, boss. I knew you wouldn't want her running around these parts all alone."

"I'm looking for evidence." Sarah wanted to get all the shouting done so she could get back to work. She didn't have time to tiptoe around Rafe's wounded pride.

He scowled and tipped his hat back. "Don't you think the authorities can do that?"

Put off by his sarcastic tone, she put her hands on her hips. For goodness sakes, she'd gone through the rigors of riding a horse again to rescue him. And he didn't seem to appreciate it one bit. "Obviously, they can't do it properly, or they wouldn't be accusing you of the crime."

Rafe leaned forward in the saddle. "What did you say?"

She frowned at his purposeful denseness. "I said, obviously not, or they wouldn't be accusing you of the crime. All three of us know there's no way you would have done it. Now, come over here. I found something."

Rafe grinned and turned to Zeke. "Why don't you head in now, Zeke? I'll take over from here."

"I can see I'm not needed." Zeke mounted his horse, sparing a smile for Sarah.

She bent down to pick up another fragment when...a shot rang out, pinging against a rock directly in front of her.

Rafe jumped off his horse, shouting, "Get down, Sarah!" He pulled the phone out of his saddlebag and tossed it to Zeke saying, "Call for help, and then get back to the ranch. I'll take care of Sarah."

Sarah hit the dirt, then sneezed the dust out of her nose. What a time for an allergy attack. Another shot ricocheted off the stack of rocks in front of her. She belly-crawled to shelter behind them and let out a scream when something stung her arm.

She twisted around. Rafe circled the trees at a low crouch. He rushed across the clearing, and another shot struck a tree next to his head. She let out a startled cry. He dove for shelter, coming to rest behind her.

She touched his arm. "Are you okay?"

He sat up. "I'm okay, but what about you?"

"I'm fine. What are we going to do? Where's Zeke?"

"He's heading back to the ranch with my phone. He'll call for help. As long as he stays behind the line of trees, he'll be okay."

Another shot pinged off the rock. Sarah pressed herself into Rafe's arms and closed her eyes.

He gritted out, "Come on, sweetheart, we've got to make a run for it. We're sitting ducks here." He pulled her toward him. "Just stay low and go in the direction I point you, okay?"

She glanced at him and knew she could trust him with her life. "What about you?"

"Don't worry about me, honey. I'll be at your back creating a diversion."

No. She frowned. "But you might get shot."

"You will do as I say." He raised an imperious eyebrow. Then, his expression softened, and he bent to kiss her. "Don't worry, Sarah." He joked, "Remember, my word is law on the Double-H. Let's go." He pulled her forward.

She got to her knees and scrambled through the brush.

He yelled and stood, then feinted to the right as a shot rang out.

She did as she was told and kept going, knowing delaying would just put Rafe in more danger. She got to her feet after reaching the safety of the tree line and turned around.

He scrambled out of the underbrush moments later.

"Thank God. I was afraid you were hit."

He hugged her tight. "I'm fine, but I'm glad you were worried about me." He pulled back saying, "We'd better get a move on before he comes looking for us."

He grabbed her hand, and they ran around the trees until they got to Umbriago. He put his hands on her waist and deposited her onto the saddle. Then he mounted behind her.

"What about Bay Rum?" Sarah asked.

"Don't worry about him. He's following Zeke." Rafe gave a twitch of the reins. "Let's get out of here."

Sarah snuggled against Rafe's warmth and tried to ignore the burning pain in her arm. She must have scraped it against the rocks. She groaned when Rafe pulled her tight and the pain intensified.

"What's wrong?" He brought his hand up. It was covered with blood. "You've been hit." He pulled up her sleeve. "Sit forward, sweetheart. I have to take my shirt off. We've got to put pressure on the wound to stop it from bleeding."

Sarah tensed as she pulled away from Rafe, and then relaxed back against his warm chest after he shrugged out of his shirt. He pressed the folded cloth against her arm. The renewed pain made her grit her teeth, but she forced herself to stay calm. She needed to be strong for both of them.

"I'm sorry it hurts, sweetheart," Rafe murmured in her ear.

Sarah was feeling woozy from the motion of the horse and her sleepless night. She closed her eyes. "It doesn't hurt that bad. Do you think we'll be okay?"

Rafe hurried the pace, keeping under the cover of trees. "Don't worry, baby, I won't let anything else hurt you."

She smiled softly and nestled her cheek against his bare chest. She placed a soft kiss on his tanned skin. "It seems funny to be called baby again."

He chuckled. "Should I be jealous? Who else used to call you baby?"

She sighed, recalling faint, sweet, memories. "My Granny Blake, but that was in a different life."

"What do you mean, a different life?"

She winced at the memory. "After my parents were killed in a plane crash, I went to live with Grandfather Maxwell. I never saw Granny again."

"Why not?"

She shook her head. "She died. When I asked about her, Grandfather told me she was dead. Even as bad as he is, he wouldn't lie about something like that."

"What do you mean bad?"

She sighed. "He wasn't a very nice man. You had dealings with him when you were trying to locate me. You saw how he was."

"He was about as cold as an iceberg. I went to the house, and he threatened to get the law on me if I didn't stop trying to contact you."

She smiled. "That sounds like Grandfather all right. By the way, I really am sorry about putting you through the whole mess back then. I thought that you only married me for my connections."

"What?"

His shocked tone made her cringe. "It seemed like a logical conclusion at the time. Of course, now I know it was a lot of bull intended to scare me off."

He frowned. "What do you mean, intended to scare you off?"

"Someone left an anonymous note on our bed. I read it and, together with the blueprint, and then hearing you tell Zeke you were ready to start the conversion? Well, it seemed like a pretty airtight case."

"How could you believe it?" He gazed at her intently.

"I could never win Grandfather's love and approval. There were always strings attached. It seemed normal to have strings attached to yours, too." Seeing his angry expression she added, "I'm sorry."

"Don't fret about it. You just need to save your strength and hang in there for me."

She was left to wonder at his meaning. Could he want her to stay forever?

Chapter Seven

Rafe held Sarah tight as they rode through the brush. She let her head rest on his shoulder.

He found himself praying she would be okay, and who could have left the note for her?

He could hardly believe it was one of his men. Most of them were like family. Tab was like an older brother. They'd grown up together on the Double-H. Zeke was like a second father to him. The newer hands didn't have much access to the house. Could one of them be working for Blackthorn? It hurt to think there might be a traitor in his midst, but he knew he'd have to be on his guard against future incidents.

More importantly, how could Sarah believe he'd married her for her family connections? He'd make it his goal to convince her it wasn't so.

"How are you doing, sweetheart?"

She sighed, nestled against him. "I'm feeling better now that we're almost home. Boy, am I ever glad you came to bawl me and Zeke out. I hate to think of what might have happened otherwise."

He tightened his arm around her shoulders. His hand was still clamped to her wound. From the looks of it, she was losing too much blood. He made for open land and kicked Umbriago into a gallop.

He craned his neck, but didn't see any signs of being followed. Whoever was taking pot shots at them must have backed off. It wasn't hard to guess who that someone was. The cowardly bushwhack fit Blackthorn to a T.

And as soon as Sarah was taken care of, Rafe was personally going to take the man apart.

Sarah put her hand up to cover his. "I'll hold it, Rafe. I'm not helpless."

"Uh-uh, sweetheart. I'm giving the orders around here. You just lie back and let me take care of you."

She sighed as he tucked her head protectively under his chin. Her revelation about her grandfather made him sick. What kind of cold-hearted man would reject the needy child she must have been? It put everything her grandfather might have told her into question, including the fact her maternal grandmother was supposed to be dead.

Rafe intended to do some checking to see if it was true.

He came in sight of the ranch and galloped Umbriago across the pasture. Zeke stood with Bob Wilson and the sheriff. Rafe noted Zeke's relieved smile and the sheriff's questioning look as he brought Umbriago to a halt.

He handed Sarah down to Zeke and slid out of the saddle, then nodded toward Wilson. "Zeke, what did you get him here for? I told you to get the law."

Zeke held Sarah out toward Rafe. "You said to get help. You didn't specify who. Besides, I figure you two have a lot of talking to do."

"Our talking is going to take place in his office Monday morning, not before." Rafe lifted Sarah out of Zeke's arms and strode toward the truck.

Wilson followed them to the pickup. "I came because I got a tip you might be nosing around the area where the wolves were found, Halliday."

"Looks like you had a mite of trouble out there, Rafe," the sheriff added sympathetically.

Rafe gave Wilson a distracted scowl. He knew the man was only doing his job, but right now he was as annoying as a mosquito buzzing in his ear. "I want to get Sarah into town for some medical attention. You two got a problem with that?"

The sheriff said, "Do you want to make out a report when you're in town?"

Rafe shrugged. "There isn't much to report. We were in the clearing where the wolves were found when someone got the drop on us from the bluff. If you two hurry on up there, you might find some evidence. That is, if you really want to find it. Now, if you'll excuse me, I need to get Sarah to the hospital."

She lifted her head off his shoulder. "I don't need any medical attention."

"I say you do, and on the Double-H, my word is law. Remember?" He heard her soft chuckle and said a prayer of thanks that she was going to be all right.

Wilson said, "That's mighty coincidental, you three being attacked where the wolves were found."

Rafe turned to look at him. "You might say that."

Wilson gave him a direct glower. "It would be a good way to divert suspicion from yourself."

Rafe took a step forward. "Why you—"

Zeke stepped between them. "Now Rafe, Bob's only doing his job."

Wilson shrugged. "In my line of work, it pays to be suspicious. Of course, it could also be someone has a grudge against you. Maybe it isn't enough they get you in trouble. Maybe they want to kill you."

Rafe turned back toward the truck. "Don't worry. I'm going to straighten it out myself. We all know who's behind it."

The sheriff said, "You wouldn't have any rash ideas, would you, Rafe?"

Rafe flashed a cool smile his way. "Who, me?"

"You don't have any proof Blackthorn was behind this," the sheriff warned. "Let me and my men take care of it."

Rafe set his jaw. "When my family is threatened, I take action."

"Be reasonable. A physical attack isn't Blackthorn's style. He'd try to run your ranch into the ground, but he wouldn't try to shoot you."

Rafe scowled at the thought, it would mean an unknown assailant was after them. At least with Blackthorn, he knew what kind of a varmint he was dealing with. He put Sarah in the truck, slammed the door, and sprinted around to his side.

"I'll take it under consideration, boys. But right now, I've got more important things to worry about."

He gunned the engine and sped off toward town.

Sarah held her breath as the emergency room doctor examined her arm. He probed the wound gently, making her wince. She glanced at Rafe, who stood grim-faced.

"You can wait outside, Rafe. I don't need you to hold my hand."

"No dice. I'm sticking with you. How's she doing, Mark?"

Dr. Phillips, a tall man with sandy brown hair and bright blue eyes, looked at Rafe. "Don't worry, your wife's going to be okay. I'll get the nurse to clean the area and then I'll put in a few stitches. What exactly happened out there?"

Rafe's jaw tightened. "Some low-down bushwhacker took some pot shots at us. Sarah got hit by one."

Mark shook his head. "Well, she's lucky he wasn't a very good shot." He turned to Sarah. "How long since your last tetanus shot?"

She flinched when a nurse swabbed the area to be stitched. "I'm not sure."

Dr. Phillips picked up a hypodermic needle. "I'm going to give you some anesthetic now. Just take a deep breath, hold still, and pretty soon, you won't feel a thing."

She bit her lip while the needle pricked her skin. She looked at Rafe and noted he was pale. Had he been hurt too?

"Are you okay, Rafe?"

"I'm fine," he said, tightening his jaw and shifting his stance.

Dr. Phillips looked over at him and chuckled. "Pal, you better sit down before you fall down."

Rafe hesitated for a moment before slumping into a chair next to the gurney.

Dr. Phillips grinned at her. "It's always the husbands that are the worse." He bent to put in the stitches then turned to Rafe. "The worst is over now, buddy. Now, all I must do is give her a booster shot, and you're out of here."

She waited for the injection, then jumped down from the exam table. She walked over to Rafe and tugged on his hand to get him to stand. "I told you it wasn't serious."

Rafe put his arm around her. "Not serious, my ass. The doctor said you lost a lot of blood. And you needed stitches."

She glanced at Dr. Phillips, and her cheeks flushed with embarrassment. It was impossible to keep Rafe from speaking his mind. The doctor was one of Rafe's friends. What did he think of them?

Dr. Phillips scribbled out a prescription and ripped it off his pad. He handed it to her with a smile. "I want you to take this antibiotic as a precaution. Make sure you take it all, understand?"

Sarah smiled. Salty-talking, high-handed cowboys were an everyday occurrence for this doctor. "Don't worry, I will."

Rafe took the prescription out of her hand. "Don't worry, Mark. I'll see that she does."

She gave him an exasperated glance as he escorted her out of the Emergency Room. The color was slowly coming back into his cheeks. Who would have thought he would faint at the sight of a needle?

She sighed when she climbed into the rusty old pickup. They could be using her nice Jeep Cherokee. But no, Rafe insisted on rattling around in this contraption. It was a point of pride for him. Her exasperation dissipated as she glanced at him. Bullheaded or not, she owed him her life.

At least she knew she could count on him when the chips were down. If only there were some way she could repay him.

Sarah picked up a stack of plates to set the table for dinner. She turned to walk into the dining room when Rafe intercepted her. He frowned, taking the dishes out of her hands.

"You're supposed to be resting," he growled with determination.

"I did take a nap. I'm all rested." She sighed at his continuing overprotective attitude. "Rafe, you can't go wrapping me in cotton wool. What happened was just a freak accident."

Hiss jaw tightened. "You aren't supposed to do any heavy lifting, and you know it."

She let out an exasperated groan. "I don't call a few plates heavy lifting."

He lifted an eyebrow. "Well, I do." He turned and carried the dishes into the dining room.

She glared at his back. He could be so hardheaded. Sometimes, she just wanted to kick him.

She waited until Rafe was holed up in his study after dinner to go in search of Zeke. Rose was busy planning the next day's shopping, so it was the perfect time to do what she had to do.

Lisa's statement about the rumors of Rafe's financial problems had nagged at her for days. Just how bad a shape were his finances? And Rafe's plan to sell part of the ranch to Jim Barclay only added to her concern. If anyone knew the truth about Rafe's financial difficulties, it would be Zeke.

As she walked near the bunk house, masculine laughter filled the air. She peeked through the window, and a lively card game was going on.

"You looking for someone special?"

Startled, Sarah spun toward the familiar voice.

Tab Whittacker leaned against the side of the building, smoking a cigarette. He gave her a friendly smile.

She let out a relieved breath. "You startled me."

Tab took a draw off his cigarette and tilted his head as he glanced at her through the smoke. "It's a nice night. I thought I'd take a stroll."

"Me, too." Sarah smiled. Thank goodness it wasn't Rafe. She'd have a tough time explaining what she was doing here without tipping him off.

"How's the arm?" He gave a pointed glance at her.

She patted the white bandage that covered the gouge. "I'll live. I guess I was lucky. Things might have turned out differently if Rafe wasn't around."

"I'd say you were fortunate." He pushed away from the wall and ground out his cigarette with the toe of his boot. "These hills can be dangerous for strangers."

She shuddered at the words. She'd always felt comfortable in the wilderness, but Tab's statement filled her with foreboding. "I take it you're pretty familiar with them."

He shrugged and looked toward the big ranch house. "Didn't Rafe tell you?"

"Tell me what?"

"It figures," he said sourly.

"What?"

"Never mind." Tab hooked his thumbs in his pockets and leaned against the house. "I've been here longer than your husband. I was born and raised on the Double-H. My pappy worked for Rafe's daddy. For a while, after Rafe's daddy passed on, I thought I might buy Rafe out. But things didn't work out."

She glanced at his handsome, weather-beaten features, and relaxed when she caught his easy smile. "That's quite a family history. It must be nice to have such deep roots."

He inclined his head. "You might say that. Course, things changed after Rafe took over from his pa."

Sarah wondered whether he meant for the better or worse. "Yes, I suppose they would. Things never stay the same, no matter where you work. I'm sure Rafe is a good boss."

"Yeah, I suppose so. Like I was saying, are you looking for someone special?"

The screen door slapped, and Zeke walked onto the porch.

"Zeke's the one I wanted to talk to."

"Mrs. Halliday?"

Sarah turned back toward Tab. "Yes?"

"There could be rough times ahead, what with your husband accused of a crime. You might want to consider clearing out."

She gaped at him. He had no right to talk to her like that. "It's mine and Rafe's private life, and none of your business. Unless you know something I don't know?"

Tabs lips thinned. "It was just a friendly warning. You being a rich city girl, you just don't fit in here, especially when times are rough for the boss."

She gave him a lingering glance as he walked away. Just what was behind his friendly warning? A dislike of her or was he just protecting his boss?

She walked over to Zeke, who was sitting on one of the porch rockers. "Good evening, Zeke. I wonder if we could talk?"

He patted the seat next to him. "Why don't you sit a spell. Rafe told me you were all right. He get that right?"

Sarah leaned back and rocked in the chair. The breeze that lifted the wisps of hair off her neck was refreshing. "I'm fine. It was just a scratch."

"Still, I don't like it," Zeke grumbled.

She smiled and looked at his wizened face. "I'm not too happy about it myself, but there's something else on my mind tonight."

He stopped rocking and glanced at her. "And just what might that be?"

She looked around. The porch was deserted, only motes of dust danced in the twilight. She remembered Rose had felt someone snooping when they'd talked about Sarah's plans to track down the site. A person couldn't be too careful because someone might be listening.

"I heard about Rafe having trouble securing a loan to open his dude ranch. He's considering selling off a parcel of the ranch for cash."

Zeke scowled. "Where'd you hear that? Has Rose been a-gossipin'?"

Sarah grinned at the ornery way he said Rose's name. "I've got my sources, and they're private." She had no desire to tell him of Lisa's confidences.

He harrumphed and leaned back in his rocker. He looked off into the distance. "You figuring on leaving him again if it's true?"

She was saddened by the tense set of his body. "No, you're not going to get rid of me that quickly." She watched his shoulders relax. "So, give. Is it true?"

He studied her. "Why do you want to know? Are you plannin' to help him out? A rich gal like you probably has more money than she knows how to spend."

She leaned back and started rocking again. "I'm not the rich woman you think I am. I walked away from my grandfather's money years ago, and I never looked back."

"Just like you ran out on Rafe," he said sourly. "You kind of got the habit of running when the times get tough, don't you?"

She'd have to confide in Zeke if she wanted his cooperation. "The reasons are totally different. I left my grandfather, the man who raised me, because there were too many strings attached to his affections. I left Rafe because I thought he married me for my family connections. Being kin to a hotel tycoon wouldn't hurt a man who wanted to open a dude ranch."

"Of all the damned fool notions, where'd you ever get an idea like that?"

"I found a note on the bed after our wedding explaining it. When I went to ask Rafe if it was true, I overheard him talking to you about the dude ranch, jumped to conclusions, and ran out, just like you said. If it makes any difference to you, I now know that the note was a lie."

"Well, it's about time. So, what're you plannin' to do about it?"

"Aside from the fact that Rafe couldn't blow me out of here with dynamite, I'm going to rescue his ranch. I've got some money saved up and I'm going to use it to start up the dude ranch. All I need to know from you is how much capital he needs to start the operation."

Zeke shook his head. "He'd never take it from you."

She nodded. "I know how stubborn he is, but I could do it on the sly. He'd never know until it was too late to stop me."

He pushed to his feet. "I don't think he'd cotton to the idea. So, you aren't going to get nothin' out of me. I don't want to talk no more."

She stood, narrowing her eyes. He wasn't going to wiggle out of helping her that easily. She was prepared to fight dirty to rescue the man she loved.

"You tell me what you know, or I'll tell everyone I saw you smooching Rose after dinner tonight."

He spat on the ground. "You been spying on me?"

She grinned, unrepentant. "I was in the right place at the right time."

He looked down. "The boss told me he needs fifty grand to make improvements before he opens. He hasn't got the money, and the bank turned him down. So, now he's fixin' to sell off some acreage to Jim."

Sarah thought about the nest egg she'd been building to start her own production company. It would be just enough.

Sarah dialed her cousin Pipi's private number. She glanced around warily to make sure she wouldn't be overheard. The kitchen was deserted.

"Hello."

Sarah sighed with relief. "Pipi, it's Sarah. Listen, because I need a big favor from you."

"You never ask for favors so it must be something important."

"Yes, it's vital."

"Name it, and it's yours."

She gave another glance over her shoulder. "I need you to take the funds out of my private account and wire them to the Shelbyville Bank for me."

"Okay, how much?"

"All of it. There should be sixty thousand dollars, all told."

"All of it! For what?"

"I'm going to help Rafe out of some financial problems."

"Are you crazy? What are you trying to do? Pay him off to soothe his pride?"

"No, I'm not crazy. I'm in love." She'd known Pipi would kick up a fuss, but she wasn't about to knuckle under. "Rafe has no idea what I'm up to. If he knew I was planning to finance his dude ranch, he'd be furious."

"Why don't you just ask Grandfather to put his ranch under the Maxwell Hotel Banner. They'd give him the seed money."

Sarah tensed at the thought. "You know better than that, cousin. I don't want to be linked to that man in any way. I'm going to help Rafe myself."

Pipi sighed, then said begrudgingly, "Well, if you've made up your mind, I don't suppose my arguments are going to dissuade you. You always were stubborn. I think that's why you and Grandfather were always at loggerheads."

"Yes, I have made up my mind." Sarah chose to ignore the comparison even though she knew it was true.

"In love, huh." Pipi grumped. "I thought you were going there to set things right, not fall under his spell again."

"You make him sound like a hypnotist. He's my Western Romeo, and helping him out is my way of paying him back."

"For what?"

Sarah gritted her teeth. She should have kept her mouth shut. "He saved my life," she said reluctantly.

"What?" Pipi screeched.

Sarah brushed the hair back behind her ear. "Keep calm, Pipi. I'm okay."

"I'm coming out there to get you," Pipi shouted.

She frowned. "Well, I'm not leaving. Don't worry about me. It was just some nut taking pot shots. Rafe has been taking good care of me."

Pipi sighed. "He is, huh?"

Sarah frowned at the doubting tone. "Yes, he is. So, now it's my turn to take care of him."

Chapter Eight

Rafe savored the last sip of his breakfast coffee. It was Monday morning, and all of the men were already at work, while he was lingering at the table, putting off the inevitable meeting with Wilson. How would Sarah react if he were actually charged with shooting the wolves? She'd said she believed him, but did she really?

He would know soon enough because he was due in Wilson's office in an hour. No doubt, if he didn't show, they'd send the sheriff out to arrest him.

He stood and walked into the kitchen where Sarah was helping Rose with the dishes.

She glanced up sharply at his approach. He could see the anxiety in her eyes, and it made him tense. What was she thinking? Then, he focused on the white bandage on her arm, and his gut twisted. She'd been shot while trying to prove his innocence. That told him she trusted him.

How could he have guessed this summer would bring such a roller coaster of emotions?

He walked up to her and pulled her into his arms. "Don't worry, sweetheart, it will be okay."

"If only I could have gathered some evidence," she whispered while caressing his back.

He luxuriated in her touch for a moment. This was right and real. "We were rudely interrupted, remember? There wasn't time to get any evidence. Besides, Wilson and the sheriff went up there. If there was anything to find, I'm sure they discovered it."

She nestled in his arms. "I'm sure they're going to realize that it's all a mistake."

"I don't want you to worry." He hugged her tighter. Her belief in him meant everything.

She nodded. "I know it's all going to blow over." She stepped out of his embrace, obviously noting he looked like a man going off to face a firing squad. "It'll just take me a minute to get ready."

"For what?"

"I'm going with you." She grabbed her purse and walked toward the door.

He frowned. "I don't think that's a very good idea, Sarah. They didn't ask you to come in."

She stood tall in the face of his repressive attitude. He didn't want her involved, but there was no way she would back down. "Tough. I want to be with you. Don't worry. I won't get in the way. Besides, I have some business to do in town later."

"What business do you have to do?"

"There are a few items I forgot to buy at Daley's Camera Shop last time."

"I could pick up any photography supplies you need," he offered.

Sarah frowned like she was fumbling for an excuse. "No thanks, you wouldn't know what to get. Besides, you owe me. You did confiscate my keys, leaving me stranded."

"Okay, I guess you can come," he said grudgingly.

Sarah sat in an uncomfortable tweed chair in a corner of the room while Rafe sat in front of Bob Wilson's desk. Rafe put on a front of confidence, but she knew he was as tense as a canary in a room full of cats.

Rafe cast a frustrated glance her way.

"How do you like that?" Rafe grumbled. "Here I am on time for my appointment, and he keeps me waiting for half an hour."

Sarah was worried, too, but strove to hide it. She needed to be supportive, no matter what happened. He flashed her the I-don't-give-a-damn smile of a man going before a firing squad.

She twined her fingers together to keep her hands from shaking. "Try to be patient, Rafe. Bob did say he was waiting for some lab results, and it would be worth our while to wait."

He sighed and leaned back in the chair. "At least you believe I'm innocent. Now we just have to convince the law." He ran his fingers through his hair. "Waiting stinks. I've never been good at it."

She smiled at his petulant, little boy tone. "Oh, I don't know. You waited six months for me."

He cast her an intense look. "That's different. You were worth waiting for."

It was his first declaration of affection, and she hugged it to her like a security blanket.

Wilson entered the room. "I'm sorry to keep you waiting so long. Ballistics had to fax me some info on the shell casings we found on the bluff yesterday."

"And...?" Rafe prompted.

Wilson slapped a sheet of paper on his desk. "The shots that hit your wife came from a rifle. A thirty ought six."

"There are plenty of those around. Heck, we've got several of them around the ranch." He looked from the paper to Wilson. "Hey, what about Blackthorn, does he own a rifle?"

Wilson smiled grimly. "He did, but he reported it stolen a week ago."

"It figures." Rafe scowled. "Blackthorn's not stupid. If he were going to do the shooting, he'd claim that he didn't have the gun."

Wilson frowned. "Rafe, we checked. Nevell Blackthorn was working on bank business when your wife was shot."

"Has he got any witnesses to back him up?" Rafe asked sharply.

Wilson sighed. "He doesn't need witnesses, Rafe, you do. You're the one accused of a crime."

"What about the rock fragments?" Sarah asked. "And the bullets from the wolves? You've had plenty of time to check on them."

Wilson turned to look at her. "They came from the same gun, ma'am."

Sarah smiled. "Then you know Rafe is innocent. Rafe was with me when the second shots were fired."

"That's true, but you two could have set this up as a ruse." Wilson shrugged. "Or Rafe could have persuaded a pal to take a shot at you."

"What a stupid thing to say." Sarah stood and stepped toward the men. She put a hand on Rafe's shoulder. "My husband wouldn't do such an underhanded thing. I have complete faith in him."

Wilson nodded. "My gut feeling says he's been set up, but I have to check the weapons on the ranch to be sure."

She glanced at Rafe. The satisfied smile he gave her took her breath away. Apparently, her trust meant a great deal to him.

He refocused Wilson. "What do you want me to do, Bob?"

Wilson sat in his desk chair. "Let's work out the details."

"I'll do whatever I have to do to get this cleared up. I want this solved as much as you do."

She smiled. It was going to be all right. "Rafe, while you two talk this over, I'm going to go take care of the business I talked about. How about if we meet at the cafe in an hour?"

"All right, sweetheart. I'll see you then."

She left the courthouse and headed at a brisk pace to the bank. She didn't have much time to do what she had to do.

She opened the front door of the bank and walked up to the teller's counter. "I have a transfer of funds that's supposed to be here this morning."

"And your name?"

"Sarah Halliday. I have a picture ID from my old bank. Of course, it's still under my maiden name of Maxwell." She slid her bank card and driver's license from her purse.

The teller smiled and handed Sarah the cashier's check. "Would you like to start an account with us today, Mrs. Halliday?"

"Yes, a joint account. I need to make sure my husband has access to this money." She endorsed the back of the check and slid it across to the teller.

A large, tanned hand dropped down on the check, preventing the teller from picking it up. She gaped up at the space behind Sarah's left ear. Sarah didn't have to look behind her to know who it was.

"Wilson and I finished our business a little early, wife," Rafe said dryly. "Isn't it a good thing I saw you in here on my way to the cafe?"

She sucked in a breath and turned around. "Rafe, I can explain."

"There's no need to explain, Sarah. I understand perfectly."

He smiled at the teller, but it didn't reach his eyes. He was obviously furious.

"My wife has changed her mind," Rafe bit out. "She'll be keeping her precious money."

"But—"

"Button it," Rafe snapped. He picked up the check, turned, and strode toward the door.

Sarah rolled her eyes and followed him. There was nothing worse than a male with a wounded ego, and Rafe's pride had just been trampled on by her money.

He jerked open the driver's door to his truck, and she dashed to the passenger side. As she hopped in, she cast a glance his way. His jaw was set. He probably did have a right to be angry, but he didn't have to be such a jerk about it. She was doing this for them, after all.

He pulled out of the parking space and started driving toward home.

"What was that all about?" Rafe bit out. "Payment for services rendered?"

"I don't know what you mean." She stared at his rigid profile, totally confused by the statement.

He cast an annoyed glance her way. "Don't play dumb, Sarah. You know exactly what I mean. Payment for a nice roll in the hay, making love, sex. I might be good, honey, but I'm not for sale."

She gaped at him as his words penetrated. "Is that what you think?" It had never entered her mind he would think such a thing. "That's ridiculous."

"Hell yes, it's ridiculous. I'm not some gigolo you can buy with your wealth. What I gave, I gave freely. So, you can keep your blasted money." He pushed the check across the cracked, blue vinyl upholstery as if it was a piece of trash. "I don't need it."

"Don't need it or too proud to take it?" Sarah snapped back.

Sarah watched Bob Wilson drive off with Rafe's rifles. He'd also taken the ones Rafe had picked up in the bunk house.

She was in a foul mood because of Rafe's stupid macho pride. He'd turned what could have been a beautiful gesture on her part into a disaster. What did he expect her to do, stand back while he floundered financially? Why should she watch him sell off part of his birthright when she had the means to save him?

Eventually, she hoped to change his mind and open him up to sharing everything with her. It was the only way to make their marriage truly work. But she was just too steamed to approach him for the time being.

Right now, she needed to lose herself in her work. It was the one area she still felt competent. She was going to get busy and complete her series.

She walked into the kitchen, carrying her camera and supplies. Rafe was at the sink, getting a drink of water. She watched the play of muscles in his back as he lifted the glass, and frowned. Why did he have to be such a big, macho cowboy? Couldn't the man bend a little?

He drained the glass and put it on the counter. He turned to look at her and leaned back against the cabinet, crossing his arms over his broad chest. "Where do you think you're going?"

She flipped her hair over her shoulder. "This is still a free country, cowboy. I don't have to stand here and be interrogated."

A nerve twitched in his jaw. "Yes, this is a free country. But there's an assassin out there, remember? It's not safe to go wandering around."

He was right, and it irritated her to no end. Still, she couldn't stand to be cooped up all day. "He missed, so he must not be a very good assassin."

He arched an eyebrow. "He didn't miss the wolves."

She recalled the revolting slides and shuddered.

"So, I repeat, where are you going?" he asked patiently.

"I need to get some work done. I have a deadline to meet." At his implacable stare, she added, "Besides, I can't handle just sitting around. And I promise I won't go anywhere near the bluff."

"Let's just hope the assassin doesn't think the same thing," he said dryly.

She frowned at his sarcasm. "Quit trying to scare me."

"I'm not trying to do anything. You're scared because there's a real possibility of danger. You can't go alone, so if you go, I go, too."

She bit her lip. The last thing she wanted was for him to tag along. How could she get any work done with him looking over her shoulder?

"You can't spare the time from work," she protested.

He pushed away from the countertop. "Don't tell me what I can't do, wife. I'm still boss around here. Where do you want to work?"

She sighed. It looked like she was going to have a tagalong whether she wanted him or not. "I'd like to take some pictures by the lake. I figured I could get some good shots of wildlife around there."

He nodded. "Yeah, you probably could, but it's pretty far out. If we go this late in the day, we'll have to camp out. Unless, of course," he said humorlessly, "you're afraid to be alone with me."

"I'm not afraid of anything." She bit her lip. She was quite uneasy at the prospect. In their surly moods they'd probably be at each other's throat the whole time.

Still, she could get some beautiful evening shots and she did have camping equipment out in her Jeep. "Okay, let's go for it. I've got all the equipment we need in my car."

"Fine, I think we could use some time alone." He turned and walked out the back door. "Let's go."

She relaxed at his statement. She could get him to see her side of things.

He opened the rear door of her Jeep, then slipped her keys back into his hip pocket.

She frowned at the telling action. He wouldn't give an inch.

She pulled out her bedroll. Underneath was a spare one. They were both attached to backpacks. She turned to Rafe. "Have you ever done any hiking?"

He took one of the packs from her. "Don't worry. I'll keep up." He picked up two canteens. "I'll go into the kitchen and fill these. What about food?"

"I have a week's worth of freeze-dried food in the packs. We won't starve. I'll find Rose and tell her we'll be gone while you're getting the water."

Rafe hobbled around the clearing, setting up camp while Sarah scouted around for photo opportunities. He had to admit, hiking in cowboy boots wasn't the smartest thing he'd ever done. But after they'd started, there was no way he was going to admit it. Sarah had known, anyhow. He could see it in the twinkle in her eyes whenever she'd looked his way.

He wiped the trickle of sweat out of his eyes, and looked off into the distance where she was checking out an ant hill. He grinned when she loosened up and smiled. She was just like an excited little kid when she worked. It showed a passionate nature reflected upon other areas in her life.

Such as her uninhibited passion in bed. The errant thought caused a tightening in his groin. He was supposed to be mad at her, not thinking about taking her to bed.

Would two fit in the sleeping bag? He rolled it out and smiled. If they slept on top of each other, maybe.

He turned and walked away from the task to gather firewood, his thoughts growing dark as he thought about her attempt to buy him off. He wanted her, not her money. Would she ever get that through her stubborn little head? But something even worse worried him. Was this pay off just a preliminary to her leaving him? He cast a frustrated glance her way. She was snapping a shot of an eagle in flight. She was like the bird, free and alone, but he wouldn't rest until he had her tethered to his side.

He had the fire going and dinner cooking when she made her way back to camp. She plopped on the ground, smiling when he handed her a cup of coffee.

"Thanks," she murmured, and took a sip.

He sat next to her. "It's been a long day. I figured you could use a cup. Dinner will be ready soon."

"I think I'm too tired to eat." She closed her eyes and sighed.

He reached over and began rubbing her knotted shoulder muscles. The tension seeped out of her. "You have to take your antibiotic on a full stomach."

She opened her eyes. "I forgot about those. I didn't bring them."

He pulled the bottle out of his shirt pocket. "I knew you would, so I got them out of the bathroom before we left."

"Figures." She gave a pointed glance at his boots. "I should have warned you about hiking in cowboy boots, sorry."

He chuckled. "That's okay, sweetheart. I'll live."

"Whatever you're cooking smells good enough to eat."

He grinned. "Freeze-dried beef stew, and applesauce for dessert."

"Yummy." She took a deep whiff. "You're going to spoil me. It's nice to have a helper along on a shoot. I'm not used to such luxury."

He rose and stirred the stew. "Sweetheart, if you play your cards right, you could have this kind of help all the time."

She smiled. "I might just take you up on that offer, cowboy."

He could have cheered, but instead, he got out two tin plates and dished their stew. She was moving toward forever, he realized.

After dinner, She started to gather their dishes, but he took them out of her hands. "I'll do that while you wash up. We want to keep that wound clean, remember?"

"I'll take you up on that offer. I think I'll go to the lake for a dip."

He turned away and grinned. She didn't know it, but he planned to join her shortly. This camping trip was serendipity. They were both a heck of a lot safer out here where absolutely nobody knew where they were. And it gave him time to cement their relationship.

He finished the dishes, grabbed a towel, and headed toward the lake.

He stopped at the water's edge. The sunset painted the water with rainbow colors, and highlighted Sarah's beauty. As she turned toward him, droplets of water looked like diamonds sprinkled over her fair skin. Her dark green eyes were fathomless and her full lips curved into a siren's smile.

"I wondered if you would join me."

"No power on Earth would stop me." Rafe peeled off his shirt and kicked off his boots.

"Good."

Her eyes widened when he slipped out of his jeans and briefs. He strode toward the water. "Do you want me, sweetheart?"

She grinned. "More than you could ever know, cowboy."

He looked at his hard flesh. "Oh, I think I've got a pretty good idea." They both laughed at the private joke. He closed the distance between them with a few long strides and bent to kiss her parted lips.

She pulled away. "It seems like the only time we get in sync is after we fight."

He traced a teardrop that trickled down her soft cheek. "Don't cry, sweetheart. We're both going through some tough adjustments now. Things will get better."

"I hope so because sometimes I hurt so bad inside, I want to die. Other times, I get so mad at you I want to kick you."

"Believe me, sweetheart, the feeling is mutual." He scooped her up with a chuckle. He kissed her mouth as her slippery body slid across his. Her breasts were tempting mounds pressing against his chest. Rafe's knees began to shake from excitement as he walked toward the bank. "We better take this on dry land before we both drown."

She laughed. "By all means. I'm not ready for a watery grave."

He carried her toward the campsite.

"But what about our clothes?"

"Don't worry about it, sweetheart. I'll go back for them later." He reached the camp and bent to lay her on top of her sleeping bag. The firelight cast shadows on her body, highlighting her curves. "You're beautiful, Sarah."

She reached up to trace a pattern on his chest. "Thank you. Every woman wants to be considered beautiful by the man she...loves."

He was exultant. She'd said aloud she loved him. He bent to kiss her, positioning himself on her so she could feel how much he wanted her. She parted her legs and he nestled between them.

"I need you, Sarah," he murmured before moving down to suck at her nipples. They were like new strawberries in his mouth, sweet and hard.

She gasped, arching firmly into his mouth. "That feels wonderful. I've been aching for your touch."

He smiled and moved down her body, scattering kisses across her taut abdomen. He stopped to dip his tongue in her navel, and she arched toward him. He chuckled at her surprised reaction and moved lower to press kisses on the insides of her thighs. He found the heart of her and stroked her with his tongue. She pressed against him whimpering. Emboldened, Rafe continued circling that little bead, teasing it until she screamed in ecstasy, arching toward him.

Then, she eased. He pressed kisses on her thighs moving back up to join her.

"Why did you do that, Rafe? I wanted to feel that when we made love."

"And you will, sweet Sarah. Just lie back and let it happen." He nibbled at her neck and cupped her breast, finessing the nipple. It instantly beaded to his touch. "You see?"

She moaned when he bent down to flick his tongue across her nipple. "Yes, I guess it is possible."

He moved to the other breast and placed his hand between her thighs. He traced slowly between the damp petals until he reached her bud.

Her legs thrashed as she opened for him.

The scent of their love was heavy in the air, and he triumphed in it. She reached out to touch him, cupping him in her hand.

He pressed himself into her hot palm, but when he almost lost control, he pulled away. He settled between her thighs, pressing the tip of his shaft against her heat. Unable to wait any longer, he surged into her.

She moved against him, wrapping her legs around his hips. "Oh, Rafe, that feels so right," she cried out in a voice raw with emotion.

He surged into her once, twice, three times, and she climaxed.

Undone by her passionate cry, Rafe followed her into bliss with a hoarse shout of love.

Chapter Nine

Something tickled Sarah's nose. She wiggled it against a warm furry pillow, opened her eyes, and realized she was sleeping with her head cushioned on Rafe's broad chest. She raised her head and realized she was halfway lying on him as they both nestled inside her sleeping bag.

She yawned and then grinned. She might not remember falling asleep last night, but she'd never forget their long, passionate night of lovemaking.

She cautiously unzipped the sleeping bag, trying not to rouse him. She smiled again. The poor guy would probably be full of aches and pains when he woke up. She wasn't exactly light as a feather.

The zipper buzzed noisily as she eased off him and lay at his side. She leaned up on one elbow and gazed wondrously at the man she loved. Her gaze stopped on that part of his anatomy that had pleasured her last night. In the early morning light, it was just a shadow of its former self, but as she looked, it started to grow.

"Taking inventory, sweetheart?"

"I just wanted to make sure we hadn't done any damage last night."

He pulled her into his arms. "And do I pass inspection, wife?"

"You'll do." She nuzzled his neck. He tasted wonderful, sweet and salty at the same time. "You know, I could get used to this." She sighed blissfully when he caressed her breast.

"I aim to see you do." He rolled onto his back, taking her with him.

She straddled him, momentarily astounded by the rapid change of position. "Don't tell me it's time for another riding lesson?"

He groaned. "That's terrible, sweetheart, but since this is a truly wonderful morning, you get to be in charge. I'm all yours."

She smiled when he reached between her thighs to touch her softly. She couldn't help moaning at the exquisite pleasure his touch brought. The breeze ruffled her hair as she arched up to give him better access to what he so ardently sought.

She reached back to touch his hot velvet shaft, reveling in her ability to excite him. There was magic between them. He loved her. He'd yelled it out last night at his climax, though he hadn't seemed aware.

She moved back, positioning herself above him, and slowly lowered herself onto him. She moved easily, filling herself with his love, slowly, exquisitely.

"You're in control this morning, sweetheart," Rafe husked. "Do with me what you will."

"Don't worry, cowboy, I'll take extra special care of you." She loved the intense look of passion on his face. She watched his expression change as she began to move. His dark hooded gaze burned with excitement.

All too soon, her own passion overwhelmed her.

She moved raggedly against him, her breathing rapid. Her thighs trembled as their sweet friction started a brush fire inside of her.

He cupped her hips, gentling her motions.

She gasped as she rubbed against him, feeling the sweet muscular contractions of her climax wash over her. She was aware of his blissful cry as he joined her. She collapsed against him.

She lay on top of him while she caught her breath. "We're right back where we started this morning."

"Was I a comfortable cushion, sweetheart?"

She raised her head and looked at him, feeling herself flush. "Sorry about that."

"Sorry? Are you crazy? I loved every minute of it. It's not every night I get to cradle you all night long." He brushed her hair back from her eyes. "So, what's on the agenda for today?"

"I'd like to get in a couple of hours of work before we head back." She rolled off him and sat up. He looked more relaxed than she'd ever seen him before. "That is, if it's okay with you."

Rafe sat up also. "It's fine with me, on one condition."

"Oh yeah, what's that?"

"That you give me a morning kiss."

His eyes glittered as she bent toward him. Nothing could spoil this wonderful morning. His lips brushed warmly against hers. She kissed him back, feeling the sweetness seep all the way down to her toes.

She pulled away and laughed. "If we don't cut this out, I'll never get any work done."

"So? Who wants to work?"

Sarah stood and smiled. "I do, cowboy, so let's get cracking."

Rafe rolled up Sarah's sleeping bag. He breathed deeply and smiled. He could still smell the traces of her scent and the perfume she wore. Things were going well, better than well. He'd told her he loved her last night, and he didn't regret it one bit. It was a new sensation because he'd never believed in that kind of hearts and flowers stuff. Sarah had made him a believer.

Still, he had to make it clear to her he wasn't going to be placated by her money. After all, she'd thought he'd married her for her family connections. How would she feel if he actually took the money she offered? It would give her too easy an out.

No, it was going to be tight, but he'd solve his financial problems by himself. He hated to part with any of the Double-H, but when it came down to preserving their future, he was prepared to go through with it.

He stuffed the clothes he'd retrieved from the beach into his backpack and tied it securely. He slipped the pack onto his back, picked up Sarah's, and headed for the rise where she was scouting for shots.

As he headed toward the sun, his thoughts returned to their lovemaking. Maybe he'd give Rose the night off so he and Sarah could have a cozy dinner for two. He smiled. It was just the kind of thing she would love.

He crested the rise and looked around. He didn't see her anywhere. Where could she have gone? She said she'd be here taking some shots of the cliffs.

Then he spotted a still, dark object lying in the tall grass, several hundred feet away. Maybe she'd dropped some of her equipment. He told himself he was just worrying for nothing, but his footsteps hurried toward the object anyway.

He drew closer, and saw it was Sarah, crumpled like rag doll in the grass.

Heart lurching in his chest, he knelt beside her, touching her warm, motionless arm. "Sarah, are you okay?"

There was no reply. He felt for broken bones, and then carefully turned her over. She gave a tiny moan, but her eyelids remained closed.

What was the matter with her? Was she shot? He couldn't see any wounds. He brushed the hair back from her forehead and his hand came away with blood.

Looking closer, he found a gash with a deep purple bruise underneath her hairline. He leaned in, placing his ear near her nose. Her sweet breath came slow and shallow into his ear.

"Sarah, sweetheart, can you hear me?" There was no response. Her face was so pale. How long had she been like this? She must have fallen and hit her head.

He looked around, but didn't see any stumps of rocks nearby, just grass.

It hit him like a sucker punch. Someone had attacked her.

His jaw tightened as he looked around anew. Whoever had done it was gone.

Damn it, he'd thought they were safe, otherwise he never would have let her go off on her own. This was all his fault. He should have anticipated the unexpected attack. He should have taken better care of her.

He shrugged the backpack off his shoulders and yanked out his cellular. He dialed the number for the local rescue service. The wait for an answer seemed like an eternity.

"Shelbyville nine-one-one, how can I direct your call?" a businesslike female voice asked.

"This is Rafe Halliday from the Double-H. I need paramedics right away. My wife has a severe head injury. We're camped out just one mile east of Jersey Lake."

"I just dispatched the Rescue Service. They'll be there as soon as possible, Mr. Halliday. In the meantime, stay on the line with me. I need to ask you some questions."

"Fine," Rafe said tightly. "Just please hurry them up."

"Please remain calm, sir. They'll be there soon. How did the injury occur?"

"Somebody bashed her on the head," Rafe said harshly, through gritted teeth. His stomach convulsed at the image, and he thought he was going to be sick.

"Are you sure?"

"Yes." He reached down to touch Sarah's cheek. "Send the sheriff, too."

"Do you know who attacked your wife?"

"I don't know for sure. I found her lying on the ground, unconscious." He stopped to take a calming breath. "But I have my suspicions," Rafe continued. Nevell Blackthorn would be one sorry man when Rafe got his hands on him.

"I'm going to assist you by phone until the paramedics arrive. Is your wife having any trouble breathing?"

"Her breathing seems to be kind of shallow, but I guess she's doing okay that way. The main problem is she's bleeding a lot. There's a big gash on her forehead."

"Mr. Halliday, I need you to apply gentle pressure to the wound to stop the bleeding. Do you have a clean cloth to place on the wound?"

"There's a clean towel in my backpack. Hold on a second and I'll get it." He searched around the contents of the pack and tugged out the towel. He never used it last night. "I've got it."

"Okay, Mr. Halliday, you're doing great. Just fold the towel into a square and use it to apply gentle pressure to the head. Remember we don't know what kind of damage might be underneath, so you need to be careful."

"Right," he said calmly when he was really shaking in his boots. The thought of a skull fracture or brain damage had him terrified.

If he lost her, he wouldn't want to live. Sarah meant everything to him. She'd finally taught him how to love.

Rafe paced the hall outside the Emergency Room. Why in blazes didn't they tell him anything? It seemed like hours had gone by since they'd arrived by ambulance.

Sarah had been whisked into the trauma bay while he had been shoved back into the waiting room. They'd even tried to keep him out of the ambulance, but he'd bullied his way on board. This was all his fault, and no one was going to make him leave her side until he knew she was going to be okay.

He couldn't stand the agony of not knowing what was happening. He quit pacing and stopped near the window. The sun still shone brightly, but his world was dark with fear and rage. How dare the slimy skunk lay a hand on her. This time nothing would save Blackthorn from his revenge, no matter what the consequences were.

She'd looked so pale and lifeless lying on the gurney. He didn't think he could bear it if anything happened to her. His gut twisted at the mind-numbing thought.

He'd brought her nothing but trouble this summer. It was his own damned love-blind fault for putting her in danger. Maybe she had been smart when she'd left him in the first place.

Footsteps came down the hall, and he turned to look.

Bob Wilson walked toward him. His face looked haggard, and his pace was slow.

Bob stopped next to Rafe and slipped his hands into his pockets. "How's she doing?"

Rafe shrugged and tightened his jaw. "They haven't told me anything yet. They won't even let me in there, but maybe it's just as well. I'd only be in the way. She's having a CAT scan right now so we should know something soon."

Bob put a hand on his shoulder. "I'll wait with you. But let's have a seat, I'm bushed."

Rafe walked with him to a row of green vinyl chairs in the waiting room and sat. It struck him as odd that Bob had showed up now.

"Hey, what are you doing here? Why aren't you at the crime scene with the sheriff's deputies?"

Bob stretched his legs out. "They've got things well under control, and I've already done my part. I thought I'd stop by and fill you in on some good news."

"Oh yes, I could use some good news right now. What is it?"

Bob grinned. "We got the guy."

Rafe relaxed and leaned back in the chair. It *was* good news. "Blackthorn?" he asked sourly.

"Not quite."

Rafe frowned at the enigmatic answer. He'd be damned if Blackthorn were going to get away with this. "What do you mean, *not quite*?"

"He had help," Bob said tightly. "A man on the inside at your ranch worked with him."

"Who? I'll tear the traitor apart." Rafe's jaw set firmly. He thought he could trust all his hands. No wonder they got the drop on them so easily.

Bob shrugged. "Too late. We already took them both in. We got a make on the rifle this afternoon. It belongs to Travis Cain."

Rafe's jaw dropped open. It was the last name he expected to hear. "Are you sure about that, Bob? He's just a green kid I hired on for the summer. What motive could he have to try to kill Sarah?"

Bob's lips thinned as he scowled. "He's Nevell Blackthorn's nephew, that's why. Didn't you check his references?"

Rafe winced. He'd just taken Travis's word. "What references? He looked strong enough and claimed to have experience. I would have found out soon enough if he were lying about that. He fit the bill." He looked at Bob. "That means Blackthorn was behind it all."

"It looks that way. Travis has admitted to spying for his uncle while he's been at the ranch. You know, giving him inside information and pulling a few pranks. You ought to have seen his gear. He's got some sophisticated electronic equipment. He said he agreed to do it because his uncle was going to pay for his next year of college. But he claims he didn't attack Sarah or shoot the wolves."

"Oh yeah? Then where was he this morning when Sarah was hurt?" Rafe's eyes narrowed.

Bob shrugged. "He said he went for a long walk, that he felt bad for what he'd been doing, spying on you and all. He said he was considering giving it up."

Rafe's jaw tightened. "That sounds pretty lame to me. Has he got any witnesses to back him up?"

Bob shook his head. "No."

"Good. I want to see them both pay for what they did. Blackthorn always thought he was above the law. I mean to make him see he's no better than anybody else. I want the son-of-a-bitch to fry."

"Don't worry, charges are already being brought against them for attempted murder. There's no way he's going to wiggle out of this one. The jerk is already complaining about false arrest, but we've got him dead to rights."

Rafe sighed and looked down. "So, my phones were bugged. No wonder he always seemed to be one jump ahead of me."

Bob nodded. "Yeah, it was a pretty high-tech setup. The kid's a computer major in college."

"Rafe?" Doctor Phillips stood in the doorway.

Rafe turned to look at Mark, who strode toward him.

Rafe tensed, bracing himself for the worst. The painful reality of the situation was like a slap in the face. "How is Sarah doing?"

"I think she's going to be okay, buddy. She's one lucky lady." Mark sat down across from them. "The CAT scan was negative. There's no fracture, no bleeding in the brain. She just has a simple concussion. Now, all we must do is wait for her to wake up."

"How long is that going to take?" Rafe asked.

"That's hard to say. Head injuries are tricky. But I think she'll regain consciousness soon."

Rafe let out the breath he was holding. "Thank God."

"Cheer up, Rafe. At least you didn't have to watch me put in the stitches this time."

Rafe grimaced. Two attacks against Sarah were two too many. He couldn't put her in that kind of danger again. Blackthorn had long tentacles.

Mark glanced at Bob. "Do you think she was hit by the same guy that shot at her last week?"

Bob nodded. "Yes, but we got him this time."

Mark shook his head. "Somebody sure had it in for her."

"It was Blackthorn," Rafe said.

Mark nodded. "I wondered. You two never did get along, even back in school. I remember when you made quarterback on the high school football team and he wound up sitting the bench for most of the season. Still, you wouldn't think an old rivalry would drive him to attempt murder."

"I think the guy's got a screw loose myself," Bob said.

Mark shrugged. "It sure seems that way." He turned back to Rafe. "We'll want to keep Sarah here under observation for a few days. We'll be moving her up to her room in a few minutes. The nurse will come out to get you first."

"Thanks, Mark."

Bob patted Rafe on the shoulder. "Well, that's dandy news, Rafe. It's good to hear your wife is going to be okay."

He sighed in relief. "It sure is."

"Oh, before I go." Bob pulled a note out of his shirt pocket. "I did that checking you asked me to. Mrs. Sarah Blake is alive and living in Durham, New Hampshire. I've got her number right here."

Rafe looked at the note. "I had a feeling that old devil was lying. So, Sarah's maternal grandmother is alive."

"I brought it along because I figured you might want to give her a call and tell her about Sarah being hurt."

Rafe clasped the note tight in his hand. This would mean so much to her. "I owe you, Bob."

Bob smiled and stood. "Good, you can pay me back by letting me handle this thing with Nevell Blackthorn. I don't want you interfering with the case we're building against him. Call the grandmother."

"I'm right on it."

Rafe walked into the lobby for privacy. He dialed Sarah's cousin, Pipi's work number first.

"Maxwell and Mackenzie law offices," the cheerful female voice on the other end of the line answered.

Rafe leaned against the wall. This wasn't going to be easy. "Put me through to Phillipa Maxwell."

"I'm sorry," the drone on the other end of the line said sweetly, "Ms. Maxwell is in a meeting right now and can't be disturbed. May I take your name and have her call you back?"

He frowned at his cell. "Listen, ma'am, this is an emergency. Tell her that her cousin Sarah has been hurt."

There was a pause. "Very well, I'll give her the message. Hold please."

Rafe listened to the music playing softly in his ear and scowled. How was he going to tell her the news? Either way, she was going to blame him, and she'd be right. Sarah wouldn't be lying in a hospital room if he hadn't conned her into coming back to rescue him. He had to make it up to her.

"Phillipa Maxwell here," a brusque, woman's voice said, "my receptionist said Sarah was hurt. Is this Rafe Halliday?"

"Yes, I'm Rafe Halliday."

"Let me tell you one thing, Rafe Halliday. If you're to blame for this, I'll kick your behind clear across Wyoming. I'll sue you until you've got nothing left but the lint in your belly button."

He grimaced at her words. They were too close to his own thoughts. "I'm to blame all right. I left her alone and someone bashed her on the head."

Phillipa gasped. "Oh, my God. How is she?"

"Unconscious." It hurt to talk about. He stared at the geometric pattern of the ceramic tile on the wall to get a handle on his raging emotions. "Sarah has a concussion, but there's no skull fracture and no bleeding in the brain. On the bright side, the doctors think she'll be all right."

"They think, but they don't know."

Pipi's apprehensive tone reflected his own fears. "That's about the size of it."

"I'll be on the first plane out there," Phillipa told him in an assertive voice.

He nodded. "Good, I was hoping you'd say that. Sarah needs her family around her now. Listen, before you hang up, I did some digging and got Sarah's grandmother's phone number."

"But that's impossible," Phillipa sputtered. "She's dead."

"No, she's not."

"But Grandfather...why that nasty old man. How could he do such a thing?"

He shrugged. "Judging by his personality, I'd say it was easy. Anyway, I'm going to call her."

"Why don't you let me do it? That way we can decide to fly out there together. I might even haul Grandfather out there with me. He's got a lot of explaining to do, and he might as well do it in person. Settling things with Grandfather would do Sarah good."

"Sounds good to me," Rafe murmured. "I suppose it would be good for her to have it out with the old grump. Just don't let him upset her. It'll be nice to have a go-between like you that Sarah's comfortable with."

"But what about you? You'd be the natural one to intercede."

His hand tightened on the phone. "I won't be here."

"Are you running out on my cousin?" Phillipa shouted.

He held the phone away from his ear until her tirade was over. "I'll wait until I'm sure she's okay, but then I have to leave."

"Why, did you find out she's not going to be wealthy after all?"

He tensed. "I'm going to ignore that because I know how upset you are. To put it plain and simple, I'm not going to hold her to me with lies anymore. All it's done is cause misery. This way, she's free to follow her own path."

"Don't act so innocent. Sarah told me before she went out on her fool's errand that you were using her connections to get funding for your dude ranch. And aside from that, she had me wire all her personal funds to give to you."

"I married Sarah because I love her. And I wouldn't accept her help. She still has the check." He tensed because the accusation reflected Sarah's own fears. He had taken advantage of her, but not in the way she feared. He'd taken all her love and given back nothing but pain in return.

Pipi sighed. "I don't want to spend any more time arguing with you. I'll be on the first plane out, and don't you dare leave until I get there. I have some annulment papers for you to sign."

"I'll be waiting."

Rafe sat in the chair by Sarah's hospital bed. At least she wasn't so deathly still anymore. Her eyelashes were like dark crescents on her pale cheeks.

She'd turned her head and murmured a while ago. It gave him hope she'd be all right.

It was dark outside, but he didn't mind sitting in the dark. It cocooned them together for the last night he'd spend with her. Leaving her was right. He couldn't hold her with lies and deception anymore. He knew she loved her career. This would give her time to pursue it.

If he was lucky, someday, she'd come back to him.

He reached out to touch her hand. Her beautiful eyes slowly swept halfway open.

"Rafe?"

"I'm right here, sweetheart," Rafe husked.

"I'm so sleepy." She yawned.

"I know, close your eyes and rest now. Nothing will hurt you anymore, sweet Sarah."

Her eyes fluttered shut.

He let go of her hand, sweeping a light caress across her fingers. He swallowed the lump in his throat and got to his feet. Men didn't cry, but he wanted to bawl like a two-year-old.

He gave her one last lingering look, memorizing her sweet features before he hustled out of the room. If he stayed one moment longer, he could never leave.

He shut the door firmly behind him. Leaving her was one of the hardest things he'd ever done, but he knew it was right. Had Sarah felt this way when she left on their wedding night? The notion haunted him.

He pushed away from the door, turned, and walked toward the nurse's station. He'd report she'd regained consciousness and then get the hell out of here before his nerve failed him. Phillipa would just have to mail the papers to him.

Rafe approached the nurse's station. He waited a moment, and when they continued to ignore him, he cleared his throat. Several nurses looked up.

The nurse closest to him frowned. "Yes, Mr. Halliday, how may I help you?"

"I wanted to report my wife regained consciousness."

Footsteps came down the hallway, and he looked up. A petite woman with red-gold hair, worn up in a twist, and an elderly lady in tow, strode toward him, followed by a tall elderly man with a thick mane of white hair.

Rafe recognized the red hair and obstinate tilt of chin from Sarah. This had to be Phillipa and Sarah's grandparents.

The redhead pushed her way to the nurse's station. "I'm Phillipa Morris, and I'm here to see my cousin Sarah Halliday."

"Visiting hours are over miss."

"I don't care," she snapped. "You take me in to see Sarah right now or I'll slap you with a lawsuit that will set you on your ear."

"Now, now," Granny Blake said, walking up to the desk. "I'm sure there's no need for argument. We've been informed my granddaughter was in an accident. We just now flew in from out of state, and we'd like to see her, please."

Sarah's grandfather nodded, glaring at the nurse. "Don't dawdle, girl. Show us the way at once."

Phillipa's foot tapped impatiently.

"I'm Rafe Halliday. I'd be pleased to show you to Sarah's room," he said, ignoring the irritated look on the head nurse's face.

They all turned to glance at him. Grandma's gaze was sympathetic, Grandfather's assessing, and Pipi looked only plain accusatory. Rafe told himself he deserved her condemnation for the deception he'd pulled on Sarah.

The grouchy nurse said, "Very well, but make it a short visit. I can't have the other patients disturbed."

Rafe took Granny's elbow. "Follow me. I was just telling the nurse Sarah regained consciousness."

"Oh, thank heaven," Granny said.

"I always knew Sarah was a fighter," Phillipa muttered.

"And why not, she comes from good stock, at least on my side of the family," her grandfather said stiffly.

"Right," Rafe replied tightly. She was a fighter, but he didn't intend to have her fight a losing battle any longer. He opened the door to her room.

Phillipa peered inside. "I thought you said she regained consciousness."

"She did, but she must have fallen asleep again." Rafe smiled at Phillipa's doubtful glance. It pleased him to know Sarah had a strong champion in her corner. "Scout's honor."

"I doubt you were ever a scout," she said, then turned on her heel and entered the room. Rafe followed them.

Granny walk up to the bed and stared, her gaze drinking in the sight of Sarah after all these years. She turned to look at Rafe while tears ran down her cheeks. "Thank you for bringing my baby back to me after all these years."

"You're welcome." A lump tightened his throat. "I wanted Sarah to have the real family she'd always missed."

Phillipa coughed.

Rafe looked at her and smiled at her disgruntled expression. "I'm not forgetting you, Phillipa. Sarah already has you and now she'll have you both." Rafe glanced at the old man, noting his imperiously raised eyebrow. "She may even have her old curmudgeon of a grandfather if he's smart."

Grandpa had the good grace to look sheepish.

"A happy family is what she's always wanted. Now did you bring those papers for me to sign?"

Phillipa opened her bag. She pulled out a document and a pen. "All you have to do is sign this and walk away." She looked up at him inquisitively. "If that's what you really want to do."

"It's what's best for Sarah. Who knows, maybe someday she'll be ready to come back to me." Rafe reached for the document and the pen Phillipa thrust at him. He scrawled his name on the line at the bottom.

"You'd wait for her?" Phillipa asked curiously.

"Forever," he said, and walked out the door.

Chapter Ten

Rafe stepped off the curb and walked toward the idling pickup truck. He opened the passenger door, and got a glimpse of Zeke's sour face before he hopped in. "Thanks for coming out this late to pick me up."

"Don't mention it." Zeke motioned back toward the lights of the hospital. "Is she going to be okay?"

"Yes, thank God. She just regained consciousness. Mark said she should make a full recovery." Rafe pulled the door shut then rolled down the window, hoping a touch of breeze would make him feel better. "Let's get going, Zeke," he said impatiently. "I want to get home."

Zeke put the truck into gear and pulled out of the parking spot. "I suppose you heard they picked up Travis Cain."

"Yeah, I did. Bob Wilson stopped by to give me the news. He said they rounded up Nevell Blackthorn, as well. The two of them were in on it together." He gazed over at Zeke. "Were you there when they came to arrest Travis?"

"I sure was," Zeke said with a scowl. "The sheriff came just as we were all sitting down to lunch."

"I never would have thought Travis was the one doing this thing." Rafe closed his eyes and said tiredly, "Thank God Wilson insisted on doing ballistic tests on the rifles on the Double-H. It uncovered a viper in our midst."

"Yeah, but it almost came too late."

"I know." Rafe thought about Sarah's brush with death and shuddered.

"It came as a shock to all of us when they came to get Travis. I never thought the kid would have it in him to shoot a person, let alone an animal. He just doesn't seem to have the stomach for it."

Rafe glanced at Zeke's puzzled expression. "How'd Travis take it when they came to arrest him?"

"Bad." Zeke shook his head. "When the sheriff walked into the dining hall, the kid turned white as a ghost. And when they slapped the handcuffs on him, he looked like he was going to cry. The kid was shaking like a leaf. He was talking a mile a minute when they hauled him out the door. He was saying he might be a spy, but he wasn't a killer."

"It doesn't sound like a pretty picture." Rafe set his jaw. The kid had that coming and more. "Travis deserves everything they throw at him. I just hope Blackthorn gets a dose of the same medicine."

"I'm not saying he don't deserve it, I'm just saying he didn't take it very well."

"I know." Rafe sighed, regretting his irritable tone. He was miserable, but he didn't have to take it out on Zeke. He looked out into the black night seeking solace for his wounded heart. "I'm sorry I spoke sharply to you, old friend. It's just that I'm a might edgy right now."

"I understand." Zeke was silent for a moment. "I picked up the ambulance call on my monitor. Poor Rose was shaking something awful," Zeke's added, his voice rough with concern. "She wanted us to rush right up to the hospital, but I told her we'd best keep out of the way. The way the sheriff put it to us later, she was in bad shape."

Rafe winced, remembering Sarah's pale face. "Mark told me she was very lucky. If she would have gotten hit just a little bit harder, she would be dead."

"Folks at the ranch will be relieved when I tell them she pulled through. Course, most of the men are out on the town tonight, so it will have to wait until morning. But we can set Rose's mind to rest right away."

Rafe nodded. "You did right to keep Rose away. They wouldn't even let me in by Sarah until they took her up to her hospital room."

They pulled into the driveway of the Double-H.

He turned to look at Zeke, face illuminated by the yard light. He looked his age tonight. No doubt, he'd suffered, too. Rafe was sorry to have put him through it.

"Do you want to go in and tell Rose the good news? I think I'd just like to go to bed."

At Zeke's eager smile, he knew the two were more than friends.

Zeke got out of the truck. "I'll take care of it. You just get a good night's sleep."

Rafe got out, too. The yard light shone on Sarah's Jeep. Rafe rattled her keys, still stuffed into his pocket. They were the last link to her.

He'd have the Jeep run up to the hospital in the morning. Then he'd have no reminders to fret over.

Rafe's alarm clock went off at four-thirty, as usual. He rolled over to shut it off, and his hand landed on the empty side of the bed. He frowned and slapped the clock. The stupid bed was way too big without Sarah to share it with.

He closed his eyes and sighed. It was better this way. He'd done his duty and stuck around to make sure she'd be okay, but then he'd caught a ride home. This was where he belonged. Sarah had her own life.

He rolled out of bed and walked to the closet. It was Sunday, the hand's day off, but he needed the routine of work to keep his mind off Sarah. It wouldn't do either of them any good if he pinned after her.

The whole mess was over. The sheriff had Nevell Blackthorn and Travis Cain in jail. Rafe intended to keep his promise to Bob and stay out of the investigation. There was nothing more to do than go on with the rest of his life. It seemed like a grim prospect.

He jerked his work shirt off the hanger. There seemed little point in getting dressed, but he went through the motions automatically.

He wandered into the kitchen where Rose was bustling about making breakfast. He stopped short, surprised she was here.

"It's your day off, Rose, what are you doing up?"

She gave him a sympathetic smile. "I figured you'd be up bright and early, with all that's on your mind. Besides, I thought you could use the company. Have a seat at the table and I'll serve you some breakfast."

He sighed and slumped in a dinette chair. He doubted if he could swallow a mouthful. He glanced out the window. A light rain was falling and trickling down the glass. The dawning light looked drab and dreary, just like his mood.

"I don't feel much like eating," he muttered.

She shook her head. "I know how you feel, boss. I don't have much of an appetite myself this morning, but you've got to keep up your strength for the missus."

Rafe blanched at her innocent words.

"When are you going up to the hospital?"

"I'm not going to the hospital." He looked away from Rose's inquisitive gaze.

"Why?" Rose asked apprehensively. "Did they tell you that she can't have any visitors?"

"No." Rafe looked away, not wanting to say out loud what he'd agonized about all night. If only Rose would drop the subject, but he knew she wouldn't. "She's not coming back."

Rose put her hand to her heart. "What do you mean, she's not coming back? I thought you said she was all right?"

"She will be, God willing, but she's out of our lives. I set her free to go back to her old life."

Rose clucked her tongue. "But she was doing so well here at the ranch. We were all getting along just ducky. I just don't believe she'd want to leave."

He shrugged and looked away from her sympathetic gaze. "Believe it or not, it's true. She only stayed here for the summer because I forced her into it. You know the snow job I gave her. And what did it get her? Nothing but trouble. Well, now I'm letting her go. She's free."

She harrumphed and put her hands on her hips. "Lord, what a load of malarkey. If ever I saw two people made for each other, it's you and the missus." She shook her head. "Why, you young people nowadays don't know a good thing when it's right in front of your face."

"I don't want to talk about it any longer." He started to stand, thinking he'd rather clean out stalls than listen to any more of Rose's scolding.

"Oh, sit back down, you hardheaded man, and I'll pour you some coffee," Rose said with a great deal of exasperation in her voice.

He didn't even seem to have the power to go against Rose's bossiness today. Rafe sat back down.

"Zeke told me Sarah woke up before you came home." Rose carried two cups of coffee to the table and sat across from him.

He nodded. "Yes. The doctor said she should make a full recovery. They'll want to keep her under observation for a couple of days to be sure. Mark said she was incredibly lucky."

Rose shook her head. "Some luck!"

"That's what I said." Rafe's jaw tightened as he thought of the pain she must be feeling. "She shouldn't have been out there, Rose. I got careless, and it almost cost Sarah her life."

Rose reached over and patted his hand. "It's not your fault, Rafe. I'm sure the missus won't blame you."

"That's just peachy," Rafe mumbled and took a sip of coffee.

She sighed. "Anyway, like I was saying, I'm glad she's going to be okay. It gave all of us quite a scare when we heard about her getting hurt. Zeke was listening to his police band radio when he picked up the ambulance call."

"I'll bet." Rafe grimaced when he pictured the scene. "What did Travis say?"

Rose took a deep breath. "I just finished laying out lunch when the sheriff came. Even though everyone was all in a tizzy about Sarah being hurt, I had my job to do. The sheriff came right to the table and handcuffed him. You could have knocked me over with a feather, I was that surprised. The boy looked like he was going to faint, he turned so white. I never would have pegged him for a criminal."

"Me, neither." He shook his head. "I guess he was the best kind of criminal because he looked so innocent."

She nodded. "They came back in and checked the phones in the house. They said they were bugged. Can you imagine that?"

He shrugged. "I guess Travis had an easy time doing that, having access to the house at meal times. All he had to do was excuse himself to use the bathroom and sneak into my study."

Rose tightened her lips. "And to think, I took kindly to that lad." She shook her head. "The boy got really agitated when they were taking him away, saying he was a spy, but he'd never shot anything in his life. He said the rifle was a birthday present from his dad and he'd never even fired it. Well, I can tell you, there was a lot of speculation after they hauled him away."

"I'll just bet." Rafe knew how cowboys loved to talk. "Just so Travis, and especially Nevell Blackthorn, get what's coming to them. That's all I really care about."

"Well, now that things have straightened out, you can wait for the missus to come back to you. I know you're in love with her. It's as plain as the nose on your face. And I know she loves you and wouldn't want to leave."

He tamped down the hope that sprang up in him at her words. "It's barely possible she might come back to me, but I wouldn't bet on it. The odds are against me."

Sarah turned her head on the pillow and carefully opened her eyes. She had a gigantic headache that seemed to throb along with her pulse. Well, at least that told her she was still alive.

She glanced at the strange walls. They were painted a sickly yellow. Where was she? She sure wasn't in her own bed. Then she noticed a person standing at the foot of the bed.

"Rafe?"

"No, it's Pipi." Her cousin stepped closer. Her mouth curved into a soft smile. "How are you feeling this morning, Sarah?"

"Terrible." She sighed. "It feels like there are little men banging away at my head with tiny hammers. I was attacked, wasn't I?"

Pipi nodded solemnly. There was a tight frown on her face. "Don't worry, they already caught the man."

"Good." Sarah sagged back against the pillow.

Pipi brushed the hair back from Sarah's bandaged forehead.

She smiled at Pipi's tender gesture. Her older cousin had always looked out for her. "I guess Rafe must have called you."

"Yes, he let me know you were hurt. I arrived in the middle of the night, while you were sleeping."

"He shouldn't have worried you. I'm okay."

"Are you?" Pipi's voice was cautious.

"Yes, I'm fine, and I'm even better now that you're here. I'm just a little sore, that's all. So, have you seen Rafe?"

"Yes, he and I had a long talk," Pipi said after a moment's hesitation.

She glanced up sharply at Pipi's evasive tone. What was wrong? Rafe might be hurt, too, or even worse, dead. "Is he okay?"

"Yes, he's fine." Pipi looked toward the door as it opened, and then turned back to Sarah with a bright smile. "I've got someone special I want you to meet."

Footsteps entered the room. An older lady entered the room.

Sarah would have recognized that dear face anywhere from pictures. "Granny Blake, is that you?"

The lady walked up to the bed and reached out to clasp Sarah's hand tightly in hers. "Yes, I'm here, baby." Granny's soft hand trembled while tears dampened her green eyes. "I gave up hope of ever seeing you again."

Sarah couldn't believe her eyes. "I must be having a hallucination caused by the bash to my head. Pipi's not real, either."

Pipi chuckled. "Oh, I'm real all right, just ask the nurse from last night. She probably thinks I'm the toughest hombre to cross her path in ages. Granny is real, too. Grandfather had us all conned."

Grandfather stepped near the bed. "I'm afraid it's true," he admitted gruffly. "I thought it best you didn't grow up under that kind of influence."

Sarah blinked at the three of them. "You mean to tell me this is real? I'm not off my head?"

"Not last time I checked, cuz." Pipi grinned. "But I can always have a shrink check you out if you like."

Sarah processed the information slowly. She stared up at Granny Blake's sweet face. The two of them shared the same eye color. That hadn't changed, but there were new lines on her grandmother's face. Her hair was now a cap of gray curls instead of blonde.

"You're alive!"

She stared at Grandfather's hard countenance, stunned. "How could you have kept us apart?"

He fidgeted, then looked away. "It was wrong, I realize that now. And I'm...sorry."

His proud face crumpled, and she noted how much he had aged.

"But, how?"

Granny shook her head. "He snatched you after your parents went down in that plane crash before I was even informed of the accident. He wanted you all to himself, so he took me to court for total custody. With all his money, it wasn't hard for him to win. I think it was his revenge on me for your mother stealing his son away."

Sarah frowned. "Stealing away. He's always said my mother had ruined my father."

"And she did," Grandfather said bitterly.

Granny gave him a quelling glare, and he piped down. "Sarah, the truth is, your dad was following along in his father's footsteps until he met my girl, Dawn. Of course, your grandfather could never accept anything less than blue blood for his son, so he rejected them both."

She brushed a wisp of hair off Sarah's forehead. "I was worried at first that your dad might desert my girl. His father had always been such a strong influence in his life. But instead, he broke away and made something of himself. You were all very happy, but the plane crash changed all that. They were coming back from a delayed honeymoon trip when they died. So, at least I had the comfort of knowing they were happy."

"Oh, Granny, I never knew any of this." Sarah glared at her grandfather. "According to him, my mother was just a cheap little tart, and my father was besotted by her. Of course, deep down, I knew differently. I had early memories of us being a happy family."

Granny smiled sadly and shook her head. "I missed you, baby child."

Sarah smiled while tears ran down her cheeks unchecked. "So many years have been stolen from us." She felt like some part of her that had been dead was now coming back to life. "I missed you, too. We've got so much time to make up for."

Granny smiled and squeezed her hand. "We will, baby Sarah, we will."

"I missed you, too," Grandfather said roughly. "It's been ten long years since I last saw you. I admit, after losing my son, I latched onto you. I know I was never good at showing it, but I loved you very much. Still do, for that matter. What I did was wrong, and I'm sorry for all the hurt I've caused. Can you ever forgive me?"

Sarah took a calming breath, swallowing the lump in her throat. She saw the lines of sorrow on his face and heard the genuine regret in his voice. This humble old man was very different from the stiff autocrat that had raised her.

She reached out to take his trembling hand. "I guess we'll have to start fresh, won't we?"

Tears misted his eyes as he glanced at her and then at Granny Blake. "We all will."

Sarah cleared the lump in her throat. "Tell me, Granny, how did you find me after all these years?"

"That nice husband of yours did some checking and got my number. Then Pipi called me last night and told me you were hurt. She chartered a plane, and before long, we were here. It was just like being caught in a whirlwind. Before I knew it, I was here looking at your sweet face."

Sarah smiled. This was just like Rafe's typical high-handed style to go behind her back. But considering the results, she didn't mind. "That was so nice of Rafe. I should be mad at him for being so sneaky, but I can never stay mad at him for long."

Granny smiled understandingly, then glanced nervously at Pipi. "Yes, he said you'd want family around you when you woke up this morning."

Sarah's heart melted. What a sweet thought. Rafe loved her. He'd shouted it at the campsite. And his actions proved it. He'd always said actions counted the most. She hugged the thought to her.

She looked around the hospital room, but didn't see any sign of him. "So, where is he?"

"He went home, Sarah," Pipi said quietly.

"Why?" she asked, knowing somehow, Pipi wasn't telling her everything.

Pipi huffed a breath. "Rafe said he didn't want to push you anymore. He said he'd conned you into staying here, which I always suspected, and that was no basis for a marriage." She pulled a document out of her bag. "He waited for me to get here and signed off before he left."

Sarah gasped.

Pipi continued, "I told him I figured it was because he found out you weren't rich, after all. That you weren't really an heiress."

"What do you mean she's not an heiress?" Grandfather asked.

"Well, you cut her off when she left the family fold, didn't you?"

Grandfather looked away. "I couldn't bring myself to do it."

Pipi sighed. "Rafe told me he wouldn't accept your money. Is that true?"

"Yes, it's true. He was majorly teed off when he found out I planned to help finance the dude ranch."

"Why didn't you come to me for the investment?" Grandfather demanded.

"At the time, we weren't exactly on good terms. I didn't want to put up with the strings that might be attached."

He looked down. "I guess I've been a little heavy handed over the years."

"Don't fret over it, Granddad, it's all water under the bridge now."

Sarah glared at Pipi. "You as much as called him a fortune hunter. No wonder he took off. This is terrible."

She closed her eyes. This couldn't be happening.

"Cheer up, Sarah," Pipi said brightly. "He's giving you an easy way out."

"I love him."

"Yes, but does he love you?" Pipi countered.

"Of course. Even a blind man could see it by his actions. Would a man who didn't love me make this noble gesture? Rafe always said actions mean more than words, and he was right."

Pipi turned to Grandfather. "You talk some sense into her. She won't listen to me."

He glanced warmly at Sarah. "I'd say Sarah knows her own mind."

"Right," Granny chimed in. "He seemed like a fine man to me."

"Darned tooting," Grandfather added. "A man after my own heart. You two love each other, don't you?"

Sarah smiled with remembrance of their last passionate encounter. "Yes, we love each other very much."

Pipi snorted. "Then why did he leave? If he cared, he would have stuck around."

"He left because he didn't want me to stay under duress. Now I don't want to hear any more of your objections, Pipi." Sarah sat up, and her head began to swim. She clung to the mattress to keep from toppling over. She had to tough it out and get to Rafe.

"What do you think you're doing?" Pipi screeched.

When the dizzy spell passed, Sarah raised her head and scowled at Pipi's panicked gaze. "I'm getting out of here."

"Good idea. Let's get back to Boston as soon as possible," Pipi placated while putting a hand on Sarah's shoulder to make her stay put. "But first, the doctors want to keep you under observation for a couple of days."

Sarah shrugged away and slid her legs off the side of the bed. "No way, I'm getting out of here now."

There was a tap on the door, and Dr. Phillips walked in. "What's going on in here, World War III?"

Pipi rounded on him with her hands on her hips. "You talk some sense into her." She peered at the doctor's name tag. "Doctor Philips. Sarah wants to leave, and I was telling her it isn't a very good idea."

Mark Phillips frowned at Pipi, then turned to look at Sarah. "Why do you want to leave now?"

"I'm okay and I want to go home. There's some urgent business I need to take care of."

Pipi snorted. "For Pete's sake, Sarah, I wouldn't call the cowboy urgent business. You don't actually mean to chase after that husband of yours? You're a heck of a lot better off without him."

"Pipi, someday, when you meet the right man, you'll understand."

"Bull."

Doctor Phillips gave a sharp whistle. "That's it. All visitors out so I can examine my patient."

Pipi glared at him and turned on her heel. She left the room with Granny and Grandfather trailing behind her.

"You'll have to pardon her, doctor," Granny said on her way out. "She's just a little overwrought."

"She's always been high strung," Grandpa added.

Mark nodded. "I understand."

After they shut the door behind them, Mark turned to Sarah. "Boy, she's really something."

Sarah grinned. "Who, Granny?"

"Uh-uh, the redhead."

She shrugged. "Pipi tends to be a little overprotective."

"Yeah, like a momma bear with her cub. So, how are you really feeling this morning?"

"Like hell, but I can handle it. I need to go home."

"I'll be the judge of that. Let's take a look." He shined a light in her eyes, then probed her forehead.

"Ouch," Sarah mumbled.

"You're going to have one beautiful shiner in a couple of days," he said, slipping his light back in his pocket.

She smiled. "Gee, thanks."

He cocked his head and gave her a once-over. "Well, you don't seem too bad, considering what you've been through. But I wouldn't advise any strenuous activity for several days. I'd rather have you here, but I guess you can go home if you're that gung-ho about it. Just don't overdo it. I don't want Rafe and the redhead to come down on me."

"Thank you, doctor." Sarah let out the breath she was holding.

He walked to the door. "You know, you're one lucky lady. A little harder and you wouldn't have made it."

Sarah nodded. She knew she had a second chance at life, and she wasn't going to mess it up this time. "Thank heaven they caught the guy."

Mark opened the door. "I heard they arrested one of the ranch hands. They also picked up Nevell Blackthorn. I hear he's making quite an argument about false arrest."

Thankfully, Bob Wilson had checked the rifles at the ranch. That was probably how they'd zeroed in on the hand. She could picture Nevell Blackthorn all huffy and trying to throw his weight around. The man definitely wouldn't take well to confinement.

But she had more important things to dwell on, like Rafe and how much they meant to each other. There would be nothing to keep her from telling him she loved him now. She felt free.

Sarah eased to the side of the bed and stood up. Keeping one hand on the bed for balance, she walked to the closet. The door opened and Pipi, Granny, and Grandfather walked in.

"So, that stupid doctor is letting you leave?" Pipi carped.

Sarah continued pulling her clothes off the hangers. "Mark Phillips is not stupid. He's very accommodating. And he's a very good doctor, to boot."

"I don't care if he's the world's best doctor. I'll accommodate him with a malpractice suit if anything goes wrong."

"Will you stop spouting off and come over here to help me get dressed?"

Grandfather left to call for a wheelchair escort.

Sarah sank on the bed while Pipi and Granny fluttered around her, helping her dress.

She put on the same jeans, camp shirt, and hiking shoes she'd worn yesterday. The scent of wood smoke on the clothes brought back memories of that wonderful camping trip and the surprise attack that followed. She really should have seen it coming, but she thought he was there on ranch business. Her last memory was of Tab's grim face as he brought the butt of his rifle down on her head.

After she finished dressing and signed the release forms a nurse had brought in, Pipi said, "I'll go call us a cab to take us to the airport."

Sarah grinned. Her cousin wouldn't give up easily. "While you're at it, call me one to take me back to the Double-H."

Pipi frowned. "But he doesn't want you."

"That's not true," Sarah said cheerfully. "He doesn't want to force me. I'm going back of my own free will."

"For a lifetime of cows and horses? You know how you hate horses, Sarah."

She put a soothing arm around Pipi's tense shoulder and pulled her close for a hug. "No, for a lifetime of love and babies. Don't worry about me, Pipi, I know what I'm doing. And no offense to any of you, but I found the love and family I've always missed right at the Double-H, in Rafe's arms. And guess what, I'm never going to leave."

Granny smiled and patted her arm. "Go for it, Sarah. Follow your heart. I did like the look of that young man you married. Besides, we've got all the time in the world to get to know each other."

Sarah let go of Pipi and hugged her grandmother. "Thanks, Granny Blake. I love you even more for being so generous."

She turned to get crushed in her grandfather's tight embrace. "Be happy," he said with a shaky voice.

She blinked away the tears in her eyes.

"If that cowboy hurts you, I'll kill him," Pipi vowed.

"Don't worry, Pipi, I know exactly what I'm getting into."

Sarah paid the taxi driver and watched him pull out of the driveway. She looked around the grounds, but didn't see anybody.

Of course, she realized. Today is Sunday, and most of the men would be in town.

She walked toward the house, hoping to find Rafe inside. She couldn't wait to see him and tell him she loved him, and she was back for good.

A loud noise coming from the barn made her stop, then change course. Rafe was already up and doing chores.

She ambled over to the outbuilding. As she drew nearer, she heard two men's voices. They sounded angry, but she was too far away to make out what they were saying. One voice was Rafe's, but she couldn't place the other one. She cautiously stepped forward, not wanting to intrude. Her eyes adjusted to the dim light as she walked to the open doorway.

She gasped at the sight that greeted her. Tab Whittacker stood with his rifle pointed at Rafe.

What was going on? Tab was supposed to be under arrest for attacking her. Unless they got the wrong man? She took a quick sidestep into the shadows and listened.

"You're lying, Halliday," Tab hissed. "I know she's dead."

Rafe stood in a loose stance, his feet apart as if ready to dodge a bullet. But Sarah knew he'd never make it at this close range.

She had to do something to save him, but what?

"No, you're just incompetent," Rafe said coolly. "You're probably the one that tried to shoot us and missed."

A horse nickered. Umbriago was in the next stall.

Could she? She really had no choice.

"Missed, my ass," Whittacker shot back. "I was trying to wing her and scare her off. When I aim at a target, I don't miss."

"So, it was you who set up Travis?"

Whittacker sneered. "You're finally catching on, Halliday. It was easy. I knew he was spying on you for Blackthorn, so he was the perfect fall guy. I slipped the rifle out from under his bunk. The kid didn't even know it was missing."

"And you shot the wolves," Rafe said grimly. "Was it Blackthorn's idea?"

"You still don't get it, do you? I did it all. Blackthorn's just a loud-mouthed idiot. It was so easy to push his buttons and get him all riled up against you. You always did give him too much credit. You should have looked to your own backyard for trouble."

"Yeah, and I would have found a yellow-bellied coward."

"Why you..." Whittacker took a step forward, then stopped. "Uh-uh, jerk. I ain't gonna be that easy. You ain't gonna get me rattled."

"But why did you wait until now to try to destroy me? And why pick on Sarah?"

"I was biding my time, but I couldn't wait no longer. You were fixin' to sell part of the ranch to set up your dude ranch. It ain't right to break her up."

Sarah cautiously inched toward Umbriago, whispering soothing sounds at him the way she'd heard Rafe do. If the horse shied, they were both in big trouble.

Umbriago stood steady, eyeing her calmly.

Whittacker was certifiable. She had to intervene before he killed Rafe.

She stepped up on a rail on the side of the stall and grabbed the horse's mane gently. She eased a leg over his bare back, all the while whispering, "Good horse," whether to soothe the animal or herself, she didn't know.

Whittacker bragged, "Why pick on Sarah? I knew you'd be easy pickings if she walked out like last time. So, that was my first step. I shot the wolves, but she didn't leave. So, I winged her. Hell, I even tried to warn her off, but she wouldn't listen. I had no choice but to kill her."

"Like I said, Whittacker, you missed."

"Bull. I didn't miss with all the other stuff I pulled, either."

"What do you mean by that?" Rafe asked in a deceptively calm voice.

"Figure it out, boss man," Whittacker sneered. "Who do you think's been causing all the problems around here? Me, that's who. I've been doing all I could to make you go under."

"You're just talking through your hat, Whittacker. Why would you do that?"

"I figured things would fall apart, and I could buy you out. But instead, you came back and dug your heels in. This ranch should be mine. I loved her. I'd never sell part of her off like you want or have a bunch of city dudes come stay here. It ain't right."

"You'll never get away with this, Whittacker."

Whittacker moved the barrel of his rifle to Rafe's heart level. "I don't care. It doesn't much matter anymore. If I can't have the ranch, you can't either."

Sarah kicked her heels into Umbriago's sides and gave a rebel yell. The horse bolted out of the stall, straight toward the men.

Whittacker turned toward her with a growl just as Rafe jumped him with a flying tackle. A shot rang out, and the rifle clattered to the floor.

Umbriago stopped short, and Sarah slid from his back. She ran forward, scooping up the rifle. She pointed it toward the fighting men as they rolled on the floor.

Good grief, she couldn't shoot for fear of hitting Rafe.

He rolled on top of Whittacker and drove a fist square into his jaw, where sagged against the floor.

Rafe stood and turned a wild glance her way. "Are you all right? You scared the hell out of me."

Sarah rushed toward him, thanking her lucky stars that he appeared unharmed. "I was thinking the same thing, cowboy. I didn't know if it would work, but I knew that I had to try it."

Rafe took the rifle from her and pointed to a coil on the wall. "Go get me that length of rope and I'll tie him up for the sheriff."

She grabbed the rope hanging on a peg and brought it back to him. He handed her the rifle, and she held it on the unconscious man while Rafe trussed him up. When Rafe walked back to her, she put down the rifle and wrapped her arms tightly around him.

"Oh, Rafe. Are you all, right?"

He pulled her close. "Why didn't I ever see what a lunatic he was?"

"Because he seemed like family. You've known him all your life."

He sighed and pulled away. "We grew up together. He was like a big brother to me."

He took her hand and walked with her out of the barn. He turned abruptly to hold her at arm's length. "Where did you ever get the courage to do that?"

She smiled and squeezed his hand. "Love can do amazing things. I love you, Rafe. With all my heart. I wanted to tell you before, but I was afraid you didn't feel the same."

"And now?"

"I know you do, and I want to shout it from the rooftops."

He grinned. "Yes, sweetheart, I love you very much. I'd come to accept the fact that I had to let you go, but I sure am glad you came back." He bent to brush a burning kiss across her lips. "You always seem to come to my rescue, sweetheart," he said warmly as he pulled away.

She smiled up at him "That's my job in life. And I want to help you some more. I want to help fund the dude ranch."

"Now, honey," he said calmly. "I told you before, I don't want your money. We can do without it."

"Am I or am I not family?" she asked with a smile on her face.

"You are," he agreed with a raised eyebrow.

"Then what's mine is yours, and vice versa. Agreed?"

He sighed. "I don't want you to think I married you for your money or family connections."

She shook her head at his troubled expression. "I don't, not anymore."

"I may be hardheaded, but I can learn. I guess that's another thing I have to thank you for, teaching me to open up and trust. Yes, I agree to let you help. After all, this is your home, too."

"It's a deal," she said before sealing it with a kiss.

Sarah walked to the table with a fresh bowl of popcorn for Mandy and Pipi to string. She set the large wooden bowl between them.

"Thanks, Aunt Sarah," Mandy said distractedly.

Sarah ruffled her hair. "You're welcome, Mandy."

Pipi grinned at her. "Yeah, thanks, Aunt Sarah."

"Don't get smart with me or I might invite that nice Doctor Phillips over to put you in your place again."

Pipi threw a piece of popcorn at her. "You wouldn't dare."

Sarah laughed and looked into the kitchen. Rose and Granny were making fudge while they gossiped. Zeke sat meekly on a chair, patiently waiting for samples. Grandfather was out organizing a sleigh ride for the ten guests that were staying there. The dude ranch had been a smashing success and created a closer bond between them all.

Sarah made her way over to the sofa and sat next to Rafe. She glanced up at Gabe and Lisa stringing lights on the Christmas tree.

"Isn't it wonderful to have all the family here for Christmas?"

Rafe chuckled and rubbed her expanding tummy. "And we'll have even more family before you know it."

She sighed dreamily as she felt the baby move. She leaned her head on Rafe's shoulder. "Four more months. I can hardly wait."

He rested his chin against her head and whispered, "I love you, sweet Sarah. Thank you again for coming to my rescue and teaching me the meaning of love."

She smiled. "You're welcome. I love you, Rafe. Forever."

HER HEART'S DESIRE

Julie Castle

Chapter One

Samantha Logan parked her car in front of her family's dilapidated summer cabin. Her fingers trembled as she pulled the key from the ignition.

Well, she'd done it this time! The morning newspapers would expose the entire disaster, complete with the glaring caption: "Runaway Bride."

Thank goodness she had found out what a lying, cheating skunk Grayson St. James had been before marrying him. No one would think of looking for her here at this old family cabin. It hadn't been used since her high school graduation party. It looked kind of sad and abandoned now. The moonlight highlighted the sagging roofline. A summer breeze and utter silence surrounded her, making her shiver. She sighed as an owl hooted in the tree, reminding her how far she was from Chicago. All part of her plan. This had been her summer fun place as a child. Now it would be the perfect place to hide until the furor died.

She walked up the rutted path, retrieved the spare key from above the door, and stuck it in the lock. It wouldn't turn. The darned thing was probably rusted. Frustrated, she threw down her bags and got a good grip on the doorknob, rattling it as she tried to force the lock.

Suddenly, the door flew open, taking her with it. She tumbled inside the pitch-dark room. Crashing to the floor with a *thump*, she let out a shriek. Then the air whooshed from her lungs.

Stunned, she desperately gasped for air as a heavy person jumped onto her back, pinning her to the floor. A mingling of woodsy cologne and testosterone washed over her as he flipped her around. She now lay pinned under his muscular, very male body, if the bulge pressed against the junction of her thighs was anything to go by.

He was too big to be her ex-fiancé, but could Grayson have dispatched some thug to retrieve her? Or even worse, had she stumbled across a squatter, a criminal hiding in the woods?

Panicked, she took a wild swing into the darkness. Her fist crunched into hard flesh and bone as she struck a glancing blow off his jaw.

It had no effect on the hulking brute on top of her. The solid wall of muscle shook off her blow with a muffled grunt. Then, he flattened her even more with his weight.

She tried to hit him again.

He blocked her move, capturing both her wrists in a steely grip.

One of his large hands began running over her trembling body. As it skimmed over her breasts, she let out a blood-curdling shriek.

He froze, his hand still cupping her breast. "Stop that damned caterwauling."

She paused. She recognized the voice, and her terror melted like ice cream on the Fourth of July. If there was anyone she didn't want to see or be felt up by in the dark, it was Jake Ramsey.

"Ramsey, what the hell are you doing here?"

"Well, if it isn't my little Sunshine. What's the matter, honey, cold feet?"

Samantha pushed against his rigid body. "Take your hand off my breast, goon."

He removed his hand, but not without a teasing squeeze. "Sorry if I offended your delicate sensibilities, Sunshine."

She frowned at his sarcasm while his solid weight slowly lifted off her aching body. He knew she hated the nickname he'd hung on her during her turbulent teens. He obviously hadn't mellowed in the seven years she'd been away.

The lights came on, and she glared at the tall, redheaded brute hobbling her way. He had a few sprinkles of silver at the temples now, but it didn't fool her into thinking the years had softened him. She'd just had a sample of his rough treatment.

He was dressed—or should she say *undressed*—in a tight pair of halfway-unzipped jeans. His feet and his chest were bare. Her gaze followed the sprinkle of hair on his chest to where it whorled around his navel and disappeared into his pants. He looked like a sleep-rumpled male centerfold come to life. That was, if one discounted the brooding expression in his gunmetal gray eyes.

She ignored his speculative gaze and focused on his limp. It was gratifying to know she'd gotten the better of one man this horrendous evening.

But why was Ramsey here? He wasn't one of Grayson's pawns. Had matchmaking Uncle Delbert gotten wind of her departure? One look at Ramsey's grim expression told her he wasn't one of Cupid's little helpers. No, her father must have found out about her premature wedding departure and sent his own goon squad after her.

Ignoring the hand Ramsey semi-gallantly held out to assist her, she picked herself up off the floor. She slanted an assessing glance his way. His stony expression was as hard to read as always.

"Did Dad send you after me?"

"So, I was right." He quirked an eyebrow, stating flatly, "You did cut and run."

Samantha brushed the dust off the seat of her pants and scowled at him. "I wouldn't put it that way. And anyway, it's none of your business."

His mouth kicked up in a triumphant grin as he sat on the arm of the sofa. "Then why did you think I came to retrieve you?"

She shrugged and looked away from his too-penetrating gaze. "Isn't rounding up wayward daughters one of your many duties as my father's hired goon?"

"That's private investigator, not hired goon," he explained, patiently adding, "I got out of the wayward daughter business when you blew town seven years ago."

Irritated by his disapproving tone, she shot him an annoyed glare, and his half-naked body again drew her attention. She couldn't help staring. She snapped her attention back to his face in time to see him smirking at her.

The jerk knew he was getting to her.

"I'm not saying another word until you zip your pants."

He smiled. "Afraid?"

"Disgusted." She glowered at him. The clashes with Ramsey as her father's henchman were a part of her rebellious teens that she didn't like to remember. Leaving home and making her way in the world without her father's money was the best thing she'd ever done.

His jaw tightened as he zipped his pants. "What happened, Sunshine? Grayson not so hot in the sack?"

Samantha closed her eyes as an appalling image of catching Grayson in the act with another woman flashed before her. "Listen, jerk-face. I am tired, cold, and hungry. I've had one hell of a rotten day, and I'm in no mood to put up with snide remarks from the likes of you. I don't care why you're here. Get out!"

He smiled grimly, showing even white teeth. "Sorry, no can do. I'm here on vacation and in no mood to be booted out of my snug bed by a spoiled little rich girl. Now, say sorry for disturbing me and run back to Daddy."

She glared at him. He was a dangerous man, but she knew he always held himself under complete control. She'd found that out the hard way once. Seven years ago, she would have let him run her off, but now she was made of sterner stuff.

She plopped onto a chair. "I'm not leaving."

"How about I throw you out?" he asked quietly.

She gritted her teeth. "How about I tell my father what a jerk you are and get you fired?"

A crackle sounded from outside. "You in the house, come out with your hands up!"

Samantha jumped at the order that was shouted through a bullhorn outside. She cast a startled glance at Ramsey. He didn't look at all surprised at the interruption.

"Who's that?"

"The police."

Samantha gaped at his matter-of-fact response. "Police! What in the heck is going on?"

"You tripped the burglar alarm, Sunshine."

She gazed at his shark-like smile gleaming in the dimly lit room and shuddered. There was no burglar alarm. Or, at least, there hadn't been seven years ago. She wrinkled her nose, noting his triumphant expression. It seemed things had changed in the interim, but why would her father go to the expense of protecting this run-down cabin they seldom used? It didn't make any sense.

"Well, go tell them there's no problem."

"But there is," he said with a relaxed smile. "Breaking and entering is a crime."

Samantha's eyes widened at the implied threat. "This is *my* cabin."

"Correction, it's your daddy's cabin. There is a distinction. Maybe a night in jail will teach it to you."

Her last ounce of civility vanished as she jumped to her feet. "I'm not the one who's going to end up in jail."

She watched the storm clouds gather in his gray eyes and took a nervous step back. She'd gone too far. Maybe it would be safer to take her chances with the cops.

She spun on her heel and ran toward the door with Ramsey's footsteps in hot pursuit.

He closed the distance, grabbing her arm as she reached for the doorknob.

She lashed out, slamming her heel against his kneecap. His long leg buckled, and he hit the floor groaning, clutching his thigh. She spared one backward glance at the look of pure astonishment on his rugged face before she tore open the door.

A bright light shone out of the darkness, blinding her and stopping her in her tracks.

"For heaven's sake, Sammy, I could have shot you!"

"Kathy, is that you?" Samantha squinted past the light as she stepped onto the porch. Astonished to see her childhood friend dressed in a police uniform, she ran toward Kathy and safety, leaving Ramsey far behind.

"Who did you expect, Santa Claus? What's going on, Wonder Woman?"

At another of his childhood nicknames, she smiled, her tension ratcheting down a few notches. "I knocked him down, Super Girl." She pointed at the fallen Ramsey with personal pride. "All you have to do is arrest him."

"I came as soon as I got word of a disturbance." Kathy aimed the flashlight beam at Ramsey, who was still lying in the doorway. "You did this?"

Samantha frowned at her old friend's horrified tone. Of course, she'd defended herself and would again in similar circumstances.

"I want her arrested for assault." He pointed an accusing finger at Samantha, grimacing as he got to his feet.

Samantha was outraged by the accusation. "Just who was chasing whom? If you hadn't turned violent, I wouldn't have had to kick you." She stepped toward him and halted, noting the dangerous glint in his eye. He was back in goon mode, and she knew better than to get too close. "As for criminal charges, how about assault and battery? That should put you away for a while."

"Will you two stop bickering so I can get a few facts straight," Kathy interjected.

"Fine." Samantha was confident Kathy would side with her. She slanted a confident smile at Ramsey and noticed he was watching her with narrowed eyes.

"Okay by me," he said, adding with an enigmatic smile. "I've got nothing to hide."

Kathy nodded. "Let's take this inside, where I can make a report if necessary."

Samantha resented his implication that she was up to no good. Her reason for being here was none of his business. She brushed past Ramsey, refusing to let him get to her as she entered the cabin and took a seat at the dinette. He slid into the chair across from her with a confident air.

Kathy leaned against the counter and flipped open her notepad. "Okay, let's have Sammy's version first" she said, clicking her pen.

Samantha recalled their frightening tussle on the floor and glared at him. "I came here for a nice quiet rest. I opened the door, and Ramsey dragged me through the doorway, shoved me, and grabbed himself a cheap feel in the process."

She bristled at his derisive snort following her last statement.

"Now, it's your turn, Jake."

She was annoyed by Kathy's friendly tone. Jake, was it? Just how cozy were these two? She slanted a glance Kathy's way, noticing that she didn't seem to be put off by Ramsey's state of undress.

"As you know, I've been on vacation for the past week. It's all entirely legal and above-board. How was I to know who was breaking into the cabin in the middle of the night? I had every right to defend myself." He flashed a calm smile Samantha's way, adding, "And do I look like a man that would, as she so crudely put it, cop a cheap feel?"

Kathy flipped her notepad closed. "I don't think there was any intentional crime committed here, just a case of mistaken identity." She slipped the tablet into her pocket and turned toward the door. "I expect you two to settle matters like civilized adults. However, I warn you both. If there is more trouble, I'll haul in the two of you and let a judge decide."

"But..." Samantha sputtered when the door closed behind Kathy. So much for an old friend's protection.

She slanted a wary glance Ramsey's way, noting his victorious expression, and fumed. She'd had just about enough macho preening for one evening. She got up and headed toward the exit.

"I don't believe it."

She jerked open the front door, aggravated by his amazed tone. "Don't believe what?"

"That you're going to be mature and reasonable about this."

She grabbed her suitcase off the porch. "Mature and reasonable, my ass. I'm staying." She kicked the door shut behind her. "We'll just have to coexist for two weeks."

Ignoring his raised eyebrow, she headed toward the ladder to the loft, but her footsteps faltered as she gazed up at the slightly dizzying height. She shook off the remnant of fear. It was only a short ladder, for Pete's sake, and she'd scaled it many times as a kid. Besides, she had her phobia under control, thanks to an excellent therapist. It was probably the stress of dealing with Ramsey stirring her hidden emotions. A good night's sleep would set things right.

He stepped forward to block her path. "Uh-uh, Sunshine. You ain't sleeping in my bed."

She stood toe-to-toe with him, openly defying him. She realized there was something new in how he looked at her now. Something more watchful, more judgmental. The feeling of being found lacking grated on her already abraded nerves. Suddenly, she was more frightened of him than the ladder, but she was determined not to show it.

"The loft has the only bed in the cabin. I figured even a goon like you would be gentleman enough to give it up for a lady."

His speculative gaze focused on her face. "You figured wrong, Sunshine. If you choose to stay, you take the couch."

She cast a sleepy glance at the lumpy sofa, exhaustion rapidly sapping her will to fight. It was most likely a delayed reaction to the series of traumas she'd experienced tonight.

"Fine." She blinked back tears that suddenly misted her eyes and turned away from him, knowing his probing gaze wouldn't miss them.

She could feel him still standing close behind her, probably trying to figure out what had brought her here, and she tried to brace herself for more questions. If he knew what was good for him, he'd walk away, unless he wanted a sobbing woman on his hands.

After a tense moment, his light footsteps climbed the ladder to the loft.

She let out a shaky breath she didn't know she'd been holding.

If it meant she would have some breathing space, she could tough out a few nights on a lumpy couch. The knowledge she would disappoint her dad again hurt, but not as much as Grayson's betrayal. After a seven-year absence, she'd come home, gotten engaged to a man her father had approved of, and it had all blown up in her face.

At least Ramsey didn't have a clue as to her real reason for being here. It would be too humiliating to acknowledge the truth. She never did find out if Grayson St. James was any good in the sack, but if what she'd seen was anything to go by, he was rather dangerous. The picture of him engaging in some hardcore sex with another woman would stay with her long after her anger from his betrayal faded.

The fact he'd never tried to do more than kiss her during their whirlwind courtship didn't fit. It made the whole scene quite unreal. In an instant, she'd learned the truth. He was only marrying her for her money.

That he didn't find her sexually attractive stung, but it shouldn't have been that much of a surprise. She'd been too busy building her business to have much of a social life, let alone a lover.

So, now she was a twenty-seven-year-old semi-virgin with a cheating ex-fiancé and a growing need for more romance. There had to be a man for her somewhere.

She ducked into the bathroom and changed into her pajamas. Then, she rummaged around her bag for her Ginkgo Biloba—just the thing for the stress she was feeling.

Finding the bottle, she quickly downed a pill. If she ever needed calming, it was now.

Jake stood next to the sofa an hour later, watching Samantha sleep. He tried to tell himself he only felt compelled to check on her because she was his employer's daughter, but he knew it wasn't true.

He'd had a soft spot for his little Sunshine since he'd come to work for her father when she was twelve. She was a lively, intelligent child who had turned into a rebellious teen. Through the years, he'd pulled her out of more scrapes than he could count, until their final confrontation that night on the beach seven years ago.

He'd dragged her out of a wild party with a bunch of her high school friends after graduation. She'd been furious. Instead of arguing, she pulled him down for a scorching, angry, melt-his-socks-off kiss that had made him hard as stone. He'd set her back on her heels with a shove and given her the lecture of her life, telling her what a spoiled little rich girl she was.

She'd left home the next day, and he'd felt guilty for chasing her away. Instead of going down in flames, she'd built a successful catering business. The expansion of that business had brought her back home six months ago. It hadn't taken long for Grayson St. James, one of Logan Industries' young executives, to sweep her off her feet.

Seeing her again at her engagement party a month ago had knocked him for a loop. Her cascade of long, dark brown hair with copper highlights was the same. The intelligent flash of her turquoise blue eyes was all he had remembered. She'd returned a full-grown, desirable woman, and that soft spot had developed into a raging attraction. It was the main reason he'd taken on this surveillance rather than delegate it to a staff member.

He'd always known she would marry someone from her level of society. Not some hard guy like him. He came from a low-income family. The eldest son of an alcoholic father who'd died in a drunk driving accident when he was twelve, he knew what it was like to grow up fast. All the same, he was happy to hear about her breakup. He'd never liked Grayson St. James. Even though he was a protégé of Delbert Logan's, and Samuel Logan viewed him with a friendly eye, Jake was suspicious. Consequently, he'd exceeded his authority to conduct some intense background checks on the man, which thus far, had found nothing.

Jake covered Samantha with the comforter he'd brought down from the loft and then turned away. He needed to keep his head on straight. It was his last mission for Logan Industries and his most important.

He was here keeping an eye on the boathouse. Logan Industries had experienced a loss of technology to other firms. Someone was trying to bring down the firm, making it ripe pickings for a hostile takeover.

While Jake's staff cast a wide net outside the firm for the perpetrator, he narrowed his sights on the executive suite. Two weeks ago, he'd intercepted an email message that there would be an exchange of information for money at the cabin's boathouse three nights from now. The message, written by Samantha's younger brother Tad, had quickly narrowed the list of perpetrators down to one.

Was Samantha mixed up with her brother in this dirty business? It didn't seem likely, but here she was, a runaway bride, and she wouldn't tell him the reason for her departure. It was too big a coincidence to ignore. After getting over his initial shock at finding her here, he realized he needed to let her stay to keep an eye on her. He'd soon know if she was trustworthy.

In the meantime, he'd ruthlessly clamp down on his attraction to her. After all, there could be no future between them.

Chapter Two

Samantha rolled over and let out a yelp as she fell off the sofa. She landed on the floor in a flurry of covers.

Stumbling to her feet, she rubbed her bruised posterior. She yawned and stretched, wincing at the kinks in her back.

The aroma of coffee lured her to the kitchen.

Grabbing a mug off the drain board, she poured herself a cup and leaned back against the counter as she took a sip. It was much stronger than she usually made it.

Wrinkling her nose, she stared down at the murky substance as the horror of the previous evening came back to her with a jolt.

Ramsey!

She groaned, and the jarring sound of a cleared throat caused her to turn her head toward the dining room. Her eyes locked with Ramsey's hostile gray ones, and she choked on a mouthful of coffee.

After a bout of flustered coughing, she dared another look. He was sitting in a kitchen chair, watching her intently. Bright sunlight highlighted a deep purple shiner below his right eye.

She swallowed a dismayed groan. "Did I do that?"

"Yup." He continued to stare at her.

She frowned at his short reply because it gave her no clue what he was thinking. Did he still intend to throw her out? If he did, what could she do about it? Despite her statement to the contrary last night, she certainly didn't intend to call her father. The fact that she'd been a damned fool where romance was concerned was too bitter a pill to share with her, no doubt, disappointed father.

She felt Ramsey's inquisitive gaze rake over her flannel pajama-clad body and cringed. She probably looked a sight. "I'm sorry I hurt you. I don't normally resort to physical violence."

He shrugged, the corners of his hard mouth kicking up in a tight smile. "Consider it a love tap. Don't worry. I've had worse."

She studied his rugged features. A faded scar ran across his left cheek, and his slightly crooked nose had probably been broken once or twice. It was apparent he'd been through his share of battles. At least he was dressed today. She wouldn't have to worry about where to look. But the navy t-shirt he wore clung to his muscular chest. She'd gaze at his eyes instead. He had lovely eyes, eyes a woman could get lost in if she wasn't careful.

"What about you?" He looked her up and down. "Any after-effects from, as you said, the manhandling I gave you?"

"Just a few bruises." Her hand moved to rub her aching back and automatically drifted down to touch her bruised behind.

His smile widened. "Where?"

"Not where they'd show." She hastily withdrew her hand, at a loss as to how to handle his teasing mood. She decided this new side of him would take some getting used to. "So, what are you doing skulking around here and giving me such a rude awakening?"

He quirked an eyebrow. "I'm hardly skulking. I'm having a leisurely cup of coffee while breakfast cooks."

She inhaled the tantalizing aroma, and her stomach let out an audible rumble in anticipation. His smile told her he'd heard. It had been a long time since she'd eaten. She'd just picked at her rehearsal dinner last night, too keyed up to eat. Bridal jitters were a warning sign she should have heeded.

Ramsey slowly got to his feet.

She couldn't help noticing the jeans he wore fit him like a second skin, giving her unmistakable proof of his masculinity. Embarrassed at her wandering train of thought, she snapped her gaze back to his eyes.

He grinned. "How about I feed you a little breakfast? Afterward, we can talk this little misunderstanding over."

She brightened at the offer of breakfast, yet still felt the need to clear the air. A thick undercurrent of suspicion remained between them. "What happened last night wasn't a misunderstanding. You jumped all over me, both verbally and physically." Glancing at his shiner, she softly admitted, "I suppose I wasn't much better. Truce?"

"Truce. If we're living together for a while, you might as well get used to calling me by my first name."

"Okay, I'll call you Jake." She watched him limp to the stove and bit her lip in dismay. Had she kicked him hard enough to do real damage? "Why don't you let me get it, Jake? After we eat, I'll take you into town to get your knee seen to. In the meantime, I've got some Evening Primrose in my bag. It helps with cramps."

He cast a startled glance her way. "No thanks. You can keep your herbal stuff. I'm fine. My knee's gone out on me before. A few days rest will fix it." He gestured toward the dinette. "Have a seat. Breakfast will be up in a minute."

She sat down. "What are we having?"

"Cinnamon French toast, one of my specialties." He slid a plate in front of her.

She poured syrup on top and dug in. She sighed in bliss after the first bite and looked up to find him grinning at her unabashed enjoyment. "I didn't know you could cook, Jake."

"One of my many hidden talents." He settled into a seat across from her. They ate in companionable silence.

He put down his fork and leaned back to sip his coffee. "So, give. Why are you here instead of off on your honeymoon?"

She blinked at him, startled by the edge of suspicion in his voice. Was he playing some good cop/bad cop routine on her? His watchful gaze told her that he probably wouldn't be fobbed off with a few half-truths, but to protect her wounded pride, she had to try.

"It's simple. I decided to call it off. I still had the two weeks off from my shop, so I decided to come here for some rest."

He continued to study her expression. His fingers drummed impatiently on the table. "So, I shouldn't expect an armed posse to come looking for you?"

"No. I left a note."

She quickly realized he wasn't buying her everything-is-okay story, and looked away from his perceptive gaze. He was the last man she'd want to share her secret with. The sting of Jake's rejection seven years ago hadn't completely faded. Grayson's infidelity only confirmed her shortcomings as a woman.

He frowned. "A note! You blew town again."

She wrinkled her nose at his gruff statement. "I didn't blow town. I made a strategic retreat. I'm not some green eighteen-year-old kid you have to worry about, Jake. They aren't going to send out any search parties. You're quite safe."

He got a faraway look in his eyes. "I remember when you left home a week before your eighteenth birthday. It gave your father quite a few gray hairs."

Her thoughts drifted back to her troubled teens. Jake had been the catalyst for her final act of rebellion. His rejection had sent her running, not away, but toward her future.

"I had to break away. It was the best thing for us, and you know it. Besides, if I remember it right, you were the one who told me I was a spoiled brat, and I ought to grow up."

He looked away. "Yeah, we both said things we didn't mean that night."

She was surprised by his regretful tone. His jaw tightened, the only sign of his tension. He'd obviously had a few mixed feelings about that evening, as well. It was a balm to her freshly wounded femininity to realize she'd affected him at least a little bit.

"Don't worry, Jake, there aren't going to be any recriminations about that night. I'm a strong, successful businesswoman now, and that might not have happened if you hadn't set me running."

He frowned. "Let's get back to the point at hand. If everything's so hunky-dory, there's no reason I shouldn't call your family and let them know you got here okay." He reached for the telephone on the counter.

She grabbed his arm, feeling his muscles ripple under her palm when he went still. "Please don't."

"Why shouldn't I call? More importantly, why did you run out on your daddy's hand-picked son-in-law?"

She glared at him, but felt the wind leave her sails when he refused to back down. "I won't marry a man I can't trust. It sounds cliché, but I caught Grayson with another woman."

"You caught old Grayson in the sack?"

She gulped. "They weren't in bed. He had her bent over one of the dining room chairs. I stopped by his apartment after our rehearsal dinner." Feeling Jake's watchful gaze on her, she turned away. "He'd given me a key, and I intended to surprise him."

"But he surprised you instead."

"That's one way of putting it."

"Who is she?"

Samantha closed her eyes. The stunning events replayed in her mind. She'd heard them before seeing it—curious thwacks, groans, and cries that drew her toward the living room. She rounded the corner and found her fiancé clad only in a black cape. His angry red erection bobbed in the air as he alternately teased and punished the blonde bent over the arm of the sofa. The woman's breathy cries begged him to take her. Grayson's laughing retort was how he'd compared his lover's hot response to Samantha's frigidity. Samantha had stood there in stunned disbelief as her tender feelings for him died. It was all based on a lie. During their whirlwind courtship, he'd restrained his desires, not wanting to tarnish their union by taking her before their wedding. His old-fashioned gallantry had touched her.

"I don't know. I saw her from behind. Long blonde hair and a butterfly tattoo on her bright red bottom were all that sunk in."

Jake reached out to touch her hand. "I'm sorry, honey." The warmth from his fingers was comforting.

"He didn't even notice me standing there. He was making so much noise whipping her. If what I saw is any indication, he's rather kinky and dangerous. He seemed completely out of control. I threw my engagement ring at him and told him what he could do with it before I ran away. He was shocked. It was almost comical. If you'd been chased by a naked man wearing a cape and carrying a strap, you'd understand why I hightailed it out of there." She squared her shoulders as she shook off the upsetting memory.

The rage she saw in Jake's eyes shocked her.

"Did that dirtbag touch you?"

"No. He tripped on his cape. I made it out of there in the nick of time."

"I'll call the cops and have him arrested."

"For what? Playing 'Captain Kinky?' There's no law against being tied up and spanked. It might spice some couple's lovemaking, but not my fiancé. Not with another woman. I don't care what wild oats he might have been trying to sow."

"I'm sorry, Samantha."

She pulled away. The last thing she wanted from him was sympathy. "Save your pity for someone who needs it. Last night's fiasco made me see that marriage isn't for me."

He shook his head. "I wouldn't say that. You're the type of woman who should be married."

Unsettled by his tender statement, she frowned. "Why, because I'm helpless? Do you think I need a man to take care of me?"

He picked up his coffee cup and smiled at her. "No, because you're warm and passionate. You have a lot of love to give to the right man. A jerk like Grayson St. James didn't deserve you."

His words of admiration surprised her. Seven years ago, he'd thrown her offer of a night of passion back in her face.

"You could have fooled me. Last time we had this conversation, you wasted no time letting me know I was less than desirable."

He shook his head. "You were still jailbait, and I worked for your old man. Anyway, the only reason you made a play for me was to get back at your father."

She felt herself blush. It wasn't true. She'd had a secret crush on him back then. It all came to a head when Jake pulled her out of an after-graduation beach party. She'd been furious at still being treated like a wayward schoolgirl.

In an instant, she'd decided bedding Jake Ramsey was the perfect way to assert her independence and had reached up to kiss him. She could still recall his shock. He froze in her embrace. Then his mouth had softened under hers, and his arms came around her to draw her to him. He'd pressed her against his erection for an instant, giving her unmistakable proof of her effect on him. Then he'd pushed her away.

She could still recall his words. *Don't tease me, Sunshine. I'm a man. Not one of those little boys you fool around with.*

The next day, much to her father's disapproval, she'd moved out.

Embarrassed at dredging up the past, Samantha changed the subject. "About our sleeping arrangements... I think it would work better if I slept in the loft. That way, your early rising won't wake me." She stretched and stifled a groan. Her back ached from a night spent on the lumpy couch.

"No."

She was startled by his abrupt denial. His teasing mood had evaporated. It seemed she'd crossed some line. Trying to mend the rift, she said, "I'd be willing to pay for inconveniencing you."

His hard mouth kicked up into a mysterious half-smile. "I doubt it. Not the kind of payment I'd want."

Did Jake want her? It would be an earthshaking revelation. She couldn't handle a man like him. Not here, not now. All her instincts for self-preservation told her to ignore his statement. She would appeal to his chivalrous side. After all, he'd been quite agreeable this morning.

"It's just that the sofa is hard on my back. Do you remember my old back injury from when I fell off a ski lift when I was sixteen? Well, it's been bothering me lately." She smiled sweetly, all but batting her eyes at him. "The gentlemanly thing to do would be to let me have the more comfortable sleeping arrangements."

A mocking smile played on his lips. "I'm not a gentleman, or have you forgotten?"

She stiffened her spine, leveling a cool gaze his way. So, he wanted to play games. Well, she didn't want to play.

"No, I haven't forgotten." She got up from the table and deliberately turned her back on him. "I'm going to shower, get dressed, and go into town for supplies. I'll keep to myself for the rest of my stay."

"I'd wait a while if I were you."

She frowned and turned to snap at him. "Don't tell me what to do, Ramsey. I make my own decisions."

He shrugged. "Suit yourself."

Walking into the bathroom, she turned on the shower adjusting the temperature. Shrugging out of her pajamas, she hopped into the shower. A second later, the spray turned from hot to icy. She let out a high-pitched shriek of surprise as needles of cold water pounded on her head.

"I told you to wait," Jake called from the kitchen. "The water heater is on the fritz."

She swore a blue streak. He'd let her freeze to teach her a lesson. Jake Ramsey was a hard-hearted jerk. Then she remembered the quilt he must have covered her with last night, and sighed.

He had her in total confusion. Maybe that was what he wanted. Just what kind of game was he playing here? Irritated, she rummaged through her bag for her supplements. She'd need them to get through this. Pulling out the bottles, she lined them up on the bottom row of the medicine cabinet, shoving his toothbrush and aspirin to the side.

She walked out of the bathroom ten minutes later, chilled but fully dressed. Thankfully, he was nowhere in sight.

She stopped by the loft ladder, peered up, and listened. There was no noise from above. He had probably gone outside. Why didn't he want her up there? What was he trying to hide? Her duty as the owner's daughter was to ensure he didn't have the loft covered with empty beer cans and girlie magazines. She eyed the ladder warily. She put her qualms about climbing the ladder to rest. She could do this. It was the perfect moment to find out what he was doing.

But what would she say if he was up there? I thought I'd take you up on your offer to have a fling? He'd probably love that, given his surprising come-on this morning. If she was going to do this, she had to be quick. It was a good thing her fear of heights was a thing of the past.

She reached for the ladder and cautiously started to climb. At the top, she stopped to peer around. The loft was neat as a pin. There were no beer cans or girlie magazines in sight. She noticed some items he must have brought with him, a laptop and a telescope on a tripod. How odd. Who was he watching with the telescope?

Tempted to see what the scope was homed in on, she hesitated. The knowledge she would be invading his privacy made her pause. She was probably being too suspicious. She'd have to face the consequences if he found out. He was bound to be furious.

Her foot wobbled on the tread, and she sucked in a shaky breath as a remnant of her old fear of heights resurfaced. She tamped down the incipient panic attack, practicing her deep breathing and repeating her mantra just as the therapist had taught her. Regaining serenity, she started to step up when a thump from below caught her attention. She looked down and froze, panic washing over her anew.

Jake stood at the bottom of the ladder, glowering up at her.

He took a step closer. "Well, if it isn't my cat burglar. I didn't know you went in for second-story work, Sunshine. Want to tell me what you're doing up there?"

She shook her head. Silently repeating her mantra, she tried to stay still.

A nerve pulsed in his jaw. "In that case, why don't you come down from there?"

"I don't think I can." She met his eyes and saw a glimmer of understanding dawn there.

He shook his head. "Don't tell me you're still scared of heights."

"I thought I was over it, but I'm not. No thanks to you." Through clenched teeth, she muttered, "Get me down from here, Ramsey."

He grinned back. "Hold still, and I'll take care of you."

She wanted to kick him for finding this situation amusing. Instead, she conjured up a picture of a dewy meadow filled with wildflowers and changed her mantra to—*I hate Jake*.

He scaled the ladder, standing with his feet on the rung below hers.

The ladder swayed, and she screamed, closing her eyes, sure they would fall.

"You're not going to fall." Jake's voice was soft and reassuring. "Can you step down with me?"

She gave a tiny shake of her head.

"Yes, you can," he said.

He smoothed her hair back. He leaned into her, letting her feel his intriguing warmth, and kissed her exposed nape.

She gasped. Her knees wobbled, but not from fear this time.

"Feel good?" he asked suggestively. "Come on, baby, let's go down."

She suddenly found herself moving with him. Every time she got frightened, his plundering lips were there to shock her out of her fear.

At last, her feet touched the floor, and she slumped against the ladder, trembling from relief and excitement.

His hands clasped her shoulders in a firm grip. He gently turned her around. A heady mix of emotions flashed in his gray eyes before his mouth came down to claim hers.

An excited languor surged through her. Her lips parted under his masterful ones. The kiss was hard and more wonderful than she'd remembered. He pressed her back against the ladder. His chest rubbed against hers. Her nipples instantly beaded into hard points. He stepped between her open legs, nestling his manhood against the juncture of her thighs. She shivered, sucking at his tongue, wriggling against him as he bumped against her. She found herself rubbing against him as pressure built inside her.

A kiss like this was what she ached for, she realized. Waves of anger, fear, and betrayal washed away under his ministrations. He groaned into her mouth and pressed tighter.

He broke the kiss, and murmured something dark and desperate as he bent to suck on her neck.

Her face burned, as well as her whole body. She whimpered against him. She tried to put her arms around him, but he held them fast, effortlessly restraining her for his pleasure. She grew wet as she shimmied against him. His erection was harder, pressing closer, and then suddenly...

She came. Orgasm wracked her body as she clung to him and cried out.

He went still, his body stiff. He pushed her back against the ladder, their mouths inches apart.

Her cheeks flamed while she gazed into the smoky depths of his eyes. Good grief, she'd practically humped the man. And, worst of all, she'd come from a kiss and some petting. She *was* the sex-starved princess Grayson had called her.

"I'm sorry. I didn't mean..." She caught the desire die in his eyes, and her protests dried.

He drew in a ragged breath. "Don't say it. I'm not your type, right?"

His mocking tone told her he didn't know how wrong he was and how close she'd come to surrender. That was what it'd be like with him, she knew, absolute surrender. At least she had the power to turn on one man. She had his hard-on for proof. But vulnerable as she was, he wasn't trying to take her. Knowing his state, she thanked her lucky stars. At least he'd maintained some control.

She eased away from him as far as the ladder would allow.

He frowned. "Don't worry, I don't take unwilling women, even if they get their jollies dry-humping me."

All her softened feelings for him vaporized. This wasn't something she wanted to joke about. He should understand that. "I won't bother you again."

"Sunshine, it was no bother. I'm ready to serve any time, any place." He traced the curve of her bottom lip, brushing it softly with his index finger.

She felt like she'd been poleaxed. She noted the dumbstruck expression on his face.

His brow wrinkled. "Why did you climb the ladder if you were so scared of heights? Was the urge to snoop just too much for you to resist?"

He was angry. Good. Maybe that would keep him from realizing she was putty in his hands. She turned away from his watchful eye and stepped forward on shaky knees.

Now was the time to rebuild the walls between them. If she was this shaken up by an unfulfilled seduction, she knew she couldn't handle a full-fledged affair. It made her consider running back home, but she'd done enough of that in her twenty-eight years. It was time to stand her ground and get her mixed-up hormones in order. Maybe she'd pick up some ginseng in town. It was supposed to boost one's stamina.

She grabbed her purse and headed for the front door. "As I said earlier, I think it would be better if we kept to ourselves for the two weeks."

"It isn't going to be that easy, Sunshine. Not easy at all."

She ignored his regretful tone. She swept out the door and hopped into her little red sports car. She peeled out of the driveway like the devil himself was at her heels. An apt description of the man she'd left behind.

All her senses were on full alert. Tingling where she had no business was ringing, she felt more vibrantly alive than she had in ages, and it frightened her. She'd sworn off men and marriage last night, and now she ached for Jake Ramsey. On the bright side, she'd learned she wasn't cold, as she'd heard Grayson refer to her last night. Not where Jacob Ramsey was concerned, anyway.

Reaching the edge of town, she glanced at her watch. It was six-thirty. She pulled in behind a police cruiser in front of the local cafe. It might be Kathy's cruiser. She wanted to get more information on what Jake was doing up here, all by his lonesome.

The cafe was half-full. Luck was on her side. Kathy was sitting at the counter. Samantha sat on the empty stool beside her and accepted a menu from a passing waitress. What she needed was a nice soothing cup of chamomile tea.

Kathy turned to smile at her. "Hey, girl, what brings you out and about so early in the morning?"

"Don't you mean who? Jake Ramsey is the most obnoxious man it has ever been my misfortune to meet."

"Oh, I don't know, I think he's kind of cute in a rough-around-the-edges sort of way."

"Cute? Are you out of your mind? He's a big Viking barbarian with an ego three sizes too big." Samantha slanted a speculative gaze Kathy's way. "Just how chummy are you two, anyway?"

"Don't worry. You can have him all to yourself. A Viking, huh? That is an intriguing picture. I can see him standing on the deck of his ship, his hair flying in the breeze as he goes off in search of plunder."

Samantha thought about the clinch she and Jake had just been in, and felt her cheeks turn red. Plunder indeed. He'd practically ravaged her, and she'd loved it.

Striving to downplay her troubled emotions, she rolled her eyes at the vivid description. "Let's not get carried away. He's a man like any other, only more macho and objectionable. By the way, you seem to be taking his attack on me in a pretty calm manner."

"He was the one I found moaning on the floor. I gave you a break last night. I could have arrested you for assault."

Samantha leaned closer to Kathy and lowered her voice. "I can explain that. I thought he was a crazed rapist."

"Rapist? My God, what did he do to make you think that?"

"Will you keep your voice down?" Samantha glanced around, hoping they hadn't drawn too much attention. "I tried to get into the front door with my key."

"The lock's been changed."

"I found that out the hard way."

"So go on." Kathy leaned closer. "Tell me the rest."

"Ramsey pulled me inside, threw me to the floor, and touched my..."

"Your what?"

"My breasts."

"Well, it would be hard to miss those," Kathy said, grinning to break the tension. "You do have a rather impressive pair. It's a good thing he's got big hands."

"Very funny. I'm not interested in the barbarian's hands or any other part of his anatomy, for that matter." She clamped her thighs together, recalling and rejecting the memory of his magic touch.

"You know what they say, big hands, big—"

"Never mind," Samantha cut in. She needed to change the subject, fast.

Kathy smiled. "Remember the breast enlargement exercise book we got ahold of when we were thirteen?"

Samantha flashed a big grin. "How could I forget our quest for curves that summer? I never did so many pushups in all my life."

"Yeah, I did build up some rather impressive biceps. Just no boobs," Kathy said, looking down at her petite curves. "You, on the other hand, grew like mad throughout the summer."

"It's all genetic, and you know it." Samantha smiled at her friend's irrepressible grin. "Let's get back to the subject at hand."

"Did he try anything else?"

"He frisked me."

"You mean, patted you down for weapons? You probably scared the poor man to death."

"Poor man?" Samantha gaped at her in disbelief. Did she think their little tussle had scared him? "Come now. He's a lot bigger than I am."

"He's also super-paranoid about prowlers." Kathy shrugged. "He had some trouble back home."

"I didn't know about the trouble back home. It explains his over-reaction last night, but doesn't clarify his strange attitude today. He's still being nasty to me."

"What do you mean, nasty?"

Samantha sighed, flashing back to their passionate embrace. "He kissed me."

Kathy rolled her eyes. "Oh, wow. That's just brutal." She leaned forward and gazed at her neck. "I see that's not all he did."

Samantha frowned. Did her reaction show? She couldn't still be glowing, could she? "What do you mean?"

"He gave you a love bite."

"What?" Her hand went to her throat. Her gaze flashed to the mirror behind the counter. Of all the uncivilized, macho tricks, the man had marked her. She watched herself blush, recalling the heady encounter. She'd been too caught up in action to care what he was doing.

She buttoned the top button on her blouse. "That just tears it." She'd have to rub the love bite with vitamin E to heal it quickly.

"It can't be all that bad. Why don't you two kiss and make up?"

"No way. The man's too complicated for me. After we kissed, he yelled at me. He's been running hot and cold and acting suspicious since last night."

"Considering how things started, there's bound to be some tension. Like my mother said, what you give is what you get back. If you treat him in a friendly manner, he'll probably reciprocate."

Samantha gave up the argument. Kathy would disagree, but she knew she had to reset boundaries for her own peace of mind or she'd tumble into his bed like a ripe plum. She wasn't ready for a man like him. Even so, he made her feel like a warm, sexy woman. It was a reaction that scared the heck out of her.

"So, what are your plans? I can put you up at my place."

"No, thanks." Samantha smiled and patted Kathy's hand. "I appreciate the offer, but I intend to stay at the cabin."

Kathy cocked her head. "What about Jake?"

Even though she feared acting like a moth to the flame, she knew she couldn't walk away. She had to settle this mess with Jake to regain control of her life. "He and I have come to an understanding. We'll share the cabin for two weeks, but keep separate."

Kathy smiled and shook her head. "Sure, you will."

Samantha ignored her amused remark. "I was wondering if Ramsey told you why he decided to come here for vacation."

"He's here on business. Or, at least, that's what the Chief said. We're supposed to make extra patrols by the cabin and offer assistance as needed."

"That's odd. This keeps getting more intriguing. What kind of business could he be conducting in the wilds of the north woods?"

"I'm not sure. He's keeping it close to the vest. I know he wired the cabin and boathouse, and we've increased our patrols."

The telescope and laptop would fit in with an undercover operation.

Samantha got to her feet. "I'm going to dig and find out why he's here."

"That's just what I'm worried about," Kathy said as Samantha walked toward the door. "Don't do anything stupid. I'd hate to have to arrest you."

As she stepped outside, Samantha heard the distinctive clunk of her defective passenger door slamming shut.

"My car!" She spun toward it.

A man wearing a blue baseball cap sprinted away and raced around the corner.

Samantha ran to her car and tore open the door. The contents of her glove box and console lay strewn across the front seats. CDs glinted in the sun. Papers were crumpled and fluttering in the breeze.

Kathy walked out of the diner. "What happened?"

"Some guy did this. He heard me coming and took off."

"Who was he?"

"I didn't recognize him. All I saw was his back. He was tall, dressed in jeans and a flannel shirt, and wearing a blue baseball cap."

"That describes half the men around these parts. We've had a rash of petty thefts lately. Did he take anything?"

Samantha cast a shaken glance over the jumbled mess. "It's hard to tell. What kind of jerk would do a thing like this?"

"I'll write up a complaint."

Samantha shivered. "I guess it was just a random act of vandalism. I'll keep my doors locked from now on."

Jake limped into the bathroom in search of aspirin for his aching knee. He opened the medicine cabinet, noting Samantha's bottles lined up on the shelf. Evening Primrose, that's what she'd offered him earlier, said it helped cramps.

Shrugging, he grabbed the bottle and took one. Reading the back of the bottle, he saw it was good for PMS and cramps. Well, it wouldn't kill him. At the rate they were going, he'd have a severe case of blue balls before the week was through. He was still semi-aroused. He'd never forget how she'd caught fire in his arms, coming, shivering against him. It was imprinted on his brain.

He walked out to the living room and punched in Samuel Logan's private number on speed dial. He paced the room's confines while waiting for his boss to pick up. No doubt, big Sam was in a foul temper by now with the wedding canceled.

"Logan here. This better be important."

Jake stifled a grin at his gruff tone. "It's Ramsey."

"Goddamn, Ramsey, you must be psychic. I was just about to call you. You've got to drop what you're doing and hunt down my daughter. She jilted Grayson and took off."

"Leave her alone. There's no need to hunt her down. She's here at the cabin."

"I don't believe it. Do you mean to tell me she ran off to meet you of her free will? The girl can't stand you."

That might be true, but she was here for the duration, judging from how she'd taken over the medicine cabinet. Jake thought back to their sweet interlude this morning when she came in his arms and grimaced. She'd regretted it the minute he'd backed away from her.

"I know it. She didn't know I was here. I've decided to let her stay and lick her wounds privately."

"What wounds?"

"Let's just say that Grayson St. James wasn't the injured party, no matter what kind of sob story he tells you." He scowled, thinking about the incident Samantha had described.

"So, what happened? What did that boy do to my baby?"

Jake hesitated. Samantha would never learn to trust him if he betrayed her confidence. He'd handle St. James personally when they returned.

"I can't tell you. I promised."

"Promised?" Samuel shouted, adding sourly, "Damn it all, I'm your employer and ordering you to tell me."

"I can't." He patiently waited for his boss to finish sputtering. "Sorry."

"Well, I'll be damned. She has you wrapped around her little finger."

Jake sighed at the grudging amusement in Samuel's voice. "Not true. I'm the one in charge around here."

"Right. Keep me apprised of the situation. That fool stake-out you insisted on come up with anything yet?"

"No." Jake relaxed, satisfied by his dismissive tone. Big Sam had enough to worry about without fretting over Tad's involvement. He'd just as soon downplay things until he knew the truth.

"Told you it was all a mares' nest. Wrap things up soon and bring my daughter back. And, Ramsey?"

"Yes, sir?"

"You take good care of my little girl. Let nature take its course."

Jake frowned at the phone. Cryptic messages weren't usually his boss's style. "What?"

"Simple. I'm through playing Cupid, boy. One lesson I learned while I spent the morning canceling the wedding and worrying about my daughter is that I'm lousy at it. From now on, she can find her beaus."

When Samantha returned, Jake sat on the sofa reading a paperback mystery novel. His foot was propped up on the coffee table, and an ice pack draped over his knee.

She felt a troublesome pang of guilt again at the damage she'd done. He'd already rejected her herbal remedy. What else could she do for him?

"Do you want me to take you into town to see a doctor?"

"Don't bother. I know what to do for it."

After putting away her groceries, she turned to face him. There was a vigilant expression on his face that set her on edge. She bit her lip. Maybe Kathy was right. She'd probably shaken him up last night.

"I'm sorry if I scared you last night."

"I wasn't scared."

She should have known he wouldn't admit to it. A bad-boy smile played around his lips again. It had been the wrong approach to take. She decided that it would be better just to come out with it.

"I know why you're here."

He went still, eyeing her warily. "What do you mean by that?"

She frowned at his innocent act. She doubted he'd been innocent since he was a baby in his cradle. "Come now. You're here on business. You're doing surveillance."

His foot came off the coffee table with a thump, the ice pack dropping to the floor. "Who told you that?"

She folded her arms over her chest, refusing to be intimidated by the big barbarian any longer. "I have my sources."

He stood and stalked toward her until he halted mere inches away. "I want an answer, Samantha. Who told you?"

She moved to the side, alarmed by his violent reaction.

His hands came down on the countertop on either side of her.

She stood trapped for his interrogation. It was a vivid reminder of the times he'd pulled her out of teen scrapes with the usual lecture on proper ladylike behavior. There was just one difference now. She wasn't going to take it anymore.

She tossed her hair back and glared at him. "Does it matter? I know the truth, and you're a big liar, Ramsey."

"Shut up."

She saw a nerve pulse in his jaw and knew she'd hit a sore point. Still, she couldn't resist prodding him further. "Make me."

He took a deep breath. "Let's settle down. There's no need to get into a fight. You'd never win, and you know it."

She bristled at his condescending tone. She had to restrain herself from lashing out at his sore knee again. "Don't be so damned patronizing. I'm not some dumb teenager you can order around anymore."

He waited a moment and then let out a heavy sigh. "Look, I know this is a rough way to find out that I'm here to haul your baby brother's ass out of trouble. You might say his life depends on me. And, if you don't want things to get complicated real fast, you'd better settle down."

Chapter Three

Jake's anger vanished. Samantha sagged against the cabinet and he cursed how she'd made him lose control.

Her hand went to her throat. "Oh, my God."

"You didn't know." He'd shot his mouth off, complicating things to no end, and she hadn't known.

He glanced at the hickey peeking above her primly buttoned-up blouse and frowned. She had him acting like a love-starved teenage kid, and he'd made a rookie mistake. The reason for his slip-up was simple. She had him rattled.

He wondered for a moment if taking her to bed would cure what ailed him. Not that she'd have him on a bet anymore.

She placed her hands on his chest and tried to push him away.

He stood fast, refusing to budge. She needed to understand the precarious situation they were in. He wasn't worried about himself or Tad. He was concerned about her. She let her hands drop to her sides and glared at him.

"Just what kind of trouble is Tad supposed to be in?"

He snapped his thoughts back into a businesslike mode. He was a professional, damn it, and she was his charge, whether she liked it or not. Her distress was palpable, but he had a job to do.

"There's been a loss of technology from Logan Industries. We traced it down to a handful of people."

A faint smile curved the corners of her lips. "Doesn't that show you it's probably somebody else?"

He saw a glimmer of hope flare in her eyes, and he sought to squelch it immediately. Hope could be a dangerous thing. "I intercepted an inter-office email that said there was going to be an exchange at the boathouse. Who else would know about the old family vacation spot?"

"Lots of people."

Her words were defiant, but Jake could sense her doubt. She wouldn't meet his eyes.

"So, what do you plan to do?"

"I'm going to catch him in the act, read him the riot act, and turn him over to the cops."

She gasped. "You can't do that, Jake. If you're right and Tad is involved, there has to be a logical explanation. He's probably trying to ferret out who's responsible."

The idea of Tad as a detective was laughable. He was too busy having fun to do anything so serious. Tad Logan was six months out of college and still in frat boy party mode. Only his father's influence had him ensconced in the executive suite of Logan Industries. "Get real, Samantha. You're grasping at straws, and you know it."

"You don't have to act like it's such a far-fetched idea." She raised her chin a notch. "I have absolute faith in my brother's integrity."

He gazed at the obstinate set of her chin. Even in the face of overwhelming evidence, she refused to back down. "You haven't been around for years. How do you know he's so noble?"

"I just do." Her militant expression softened. "Did you ask Tad what was going on?"

"And tip my hand?" He shook his head. "Now you see why I tried to get you to leave. You shouldn't be here, Samantha."

That wasn't the only reason. It was unlikely, but things could turn nasty. She didn't belong in the line of fire. Now that he knew she wasn't involved, she had to get out.

"Oh, my God." Her eyes widened. "You're afraid of trouble, aren't you?"

"I didn't say that." Damn, but she could read him like a book.

"You didn't have to."

Her concern, of course, was all for her brother. "It's a distinct possibility. I want you to leave and keep your mouth shut."

"No way. I'm not leaving. I'm going to stay and look after my brother's interests."

"I'm perfectly capable of looking after your brother."

Her eyes narrowed as she glared at him, her hands on her hips. "Yeah, and help him right into a jail cell. No way am I going to leave him to your tender mercies. I'm staying."

"I'm not the heartless bastard you take me for." He brushed a wisp of copper-highlighted hair off her flushed face. "A little time in the slammer just might straighten your brother out."

She swatted his hand away.

He frowned at the meaningful action and let his hand drop. "I doubt it would go that far. Your father wouldn't want his son locked up."

"No, he'd cut him off from the family and the business. Tad's always been the apple of our father's eye. He couldn't stand the isolation. You can't just throw him to the wolves. If you're right and he is involved, there must be some mitigating circumstances."

"Drink, drugs, gambling, a woman. Any one of them could be the catalyst for a man's downfall. But they're just excuses. A man has to be fundamentally weak to let them consume him."

She wrinkled her nose. "From your tone, I can tell you'd never let yourself be that weak."

He quirked an eyebrow in response to her scathing tone. "Drink, drugs, and gambling aren't a problem. But a certain woman I know is driving me crazy right now."

"Very funny." She frowned at him. "Does my father know what you're up to?"

"He knows I'm here."

"He doesn't know you're here waiting for Tad, does he?"

"I didn't see any reason to alarm him." Hope sprung to life in her sparkling turquoise eyes, and he once more sought to tamp it down. He had enough trouble on his hands without Samantha's involvement. "He knows Tad is on the short list of suspects, but I didn't apprise him of the stake out because he had enough on his mind with marrying you off." He knew he'd hit a nerve when her gaze dropped, and he called himself a ruthless son-of-a-bitch. This dose of cold water was for her own good.

She sighed. "And what did he think about Tad being on the list?"

Jake hesitated, surprised by her rapid recovery. She wouldn't be diverted so easily. "He doesn't believe it, either. Says a Logan wouldn't cheat, especially his golden boy, Tad."

"He's right. They've always been close. There's no way Tad would betray him." She flashed a victorious smile his way. "That should tell you you're pursuing the wrong man."

"Possibly. It would be best if you weren't here when it happens, whichever way it comes down. Now that I know you're not involved, I need you to go home if you agree to keep your mouth shut."

She frowned. "So, you thought I was in on the thefts."

"I wasn't sure. It was a strange coincidence, you showing up here the other night."

"You ought to be happy I'm here. If you're right and Tad shows up, I'm probably the only one he trusts. Face it, Ramsey. You need me."

He saw past the smoke screen she was trying to throw out. He didn't trust her suddenly friendly smile one bit. "What makes you think I need you?"

"For starters, I'm another pair of eyes."

"I don't need another pair of eyes. I've got the boathouse wired. If anyone tries to get in, I'll know it."

She slanted a sour glance his way. "Like you knew when I tried to get into the cabin last night."

"Something like that. Only this time, my intruder won't be a beautiful, if irritating, woman."

She rolled her eyes. "What a sweet talker you are. If Tad is involved, he's probably a little part in this. I can talk to him and convince him to help you get to the bottom of this fiasco. So, you need me, right?"

He shrugged. It probably would be better to keep her where he could keep an eye on her. With any luck, the proximity might ease his way into her bed. "I know when I'm fighting a losing battle. You can stay as long as you promise to keep out of the way. And obey my orders."

"Of course."

Samantha jotted down a name on her short list of suspects with a sigh. She was grasping at straws, and she knew it. A cranky secretary and a grumpy gardener weren't much of a line-up. She had to admit, a born detective, she wasn't, but she had to try. She absentmindedly sketched a crooked maze. That's what this whole mess was.

Jake's footsteps rumbled in the loft. He'd disappeared there after supper. Whatever he was up to probably wasn't suitable for her brother.

She picked up the list and headed for the ladder to the loft. If Tad was involved in this mess, she had to find out as soon as possible to help him. Jake might believe him a criminal, but she knew he was just a fun-loving kid.

She stopped at the bottom of the ladder and looked up. Images of her earlier panic attack flashed through her mind. A cold sense of dread settled in the pit of her stomach. She had to keep her fears at bay if she was going to help her brother.

She put her hand on the ladder and closed her eyes, visualizing her dewy meadow. She imagined herself walking among the wildflowers, and her tight muscles began to relax. She climbed, silently repeating her new mantra—*Jake Ramsey is my partner. I hope I can trust him.*

And then, suddenly, she was at the top. She didn't risk a glance down, not wanting to push her luck. Instead, she quickly stepped into the bedroom.

Jake looked up from his seat at the computer. He frowned at the interruption and closed the laptop. "What's up?"

She was taken aback by his continued secrecy. She knew all about his mission. There was no longer a need for him to hide what he was doing. "I thought we should talk about how we're going to conduct this stakeout."

"We?" He yawned, stood, and stretched.

She frowned at his less-than-cooperative tone. "Yes, *we*. I'm your assistant, remember?"

"I agreed you could stay, but I never accepted your offer of help. I told you that I work alone, and I also told you before my room is off-limits."

She frowned. He was the most hardheaded man she'd ever known. "There's no need to keep secrets anymore. If I'm going to help you, I need to know what's happening. I'll be a good assistant. You wait and see." She thrust the paper at him. "Here, I made a list."

"A list of what?" He yawned and took the paper.

"Other suspects."

He glanced at the paper and cocked an amused glance her way. "You think Mrs. Johnson and Ned, the gardener, are part of a den of industrial espionage agents?"

She sighed. "It's a long shot, but you must admit, they're not the friendliest people on the planet."

"Mrs. Johnson retired late last year, long before the losses began. She's now being cranky down in Florida, I believe. Ned doesn't have the access needed to pull off the thefts." He looked up and grinned. "The maze you drew is a nice touch, though."

"I tend to doodle when I'm tense." She snatched the paper back. "Let's get back to the business at hand. What can I do to assist you?"

"I know one sure tension reliever, but I don't think you're ready for that yet."

She backed away. "You're right. I've decided we need to keep this on a business-like footing. What happened this morning was an aberration. Two stressed people in close quarters."

A nerve pulsed in his jaw. He reached out to snag her. "Let's put your theory to the test."

He silenced her shriek with a kiss.

She went still for an outraged moment, then slowly her anger melted under his passionate onslaught. She opened her mouth to his demands, slipping her tongue into his mouth and tasting him. Her arms wrapped around his neck as she trembled against him.

Suddenly, he set her back on her heels, pushing her away. "There you go, partner. Nice and business-like."

She blinked at him, shimmering with unsatisfied need. He was up to his old tricks, probably trying to teach her a lesson. "And I don't want you giving me more love bites."

He rolled his shoulders. "Look, we can't be in the same room without fighting or wanting to jump each other's bones. So, why don't you head back downstairs and go to bed? I can handle things up here."

He was wrong. She could control herself if she tried, and he needed her help, even if he wasn't willing to admit it. She didn't like his attempt to push her away. He wasn't going to get away with it.

"I can see you're dead on your feet. How much sleep did you get last night?"

He shrugged. "Not much, between keeping watch and coming down to check on you. I'm getting too old for this stuff."

"That reminds me." She crossed the distance between them to place a hand on his arm. "Thank you for covering me with the quilt last night. I would have frozen without it." She was pleased a startled smile curved the corners of his hard mouth.

"You're welcome."

Encouraged by his warm tone, she hurried to say, "You may as well relent and let me help you, Jake, because you're stuck with me. If we try, we're both mature enough to control ourselves."

He shook his head. "Okay. If that's what you want, have at it. I remember how stubborn you can be. If you're determined to help, I know there isn't much chance of me changing your mind."

She smiled at his grudging tone. "No chance at all." She glanced at the telescope, focused on the boathouse next to the lake. "What do we do now?"

"Wait."

"What do you mean, wait? Aren't we going to put our heads together and come up with a plan of investigation? One of us could patrol the grounds while the other does some nosing around on the computer. And, of course, we should come up with code names."

He shook his head. "Hold it right there, Sunshine. All we're going to do is sit tight and keep a low profile. Surveillance work tends to be rather dull and tedious."

She wrinkled her nose. He seemed to be enjoying her disappointment. He was wrong if he thought a little boredom would make her quit.

"It would seem."

"The only code word we'll need is a panic code."

She frowned at his suddenly serious expression. "What do you mean by a panic code?"

"Simple, if you hear me say it, duck. If I hear you say it, I'll know you need my help fast."

"I think I resent that. I can handle a crisis just as well as you can."

"Tough. If you want to play, it'll be by my rules."

Gazing at his firm expression, she knew she was beaten. If he wanted to treat her like a weak female, she'd have to go with it for now. "Okay, I get to pick the words?" She glanced out at the gathering clouds. "How about stormy weather?"

He nodded. "It'll do. If you're determined to help me, you might as well take first watch."

She glanced out the window, noting the gathering darkness. "What should I look for?"

"Take a good look around every once in a while. If you see anything out of the ordinary, wake me. I've got the buildings wired, so the alarm will go off if anyone enters. I'm going to turn in. Wake me at three, and I'll relieve you."

Was it okay to leave her post for a few moments to get her book and a cup of coffee? She heard the clunk of his boots hitting the floor as she turned around to ask him.

Averting her eyes to give him some privacy, she glanced at the laptop and reached for it. Maybe there were some games on it to keep her occupied. "What's on this?"

"Just some personal notes." He reached past her to shut down the machine. "Keep your hands off my things."

Stung by his sharp tone, she turned to frown at him. It was plain that he was still keeping secrets. What did he think she was going to do? Go out and blab his secrets to the bad guys? "Fine, you don't have to get huffy."

He raised an eyebrow in reaction, but didn't reply. After a moment, the corners of his mouth kicked up in a reluctant grin. He started to unbutton his shirt slowly.

All too aware of the power of his teasing smile, she couldn't take her eyes off him as he stripped. She gazed at his hair-roughened chest, topped by tight pink nipples, and followed the hairline down to where it whorled around his navel and disappeared into his pants. He was semi-hard, judging by the bulge in his pants. Her mouth went dry.

Gone was the goon of a few moments ago. In his place was this blatantly sexy man. Jake's muscular physic was a walking advertisement for hot, relentless sex. And the hungry look in his eyes made no secret he wanted her. He unsnapped his jeans.

She swallowed hard. "What do you think you're doing?"

"I'm getting ready for bed." His jeans hit the floor, and his smile widened. "I usually sleep in the raw, but I'll leave these on to accommodate your tender sensibilities." He pointed to the briefs that covered and cupped his manhood.

"Gee, thanks," Samantha retorted sarcastically. She turned away, telling herself to get a grip. She'd seen other good-looking, hunky men, and there was no reason to go crazy about this provocation.

"No problem," he replied with a chuckle. He climbed into the old iron bed, and the springs creaked in protest. "Do you mind switching off the overhead light, partner?"

She bristled at his amused tone. He probably thought she was a prude. Just because she didn't have a lot of experience didn't mean she was prudish, just selective.

A rueful smile curved her lips as she switched off the light. What a mess. She was hot for the man who wanted to throw her brother in jail. She sighed, walked over to the desk lamp, and switched it on.

Jake sat up in bed, instantly alert. "What's the matter? Is someone out there?"

She was startled by his reaction. It brought home the fact that this wasn't a game. "No. I didn't mean to alarm you. I didn't feel like sitting in the dark."

"Suit yourself." He lay down and rolled over, turning his back to the light.

She pulled the desk chair over to the window, sat down, and stared into the night. The full moon illuminated the weird shapes of the dock and pines, and highlighted the inky ripples on the lake.

An hour later, gentle snoring came from the bed. She yawned. This stakeout business was murder. She'd like nothing better than to crawl into that nice soft bed. She had to do something to keep alert.

She felt tempted to go down and put on a pot of coffee, but she didn't want to leave her post. Jake might not hear the alarm if an intruder tripped it. She couldn't take the risk of letting the bad guys slip away.

Yawning, she paced the room, stopping before the window to stare into the darkness. All was peaceful. She stifled another yawn and began to walk again, stopping in front of the computer.

Why was Jake so adamant about keeping her hands off his computer? Did it contain a file on Tad? She glanced at his moonlit silhouette. He was a secretive man, which meant he didn't always see all sides of an issue. Maybe there was something here she would have a different angle on.

After a final hasty glance at the bed to ensure he was still asleep, she slipped into the chair, flipped on the screen, and reached for the mouse. She started reading what she'd assumed to be a dossier and blinked.

This wasn't a clue. It was a mystery novel. "The Case of the Purloined Pearls," by Ramsey L. Jacobs. Could this be the work of her very own Jake Ramsey? The answer was obvious.

Being a mystery lover, she'd read Ramsey L. Jacobs's previous novels. She had one in her suitcase downstairs. He was good in a gritty, dangerous, masculine way. The stories were all Jake. She could see that now, and he could write a page-turner that kept her riveted. Who would have thought he had a creative side?

He'd kept his talent under wraps, but why? She'd want to shout it from the rooftops if she were a successful novelist. Then she remembered the mysterious buzz about the author. Ramsey L. Jacobs never did interviews. His best-selling mystery novels carried no author's photograph or biography, just a veiled suggestion that his line of work wouldn't allow such revelations.

A wild speculation from reviewers concerning his true identity ran the gamut from clean-cut FBI agent to down-and-dirty gangster. His publisher had kept his secret very well, but all would be revealed at a Bookseller's Gala in Chicago in several weeks. What a coincidence. Her firm, Samantha's Special Affairs, was coordinating the event.

It must've been why Jake had made several comments about early retirement. He was going to move on to new horizons. They were horizons that didn't include her. It wasn't right to invade his privacy like this. She'd just read one more page and then stop.

Sometime later, a hand clamped onto her shoulder and made her jump. Her gaze followed Jake's big, rough hand and traveled up his tanned arm to focus on his exasperated scowl.

She should have stopped at one page.

"I ought to have known you'd never do as asked."

She'd pushed her luck too far this time. Still, she couldn't help resenting his world-weary tone. "I apologize for invading your privacy. I'm very sorry."

A nerve pulsed in his tight jaw. "Sure you are, now that I've caught you in the act. I should have known better than to try to keep a secret from a woman."

Who had made him so distrustful of women? She gazed up at the harsh planes of his face, realizing that, while he knew her well, she knew nothing about him.

"Why didn't you tell me you were Ramsey L. Jacobs?"

"Because it's none of your business, Miss Snoopy Nose." He reached beyond her to switch off the screen.

"On the contrary, remember my mentioning the big events I'm catering? Well, my firm is handling Poole Publishing's Bookseller's Gala." She noted the surprised look on his face as she leaned back in her seat. "You don't have to be so touchy about this. I can assure you, your secret is safe with me."

"I'm not touchy." He let out a weary breath. "Some assistant you turned out to be. The red army could have rowed across the lake, and you wouldn't have known it."

"I'll have you know, I took periodic looks outside. Nothing moved but a couple of deer." She'd followed his instructions to the letter. Except for keeping out of his stuff. "I had to do something to keep awake. Remember, I'm not used to these all-night stakeouts like you are."

He shook his head. "That's no excuse for disobeying my instructions."

Anger flared for a moment, but then she sighed, feeling exactly like the Miss Snoopy Nose he'd called her. "When I saw a new Ramsey L. Jacobs novel, I couldn't resist. I'm sorry for intruding on a touchy issue for you."

He shrugged. "I'd appreciate it if you'd stop referring to me as touchy."

"Fine." She stifled a grin at his wounded tone. He didn't like being called sensitive.

He frowned, his brow wrinkling. "It's your turn to catch some sleep. I'll keep watch."

"I'm a big mystery fan, you know."

He went still and slanted an enquiring glance her way.

Encouraged by his interest, she continued, "I've read two of your previous books. They were excellent."

"You don't say."

She nodded, noting his edgy tone. He probably wasn't used to sharing this area of his life. "This book is good, too."

He continued to look at her, an eyebrow raised. "Good?"

"Great. It's just that your hero is so stiff and stuffy. He needs a life outside the case. A little romance."

He frowned. "He's a loner. Detective Murphy is supposed to be alone."

She shrugged. "Well, that's just my amateur opinion. Even so, I'm a big fan."

"Thanks."

She detected the hint of a blush on his face as he seemed to soak up her praise reluctantly. Did her positive opinion mean that much to him? "So, why the pen name and all the secrecy?"

"Being thought of as a creative person isn't advantageous to the business-like reputation I need to convey at Logan Industries. Consequently, I separated the different areas of my life until I was ready to leave my job."

She substituted goon-like for business-like, but she got the picture. "That's why you're leaving? To pursue your writing career?"

"That's one of the reasons, but I'm mainly tired of the old routine. I need new challenges." His mouth kicked in a wry grin. "And let me tell you, spending a week with you without killing you or making love to you will be an exciting challenge."

"Thanks a lot." He'd probably used the comment to get a rise out of her, but she wrinkled her nose, refusing to be baited by his mention of making love. At least she was satisfied knowing she'd shaken him up, too.

He studied her mild reaction and then shrugged. "Go to sleep, Samantha. I'll take the next watch."

She climbed into bed. "You'll wake me if anything happens?"

He pulled the covers over her, tucking her in. He bent over, his hands on either side of her, and pressed her down onto the mattress as he kissed her. His lips brushed against hers, and he nipped at her lower lip until she opened her mouth to his marauding tongue.

Pulling away, he said, "Don't worry, Sunshine. I'll take care of everything."

She watched him walk away, stunned by the intimate gesture. Smiling, she closed her eyes. Her lips tingled from the kiss. The pillow still carried his scent and his warmth.

She pictured herself frolicking through her dewy meadow as she fell asleep. But this time, she wasn't alone. Jake was by her side.

Two hours later, the click of the screen door snapping shut jolted Samantha awake. Before she sat up and looked around, she knew Jake was gone.

She rolled out of bed, slid into her shoes, and ran to the window.

In the dark, a boat scuttled across the lake toward the boathouse. Was the bad guy coming two days ahead of schedule?

Looking closer, she could see the shadow of a man hiding behind the shed. Probably Jake, she surmised. She had to hurry down there. No matter what the future brought, she would protect Jake and Tad. She clambered down the ladder, totally forgetting her fear.

She made her way off the porch and toward the shed, keeping in the shadow of the tree line.

Jake turned at her approach. His stern expression let her know she wasn't welcome.

"I thought you were going to wake me," she whispered as she crouched next to him.

He frowned at her, his shoulders rigid. "I told you I'd take care of things. Go back in the house, Samantha, while there's still time."

"I'm staying." Short of him tying her hand and foot, there was no way she would comply with his order.

His frustrated scowl told her he read her intentions perfectly.

"Why do you think he's here ahead of schedule?"

"We don't know his agenda, but I don't consider this early invasion a good sign. Go back to the house. I don't want to worry about you being in the line of fire."

She bit her lip. Would she be a hindrance? At that moment, the problem was taken out of her hand when the boat's engine stopped.

"Too late," she whispered.

He clamped a restraining hand on her shoulder. "Stay here while I go check this out."

She nodded as his will came close to breaching her defenses. The only way to get him to back off was to capitulate. She schooled her expression into one of submission.

"Fine. I'll stay behind."

His eyes narrowed. "You'd better, or I'll paddle your ass so hard, you won't be able to sit for a week."

She glowered at him. "My hero." When he continued to glare, she let out a sigh of defeat. "Fine. Just make sure you're extra careful."

"Don't worry. I'm not going to do anything to your brother."

"It's not just Tad I'm worried about, Jake. I care about you, too, you hard-headed jerk."

His eyes widened and a startled smile emerged. His pleased reaction told her she might just as well have said she was crazy about him.

He bent to brush a quick, burning kiss across her lips. When he pulled away, she blinked at his fierce, totally macho smile. "What was that for?"

"For being worried about me. It's a new experience for me." He turned and moved away to blend into the shadows, heading toward the boathouse.

Stunned by his outburst of affection, she hesitated for a moment, and drew her wits back together. They still had a crisis to overcome, and she was well-known for being calm. She'd do her best to stay out of Jake's way, but she had to be close enough to help. She sprinted to the corner of the shed and glanced at the pier.

The boater was tied to the dock. In the dark, she couldn't tell who it was.

She had to get a little bit closer. A few quick steps took her back to the gloom of the tree line. She picked her way through the pines until she reached the boathouse. Holding her breath, she glanced left and right, but didn't see Jake. Was he hiding inside?

She made a quick dash to the door. As quietly as possible, she turned the handle. It turned silently and effortlessly. Jake must have oiled it for just such an occasion.

The darkness inside the room was oppressive. The moonlight shining through the dusty windows gave only a tiny bit of illumination. She didn't see Jake.

Just then, the door on the dockside began to squeak.

She quickly stepped inside, closed the door, and dove for the shadows.

Footsteps rang on the concrete floor as the intruder stepped inside. A flashlight beam split the darkness.

"Is anyone there?" the trespasser shouted.

She gasped and sprang to her feet. "Tad?"

Suddenly, a *thud* rang out, followed by Tad's outraged male bellow.

She scrambled out of her hiding place. The fallen flashlight illuminated Tad and Jake wrestling on the floor, struggling for domination. She rushed over to grab the flashlight and beam it at the fighting men.

"Stop it immediately, you idiots."

Jake hesitated for a moment, frowning at her.

Tad threw a wild punch, landing a glancing blow off Jake's chin, then looked at Samantha and released a startled gasp.

"Sis, what are you doing here?"

She gazed at her little brother in horror. How could he have betrayed their father this way? "That's what I want to know. How could you be disloyal to Dad this way?"

"Stay out of this, Samantha." Jake rolled to his feet. "This is police business now." He bent to jerk Tad up by his collar.

"Police," Tad gasped. He reached for his dropped attaché case. His feet stumbled for a steady footing as he jerked out of Jake's grasp.

She willed herself to calm down. Tad's shocked reaction at the police mention wasn't that of a criminal.

"Before we take this any further, I suggest we go inside. I need to fix you both up with ice packs for your wounds."

Jake pushed Tad forward. "All right, Tad, let's follow the lady."

She noticed Jake's limp as he followed a glowering Tad. His knee was acting up again, thanks to the tussle with her brother. The Logan family was responsible for causing him much pain this week.

"Your knee's bothering you again."

"I'm okay. Maybe you can give me one of your Evening Primrose pills."

"Sure thing." He had to be hurting badly to ask for one. Noting the grim set of his mouth, she knew he was far from okay. She walked up to him and put her arm around his waist. His taut muscles rippled at her touch. "Lean on me."

Tad turned, scowling. "You two are pretty cozy."

Tad's scornful glare raked over the two of them, and her temper boiled over.

"You have no right to question my conduct after the stunt you pulled tonight." From the corner of her eye, she noticed Jake's masculine, self-satisfied smile and sighed. *Men!* She thought about moving away, but Jake seemed to read her thoughts and clung even closer to her side.

They followed Tad through the cabin door. "You've got a lot of explaining to do, Tad."

"But…"

She let go of Jake and rounded on her brother. "Have you been stealing from the firm? I told Jake it couldn't be you, that there had to be some explanation, some mitigating circumstance."

"Why don't you both leave me alone?" Tad backed away. "I haven't done anything wrong."

Jake held up a hand. "Hold the interrogation while I make us some coffee. I think we're going to need it."

She cast a concerned glance Jake's way. Was he hurt worse than she'd thought?

"I'll go get those pills." She rushed to the bathroom and got the bottle, then ran back to the kitchen with it.

"Thanks." Jake took the bottle from her. He glanced at Tad. "Want one kid? They're good for cramps."

"No, thanks."

"I'll pour the coffee," she stated, looking for something to do. She glanced at Tad, standing close to the door. He wouldn't meet her eyes.

He *was* guilty. She still couldn't wrap her mind around that horrifying fact. Heartsick, she turned back to the coffee maker.

Jake looked at Samantha and took the cups out of her hands. "I'll do that, Sunshine. You sit down." He turned to look at Tad. "Well, why don't you tell us what's been going on."

Tad set his attaché case in the corner and then dropped into a chair. "What makes you think anything is going on? This is my family's cabin, after all. I'm here on vacation."

Jake chuckled. "Boy, does that ever sound familiar. Seems to run in the family."

She chose to take the high road and ignore Jake's comment.

Tad frowned at her. "What are you doing here, sis? Grayson's been pretty tight-lipped about the whole thing. Pop's got the goon squad out looking for you." Tad looked up at Jake and blanched. "No offense intended, Mr. Ramsey. It's just a family joke between us kids."

"I'm well aware of that. Samuel didn't need to worry about your sister. She's in good hands."

Tad scowled, watching her smile as she took the mug Jake handed her. "I'm not so sure of that. Has he been bothering you?"

His accusatory tone was the last straw. She had nothing to apologize for. Grayson was the one who had betrayed her, but that wasn't a subject she would discuss right now. "I'm fine. I'm a big girl, Tad, and I can take care of myself."

Jake shoved a mug Tad's way. "This is getting a bit off base. I believe you were going to tell us what you're doing here, Tad. And spare me any of your cock and bull stories. I know you're not here on vacation. I intercepted your email about the drop."

Tad gulped. "I don't know what you mean."

Jake pointed at the attaché Tad had leaned against the wall. "How long have you been stealing from your father?"

Samantha tensed, dreading her brother's answer. She glanced at the attaché he'd brought with him, and her heart sank. At his continued silence, she turned to glance at him. His outrage seemed to evaporate right before her eyes. He now looked like the scared kid he was.

"This is the first time." Tad's voice broke. "I promise."

"I find that hard to believe. The losses have occurred for six months since you joined the firm."

"I swear, this is the first time. And, anyway, I didn't steal anything."

Jake shook his head. "Oh sure, you were going to sell false information."

Tad nodded. "That's what I was going to do." He got up and retrieved the attaché, opening it to pull out a manila envelope. "I swapped the file they wanted."

Samantha noticed Jake's intrigued expression and hope bloomed back to life. Her faith in her brother's innocence wasn't misplaced, after all.

He handed the envelope to Jake. "I was trying to buy some time. I could turn them in if I could catch the blackmailer."

"Blackmailer?"

She gasped. "You're being blackmailed? Why? About what?"

Tad shook his head. "Not me. A friend of mine was blackmailed. I've got to help her. I'm her only hope."

"Her?" Jake asked dryly.

"Who is she?" she asked.

"I promised I wouldn't tell."

"You don't have any choice," Jake stated flatly.

"You can't make me talk. I don't care what you do to me, Ramsey."

She shook her head. "Can't you see, Tad? The best way to help your girlfriend is to let a professional take care of it. Even if you don't like Jake, you must agree, he's good at his job."

Tad hesitated a moment, then sighed. "She works at Logan Industries. Her name is Jennifer Mitchell."

The name sounded familiar. She wracked her brain for a face to go with it. Oh yes, she'd met Jennifer a few weeks back when she'd visited her dad. She was cute and blonde, just her kid brother's type.

"Uncle Delbert's new secretary. I had no idea you two were an item."

"Nobody does. Jenny wanted it to be our secret."

Jake frowned. "So, what does this alleged blackmailer have on her?"

"It's all a big misunderstanding."

"Of course, it is," she broke in, ignoring Jake's raised brow. Couldn't he see that a gentle approach would work best? She reached out to touch her brother's hand. "We only want to help. Answer Jake's questions, okay?"

Tad nodded and leveled a defiant glance at Jake. "She took some petty cash, but she would put it back soon. Honest."

Jake frowned. "How much?"

"Seven thousand dollars."

"That was fast. She's only worked for the firm for three months."

"She had car problems, and she needed quick cash. She meant to put it back, but now it's too late."

"Is it, Jake?" She cast a curious glance his way. He was the head of security. Didn't he have some leeway over things like this?

Jake's jaw firmed. He glanced resolutely at Tad. "I'm not making any promises, but we may be able to work things out. We'll deal with it when we get back to town. That's the best I can do."

Tad nodded eagerly. "I never thought to ask. I didn't think—"

"That the goon would understand."

"Yes, well..." Tad turned to look at Samantha.

"That still leaves the matter of the man you're supposed to meet, Tad, if he shows up. Are you sure you don't know who you're dealing with?"

"Jenny said she didn't have a clue who it was. Otherwise, I would have punched the sucker out."

"Right." Jake nodded.

"Oh, great. Don't you two know violence never solves anything?"

"I could call Jenny and ask again."

"No, I don't want to tip anyone off." Jake's jaw tightened. "Someone served you up like a fall guy on a silver platter. I think it's important to play this out."

"What do you mean, served me up as a fall guy?"

"It isn't a coincidence I'm here, kid. Logan Industries suffered a loss of technology for the last six months. We were closing in on the culprits when somebody blackmailed your friend Jennifer, and you were set up to take the fall. The question I'm asking now is, by whom?"

Tad shook his head. "I can't believe it. You must be mistaken."

Jake picked a paper off the counter. "It's here in black and white. Whoever they were, they sent copies of your email to me."

Tad's jaw dropped as he scanned the paper. "But who? Why?"

"It could have been someone trying to divert suspicion. Or it could have been someone out to hurt you or your father."

She chilled at Jake's grim deduction. It was true. Setting Tad up for a fall would be the perfect way to destroy their father. Jake wouldn't let that happen. He was too good at his job to let the crooks slip away. She had complete faith in his abilities, but now realized it went further. He cared personally for her family.

Tad went pale. "What can I do to help?"

"Cooperate."

Samantha nodded. "Yes, listen to Jake. He's the only one who can untangle this treacherous mess."

Tad turned to gaze at her. "Speaking of messes, it brings me back to what I asked earlier. What are you doing here, sis?"

Darn, she'd hoped he'd forgotten that question. Seeing his concerned expression, she sighed. "If you must know, I'm hiding out."

Tad's eyes widened. "From what?"

She hesitated, not wanting to discuss her tragic love life with her kid brother.

Jake scowled, then bit out, "Grayson St. James."

"Why does she have to hide from him?"

Tad's outraged tone was worrying, and she didn't want her brother to do anything rash.

She smiled, hoping to soothe him. "Let's talk about this later."

Jake frowned. "She's hiding from her crumb of an ex-fiancé because he's certifiable."

"What?" Tad turned a startled glance her way.

Fixing Jake with a repressive glance, she tried to find a suitable way to explain things. Tad, she knew, wouldn't rest until he knew the truth. His protective instincts were on alert.

Finally, she opted for the truth. "I caught him in bed with another woman."

"That son-of-a-bitch. I'll kick his ass."

"You'll have to stand in line for that pleasure." Jake's smile was savage.

Tad gazed at him with new understanding, then turned to her. "Does Dad know?"

"No, and don't you dare tell him. I'll handle it my way. I warn you both now. I won't tolerate any violence." She saw the conspiratorial look the men shared and almost groaned.

"Who was she?"

"That's what Jake asked me. What is it with you, men? The *who* doesn't matter, the *what* was enough to send me running."

Chapter Four

Samantha came awake slowly, enveloped in Jake's scent. She reached out to find a cold, empty pillow next to her. Of course, she was sleeping solo in the loft while Tad and Jake bunked downstairs.

She recalled the turmoil of last night and sighed. Poor Tad, to get pulled into this mess. She approved of his desire to protect his girlfriend, even though she questioned the girl's morals for stealing in the first place. Time would tell what would happen to their budding relationship. She knew it hurt to have his romantic dreams shaken. She could only hope this rough patch would be the start of their maturity. As for her love life, she'd seen a new side of Jake last night. The trauma seemed to have given their budding relationship wings.

A soft footfall alerted her to another presence.

She glanced over to find Jake wrapped in a towel, still damp from the shower. She met his eyes and could feel herself blush, imagining what that skimpy towel barely concealed. The man wasn't shy about his body. And a magnificent body it was.

"You could at least knock," she grumbled, sitting up.

"There's no door." He smiled.

"A mere technicality." She warmed to his good humor. "Did you leave me any hot water today?"

"It'll be ready in about twenty minutes."

She glanced at his leg and gasped. His knee was marred by a yellowing bruise and crossed by a spiderweb of faded white scars. "Did I do that?"

Jake looked at the injury and shrugged. "Not a pretty sight? Don't worry, you're only responsible for the black and blue marks. The scars are from a previous battle."

"That's terrible. Oh, good grief, it must have hurt." She was surprised by his matter-of-fact tone. "What happened?"

"When I was fourteen, my old man killed himself in a drunk driving accident and damned near took me with him. It reminds me daily how important it is to keep a tight rein on your weaknesses."

She gazed at the resolute planes of his face with new insight. He'd been through more torment than she could even fathom, yet he'd come out of it healthy and strong. It spoke volumes about the kind of man he was. "I had no idea. I'm so sorry you had to feel that kind of pain."

He gave a negligent shrug. "My father was an alcoholic. After he died, I quit school and got a job to help my mother make ends meet. Once my brothers and sisters finished high school, I joined the Army and completed my education."

His tense posture told her opening himself up like this wasn't easy. He guarded his privacy the way some men might protect a priceless jewel. She was honored he trusted her enough to share his painful history with her.

"After my stint in Special Forces, I joined the Logan Industries security team. Over the years, I worked my way up to head goon while pursuing my once secret love of writing." He chuckled at her embarrassed flush. "Not many people know my life history, but I feel I can trust you."

"Thank you for believing me capable of keeping your secrets."

He smiled at her. "I believe you can do many things, including holding my future in your hands. In the meantime, we can have a little strategy session after we wake Tad up. We've got a lot of planning to do."

He pulled fresh clothes from the dresser, then turned to head down the ladder.

Did she hold their future in her hands? It was an intriguing thought.

"Time's wasting, sweetheart. So, get a wiggle on."

She chucked a pillow at him. "Get out of here, and I will."

He laughed and carried the pillow back to the bed. Sitting on the edge of the bed, he put the pillow back behind her head.

His gaze darkened as he leaned down to brush a quick kiss across her lips. "You're certainly in a playful mood this morning. Care to tell me why?"

"Must be the stimulating company I'm keeping." She smiled and put her arms around his neck. Amazed by her boldness, she stated, "Why don't you give me a proper good morning kiss?"

"My pleasure." He pressed her back into the pillows. She sighed as his mouth slanted over hers, the kiss warm, sure, and oh-so-perfect. She melted into his embrace, her breath quickening as he trailed a river of scorching kisses down her throat and into the hollow between her breasts.

The sound of the shower turning on downstairs broke the spell, reminding her they weren't alone. She tensed in his arms.

Jake went still, and then pulled away. "What's wrong?"

"Tad's up." She bit her lip and looked away, feeling self-conscious. She did want to nestle, but not with an audience downstairs. She started to wriggle out from under him.

"Easy, baby," he said, holding her still.

"I'm not equipped to handle this. Maybe I need to take some lessons." She tried to lighten the embarrassing situation.

"I'm not pushing," he hastened to assure her. "We'll take things slow." His eyes twinkled. "One love lesson at a time." He carefully pulled his body away from hers. He sat up with a groan, running a shaking hand through his tousled hair.

Shea gazed into his passion-darkened eyes, and knew he was feeling frustrated, yet he could reign in his desire. It only reinforced her good opinion of him.

He reached out to brush a wisp of hair off her flushed face. "Later."

She watched him go, hugging the promise to her like a prize. He'd started a fire in her that only he could put out.

Jake poured a cup of coffee and set it in front of Samantha. Her smile reassured him. After she'd pulled back from him this morning, he'd feared she might turn away from him altogether.

Tad sat next to them, wolfing down a second stack of the buttermilk pancakes Jake had whipped up.

"Want me to mix up some more?" Jake offered.

"No thanks," Tad said mid-bite. "This should do it. These are great, by the way. I'm surprised..."

"That the goon can cook?" Jake chuckled at Tad's embarrassed flush. "Don't worry about it, kid."

"You said we needed a strategy session," Samantha steered things along.

"That's right. We've got some work ahead of us." He glanced from Samantha's open gaze to Tad's suddenly cautious one.

Tad's fork clattered to his plate, betraying his tension. His gut told him Tad was telling the truth, but he wouldn't be wholly crossed off the list of suspects until his story was checked out. In the meantime, Jake intended to keep close tabs on him. He couldn't afford to drop the ball now and let down his guard.

He'd take whatever steps he needed to solve the case. Hopefully, by the time he was done, Samantha would still be by his side. In addition to the allegiance, he felt for his boss. This went deeper than his loyalty to Logan Industries. He wanted to stay here and teach sweet Samantha all the love lessons she could handle. He'd come to a startling realization last night. He needed her like a thirsty man needed water. And despite their age and class differences, he intended to go after her.

"What kind of strategy session?"

Jake turned his focus on Tad. It was too great a coincidence that blackmailing was going on alongside industrial espionage. He wasn't sure how, but instinct told him the crimes were linked. While Tad viewed Jennifer's actions with a loving eye, Jake had to be more critical. She might not be the victim Tad thought. Time would tell, but until he knew for sure, he had to ensure Tad's cooperation.

"We need a long-range plan, Tad."

Tad's jaw tensed. "Such as?"

"Some things I need to do during this investigation may upset you, but I'm going to need you to step back and give me a free hand."

"You're talking about Jenny, aren't you? I'm telling you right now, she would never have set me up."

"Probably not, but her role in this has to be investigated."

Tad sighed. "I suppose, but you'll be wasting your time. You haven't changed your mind about giving her a break, have you?"

Samantha shook her head. "Of course not, Tad. When Jake makes a promise, he keeps it."

Jake felt bolstered by her fervent approval. "No, I haven't changed my mind. In the meantime, we've got the drop to deal with."

Tad nodded. "Right, I'll go ahead with it as planned."

"No, it's too dangerous." Samantha looked at Jake for backup. She seemed relieved at his nod.

"I agree. I'll make the drop instead of you. We're about the same build. If they show up, the crook won't be able to tell the difference in the dark."

She nodded. "I don't like that you are risking your neck any better, but at least you've got some experience. I'm just hoping the creep won't show up. You don't think he will, do you?"

"Probably not, unless they arranged for another patsy to complete the scam. They're probably watching and freaking out because Tad came here early. I've got to convince them I believe you're guilty, which brings me to the second part of our plan. Tad, I'm afraid you'll have to go to jail."

"What!"

Samantha was obviously shocked by the suggestion. "That's out of the question. You said he was innocent. How can you, in good conscience, put him behind bars?"

Jake's jaw tightened. She still didn't trust him, but he hadn't given her much reason to do so.

Tad leaned forward. "He's probably right. With me out of the picture, they might drop their guard."

She bit her lip and slanted a worried glance at Tad. "Are you okay with this?"

Tad nodded. "I want this whole mess cleared up. I think I can trust Jake not to betray me."

She turned to Jake. "All right, go ahead and call. But, please, I don't want Dad to find out about this until we know who's behind it."

"No problem. Kathy will work with us to help us cover our tracks."

Jake dialed and was patched through to Kathy, who was out on patrol. "Yeah, Kathy, Jake Ramsey here. Say we've got a situation here and need your help. No, Samantha's okay. It's something else. Okay, we'll see you."

"When's she coming?" Tad asked.

"She'll be here in about ten minutes. I'm afraid you'll have to spend the night in jail to make it convincing."

Tad nodded grimly. "I'd better pack my things."

Jake smiled in sympathy. "I've heard that the local jail serves fine cuisine. Kathy will spring you tomorrow evening, and you can help her patrol the area. You can point out anyone from Logan Industries. In the meantime, I'll set a trap for your alleged blackmailer if he shows up. I'm proud of you, kid."

Samantha leaned forward. "Me, too. Nobody can say my brother isn't made of strong stuff." She turned to Jake. "What about me? What can I do to help?"

Jake knew she was feeling left out, but that was too bad. Even though there was little chance of them showing up, he didn't feel good about letting her be involved. "I want you to go with Tad and Kathy."

"They don't need me. I'll be nothing but a third wheel." Her nose wrinkled as she frowned at him. "I'd be more useful here. I could be your lookout. I promise to stay out of your way."

"You promised that last night and then disobeyed."

"That was then, and this is now. I need to do this, Jake. Please don't deny me."

His resolve melted in the face of her determined smile. "Okay. You can act as a lookout, but only from a distance. You can take a post up in the loft and watch through the telescope. We can keep in constant contact by two-way radio."

Samantha put away the last of the supper dishes. Tad was cooling his heels in jail, and Jake was up in the loft, conferring with his staff at Logan Industries. She knew he was also planning to call her father to call off the posse looking for her.

She felt guilty for causing such a mess. When she'd run away that night, she thought her dad would read her note the next day and let her have some time to lick her wounds. Who knew he'd have the goon squad out looking for her? But, according to Tad, he had. And, all this time, she was here, safe and sound, with the head goon.

The thought of Jake harshly explaining why she'd run off made her cringe. How would her father react to the news of Grayson's infidelity? A small part of her said he would find a way to blame her. The one time she'd sought to please him in her life had turned into a disaster.

The first thing she'd have to do when she went home next week was try to smooth things over with her father. But he had to let her be herself. If she could grow out of her rebellious teens and become a successful businesswoman, he could also learn to bend a little.

During all the turmoil of the last few days with Jake, she'd almost forgotten the cheating scoundrel who had driven her here into hiding. Thoughts of Grayson melted into insignificance when Jake had kissed her. Now reality had smacked her in the face, and her cheating ex-fiancé was on her mind. The gleam of fury in his eyes before she'd turned to run away from him had been terrifying. She'd make sure they didn't cross paths again when she went home.

She started to pace, coming down with severe cabin fever. Suddenly, the walls of the cabin were too confining.

She walked onto the porch, hoping the fresh air would help. It did. Her tension slipped away as she watched the setting sun create a rainbow of colors in the evening sky.

She strolled down the path leading to the lake. A walk was just what the doctor ordered to relieve her stress.

Going along, she tried to sort out her emotions. Were her tender feelings for Jake genuine, or was she seeking comfort on the rebound? Having been burned by love once, she wasn't eager to make a second mistake. But now she knew what she'd felt for Grayson hadn't been love. Infatuation maybe, but not love. Jake Ramsey was different. He was a sexy, compelling, sometimes maddening man. Her head said she would be a fool to jump into a relationship with him, but her heart said leap.

Stumbling over a root, she regained her footing and turned her mind to less troubling subjects. She crunched through the overgrown path, focusing on her pristine surroundings. Tomorrow, she'd come down here and do some trimming. She smiled when the birds sang and took a deep breath of the cool, refreshing air. This was just what she needed to restore her composure.

Dark clouds started to gather on the horizon, and the wind picked up, making her shiver. A storm front was rolling in.

She stopped in her tracks and looked back. She'd walked farther than she'd intended to, lost in thought. The cabin was far out of sight.

As she stood peering through the darkening pine forest, looking for a familiar landmark, an uneasy prickle of awareness crept up her spine. She told herself it was just nerves, but try as she might, she couldn't shake off the sensation that someone was watching her. It was palpable.

It was then she noticed how quiet the forest had suddenly become. The birds were silent.

She darted an uneasy glance around the dark forest, but didn't see a soul. Even so, she couldn't shake off the sensation of evil eyes on her.

A branch snapped, the sound ricocheting through the forest.

She spun in that direction. A ghostly man's shape lurked in the shadows.

Had Jake followed her? "Jake, is that you?"

The only reply was the wind whistling through the pines.

She stood frozen as the shape morphed back into the shadows like a ghost. It was not Jake.

She suddenly got a horrible feeling. Would it be safer to go back and risk running into whatever it was? Or should she blaze a new trail into the unknown?

A clap of thunder broke her stalemate. Cold raindrops poured down on her, chilling her to the bone. She had no other choice. She'd risk the trip back. It was better to face a ghost than get lost in the darkening woods.

With chattering teeth, she sprinted toward the cabin, heedless of the wet branches slapping at her. Her only thoughts were Jake and safety.

As she broke through the forest and caught sight of the cabin, a giddy rush of relief surged through her.

A man's low-pitched laugh echoed from behind her.

A shiver of dread ran up her spine. He'd followed her, and he wanted her to know he was there.

She had to get away.

She didn't risk a look back. Instead, she picked up her speed, racing toward the cabin and Jake's welcoming arms.

She clambered onto the porch, soaked to the skin and trembling. So close to safety, she turned, and thought the mist-shrouded form was in the woods. She blinked, and it faded away.

Had she just imagined it? Maybe her nerves were playing tricks on her.

Jake jerked the door open. "Where were you? I've been going nuts trying to find you."

She frowned at him, noting his fierce scowl and greeting that shot welcoming all to hell. Then, she noticed his wet hair and soaked tennis shoes, and felt her outrage melt. He must have been out searching for her.

"I was taking a walk," she replied through chattering teeth.

"Of all the crazy things to do. I don't want you going off on your own anymore."

He pulled her into the cabin. Stopping to grab a towel from the rack, he ran it over her shaking body. Then he started to unbutton her soaked blouse.

When he finished, she shrugged out of her blouse, recalling his promise as a small bonfire rekindled in her, submerging her remnants of fear. If there was any time she needed the comfort of his touch, it was now. It was time to listen to her heart.

She watched his eyes darken with desire when his gaze dropped to her breasts. Her pink nipples were visible through her wet silk bra. She reveled in her ability to turn him on. Abandoning all modesty, she slowly and deliberately undid the back clasp, let it slowly slide down her arms, and then tossed it on the floor.

He muttered a sensual promise as he pulled her into his arms for a hard, claiming kiss.

She clung to him desperately, seeking all he had to give. She burned for him. He was her destiny. She knew that now, surely as she knew her name.

He eased away, unzipping her jeans, and pulling them off, along with her panties. He scooped her up in his arms and carried her to the sofa, placing her gently on it.

She eagerly watched him shed his clothes. Then, he was on top of her, his hot mouth teasing the aching peaks of her breasts.

She cried out, pressing against him. She needed him inside her. Now.

He groaned. "Easy, baby. Love lesson number one, never rush."

She murmured her agreement as her mouth sought the warmth of his neck. She tasted the tangy heat of him. His low, rumbled sigh reminded her of a big cat. She rubbed against him, encouraged him, and reached to cup his manhood.

His gasp of pleasure excited her. He made her feel like a complete woman. He moved in her hand and then pulled away.

She gazed up at him, stricken. "What's the matter? Wasn't I doing it right?"

"You were doing it too well. I want to take my time and pleasure you properly."

She muffled a cry of delight as he touched her slick, wet flesh, caressing her to madness. She writhed against him, overwhelmed with need.

He moved, covered himself with protection, then settled between her legs. He started to enter her.

She gasped at his fierce possession, crying out at the almost too-full connection between their bodies. He was too big.

"We don't fit."

"Shh. Give it a few minutes, Sunshine. You're so tight. As soon as you relax, things will work just fine."

"I don't know." She flashed back to Grayson's harsh dismissal of her sexual charms that night. It was the exact opposite of the way he'd acted during their courtship. "Maybe Grayson was right. Maybe I don't have what it takes to satisfy a man."

Jake went still, and gazed down at her, frowning. "That turkey was wrong. Love lesson number two, never doubt my desire for you. You're every inch a woman. My woman." He bent to kiss her, silencing any protest she might have made.

She relaxed as the kiss continued.

His hand ran up the side of her trembling body, and she moaned when he cupped her breast. Then, he caressed the exquisitely sensitive spot at the apex of her thighs.

She sighed, melting into his caress. This was going to work, after all.

Ever so gently, he began to move. As they rocked together, sparks of pleasure shimmered through her. Her fingers slid into his thick hair, and she deepened the kiss. Her fingernails lightly scored his back as his deep thrusts drove her out of her head.

"That's it, Sunshine," Jake rasped. "Go wild for me."

A crescendo of pleasure washed over her, and she rode on wave after wave of bliss. "Jake."

She heard her name on his lips as he exploded inside her, then he went still.

He lay motionless for a moment, his breathing harsh. Bending to brush a brief kiss on her lips, he reversed their positions, flipping her over to lie on top of him.

She snuggled in his strong embrace, feeling loved and safe.

As she listened to his heartbeat, thoughts of being chased in the woods intruded. Jake would probably be angry, but she had to tell him. Knowing she couldn't put it off any longer, she exclaimed, "I think someone was following me."

He suddenly went still. "What did you say?"

"When I was walking in the woods, I got this creepy feeling someone was watching me. It was getting pretty dark by then, but I thought I saw a man for a minute. Then it started to rain. As I ran back to the cabin, I heard him laugh." She shuddered at the memory.

She gazed down at Jake. Did he believe her, or did he think she was hysterical?

His grim expression told her he believed her, all right.

She hurried to reassure him. "It was probably some teenager with a twisted sense of humor, just like the vandal in town the other day."

He slanted a searching glance her way. "What else haven't you told me?"

"Nothing." She shrugged. The incidents were unrelated, but she didn't want to keep any secrets from him. "Someone rifled through my car when I was in town yesterday. Kathy figured it was just some kids raising heck. They didn't take anything, so I let it drop."

His brow wrinkled as he frowned at her. "She's probably right, but I'll still wrap you in cotton wool while we're here."

She sighed, settling on top of him and resting her head on his chest. That sounded perfect to her. She'd like nothing better than to be wrapped up in him.

The next evening, Kathy sat down at the dinette table and flicked a long-suffering look Jake's way. "I'm still not thrilled about involving these two civilians." She gestured to Samantha and Tad.

Jake nodded. "I agree with you, but they involved themselves. I figured it would be better to have them where I can keep an eye on them."

Samantha frowned at the pithy exchange. "I, for one, don't appreciate being talked about like I'm not here. What am I supposed to do? Sit around here twiddling my thumbs?" Jake's caution had escalated a hundredfold because of her disclosures last night.

He turned to her. "I've been thinking about that. I changed my mind about your duties. Could you go with Kathy and Tad? I'm not leaving you here all alone."

"No fair. You promised me I could help. Besides, we have your two-way radios. So, I won't be alone. You and I will be in constant communication."

He hesitated for a moment and then sighed. "You win. I suppose you'll be safe enough here. You can watch my back, but nothing else. If you see anyone coming, you're to warn me and stay put. I don't want a repeat of your boathouse caper."

She smiled and gave him a sharp salute. "Yes, sir. I can obey orders. You wait and see."

He scowled at her attempt at humor and turned to Tad. "You and Kathy had better get going. We've got an hour until the appointed meeting. We'll give him ample time to show, and we'll meet back here to plot out our plan of attack."

Samantha stood, walked around the table, and into his arms. "You will be careful, won't you?"

Jake smiled as he embraced her. "Don't worry, Sunshine. I won't take any chances." He leaned down to brush a scorching kiss across her lips. Drawing back, he whispered, "I want to stay healthy to teach you love lesson number three. It's a pure delight."

Her cheeks heated as she watched him walk away.

Tad and Kathy were staring at her. Kathy had a big grin on her face, and Tad looked stunned.

She shrugged. They were a couple now. Soon everyone would know.

Kathy stood. "Okay, Tad, how about you and I get this show on the road."

"Be right with you." Tad hesitated a moment. "Be careful, sis."

He was referring to more than this evening's adventure. "Don't worry about me, Tad. I'm in excellent hands."

Kathy flashed a mischievous grin. "We saw."

Tad shook his head. "I can't get over it. You and the goon."

"Please don't call him that. He happens to be a very nice man."

"Yeah. When it suits him to act that way." Tad turned and walked away.

Samantha ignored the statement and grabbed a thermos off the counter. She had a job, so she might as well get to it. She headed for the loft ladder, taking a moment to make sure to keep panic at bay, and then began to climb.

She took her place by the bedroom window and got ready for a long, slow night. She peered through the telescope. Nothing moved except the inky ripples of waves on the lake. It was a chilly evening. Shivering, she pulled her sweater tighter.

Something in the room went *snap*.

Startled, she looked around. She was the only one in the room.

She heard the sound again, and realized it was coming from the two-way radio Jake had left on the nightstand. It made a crackling noise.

She reached for it, pushing the button. "Jake, is that you?"

"Who else?"

She smiled at his reply. "I don't see a soul moving out there."

"It's a bit early yet. Sit back, relax, and keep watch. Let me know if you see anyone approach. It's probably a wild goose chase, but if he does show, I expect him to come by boat."

"Okay." She sighed.

It was going to be a long, boring night. Extended cloak-and-dagger work like this was far from her comfort zone. On the bright side, once they solved this mystery, she looked forward to building a relationship with Jake. She opened the thermos and poured herself a cup of the steaming brew. The coffee's aroma helped to fortify her spirits.

As she lifted the cup to her lips, she heard the distant hum of an outboard motor.

Good grief, someone was coming. She spun toward the window, splashing her hand with hot coffee. Wincing at the stinging burn, she set down the cup and turned to peer out the telescope. A distant motorboat slowly made its way toward the boathouse. It was running without lights, and in the dark, it almost blended in with the water.

She reached for the radio, excitement and dread warring within her. "Jake, I see them coming."

No answer.

She frowned. Where was he? Could something have gone wrong so soon? "Jake, are you there?"

"Yes, I'm here. I hear the boat, too. How far away is it?"

"About fifty yards." She kept her gaze riveted on the dark boat scuttling toward them. Its stealthy approach seemed very menacing in the dark of night.

"How many people are in the boat?"

"It's hard to tell. It's running without lights. I can see the silhouette of one man."

"Okay, stand by."

"Be careful, Jake, whatever you do. Your life is worth more than this case."

She was frozen with apprehension while the boat crept toward the dock. The pilot blended into the darkness like an apparition. Had Jake been right? Was this a new fall guy? Or was it someone more sinister?

The motor shut off, and the boat glided up to the dock. This was where she'd helped out last night, but this time, Jake wouldn't be dealing with an innocent kid like Tad. She felt a strong need to run outside and help, but knowing she could ruin everything kept her at her post.

"Jake, he's out of the boat and heading your way."

"Thanks, Sunshine," Jake whispered back. "Now, let's maintain radio silence. And remember, don't get any bright ideas about coming out here to help me. If things look bad, call the cops."

She waited breathlessly for some sound to tell her Jake had the upper hand, but there was only silence. She bit her lip, knowing she couldn't call out to him for fear of giving him away. She kept her eyes glued to the telescope and listened hard.

"I've got him, Sunshine," Jake stated. "I'll bring him up to the cabin."

A sound came from behind her.

She turned. From the corner of her eye, she caught a dark figure, a whirl of motion in black and gray.

A crash of pain blinded her, knocking her to the floor, and her world went black.

Chapter Five

Jake entered the cabin, the suspect in tow. The first thing he noticed was the utter silence. The second thing was that the place was trashed. Cabinet doors hung open, and drawers turned upside down.

His heart sank as he silently prayed Samantha was hiding safely upstairs. Only five minutes ago, he'd talked to her on the radio. But five minutes could be an excruciatingly long time. Her story of being hunted in the woods had new and horrific meanings.

"Samantha," Jake yelled.

There was no reply.

He nudged the prisoner toward the dinette. "You better pray she's still alive, dirtbag." He pulled a pair of handcuffs out of his back pocket and secured the prisoner to the table leg.

He ran toward the loft. Samantha wouldn't desert her post voluntarily. He didn't want to think about what her silence might mean. She'd come to be everything to him in the few short days they'd been together.

He quickly scaled the ladder. Coming to the top, he noted Samantha was gone. The loft was torn apart. Dresser drawers were emptied and dumped on the floor, the contents strewn everywhere, and his laptop was missing. Was this a robbery gone wrong?

The answer didn't matter because Samantha was missing.

The aroma of coffee broke through his despair. He glanced at the thermos, but it was closed. So, where did the scent come from anyway? Then he noticed a puddle of spilled coffee on the floor near the window by the corner of the bed.

He stepped forward to investigate, and froze. Samantha lay crumpled like a rag doll on the floor beside the bed. It looked like someone had tucked her back there, hoping she'd go unnoticed.

"Good God." He hurried to her side. As he reached for her, he made a silent vow to kill the bastard who had dared to touch her.

He brushed the hair away from her face. She was out cold, but she was alive. His gut twisted as blood trickled from a nasty gash on the side of her head.

"I'm so sorry, Sunshine." He swallowed the lump in his throat. He should never have left her alone. He'd thought it would be the safest place for her. All the action was supposed to occur at the boathouse. His miscalculation could cost her.

The front door clicked. Jake went on instant alert, pulling the revolver out of his shoulder holster. Either the prisoner had Houdini's escape skills, or Samantha's assailant was still in the house.

"Hey, where are you guys?" Tad shouted from below.

Jake slipped the revolver back in its holster and rushed back to Samantha's side, shouting, "We're up in the loft. Get up here. We need your help."

"Who tore up the downstairs?" Tad asked, entering the loft. His eyes widened as he looked at the wreckage in the bedroom. "Holy cow. Somebody did a number on this place."

Kathy climbed the ladder. Her brow wrinkled as she surveyed the damage. "Is Samantha okay?"

"No." Jake watched Tad's jaw drop. "Someone bashed her on the head. Kathy, call for medical assistance. Tad, hand me that stack of clean tee shirts. We need to stop the bleeding."

Tad hurried to the corner and picked up the stack off the floor. He returned to Jake and handed them over, saying, "You said we'd be safe." He paled as Jake pressed a shirt against her bloody forehead.

"I was wrong. I'm sorry." Jake slanted an assessing glance Tad's way while he gently pressed the compress to Samantha's forehead. "You'd better sit down before you fall, kid."

Tad sagged onto the bed. "Is she going to be okay?"

"God, I hope so," Jake replied grimly.

Samantha shifted away from Jake's touch, moaning.

"Shh," Jake crooned softly, reaching out to brush a tendril of hair away from her ashen forehead. "You'll be okay, Sunshine. I won't let anything else happen to you."

Jake paced the exam cubicle in the Emergency Room, waiting for the doctor to return. He stopped to gaze at Samantha, lying so still on the gurney. Her eyes sleepily swept open.

"What happened?" she murmured.

"Someone assaulted you."

"Who?"

"That's what I was hoping you'd tell me."

She shook her head and then winced. "It happened so fast. I saw a shadowy figure, a blur, and then wham. Sorry."

"I'm the one who's sorry for leaving you in jeopardy."

The cubicle curtain slid open, and Dr. Adams entered the area.

Jake glanced up at the older, bespectacled doctor. His calm demeanor was reassuring. "How's she doing, Doc?"

"The CAT scan was normal. No skull fracture or brain bleeds. So, I'd say it's just a concussion."

Jake felt a heavy weight of despair lift off his shoulders. "Thank God."

"It is good news, considering the severity of the blow she received. I'm going to stitch her wound, and I'll want to keep her here overnight for observation."

Jake wanted to hug the gruff old gent. Instead, he settled for a handshake. "Thanks, Doc."

Dr. Adams stepped toward the gurney and injected Samantha's wound with a numbing agent. "Little Sammy Logan, I treated you for a broken arm and eating too many green apples as a child, but I never expected to see you as the victim of a crime. What happened?"

"Jake and I are on a case, and I messed up."

"A case?"

"Jake works for my dad at Logan Industries as head of security. I was helping him with a stakeout. We were getting to the exciting part, and someone got the drop on me."

Jake's shoulders tensed gazing at her confident smile. She'd run blithely back into jeopardy if he didn't nip her interest in his case in the bud.

He looked at the doctor, who was now peering suspiciously at him through bifocal lenses. "Don't worry, I won't let her assist me anymore."

Samantha frowned and looked at him. "But..."

"Hush," Jake said softly, "we'll talk about this later."

He walked out to the waiting room to find Tad. He dropped into a seat next to him. "She's going to be okay. She has a slight concussion, so they want to keep her overnight."

Tad let out a sigh. "Thank heaven. I was going nuts, imagining the worst."

Jake patted him on the shoulder. "Same here."

"Well, I always knew my sister had a hard head." Tad gave a mirthless chuckle.

Jake smiled back tightly, thinking of her dogged determination to help him. "She's one strong-minded lady, all right."

Tad nodded, cleared his throat, and added softly, "What I said back at the cabin about this being your fault? Well, I'm sorry. This wouldn't have happened if I hadn't gotten involved in this blackmail business. I should have talked Jenny into turning the matter over to you."

There was plenty of blame to go around. Nevertheless, he'd screwed up and let Samantha come to harm. It was a mistake he wouldn't make again.

"Let's go to the police station and find out what Mike Bridges, a Logan Industries janitor, was doing at the boathouse tonight."

Jake ran an impatient hand through his hair, listening to the litany of denial Bridges was spewing.

Mike Bridges blinked his pale blue eyes and turned to snap at Kathy. "I already told you a million times. I was out doing a little boating. How did I know some dumb gorilla would take offense at me tying to his dock?"

Kathy scowled. "Right, and I'm the queen of Sheba, just taking a ride on my barge."

Jake pinned Bridges with a relentless gaze. "You're in this up to your ears, Bridges. If you don't want to get charged with accessory to attempted murder, you'd better spill it."

Bridge's jaw dropped. "But they said I wouldn't get in any trouble."

"Who?" Jake asked in a deceptively calm tone of voice.

"I don't know."

Jake slapped his hand on the table, making Bridges jump. He leaned in, closing in for the kill. "Cut the crap, and tell me what I want to know."

Bridges gulped and backed away. He looked at Kathy, panicked. "He can't talk to me like that. That's police brutality or something."

Kathy smiled back at him. "I didn't hear a thing."

Bridges paled. "Okay, I'll tell you what you want to know. Just get him to back off."

Kathy leaned forward and switched on a tape recorder. "All right, talk."

"What I said about this being a job was true. I was cleaning some offices one night a week ago when someone asked if I'd like to make some extra money running errands. It was good money, so I took it. But you've got to believe me, I didn't know it involved any of this. I was supposed to pick up an envelope and bring it back to work on Monday."

"Who hired you?"

"I don't know their names. They were a couple of suits from work. A man and a woman."

Tad leaned forward. "A woman?"

Bridges grinned. "Blonde and stacked just the way I like them. The geezer hung back and let her do all the talking. And, man, that babe could talk the birds out of the trees."

Samantha opened her eyes, awakened by the nurse making her morning rounds.

"How are we feeling?" she asked sympathetically.

"We feel like we were hit by a Mack truck." Samantha smiled and winced, adding, "But we will recover."

"Any nausea?"

"No. I'm starved, as a matter of fact."

"Well, that's a good sign. I'll get you breakfast after the doctor makes his morning rounds."

Half an hour later, Dr. Adams walked into the room. "The nurse tells me you're doing better this morning."

Samantha smiled at him. "That's right. So, how about it? Can I go home?"

He looked at her eyes using a small light and examined the cut on her head. "It looks fine. You're free to leave if you promise to take it easy for a few days. You aren't up to any more late-night confrontations."

"I'll be careful, cross my heart."

"You sure are anxious to get out of here."

"I'm eager to get back in the swing of things. I need to help Jake finish up the investigation."

Dr. Adams shook his head. "You're in no shape to do anything like that, Sammy Logan. I thought you were off the case from what I heard last night."

"That was just the stress talking last night. I know Jake didn't mean it." Noticing the doctor's frown, she hurried to reassure him. "Don't worry. I promise that I'm simply going to be an armchair advisor."

"See that you keep that promise," Dr. Adams said, walking out the door.

A few minutes later, Samantha was choking down lumpy oatmeal when Tad walked into the room.

She smiled and put down her spoon. "They're going to spring me this morning. I can't wait to tuck into some real food. If I play my cards right, Jake will make me one of his special omelets."

Tad looked away. "I'll go see about signing you out."

She blinked at the vacant spot where he had stood moments before. Why was he acting so nervous? Was he worried she blamed him for her injury?

She'd reassure him there were no hard feelings once they returned to the cabin.

Samantha buckled her seatbelt and breathed in the refreshing crisp morning air. The bright sunlight enhanced her upbeat mood. She could hardly wait to get back home to Jake. Instead of being unsettled by the notion, she felt warmed by it.

Tad pulled out into traffic, then drove at a low rate of speed. He came to a complete stop as the stoplight turned yellow, earning a blast on the horn from the car behind them.

She slanted a curious glance his way. It wasn't Tad's style to poke along. "You don't need to slow down because of me. I'm not that fragile."

"Right," he muttered and eased into traffic as the light turned green.

She was surprised by his lack of reaction. Maybe it was just as well. Her head was beginning to throb. She dared a look in her visor mirror, noting the purple shiner highlighting her left eye and the row of stitches on her temple. She touched her forehead and winced at the stinging pain.

It was a good thing Jake had been around to help her. He seemed to be rapidly turning into her guardian angel. She wondered how he'd like to sign on for a lifetime job.

No, she wouldn't think about forever. She'd be satisfied with the here and now.

Tad pulled into the rutted driveway, and her head throbbed with each bounce. He switched off the engine, got out, and sprinted around to open her car door before she even got it together enough to unbuckle her seatbelt. This head injury had slowed her down more than she cared to admit.

She allowed Tad to help her out of the car. "Boy, is it good to be home. This little setback won't keep me down for long."

"I'm glad to hear it," he replied as he helped her navigate the bumpy front walk.

"I can hardly wait to get back to the investigation. After last night, it's become even more of a personal quest to catch the jerk terrorizing us."

He stiffened beside her, and she decided he was probably feeling guilty again.

To change the subject, she said, "I was surprised Jake didn't come to pick me up. Is he out working on the case?"

He opened the front door and cleared his throat. "Yes, he's busy right now."

Samantha looked around the living room as he steered her over to the sofa. Something seemed to have changed while she was away, but she was too tired to figure it out. She smiled while her brother fluffed a pillow and tucked it behind her back.

She patted the seat next to her. "Sit down and tell me what Jake's up to now."

He turned away. "I'll fix you a nice cup of tea."

She watched him scurry away, her tension building. She didn't need a house to drop on her to tell her something was very wrong. She surged to her feet and wobbled a moment as a wave of dizziness washed over her. After a few minutes, the feeling passed, and she relentlessly tracked Tad into the kitchen.

He shot an alarmed glance her way as she approached. "Something wrong?"

"You know darned well something's wrong." Samantha's toe tapped impatiently on the faded linoleum. "I want to know what's going on, and I want to know now."

He sighed. "I told Jake this wouldn't work."

"What?"

"Keeping you on ice." Tad shrugged. "I'm supposed to keep you out of trouble."

She frowned as his words washed over her. Jake had another think coming if he thought she would stay cosseted like some hothouse flower.

"He seems to have forgotten we're a team."

"Not anymore," Tad said, his brow furrowing.

"So, he wasn't bluffing last night." She frowned. Jake had tried to protect her, but she wouldn't let him shove her aside so quickly. "No way. I'll get him to see things my way when he returns. When is he coming back?"

"He's not."

"What!" She slumped into a dinette chair.

"He cleared out last night. He told me to tell you you're through. After the fiasco last night, I think you're better off staying out of it. This is your chance to make a clean break from the goon. Take it."

She couldn't believe it. Jake had probably broken up with her to protect her, but what if he'd meant it? Either way, she had to see this through to the bitter end.

"I can't. Whether he wants me or not, he's stuck with me. It's personal now, and I have a duty to our family to see this crisis through."

He shook his head. "There's much more to this than a sense of duty."

She sagged in her chair. "I'm in love with him, but I'll get over it."

Chapter Six

Samantha glanced at Tad's solemn expression as they drove toward their father's estate. He was probably bracing for the upcoming disclosures he'd have to make to their father. As for her, she intended to put the proper spin on things before Jake had a chance to label things in harsh black and white.

She also intended to find out how Jake felt about their relationship. Had she been a fool to give her heart and body so quickly? He had touched her deeply, had made her want to take the risk, and now he was gone. Had he left to protect her? Or, as Tad had said, was it a way of breaking off their budding relationship?

She knew Jake enjoyed their mind-blowing sexual encounter as much as she had, but he'd never said he loved her. In retrospect, she couldn't help dredging up Grayson's derisive evaluation of her shortcomings as a mate.

However, there was more at stake here than her on-again/off-again love affair with Jake. Clearing her brother's name would have to take precedence. When she'd vowed to stay involved with this case, she'd meant it. She would clear her brother's name and assist Jake, come hell or high water.

They turned into the driveway of their father's estate. The house's white colonial façade looked cold and forbidding in the fading daylight. She hoped it wasn't an omen of what was to come.

Tad switched off the ignition and turned to say, "You don't have to do this, sis. Dad's liable to be still freaked out about your disappearing act. I can face the music alone. I think Jake's right, and you should stay out of it. Or, as he put it," Tad added with a grin, "be a nice little lettuce and stay in the icebox."

Samantha rolled her eyes. "Jake is not right. Number one, I belong in the thick of things, where I intend to stay. And two, I do not appreciate being referred to as produce."

"We might as well get this over with," he said reluctantly.

"Right." Time was of the essence if they were going to beat Jake to the punch.

She opened her car door and got out.

She thought about protesting when Tad rushed around the car to take her arm. Instead, she leaned on her brother, walking up the sidewalk on rubber band legs. Adrenaline, she realized, was the only thing keeping her going right now.

"I guess this is what they mean by bearding the lion in his den."

"Just remember, his roar is worse than his bite," she replied with a smile, appreciating his attempt at gallows humor.

Their father was firm, but fair. A self-made man, he'd always expected model behavior from his kids. Samantha had always fallen short of the mark, but Tad was his pride and joy. This was going to be tricky.

Mrs. Reynolds, the housekeeper, opened the door. Her eyes widened, giving Samantha and Tad a curious once over. "Well, if you kids aren't a sight for sore eyes. Your folks will be so happy to see you."

Samantha relaxed at the warm greeting. They must have gotten here first. Score one for the Logan kids. She and Tad walked through the foyer and into the elegant sitting room to find their stepmother, Carol, a tall, elegant lady with aristocratic features and lovely silver hair, reading.

Carol put down her book and rushed over to greet them, hugging them. "I'm so happy you're both here. Samuel and I have been going crazy, wondering where you went." She pulled back, looked at Samantha's black eye, and froze, seemingly horrified. "Samantha, my dear, are you alright?"

She knew the stitches on her forehead and her shiner weren't pretty. She avoided Carol's sympathetic gaze, fighting the stupid tears that suddenly welled in her eyes. All the while, she told herself to get a grip. The concussion was turning her into a basket case.

"It's a long story. I'd rather not go into it now, if you don't mind."

"Of course," Carol replied gently. "When you're ready, we'll have a heart-to-heart talk about everything that's happened."

Samantha read the curiosity and concern in Carol's voice. She knew there wouldn't be any recriminations from her about the wedding that wasn't. However, her father was another story. She wasn't quite sure what his reaction would be to the loss of his handpicked son-in-law.

"We need to see Dad. Is he at home?"

"He's in a private meeting in the den. Can I get you anything while you wait?"

She cleared her dry throat. "Something cold to drink would be nice. Iced tea if you've got it."

"Same here," Tad echoed, "but make mine with something stronger. I think I'm going to need it."

Carol smiled. "Sit down and relax. I'll be right back with the refreshments."

Samantha paced the pearl gray carpet. It was almost the same color as Jake's eyes, she realized. That errant thought brought her up short. She needed to focus on the job at hand and not her one-time lover. She just hoped her father wouldn't come down too hard on Tad. He had made some mistakes, but he'd learned his lesson the hard way.

Carol returned carrying a silver tray of frosty drinks. "Help yourselves, kids."

Samantha snapped open her purse, getting out her bottle of pain medicine. Her head was starting to throb. She grabbed a tall glass of iced tea and downed a tablet with a long pull on her drink. She frowned into the glass, realizing it wasn't the iced tea.

Carol gazed at Samantha with concern. "You look kind of pale, honey. What are you taking the pill for?"

"She's got a concussion." Tad's voice was tinged with guilt.

"What happened?" Carol glanced questioningly at the two of them.

Samantha tried to think up a good excuse. She didn't want Carol to worry. "It's nothing—"

"She was attacked by an intruder at the cabin last night."

Carol gasped, her hand going to her throat.

Tad's shoulders slumped. "It was all my fault. That's what I intend to tell Dad."

Samantha rolled her eyes at his dramatics. So much for trying to sugarcoat the facts. She should have known her boy scout of a brother would insist on taking all the blame. She took another pull from her drink while Tad filled Carol in on all the horrific details.

Stepping away from them, Samantha strolled toward the den. If she was lucky, perhaps she could get the jump on Tad and her watered-down version of the truth across first.

Her father's loud booming voice, obviously in a heated conversation, stopped her short. Oh great, he was already angry. She'd hoped to find him in a good mood. She shifted her gaze to look through the open doorway between the rooms. A man was standing across the desk from her father. His back was turned to her, but she recognized Jake's red-gold hair and wide-shouldered stance even from the behind.

Drat, he'd gotten here first.

Her father looked up at that moment and saw her standing there. He said something, and Jake spun around to look at her.

She fought the urge to turn and flee from his irritated gaze. Gone was her lover of two nights ago. In his place was the goon. She found herself ensnared and held motionless by his compelling gray eyes, nevertheless. She felt as if she was standing in quicksand.

She broke eye contact and turned her attention to her father. He looked a bit haggard. She felt a pang of regret for any pain she'd caused him. What had Jake been telling him?

She took another long sip of her drink before entering the room. From the corner of her eye, she noted Jake's watchful gaze following her every movement. Like a field mouse watched by a hawk. Jake didn't seem happy to see her, but she hadn't expected him to welcome her with open arms. She stepped through the doorway and into the lion's den.

"Hello, Samantha," Dad said gruffly. "It's good to see for myself that you're in one piece."

"I'm fine, Dad," she stated, surprised by her father's emotion. She flicked an inquisitive glance Jake's way. Her presence had probably messed up his plans. But just what were those plans? "Mr. Ramsey." With a nod of her head, she acknowledged his presence.

"We're back to Mr. Ramsey now." His mouth kicked up with reluctant humor.

"Would you prefer goon?" Samantha asked sweetly.

"No," Jake replied solemnly. "I'd prefer to return to a first-name basis, if you don't mind, Sunshine."

"No problem," she said with deep regret. The last time he'd called her that they'd been making love. Was he trying to remind her of that sweeter time? She couldn't relent. For her brother's sake, she had to see this through.

Her father cleared his throat. "Samantha, if you're through sparring with my Chief of Security, I propose we get down to business. Your brother's got a lot of damage to fix."

"Fine." Jake had told him about Tad's involvement. She pinned Jake with a steely gaze. "Well, Jake, as you can see, the lettuce has hopped out of the icebox. And my question is, what kind of crap have you been telling my father?"

"Samantha Katherine Logan," Dad reprimanded harshly. "I'm surprised at you using that kind of language. Jake is a friend and a valued employee. I can assure you, anything he tells me is the truth."

She continued to scowl at Jake. She was in no mood for a dressing down by her father, which was what her hostile reaction had brought her. She was confused, angry, and just the slightest bit unsteady.

She swayed a bit on her feet, and Jake reached out to grasp her arm and steady her.

She pulled away and noticed a flicker of distress cross his rugged face. Her heart sank. She hadn't meant to cause him pain. She just wanted to make sure her brother was protected.

Jake's mouth compressed into a firm line as he eased her into one of the leather Windsor chairs facing her father's mahogany desk. He took the cool glass out of her limp fingers and raised it to his nose.

"Liquor," he stated harshly. "You're not supposed to drink when recovering from a head injury. Don't you have better sense than that?"

Samantha gave him a half-hearted glare. He didn't have to sound so darned superior. She hadn't thought about it until it was too late, but she wouldn't admit that to him. "I don't need you to babysit me."

"Oh, but I think you do." His smile was harsh. "But—"

"He's right, Samantha," Dad cut in. "Jake told me about Tad's involvement in the thefts."

"In Tad's defense," Samantha began her plea.

"Don't worry, honey. I understand there were extenuating circumstances. I may be a hard-headed old man, but I can learn." He offered a tender smile. "I love you and Tad very much."

Astonished, Samantha blinked at her father. Since when had he ever apologized or said he loved her? She'd always known there was affection there, but it was never expressed.

"I love you, too, Dad." Her father's startled smile warmed her heart.

She owed Jake an apology. Turning to look at him, she said softly, "Thank you."

"You're welcome."

"Jake has also filled me in on why you fled your wedding and, more importantly, on the events at the cottage."

Her smile faded. Had Jake told her father about her finding Grayson in bed with another woman? He'd led her to believe he'd let her broach the subject in her own time. His high-handed tactics were irritating. But, in a way, she was glad she didn't have to talk about it. Still, it wasn't very pleasant. Had Jake filled him in on the Captain Kinky part? Her face grew hot while feeling distinctly uneasy about discussing such a personal subject with her dad.

His voice broke in on her musings. "I was, of course, upset about St. James's infidelity. I'm sorry, honey, but don't you worry. I'll deal with him."

The idea of Grayson being fired appealed to her, but did she want to be responsible for ruining his career? She knew her dad had the power. "You don't need to fire him on my account. Let him stand or fall on his merit."

"Let me worry about his job performance, or lack thereof. St. James is the least of our worries. What concerns me more is the fact that someone attacked you. I'm not going to sit idly by and let it happen again. So, in short, I want you under Jake's protection until we get the individuals involved in the thefts and attack on you arrested. He has agreed to stay with the firm until the case is solved."

Jake flashed her an apologetic smile. "That's right, Sunshine, you get to be my last case."

Oh great! It was probably the least romantic prospect she could imagine. She didn't want to be an obligation to him. She wouldn't keep him by her side with strings attached.

Slowly and wobbly, she got to her feet. "No, thanks. I'm going to take care of myself from now on."

She turned to collide with Jake's hard chest.

His arms came out fast to hold her. "No way, Sunshine. This little lettuce is not getting out of my sight."

"Like hell." She was annoyed he treated her like a wayward child. However, even in her fury, she couldn't help responding to his nearness. Inhaling his natural, masculine scent, she was transported back to the night she'd nestled in his arms. Would she have the chance to go back? He'd liked her, lusted for her, but didn't love her.

Looking over her shoulder, she found Carol and Tad standing in the hall. He had a militant expression on his face, and Carol looked concerned.

She hated the distress she was causing them by rejecting Jake's protection. She turned to glance at her father, and worry lines bracketed his mouth. He seemed to have aged overnight.

Jake had her trapped in his web, and he knew it., Glancing up at his victorious expression, she had no choice but to become his last case.

Samantha slid into the passenger seat of her car as Jake got behind the wheel.

He turned the key in the ignition and smiled. She gazed back at him, confused and off balance. She wasn't sure she wanted him with her day and night. He'd too easily manipulated her.

She slumped back in her seat with a huff. He may have gotten his way, but she didn't have to like it. Jake Ramsey was a dirty fighter.

He pulled out of the driveway. She threw him a cutting glare as he eased into traffic in the wrong direction of her apartment. Oh no, he was taking her to his place. It would be on her turf if she had to deal with him.

"I'm not going to your place," she stated flatly.

His jaw tightened before he let out a sigh, flipped on the turn signal, and turned toward her apartment building.

He seemed determined to remain calm and business-like. She wrinkled her nose because his exaggerated patience just made her more mad.

"You know where I live. I wouldn't have thought that would be any of your business." She was unable to resist the temptation to keep on baiting him.

"I keep tabs on all the Logans," Jake responded evenly. "It's part of my job as the head goon."

He pulled into a parking spot next to her building.

She started to unbuckle her seatbelt, but his touch on her hand stilled her action.

"We need to talk about why I left."

She heard his less-than-apologetic tone and frowned. Didn't he know how torn up she felt? Or didn't he care? The last thing she wanted from him was a half-hearted excuse.

"No, we don't."

He nodded. "Maybe you're right. We can hash this over better inside."

She got out of the car. Walking up to her front door, she fumbled in her bag for her key. As far as she was concerned, there was nothing to discuss. If he'd walked away to protect her, the sight of her should have made him soften. Instead, he was angry and on edge, hardly the gallant lover she'd built him up to be.

He took the key out of her hand and put it in the lock.

She didn't like his high-handed attitude, but kept mum. She didn't want to give the neighbors, some of whom were her clients, a free firework show that was sure to follow. Mrs. Morley was probably peeking at them now from two doors down through her lace curtains.

Jake opened the door, and she was about to step past him inside, when he blocked her move by putting an arm across the opening. "Stand back while I check it out."

"Oh, please." She rolled her eyes at his dramatics. "Is this necessary?"

His steely gaze quelled her protest. He was in goon mode again, and the best thing she could do was stand aside.

"Yes," he replied briskly. "Despite the screw-up last night, I know what I'm doing."

She wasn't questioning his abilities, but he seemed to have taken her comment that way. He pulled a gun out of a shoulder holster under his jacket, and she shivered.

"This isn't a game, Sunshine. Now stand back and let me make sure nobody's left you any nasty surprises."

She waited wide-eyed from the doorway as he checked her apartment. He looked around doors and poked into closets, while she shuddered at the possibility that the person who'd attacked her could hide in her apartment.

He finally strode back to her, slipping his gun into the holster. "The apartment is secure."

She silently brushed past him, suddenly overwhelmed by emotion. Too much had happened to her in too short a time to deal with it all calmly.

"Damn it, Samantha, won't you even look at me? We need to talk about us."

She noted his irritation, but didn't respond to it. "I'm not sure there is an us. I need some time to think about all that's happened, Jake. Don't push me for more than I have to give."

"I guess I can understand that." He sighed with a note of resignation. "Show me where I can bunk for the night."

She turned to show him to the guest room, but her world swung on its axis.

"Oops," she cried.

He reached out to catch her when she would have fallen to the floor. "I think that drink is catching up with you, Sunshine."

Sleepily, she realized he was right. The drink she'd guzzled and the pain medication had done her in.

How humiliating!

As he laid her on the bed, she realized Jake was coming to her rescue again. Things would be better tomorrow, she reassured herself. There was nowhere to go but up.

Chapter Seven

Samantha awoke with a splitting headache. She rolled over carefully and tried to fall back to sleep. The horrid little men swinging pitchforks inside her head wouldn't let her return to the oblivion of slumber.

Sighing in defeat, she slowly sat up. "I might as well get this over with," she croaked.

Good grief, she sounded like she'd swallowed a mouthful of cotton balls. She was turning into a drunken sot, thanks to Jake Ramsey. If the sight of him hadn't shaken her up, she wouldn't have drained her Long Island iced tea without thinking of the consequences last night.

She stood and wobbled as her head swam, then moaned as the movement brought instant pain. *Help!* Her poor head ached as if a mule had kicked it.

Then, she felt a chill, and glanced down to find she was naked. She'd been in no condition to undress last night, so she could only conclude Jake must have stripped her.

Her cheeks burned with embarrassment. He was taking way too many things for granted. She'd have to ensure he understood the conditions she intended to place on him. He would have to play by her rules if she were to tolerate his presence. She reached for her robe, belting it loosely around her queasy middle. The peach and white striped terrycloth robe was the oldest and most comfortable garment she owned, and right now, she needed the small measure of comfort it gave her.

Her head throbbed with each step she took as she carefully made her way out of the bedroom. Her stomach's flip-flopping made her slow her pace to appease its quivering. She vowed never to mix medication and alcohol. One experience like this was quite enough.

Relentlessly plodding through the living room on her seek-and-destroy mission, she heaved a sigh of relief when Jake was seated at the kitchen table. His sympathetic smile at her approach didn't improve her mood.

Scowling, she stepped into the doorway and sagged against the jamb. "All right, Ramsey, we have to get a couple of things straight."

From the corner of her eye, she caught a flash of movement that let her know they weren't alone. She turned her head, dismayed to discover a beautiful strawberry blonde standing by the sink pouring coffee.

Jake patted the chair next to his. "You'd better sit down before you fall, Sunshine. You look like hell, by the way."

Samantha took her gaze off the blonde and turned to frown at Jake. He didn't have to sound so cheerful. This kind of helpful input was the last thing she needed. However, seeing that her knees were as rubbery as wet noodles, she gave up the battle of standing upright and slid into the chair. Groaning, she laid her throbbing head on the hardwood of the table.

"Stop teasing her, Jacob," the blonde scolded in a melodic, southern drawl.

Terrific, Samantha thought sourly, staring at the wood grain. They were both from the south, probably childhood sweethearts. Maybe she was here for the awards ceremony. But fathoming what the woman was doing in her kitchen took more effort than her foggy brain could manage.

"Can't you see she doesn't feel well?" the blonde said sweetly.

Great, she even sounded nice. What a rotten start to her day. She wasn't about to give Jake the satisfaction of thinking she was jealous by asking who the blonde was.

"I think I'm going to die," Samantha mumbled into the woodwork.

The chair scraped as Jake got up. Good, maybe they were going to go away and leave her alone.

No such luck.

Jake put a cup of steaming coffee in front of her. "This should fix you up," he replied as he handed her one of her pain pills.

Samantha downed the pill, followed by a fortifying sip of coffee.

Jake sat back down. "In case you're wondering, I had Laura come in early this morning to install an alarm system."

Samantha choked on a mouthful of coffee. "Alarm! I never agreed to have an alarm installed. I don't want one, and I will certainly not pay for one." First, waking up nude, and now this. It was too much. It wasn't so much that she objected to the idea of tighter security, but Jake's actions were too high-handed to be tolerated.

His jaw firmed. "This isn't up for debate. I think you need one, so I'm having it installed. Don't worry about the cost. Please trust me to do my job properly this time around."

She watched the cool mask of professionalism cover his face, and her heart sank. He thought he'd screwed up at the cabin and was in goon mode again. "I do trust you. And, just for the record, it's not the cost I object to. It's the autocratic way you went about it."

He raised an eyebrow, and she saw red.

"Just because we slept together doesn't give you the right to tell me what to do."

She instantly regretted her outburst when she remembered the blonde was listening, who flashed an embarrassed glance her way.

Laura's eyes were the same smoky silver as Jake's. Were they related? Her guess was confirmed a moment later.

"Thanks for clearing that up," Jake said dryly. "By the way, in case you're wondering, Laura is my kid sister."

"Pleased to meet you," Laura chirped. "Don't let him buffalo you, honey. Stick up for your rights."

Jake swatted at her. "Don't you have some work to finish, baby sister?"

Laura easily dodged his slap, sticking her tongue out at him. "Slave driver," she called out as she headed for the living room.

Samantha waited for Laura to get out of earshot and then turned to Jake. "We need to set up some ground rules if you're going to stay here."

His eyebrow arched. "Such as?"

"Such as this." She pointed to her lack of attire.

"Your robe?"

She wasn't pleased with his innocent act or the grin that followed. "You know darned well what I mean. You had no right to undress me last night."

"You were in no shape to remove your clothes yourself." He smiled. "Besides, you asked me to."

"I did not!"

"How do you know? You were so blotto, a brass band could have marched through your bedroom, and you wouldn't have realized it." He frowned, growing serious. "The truth is, you were sick last night. I rinsed out your things and changed the sheets, all of which I'm sure you don't remember."

Appalled, she blurted out, "I'm sorry. I didn't know."

He shrugged. "Don't worry about it. It's all in a day's work for us goons. However, we need to talk about the dangers of mixing prescription medicine and alcohol."

She held up a hand to forestall the lecture that was sure to follow. "Please. You don't need to remind me. It was a mistake and not one I'm going to repeat. Frankly, I'm not up for one of your lectures for wayward girls this morning."

She got up and headed for her bedroom before he could argue. Jake's father's alcoholism made this a hot-button issue for him, but it was just a one-time mistake on her part. She understood his concern, but that didn't stop her from resenting his scolding.

Jake watched her walk away and shook his head, wishing there wasn't so much bad blood between them. He'd left her behind to protect her, but she wouldn't believe that now. He would keep her safe, regardless of her disapproval. He just hoped their attraction would mend their relationship over time.

He walked into the living room and stopped to admire Laura's technique as she finished wiring the alarm. His kid sister was a whiz with electronics and was at the university's top of her engineering class. She had no connection with Logan Industries. Given the circumstances, using one of his staff members was out of the question.

She looked up and grinned. "Seems your girlfriend is a tad grumpy this morning. Was it something you said or did?"

He shook his head. She wouldn't get him to rise to the bait that easily. "You're here to work, not to ask prying questions."

She laughed out loud at his forbidding glance. "It's obvious you're crazy about each other."

He gave up the battle. So much for intimidating his kid sister. He should have known the only way to get Laura off his back was to level with her. "We did have something going, but things got complicated, and the lady doesn't think much of me."

"Well, anyone could see the sparks between you two. I like her, but it was dirty pool not telling her who I was from the beginning. Did you see the looks she kept shooting at me?" She grinned at him. "I wouldn't blame her if she never fell in love with you."

Jake thought back on his and Samantha's tender moments at the cabin. "Oh, she loves me, all right. At least, she did. She doesn't like me at the moment, but I'm working on it."

Samantha's bedroom door opened, and Jake watched her stride briskly, if a bit gingerly, back into the kitchen, fully dressed. She grabbed her purse and keys off the counter and said a bit too brightly, "I'm off to work. I'll leave you two to get on with your high-tech stuff."

He noted her animated expression. She wanted to put some breathing space between them. Going back to her routine seemed like the perfect buffer zone. He wondered for a moment how to break the news.

"I'm sorry. I can't allow that."

"You what?" She glared up at him, hands on her hips. "I already told you. I won't blindly obey your orders. If you want my continued cooperation, you'll have to lighten up on the goon routine."

Jake shook his head and watched her eyes spark with outrage. "No. You can't go back until my people have had a chance to check things out. Besides, you're still on vacation."

"Damn it, Jake, you can't wrap me in cotton wool to keep me safe. The trouble is at Logan Industries. You should be there working on the case, not babysitting me. I'll be fine. Samantha's Special Affairs isn't exactly a hot bed of industrial espionage and intrigue. Vacation or not, I want to go to work."

"I have people I can trust running down leads at your father's firm. My place is at your side until we get this cleared up." He knew she thought he was overprotective, but he wasn't about to let her risk her life again. Still, he hated to see the fire of defiance dim in her eyes. "I'll make a deal with you. You can go to work on the condition I go with you. Are you willing to go along?"

She scowled at him, her fists balled impotently at her sides. "What other choice do I have?"

"None."

She shrugged. "Fine." Jake pulled his keys from his pocket as they entered the parking lot behind her condo. "I'll drive." He pushed the remote to unlock the doors of his dark blue sedan.

Samantha cocked an annoyed glance his way. "I didn't even want you to come along. The least you can do is let me drive my car."

She eyed his nondescript vehicle scornfully. No doubt, she thought it lacked the dash of her red sports car, but it was much safer.

"Listen, Sunshine. It makes sense to do it my way. My vehicle has a few little extras that yours lacks."

She rolled her eyes. "Don't tell me. It's equipped with secret agent devices, right?"

He grinned at her scornful tone. The fire had certainly not dimmed in his sweet sunshine. "Not exactly, but it does have a few safety devices your car lacks. Besides, it would be best if you kept a low profile for the next few days. Your red rocket over there practically screams *come and get me* to the bad guys."

"I guess you're right," she muttered, sliding into the passenger seat of his car.

Samantha wondered what her staff would make of Jake's heavy presence as they pulled into her shop's parking lot. He didn't exactly fit the bill as a soda jerk. She shot an uneasy glance his way.

He turned off the ignition and turned to look at her. "What's the matter?"

She wasn't even sure of his status in her life. First, he was the goon, and then, he'd become her lover, and now, what? Her keeper? Bodyguard? Her father's hired gun? The idea irritated her. No, he'd have to stay in the background for the time being.

"You don't need to come in with me."

"The hell I don't." He swung out of the car, and a few quick strides brought him to her door. He opened it. "Until this is solved, I'm going to be your shadow."

She slanted him an annoyed look, but knew he wouldn't relent. He'd stick by her side to the bitter end, no matter what she said.

"How am I going to explain you to my staff?"

"So, that's what's bothering you?" Jake flashed a suddenly bright smile. "Don't fret. I'm sure you'll come up with something."

Head clerk Monica Brown, a plump, motherly, middle-aged woman, looked up in surprise when they entered the shop. "Samantha, how are you? I didn't expect to see you back so soon."

She smiled, hoping to reassure Monica and divert any embarrassing questions about her canceled wedding. "I'm fine. I decided to come back early."

"That's probably best." Monica nodded. "You need to keep busy to take your mind off things."

Gary Bates, a junior clerk and college student, carried a box of supplies from the storeroom. "Hey, boss lady, it's good to see you back." He handed the box to Monica and walked to Samantha, casually placing one of his gangly arms around her shoulders as he gave her a friendly hug. He turned to look at Jake. "Who's the new guy?"

Samantha smiled. The young man was as friendly as a puppy. Then she glanced at Jake to find him scowling at the innocent embrace.

She frowned at him.

Jake seemed to get the message. He flashed her a subdued smile. Pleased by his reaction, she hugged Gary back and stepped away.

"Everyone, this is Jake, a new employee. Gary, why don't you acquaint him with operations? And then you can put him on start-up detail."

"Sure thing, boss." Gary smiled at Jake. "Come with me, and I'll give you the two-cent tour."

Samantha watched them walk away, relieved. So far, so good. Her morning staff seemed to accept Jake as one of them. She walked to the front of the shop to raise the shades and unlock the front door.

Monica gazed at her with an anxious look. She wasn't up to discussing her fiasco of an engagement.

Samantha turned to face her, striving to appear calm and serene. "So, what's on today's list of events?"

"You're sure you're alright?"

"Quite sure." Samantha placed a reassuring hand on Monica's arm. "My marriage to Grayson St. James wasn't meant to be. I had a lucky escape, but thanks for worrying about me."

Monica let out a sigh of relief. "You're welcome. I'm glad to see you've got such a good attitude."

"Thanks. Let's go over today's agenda, okay?"

Monica smiled and ticked off on her fingers the day's schedule. "We have the faculty tea, Billy Henderson's birthday party, and the Marshall wedding shower. We've got five dozen petit fours, finger sandwiches, and the tea things set up with Marsha and Rose to serve."

Samantha nodded. "Sounds perfect."

Monica smiled. "Glad you approve. Next, Mark is coming with me as "Happy the Clown" for the birthday party. He can help me ride herd on the little devils."

"Sounds like fun." Murphy's Law prevailed at children's parties. Anything that could go wrong, usually did.

Monica shook her head. "Right. Finally, we have a new dancer coming in for the shower. He's a senior at the university, majoring in performing arts. I auditioned him myself, and he's good. A little bit nervous, but good."

"Naughty girl." Samantha chuckled at Monica's blissful expression.

"I might be married, but I can still look."

The front bell jingled. Samantha turned.

Grayson St. James entered the shop, and she groaned. Oh, good grief, how did he know she was here? She was still supposed to be on their honeymoon. What a crummy morning this was turning into.

He flashed a confident smile, striding toward her. "Thank heavens I found you. I've been searching everywhere for you, sweetie pie."

Her stomach curdled at the pet name. She wasn't buying his apologetic tone.

"I'm so sorry about what happened. Tell me my girl's okay." He leaned forward to kiss her.

Startled, she turned her head away so the kiss landed on her cheek. She cringed, pulling away. "I'm not your girl anymore. I think the fact I ran away from you that night made it clear. I'm not into your fun and games, so why don't you turn around and leave!"

Her mouth turned dry as Grayson faltered, his smile slipping. Was he going to cause a scene? Maybe she should have listened to Jake and stayed home. Seeing Grayson's lying, cheating face brought back the humiliation afresh.

He reached out to take her hand, bringing it up to brush a kiss across her knuckles. "I'm sorry if I hurt you, sweetie pie. It was the first time, the only time, I swear. I admit I was a curious fool. Please say you'll forgive me."

He wasn't going to make this easy.

Samantha swept an irritated glance over him. She noted his handsome face, precisely styled blond hair, and crisply tailored suit, wondering what she had seen in him. He looked like a low-rent clone of a young Robert Redford.

She tried to tug her hand away, but he tightened his grip, pinching her fingers. She glared at him. Was the man just plain dense? His intense scrutiny scared her just a little bit.

"It's over. Please leave."

"Take your hand off her, St. James."

Jake's firm demand came from the back of the shop. The immense relief she felt surprised her. Yes, she wanted to handle this herself, but it was nice to know she had backup if she needed it.

Grayson dropped her hand as if scalded.

She wiggled her fingers, trying to get the blood back into them, grateful for the intervention. Hired guns had their uses, after all.

Grayson glared at Jake. "Ramsey, what are you doing here?"

"That's what I was about to ask you." Jake walked up behind Samantha and slipped an arm around her waist, drawing her close to his side. "The lady doesn't want you here. Beat it."

"This is none of your business." Grayson's lips thinned as he glowered at their embrace. "Samantha is my fiancée. I'm sure he wouldn't be very pleased if her father found out she was consorting with one of his lower-level employees."

"He knows and approves. He also knows all about your sexual quirks, and he disapproves." Jake's smile was frigid. "You're on fragile ground, St. James. I wouldn't push my luck if I were you."

Samantha bit her lip as she listened to the heated exchange.

Monica and Gary were standing in the back of the shop, mouths agape.

The men were putting on just the kind of show she'd wanted to avoid. She placed a hand on Jake's arm. "Why don't you return to what you were doing, Jake? I can handle this."

He hesitated a moment. "You're sure?"

"I'll be fine." She felt bolstered by Jake's concern, but she needed to handle this mess with Grayson all by herself. It would put a fitting end to this fizzled romance. Closure was what the self-help books called it, and boy, did she ever need it.

Jake fixed Grayson with a cool gaze before turning toward the storeroom. "I'll be in the back. If you need me, yell."

She watched Jake walk away, elated by his confidence in her. Maybe he was learning to give a little. It was a comforting thought.

Steeling her resolve, she turned to face Grayson, his troubled gaze remained firmly fixed on Jake's retreat. She cleared her throat, drawing Grayson's attention. His suave smile returned as he gazed at her. Damn the man for thinking of her as such a pushover.

"Samantha, sweetie pie, please give me a chance to talk to you. After what we meant to each other, I hope you can at least give me that."

She was shocked. All the time she'd known Grayson, she'd never heard him beg anyone for anything. Maybe he needed closure, too. She couldn't talk about their faded relationship now. Not with things in such turmoil.

"After we've both had a chance to cool off, we'll talk."

"Thank you," he said, then turned. At the door, he stopped to say, "I'll pick you up for dinner tonight."

"Hey," Samantha yelled after him, but he was already gone. Of all the nerve! If he thought he'd maneuvered her into a date, he had another think coming.

Jake carried some ice cream refills to the counter. "I see you got rid of him. Did everything go okay?"

"Just fine. I'll talk to you about it later."

She'd call Grayson at work and tell him not to come, so there was no need to inform Jake about her lack of success. She didn't want him to lose confidence in her.

An hour later, she was doing inventory in the storeroom when Jake's strong arm slipped around her waist. She snuggled against his muscular body.

"Guess who?" he whispered, bending to nuzzle her nape.

"Grayson," she said, chuckling when he grumbled in response to her teasing. The fact that she could joke about him meant she'd relegated him to history. What do you know, she'd gotten closure on her own.

"Guess again."

"This isn't very professional, Jake." She leaned into his strength, all her previous objections fading away. She owed it to the both of them to at least give their budding relationship a try. Smiling, she all but purred at the sensation his plundering lips caused.

Monica poked her head around the door. "Samantha, the stripper is here."

"Stripper?"

Samantha flushed, seeing Monica's sparkling eyes as she viewed their embrace, and stepped away from Jake's arms. Oh boy, she was sure to be in for some razzing later.

"Send him into my office."

"*Him*?" Jake sputtered.

Samantha turned to face him. "Yes, a male stripper hired for a bachelorette party this evening." She noted the startled expression on Jake's face. "It's part of my business. He's new and needs a bit of coaching before his debut."

His eyebrow quirked. "Let Gary coach him."

She crossed her arms, standing up to his disapproval. "No, that wouldn't do, at all. The man needs reassurance he can perform in front of women."

"Then how about Monica?"

"Listen here, Jake Ramsey. This is my business, and I'll run it as I see fit. Now, go out front and help Gary while I get on with things." She watched him hesitate for a moment before breaking into a rueful smile.

"You're the boss." He shook his head. "Just see that all you do is watch." He leaned down to brush a scorching kiss across her lips, then walked out.

Samantha sagged against the shelves, still tasting his sweet mouth on hers. Gathering her senses, she straightened and headed toward her office. His kisses still packed the same punch, and no buff hunk would take him off her mind.

Inside her office, a tall, dark, good-looking man dressed in a police uniform stood next to her desk. The ladies would go for this one.

"Thanks for coming in, Lance."

"Glad to meet you." He held out his hand.

She shook it. "Nice costume. Did you bring your music?"

"Sure did," he said, grinning.

"Well, let's get to it, then. And remember, you're there to entertain, and that's all. Look, but don't touch, if you know what I mean."

Lance popped a tape into the player while Samantha sat behind her desk. He started a sexy bump and grind.

She admired his sexy style. "You're doing just fine, but slow down a little. There's no rush. That's right, make eye contact. Okay, now start to unbutton your shirt. That's terrific, slow and teasing. Now turn and let it slip down your body. That's great. Back around and unsnap your pants."

"That's good enough, kid." Jake walked through the doorway, stopping to turn off the music.

"Was I any good?" Lance asked Jake while he slipped on his shirt.

"You're a natural, kid."

She smiled at Lance, knowing he needed reassurance. "You were just fine. You're going to do a fabulous job tonight."

"You'd better get going, so you can practice at home." Jake popped the disc out of the player and handed it to Lance, ushering him toward the door.

"I thought you would let me run my business my way." Samantha leaned back in her desk chair, shaking her head. The man was so jealous it was amusing. "That was a pretty pitiful way of letting me be in control."

"So, sue me."

Monica tapped on the door. "We just had two employees call in sick. Mike's got the flu, and Sharon can't come in for her afternoon shift. What do you want me to do?"

"Well," Samantha said, grinning at Jake. "I've got a perfect replacement for Happy the Clown, and I can take your place as his assistant while you stay in the shop for the afternoon."

Samantha smiled at Jake as he drove the company van toward Henderson's suburban home. He looked funny, wearing clown makeup, a big red nose, and a fluffy wig. Dressed up as Little Bo Peep, she had to admit, she looked just as ridiculous. What amazed her was Jake hadn't pitched a fit over clown duty.

Mrs. Henderson, a frazzled mom, met them at the door. "Thank heaven you're here. I was about ready to pull my hair out."

There was a dull roar of a dozen six-year-olds wreaking havoc in the backyard, and she smiled. "Never fear, Mrs. Henderson, Samantha's Special Affairs to the rescue."

Three hours later, she dragged her way to the van and limply hopped inside. She eyed Jake's fresh-as-a-daisy clown costume sourly. "How can you be so peppy after what we went through?"

He smiled, pulling out of the driveway. "It wasn't that bad."

"Maybe for you," she grumbled.

He chuckled. "Well, you're the one who set up the ground rules. Whoever makes a mess has to clean it up."

"That was when I figured you'd be the one making the messes." She wrinkled her nose at the disgusting memory. Shoveling pony poop was not in her usual job description.

He shook his head and chuckled. "You should have brought a diaper for the pony. Everyone knows a pony that eats a gallon of ice cream will make a mess."

"I was too busy organizing the games to notice until it was too late. Besides, I still maintain the pony wrangler was negligent. He's the one who should have been on clean-up duty. He had no business wandering away. If he wants me to renew my contract with him, he'd better buck up his ideas of service."

They'd turned in the opposite direction from the shop.

"Where are we headed?"

"Logan Industries. I told your father we'd check in."

She glanced at her rumpled costume in horror. "Like this?"

He shrugged. "Sure, why not? It's after hours, so we won't have to worry about unfriendly scrutiny."

She bit her lip. "He already thinks I'm a kook. Now, he'll be sure of it."

He frowned and shook his head. "He doesn't think anything of the kind."

She knew better. Her father disapproved of just about everything she did. He had approved of her engagement to Grayson, and look how that turned out. Lacking the energy to argue her case, she sagged in her seat.

Maybe it would be good to see the scene of the crime. Despite her misgivings, she was curious to learn what her father had discovered. For Tad's sake, she hoped Jennifer had been duped, but she didn't believe it. Once in custody, Jennifer was sure to be a fountain of information. And, hopefully, she could lead them to the source of the thefts.

Jake stopped the van in his slot at Logan Industries and turned to look at her. "Don't worry about the costume you're wearing. I think you look kind of cute."

She slanted him an irritated glance. "You've got to be kidding." She had no choice but to go in like this, seeing that she was only wearing her bra and panties under the costume. He was lucky he'd been wearing street clothes under his baggy costume.

Jake grinned and opened his car door.

She grabbed at his flapping coattails, trying to avert disaster. He looked even wilder than she did with his clown costume, makeup, and big red nose. "Take off your costume," she shouted as he sprinted around the car to open her door.

"No time." He smiled as he half-helped, half-tugged her out of the van.

She reluctantly fell into step beside him. Oh well, this was her line of work. If she were to stay in the area, her father would have to get used to seeing her in all sorts of get-ups.

Jake gave her a reassuring smile as he ushered her into the building. "Cheer up, Sunshine. It's not so bad."

Their footsteps rang as they walked down the office building's marble halls. Samantha glanced in askance at the few executives still working. Hopefully, they wouldn't recognize Jake. It wouldn't do his formidable reputation any good to be seen as a clown.

Her father's executive secretary, Eleanor, burst out laughing at the sight of them. "Oh my," she said, wiping her eyes. "I do apologize, but you startled me. Go on in, Samantha. Your father is expecting you."

She started to follow Jake into the inner office.

He stopped, turned, and said, "You can stay here and visit with Eleanor if you like. I'll go speak with your father."

Samantha knew he was giving her an easy out because of her discomfort, but she couldn't take it. She'd vowed to stay on top of this mystery until they solved it, and she wasn't going to give up now.

"No, I'll go with you."

"I'll make some coffee," Eleanor said with a smile. "It looks like you could both use a cup."

"Thanks." Samantha followed Jake into the inner office.

Her father sat at his desk looking at a piece of paper, and Tad occupied a wing chair across from him. One look at her brother's solemn expression told her the news wasn't good.

She cleared her throat, and they both looked up. She was buoyed by the twinkle in her father's eye as he looked at the two of them.

"Well, Jake, I see you're right in the swing of things," Samuel stated with a grin.

"Yes, sir. I always knew she'd turn me into a clown someday."

She shot him a repressive glance, but gave up the battle when he grinned at her. Men, who could understand them? She'd expected her father to be appalled at their appearance, and he gave every impression of being amused. Tad even cracked a smile.

"So, what's new?"

Tad's smile vanished. "Jennifer's gone."

"I thought I told you not to contact her." Jake scowled.

"You did." Tad's shoulders sagged. "I wanted to make sure she was okay. I dropped by her place. She's gone. According to her landlord, her apartment's been empty for a week."

Samantha gasped. "That's right before I was attacked."

Jake stiffened beside her.

Could the high-pitched laugh from her stalker have been a woman's voice? She'd had the impression the blurry figure in the woods was bigger and male, but fading light could play tricks on a person.

"I know you're probably wondering if Jenny is involved in attacking you, sis. But she couldn't be. Jenny isn't capable of that kind of thing. I think it's more likely she ran away because she was scared."

Jake frowned. "I'll have my staff scour her apartment. They should pick up something about her location."

"Sounds like a good idea. I already had them start on her office." Samuel stated with a nod.

There was a knock on the office door. Delbert Logan stepped through the doorway. "Hope I'm not interrupting anything."

Samuel looked up. "What's up?"

"I just wanted to tell you the sales figures are delayed a week. My secretary was out today, and the temp they got me is a bit slow," Delbert replied with a smile. He turned to look at Samantha. "Samantha, dear, is that you?"

"Yes, it's me." She couldn't help feeling uncomfortable. He'd been instrumental in her doomed engagement, introducing her to Grayson and playing matchmaker. She only hoped this wouldn't wreck her close relationship with her uncle.

He peered at her closely, his gaze focusing on her sympathetically. "Are you all right? I've been concerned about you since you ran away."

Samantha bit her lip at his choice of words. No doubt Delbert thought she'd flipped her lid after Grayson's infidelity, and her shocked reaction now didn't help. "I'm fine, Uncle Delbert. Back at work, as you can see by my costume."

"Well, that's good to hear. We must have lunch sometime and talk it all out. If you ever need any help, come to me." He cast a quizzical glance at Jake.

Samuel stood. "I'll see you on Monday then, Delbert."

"Yes, Monday," Delbert stated before he walked out.

Samuel waited for Delbert to get out of earshot, then picked up another piece of paper off the desk, handing it to Jake. "Your staff found this behind Jennifer's desk a few minutes before you arrived. It must have slipped back there without her noticing."

Jake smoothed out the crumpled note. "Looks like a list of tasks. Pick up tickets. Meet with Jimmy. L.V." He handed it to Tad. "Is this her handwriting?"

Tad frowned. "Yes."

He glanced at Tad sympathetically. "Do you know a Jimmy?"

Tad shook his head. "No."

Jake shrugged. "Maybe she ran off with him."

Chapter Eight

"Samantha, do you want pasta or an omelet for dinner?" Jake asked from the kitchen.

"Surprise me." She stretched on the sofa and closed her eyes.

It had been an exhausting and troubling day between the Henderson party and the meeting with her dad. Jake had volunteered to cook dinner, and she'd gratefully taken him up on his offer.

"Here you go." Jake stood in front of her. "I thought you could use this."

She opened her eyes to find him holding out a glass of lemonade. He wore his clown costume, though he'd removed the big red nose and greasepaint. He had an annoying habit of sneaking up on her. She idly wondered if she could break him of it as she reached for the glass.

"You were right. Thanks. Thank you again for making dinner."

"You're welcome, Sunshine." He bent down to place a quick kiss on her lips. "Dinner will be ready in half an hour. In the meantime, I'm going to get cleaned up."

She watched him walk away, thinking that, despite his sometimes high-handed tactics, it was amazing how well Jake could fit into her life when he tried. But was it enough to build a relationship on, she wondered?

The shower started. A moment later, the doorbell rang.

She got up to answer it, stopping to peer out the peephole. Oh, good grief! Grayson stood on her doorstep, leaning heavily on the bell. Given the crazy afternoon, she'd forgotten to call and tell him not to come.

Maybe if she pretended, she wasn't home, he'd go away.

He pressed the bell again for an extended ring.

Groaning in disgust, she pushed the sequence of buttons on the control panel that Jake had taught her to disable the alarm. Before Jake came out to see the commotion, she had to get rid of her ex. She didn't have the energy to deal with two outraged male egos. Jerking the door open, she frowned at the man on her doorstep.

Grayson thrust a bouquet into her hand while flashing a suave smile. "Here you go, sweetie pie." He stepped forward, forcing his way inside.

Samantha scowled and took a step back. She understood the need for closure, but this invasion was too much. "Hold it right there, buster. If you didn't notice, I haven't invited you in, Grayson. I'd like you to go. Now!"

His handsome face showed a flash of cold anger before it resumed its smooth façade. "You said you wanted to talk." His tone was confident as he leaned forward to kiss her.

She dodged it. "I meant far in the future, and you know it."

His wounded expression was the last straw. She knew now she'd never had the power to move him. He was probably just worried their split would hurt his standing in her father's company, and as far as she was concerned, he could stand or fall on his merit. Grayson St. James wasn't her problem anymore.

Her problem was, thank goodness, busy in the shower.

"I've been waiting for you to wash my back, darling."

Grayson's jaw dropped as he gazed beyond her. She spun around, already knowing what she would find.

Jake stood in the middle of the living room, naked but for a towel wrapped around his hips. Sunlight glistened on the water droplets on his chest.

"So that's why you tried to get rid of me," Grayson hissed.

She was too busy frowning at Jake to pay much attention to Grayson's accusation. Jake stood resolutely with a dangerous glint in his eye. She'd wait until she got rid of Grayson to deal with him.

She turned back to confront him.

He glared at Jake and took no notice of her. This situation was rapidly spinning out of control. Grayson had no hold on her anymore, and it was high time he accepted that fact. Determined to resume control of the situation, she waved her hand in front of Grayson's face to draw his attention.

After a moment, he slanted a scornful gaze her way. "Samantha, sleeping with the hired help is so low class!"

Her sense of outrage boiled over as she stalked up to him. How dare he criticize her? "You ought to know. What did you do, sleep your way through Logan Industries? At least I love a man before I sleep with him. I thank my lucky stars I had the good sense not to sleep with you, jerk."

Grayson's eyes widened in alarm, and he backed away. He scuttled toward the door and safety.

She caught up with him in the doorway. "Get out of my house!" Reinforcing the demand with a shove over the threshold, she threw the bouquet at him. It felt oh-so-good to toss him out of her house. It was payback for the humiliation he'd put her through.

Grayson went still, the bouquet bouncing off his chest. "Sweetie pie, please don't be hasty. I'm sorry if I made you mad. It's just that seeing Ramsey naked in your house made me crazy."

"Sorry, my ass. And as for crazy, yeah, I think you are." She shook her head as she watched him try to backpedal. He had a hidden agenda. She realized that now. She wasn't falling for his apologetic act again. "Tell me what you came here for."

He hesitated, shifting a nervous glance at the ground. "About my job."

She sighed as her suspicions were confirmed. She'd always been just a commodity to him on his climb to the top of the corporate ladder. "You can stand or fall on your own merits, Grayson. As Rhett Butler once said, 'Frankly, my dear, I don't give a damn.'"

His suave mask melted as he scowled at her. "I don't know what I saw in you, you spoiled little bitch." He turned and stalked away.

"Vice versa, believe me!" She slammed the door and then spun around to look at Jake.

He had the pleased expression of a tabby cat with a bowl of cream. "Good work, Sunshine."

She was irritated by his confident tone. "You are not off the hook just because I threw that jerk out." She put her hands on her hips. "The stunt you pulled made me look like a fool."

"No, it didn't." He walked back toward the bathroom, then stopped to glance at her from the doorway. "It made you look like a woman who knows to get rid of unwanted males before they get pulverized." He added sternly, "After I get dressed, we'll talk about not disabling the alarm to open the door for low-life ex-fiancés."

"Don't worry. After the reception we gave him, I doubt Grayson St. James will trouble us again."

"Samantha, aren't you ready yet?" Jake called from the living room the following evening.

"I'll be right there."

She stood in front of the mirror, putting the finishing touches on her makeup. Her hair swept back in a chignon, and diamond studs glittered in her earlobes. She wore an elegant silver gown. It was the same color as Jake's eyes, so she'd chosen it. She wanted tonight to be a success for him. He was moving away from his old life, but she had reason to hope his new one contained her.

Jake was pacing the living room. He stopped and gave her an appreciative once-over when she came out of the bedroom. He let out a wolf whistle. "Samantha, you are undoubtedly the most beautiful woman I've ever seen."

The compliment warmed her. "Thank you." She swept an appreciative gaze over him in his perfectly tailored tuxedo. He looked every inch a successful novelist on the way up.

He held out his arm. "Well, shall we?"

She smiled and linked her arm with his. "Lead the way."

He escorted her into the convention hall at a local five-star hotel. She was there an hour early to fix any problems that might occur.

"I need to check on things. Why don't you have a drink at the bar? I'll join you in half an hour."

Jake gazed around the room. Staff bustled around, setting up the area. He nodded at Monica and Gary as they placed floral arrangements on the tables.

"Okay, I guess you can't get in any trouble here. I'll meet you in half an hour. It'll give me time to check in with my editor, Mike Barnes. He's probably lurking around the bar."

She could feel his tension. It was an important night for him. Win or lose, being nominated for an award was an honor. Coming out of anonymity was a big step for him, too. "Don't worry, Jake. I'm sure that the evening will be a huge success. The press is going to be very impressed with you."

"Right." He brushed a kiss across her lips and turned. "Remember, I'm just a shout away if you need my help."

She watched him walk away, thinking what a difference a few days could make. Just a week ago, she was an inexperienced late bloomer. Now she was every inch a woman. Jake's woman. She smiled at the thought, but reminded herself she had a business to run. Even though she wasn't supposed to work this evening, she wanted to ensure the event ran smoothly.

She walked toward Monica, who stood by the head table, clipboard in hand, directing the activities.

She looked up at her approach and gave Samantha's formal attire an appreciative once-over. "Nice dress."

"Thanks." Samantha smiled at her surprised reaction. The gown was very feminine and, at the same time, elegant. Her new confidence was attributable to one man. Jake. "So, how's it going?"

Monica frowned. "Not so good. Someone spilled bleach on our red table linens." She took the lid off a plastic bin and pulled out a red napkin, now marred with white and pink splotches. A strong odor of bleach wafted into the air. "The whole batch is like this. The laundry swears they had nothing to do with it."

Samantha gazed at the mess, alarmed. The whole bin was a complete loss. "Oh no! We don't have time to bring in our backup supply."

"Don't worry, boss. All is not lost. The hotel has agreed to let us use theirs for a small fee. So, I guess white linens will have to do."

"Right." Samantha relaxed. "Are there any other mishaps I should be aware of?"

Monica winced. "The florist delivered lilies instead of the roses we were expecting." She handed the statement to Samantha. "He said you changed the order. Did you?"

Samantha glanced at the bill in frustration. "Of course not. Someone must have messed up at Parkinson's Floral. It's too late to get new flowers delivered."

"Don't panic, boss. Gary, Rose, and I did a little creative arranging. We'll make do."

She gazed at the sparse but colorful arrangements. "Thanks. You three did great, considering what you had to work with."

"Thanks."

"You're welcome. Thank you for all your hard work. You guys are absolutely the best staff ever."

Monica looked at her inquisitively. "So, what are you doing here? You not scheduled to work this function."

"Jake is one of the nominees. I'm here as his guest."

Monica's eyes widen. "The new soda jerk is a mystery writer?"

"Yes." Samantha felt herself blush under the knowing gleam in Monica's eye.

"He's your boyfriend," Monica said, breaking into a delighted grin. "No wonder Grayson got so hot under the collar when he saw his arm around you the other morning."

"Jake and I have been seeing each other since I broke off my engagement." Samantha recalled the scene at her apartment and sighed. "Grayson isn't taking it very well."

"Don't worry about what that bozo thinks. When it's right, it's right. St. James was wrong for you, but Jake is right. You two generate enough heat to start a bonfire."

Her cheeks heated again, but she didn't decline the statement. She could no longer deny, even to herself, how she felt about Jake. "As long as you have the situation well in hand, I'm going to go meet my date."

"Have a great time," Monica called out.

She stepped out of the ballroom and into the shadows, making her way down the corridor. In the hidden doorway of a nearby room stood a cloaked shape.

She shivered, stopping in her tracks. The ghostly image transported her back to the stalker in the woods. The form separated itself from the darkness, and her terror evaporated.

"Uncle Delbert. What are you doing here?"

He smiled, his genial, round face crinkling. "Well, fancy meeting you here, Samantha. How is my favorite niece this lovely evening?"

"I'm just fine. I'm on my way to the bar to meet a friend."

"I was looking for the bar. I'm supposed to meet a buyer there for a little afterhours socializing."

"You're heading in the wrong direction," Samantha replied with a smile. He'd always been a bit bumbling. "Follow me, and I'll show you the way."

Delbert fell into step at her side, gallantly taking her arm. "I was so sorry about your falling out with Grayson."

She stiffened. She had hoped he'd decided to let the subject drop. Maybe he felt a sense of obligation having played matchmaker for the two of them. Had he deliberately hunted her down now to try to patch things up?

"Some things don't work out. Our parting will turn out for the best. You'll see."

"I can't agree, my dear. Why, if you could see the poor lad's face. All he does is mope around since you jilted him. Please give him a chance to make things right."

So, he was here on false pretenses. No amount of well-meaning persuasion on his part would induce her to change her mind. He was in the dark about Grayson's obnoxious visits yesterday and his kinky sex life.

"I have seen his face."

His eyes narrowed as he studied her mutinous expression. "You have?"

"Yes, indeed. Twice, as a matter of fact, and Grayson certainly didn't look forlorn. He looked like the cheating jerk he was. You're wasting your breath if he sent you here to plead his case. It's over!"

Delbert blinked rapidly and patted her hand. "Very well, my dear. I don't want to upset you."

"I'm sorry if I sounded harsh, but it's been an upsetting time for me lately."

"Just as you say, my dear. I understand you've had a difficult time with Grayson's recent error in judgment and the trouble up north. Rest assured, you won't hear another word out of me."

She let out a sigh of relief at his sympathetic tone. She was happy Grayson St. James was out of her life for good. "Thank you for being so understanding."

Delbert's kindly gaze lingered on Samantha's smile for a moment before slanting to Jake, seated at a corner table. "You're seeing Mr. Ramsey now?"

She bit her tongue. *No more matchmaking. Please!* Their relationship was complicated enough without any of Delbert's meddling. For whatever reason, he seemed even more anxious to marry her off than her father. It was time to set some boundaries.

"Yes, we're seeing each other, and it's going very well."

Her uncle hesitated. "I'll go to the bar and wait for my buyer. Remember to be careful who you give your heart to, my dear. You never know whom you can trust. Have a lovely evening, Samantha."

"Thanks." She watched him walk away, wrinkling her nose at his cryptic warning.

He was probably worried Jake was taking advantage of her while she was on the rebound. Nothing could be further from the truth. Jake had been a perfect gentleman since that night at the cabin. As a matter of fact, the sensual tension between them was so sharp at times, it could cut with a knife. Their sexual stalemate would have to end soon.

She walked over to Jake and caught him gazing at Delbert sitting at the bar.

"Did you talk to your editor?"

"Sure." Jake turned his attention to her. "He gave me the usual patter about publicity being good for my career. I'd just as soon stay incognito. Dressing in a monkey suit is not my idea of a good time."

"You're the best-looking man in the room, handsome."

A startled smile kicked the edges of his hard mouth.

"What were you doing with Delbert Logan?" He cast a curious look her way.

"I found him wandering the hall, lost. He was looking for the bar. You know Uncle Delbert. He's got a poor sense of direction."

Jake's brow wrinkled. "Wandering the hall? Is he here for the awards ceremony?"

"No. He's meeting a buyer for a little afterhours fun."

He raised an eyebrow. "Male or female?"

"He didn't say, but I'd bet it was female. He's a born romantic, my Uncle Delbert."

"What was all the yelling about?"

"I wasn't yelling at him. I was reiterating the fact that Grayson and I are through. He was playing matchmaker for Grayson and me. He seems to be taking our split personally."

He frowned. "Do you want me to have a word with him?"

She shook her head. "No, I think he got the message. He meant well, but I've finally convinced him to drop it."

Samantha circulated the ballroom after the awards ceremony by Jake's side. He'd won in his category, as she'd predicted. It felt good when he'd stayed by her side, wordlessly showing they were a couple. She reveled in the occasional touch of his hand on her arm when he introduced her to friends and colleges. The secret smile he had just for her.

On the ride home, she sat back in her seat and smiled. The evening had been a complete success for Jake and her business. Her client list was sure to grow, and his peers had acknowledged Jake's accomplishments. Best of all, he'd publicly acknowledged her place in his life.

He parked the car and turned to look at her, his expression softening. "Your hair shines in the moonlight." He leaned across the seat to capture her mouth with his, his tongue coaxing and demanding a response.

She melted in his embrace. Their love was right, come what may. They'd go back to the rhythm of the magical night at the cabin before things got complicated. They'd return to the way things were before, warm, loving, and passionate.

He broke from the kiss and looked questioningly at her, his hands moving down to skim over her arms. Feeling her tremble, he asked, "Cold?"

"No," she whispered.

She gazed into his stormy gray eyes, drinking in the heat of his desire. She moved forward, slipping her arms around his neck and tugging his head down to hers for another kiss. "Please don't stop."

He smiled. "There's no power on earth that could stop me, but I think we'd better take this inside before we give your neighbors a free show."

He tugged her out of the car, stopping to drop a scorching kiss on her lips, then scooped her up and carried her to the steps. He took the key from her, opened the door, and reset the alarm. He held her close as he walked through her apartment to the bedroom. Setting her down next to the bed, he reached behind her to unzip her gown, letting it slide off her shoulders.

She stepped out of the pool of silver fabric and stood unashamedly in front of him, clad only in skimpy silver underwear. She reached behind her, unhooked her bra, and let it slowly slide down her arms.

He sat on the bed, his body tensing. A slow, appreciative smile curved his lips.

She reveled in her strip tease. She let the bra linger over her breasts for a teasing moment before tossing it aside. Then she curled her fingers into the waistband of her matching panties and inched them down, shimmying out of them and kicking them aside.

She stood before him totally and unabashedly naked, and flashed a shameless grin. "See something you like, cowboy?"

He smiled. "One or two things."

She pouted and playfully reached out to loosen his bow tie. "Is that all?"

Chuckling, he stood and shrugged off his tux jacket. "If pressed, I can think of a few more." He ripped his shirt off and bent to nibble on her ear, whispering, "I'm crazy about each delectable inch of you, Sunshine."

She sighed blissfully, his warm breath causing the most scorching sensations to course through her body and curl her toes. Practically purring, she curved closer to him, running her hand through his hair. "You've still got too many clothes on."

While trailing a line of kisses down her throat, he quickly unzipped his pants. Then, he scooped her in his arms and laid her tenderly on the bed. He slid in beside her, swirling his tongue around her nipple.

She arched toward him. His talented mouth tugged on her tight nipple, giving it the most exquisite attention. She cried out. It was beautiful, so wonderful. Her fingers curled into his thick dark hair as she held him to her, trying to hurry him along. She needed him so much.

He pulled back. "Don't rush me, Sunshine. I do my best work when I go slow."

Slow wasn't what she wanted. She ran her hand down his body, touching his erection. He groaned, surging forward under her ministrations.

That was more like it. She wanted him just as hot for her. She could feel his leashed power as his hot velvet shaft pulsed in her hands.

He caressed her, tracing fire lines down her quivering abdomen until he reached her inner thighs.

Her legs opened for him. His teasing touch tempted her, leaving her wanting more. She needed him, had to have him. Finally, his fingers found her femininity when she'd thought she'd go mad from need. She gasped as he inched first one and then two fingers inside her. She knew she was wet, her body weeping for him.

"Oh, yes." She arched against him, her hands running down his back to knead his tight buns. He bucked against her, and she reveled in her power to excite him. "Now, please."

"Yes. I can't wait any longer, either." He surged between her thighs, entering her, filling her intimate center.

She cried out at the sensation his possession ignited in her. His stiff shaft moved in and out, rubbing against her most sensitive spot, sending a thousand shards of pleasure through her. She wrapped her legs around him and pulled him deeper, making him groan. She trembled, shivering, as shimmers of orgasm overtook her.

He groaned as he thrust into her one more time, crying his triumph. He went still, his breathing slowing too normal. "I think those love lessons have created a monster. Lord, Sunshine, you'll wear me out."

"As long as you're with me, I won't complain." She smiled at him, noting his surprise at her words.

He grinned. "Demanding little cuss, aren't you?"

"When I see something I want, yes."

He had a satisfied expression as he rolled to the side, taking her with him.

She nestled against him with a smile. They'd had a breakthrough in their turbulent relationship. She drifted off to sleep, confident their troubles were all behind them.

Chapter Nine

The phone rang, jolting Samantha awake. She leaned over Jake to answer it. "Samantha, honey," her father said. "Let me talk to Jake."

She glanced at Jake's sleep-rumpled, sexy naked body lying beside her. She tugged the sheet up to cover her breasts. It was amazing. Her father's gruff voice made her feel like a wanton teenager caught in the act. "I'll go see if I can find him." She put her hand over the mouthpiece and thrust the phone at a grinning Jake, who seemed to read her reaction very well. "It's my father."

He ran a caressing finger over her cleavage before taking the phone. He held his hand over the receiver. "Good-morning, beautiful. Why don't you fix a pot of coffee while I take this? Then we can spend the rest of the day in bed. We need to work on love lesson number ten."

She slid an appreciative glance at him before getting out of bed. She belted her robe around her. "I can't wait."

He took his hand off the receiver. "Hello, Samuel. Samantha came to my room to tell me you were on the phone. What can I do for you?"

She winked at him and walked out of the bedroom, making her way into the kitchen. She put a filter in the coffeemaker's basket and reached for the dark roast blend Jake liked so much. She'd surprise him with breakfast in bed, and then they'd spend the day in other pleasurable pursuits, maybe love lesson number ten. She tingled at the prospect.

The bedroom door opened. Shoot, so much for surprising him. He could whip up one of his excellent omelets while she toasted some English muffins.

He walked up behind her, slipping his arms around her waist. He pulled her against him, bending to nuzzle her nape. "Sorry, Sunshine, I'll have to skip breakfast."

The tendrils of hair that had escaped her topknot stirred when he breathed. She arched her neck, loving the warm sensation he created. "We could eat breakfast after." Rubbing against him, she realized he was already dressed. What a waste of time. She'd have to take them off him again.

"I wish," he said with regret. "I'm afraid duty calls. Samuel has a lead on the broker for the dummy stock sales. I've got to go to work and run down a few leads. This time, I think we've hit paydirt."

She was disappointed, but knew his duty to the firm came first. Whatever it took to wrap up this caper was worth it.

She turned to face him with a bright smile, eager to be in on the clincher. "I'm going with you. It'll take me ten minutes to get dressed."

He went still. "No."

She set down the coffee scoop and slanted a curious glance his way. Why the sudden change of mood? "You can't mean that. Remember, I'm your partner. You can't just up and leave me here to twiddle my thumbs."

He faced her displeasure calmly and firmly. "I meant every word of what I said. Stay out of this, Samantha."

She wrinkled her nose as she frowned at him. Why was he being such a jerk suddenly? They'd had this argument before, and she'd won. They were partners whether he liked it or not. It wasn't fair of him to try to change the rules now. Was there more to her father's phone call than he was saying? The thought scared her a little.

"Why should I stay out of it? We're talking about white-collar crime here, not murder incorporated."

He arched a brow. "Have you forgotten being stalked and attacked at the cabin?"

"Of course not." She sighed. His closed expression told her she had little chance of changing his mind, but she had to try. "Those were just random acts of violence. Everything's been fine since we returned."

He shook his head. "In this case, I'd rather be safe than sorry. You're staying home. Period. End of argument."

She scowled at him. How dare he think he could order her around? That wasn't his function anymore. He'd better learn that fact fast, or he'd be out on his ear.

"I'll go on my own then."

A nerve pulsed in his tense jaw. "You do, and I'll see to it that you can't sit down for a week."

She gaped at the barbaric threat. Gazing at the steely look in his eye, she suddenly decided she wouldn't put it past him to resort to spanking her.

She automatically backed against the counter. "Lay one hand on me, and you'll draw back a bloody nub."

The tension seemed to roll off him as he flashed her a startled grin. "Bloody nub? Don't be so dramatic, Sunshine. I've got to go. I don't want to keep your father waiting."

She fumed, but realized she was just as unreasonable as he was for her reactions. She was worried about his safety. But the best way for him to stay safe was to focus all his energy on the task at hand. She'd probably be a distraction if she were there.

"Fine, go. Please save me from the bad guys. I'm a weak lady who needs a big strong hero like you to save me."

He flashed her an apologetic smile as he walked toward the door. "I'm not falling for that for a minute. Don't you dare try to follow me down there. I told the security guard to bar you from the building until further notice."

She scowled as she followed him to the door. "That's just peachy."

He brushed a quick kiss across her lips. "I'll make it up to you when I get back."

"I might not be here."

He stopped in his tracks and turned to slant a panicked glance her way. "Don't even joke about walking away, Sunshine."

"I just meant that I might go into the shop." She read the look in his eyes and knew he was concerned for her safety. "Alright, I'll stay put until you get back. I guess you should get going."

"Later," he said, walking out the door.

"Yes."

He pulled out his cell phone. "I'll call Laura to sit with you."

She didn't relish the idea of company right now. Her emotions were too raw.

"No, thanks." When he hesitated, she reassured him. "I don't need a babysitter, Jake. I'll be fine."

"I hate to leave you alone." He gazed at her rebellious frown and slid his phone back into its holster. "Okay, you win. I guess I've pushed my luck far enough this morning. Just make sure you set the alarm. And don't forget the panic code."

She smiled, hoping to reassure him. "I won't forget. Thanks to you, I have my new alarm system to protect me. You need to leave now, or you'll be late."

He glanced at her appreciatively. "You're something else, Sunshine. I'll make it up to you when I get back. Get ready for love lesson number ten."

She locked the door behind him and slumped against it. "Dear Lord," she prayed, "please don't let anything happen to him."

She paced the confines of the living room for a moment, and then went into the bedroom to get dressed. Stewing over Jake's mission wasn't going to do either of them any good.

As she pulled on her clothes, she couldn't help worrying about him. He was fast becoming the most important person in her life. She should have told him she loved him, but now she might never get the chance. His concern for her safety made her wonder about his. Could he be right? Could the attacks on her be related to this case? Maybe she should drive to Logan Industries and lurk around outside.

She wandered back into the living room, and a tap on the door jolted her out of her reverie. Had Jake called Laura anyway? It might be nice to have someone to talk to.

Suddenly glad for the company, she hurried to the door and tore it open. She realized her mistake in an instant, but by then, it was too late.

"Oh, my God." She gasped and backed away.

Grayson stood on the step, pointing a black revolver at her heart.

Her eyes widened as she took in the anomaly of her usually dapper ex-fiancé, dressed in a ratty flannel shirt, worn jeans, and a blue baseball cap. It was the same combo her stalker had worn. Suddenly, it all came together. The random acts of violence she'd experienced after leaving him hadn't been random at all. He'd probably worn the clothes again for effect. Her rejection must have unhinged him. The smirk on his face told her he was enjoying himself, the creep.

Jake pulled into his parking slot, walked through the front door, and headed for Samuel's office.

Tad bumped into him in the hall and fell into step beside him. "I'm surprised to see you leave Sammy's side. What's up?"

"Samuels got a lead on those stock sales."

Samuel looked up as Jake entered his office with Tad on his heels. "You made good time, Jake. Did you come solo?"

"Yep. I had a tough time, but I eventually made her stay home. I had to threaten to turn her over my knee."

Tad let out a whoop of laughter. "I'd like to see you try it. You'd draw back a bloody stump."

"That's pretty much what she said," Jake admitted wryly.

"I could have told you my darling daughter doesn't take discipline well. I tried after she ran into traffic when she was six. She bit me. Hard! But let's move on to less amusing subjects. Here's the full report."

Jake took the paper Samuel handed him. He glanced at the investigator's report, and his shoulders tightened. Somehow, he wasn't surprised. He'd always thought it was an inside job.

"The money trail from Sun-Worthy Investments led straight to Delbert Logan."

Tad gasped and peered over Jake's shoulder at the document. "Uncle Delbert? I don't believe it. He's been so nice to me since I came to work with him. He always welcomed me into his office to chat or visit Jennifer."

Jake frowned at the disclosure. The whole murky scheme was starting to come into focus. Delbert had probably dangled the sultry Jennifer before Tad like a tempting bait. But why did he try to discredit Tad? Was it jealousy, or something darker? Or did he simply need a fall guy?

"Figures don't lie, kid. You must admit, he's been acting a little strange now that his retirement date is growing nearer." Samuel heaved a heavy sigh. "I can hardly believe it myself. He's always been my most trusted and loyal employee. He's family, my second cousin. Delbert came to work for me right after I took charge of the firm from my father forty years ago. Do you think he's the one who's been selling our secrets to the highest bidder?"

"That's what I'm about to ask him." Jake took the report out of Tad's hand and turned to Samuel. "Call the police and have them meet me in Delbert's office. He has a lot of explaining to do. And I want the cops here when he spills his guts. Something tells me he wasn't in this alone."

Chapter Ten

Samantha gasped and took a step back. "Grayson, what on earth are you doing here? The need for closure I can understand, but this is just plain pathetic."

"Closure, my ass." He sneered while brandishing the gun. "Do you think I was really in love with you? It was an act. All I want is your name on a marriage license, and I'm not fussy about how I get it. We're going to Vegas to get married, sweetie pie. It's all part of my master plan." He chuckled.

Appalled, she gaped at him. Did he think he could get away with forcing her to marry him? He had to be bluffing. "Some master plan. You're a fool if you think I'm going to marry you."

He glowered at her. "That's exactly what you're going to do if you don't want me to put a bullet in you. Jenny could assume your identity if you force my hand. She'd be quite convincing with a little hair dye and your ID. She's done it before. She's quite a good little actress."

He wasn't bluffing. Samantha cringed at the chilling threat. She suddenly did not doubt he would cheerfully carry it out. He was crazy. She could see that now. His suave mask had lifted to reveal the monster inside.

Still, she had one trump card he couldn't beat. "No one in their right mind would believe I married you of my free will."

He thrust a pad of paper into her hand. "Sure, they will. You're going to leave one of your famous notes. Remember, you have a history of leaving notes and running away when the going gets tough. After the spat you and Ramsey had this morning, you decided to dump him and elope with me. Play along, and you'll keep breathing."

She cast a desperate look at the alarm box in the next room. It was too far away to push the panic button. She wished she was packing a gun.

Grayson grinned. "Once we're married, your shares will be mine to control. And, with dear Uncle Delbert in my hip pocket, Logan Industries will finally be mine. Now write, before I have to get nasty. And don't try to mess with me. I'm all out of patience as far as you're concerned."

Nasty. He'd been nothing but evil. So, it was all about shares. Lives would be destroyed in Grayson's quest for power. What was the connection between him and Delbert?

She picked up the pen and reluctantly scrawled the words Grayson dictated. At the bottom of the page, she tried to make a doodle of an umbrella surreptitiously. Umbrella. Stormy weather! She could only hope Jake would make the connection. Hopefully, he would read between the lines and come to her rescue.

Grayson snatched the paper away, smearing ink across the bottom. "I told you not to try any cute stuff, bitch."

"I'm not. Honest. I tend to doodle when I'm nervous, remember?"

He scowled, glancing from the note to her. "Yeah, I remember the doodle of a skunk you made on your note to me." He jerked her toward the door, stopping to slap the note on the countertop.

She thought a skunk described him to a T as she walked beside him, propelled forward by the gun pressed against her side. They stepped out the door and headed toward a brown panel van parked at the curb.

Mrs. Morley from two doors down was fetching her mail.

Grayson stiffened beside her and slid the gun around to jab painfully into the small of her back.

"Good morning, my dears." Lovely day, isn't it?"

Samantha put a bright smile on her lips. There was no way she could let this sweet old lady place herself in the line of fire. "Yes, it's a nice day. Looks like rain later, though."

Mrs. Morley looked up at the blue sky. "I don't think so, dear. There's not a cloud in the sky."

Samantha could feel Grayson's finger twitch on the trigger. She stiffened. To Mrs. Morley's eye, it probably looked like a romantic embrace.

Hoping to calm Grayson down, she said, "Right you are, Mrs. Morley. Those weathermen are usually wrong."

Grayson relaxed beside her, and she slanted an assessing glance his way. Would he get the umbrella and storm connection?

He bestowed his most brilliant smile on Mrs. Morley. "You might as well be the first to know, ma'am. Samantha and I made up, and we are in the process of eloping. Isn't that right, sweetie pie?"

She thought of the carnage that might result from the wrong answer and murmured, "That's right."

"How wonderful," Mrs. Morley said with a bright smile. "Don't let me detain you two lovebirds from Cupid's work."

Samantha watched her neighbor go back inside with a sinking heart. Now she was alone with the monster, and he'd already laid the groundwork for his claim of elopement.

Despite his promise to keep her alive, she knew her life would be worthless once she signed that marriage license.

He yanked her forward, and she stumbled toward the van. He prodded her to slide open the cargo door. She peered into the dark, dusty bay. It was separated from the driver's compartment. Riding in there would be like riding in a metal tomb.

She slanted a rebellious scowl his way. "I'm not sitting back here."

"Don't give me any of your lip." He gave her a hard shove into the cargo bay.

She slammed hard against the wall, seeing stars for a moment, before he slid the door shut, enveloping her in darkness.

She shivered as the oppressive isolation settled around her, then forced herself to calm down. She closed her eyes and visualized her dewy meadow, but this time, Jake was battling Grayson to protect their wildflower realm. Jake would decipher her clues and come to her rescue. Until he did, she'd have to keep her wits about her to escape this unscathed.

They drove for hours, and the temperature soared in the cargo hold. She coughed at the fumes that leaked inside. Good Lord, did he intend to asphyxiate her instead of shooting her?

Suddenly, he jammed on the brakes, and she hurtled toward the front, slamming against the wall with a *thump*. "Ouch!"

She went still and held her breath, trying to pick up sounds from outside. Was it Jake? Had he intercepted the van?

The door flew open.

She blinked against the sudden brightness, then felt her hope vanish. Grayson stood outside, leveling his gun at her again.

"Get out."

She slid to the edge of the door and sat for a moment, gazing out at her surroundings for help. There was none in sight. They were alone, parked at the edge of an airstrip. Several Logan Industries' jets sat at the ready.

But then, someone walked out from a small outbuilding. Help at last. As the figure approached, she could see it was a blonde woman dressed in a miniskirt and a halter top.

"Jennifer," she groaned.

"Got it in one, sweetie pie," Grayson said with a chuckle. He waved the gun ahead. "Move it before I change my mind and leave you here. You'd cook in that tin can before anyone found you."

She scowled at him, but quickly hopped down. She wouldn't put anything past him. The jerk was certifiable.

"I see you brought the goods." Jennifer grinned. "Good work, honey."

"Have I ever failed you, babe?"

"Not so far." She slid a critical gaze over Samantha. "She doesn't look any worse for wear."

"Well, it wouldn't do to have my fiancée all marked up for the wedding. People might think she was coerced."

Samantha scowled at the two of them and bit back her hostile retort. Their mocking exchange made her see red. She'd bide her time and wait for a chance to escape or rescue. Then, she'd be the one laughing.

In the meantime, she'd have to act as cowed and intimidated as she felt. It wouldn't be hard.

Jake tore into Delbert Logan's office, holding the damning paper. He'd finally gotten past the false front Delbert had put up and found his culprit.

Delbert looked up from his computer and gulped. "What can I do for you, Jacob?"

"For starters, you can tell me why you've suddenly turned traitor on Samuel Logan," Jake said, eyeing the man's discomforted reaction.

Delbert's face turned red. "I don't know what you're talking about, Ramsey. I've been a loyal employee since I came here forty years ago."

He saw past the older man's bluster to the outrage beneath. "But you're more than an employee. You're a trusted member of the family."

"I used to think so," Delbert muttered, "and then they started trying to force me out. Forty years of loyal service for my cousin, and what? A gold watch and a condo in Miami for my reward? I don't think so."

"I'm still trying to figure out who put this bug up your butt." He watched Delbert shuffle the papers on his desk nervously and knew that he'd hit a nerve. This seditious scheme hadn't come from Delbert. Someone had put him up to it, but to what purpose? The shares he'd just accumulated were barely enough to make a ripple. "I also wonder why you thought your thousand shares were enough to make an impact."

"I might not have enough shares on my own, but added to Samantha's, I'll have a majority." He smiled and eased back in his desk chair.

Samantha s shares! She'd always had a soft spot for her uncle, but he didn't believe she'd turn against her father, even if they didn't always get along. "You don't expect Samantha to hand them over to you, do you?"

He smiled genially, his eyes twinkling. "I'm confident things will work out that way. You wait and see. Love will find a way."

"Love?" Jake scowled as he suddenly got an awful feeling. "What do you mean by love? What are you up to, old man?"

Delbert shrugged. "Who says I'm up to anything? I've been told Samantha and Grayson have rekindled their romance, and I couldn't be more pleased." He beamed at Jake, warming to the tale. "You shouldn't have wasted your time interfering with their romance, Jacob. Samantha and Grayson belong together. If you were a parent, you'd understand just how proud I am of my son."

His son? St. James was more than a protégé to the man. He was his son.

Suddenly, the whole sick scheme came into focus. Delbert was living in a fool's paradise if he expected Samantha to fall back into Grayson St. James's arms. Somehow, he had to make the man understand. "Face the facts. She wouldn't have him on a bet."

Delbert slanted a sly gaze at Jake. "I wouldn't be too sure of that if I were you. You can ask her if you don't believe me."

Jake stiffened, realizing something was up. He turned on his heel, leaving Delbert in the care of his security staff.

He punched in Samantha's number on his cell phone as he drove toward her apartment. She didn't pick up.

She was gone. He knew it in his gut.

He noted Samantha's car was still in her apartment's parking lot as he pulled up to the building. He ran, punched in the sequence on the alarm, and entered the condo shouting her name.

There was no reply, confirming his fears. She'd vanished.

He walked inside, looking around. There was no sign of a struggle. Everything looked as it had when he'd left this morning except for a scrap of paper on the counter. He picked it up and read the note written in her handwriting.

Jake, it's over. I realized we weren't meant to be together. It's Grayson I love. We're going to be married. Please don't try to stop me.

Samantha.

He sagged in the chair in disbelief. It couldn't be true.

Then, he noticed the smudge on the bottom of the page. He picked it up and peered at the doodle. Samantha always doodled when she was tense.

An umbrella.

Stormy weather.

Samantha was in trouble.

He sprang to his feet and ran to the door while pressing the speed dial on his cell for Samuel Logan's office. "Sam, Ramsey here. Grayson's snatched Samantha. Delbert probably knows where they are going. Does Grayson St. James have one of the corporate jets on standby?"

Sam confirmed.

"I'm heading for the airport now. Have some staff meet me there for backup and call the police."

Jake shut the door behind him and reset the alarm, although it was rather pointless now that Samantha was gone. He started down the walk when he spotted one of her neighbors.

"Well, hello, Jake," Mrs. Morley said. "Are you here to water Samantha's plants?"

Jake slowed to glance at the friendly neighbor, who was watering the begonias in her window box. Maybe she knew something.

"Have you seen Samantha?"

"Oh, so you don't know." She beamed, touching her hand to her heart. "It was so romantic. I saw them less than an hour ago. She and that handsome fiancé of hers have eloped."

His mouth went dry. "Eloped?" St. James must have used deadly force to get her to comply.

"Yes, indeed. You couldn't have gotten a feather between them, holding each other so tight, they were."

He frowned as the image formed in his mind. "Did Samantha have her arm around him?"

Mrs. Morley's brow wrinkled. "No, come to think of it, she didn't. She just stood there, kind of stiff. It was probably just wedding jitters. Funny thing, though, she warned me about rain."

"Stormy weather." It confirmed the doodle on her note. *The panic code*!

Ice flowed in his veins. Samantha was in big trouble.

Jake dashed to his car and high-tailed it toward the private airstrip Logan Industries used.

He could only pray he was in time. He had a sick feeling once Samantha became Mrs. St. James, Grayson would kill her.

Samantha slanted a curious glance at Jennifer while they waited in a control shack for the jet to get fueled. Gold hoop earrings swung in her ears as she hopped up on a table while pointing the gun in Samantha's general direction.

What was Jennifer getting out of this? She seemed bored to tears as she stood guard over Samantha.

Jennifer noticed Samantha watching her and scowled. She waved the gun lazily in Samantha's direction. "Don't get any bright ideas, rich bitch."

She froze in the folding chair she was sitting on, terrified the gun might accidentally go off. "Don't worry. You have nothing to fear from me."

She smirked, plopping the gun down on the table, and picked up a fingernail file. "You bet, I don't. God, I can't wait to blow this town. Bright lights! Casinos! Vegas is where it's at."

"You don't say."

Samantha glanced out the window. Grayson was on the tarmac getting the plane ready. Jennifer continued to shape her long, red nails when she turned back. She didn't relish getting on the jet with these two psychos. If only Jake would arrive.

"I do say," Jennifer said with a chuckle. "What do you say, honey? Want to spend your wedding night with me instead of Grayson? I can arrange it. Or maybe you'd like to try a threesome."

Samantha shuddered at the thought of sharing the same bed with these two monsters. "No thanks."

"You don't have to act like you smelled something bad. You know, I don't like you." Jennifer scowled, picking up the gun again. "If you hadn't freaked out when you caught us in the act, we wouldn't have had to trail your sorry ass over half the countryside. You've been more trouble than you're worth, lady. I told Gray we should have moved on to the next score long ago."

So, they were a couple of con artists. Somehow, it didn't surprise her. "As long as we're laying our cards on the table, why did you attack me at the cabin?"

"That was Gray's idea. At first, he thought he'd scare you back to him. When that didn't happen, he decided to snatch you, but that pain in the ass Ramsey kept getting in the way."

Samantha frowned. "Another thing, why did you have to pick on my brother?"

Jennifer shrugged. "We figured while waiting for the golden goose, we might as well score a little cash. Stuffy old Daddy Delbert got suspicious and freaked, so we had to set up a fall guy. Hot-to-trot Tad was an easy mark."

Samantha frowned at the easy mark slur, and then the words *Daddy Delbert* sunk in. "Delbert is your father."

"No, stupid, he thinks he's Gray's long-lost father. Gray's mother had a fling with him when she was passing through town. Gray decided to con him, and viola. The ripest plum on the tree just fell into our laps. He was so hungry for a family. The old man was pissed about having to retire, so it didn't take much to fire him up."

From the corner of her eye, Samantha thought she saw someone walking behind one of the jets. It was Jake, she realized, as he came closer.

She inched closer to the table and the gun that rested upon it, thanking her lucky stars Jennifer was too busy shaping her nails to notice.

The faint wail of a siren intruded.

Jennifer stopped filing her nails, turned to look out the window, and let out a shriek. "Shit, it's Ramsey."

Seeing her options vanish, Samantha jumped up and flipped the table with all her might, sending a swearing Jennifer crashing to the floor.

"Damn it to hell." Jennifer sputtered, reaching for the gun.

Samantha lunged and snatched it away. "Freeze, you psychopathic slut." She surged to her feet, holding the gun on the other woman. "You'll sit there and shut up if you know what's good for you."

The siren grew louder.

She flicked a glance out the window. Grayson must have heard it, too, because he spun around in that direction. She caught a flash of movement to the side of her in time to catch Jennifer running out the door.

The gun shook in Samantha's hand, but she couldn't bring herself to shoot. Bucking up her courage, she lit out after the other woman, yelling, "Stop!"

"Screw you." Jennifer shrieked while racing toward the jets.

Samantha chased her across the tarmac. Thankfully, Grayson seemed too focused on the sirens to notice until they were beside him.

Jennifer ran up to him.

"What in the hell are you doing out here? You're supposed to be guarding her."

He gazed past her to Samantha, and his jaw dropped. "Oh, I see. Baby got cute!" He reached into his boot to pull out a knife and advanced on Samantha. "Drop it."

Jake emerged from the side of a jet, his revolver pointed at Grayson. "My words exactly, moron. Drop the knife. Now!"

"Go to hell, Ramsey." Grayson spun and lunged at Jake, slashing at him with the knife. He drew first blood, opening a gash on Jake's arm.

Jake feinted to the side, kicking the knife out of Grayson's hand and knocking him to the ground just as the police drove up. He placed one booted heel on Grayson's throat, pressing hard enough to make him freeze. "One more false move, and it's all over for you. Got it?"

Grayson coughed, giving a little nod.

"Good!"

Jennifer stepped to the side and started to scuttle away.

Samantha stepped forward, stopping her at the point of a gun. "Not so fast. The police will have plenty to say to you, too."

Several other squad cars arrived on the scene, and Laura hopped out of one.

She ran forward. "Are you two okay?"

"I'm fine," Samantha replied, "but I can't say the same for my hero. How bad is that arm, Jake?"

"It's just a scratch." He shrugged.

A patrolman came up. "Paramedics will take care of that, sir."

Jake let them wrap his arm, then walked over to hug Samantha. "How about you? Are you all right, Sunshine?"

She nestled against him. The warmth of his embrace seeped strength back into her bones. "I'm fine now that you're here. Thank you for rescuing me."

"You're most welcome." He bent to give her a thorough kiss.

A black Lincoln tore onto the tarmac. Tad and Samuel jumped out just as the squad car containing Grayson and Jennifer pulled away.

Samuel rushed over to them. "What happened?"

Samantha stepped away from Jake's embrace and into her father's. "I'm fine. Jake came to the rescue, as usual. Grayson wanted to kidnap me and force me to marry him. He wanted to gain control of my trust fund stocks. He and Delbert planned to oust you from the board and take over the company."

"We have Delbert in custody. He can't hurt you anymore."

She inhaled the mingled scents of tobacco and leather as her father hugged her. She gazed at the new lines on his face, knowing she'd put quite a few of them there during this crisis. Despite their many differences, they had found common ground. If he could change, then so could she. She gave him a quick kiss on the cheek as she stepped away.

"Everything's under control, sir," Jake confirmed. "The authorities have Grayson and Jennifer."

"That's fine." Samuel cleared his throat uncomfortably.

She smiled at her father, knowing he wasn't used to such public displays of affection from her. Then she glanced at Tad, who hovered a bit tensely in the background.

"Jennifer was in on the whole thing, Tad. I'm sorry."

"It's okay, sis. I'm well over her."

Laura stepped up and put her hand on Tad's shoulder in a gesture of comfort.

Maybe Cupid would strike twice for their families. Although Jake hadn't said the three little words, she was sure he did love her.

Two weeks later, Samantha sat alone in her apartment, eating dinner. Jake had made himself scarce since Grayson's arrest, and she consoled herself with the excuse he was busy helping the prosecutor build a case against Grayson and Jennifer.

There was a long line of warrants against the two. They had tried something like this before. Even worse, DNA tests proved Grayson wasn't Delbert's son. It had been a con from the word *Go*. Once he'd told the truth, Delbert had collapsed with guilt and was helping the police wrap up the case.

Tad and Laura were an item, and Samantha was living the life of a nun, eating dinner alone.

Sometimes life wasn't fair.

Her doorbell rang.

She went to answer it. She punched in the code, thinking wryly that at least she'd gotten an alarm system out of the deal.

A delivery person stood on her doorstep. He held out a clipboard for her to sign. "Special delivery for a Samantha Logan."

"I'm Samantha Logan. What is it?" She glanced at the rectangular box he handed her, curious.

"I don't know, ma'am."

She closed the door behind him and carried the box into the dining room. It was heavy for its size. What could it be? She hadn't ordered anything. Then she noticed the return address as Poole Publishing.

"Jake's publisher," she muttered.

It must be for him. But, no, as it had been addressed to her. Curiosity rising, she ripped open the package and out popped a book. 'The Case of The Purloined Pearls' by Ramsey Jacobs, hot off the presses.

Why did they send a copy to her?

Intrigued, she sat in a chair and opened the book. She began to read.

It was different than the book she'd read on his computer up north. Jake had introduced a new character, a kooky, free-spirited woman with long dark hair and blue eyes. She and Detective Murphy worked together to solve the case.

Tears misted Samantha's eyes as she turned the page and glanced at the dedication. *I dedicate this book to my darling, Samantha. Without her lessons in love, I would have been unable to complete this work. I love you, Samantha, with all my heart.*

She hugged the book to her. The doorbell rang once more. Could Jake have sent flowers, too? She rushed to the door and tore it open.

Jake stood there.

He glanced at the book she held in her trembling hands and watched a tear run down her cheek. He reached out to brush it away, lifting it to his lips.

"Sweet, like you." He sank to one knee. "I love you, Sunshine, with all my heart. Will you marry me?"

"Yes," she cried, her knees growing weak. "You are my heart's desire," she confided.

Mrs. Morley peered at them from her begonias. "Twice in one week?"

He scooped Samantha in his arms, chuckling. "What can I say, Mrs. Morley? She's a very popular girl."

"I'll say." Mrs. Morley grinned. "What's your secret, Samantha?"

"Plenty of vitamins and a few love lessons," Samantha shouted as Jake carried her over the threshold.

SERENA'S WEB

Julie Castle

Chapter One

Serena McLain's hand trembled as she reached out to ring her father's doorbell. The chimes echoed on and on inside his elegant two-story colonial house. Her heart sank. Just as she feared, there was no answer.

It had been four days since he'd seemingly vanished off the face of the earth, an eternity for a man who usually checked in every day. Especially when he was working on a hot project like the exposé he was writing on Gerald Grayson. When he'd failed to show up for her son's birthday party last night, her concern had rapidly turned to fear.

He would never have missed Sammy's fifth birthday party.

A rivulet of sweat trickled down the back of her sunflower-printed sundress as she stood, edgy, in the hot June sun. Tugging open her matching yellow tote with the pansies she'd embroidered on it, she rummaged through the cluttered bag for her dad's duplicate keys—the ones she used when he was off on his many research trips and book-signing junkets. Her sense of urgency escalated as she pawed though glue sticks, markers, and extra tissues. Also, Joey had sent her the latest package and the can of Mace she'd bought to ward him off.

Sunlight glinted off the small blue healing crystal attached to her father's key ring. *Thank God.* Fishing them out, she approached the door, the keys jingling in her trembling hand. She'd take a quick look around. If her dad wasn't here, she'd march right down to the police station.

Grasping the keys tighter to stop their clattering, she took a deep calming breath, letting the crystal absorb her fear and soothe her mind. Closing her eyes, she visualized a tropical sunset, her coiled muscles beginning to relax. Repeating her mantra happi-ly-ever-after, she felt in control once more.

Serenity reclaimed, at least temporarily, she reached for the doorknob. Her damp palm slipped, turning the knob, and the door creaked open. She gasped, staring at the swinging door in shock. It was unlocked! Her dad wouldn't leave his home unsecured like this. She'd been right to worry.

"Dad, are you here?"

She peered through the small opening, taking in the utter stillness. Then there was a sound, a faint click, followed by a grating whir. Was someone there? Inching closer, she listened hard. Her overheated face felt a whoosh of cool air, and she realized it was the central air kicking in.

Telling herself to get a grip, she walked into the foyer of her old family home. Paper crinkled under her feet. She looked down at the pile of mail shoved through the mail slot. What in the world? Squatting, she picked up the letters, noticing they'd been slit open. She placed them on the hall table, unnerved. Someone had rifled through her father's mail. He wouldn't leave it lying haphazardly on the floor like this. The earliest postmark was from four days earlier.

Her stomach clenched. She had a missing father, an unlocked house, and tampered mail. It meant breaking and entering, at the very least, maybe worse. Her gut instinct to leave Sammy home with a sitter had been right. She didn't know who or what she might encounter, but she had to search the house.

A boost of confidence rose in her from taking that self-defense course at the gym last week. Assertiveness had been the main crux of the rape prevention class, with a bit of karate thrown in for good measure. That, coupled with the yoga she'd been practicing for years, would see her through this crisis.

Firming her resolve, she headed straight for her father's den. If he was home, that was where he'd be, maybe so engrossed in work that he didn't hear her.

The scent of his cherrywood tobacco still hung in the hallway's air, soothing her jangled nerves. She approached the cozy bookshelf-lined room, crying tentatively, "Dad, are you there?"

There was no reply. Turning the corner, she stopped dead in her tracks. Someone had torn the place apart. Her father's books were scattered, yanked from the shelves. Papers spilled out of his open desk drawers. And his computer was gone. Good grief, he'd been vandalized and robbed!

Where was her father? Maybe he'd interrupted the burglars and been hurt in the process. No, she wouldn't let herself believe that. She had to think positively. There was no indication of a struggle, no blood anywhere. He might have chased them off and still be chasing them. The blinking red message light on his phone caught her attention.

Maybe he'd left a message. Serena rushed across the parquet floor to the phone and pushed the play button. She heard her voice on a recorded message she left this morning. "Dad, are you there? I'm getting worried. Please get back to me." *Beep.* "Dad, this is Serena. I've been trying to reach you. I need to talk to you, so give me a call." She'd left that message three days ago after he'd failed to show up for dinner at her house. She'd wanted to tell him about Joey resurfacing.

It seemed stupid to worry about her itinerant ex-husband now, but one look at Joey's strung-out face when he'd shown up on the last day of school two weeks ago had sent her running to that rape prevention class. The drug use that separated them six years ago had only worsened, reducing the bright-eyed idealist she'd once loved into a bitter shell of a man. He'd pulled her stiff body into his arms, groping her while demanding money. He'd read one of her father's books and knew he was making good money. It was only fair she should share. Luckily, the principal had noticed the altercation and had Joey ejected from the building.

He'd started sending her creepy gifts, like the poem about the key to his heart nestled in her bag. She was saving them up to get a restraining order.

Beep. "Sam, Frank again. Where in the hell are you? Regency is chomping at the bit to get your book. Call me back, pronto." She recognized the irritated voice of her father's literary agent, Frank Gorman.

Beep. "Samuel, you old dog. It's Frank. I'll meet you, usual spot, ten-thirty. You can buy the drinks this time. You need an excuse to spend some of that sweet advance you got for Grayson's Malice."

When had this been left? Four days ago. The day her father had vanished. Maybe Frank knew where her father was.

She glanced at the desk calendar. The date was circled, but there was no indication of where he'd gone. She spotted the outdated Rolodex on the floor and picked it up, flipping through it for The Frank Gorman Literary Agency. Fighting back a growing desperation, she reached for the phone and punched in the number.

"Gorman Literary Agency."

"Hello, I'd...like to..." she stammered.

"Slow down, honey. I can hardly make out what you're saying."

Serena took a calming breath, willing herself to slow down and focus. "Sorry," she wove her finger into the telephone cord, twisting it, as she enunciated clearly. "I need to talk to Mr. Gorman, please."

"I'm sorry, he's rather busy at the moment. If you'd care to leave a message..."

She frowned at the phone. This honey-voiced secretary was not about to stop her. "Ma'am, this is important. I know he'll want to speak to me. It's about my father, one of his clients, Samuel Carlson."

"Big Sam. Why didn't you say so in the first place?" The secretary chuckled, "sorry for the brush-off, sweetie. Writers can be a pesky crowd. You must be Serena. I've heard a lot about you and your little boy Sammy. Sam is proud of both of you. So, how's your father?"

Serena glanced at the ransacked office. Missing, hurt, worse? No! She wouldn't let herself go there. It would hurt too damn much. "I'm not sure how my dad is," *or where he is,* she thought silently, "that's why I want to talk to Mr. Gorman."

"Hold on a second, sweetie. I'll put you right through."

Serena waited, anxiety churning in her stomach, making her uneasy. Frank Gorman was her best hope of tracking down her father. Hopefully, her father had checked his messages and made contact with him.

"Frank Gorman here. Where is that old reprobate? You can tell him for me, missy, I don't appreciate being stood up."

Her knees buckled as her worst-case scenario was voiced. She sagged in the leather desk chair, her last glimmer of hope melting away. Her father had never called Frank back. "So, he hasn't called you?"

"No, he hasn't," he said, grumbling, "I sat cooling my heels in that bar for two hours Monday, waiting for him to bring me his book."

"Oh God, no." With a sniff, she blinked back the tears threatening to fall. Had he been hurt, or...

"What's wrong?"

She brushed tears away from her eyes. Falling apart wasn't an option. "Dads disappeared. He's been missing for four days. And you're the last appointment in his date book."

"Damn, that son of a bitch must have him."

The possibility of abduction hadn't occurred to her, but it made sense. She knew the son of a bitch he was referring to by his tone. Gerald Grayson had been doing all he could to block her father's unauthorized biography. But kidnapping? Would he go that far? "You said Dad was bringing you his manuscript. "That means Grayson's got it along with my dad. He's already won."

"Not necessarily. Your pop told me he'd taken out insurance. He's got a copy stashed away for safekeeping. If he doesn't check in weekly, the book will go to a trusted party. The book will get published despite Gerald Grayson's evil manipulations."

"Insurance?" Her dad really must have been concerned. She was glad his work would go on, but it was small comfort in the face of losing him. If Gerald Grayson was holding him somewhere while he searched for the copy, it meant her father was still alive. That was the hope she needed to cling to now. Maybe the person her father sent the copies to could help. "Who's got it?"

"He didn't tell me who's holding it. He didn't want me to take the risk. He said Grayson was one of the most ruthless men he'd ever written about."

Why hadn't he told her all this? Maybe because she'd been preoccupied with the end of the school year, Joey's reappearance, and her classes at the gym. He hadn't let on to her, other than his usual fatherly warning to be careful. "Why didn't he tell me any of this?"

"He probably didn't want you to become a target."

A tear trickled down her cheek. She brushed it away, and a slight movement caught the corner of her eye. She froze, her breath catching in her throat. Was someone there?

Turning her head cautiously, she saw it was only the drapes fluttering. She let out a sigh of relief and told herself to stop acting like a scared rabbit. Whoever had done this was long gone.

"Hello. You still there, Serena?" Frank's worried voice broke through her musings.

"Sorry. Yes, I'm still here. I'm calling from my dad's place. It's ransacked and his mail is opened. I think they must have been searching for my father's copies. He told them about it, but hasn't revealed where it is. Why else would they go to all that trouble?"

Frank gasped, then yelled, "Good God, girl, get the blazes out of there! They might come back!"

They'd search her home next. Sammy was in danger. "My house. They could go to my house next. I've got to call my sitter and make sure she takes Sammy to her place."

"Do it, and then get the hell out. And remember, keep me informed."

She hung up and then punched in her home number. Hopefully, Mrs. Monroe would be nearby sipping her morning cup of tea.

"Hello?"

"Mrs. Monroe, I don't have time to explain, but would you take Sammy to your place and keep him there until I return?"

"Of course, my dear. Is everything all right?"

"Not really. Dad's home has been broken into, and I'm worried the burglars might be headed to my place. I don't want you and Sammy there, just in case. But please keep it light. I don't want to scare Sammy."

"Oh, goodness. We'll go right away. Don't fret, dear. I won't alarm Sammy."

"Thanks. I'll come to your house after I talk to the police. Wait for me there." Serena hung up, glancing at the growing shadows in the corner of the room. She felt vulnerable sitting alone in the burglarized house. Jumping up, she turned and headed for the door. She'd go directly to the police station. Surrounded by officers, Grayson couldn't touch her.

Jumping into her Volvo, she cranked the ignition, jamming her foot on the gas pedal. The engine sputtered and died. Muttering a curse, she took her foot off the accelerator. All she needed was a flooded engine. She could picture Gerald Grayson himself, leaping out of the juniper bushes to attack her. Taking a calming breath, she carefully started the car and drove off. Making fast time to the police station, she parked right in front and went in.

Scared but determined, she marched to the front desk, approaching the man behind the counter. He was slowly filling in the blanks on a crossword puzzle. He didn't even bother to look up, damn it. Frowning at the top of Sgt. Murphy's balding head, she cleared her throat to get his attention.

He filled in a word and looked up, fixing her with a disinterested frown while putting his pencil down. "Yeah?"

Her anxiety dissolved into exasperation. Didn't the man even want to do his job? Her toe tapped on the marble floor. "I need to file a missing person report."

"We can't do that until the guy's been gone over forty-eight hours, lady. Why don't you give it a few more days?" He looked back down at his crossword puzzle, picking up his pencil again.

Smacking her hand on the marble counter to regain his attention, she leaned forward, enunciating very clearly. "It's been way past two days. Gerald Grayson kidnaped my father."

His head popped up, and he frowned at her.

Seeing his doubtful look, she became indignant. Just because Gerald Grayson had more money than God didn't make him above the law.

"I'm serious." Hearing assorted gasps from the people within earshot, she passed a scathing look over them. They had no idea what she was dealing with right now. A policewoman stared at her, a janitor watched her guardedly, and a big older detective came tearing out of an office with 'Detective Sinclair' lettered on its door.

"What in the holy hell is going on out here, Murphy?" he complained.

The desk sergeant shook his head. "The lady wants to file a kidnapping complaint."

His tone of voice said he thought she was a nut. Her spine stiffened at the insult. "Also, burglary and tampering with the mail." Hopefully, the detective would want to do his job. "My father's been kidnapped by Gerald—"

"Let's take this inside, ma'am," Detective Sinclair cut in quickly. He frowned, the lines on his beefy face deepening. "Step into my office, and I'll help you."

That was more like it. She gave a told-you-so look to the desk sergeant. The police-woman returned to her filing, but the janitor stared at her with a frown. The curious look on his stubble-covered face was troubling. Why was he so interested in her affairs? He looked away when she returned his stare and started buffing the floors again. She followed the detective into his office.

He walked behind his desk. "Have a seat, ma'am."

She sat on one of the straight-backed chairs and waited for him to settle into the worn chair behind his desk. Finally, she'd get some help.

He leaned back, his chair squeaking, and clasped his hands over his round middle. "Now, what's all this about your father being missing?"

"He's not just missing. Gerald Grayson kidnaped my father."

He raised a brow. "Kidnapped, you say. You got a ransom note?"

"No."

"Well then, you see it happen?"

She bit her lip, his gruff tone sinking in. The word 'no' hung on the tip of her tongue, but she didn't want to say it. He might take it as an excuse to dismiss her. The problem was, she'd never been any good at lying. "No, I didn't see it happen. And, no, I don't have a ransom note. But that doesn't make it any less real."

"Then how do you know it happened?" he asked.

"Gerald Grayson doesn't want a ransom, he wants my father silenced, and the book he was writing stopped."

"Says who?"

Her father's life hung in the balance, and the detective played games with her. She wouldn't tolerate it one second more. Raising her chin, a defiant notch, she glared at him. "My dad disappeared four days ago on his way to deliver the book to his literary agent, Frank Gorman. Grayson would do anything to prevent its publication."

Sinclair shook his head. "Ma'am, sounds like it's all speculation on your part. Without proof, you can't accuse an important man like Mr. Grayson of kidnapping. You could get in a lot of hot water, young lady," he fixed her with a repressive scowl, "take my advice and wait a while. Your father will probably show up sheepish for going out on a bender. He probably does this kind of thing all the time."

"He does not." Her father had never gone on a bender in his life. And there was the issue of the break-in. They couldn't sweep that under the rug. Either he didn't believe her, or he was scared of Gerald Grayson, probably both. "Do I have to go over your head to get some action?"

"Now, simmer down, lady. Don't get hysterical on me. If you insist, I'll file a missing person report." He pulled a form from his desk drawer and handed it to her. "If you want to fill this out at home—"

"I'll fill it out now." She pulled a pen from her tote bag and completed the blasted form. Thrusting it back at him, she fumed when he only scanned it for a moment and then pressed a buzzer.

"Jacoby, come in here. I've got some filing for you to do," he looked at Serena, "happy now?"

"No." She listened to his disgruntled snort, and her spine stiffened. "I expect more than a few inquiries. I demand an investigation. Will you take this seriously, or do I still have to go over your head?"

He stilled, fixing her with an irritated stare. "Fine. When did all the alleged crimes take place?"

She hesitated, surprised by his rapid flip-flop. "I just discovered the burglary. His computer and discs were stolen, his mail opened, and he's been missing four days."

His glance was sharp. "Any idea why they'd just take the computer and disks?"

She hesitated. Telling him about the copy of her father's book in safekeeping was probably not in her father's best interests. Besides, he had kept it a secret for a reason. She wouldn't betray his confidence.

"No."

"Hmm," he said, watching her.

She almost squirmed, feeling like a bug under a microscope.

"As I said, I'll send someone out later."

She wouldn't be palmed off with a vague promise like that. "Not good enough. I've watched CSI enough to know you must send a forensics team to my father's house." Gauging his tight-lipped reaction to her outburst, she bluffed. "Look, Detective Sinclair, tampering with the mail is a federal crime. Do you want me to go to the feds?" Watching his hands tighten on the arms of his chair, she held her breath. He probably wanted to wring her neck.

Loosening his white-knuckled grip, he bit out, "I'll send a team to his house. But this is the end of it, lady. I don't want you bugging me anymore."

Choosing to ignore his stern demand, she got to her feet. "I'll be at my father's house waiting for them. You've got the address." Feeling his sour gaze, she turned and headed for the door with as much decorum as possible.

"Miss McLain."

She forced herself to stop. No way would she let him think she was running. Turning to look back at him, she strove for a confident expression. "Yes?"

"Take my advice. Don't make any more wild accusations against Mr. Grayson. He's got friends that might take offense."

Was he threatening her? His bland expression left her in doubt and nervous. As much to reassure herself as to defy him, she replied, "Detective Sinclair, you do your job, and I'll do mine."

Rushing out of his office, she crashed headlong into someone.

Muscular arms wrapped around her as she bounced off a rigid body. She grabbed at his biceps, his muscles rippling under her palms as her world tilted. Her pelvis pressed against his, their legs entangled.

Gazing into a pair of intense chocolate eyes, she was trapped for a moment, intrigued despite her predicament. His whole body seemed to tighten against hers. Was he growing aroused? Her cheeks flamed with embarrassment.

He frowned, setting her back on her heels and letting go of her waist. She uncurled her fingers from his arms, mortified.

What must he think of her, clinging to him like that? The spell broken, she noticed the stubble and bandana. It was the grumpy janitor, the one who'd scowled at her earlier. He was frowning again, a seemingly perpetual state for him.

Struggling for something to say, she blurted, "I hope I didn't hurt you."

He stared past her, his frown deepening. "Next time, watch your step, lady."

She took a startled step back. The surly janitor could at least have the good manners to look at her. Stepping past him, she fled without a backward glance.

FBI field agent Mark Riley took his eyes off Sinclair, who was grumbling at someone on the phone. He turned in time to see Ms. Serena McLain hurry away, her blonde curls bouncing. The fluttery, flower-printed dress she wore waved in the breeze as she fled. She was a complication he didn't need, he told himself as he turned and ducked into his janitor's closet.

He opened his laptop and hacked into Sinclair's files. As he'd suspected, somebody didn't file the missing person report. Knowing Detective Sinclair, it probably never would be. Ms. McLain could wait until the cows came home for help, and not get it. And if she made too much fuss, they had ways of silencing her.

The Agency had known Samuel Carlson was doing a story on Gerald Grayson and hadn't interfered because he'd kept Grayson occupied while they built a rock-solid case against him. The inter-jurisdictional team he was a part of had put their egos in check to work together.

But they hadn't known Samuel Carlson was missing, probably dead, Mark surmised. And Ms. Serena McLain, although she didn't know it yet, had just stepped into a hornet's nest. Her accusation would accelerate things. No doubt his boss, Agent-in-Charge Thom Whittaker, would salivate at the prospect of a quick wrap-up to this investigation. Forcing Ms. McLain's cooperation would fit his boss's penny-pinching leadership style. He wouldn't mind putting a bow on this case early, either. Out from under Whittaker's thumb, he'd have a chance to secretly investigate the disaster that went down last year.

He was lucky to have spotted Ms. McLain. Who knew a plum like this would fall in his lap, literally? Her soft curves had felt good, too good, pressed tight against him. Her perfume was tantalizing. He put his semi hard-on down to the fact he hadn't been laid in six months. She'd felt it, too. He hadn't missed the shocked look in her blue eyes. A distraction like her? He didn't need it on his climb back to the top of the agency.

Time would tell what Grayson's next move would be. In the meantime, Serena McLain would need protection. Her feisty exchange with Sinclair was troubling. It just might get her killed.

He called his partner. "Eagle. Put a tail on Ms. Serena McLain. Her father's gone missing. She was just here, shooting her mouth off to Sinclair. When Sinclair tried to stonewall her, she threatened to go to the feds. You know they aren't going to take that lying down."

"Right."

"Her father's residence was searched, and his computer and discs were taken. They were probably looking for the book he was working on publishing. Gerald Grayson wouldn't want that falling into the wrong hands. She's supposed to meet the cops at her father's home. Send out a forensic team, and make sure that tail sticks close."

Serena stood at her father's front door, watching the crime lab technicians drive away. Captain Brown had told her they'd managed to lift a few smudged fingerprints. His professional manner erased the bad impression Detective Sinclair had given her of the local police. The crime lab would come through even if Detective Sinclair was the world's worst cop.

She shut and locked the door behind her and headed for her car. It would feel too creepy to stay alone inside the empty house. She shivered when she glanced back at the growing dusky shadows in the recessed doorway. Would she ever feel safe here again? She didn't have time to worry about it now. She had to get home and check on Sammy.

As she drove, she popped a CD of new-age music in the player, hoping its mellow sounds would soothe her.

It would be tricky explaining to her five-year-old where his beloved grandpa was. He was already asking why his grandfather hadn't shown up at his birthday party. Swallowing the lump in her throat, she tried to focus on the music.

Changing lanes twice, she noticed a van behind her doing the same thing. Was she being followed? She glanced at it through her rearview mirror, glancing nervously at the man behind the wheel. He made eye contact for a moment and then lagged back. Was he acting suspiciously? It would have seemed like an incredible thought yesterday, but now the rules had changed. She couldn't bring trouble home with her. Speeding up, she took a left. The van kept going straight. She let out a sigh of relief and turned toward home.

She pulled into her parking spot next to her Paradise Park Town Homes building and turned off the engine. Sitting there for a moment, looking out at the quiet parking lot, she suddenly realized how alone she was. It was just her and Sammy against the world. Nervous but determined, she got out of the car, half expecting Grayson to leap out from a parked car and grab her. Hurrying down the sidewalk to her two-story townhouse, she took in the modern building's angles and recessed entries with new eyes. It had never occurred to her before, but there were plenty of shadowy places for an assailant to hide.

Shivering, she tamped down her fear. Nonsense, this was home, a secure port in the storm her life had become. It'd taken her years teaching kindergarten at Holmes Elementary to save money to buy her cozy townhouse. She wouldn't let Grayson make her afraid of it. That would be letting the bastard win.

A knot of tension formed in her neck as she opened her front door. She stepped cautiously into the entryway and noted things looked normal. The living room was still strewn with Sammy's toys, dump trucks, and action figures. Mrs. Monroe's full teacup sat on the end table.

She walked through the dining room and into the kitchen, letting out a sigh of relief. Mrs. Monroe had cleared out quickly, but everything looked perfectly normal.

Rolling her shoulders to ease the remaining stress, she turned to go upstairs. Sammy's bedroom was just as he'd left it—the bed made, his Spiderman action figure in its place of honor on the dresser. She smiled, feeling inordinately better, and walked down the hall to her room. Standing in the open doorway, she saw that it, too, was undisturbed. The double bed was still neatly made with the white lace duvet cover. Sunlight shone cheerily through the lace-draped windows, illuminating the three healing crystals on top of her dresser. She walked across the pearl gray carpet to her bed and sagged on it.

Catching a glimpse of herself in the mirror, she made a face, taking in her shaken, unusually pale reflection. That would never do. She didn't want to worry Sammy. She walked into her adjoining bathroom and applied some fresh blush.

She turned and headed toward the third bedroom, which she'd converted into an office. The office was where it had all gone wrong at her father's house. Her nerves prickled in nervous anticipation, and her footsteps faltered.

The rest of the house was undisturbed. There was no reason to be afraid, but still, she couldn't dismiss her fear.

She closed her eyes and took a deep breath, visualizing a tropical sunset. She relaxed a bit, silently repeating her mantra happily-ever-after. Someday, she and Sammy would go on their trip to the tropics and have a great time. She'd been saving up for years. She continued down the hall with purpose and pushed open the door.

She let out a sob as she surveyed the carnage. It was ten times worse than her father's had been. Her desk wasn't just open—it was smashed into little pieces. She stood there, gaping. She supposed the little desk, made of cheaper material, had been easy to destroy. Piles of paper littered the floor, and lesson planners and textbooks were ripped and destroyed. And her laptop was gone.

Why had Grayson done this? Had he been looking for the hidden copy, or was he trying to scare her off? It wouldn't work. This invasion made her more determined to get to the bottom of things. Thank God she'd had the foresight to warn Sammy's sitter. She needed to get to Mrs. Monroe's to check on him.

Just then, she noticed the white message light on her phone was blinking. Was it her father? She picked her way over the rubble to the phone and pushed the play button. "Keep your damned mouth shut and stop running to the cops, you stupid bitch. We have a deep hole to bury you if you don't wise up."

A chill ran down her spine as she listened to the threat coming from a raspy male voice. She stood frozen for a second, then turned and fled, running the hall length and down the stairs. Grabbing her bag off the table, she rushed out the front door.

Grayson knew she'd gone to the police, which meant she couldn't trust the cops. She'd have to go it alone.

Hurrying to Mrs. Monroe's townhouse, she scanned the grounds looking for the culprit. Although, what she'd do if she caught him, she didn't know. Even with her new self-defense skills and mace, she didn't fancy her chances of arresting a thug.

She rang the bell, flicking a wary glance over her shoulder. Hearing the latch click, she turned to see Mrs. Monroe opening the door.

Serena let out a sigh of relief, stepping into the sanctuary.

"Come on in, dearie." Mrs. Fern Monroe, a tall, white-haired lady dressed in a red pantsuit, stepped back a pace. She looked at Serena, concerned. "Is everything all right? You look white as a ghost."

The blush she'd put on hadn't cut it, especially after the shock she'd just experienced in her trashed office. Serena shut the door behind her and sagged against it. "I'm fine. How's Sammy?"

"He's just fine and dandy. See for yourself." She motioned toward the living room.

Serena glanced at Sammy. He was sitting on the living room floor, watching a video, eating a peanut butter sandwich, and feeding bits of it to Fern's dog, Mr. Bartholomew. The schnauzer sat patiently, waiting for tidbits as he gazed at her son in adoration.

Serena smiled at the sight. Thank heavens she'd had the presence of mind to phone her sitter. She shuddered to think of them being in her home when it was invaded.

Mrs. Monroe stepped up beside her. "Sammy thinks coming to my place is a treat. 'Wizard' is what he called it."

"Thank you for reacting so quickly."

"You're not a girl to push the panic button for no need, so we took it on the lam. Come in the kitchen. I've just put on the kettle for tea."

Following her into the cheery kitchen, Serena tried to decide what to tell her. She didn't want to frighten the neighbor lady. However, she wanted her to be on guard in case Gerald Grayson's thugs returned.

She took the teacups from the glass-fronted cabinet and put them on the tea tray. She felt more vital by the moment, her equilibrium returning as the scent of earl grey wafted in the air. She made up her mind while carrying the tray to the breakfast nook. The truth was best.

Mrs. Monroe poured out the tea, sitting down. "All right, dearie, tell me all about it."

"My house was vandalized, and my laptop was stolen."

Fern shook her head. "You were right to be concerned, then. It must have happened after I left. I'm ever so sorry."

"Thanks. I'm just glad you two were out before they hit. Can I use your phone?"

"Of course, dear. Are you going to call the police?"

"No. I don't think the local police can be trusted right now."

"I don't blame you a bit. Why, I called them two days ago when my flowerbed was rampaged, and poor Mr. Bartholomew terrorized, and it didn't do me a bit of good. They were insulting. If you want my advice, you should get a big watchdog. He'd keep the burglars away."

Serena nodded, vaguely recalling Fern's messed-up flower bed a few days back. At the time, she'd been too worried about her father's lack of contact to pay it much mind. Mr. Bartholomew had barked himself hoarse that night. Come to think of it, Serena had noticed scratches on the trim around one of her windows the next day, too. She hadn't thought much of it at the time. Could it have been Grayson's thugs trying to break in? Maybe the dog's barking had scared them off. "I'm sorry about your flower bed."

"Thank you for your concern. Now, what can I do to help with your situation? If you'd like his number, I have a friend who breeds Dobermans."

Serena smiled, picturing Sammy playing with a puppy. "Thanks, I might take you up on that later. I told Dad's literary agent I'd keep him informed."

She reached for the phone on the counter and dialed Frank Gorman's number. He'd offered to help. Maybe he could recommend a private eye.

Chapter Two

Serena parked her Volvo on a quiet beach lane and glanced at Rupert Morris as he bolted from the car. The PI Frank had recommended was in his mid-fifties and looked like an aging boxer with bulging muscles turning to paunch and his aggressive manner. His rented tux barely contained his bulky body. Noting the eager expression on his hawkish face, she had a sneaky suspicion his previous work had been getting the goods on cheating spouses. Would he have the finesse to pull this off? It was a good thing she'd insisted on coming along. When they crashed the party at Gerald Grayson's lakeside estate to search for her father, he might need a restraining hand.

She got out of the car and glanced at her ice-blue silk gown, hoping she'd chosen wisely. They needed to blend in with the wealthy guests. Her blue tote bag with the flamingo she'd bejeweled on it matched her gown. She'd dumped the contents of her yellow one into it, including her can of mace. She planned to defend herself if necessary.

Rupert looked at her. "Let's get moving, Miss McLain. Time is money." He started cross-country.

"Wait up," she called, tottering after him in evening sandals.

He stopped and looked back, casting a skeptical look at her feet. "Once we hit the beach, walking in those shoes you're wearing should be easier."

Serena nodded, listening to the tinkle of music from the party floating on the night breeze. She followed the PI around the weed-choked edge of the property, lifting her skirt so it wouldn't get tangled in the brambles. She looked curiously at him when they came to a retaining wall. Did he mean to climb it?

"What now?"

"Now, we climb," he hesitated, fixing her with a doubtful look, "are you sure you're up to it?"

She smiled, hoping to disabuse him of any notions of leaving her behind. He'd been trying to get rid of her since she'd volunteered to come along. She wouldn't go. If her dad had left any clues behind here, she'd be the one who'd recognize them. "Don't worry about me. I'm tougher than I look."

"You're the boss." The PI scrambled up the wall and then reached down. "Take my hand. I'll pull you up."

She latched on as he hoisted her up with brute strength. She winced, jamming her tender toes into the nooks and crannies for purchase until she was at the top. "Thanks."

"You're welcome."

"Do we look okay?"

Rupert used his handkerchief to rub dirt off his hands. "None the worse for wear, I think."

"Okay, I'm ready," she stated with a nervous smile, getting caught up in the adventure. "Hold it," she said when the PI started to step away, gaining a curious stare from him, "I need a moment to prepare, okay?"

"Okay," he replied, throwing her a probing glance.

She closed her eyes, blocking out his inquisitive study, needing to center herself for the task ahead. Letting out a slow breath, she visualized her tropical sunset, her mantra coming silently to her lips, *happily-ever-after*. A sense of tranquility fell over her. She was ready.

Opening her eyes, she noticed the PI studying her, his brow wrinkled. No doubt, he now thought he was working for an oddball. "Just a little meditation," she mentioned, adding at his continuing doubtful look, "it helps me focus."

"Whatever floats your boat, lady. Just follow me. Do what I tell you, and we'll be okay."

Serena followed him across a strip of white beach sand. Sand trickled into her sandals, crunching between her toes. She tried to kick it out, then hurried to catch up with the PI as he strode past the terrace, glancing at the partying crowd through the French doors. The prospect of crashing this bash made her edgy.

"When we get in there, watch out for the guys dressed in blue suits and wearing earpieces. They're Grayson's security crew."

The kitchen door creaked open.

"Shh." Rupert grabbed her and tugged her behind the shrubs.

Serena froze, crouching beside him. Was it a security guard? She peeked around.

A waiter carried a big trash bag toward the dumpster.

She relaxed.

"Now's our chance," Rupert hissed, grabbing Serena's arm and tugging her towards the door.

She felt like her arm was being torn from its socket as she ran to keep up with him. He snagged the door just as it was closing and towed her inside.

When he let go, she rolled her shoulder, wincing at the pins and needles sensation, and glanced at the commotion in the kitchen. A chef labored over a large stove, stirring something fragrant, while his kitchen staff set up trays of canapés. Some of her tension eased when she realized they were too busy to notice their unauthorized entry.

She hurried to catch up with Rupert, who was getting in line with the servers.

The chef stepped away from the stove and turned, frowning when he saw them. "What?" His brow wrinkled as he gave them a quizzical look.

Serena groaned, doing her best to blend into the wall behind the PI, listening to his heavy German accent. Were they caught already?

A crash caught her attention as one of the kitchen workers dropped a tray. The chef turned to chew him out, and she let out a sigh of relief. The staff seemed to be in utter chaos. It was a move in their favor. Thankfully, the chef did not give an alarm, and the rest seemed too busy to provide the intruders with a second glance.

Tuxedo-clad servers lined up to whisk away the trays.

Rupert slipped into line and picked one up. Serena slunk into place next to him, and they were off.

They rushed out of the kitchen and into the open-concept great room, crowded with guests. An orchestra was set up on a stage, serenading the group with dance music.

Rupert put his tray on a table. "Let's go."

She hurried after him, skirting the edge of the floor and ducking behind the staircase. She looked past the marble and wrought iron to the landing above.

Rupert followed her gaze. "We need to get up there to search, but let's check the first floor first."

"Okay."

"Grayson's got a media room and game room to the right. It would be best not to raise any suspicions by strolling down there. Take a walk and check them out. I'll go left, checking the mudroom, servant's rooms, and garage. We can meet back here and then head upstairs."

"Fine." She watched the PI stride away and winced. His aggressive stance didn't exactly blend in with this high-spirited yet sophisticated crowd.

Tamping down second thoughts, she turned and started to walk away, doing her best to act casual.

Trying to act the part of a guest, she took a glass of wine from a passing waiter and headed for the media room. She stopped in the open doorway and glanced back. Nobody was watching her. Relief surging through her, she turned to enter the shadowy media room.

It contained an actual movie theater. She stopped, passing an incredulous gaze over the full-size screen and theater seats. Who heard of having something like this in one's home? Gerald Grayson had to be richer than a king. Going up against him wasn't going to be easy.

And then she heard a sound—a rustle, a whisper. She wasn't alone.

"Ahh."

The low-pitched groan made her jump, goosebumps breaking out on her arms. Someone was being tortured?

"Oh."

She focused her gaze on the shadows that seemed to blend in the seats down front. Stepping forward, she forced back her fear. Maybe she could save the poor soul.

As she neared the moving figures, she realized it was a man and a woman. She was sitting on his lap, and they were... Oh good gravy, they were making love. Her cheeks flamed as she averted her gaze. She forced herself to stay in place, glancing in all the corners of the room to ensure no sign of her father before fleeing.

Making her way into the hall, she headed toward the game room, fanning her face to cool her blush. The torture she'd been prepared for. Public sex she hadn't been. Walking through the open archway to the game room, she deliberately refocused her thoughts, listening to the beeps and crashes from the video games. Gazing around the well-appointed space, she confirmed the mobster lived well. And apparently, he had a penchant for video games.

The latest arcade machines flanked the room, and there was no lack of players for them. About a dozen other guests, mostly male, had moseyed down here. Two guests, jackets off, sleeves rolled up, were playing pool. Their blue suits and earpieces told her they were part of his security crew. One of the players, a middle-aged man with salt-and-pepper hair, gave her a come-hither smile and winked.

Oh no, this wasn't the time to be hit on by one of Grayson's greasy associates. She started to turn away.

"What's the matter, sweet thing?" he asked, reaching out to grab her arm. "Whitney and I are almost through with our game. Stick around and have a drink with me."

Serena froze, her arm manacled by his sweaty palm. He was standing close enough for her to smell his boozy breath. "Sorry, I have to leave."

"I haven't seen you around here before. What's your name, sweet thing?"

How could she get out of this without raising a red flag she didn't belong? She turned, giving him the friendliest smile she could muster. "Keep calling me sweet thing. I like it."

He let go of her arm, smiling at her with a lustful glint in his eye. He thought he was about to get lucky.

She took a small step back. "I have to go to the powder room, handsome. So, how about I take a rain check on that drink?"

"I'll be waiting, sweet thing," he replied, looking her up and down with an appreciative leer.

She turned and walked out of the room, feeling his hot gaze on her the whole way. It'd be a cold day in hell before she'd return, but he didn't know that. Once she was out of his line of sight, she rushed back to the staircase.

Rupert was there pacing back and forth. He stopped when he saw her and turned to frown at her. "What kept you?"

"One of Grayson's security crew who thinks he's God's gift to women."

"Yeah, I know the type," his frown faded to be replaced by an inquiring stare, "did he recognize you?

"I don't think so."

He shrugged. "No harm done then. You find anything?"

She thought of the affair she'd encountered. "No." The PI gave her a curious glance, but thankfully, didn't ask about it.

"Me, neither. Ready to head upstairs?"

She nodded. It was the most likely place they'd hide her father. "Yes."

"I'll go up first and start with the rooms on the right. If that doesn't alert them, you follow in five minutes and go left. We'll meet in the middle."

She nodded.

"Remember, five minutes."

Watching him go, she suddenly felt vulnerable. She peeked at the crowd from the staircase rails, ensuring Grayson's thugs didn't observe his flight up the stairs. She noted one or two passing looks, but none of the party guests seemed alarmed by his trip upstairs. Good.

She scanned the crowd, but didn't see Gerald Grayson. His snow-white hair and erect bearing would have been hard to miss.

She noticed a few more of his security team on the crowd's edges, but they didn't look up. They'd have to be extra careful to elude their notice the rest of this evening, lest they raise his suspicions they weren't bona fide guests.

She checked her watch. Only four minutes had passed, but that was long enough. She started up the staircase, holding her long skirt so she wouldn't trip on it. That would be all she needed. Taking a header in front of Grayson's cronies would be a disaster.

Reaching the landing at the top of the stairs unscathed, she let out a sigh of relief. The PI was not in sight. She hoped he was as skilled at his job as he'd claimed. Turning to go down the hall, she stopped by the first closed door. Holding her breath, she quietly turned the knob. She could swear she was looking for the powder room if someone was inside. It was a plausible excuse. Inching the door open, the bedroom done in beach tones looked unoccupied.

Relieved, she quickly slipped inside, shutting the door behind her, and got to work. She went to the dresser and pulled out each drawer, finding them bare. It had to be an unoccupied guest room. The place was sparkling clean down to its empty wastebasket. There were no clues. Her spirits were just a little bit dampened. She peeked out to make sure the coast was clear.

Rushing down the hall to close double doors, she quietly slipped one open and entered what had to be Gerald Grayson's library. The massive book-lined room held a roll-top desk, leather wing chairs, and a wet bar. It could take hours to comb through everything. She'd take a quick look, hoping to hit pay dirt, and later enlist her PI's help. Feeling her confidence return, she went straight to the desk. Hopefully, the mobster felt secure enough in his home to keep it unlocked. She grasped the handle on the roll-top and tugged.

It rolled open without making a noise, which confirmed a theory. Gerald Grayson thought himself immune to burglars. A blotter and desk set were inside, along with a calendar. She looked at the date her father went missing. Grayson had put down a golf foursome at Haley's Point. So, the man had an alibi. She wasn't surprised. A mob boss like him wouldn't do his dirty work. He'd probably had his security crew kidnap her father.

She tried the first drawer, finding it equally unlocked and containing office supplies, pens, and Post-its.

Tugging the next drawer, she spotted envelopes, stationery, and a small black book. She reached for it with trembling hands. Could this be the clue she was hoping for? Was it the mobster's date book? Hope bloomed anew inside her. Picking up the small leather bound pad, she tore open the cover and stared at the gibberish written there. It had to be some code consisting of strings of letters and numbers, which didn't make sense to her. She slipped it into her tote bag, ignoring her conscience's slight tingle of guilt. She didn't usually approve of theft, but these weren't regular times.

Moving to the next drawer, she came across a stack of explicit bondage magazines. The mobster had some sexual kinks. It didn't surprise her. Wrinkling her nose, she went through the pile, looking for clues. She gave one last appalled glance at the previous cover, featuring a seemingly terrified, naked woman. Shuddering at the image of the bound and gagged model, she slammed shut the drawer.

She couldn't let such horrendous things shake her resolve. Renewing her determination, she stood and walked to the bookcases. The floor-to-ceiling oak shelves were lined with leather-bound classics that looked like they'd never been read. Grayson probably put them out for show. The magazines were, no doubt, what he read.

Damn it. She wasn't finding anything here.

One book did look worn, the dust jacket torn. She pulled it out. It was one of her father's earlier works, an unauthorized biography of J. Edgar Hoover. She sighed, seeing her dad's name on the cover, and opened it. Specific passages had been circled and highlighted. Serena noticed they were the unflattering parts about Hoover.

Grayson was worried about the unauthorized biography her father was doing of him for a good reason. Her father was very good at what he did. Grayson could sue for liability if he didn't like what her father wrote, but he probably wouldn't want the additional bad press. She couldn't bear to put the book back on the mobster's shelf. He didn't deserve to put his dirty hands on it. She clutched the book to her.

Footsteps sounded in the hallway.

She froze, her breath catching in her throat. Had they been discovered? She glanced at the window, knowing it was her only means of escape. It would mean a second-story drop. Moments passed as she waited breathlessly. Nobody came tearing into the study after her.

She tiptoed to the door. Hesitating with her hand on the knob, she listened hard. Maybe it was too quiet, but she couldn't stand here like a statue.

Clutching her dad's book like a shield, she gingerly opened one of the double doors and peeked out. The hallway was empty. Her nerves were probably going haywire. She ran down the hall toward the room at the end. It was the only one she hadn't searched for clues.

Rupert was probably there, taking his time. After all, he was a pro at this kind of thing. She reached for the doorknob, but there was a sound from inside, and then a sneeze.

She froze as goosebumps broke out on her arms. Had that been Rupert? He should know better than to make noise. She turned the knob and started to open the door.

"No!" Rupert yelled.

Startled, she hesitated with the door ajar. Why was the PI telling her no? She stepped forward, peering around the half-open door into the dark bedroom. Her PI stood on the balcony surrounded by several dark-suited men. Grayson's security squad!

And then, catching a flash of movement at the edge of the mob, she found Gerald Grayson himself. He stepped forward, pointing a gun straight at her PI's heart.

Oh no! They'd been caught. Detective Sinclair was, no doubt, on his way. She did not doubt Grayson would press charges.

Someone sneezed again.

She jumped.

Rupert cried out, and a red stain spread across his white shirtfront. He collapsed against the balcony railing.

A scream caught in Serena's throat. In stunned disbelief, she watched one of Grayson's henchmen toss the PI over the railing like trash.

"No," she gasped, suddenly finding her voice as she stood, frozen to the spot.

One of the accomplices turned toward her. In shock, she noticed it was the man who'd hit on her in the game room.

His eyes narrowed. "Hey, Mr. Grayson, we got company."

Grayson spun toward her.

Serena came out of her stunned paralysis, turned, and raced down the hall.

Thundering footsteps behind her hastened her flight.

"Hey, where ya going, sweet thing?"

Cringing at the memory of their brief encounter, she took the stairs at a dead run.

Another sneeze, and the railing under her hand exploded from a bullet. Splinters stung her palm.

Crying out, she pulled her hand away and half-ran, half-stumbled the rest of the way down the stairs. The dance music kept playing, and couples still crowded the floor. They seemed to be unaware of the carnage upstairs. She barged through them, realizing with a sick feeling the silencer had muffled everything.

She headed for the open French doors and safety, sprinting across the dance floor.

Someone stepped into her path a few feet from the door. She crashed into him, letting out a scream of alarm.

Her heart skipped a beat until she noticed it was a waiter, not a gunman out to kill her. The tray he was carrying crashed to the floor, splashing champagne into the air.

She gave him a shove and kept going, escaping into the cool night air. Trembling in the flagstone courtyard, she looked back at the dancers. A few of them turned curious glances her way, but she pretended not to notice.

More importantly, Gerald Grayson and his minions weren't in sight. Maybe she'd eluded them. She wasn't going to question her luck. Instead, she ran across the terrace to the beach.

She had to find Rupert. He had to be lying on the sand below the balcony. She prayed she wouldn't be too late to save him. All the while, she knew it was probably a lost cause.

Mark watched Gerald Grayson's brightly lit beach estate through night-scope binoculars. Seeing figures on a second-floor balcony, he focused on them. There was a flash of a weapon's fire. Moments later, a body fell from the balcony.

Thinking it was Ms. McLain for a moment, his gut twisted. Damn Whittaker's incompetent hide! Things had turned to shit, just like Mark had predicted.

But Ms. McLain raced out of the back of the house like her tail was on fire. He let out a breath he wasn't aware he'd been holding.

He picked up a call from the house, thanks to a wiretap. He listened in, recording Grayson's voice.

"Sinclair, we've got a fouled-up situation here," Grayson said.

"What's wrong?"

"That damned McLain woman was at my residence with some private dick. My staff found him searching my room. I got rid of the gumshoe, but she's running loose on the beach. Now that she's off my property, I need you to take care of her."

"I'll take care of it, but it'll cost you. I ain't sure being on your payroll is all it's cracked up to be."

"Are you trying to hold me up for more money, Sinclair?"

"Ah, no. No, I guess not. I've had a few tonight. Sorry, Mr. Grayson."

"I'll overlook it this time, but remember, you can be replaced."

"Yes, sir. I'll be there in five."

Mark called Bob. "It's on. Grayson popped the PI and tossed him off a second-floor balcony onto the beach. Ms. McLain ran out to find him, and I just intercepted a call from Gerald Grayson himself. He ordered Sinclair to come to take care of her."

"I'll send a forensic team and bring in her son."

"Right. I'll bring her in. See you at the safe house."

Chapter Three

Serena ran along the tide-washed beach, frantically searching the dunes behind the house. She could be rushing into a trap, but she had to help Rupert. He'd fallen from a balcony at the far end of the house, so he should be a little farther down.

She spied a shape ahead in the moonlight and rushed forward, saying a silent prayer he'd survived. A litany of *please, God, let him make it* rang through her head. Her hesitant steps drew her closer until she reached the still figure lying face up on the sand.

Rupert Morris lay in a pool of his blood. His lifeless eyes stared blankly at the starry sky.

"Oh, no." She sobbed, sucking in a deep breath, only to draw in the distinctive smell of blood. Coughing and retching, she turned away, clutching in cold fingers the book she'd taken.

Hasty footsteps crunched in the sand behind her.

She spun around. A flashlight beam hit her face, momentarily blinding her. Shielding her eyes with her hand, she stiffened, expecting a bullet to tear through her at any moment.

"Miss McLain, want to tell me what you're doing here?"

Serena knew that harsh voice. Detective Sinclair.

She watched him walk closer, relieved, until it occurred to her, why was he here. Was he working for Gerald Grayson, paid to clean up this mess?

Of course, he was. It was the only explanation for his sudden presence.

Her fear turned into anger. He couldn't sweep murder under the rug! Rupert was dead, and Grayson was responsible. "What can I say, Sinclair? I was at the right place at the right time. I saw Gerald Grayson kill Mr. Morris."

Sinclair glowered. "Don't get smart with me, bitch. I've got half-a-dozen witnesses back at the party that says you killed him."

Bitch. She'd heard that word growled on her answering machine in the same husky tone. He was the one who'd left the threatening message. "All of whom happen to work for him. Like you." She didn't bother to keep the scorn out of her voice.

He transferred the flashlight to his left hand, flexing the fingers of his right.

"I warned you before about making false accusations." He smiled, making unattractive furrows line his beefy face. "I guess you're a little dumber than I thought."

Outraged, she spat out, "I'm smart enough to know a dirty cop when I see one."

"You're going to regret saying that, bitch." He drew his gun.

She stared at his twitchy right hand and shuddered. He wouldn't shoot her in cold blood, would he? She should have shut her mouth and gone over his head, but it was too late. His threatening stance said he would kill her without batting an eyelash. He only had to doctor the crime scene, claim self-defense, and get away with murder.

"Not so cocky now, are you?" Sinclair chuckled.

She took a deep breath, making a concerted effort to relax as she took a fluid stance. The karate she learned was no match for a bullet, but it, coupled with the little can of mace in her tote, was her only hope. If only she could get to her spray unobserved.

Her hand snaked into the bag's opening as she kept a watchful eye on Sinclair. He was smiling. A cruel smile. Fingers searching, she felt for the can and then touched it, the metal cool on the muggy evening. Her hand closed around the small can, and she started to raise it.

"I'll take over, detective." A smooth masculine voice came from behind Sinclair.

She jumped, startled by the unexpected voice, dropping the can. The bag slipped off her shoulder, plopping on the sand. Was it one of Grayson's henchmen here to finish her off? She might have been able to disable Sinclair, but two against one was impossible. And besides, now she was unarmed.

She noted Sinclair's disgusted scowl as he reluctantly holstered his weapon and felt some of her dread ease. This interruption wasn't welcome.

She spun to look at the newcomer, giving the stranger a wary once over. Her rescuer wore dark slacks and a shirt. His feet were shod in dark boots. He blended in with the night. If she didn't know any better, she'd guess he was one of the men in black, straight out of the movie, a secret agent sent to save her. Whoever he was, she owed him her life.

Sinclair stalked toward the stranger, his gait stiff with frustrated energy. "What in the hell are you doing here, Riley? This isn't in your jurisdiction."

"It is now." The man drew Sinclair aside, walking with him a few yards down the beach.

She tried to make out their muted conversation. From Sinclair's hostile tone, she could tell he was livid like a vicious dog denied a delicious snack. She took the opportunity to get an eyeful of her liberator without him noticing. From Sinclair's jurisdiction complaint, she knew he was a cop. There was something vaguely familiar about him, but she didn't recall seeing him at the police station.

He had wavy dark hair and an athletic build. Standing several inches shorter than Sinclair, her rescuer still reflected a substantial presence. An aura of command emanated from him. It showed in his confident stance and the determined thrust of his jaw. It was an aura Sinclair reluctantly responded to.

Thank God for an honest cop. She was saved, but couldn't say the same for her poor PI. She glanced at Rupert's body, falling apart as a sob shuddered through her. At least she was now dealing with an honest public servant, not a sham like Sinclair. Her rescuer would see Gerald Grayson held responsible for his evil actions. She blinked back tears, glancing up at the two men.

Sinclair stepped back, and his arms dropped impotently to his sides. He shot her a nasty look before walking away. She knew his glare implied a threat. She retreated, her breath catching in her throat.

"Ms. McLain, I'd like a word with you."

Serena took her gaze off Sinclair to glance at her rescuer, who was now striding up to her. As he grew near, she noted the sharp planes of his face. His dark hair had a few silver glints that caught the moonlight. A quick intelligence was evident in his brown eyes. He smiled. His mouth was slightly crooked, his eyes bright and watchful.

She choked back a sob, determined to be strong. "Yes."

He held out his right hand. "Mark Riley, FBI Special Agent, ma'am."

His honey-smooth voice calmed her. She glanced at his blunt-tipped fingers, and she had the crazy notion shaking hands with him could lead her into peril.

She shook off the thought of post-traumatic stress and reached out to shake his hand. "Call me Serena." She loosened her grip after politely shaking his hand, but he didn't. He jerked her forward, snapping handcuffs on one wrist and the other. Her book fell out of her limp fingers, dropping onto the sand.

"Ms. McLain, I'm placing you under arrest for the murder of Rupert Morris."

"What?" Serena blinked at the handcuffs now manacling her wrists, stunned, and then glanced at him.

He ignored her question, scanning the dunes instead. What was he searching for, anyway? She glanced at the deserted beach, confused.

Riley tugged on her arm. "Come on, Ms. McLain. Let's get going."

She stumbled. "This is crazy. Aren't you supposed to read me my rights or something?"

He glanced over his shoulder again. "Just shut up and get moving."

She couldn't believe his rapid change of attitude. "I didn't kill Mr. Morris. He was a private investigator I hired to help me look for my father." She frowned when Riley ignored her and started walking. Wasn't anything she said getting through? She looked at the PI's crumpled body. "What about Mr. Morris's body? You can't leave him lying there." She stumbled over the book she'd dropped.

He pulled her back to her feet. "The crime lab is on its way." He gave her arm another tug. "But we're out of here, now."

"Not without my book and bag." She dug in her heels.

"Blast it all, Ms. McLain." He bent and picked them up, slinging her bag over his shoulder and then tucking the book under his arm like a football. "Fine. I've got your stuff. Now move it, lady!"

She gritted her teeth and trotted alongside him. He might have looked comical carrying a purse if she wasn't so angry. She was sure he'd toss her over his shoulder caveman style if she balked. Just wait until she got the chance to contact her lawyer. She would sue the pants off him and the whole blasted FBI for false arrest and unprofessional conduct. There had to be some code by which he was supposed to conduct himself.

Her evening sandals churned the sand under her feet as he practically dragged her up the slope to the road. Reaching the top, he pulled her toward a dark sedan.

Riley jerked the passenger door open and shoved Serena inside, tossing her book and bag between the seats. He ignored her furious sputters and scanned the street. Slamming her door shut, he ran to the driver's side, slid into the vehicle, and locked the doors.

Her eyes widened when she saw several stealthy figures on the beach. Were they Grayson's men? Yikes. She was suddenly glad she was with an abrasive FBI agent, even if it meant she was under arrest. Once at the agency's station, she'd explain everything. But she'd need her car to drive home later. She didn't fancy coming back here to pick it up. "My car. Can you have it brought to the police station?"

Riley gunned the engine, peeling away from the curb.

She scowled at him when he didn't answer. "Did you hear me?"

"Loud and clear, lady. Don't worry about your car. We already impounded it." He stomped on the gas pedal, focusing on the road. Driving fast with a few quick turns, he kept watch out his rearview mirror. After a few miles, he relaxed and looked over at her.

Of course, they impounded it. They thought she'd killed Rupert. But she hadn't done it. Somehow, she had to get that through to him. "You've got to believe me. I didn't kill Mr. Morris. You're letting his killers get away by doing this."

Her hands trembled, and she clasped them together in her struggle to stay calm.

Poor Rupert. Grayson had shot him in cold blood. She'd expected the two of them to get kicked out if caught at the party, maybe even arrested, but not shot.

Wincing as her wrists rubbed painfully against her tight handcuffs, she couldn't help wondering if the mobster had a pipeline into the FBI. What else would explain her arrest on such flimsy charges? The authorities couldn't let Grayson go unpunished by hanging the crime on her. She'd fight it with every breath in her body. Pushing back tears of frustration, she concentrated on slowing her breathing, determined to keep her composure.

Riley frowned when he glanced at her. "Burglary is a crime, Ms. McLain. So is trespassing."

She ignored his pithy statement. He knew they'd crashed the party. He knew her name. Hell, he seemed to know every move she'd made lately. Why would the FBI be interested in her? She bit her lip as the unsettling possibilities flashed through her mind. Whatever the reasons for their scrutiny, it seemed she was in big trouble.

"Where's that crime lab you talked about?"

"It's on its way. Don't worry about it. They'll take care of the body."

"The body. How can you be so blasé? That's my private investigator lying dead down there. His name was Rupert Morris," she blinked back tears that sprang to her eyes, "he was working for me, so I guess you're right. I am responsible."

"Right."

His distracted tone had her glance at him as he drove past the city marker and turned onto a dark, two-lane road. Something didn't add up. Federal office buildings weren't out in the boonies.

She turned to look at his rugged visage. "Where are you taking me?"

He frowned. "Sit tight and shut up."

Shut up. Would a real agent talk to her that way? She glanced at the woods they were entering, knowing something was very wrong. "I've seen enough police dramas to know you don't take a suspect for a leisurely drive in the country. Stop this car at once."

Her heart sank when he ignored her demand and sped up instead. Could he be in cahoots with Sinclair? He hadn't even shown her his badge. He was probably a fake. Glancing at his focused concentration as he drove, she considered her options. She could leap from the speeding car to get away. Fear of breaking her neck kept her still.

Her mace! She'd have a chance if she could reach the tote lying in the crack between their seats. *A snowball's chance*, a little voice stated, but she had to take it.

She leaned to the left, reaching for the handle. Her fingers brushed against it, just out of reach. Suddenly, he cut the wheel to the left, and the car careened around a corner.

She cried out, thrown against him. Bouncing off of his hard body, she grabbed the purse. Snagging it, she murmured to distract him, "What are you trying to do, drive me to death?"

"Sorry."

She frowned at him. He didn't sound sorry. He looked like a man bent on destruction.

Inching the bag onto the edge of her seat, she kept her eye on him. He didn't notice. Ever so slowly, she reached into her purse, looking around for mace. Her fingers brushed over the healing crystal. She rubbed it, closing her eyes, trying to focus. Moving on, she located the small canister and palmed it. Lifting it onto her lap, she kept it concealed in her hand. Now, all she needed was to wait for the right time.

He slowed to take the next turn, and she struck. She lifted her cuffed hands, letting him have it, pressing down the button with all her might.

It hit him in the face. She closed her eyes when it drifted back her way.

"What the fuck," he growled, the car careening into the ditch as he slapped the can out of her hand. The vehicle came to a shuddering halt, lodged under a weeping willow tree. He switched off the headlights, plunging them into darkness. "Are you trying to wreck us?" He turned to look at her.

"No, just you." She glared at his shadowy visage, hoping his eyes were teary. Hers were teary, too, but for a different reason.

Damn. She was disarmed, at his mercy, and he was undoubtedly fresh out of that. Now what? Maybe if she kicked him in the genitals, it would disable him, but she wasn't sure she could locate them in the dark.

He grabbed her wrists, towing her toward him. "Are you nuts, lady?"

She shrunk back as far as the anchor of his arm would allow. "No. I don't like Gerald Grayson's goons." At that moment, her attention was caught by a car speeding toward them. If she could flag them down, she might stand a chance. She flailed against him, shouting, "Help!"

"Shut up," he hissed, shoving her down and flattening himself on top of her.

She struggled, starved for air, flattened under his weight. The fight went out of her when she heard the car speed by and drive away. She was doomed.

When he moved, she sat up, gasping for air as she waited for the inevitable. He was going to kill her now. She was sure of it. Even as she thought it, he shook his head and started to drive. They were in the ditch now, so they were bouncing over ruts.

"Why don't you say something," she demanded. Anything would be better than his ominous silence.

"No time to talk. We've got to get out of here. I'll deal with you later." He started the car up a gradual slope and eased back onto the highway, going in the opposite direction.

Startled, she tried to make out his expression in the shadows. Why hadn't he pounced? He could have done her in, then and there, if he'd wanted to.

He glanced out the rearview again, and it hit her. Grayson's accomplices must have been in the speeding car. Was she a pawn in some rival gang warfare?

"Are we being pursued?"

"We were. I lost them, no thanks to you. I'm making sure they don't resurface."

She craned her neck to peer out the back window at the dark country lane. The road behind them was empty. "I don't see anyone."

"They're probably halfway to the next county by now." Riley turned into the driveway of a small ranch-style home. A chain link fence surrounded the yard. Pine trees sheltered them, creating a gloomy shade around the place. He switched off the engine and turned to look at her.

She shrank back, troubled by his intense gaze. By the glow of the porch light, she could see his face was red and blotchy. He had to be madder than hell. Was this the part where he pounced? Her hands itched to get at her mace again, but he'd tossed it in the backseat.

He frowned. "What the hell did you think you were doing, nosing around Grayson's compound?"

She froze, startled by the intensity of his words. A sneak attack she'd expected, to be bawled out for her investigation, she hadn't. What was he up to, anyway?

She plastered herself against the car door, avoiding even an accidental touch as he took up a significant portion of the front seat. "You're not going to intimidate me with this good cop, bad cop routine, so cut it out. I don't believe you're a cop at all. You never showed me your badge, and I'm not saying one more word until I see it."

He reached into his pocket, pulled out a badge, and flipped it open. "I'm for real, lady. You would have ended up dead without me, so answer my questions civilly, if you please."

She bit her lip. He was a real agent, and she'd attacked him. What kind of sentence could she get for that? And then there was the matter of Rupert's killing. Was she really under arrest for his murder? She was innocent, but it didn't seem to matter to this guy. His scowl said she was in big trouble.

"I didn't kill Rupert Morris, honest."

"I know it."

He believed her? What a relief, but his enigmatic expression told her he didn't share her comfort. It also didn't give her any inkling of why the FBI kept tabs on her. She wasn't the sort of person the government would be interested in, but... The mobster that kidnapped her father was. Was this all about Gerald Grayson? It was the only explanation that fit.

There was only one way to find out.

"I suspect you already know I was searching for my father. Gerald Grayson is holding him captive somewhere."

"Possibly."

Her eyes narrowed. He knew this already, and he didn't seem interested in her father's location. Why had he been on the beach, ready to rescue her when she'd needed him? The FBI had to be following her.

She gazed into his chocolate-brown eyes. She'd seen those intense eyes before, but where? She glanced down at his hard body, dressed all in black.

The janitor, the rude one she'd bumped into at the police station. She remembered his body's reaction very well. It had shocked her at the time. It certainly wasn't professional FBI behavior.

"If you aren't on Grayson's payroll, what were you doing playing janitor?"

He hesitated a moment, then heaved a heavy sigh. "That's one for you, lady. Sinclair didn't even recognize me. I might as well tell you. I'm part of an inter-jurisdictional task force investigating Gerald Grayson's links to organized crime. And you, Ms. McLain, may have just blown things a mile high. Thanks to your meddling, I've been assigned to keep you alive while we move to indict. How I do that is up to you. Stop asking questions, obey my orders, and we'll get along fine. Try any more crap like the pepper spray, and I've got a nice cozy jail cell waiting for you."

She gaped at him, for once speechless. Having Gerald Grayson behind bars could be the answer to her prayers. The FBI would surely be able to help her find her father, but it would be up to her to make him a priority. But was it true? She'd been lied to so much, she didn't trust anything on faith anymore.

"I'm not going to say a word until I get a few guarantees."

A nerve pulsed in his jaw. "Why don't you pipe down? Just be grateful I was there to save you."

Serena wrinkled her nose. She didn't like his attitude. It didn't bode well for them to be able to work together. She *was* grateful, but finding her father took top priority.

"Gee, thanks for saving me, you big strong FBI agent. Now, why don't you take off these cuffs? You can go back to playing dress up and I can get back to the business of finding my dad."

"Sorry, no can do," he said, watching her closely. "As I said, we intend to keep you on ice until our investigation is over."

Keep her on ice? Stunned, she stared at his resolute expression. "You can't be serious. I have a child to take care of and a job. There's no way I'd agree to stay here."

Riley's lips pressed into a hard line. "You can and will if you don't want to end up dead like the PI you hired."

His warning chilled her, but leaving her son was impossible. She'd take her chances, put in the best security system on the market, and buy a gun if she had to, much as she disapproved of them. No, better yet, she'd get a guard dog and sign up for more self-defense lessons.

"Thank you for the offer, but I can't accept."

"You don't have any choice. Don't forget there's a charge of assaulting an agent hanging over your head. I'll prosecute if I have to."

"You can't mean that."

"Take a good look at my burned face. You're lucky I'm a peace-loving man. Most guys wouldn't have taken it so lightly."

Lightly? He'd darned near pulled her arm out of the socket with the force of his slap. That didn't include scaring her half to death and then squishing her with his hulking frame. Of course, he'd also saved her from Grayson's goons. She couldn't deny that, but it didn't mean she'd follow his orders blindly. There was no way she'd drag her son into this mess. Sammy couldn't handle this kind of cloak-and-dagger business.

"I won't leave my son."

He gazed at her, his force of will unyielding. "It wasn't an offer. You won't have to leave your son behind. We'll bring him to you."

She narrowed her eyes, hearing his firm tone. It was as if he wasn't hearing her. Well, he couldn't make those kinds of demands on her and get away with it. "No. He's only five years old. He'd be scared to death."

The screen door slammed, and she looked toward the house.

"Mom!" Sammy ran onto the porch. "It's wizard here. Can we stay for a while?"

She gasped. He had a set of binoculars hanging around his neck and a big smile on his impish face. An older male agent dressed in a dark suit stood behind him with a hand on his shoulder.

Of all the underhanded actions, how dare the FBI do this to her?

Choking back a sob, she whirled to confront Riley. "How could you do something this callous? I'm a taxpayer, and you work for me, damn it." In the face of her outrage, he didn't even flinch. He was like granite. There was no getting through to him, she realized with a sinking heart. His stony expression didn't ask for understanding or forgiveness. "You bastard."

Chapter Four

Riley inclined his head, acknowledging the title of bastard.

Tears misted Serena's eyes, and she blinked them away. It wouldn't do to show weakness in front of a man like Mark Riley. She sensed he would take any advantage he could get.

"I saved your life, Ms. McLain. It would pay for you to remember that. You've been through a lot tonight, but getting hysterical isn't helping matters. We brought your son here to protect him."

"Listen, you robotic jerk. I'm not hysterical. I'm angry, and only the fact that you're the law is keeping me from demonstrating that fact. How did you get Sammy? He was with Fern, his babysitter."

He shrugged. "I called to have him picked up right after I intercepted Grayson's call to Sinclair. Agent Wilson told Mrs. Monroe you'd been in an accident. She was very cooperative. People generally are when they see our badge."

Fern would probably have a heart attack from the stress. "You told her I was hurt? She's probably called every hospital in the area to check on me. How could you scare her that way?"

"We weren't trying to scare her. We gave her a good cover story. She thinks you were involved in a fender bender out of town. She won't be making any calls. It's nothing personal, ma'am. We're just doing our jobs."

Nothing personal? She considered messing with her son very personal, indeed. "If you put my son in danger because of this, I'm going to make you very sorry."

He raised a brow. "If you understood the kind of hardball Grayson plays, you'd keep your trap shut and be grateful for my help."

She fell silent, knowing it was true. She owed the robotic jerk her life. It was a deal with the devil, but she had few other choices. "Unlock these handcuffs, and we'll talk. I don't want my son upset by them."

He shook his head. "No. Not until I get a few guarantees. I want your word you'll cooperate."

Damn it all. He wouldn't give an inch and seemed utterly unmoved by her distress. The only sign he picked up on was a slight stiffening of his shoulders that she'd noticed. Or, it might have been from the pain in his burned face. He was too darned hard to read.

"Yes, I'll cooperate."

"Good." He slid across the seat, grabbed her bound wrists, and bent to unlock them.

She tensed, startled by the sudden move. He was so close she could count the bristles in his five o'clock shadow. She gulped at his red eyes. They probably hurt a lot. She did regret spraying him, but he probably wouldn't believe her if she said it.

Taking a deep, calming breath, she closed her eyes, seeking her calming place, her tropical sunset, but it wouldn't come. His presence kept intruding, his touch, his nearness, the woodsy cologne he wore with a masculine backdrop.

He backed off a little.

Her eyes popped open to find him staring at her, troubled. Now he really would think she was a hysterical female.

His brow wrinkled. "You're not going to pass out on me, are you?"

So, that's what he was worried about. He didn't want a fainting woman on his hands.

"No. It's just a little meditation."

"No need for that mumbo jumbo." He raised a brow. "Keep calm, Ms. McLain. Try to remember we're on your side."

"I am calm."

He disapproved.

She wasn't surprised. Her dad didn't believe in it either, but it did give her a source of serenity, and she deeply needed it now.

He shook his head. "Yeah, right."

She held her bound wrists steady, breathing deep to slow her racing heart, her tension dissipating.

Riley finally succeeded in unlocking her cuffs.

She scrambled frantically for the door the moment her hands were free. She needed breathing space now and desperately needed to hold her child.

Riley locked the doors. "Sit still. We have to talk."

"About what?" What was he trying to pull now? She slanted a suspicious glance at him, noting his implacable expression. "I already agreed to cooperate."

"We have to get our stories straight."

Her eyes narrowed. So, he was admitting he'd gone too far. It was small satisfaction. "Afraid I'll turn you in for your outrageous behavior?"

"No, I was thinking about your son."

She hadn't expected him even to give Sammy a second thought. Were there more disclosures to come? If he even considered separating them, he could think again.

"What about him?"

He shrugged. "Right now, he thinks he's on a great adventure. If you come out of this car all weepy, he will be a heartbroken boy."

What he said made sense, much as it irritated her to admit it.

She looked at Sammy, who was playing on the porch. He was having fun with the older agent, peering through binoculars.

She closed her eyes. "All right, what did you tell him?"

"You were helping the police look for his grandpa, and the two of you were here on a little vacation."

When she'd started this quest to find her father, she'd taken great pains to keep it from her son. He'd had enough disruptions in his young life without giving him one more thing to worry about now. She hated like hell the thought of dragging him into it. Moreover, she didn't want Riley's hard-edged tendencies to rub off on Sammy. But it wouldn't be so bad if the FBI could help her find her father.

"I want a few guarantees of my own."

"Such as?" He inclined his head, studying her.

She returned his intense gaze. She was a mother protecting her child and wouldn't let him intimidate her into submission. "First, I don't want Sammy involved with any agents. He doesn't need another male role model to walk out on him."

"Okay," Riley shrugged, "I'm here to protect him, not be his pal."

She studied the agent's rugged visage, realizing Riley wasn't a family man. He was an FBI robot. "Good. Second, I want the agency's help to find my father."

"We'll do what we can."

His jaw tightened, and he sighed, knowing she'd pushed him as far as she could.

"Fine, I'll accept that."

"Okay, it's a deal then." He unlocked the doors.

She grabbed her father's book, the tote off the floor between their seats, and jumped from the car. Rushing up to the porch, she was careful to smile for Sammy. There was no need to let him in on her problems.

"Hey there, tiger. How are they treating you?"

Sammy gave her a gap-toothed smile. "Great! Agent Bob brought me supper and a bunch of toys. He even let me try out his binoculars, see?" He pointed to the set hanging around his neck.

"I see." She dropped to her knees as Sammy ran to her. She hugged him, forcing back tears. Counting her blessings, she forced herself not to fall apart. Since her dad's disappearance, she and Sammy had been alone. She had to stay strong for him.

He wiggled out of her tight grasp. "Aw, Mom. I'm too old for that stuff."

She stood and smiled at his gap-toothed grin. He'd already lost one of his baby teeth. "Right. You just turned five," She ruffled his hair, "I'm just happy to see you. I missed you."

Riley touched her shoulder, and then leaned forward to slip the can of mace into her bag. "Come in the house. Sammy can play, and we can talk."

She glanced at him, amazed he'd returned it to her. Was it an act of faith or did he think she might need it?

Confused, she put her arm around Sammy. "Come on, let's go inside."

The older agent held the door open for them and waved her toward the dinette set in the small kitchen. With Sammy standing by her side, she took a seat and watched the older agent follow them. He seemed much more the kindly, fatherly type than agent Riley. He came to the table last, and the senior agent gave him a long, quizzical glance.

"What happened to you?"

Riley shot her a telling look, then glanced at Sammy. "Pepper spray. I'm going to go clean up." He strode to the back of the house.

Serena watched him go, glad he hadn't said she'd done it in front of Sammy. She turned to glance at the other agent. Would he think she was a menace, too?

The older man smiled, walking up to shake her hand. "I'm Special Agent Bob Wilson, Mark's partner."

She shook his hand, looked into his kind gray eyes, and felt tears come to the surface again. She blinked them away. "Nice to meet you." Her cheeks heated at the foolishness of her statement.

Agent Wilson smiled. "Don't worry about it. I know it's been a hard night." He poured a cup of coffee and then placed it in front of her. He turned to tousle Sammy's hair. "Why don't you go play with those toys I bought you, sport."

Sammy grinned at him, then turned to her. "Is it okay, Mom?"

Striving to hold her emotions in check, she smiled. She didn't want to give him the idea there was anything to worry about. "Sure, go ahead. I'll be right here if you need me."

"Okay." He ran off into the living room.

"Kids are resilient creatures," Agent Wilson stated.

"I know, but it wasn't right to bring Sammy here. I tried to tell your partner that. I've taken great pains to keep him clear of Gerald Grayson's tentacles, and now you've probably brought him to the attention of the monster who kidnapped my father."

Agent Wilson flashed a sympathetic smile. "After all the trouble you've caused him since your father went missing, he's undoubtedly compiled a complete dossier on you. He wouldn't hesitate to use your son to keep you in line."

"You're probably right." She trembled at the implication her son was in danger.

She gazed at her coffee. How could an evening that had started with such hope become a disaster?

"Sorry for the strong-arm tactics." Agent Wilson sat with her. "We had to act fast."

She laid the book on the table and clutched the coffee mug, letting the warmth seep into her fingers. "Why didn't your partner say that? I wouldn't have had to spray him."

"Heat of the moment, I suppose." He shrugged.

"I'm not usually a violent person." She cringed, thinking of agent Riley's burns. They'd looked terrible. "I hope I didn't do him any permanent harm."

"Don't worry about Mark. He'll live."

"He's right about that," Riley cut in dryly.

He stood at the counter.

She hadn't even heard him coming. The man had the light footsteps of a cat, and it was unnerving. She frowned at him. His face wasn't as blotchy, but his eyes were still bright red. The stuff she'd bought through back channels had worked.

"What's with the book?" He glanced at it on the table.

She laid her hand on its torn cover. "It's one of my father's books. I found it in Grayson's library. He's highlighted certain sections. I couldn't bear to leave it there."

He shook his head. "That's just great. Theft in addition to everything else."

Agent Wilson shot him a curious glance, then turned back to Serena. "I need to ask you what you saw tonight, Ms. McLain."

She ignored Riley's comment about theft as he lurked in the corner of the room, watching her. She wrinkled her nose at his enigmatic expression. His macho, cock-of-the-walk attitude wouldn't cut any ice with her.

She turned to Agent Wilson. "I'll complete a full report, of course. Rupert Morris's killer has to be prosecuted."

"Did you witness the crime?" Riley asked. "Did Grayson do it himself?"

She shuddered as the horrific scene replayed in her mind. "Yes, I saw it happen. Gerald Grayson was up in his bedroom with a group of security guards. He shot Rupert."

"Hold it, please." Agent Wilson put a small tape recorder on the table. "Start from the beginning, Miss McLain. I need to get this documented. Please, tell us everything that happened tonight."

"Okay." She took a deep breath, trying to organize her thoughts. "I hired the PI after my father went missing. We decided to search Gerald Grayson's home during the party, thinking it would give us plenty of cover. We entered the house through the kitchen door. Rupert got in line with the servers, and we thought we slipped into the party unnoticed. We separated to search the downstairs—"

"Find anything?" Riley interrupted.

She thought of the sexually adventurous couple she'd walked in on in the screening room. And then she'd been hit on by one of Grayson's pool-playing hoods. It hadn't been a good beginning.

He cocked his head, studying her reaction. "Why the hesitation?"

She frowned, shaking off her embarrassment. So, he wanted all the dirty details. "Nothing important. I walked in on a couple in the throes of passion in the screening room. After, one of Grayson's men hit on me in the game room."

Riley raised a brow, casting an appreciative glance over her blue satin evening gown. "I see."

Let him think whatever he wanted. She hadn't enjoyed the hood's attention. "Right. After searching downstairs, we went upstairs separately to find clues as to where my father was being held. I was in the den looking for evidence. That's where I found the book. I came up empty and was going to find him when I heard a noise. I thought it was a sneeze."

The agents exchanged a knowing glance. Of course, it had been a silencer she'd heard.

"Go on." Agent Wilson nodded.

"When I opened the door, three of Grayson's men were cornering Rupert on the balcony. I noticed Gerald Grayson himself. I recognized him from his picture in the newspaper. He's the one who shot him. One of his hoods tossed poor Rupert over the balcony railing." She choked back a sob. "I froze, stunned. It seemed like time stood still. And then, one of them saw me."

"You should have run," Riley commented, frowning.

She cast a defiant glance at him. "I did, eventually. And yes, one of the hoods was the man who'd hit on me in the game room earlier. I could hear the pack of goons chase me down the hall, and one of them took a shot at me. They missed, hitting the handrail next to my hand." A twinge made her glance at her hand, and she noticed a few embedded splinters sticking out of her skin, surrounded by dried blood.

"You're injured." Riley scowled. "I didn't notice it in the dark. Why didn't you say something? I'll clean it after we take your statement."

She put her arm on her lap, and the anger on Riley's face gave her pause. Why was he upset? It was her arm. Maybe he didn't want his perfect record messed up with an injured civilian.

"I can take care of it myself." She didn't want to be taken care of by him. It was too personal. "I wondered why they'd given up the chase when I escaped to the beach unscathed. When Detective Sinclair showed up to shoot me, I knew. You arrived to save me. Thank you."

Riley inclined his head, looking away with apparent embarrassment. "You're welcome."

She turned to Wilson, pushing away the undercurrent of emotion that passed between her and Riley. It seemed he was startled by her gratitude. He saved people for a living. He should be used to it now. Anyway, they were practically strangers, for goodness, sake. Why should his moods mean anything to her?

"As I was saying, Detective Sinclair cornered me on the beach. He would have shot me if your partner hadn't been there to interfere. You know Sinclair is corrupt, don't you? Is that why you guys were staking out the police station?"

Agent Wilson shrugged. "Sorry, I can't discuss agency business, ma'am." He switched off the tape recorder and turned to frown at Riley. "What gives?"

He put a hand up in self-defense. "Sorry, partner. The little lady put two and two together. I'll say one thing for her, she might be a lousy investigator, but she's a lot sharper than Sinclair."

"Lousy investigator. Let me tell you one thing, mister. My father's life is at stake, and I'll do whatever I have to in order to find him." She glanced from Riley to Wilson while they looked at her with varying shades of surprise and amusement. She bristled, adding, "If it means crashing Grayson's party or spraying a high-handed agent with mace, that's what I'm going to do."

Riley's slight smile faded as he shot her a curious look. "Do you think Grayson would keep your father alive this long?"

"I know it. My father anticipated Grayson's tactics. He made a copy of his unauthorized biography of Gerald Grayson and hid it for safekeeping. He was going to hand-deliver his manuscript the day he disappeared."

Riley nodded. "Go on."

"I wasn't worried until he failed to attend Sammy's birthday party. He would never have missed that without calling."

"That makes sense," Wilson responded.

Encouraged by his understanding tone, she continued. "I went to his house and found his office ransacked, his mail opened, and his PC and discs missing. They were looking for a copy of the biography and his notes. The fact they did the same thing to my home later that day told me they didn't find them."

The agents exchanged a glance. They knew about her break-in. They'd been following her, of course.

"Grayson probably won't kill my dad until he gets his hands on the copy. I know Dad. He'll never tell where it is. We must find him before Grayson runs out of patience and kills him anyway."

Riley frowned. "Sounds like pretty flimsy reasoning."

She turned to confront him. "I know Sinclair sat on the missing person's report I filed, so my question is, what are you two going to do about it?"

"We've already issued an all-points bulletin for your father, Miss McLain," Agent Wilson replied.

"Where are the copies?" Agent Riley asked.

She sighed and looked away. "I wish I knew. Unfortunately, Dad wanted to keep me out of it. His literary agent is the person who told me about it. He said a third party has it and is supposed to mail it to a trusted person. I don't know whom. I assume it's still in transit."

"Miss McLain, rest assured that we have agents out looking for your father now," Wilson consoled. "Every effort is being made to find him."

"Fine." She sat straighter. "Oh yes, when I was searching Grayson's study, I found this." She pulled the datebook out of her bag and slid it across the table. It's full of gibberish. Some code, I figured."

She stood on wobbly legs. She couldn't face any more questions. Not tonight. "Excuse me. I want to check on Sammy."

Agent Wilson stood and pulled out her chair. "We took the liberty of bringing a few things from your home. You and your son have the two bedrooms at the end of the hall."

His old-world politeness reassured her. From the corner of her eye, she caught Riley watching her, studiously as a cat would a mouse. She didn't like being a mouse.

She bestowed the best smile she could muster on Agent Wilson. At least he was a gentleman. "Thanks for being straight with me, Agent Wilson."

Mark watched her leave the room. The tight feeling in the pit of his stomach surprised him. So, she thought he was too detached? Didn't she know robots had their uses? They didn't feel pain and worked until they dropped.

"The lady doesn't like you."

He turned and noted the teasing glint in his partner's eyes. "I noticed. By the way, the feeling is mutual."

Wilson patted him on the back. "Good. It'll help you stay objective. You don't need to give Whittaker any more ammunition to use against you. I'm surprised she recognized you out of your janitor duds."

"Me, too. She has a keen eye, even if she is a major pain in the ass."

"What do you think her father's chances are?"

He shrugged. "I would have said slim to none, but given her disclosure tonight, I'm more optimistic. Damn, if we could get our hands on a copy of his book, it would aid our investigation. Her father is a highly rated biographer. His book is probably full of leads."

Wilson picked up the datebook. "At least we've got this, thanks to Ms. McLain. I'll hand it over to decryption. Maybe they can make some sense of it. What do you think?"

"A record of payments is my best guess. The technicians should be able to decipher it."

Wilson nodded. "How are your eyes?"

"I've had worse." Mark blinked away the sore feeling. His eyes were paining him now, but he knew from experience they'd be worse in the morning. "It's a good thing for me it wasn't the real thing. I wonder why she's carrying around fake mace."

"You drew first watch, so I'll let you find out. See you in the morning." Wilson looked back toward the bedrooms. "Think you can handle her?"

"Don't worry. I won't screw this one up." Mark shrugged and then rammed his hands in his pockets. "Piece a cake."

He grimaced at Wilson's answering grin. Yeah, famous last words. His face itched, his eyes felt like someone had thrown sand in them, and he had a powder keg of a woman sleeping under this roof. He'd have to do his best to live up to them. Their lives were riding on it.

After Wilson drove away, Mark paced the confines of the kitchen, listening to the soft sounds of Serena putting Sammy to bed. He put on a fresh coffee pot and shrugged off his jacket, getting set for a long night. When things went silent, he walked down the hall to make his hourly patrol. As he passed the bathroom, he heard the water running and a soft groan.

On alert, he quickly pushed open the bathroom door. Serena was standing by the sink, trying to scrape out the splinters with a fingernail file. And she was shaking.

His gut twisted. "Let me," he stated, not letting her frown get to him. He grabbed her arm, ignoring her protests, and steered her toward the toilet.

"This isn't necessary. I was taking care of it." She tried to shrug out of his grasp.

"I'll be the judge of that." Sitting her down on the closed lid, he turned to open the stocked medicine chest.

She gazed at the overflowing shelves. "Wow, you've got enough to fill a drugstore."

"We try to be ready for all emergencies." He got a pair of sterilized tweezers, using them to ease the ragged shards of wood out of her arm. Blood trickled from the wounds. "Sorry," he replied, jerking out a huge one and hearing her suck in a ragged breath.

"Hold it a minute, okay?"

He looked at her, watching her close her eyes and take a slow breath, her arm going fluid under his hand. She'd done something like this out in the car. Said it was meditation, he recalled. Even if he thought it was bunk, she seemed to be revived by it.

Her eyes popped open, and she nodded, giving him a small smile.

It felt like she'd popped him in the chest.

"I'm ready now. You can continue."

He looked back down, going after the worst shards as quickly as possible. She held her arm steady. The only indication it hurt was the occasional sudden catch of her breath.

Pulling the last shard out, he stood her up and steered her towards the sink. She was a bit shaky, probably dead on her feet after her ordeal, but he needed to clean her wounds. He didn't want it to get infected.

"Hold your arm over the sink so I can clean it properly."

She complied, shooting him a sidelong glance.

"This might sting a bit." He opened a bottle of peroxide, poured a good amount over the wound, let it bubble, and repeated the process.

She flinched, but didn't so much as let out a peep of protest. She was one tough woman. He had to give her that, even if she was misguided. Her father had to be dead, and the sooner she reconciled herself to that fact, the sooner she could get on with the rest of her life.

"Sorry."

"I'm okay."

He applied antibiotic ointment to the wound, put a gauze square on it, and taped it. "I'll check it in the morning. We want to make sure it doesn't get infected." Which could lead to sepsis.

She gazed at him, licking her bottom lip nervously. "Thank you."

"Don't mention it." Damn, but he couldn't tear his eyes off her mouth. "I'm just doing my job, ma'am."

She nodded and turned away. "I'd better go check on Sammy."

Chapter Five

Serena woke to the sun streaming through Sammy's bedroom window. She sat in the stiff-backed chair and rolled her neck to work out the kinks. After frequent trips to check on her son, she'd given up on sleep and camped out in his room to keep an eye on him.

She looked over at her son, recalling the trauma of the previous evening. She'd witnessed Rupert Morris's murder, and now she and Sammy feared for their lives. It all seemed like a bad dream, but the realist in her told her it was all too true. She didn't have the luxury of escaping reality. She had a little boy to think about, and she had to be strong for him. Since her father's disappearance, she was all he had left.

Even so, she hung on to the hope her father was still alive. Unfortunately, given Riley's negative attitude last night, she wasn't sure she could trust him to expend much effort to look for her father.

She stood, brushed her hair away from her face, and cinched her robe tight around her waist. She looked at Sammy, curled up in bed, sound asleep, and tears misted her eyes. He clutched Spiderman, his favorite action figure, in his little hand. Had she placed her son in mortal danger by trying to save her father herself? It was a trade-off she couldn't reconcile because it was too terrifying to contemplate.

She straightened Sammy's covers and smoothed back his hair, and he murmured in his sleep.

She smiled and backed out of the room. She might as well let him sleep a little longer. It would give her more time to figure out what she would tell him. The novelty of the previous evening would have worn off. He'd be full of questions for which she wasn't sure she had the answers. She softly shut the door behind her.

A thud rang boomed from the front of the house.

She froze. Was it Riley making that racket, or was it one of Gerald Grayson's henchmen breaking in? She couldn't take a chance on calling out to Riley and being wrong. She'd have to investigate. If she spied the bad guys, she'd grab Sammy and run. Protecting her son was paramount to her, and to hell with the FBI.

She crept down the long hallway barefoot, grabbing a broom that leaned in the corner. Armed, she made a silent beeline for the kitchen.

Another thud, accompanied by a man's groan.

She stopped in her tracks. She hadn't imagined it. Her pulse quickened, and she let out a little gasp of fear. Was her thundering heartbeat audible to the intruder? Listening carefully, there was silence now. Working up her courage, she pressed on. The element of surprise was on her side. She raised the broom overhead and inched around the corner of the kitchen.

A blurred figure rushed toward her.

She screamed, swinging the broom, only to have it pulled from her hands. Then, she was flattened against the cabinet, staring down the business end of a gun. She looked past it to Riley's frowning face.

Thank God.

He straightened slowly and lowered his weapon. "Good Lord, woman. Next time give me some warning. I could have shot you!"

Shot me? She slumped against the counter as his unsettling words sunk in. "Aren't you being a little trigger-happy?"

He frowned. "I don't think about shooting civilians, if that's what you're asking. I was doing my job, ma'am. When I tracked movement a moment ago, I took positive action. I thought you were still sleeping in the chair next to your son."

He must have checked on her through the night. The knowledge was reassuring, but didn't offset the chill she'd gotten looking at the gun in his hand.

"I thought you were one of Grayson's men." She barely noted his frown because she couldn't tear her deer-in-the-headlights stare off his weapon.

He slid his gun back into his shoulder holster, and she breathed a sigh of relief. Then she noted his stiff-legged stance. Were his feelings hurt?

His usually stern mouth suddenly kicked up into a smile.

"What's so funny?"

"You. You look like an avenging angel with your bare feet, white robe, and gold curls. You're enough to scare any felon to death."

She snorted and flipped her hair over her shoulder. "You're such a comedian. I would appreciate it if you'd keep that gun out of sight. I don't want you scaring Sammy with it."

His smile vanished. He turned and picked up his suit coat from the back of a dinette chair.

She was surprised by his suddenly glum expression. He looked like he'd been kicked in the seat of the pants by her sharp words.

She quickly looked around the messy kitchen when he slipped the coat on and turned back to the sink. "So, what was all the noise about?"

"I was trying to make coffee."

She noted his brusque tone and stared at his rigid back. The hurt feelings she'd thought she detected a moment ago were just wishful thinking on her part. She'd been right last night. He was half robot.

She glanced at the coffee grounds littering the floor. "I see you're having a little trouble."

"How observant."

She ignored his sarcasm and stepped forward. She discounted his lousy mood as wounded male pride. After all, would a real pro let someone almost get the drop on them?

He thrust the filter basket into its slot and turned on the coffeemaker. Grounds were littering the countertop. There was a scratch on his knuckle and an old hand crank can opener lying in the sink.

"Can opener problems?"

"Yup." Riley reached for a sponge and wiped down the counter.

She watched him, irritated when he continued to ignore her. She gestured toward the broom. "You might want to try the broom on the floor."

He tossed the sponge into the sink and scowled at her. "That's right. Keep poking the bear."

She smiled at his disgruntled expression and walked to the dinette. It was nice to see his implacable FBI persona slip. She sat and watched him sweeping the floor. It was a novelty to see him do housework. Her ex, Jeff, certainly had never gone out of his way to help out.

"So, from that little quip, I take it to mean you're a little wild and a trifle dangerous," she teased.

He swept the pile of grounds into the corner and rested the broom against the wall. His jaw was set when he glanced at her. "What it means is that I have to babysit you, but I don't have to like it. We'd be better off if you tried your best to be nice."

She bridled at his curt tone. "Nice, huh? I wouldn't count on it if I were you. I'm not particularly thrilled to be stuck here with you, either. Remember my warning. If you do anything to hurt my child or me, I'll make you very sorry."

"Mom, what's for breakfast?" Sammy called from the hall.

She turned a troubled glance at Sammy's way. Had he heard them arguing? His gap-toothed grin told her he hadn't.

"We've got several kinds of cereal," Riley replied, stepping forward. "But how about we play a game first?"

"Wizard."

She turned to look at Riley, confused. "A game?" She certainly hoped it didn't have anything to do with guns. This morning's demonstration made her permanently shy away from them.

"Sure." He gave her a meaningful look. "It's my version of hide and seek."

"Oh." The game must be another safety measure, she guessed. She was thankful he was keeping things light so as not to scare Sammy. Maybe she'd misjudged Riley, after all.

"Follow me." He led them down the hall. "I'm going to show you our special hiding place. Then, later on, if your mom or I say hide, stop whatever you're doing and go there. Okay, Sammy?"

Sammy nodded. "Sure, it's easy."

Serena and Sammy halted behind Riley when they reached the broom closet. She glanced at him curiously. Surely, they couldn't hide inside the small, cramped space.

He opened the door to the closet. A broom and mop hung on hooks on the west wall. "Here's what you do. Give the left hook a pull." He gave the mop hanging on the hook a tug. The far wall slid open to reveal space behind.

"Wow," Sammy said in awe.

"Go on in." Riley ushered them inside.

"Very nice." Serena looked around the secret, windowless room. The lights automatically turned on. It was spacious and well-lit with bunkbed cots and some chairs. She glanced at the large cabinets on the far wall. They probably contained enough weapons to hold off a minor siege. She was glad Sammy was too busy bouncing on a bunk bed to notice.

Riley walked up to Serena, his gaze purposeful. "We're going to practice that drill several times to ensure it's fully ingrained."

From his intense tone, she knew he was trying to reinforce the idea that this wasn't a game. "I understand, and I appreciate your efforts." She gazed into his warm brown eyes, suddenly reassured by his training and expertise.

"Do you?"

Flustered, she took Sammy's hand. "Time to get dressed, son."

She led him from the room, feeling Riley's gaze following her. It was time to distance them from the robot.

Mark poured himself a cup of coffee and sat down. He'd made a friendly gesture, and she'd run like a scared rabbit. Let her hide out in her room. He wouldn't have to worry about offending her with his trigger-happy tendencies.

Bob came to relieve him promptly at seven a.m. He slapped a folder in front of Mark and poured himself a cup of the brew.

He picked up the dossier. "I take it this is all there is to know about one Serena McLain."

Bob nodded and walked over to the table. "She's a first grade teacher. She was married once to Joey McLain. He walked out on her shortly before Sammy was born. He's bounced in and out of prison, mostly on drug charges. His last release was six months back, and his last known address is a rooming house on State Street. What she said about her father checked out. Samuel T. Rowan, an award-winning author and investigative reporter was working on an unauthorized biography of Gerald Grayson. He vanished five days ago on the way to meet his literary agent."

"That fits her story."

"So, how are things around here?"

"Rocky."

"I'd say it's got something to do with her natural animosity toward you." Bob grinned. "You were getting in her face last night."

Mark couldn't help smiling when he recalled her feistiness. There was friction that made them strike sparks off each other. "Hey, that's my job. So, are there any new developments?"

"Grayson's got his men mobilized to find our little witness. He also has his PR men doing damage control after last night's fiasco. She caused quite a commotion when she tore through the dance floor. He's spread the story that she's a crazed guest who fought with her boyfriend. Also, Sinclair is demanding we turn her over on murder charges. He claims he took the murder weapon off her before you arrived on the scene. Agent In Charge, Whittaker, sold him a bill of goods about holding her under Federal Arrest."

"At least our boss is good at something. Sinclair and Grayson don't know we're preparing to move against them."

"Right."

"Good, maybe they'll make some more bonehead mistakes.

You know, it's not like Grayson to have someone iced during a party where the guests could see it."

"From Serena's story, I'd guess it sounds like a crime of opportunity. The PI probably saw Grayson doing something he shouldn't, and he had to be silenced. Either that or Grayson thinks he's a law unto himself."

Bob glanced at the debris on the floor and seemed to brace himself for a good-natured interrogation.

Mark was still slightly stunned Serena thought he'd threatened her and Sammy. He was there to protect them, not hurt them. He might be a little unpolished, but he wasn't a monster. Or, as she'd called him, a robot. He had feelings like everybody else. Right now, he felt tired and ticked off.

Bob smiled. "It looks like you had an interesting morning."

He might just as well get the inquisition over with. "You could say that. Miss Prissy is in her bedroom sulking."

Bob's eyes twinkled. "You came to blows that soon, huh?"

Recalling her near attack earlier this morning, Mark shrugged. "Almost."

Bob put down his cup. "Hey, buddy. I was kidding."

"I wasn't."

"What happened?" A frown wrinkled Bob's brow.

"She heard me making a little noise here this morning and decided I was one of Grayson's friends."

"She almost got the drop on you."

"She came at me with a broom." Mark smiled. She'd reminded him of a rumpled guardian angel with gold curls, a white robe, and sparkling blue eyes. "I just about died laughing."

Bob smiled. "So, was she offended by your amusement?"

Mark recalled her shocked reaction to his weapon. "That's not all that offended her. I had my suit jacket off."

Bob glanced at the slight bulge under Mark's jacket. "She saw the holster?"

Mark's jaw tightened. "She saw everything. I drew down on her. She was about two seconds from being toast."

Bob slammed his coffee cup down. "What?"

Mark eyed his partner's angry expression. He felt damned guilty about it, too, even though he knew it was part of his job. "Well, what would you do? I hear stealthy movement, and suddenly, somebody comes around the corner wailing like a banshee."

"I see what you mean."

"I thought you might." He got up and headed for the door, carrying the dossier. Hopefully, studying it would give him an edge in dealing with Serena. The way things were going, he'd need all the help he could get.

"So, she gave you hell?"

Bob's amused question made him stop and turn. He thought back to her irrational threat and scowled. "She also warned me away from contact with her and the boy. Said if I hurt them, I'd be very sorry." Mark noted Bob's sympathetic expression. "I'll be back to relieve you in twelve."

Serena looked out her bedroom window as Agent Riley drove away. She wasn't a coward, but she considered avoiding him the better part of valor. The less she saw of him, the better.

She dropped the curtain and walked out of the bedroom. Bob Wilson was in the kitchen, using the broom and dustpan to clean up Riley's mess.

"I see Riley didn't clean up after himself."

Wilson smiled at her. "Yeah, he said he had a little trouble."

"You might say that." She poured herself a cup of coffee. The aroma had been luring her while she'd been hiding out. She had to admit, Riley made a mean cup of coffee.

She walked to the dinette, Wilson watching her, his gray eyes sparkling with curiosity. Something was bothering him. She could see it in his eyes.

He slanted a concerned look her way, went to the refrigerator, and pulled out the cream. He carried it to the table and then sat across from her. "He also said you got the drop on him."

So that's what was bugging him. Wilson's concerned attitude annoyed her. She hadn't hurt his precious partner, only his pride. "Well, what was I supposed to do? I heard some weird sounds, and nobody was around to protect us. I had to investigate."

He grinned and stirred cream into his coffee. "I bet you scared the heck out of him."

She recalled Riley's startled expression and nodded. "He did jump, but he was a jerk afterward. Talk about overreacting."

"Sorry about that. I'm sure it wasn't anything personal, Miss McLain. It's the training. We're trained to react instantly."

She didn't buy the feeble excuse. As far as she was concerned, Riley was as unprofessional and abrasive as they came. "That's putting it mildly. The man doesn't seem to have any feelings."

He looked at her sympathetically. "He has feelings, but it's his job to suppress them, don't take it to heart."

She looked away from his curious glance. It was stupid to let Riley get to her the way she did. If she were smart, she'd start putting up walls right away.

"He seems to lose it around you." He watched her curiously. "I wonder why?"

The warm feeling in her cheeks let her know they'd turned red at his speculative tone. She had nothing to apologize for, but couldn't help blushing like a schoolgirl. She scolded herself to get a grip and straightened her shoulders.

"I have no idea. We hate each other.

Mark let himself into his apartment and headed for the bedroom. He needed some sleep. Maybe then he'd be better equipped to handle Serena.

Damn, but the woman could push his buttons.

She wasn't even his type. He usually went for leggy brunettes, not curvy innocent blondes. Maybe once the case was over, he could ask her out on a date and get her the hell out of his system.

He flicked the remote, closed his drapes, and climbed into bed. His head hit the pillow, and he was out like a light.

He was running, chasing Serena down the beach. He caught her and pulled her into his arms. She laughed at him. Her silky dress vanished, and they were naked. They sprawled on the sand, kissing, his leg slipping between hers as he cupped her breast. He suckled on her strawberry-peaked nipples like a starving man as she rubbed against him, moaning his name.

The phone rang.

Mark opened his eyes and groaned. He rolled over and reached for the phone, his erection harder than a marble pillar. Damn, he hadn't had a wet dream since high school. She was messing with his head.

"Hello."

"Hey, Mark, how's it going?"

He relaxed when he heard his co-worker's voice. "I was sleeping, Ron. What's up?"

"Thought you might like to know. Somebody's out for your job."

He was instantly alert. "What?"

"Yeah, I was in the gym last night and heard one of the new guys asking Whittaker about your case. He wanted to be assigned to it badly and slammed you pretty hard. He didn't get anywhere. You know what a stickler Whittaker is about going through proper channels. He's either very ambitious, or he wants to penetrate your security. Either way, I thought you'd like to know."

"Thanks." He hung up and frowned, rolling out of bed. To hell with his job. He didn't like the idea of someone trying to find the safe house. He'd better talk to Whittaker right away.

Later, he let himself into the kitchen door at seven that evening. Bob was drying the dishes and grinned. "I see our little witness has got you hopping."

Bob threw the dishtowel at him. "These are my dishes, Riley. She already did her own."

He folded the towel and hung it on the bar. "So, how have things been in this little piece of heaven?"

"Fine. Anything new on your end of things?"

"I got a call this morning from Ron Marks. He overheard a new agent ask Whittaker to assign him to our case. The guy's either out for my job or a threat to security. Either way, I don't like it." Mark frowned. "I went to see Whittaker, and he brushed it off, said I was overreacting. So, I did some nosing around on my own and picked up speculation about our possible location. Luckily, it was way off base, but we'll have to be on our guard. We might have a mole in the department. Consequently, I've got a few of my associates checking it out."

Bob leaned forward. "Manny the Toad?"

"For one. He's always proved reliable in the past. Thank heavens for an honest snitch. It may give us the edge we need."

"Right," Bob replied, adding grimly, "we'd better hold off going to Internal Affairs until we know for sure."

"So, what did you do today?"

"I helped Sammy put a model airplane together, and we played dump truck." Bob smiled. "Did you know about action figures?"

"You'll have to get one for your grandkid." Then he remembered Serena's warning and frowned. "I thought the kid was off limits to us."

Bob shook his head. "Riley, I think that restriction applies to you. As I said before, the lady doesn't like you."

He thought about her overreaction to his service revolver and scowled. For Pete's sake, he had to carry. It was part of his job. "Did she cry to you about our showdown this morning?"

Bob fished his car keys out of his pocket. "Not really. She's one tough cookie. You know that from her dossier."

"Yeah, I guess she needed to be. Raising a kid on her own couldn't have been easy. What kind of a jerk would walk out on his pregnant wife?"

Bob shook his head as he put on his jacket and walked toward the door. "My sentiments exactly. Serena's a nice woman. Maybe when the case is over, you can ask her out."

Mark frowned at the suggestion that had been close to his own thoughts. Even if his attraction did show, it didn't matter. Attraction was a two-way street, and the woman couldn't stand him. "You know the code, Wilson. Business and pleasure never mix. Besides, we can't stand each other."

"Things change. Never say never, Mark. I'm out of here. Marion's expecting me."

"Say hello for me and tell her I'll take her up on that dinner invitation one of these days."

"I will, and by the way, she's got a niece she'd like you to meet."

Marion was determined to marry him off, but Mark needed to concentrate on rebuilding his career. "Tell her to stop fixing me up. You know I'm too busy to date."

Bob grinned back. "I'll tell her, but you know it won't do any good. See you in the morning."

"See you in twelve."

Mark hung the damp dishtowel on the edge of the sink. From the corner of his eye, he caught Serena walking into the room. She glanced at him cautiously and backed away like she thought he might bite.

Her anxious reaction ticked him off. He turned toward her.

"Hello," her voice was tense, "is Wilson still here?"

"No, he just left. I'm on duty now." He noticed her apprehensive glance and bit back a curse. He walked toward her, determined to have his say so he wouldn't have to remain in her presence. "I'd like to brief you on the case."

"I was going to run Sammy's bath. Can it wait until after I put him to bed?"

Her tone was curt, but her glance was pleading. He wasn't out to scare her kid, for Pete's sake. What kind of an ass did she think he was?

He sighed and walked around her. "Sure."

He strolled into the living room. The evening paper was spread across the sofa, and Sammy was on the floor playing with his model airplane.

Sammy smiled, his blue eyes bright with curiosity. "Hi."

Mark shoved the paper out of the way and sat. "Hello." He hadn't slept well. Thoughts of the case, the mole, and Serena had kept intruding.

Sammy held up the model plane. "Bob helped me put this nifty plane together."

He smiled at the proud little voice. "Yes, he told me. It's nice. I had one like it when I was your age."

The boy held up a page of decals. "We didn't have time to put these on. Do you think you could help me do them?"

He grinned at the coaxing tone. The kid was a charmer, all right, just like his mama. "Bring them here. I'll see if I can help."

Sammy carried the plane and decals over. With Mark seated, they were eye-to-eye. He took the plane and sheet of decals from the boy's hand. He could feel Sammy's curious gaze on him as he worked. It didn't bother him, even though he hadn't spent much time around kids.

Sammy eyed him closely. "Are my mom and me going to be okay?"

Mark looked at him, noting the fear in his eyes. Had there been some contact he didn't know about? "What makes you ask that?"

Sammy frowned, his freckled nose wrinkling. "I saw mom crying last night, and today, she didn't seem very happy. I'm the man of the house 'cause my dad's not around, and it's my job to take care of her."

Mark flashed him a reassuring smile. "Did your mom tell you that?"

"Nope, she still thinks I'm little. My friend, Jeremy, told me he's divorced, too. I'm five, you know."

"I know. Happy birthday." He ruffled the boy's blond hair. "Don't worry, Sammy, your mom will be fine. Bob and I will see to that."

Sammy hugged him, his little arms circling Mark's neck. "Good. I have to take care of my mom now 'cause my grandpa's gone, and it's a big job."

Stunned by the kid's open affection, Mark sat stiffly in his embrace for a moment, then drew away. Patting the boy on the back, he swallowed the lump. "I know about your grandpa, son. I'm sorry he's gone. I bet he was a great guy."

Sammy nodded, his little face crumpling into a frown. "He was my pal. Now I don't have one, except Jeremy, and I'm mad at him."

He ruffled the kid's hair, earning a small smile from him. "You've got Bob, and I'll be your pal, too."

Sammy tilted his head. "Promise?"

"I promise. But you've got to promise to tell me if you ever get worried again." Mark held out his hand. "Do we have a deal?"

Sammy grinned and shook his hand. "Deal."

Serena was watching them. She didn't look angry, but bemused and overwhelmed by emotion. She blinked her eyes as she walked toward them.

Her voice was soft. "It's time for your bath and bed, Sammy."

Sammy groaned. "Aw, Mom. Mark was helping me with my airplane."

Serena smiled and nodded toward the bedrooms. "There'll be plenty of time for that tomorrow. It's already past your bedtime. Come on."

Sammy took the plane from Mark and gazed at him solemnly. "Remember your promise."

"I will, kid. Now, listen to your mom."

He sighed and walked away. "Okay."

Serena tucked Sammy into bed, fresh from his bath, and dressed in Spiderman pajamas. She stood next to him as he said his prayers.

He finished by saying, "God bless Mom, Grandpa, Bob, and my new friend Mark, and help them keep us safe. Amen."

She bit her lip. She had mixed emotions about him getting so close to these dangerous men. At least he felt secure, and that was the most important thing.

She bent down to kiss his forehead. "Goodnight, Sammy."

He closed his eyes and curled on his side. "Goodnight, Mom. I like Mark. He's okay."

She shut the door and leaned against it. "Yes. I guess he is."

She walked back to the living room, where Riley waited for her. She was curious to find out about the new developments.

Riley was sitting where she had left him. He motioned to the sofa. "Come and sit down, Ms. McLain."

She hesitated a moment. Did she want to get that close to him? It seemed wrong to refuse after how he'd treated her son. She sat on the other end of the sofa.

She glanced at his arm, stretched across the top of the cushion. It would only take a slight movement on his part to reach down and touch her with that strong and comforting hand.

She shook off the thought and sighed. She'd been alone too long. It made her vulnerable to the first hunky man who came along. She'd heard about women falling for their captors, which is kind of what Riley was. Inching away, she decided to set boundaries to prevent it.

"What's going on, Agent Riley?"

He smiled softly. "You might as well call me Mark. Sammy already does."

"Okay, if you'll call me Serena."

"All right, Serena. I need to ask you a little more about the copy your father hid. Now that you've had a chance to sleep on it, have you remembered anything else? Did he give you any clues to its location?"

She shared his frustration. The book would give her leverage. "No. I wish he had, but he wanted to protect me. Don't worry, if I think of anything, you'll be the first to know. I've wracked my mind to think who he'd send it to."

"Did he have any safety deposit boxes?"

"No, not to my knowledge. I hadn't considered that possibility. Do you think he could have stuck it somewhere like that?"

"Maybe. It's my job to play all the angles."

"According to Frank Gorman, it was to be mailed out, so I just assumed it was in the mail." She felt her hope build. It would have been like her dad to keep a secret safety deposit box. "Dad did all his banking at First National on Main Street. You could check if he opened a box."

"We did. There's nothing there. We thought you might know of any alternate banks he used. Or aliases."

"No, sorry." Her shoulders sagged. Darn it all, why did her dad have to be so secretive? It could cost him his life. "What next?"

"We served a warrant this afternoon for Gerald Grayson's business files."

"Is that all?" She sighed, distressed at the slap on the wrist. She wanted Gerald Grayson behind bars.

"Small steps, Serena. The Treasury Department got Al Capone on tax evasion. It's the first step in toppling the man. If there's anything to find, we'll uncover it. We're also moving to indict for Rupert Morris's death. They're still claiming you did it, by the way. Sinclair is screaming for your blood."

Sinclair wanted to silence her. She wasn't surprised, but it was still frightening. Her shoulders slumped as she looked at the floor.

"Are you okay?"

All Serena could do was shake her head because she was so close to tears. She looked up, finding Mark's brown eyes full of compassion. A sob escaped her.

He moved closer and pulled her to him. He pressed her head against his shoulder as she cried. "It'll be all right, Serena. Just give it time."

She sniffed, embarrassed by her lack of control. "I'm sorry for falling apart. This is so embarrassing."

"Honey, you can't be strong all the time." He placed a hand under her chin and tilted her face to look at him. "Feel better now?"

Her breath was trembling as she looked at him. His gaze was so intense her heart fluttered. "Yes."

Her lashes swept shut as his sensual mouth lowered to hers. His lips brushed against hers, hot and sweet.

She kissed him back, hungry, starving for him. Her mouth opened under his, and he deepened the kiss. He pulled her closer, crushing her full breasts against him. She moaned, breathing in his crisp, woodsy scent, loving the feel of his strong arms around her. Her nipples hardened against his chest. She moved, dragging them against him, and whimpered.

He pulled away, letting her go.

She gazed up at him, overheated and confused. Her lips burned, and her nipples were hard and tingly. Her head swam with mixed emotions as she looked at the rueful expression on his rugged face.

He gazed deep into her eyes, concerned. "Go to bed, beautiful. I'll watch over you."

Chapter Six

Serena stood under the full force of the shower the following day, rinsing soap off. She wouldn't look like a wild-eyed fanatic this morning if she could help it. Today didn't seem nearly as ominous as yesterday. Mark would make sure she and Sammy were safe.

She dressed and went to the nightstand to get the key she'd been carrying in her purse. It had come with the toy car the other day and a poem about the key to his heart. She'd assumed it was from Joey. Maybe she'd been wrong. If it was from her father, it just might be the safe deposit key they were looking for. She was sure Mark would do his utmost to find her dad if there was a clue.

Making her way down the hall, she stopped to peek in on Sammy. He was sound asleep. She tiptoed out of the bedroom and headed toward the kitchen.

Mark was wiping the counter, jacket removed, his holstered gun in plain sight. She stopped. The sight of his weapon still had the power to unnerve her. He was a dangerous man in a dangerous profession. She couldn't let the kiss they'd shared blind her to that fact. She bit her lip. Not that she'd read anything more into their kiss than a need to comfort on his part.

She walked to the cabinet and got herself a mug, her stomach doing flip-flops. "I see you didn't give yourself an injury this morning."

He leaned against the counter and looked at her. "No, I didn't have to ward off any antique can openers or crazed mothers today."

She shrugged and carried her cup of coffee to the dinette, noting the wary tone behind his attempt at humor. Did he share her awkward feeling? Or, more likely, was he waiting for her to set the tone? He didn't have to worry. She wasn't husband hunting.

"Sorry about that. I guess I overreacted."

"I can't blame you. You're smart enough to know what danger you're in." He caught her staring at his gun and frowned. He pulled his suit jacket from the chair and shrugged into it.

His acknowledgment of her competence gratified her. After her run-in with Sinclair at the police station, she'd half-expected all law enforcement officers to display the same condescending attitude. It was refreshing to deal with one who didn't talk down to her.

"Well, at least I can count on you to protect Sammy and me."

"Thanks." He sat across from her. He gazed into his coffee mug, his jaw tightening. "I want to warn you, never count on anything or anyone, Ms. McLain. You never know when they might let you down."

So, they were back to the formality of last names. What private demons lay behind Mark's bitter words? She frowned at his closed expression. Was he a Peter Pan-like Joey, determined not to grow up? Or, more likely, he was commitment-phobic. But she'd never asked for one. The thought that he assumed she was out to snare him ticked her off.

"Last night..."

"About last night." He looked directly at her, and his expression was grim. "It didn't mean anything."

She wrinkled her nose, digesting his gruff statement. She hadn't expected a declaration of love, for Pete's sake. Did he think she was that needy? "I didn't mean—"

He held up a hand. "No, let me finish. Sometimes women fall for agents whose duty is to protect them. There's no shame in it, Ms. McLain, but it doesn't mean anything. I can't let it mean anything."

She slanted a sour glance at the concerned expression on his face. "You don't have to worry about me going all gooey-headed over you, Agent Riley. I'm well aware last night was an illusion. Thank you for being kind when I needed a shoulder to cry on."

He visibly relaxed, and she frowned at the expressive gesture. He didn't have to be that relieved.

He nodded in agreement. "You're welcome." He leaned back in his chair and smiled. "I'm glad we understand each other."

"So am I." She looked away, tension creeping over her body, making her shoulders ache. She didn't need this kind of complication any more than he did. It was a stupid time to develop feelings for this vastly inappropriate man. She was usually much more level-headed when it came to romance, but there was something that drew her to him. She could only hope her bemused feelings were a temporary anomaly. "I'm sure I'm not your type, and you're certainly not what I have in mind for a mate."

His eyes narrowed. "That's just peachy, then." He turned to look at the back door while it was being unlocked.

Bob Wilson walked in carrying a folder and a brown paper sack. "Top of the morning to you both," he chirped, setting the paper sack and file on the table.

Mark gave a curt nod.

Serena smiled at the welcome interruption. "Good morning, Bob. Did you have a nice evening?"

"I'll say." He let out a discreet belch. "All except for a new stuffed cabbage recipe my wife tried on me. It kept me up half the night, but that was good because I got some work done."

"What's got you so happy, partner?"

"Grayson was arrested this morning. He's being brought up on racketeering charges, and the homicide charge from the PI's death will be icing on the cake." He pushed the file toward Mark.

He picked it up, glancing over the top of the folder at Serena. "It looks like your stay with us will be over soon, Ms. McLain."

It was what she wanted, but her father was still missing. She was still waiting for some good news on that front. Were they actively searching as they'd claimed? She wanted to see some action, something to pin her hopes on. Glancing from Bob to Mark, she gauged their pleased expressions. Had they forgotten about her father in this rush to prosecute?

"You agents work fast, and I'll be glad to get Sammy out of danger. But what about my dad? Are you any closer to finding him?"

Mark's shoulders tensed, and she knew the answer before he said it.

Bob shook his head. "I'm sorry, Ms. McLain, Gerald Grayson isn't cooperating, and our search hasn't turned up anything thus far. We are having more luck with Detective Sinclair, however. He's cut a deal, giving us plenty of ammunition to use against Grayson."

"Good, although I hate to see him get off after threatening me. Can't you guys lean on him and see if he knows anything about my dad?"

Bob nodded. "We're working on it, but we must observe due process. He has rights."

She cast a pleading glance at the agents. "What about my father's rights?"

Mark took a step closer, his expression softening. "We're on your side. Don't fret, ma'am. We won't quit searching."

She sighed. Maybe he wouldn't quit for now, but what about when he moved on to the next case? She'd be on her own again.

Bob nodded. "He's right. We'll do all we can to help."

She glanced at Mark's preoccupied expression as he pored over the file. He'd already moved on in his mind. Maybe it was a lucky escape for her. She would nip her misplaced feelings for him in the bud and do everything she could to find her father.

"I know this is a question I never raised before, but what about when this is all over? Do you think there will be any reprisals from Gerald Grayson for me testifying against him?"

Bob shook his head. "While I can't give you any promises, that's not in Grayson's usual bag of tricks. He'll want to remain the picture of an innocent businessman. Knocking you off after you testify would hurt his image. In my professional opinion, your danger point is now. Grayson would probably do anything to prevent your deposition before the grand jury. After that, you should be able to go home. Of course, the agency will take the proper precautions to ensure your security."

Mark put down the file and reached out to pat her hand. "If we thought he'd be a serious threat afterward, we'd stick you deep in the witness protection program."

She balled her hand into a fist under his palm. His matter-of-fact tone hurt more than his words. Didn't he understand? Losing her identity would be a nightmare. He was turning back into a robot right before her eyes.

Mark held onto her hand. "Does this news discourage you from testifying?"

She tugged her hand away, noting the guarded look in his eye. "It doesn't make me happy, but it won't keep me from testifying. I need to rescue my father and keep Sammy safe. I don't want Gerald Grayson to be able to hurt us again. All I ask is that Sammy is kept out of danger."

"Speaking of Sammy, where is the little rascal?"

Serena turned to smile at Bob. "He's still in bed."

He opened the paper sack and pulled out coloring books and crayons. "I picked these up on my way over. I'll take them into him."

"Sammy will love them. Thank you."

"Yeah, partner," Mark teased. "you two kids can have fun coloring today."

Bob head toward Sammy's bedroom and Mark's chair scraped the floor as he got up. "I might as well head for home and get some sleep."

She turned toward him. "Mark?"

He stopped and turned to glance at her. "What?"

"Do you think they'll find my father alive?"

She noted the flash of sympathy in his eyes as she stood and walked toward him. He obviously didn't think so. She could read it in his sober expression. He'd never believed her assertion that Grayson was keeping her father alive until he got the copies.

"Do you want it sugar-coated?"

"No." She held her head high, bracing herself for his words.

He nodded. "No. I don't think he's alive. You need to accept the fact he's probably dead." He hesitated, watching her, then shrugged. "Okay. If you're right about the copies, I suppose there's always a chance."

She nodded, blinking away the tears that misted her eyes. "That's the hope I'm clinging to, but thank you for being straight with me."

"All I can promise is that we'll find him if he's still alive. I'll see to it personally."

She smiled. "Thank you. I have something for you."

"What?" He glanced at her cautiously.

She held out the silver key. "This came in my afternoon mail the day Rupert Morris was killed. I threw it in my purse because I thought it was from my ex-husband. Our conversation last night made me remember it this morning."

He took the key, turning it in his hand. "It doesn't look like a safe deposit box key, but whatever it goes to, we'll track it down."

She smiled, feeling hope bloom anew. "Thank you, Mark."

"Don't be so confounded grateful. I'm not Superman, you know."

"I think you are." She touched his arm.

"Oh, hell." He dipped his head to kiss her.

Her mouth opened under his, tasting the coffee he'd drank and the passion he kept buried. His mouth bruised hers for a moment before he suddenly pushed her away.

She rocked back on her heels, opening her eyes, only to find him striding out the back door.

It locked firmly behind him.

"Uh-hum." Bob cleared his throat.

He'd caught them. What did he make of their kiss? The sober look on his face told her he disapproved.

"Mark left," she stated inanely.

"I see. Leave him alone, Serena. He doesn't need complications. At least, not right now."

Serena's heart sank. Had she been throwing herself at Mark? Maybe a little, if she were honest with herself. But kisses were a two-way street, and Mark had started this one.

She glanced at Bob's tense expression. Why did he think she'd cause trouble? It was an unsettling question. "Why would getting close to me cause a complication?"

"There's a certain code we agents live by. Kissing a subject is going way over the line." He flashed her an intense gaze. "You could issue a complaint against him if you like."

His explanation made sense, but Mark hadn't done anything she didn't want him to. "No, I wouldn't do that."

She noted his relieved smile. He and Mark were good friends. It was nice to know they looked out for each other's best interests.

"Thanks for the warning. I'll leave him alone."

Bob smiled, relaxing. "Thanks. I'm sorry if I sounded harsh. I didn't mean to hurt your feelings. It's just that Mark's a good friend, as well as a partner. I need to look out for you both."

She nodded, appreciating his fatherly tone. "Thanks. Did you see me give him the key?"

"Yes. Don't worry, Mark will run it down."

"I know he will."

"You didn't trust us at first, did you?"

She'd looked at them as more of a hindrance than a help. And Mark's prickly ways had raised her hackles from the start. "Mostly, I didn't trust him."

"You've nothing to fear on that count. Mark is eminently trustworthy, but—"

"Hey, Mom," Sammy burst out of the bedroom. "What's for breakfast?"

"Hey, tiger." She turned to look at her son, wondering what Bob had been about to say. "How about some pancakes?"

"Yummy."

Serena was cooking dinner when the phone rang. Out of force of habit, she reached for the cell Bob had laid on the counter.

"Hello."

Bob stopped mashing potatoes and snatched the phone out of her hand.

She frowned, and then realized the blunder she'd made. "Sorry," she mouthed.

He nodded. "Hello. Yeah, she forgot." He glanced at her. "It's Mark." He turned back his cell phone. "They what? What did they find?"

She put down her wooden spoon. Something had happened, she could tell by his sudden all-business tone.

"I'll take care of things here. Okay." He hung up.

"What happened?"

He smiled at her. "They matched the key you gave us to a lock."

She froze. "And?"

"It fits a locker at the bus station. It contained your father's copy on computer discs."

She grinned. Thank heavens. Finally, this was a break in the right direction. "Now what?"

"We wait." He gazed at her sympathetically. "The agency is processing the locker for evidence. Hopefully, it'll lead us to him and give us some leverage to get him out. Mark is coming here early. We've got a lot of work to do."

That sounded good to her. She was eager to get on with the search. "What can I do to help?"

Bob picked up the potato masher again. "Nothing right now. We need to wait until Mark gets here."

She frowned, feeling an edgy need to be in on things. "But I want..."

Sammy wandered in and looked at her. "What's wrong, Mommy?"

"Mark found Grandpa's lost book."

"Yippee." He shouted, then slanted a curious look at her. "I didn't know it was lost."

"I guess I forgot to tell you," she replied, searching for an explanation he'd buy. She was relieved when he thought about it for a moment, then nodded.

"Did he find Grandpa, too?"

She smiled. "Not yet. He's still working on it."

"Ms. McLain, it might be better not to build the boy's hopes up too much right now," Bob stated gently.

She winced. He was right. Just because they'd found the copy didn't mean they'd recover her father so quickly. "Bob's right. Let's talk about something else. Like tickling."

She tickled Sammy's sides to distract him. He erupted into giggles, squirming.

"How about some supper?" Bob went to the oven and took the chicken out.

"I'm starving," Sammy countered.

"Why don't you sit down then, sport? It's almost ready."

She started to regain her equilibrium. It wouldn't do to let Sammy worry. She put the mashed potatoes in a bowl, then placed it on the table along with steamed broccoli and cheese sauce. She sat across from Sammy. She smiled at Bob when he sat down, glad he was around to guide her.

She cut Sammy's chicken and broccoli into small, bite-sized pieces and let him spoon some of the cheese sauce he liked.

The kitchen door opened, and Mark walked in. He flashed a wary look Serena's way and then glanced at Bob. "You tell her?"

She didn't appreciate him talking about her as if she weren't there. She gave a pointed look at Sammy, hoping Mark would understand and not upset Sammy. "Yes, he told me. We're going to talk about it later."

Bob nodded. "That's right. Everything still okay?"

"Yup."

"Have a seat and join us for dinner," Bob invited.

"Yeah," Sammy said with a mouthful of mashed potatoes. "There's lots to eat."

Mark hesitated.

Eating her cooking wouldn't break his stupid code. "Go ahead and grab a place setting," she added softly. "I made plenty of food."

He got a plate from the cupboard and silverware out of the drawer, then carried them to the table. He sat on Serena's left and took large helpings of everything but the broccoli. "Smells good, Bob. This is better than the stuff you usually throw together."

Bob grabbed a chicken leg. "Serena cooked it."

"My compliments to the chef." Mark smiled.

"Mom, I finished my broccoli." Sammy looked at Mark. "Aren't you going to eat your broccoli?"

"Do you think I should?"

"Mom won't give you any dessert unless you try it. That's what she always says."

Mark grinned at her. "Is that so?"

She smiled back at him. "Those are the rules, Agent Riley."

"In that case, I'd better try it." He spooned some on his plate.

"If you put lots of cheese sauce on it, you can't taste it," Sammy advised.

Mark smiled and slathered cheese sauce on his. "How's this?"

Serena looked at the river of cheese sauce he'd poured. "That's how Sammy usually likes his. I'll get dessert." She gave Sammy a piece of chocolate cream pie, then served slices to the men.

"Wow, my favorite," Mark stated.

"You and Sammy have something in common."

Her boy all but inhaled his favorite dessert and grinned.

"Slow down, Sammy, or you'll get a tummy ache." She carried her slice of pie back to the table and sat.

"I'm all done, Mom." He stood.

"Okay, you can be excused."

He ran into the living room to play with his toys.

"Okay, tell me about the locker." She looked at Mark.

He put down his fork. "The copies were there, just like you said, but they're on discs. And they found a note addressed to you." He handed her the envelope. "Sorry. We had to open it."

She opened the envelope and read the message in her father's messy handwriting. Tears misted her eyes. She blinked them back to read.

Dear Serena,

If you're reading this, it means something's happened to me. Sorry for the cryptic message, but I knew you'd understand. You and Sammy are my heart. Make sure my editor gets the copies of my book and notes so Grayson doesn't win.

Love forever,

Dad

The story he used to tell her when she was a tot came back to her, about the princess looking for the key to her heart. Why hadn't she made the connection earlier? The delay weighed heavily on her mind. She looked up at Mark as tears flowed unchecked from her eyes.

He reached out to touch her hand. "Agents have started looking through your father's discs for clues."

She pushed away her uneaten desert. "I can be ready in half an hour."

He frowned at her. "For what?"

She blinked at him. She couldn't just sit here when the search was happening. She wanted to see the site for herself and look for clues. "To go search with them, of course."

"No." His jaw tightened as he shook his head.

"You can't mean that." She glanced from Mark's closed expression to Bob's apologetic one, and scowled.

"I mean exactly that. You're in protective custody for a reason, Serena. Grayson's men could be watching the field office, hoping to catch a glimpse of you."

She hesitated. He was right, much as she hated to admit it. "I have to do something. I might pick up some clues the agents might miss."

"We do need your help. We made copies of the discs, and I brought them along. He seemed to use a kind of shorthand we're having trouble deciphering."

"Okay." Glad to be able to do something, she smiled. "But, once we figure out where he might be, I want to look for him."

"You're not in any position to make demands."

"Give up the forbidding robot act, Agent Riley. Stop trying to scare me out of it."

"Somebody's got to scare some sense into you." Mark scowled. "It might as well be overly macho, robotic me."

Bob cleared his throat. "I'm sorry, Ms. McLain. Mark's right. We can't allow you to go unless we get it cleared by our superiors."

She smiled at Bob. At least he saw her side of things. "Will you try?"

"Not until the area is hopping with agents," Mark bit out.

She flashed him a resentful glance. "Fine. In the meantime, get me the discs to decipher."

He frowned. "I'll get them."

She got up and started to clear the table, putting her dessert back in the fridge. Bickering with the agents would get her nowhere fast. She'd keep her part of the bargain and hoped they'd act quickly enough to save her father.

She started washing the dishes when Mark's footsteps came behind her. She looked over her shoulder at him, up to her elbows in sudsy water.

He set two flash drives on the counter, well away from the water. "Here they are."

She gazed at him, astounded by his new conciliatory tone and soft expression. "Thanks. After I finish the dishes, I'll get right to it."

He edged her aside. "I'll do this. Bob's setting up a laptop in the other room for you. Use it to help your dad. I'm sure he'd be happy to know you tried."

She wiped her hands on the dishtowel and cast a grateful glance his way. "You're a good man, Agent Riley. Thanks." She watched him look away, apparently uncomfortable with her praise.

"You're welcome."

She grabbed the discs and went to the living room. Bob had the laptop set up on the desk.

He stepped aside. "Here you go. Let me know if you need anything."

"Thanks."

Mark rinsed a plate and turned when Bob came back into the kitchen. "You get her started?"

"Yup. She should be at it for hours."

"Good. I'd rather keep her occupied than have her fight us to go out and investigate."

Bob dried the plate and put it in the cupboard. "Your sources turn up any moles yet?"

He frowned. "The agent who was bucking for my job transferred in from DC six months back. I went to Whittaker, asked him to investigate, and he flat out told me to drop it. He thinks I'm nuts for even suggesting there might be a problem. All the same, I've put out some discreet feelers of my own."

"Good. We will have to go outside the chain of command in this case. We both know Whittaker doesn't have much faith in your judgment since the incident last year. He will take whatever you say with a grain of salt."

"I suppose he's got a right to question my judgment. It was a screwed-up mess. Having the subject's wife shoot him during my watch was a friggin' disaster."

"In your defense, Whittaker was the one who'd set up the visit. She wasn't off the subject's visitation list. We never expected her to try killing her hubby for ratting out her pop."

"There's plenty of blame to go around. I should have been more careful. That's what they pay me for. I patted her down, but I never felt her weapon. No one was more surprised than me when she shot him. I always wondered if the gun was planted in the room somehow. But that's all water under the bridge. The important thing is Ms. McLain and her son. We may have to separate if our security is breached."

"Right. We'd better make backup plans for emergency egress, just in case. We'll catch hell from Whittaker for acting on our own, but I'd rather have a live subject than a dead one."

"Same here. But I'll catch hell, not you. There's no need for you to risk your pension. You can take a leave of absence. I'm already on his shit list. There's no sense getting you in Dutch, too."

Serena used the password and opened her father's notes. Tears came to her eyes when she saw his detailed work. He had to be alive. She couldn't let herself believe otherwise.

Standing, she went to get Mark. She'd show him how to open the files so he could pass them on. She stepped into the kitchen where Mark and Bob were speaking in hushed tones.

"I've got an old fishing shack we could hole up at," Mark stated, adding, "it's within an hour from my folks' summer house."

Bob nodded. "Good. I've been planning that trip to Florida. I could go now if need be. It would work as a diversion."

Were they planning time off or their next mission? Intrigued, she stepped into the kitchen. The men fell silent and turned to look at her.

Bob smiled. "You find anything?"

"A little. I thought you might want me to teach you my dad's code so you can pass it on to the investigators."

Mark stepped forward. "Let's go."

Serena turned on her heel and headed back to the living room. She was still mulling over what she'd overheard. No doubt, they'd be breaking their code of conduct if they let her in on their plans. "First, Dad's password combines our birthdays—twelve for Sammy, nineteen for me, and thirty for dad. His notes are now in his own brand of shorthand, based on a numeric code." He gazed at the screen and then at the pad she was writing on.

Bob placed a coffee mug on the desk. "Here you are, Ms. McLain. Nice fresh java."

"Thanks." She ripped off the list she'd been compiling and handed it to him. "This should give you a starting point."

"I'll pass it along," Bob replied. He turned to Mark. "I'll give you a call if I hear anything. Remember the red alert code. Egress."

Mark nodded. "I'll be ready."

She frowned at the two of them. Was this cryptic conversation about what she'd overheard? "What are you talking about?"

"Code words." Mark watched her cock her head, seemingly considering for a moment.

"Fine. Keep secrets if you want." Serena turned back to the computer.

After ten, Serena went to check on Sammy. He was curled up in bed, sleeping. She pulled up his covers and tiptoed from the room.

She'd gone through her father's notes and was halfway through his manuscript. It was spellbinding work, as usual. Mark had called in the complete list of Grayson's haunts and hangouts that her dad had uncovered. She could only hope they'd lead to her father's safe return.

Mark had left her alone. Thank heavens, at least she could concentrate. She couldn't risk a repeat of this morning's kiss.

Her stomach grumbled, and she realized she was hungry. She'd only picked at her dinner. A snack would help. She turned toward the kitchen.

Mark was eating a piece of pie at the table and looked up.

She walked to the fridge. "I think I'll join you. Is there any pie left?"

He smiled. "I saved you a piece."

"Good." She sat at the opposite end of the table and took a bite, savoring the creamy chocolate flavor.

He was focusing on her mouth. Face hot, she put down her fork and picked up her coffee cup.

"Good pie," he commented with a hint of a smile, devouring his slice. "You're one heck of a cook, Serena."

"Thanks." She soaked up his praise. She watched him drink his coffee, his large hands wrapped around the cup, remembering how wonderful they'd felt when he'd touched her. She gulped. "So, how long do you think we'll need to remain here?"

"I'm not sure." He shrugged, gazing at her intensely. "But I expect a break in the case soon."

She felt the intensity of his gaze. Was he going to miss her? It was a balm to her femininity to know she wasn't the only one affected by this enforced nearness.

He looked her in the eye. "It's not over yet, Ms. McLain. I think we'd both be better off taking this encounter slow. Only one day at a time. You never know when life will throw a crimp in your plans."

Chapter Seven

Mark watched Serena hurry off to bed, telling himself he was lucky she ran. Damn, he wanted her like he wanted no other woman.

He had other subjects fall for him. Not that he thought he was anything special in the romance department. Subjects were frightened and vulnerable. It was natural for them to develop feelings for the agent protecting them, even a rough-edged robot like him. But none of them had ever tempted him the way Serena did with just a look. Only a jerk would take advantage of that because he knew she wouldn't want him in the real world.

In real life, she'd probably never give him a second glance because of his dangerous profession. In the corner of his mind, he still hoped there might be something he could salvage when this was all over.

Yeah, and pigs would fly someday soon.

He turned off the lights and walked through the dark house to make his hourly perimeter patrol. He stopped by the main circuit board. All the windows and doors were wired. If someone opened a window, an alarm would go off, sending a panic signal to headquarters. The doors had another nasty little surprise, enough of a charge to knock a burglar into next week.

Grayson wasn't a run-of-the-mill burglar. He was pure evil.

Mark stopped by the front door. The light on the sensor blinked green. All was secure.

He shrugged out of his suit coat, draped it on a chair, and slipped into night vision glasses. Peering out into the yard, the full moon cast a frosty glow on the chain link fence.

A motion drew his focus.

An orange and white tabby cat slunk across the grass.

It was just a cat on the prowl. "Good hunting," he muttered.

Even off his game because of his feelings for Serena, there was still a prickling at the nape of his neck. His early warning system still worked. His gut instinct told him something was going to break soon.

He'd have to be extra vigilant tonight. Walking down the hall, he turned into Sammy's room. He kept sleeping, oblivious to Mark's presence.

He walked to the window and checked the sensor, then looked outside. The darned cat seemed to be following him, probably stalking something as it slipped into the shrubbery.

Turning, he stopped and looked at the boy. Sammy had kicked the covers down. Mark pulled them back up, vowing not to fail him.

After checking the bathroom, he moved toward Serena's room. Peering from the doorway, he noted she was sleeping as usual. Her back was turned to him, her breathing soft and even.

Slipping into the room, he walked to the window, gazing out into the darkness. Nothing stirred in the backyard. Turning to check out her closet, he noticed her bag still sat packed and ready by the bed. It was her way of asserting her independence, he knew. She wanted to be able to run home the instant this was over. He couldn't blame her for not liking her movements controlled this way.

He turned to go, but she was awake and watching him.

Startled, he took off the night vision glasses, not wanting to alarm her. "Just making my patrol."

"I see."

There was an uncomfortable look on her face. She probably wondered if he was there to carry on where they'd left off. Her covers had slipped, affording him a good view of her curves under her white cotton nightgown.

God, she was beautiful.

"And is everything secure?" She pulled up the covers.

When she moved, the nightgown had slipped off one shoulder and dropped to display even more of her cleavage.

He couldn't tear his eyes away. "So far."

"That's good," she replied a bit breathlessly.

He knew she was just as aware of the sexual pull between them as he was. The air felt charged with it.

Stepping back from her was hard, but he did it. "Sleep well, Serena."

"I'll try. I'm a bit restless tonight."

"Same here," he acknowledged wryly. He was tied up in knots, and she was the reason. "I'll keep watch. You know what to do if anything goes down."

She sighed. "Yes, indeed. We practiced the drill enough today to imprint it on my brain. Why? Do you think something might happen?"

He hadn't meant to scare her. "There's nothing to point to that, but I still want you to be ready if it does."

"Okay. Take care."

He nodded, turned, and walked away.

Stalking down the hall, he went to the kitchen and checked the back door. The sensor blinked green. All was secure.

Maybe his gut was playing tricks on him, reacting to the divided loyalties he felt with Serena. His need for her was way over the line.

He poured himself a cup of coffee.

A soft rustle from outside made him freeze, his internal warning system going off big time. The hair on the back of his neck stood on end. Someone was out there.

He put down the mug and pulled out his gun, putting his night vision glasses back on. Another sound drew him to the front door.

There were two of them. He could see their heat signatures through the picture window. He stepped closer, careful to keep out of sight. One held a lock pick, crouching in the shrubs near the front door.

They'd get a very unpleasant surprise if they managed to open the door.

He pulled out his phone and called Bob. "Eagle, I've got company."

"Shit, how many?"

"I count two by the front door." Mark frowned. "I'm going to take care of them and get the hell out of Dodge right away."

"Good. Reinforcements are on the way. I'll inform Whittaker and take it from there, Domino."

"Right." Mark hung up.

Backup was coming, but the field office was fifteen minutes away. He didn't have the luxury of waiting. He had to take them out before they could harm Serena or Sammy. Damn Whittaker for his cost-cutting campaign. If two of them were on duty, he wouldn't be in the position of pushing back intruders alone.

He rushed to the back door and looked out. It was clear. He disabled the alarm, slipped out, and reset it behind him so Serena and Sammy would know if anyone entered. Keeping to the shadows, he walked around the house to the carport.

The intruders, dressed in ragged jeans and tee shirts, seemed to be arguing as one tried to jimmy the front door's lock. Grayson had to be scraping the bottom of the barrel when he hired these two bozos.

Mark crept behind his car and around behind them.

"Damn it, Scott, speed it up. Can't you get that damned door open?"

"A lot, you know. I got it now."

The other guy jerked the door open.

A flash knocked them both off their feet.

Mark rushed them in the confusion that followed.

The one named Scott grunted, rolled to his feet, and started shooting wildly.

The other guy took off running down the gravel road.

Wincing when a wild shot grazed his arm, Mark took steady aim, hitting Scott in the leg. He dropped like a stone. Spinning, Mark aimed at the fleeing man and fired two shots. The guy groaned, but kept going.

Mark couldn't pursue him and leave Serena and Sammy unguarded. Walking to the fallen man, he holstered his weapon, noting blood gushing from a hole in Scott's thigh. He whipped his handcuffs out and cuffed him to the porch railing. He didn't want to bring the scum into the house.

"Hey! Let go 'a me!" He tried to wriggle away. "I'm gonna sue you, asshole. I wasn't doin' nothin' wrong."

Tugging the guy's belt off, Mark slipped it above his bleeding wound, making a tourniquet. "Shut up and sit still if you don't want to bleed to death." He tightened the belt, listening to him groan. He stood. "That ought to hold you till the Feds get here."

A window siren went off, and a shot rang inside the house.

Mark's heart went cold as he sprang to his feet, drawing his weapon. Had Grayson pulled a diversion, sacrificing this cannon fodder so that he could sneak in the back door? He should have known.

"God Damn, it all."

He rushed through the front door. One glance at the circuit board told him someone had opened Serena's window.

He raced down the dark hall and tore open her door.

Moonlight spilled through the open window, illuminating Serena's still shape in the middle of her bed. She had the covers pulled up.

"Serena, are you okay?"

There was no reply. She didn't even flinch. He smelled the scent of gunpowder and saw the bullet hole in the bedspread. A seething pit of despair opened inside his stomach.

God, she was hit, and it was his fault. But it might not be too late.

He reached out for her, his hand shaking, and tore back the covers. She wasn't there. Pillows had been piled up, imitating her shape under the blankets.

He let out a sigh of relief as his heart started beating again. Thank God. She must be hiding out in the hole. He ran to the window, but Grayson's assassin was long gone. He shut the window and reset the alarm.

He picked up her suitcase and rushed down the hall, stopping to grab Sammy's suitcase from his unoccupied room. He had to give her full marks for sticking to the escape plan. Her quick reaction in the face of fire was impressive. Grabbing Sammy's Spiderman figure off the dresser, he turned and raced to the broom closet, tore open the door, and pulled down the mop hook on the wall. The secret panel swung silently open.

Serena stood in the secret room, her broom in her hands, ready to strike, Sammy behind her, peeking out at him. It almost made him smile.

"Good work, you two." He crouched in front of Sammy, handing him Spiderman.

"Thought you might need this."

Sammy clutched it to him. "Thank you."

"You're welcome." Mark gave the kid what he hoped was a reassuring smile and then turned to look at Serena. The echo of fear was in her eyes, along with a grim determination. She was a fighter. "You okay?"

"I am now."

He took a step closer. "Come on. We've got to get going."

She bit her lip, glancing at his drawn gun. "What happened? I heard a—"

"Our security's been breached. We have to go now."

"Okay." She nodded and took Sammy's hand. "Lead the way, Agent Riley."

He turned and led them out of the safe room. When they reached the living room, he grabbed his laptop and led them to the front door.

Serena hesitated. "Aren't we going to wait for help?"

"No. This place isn't secure, and I'm not taking any chances." He crouched to Sammy's eye level. "You okay, pal?"

Sammy looked at the gun in his hand. "Will you shoot the bad guys if they bother us?"

Mark nodded. "Yes, I will."

"Good."

Mark smiled to reassure the boy, then ruffled his hair and stood to look at Serena. "My car's in the carport. We'll go out the back door. I'll stay on the outside to cover you."

She hesitated. "I don't want you hurt, either."

"I'll be fine." He disabled the back door alarm, opened it, and reset it. A quick scan told him the area looked clear. Still, he wasn't taking any chances. He motioned for Serena and Sammy to come out and stood between them and the yard. They'd have to go through him first.

He led them to the car and opened the driver's side door, pushing Serena into the front. She slid over. He helped Sammy in the back. "Buckle your seatbelt, pal."

He backed down the driveway.

Scott was still cuffed to the railing and swearing a blue streak.

"Who's that man?" Sammy gasped. "He said the 'F' word."

Mark cast a quelling look at Scott, who shut up in response. "A bad guy."

"Did you shoot him?" Sammy asked, intrigued.

"Yes, I did." He winced when Serena stiffened beside him. He should have known she'd react that way. It probably confirmed the violent, macho tendencies she claimed he possessed.

"Good." Sammy leaned back, relaxed.

Mark almost smiled. At least the kid appreciated his firearm skills.

Driving down the gravel road, he kept the headlights off until he turned onto the highway. Several agency cars drove past him toward the house, but he kept going. They could take care of Scott. Bob would smooth over the rest. Mark and his subjects would make a clean getaway.

Serena perched stiffly in the passenger seat, terrified. She kept a wary eye out for danger as Mark sped down the dark lane with the headlights off. They were driving bat-blind for a reason, she told herself. He thought someone was after them.

She looked over her shoulder, but didn't see anyone. Were they in the clear, or were Grayson's thugs lying in wait? Chilled by the possibility, she slanted a glance at Mark.

He drove with a single-minded intensity that was reassuring. His instincts were keen, and she implicitly trusted his decision to pull them out. She'd been impressed by his warrior's prowess tonight. The fact that he made Sammy feel safe was the icing on the cake.

He cut off the gravel road and bounced them onto the two-lane highway. She squealed at the unexpected action, bumping shoulders with him. "Sorry," she stated, sitting back. She turned to look at Sammy. "You okay back there?"

"I'm fine, Mom. That was fun, Mark. Do it again."

"Maybe later, kid." He grinned and switched on the headlights.

At her son's sparkling eyes, she let out a sigh of relief. Thanks to Mark, Sammy was a bit over-stimulated, but he felt secure. Although she didn't like guns, she was thankful to have Mark nearby. They owed him their lives. Thank heavens Sammy was looking at this as an adventure. She cast another glance back at him. He looked sleepy, but not alarmed, for which she was grateful.

"Try to get a little sleep, son."

He yawned. "I'm not tired, Mom." His eyes drifted shut.

Now that Sammy knew everything was normal, he was fighting to stay awake.

Smiling, she turned and sat back against her seat. She buckled her seatbelt and turned to look at Mark. Had he known there might be a need to flee? His overheard discussion with Bob came back to her. Is this the emergency egress they'd been discussing? She could barely grasp all that had just happened, but she felt Mark was ready for it. Why hadn't he shared the information with her? She'd have been prepared, too. As it was, they'd gotten away by the skin of their teeth. FBI code or not, it hadn't been fair to keep her in the dark.

Recalling the evening's terrifying events, she tried to sort them out in her mind. First, Mark had come into her room, making his rounds. Lying there in front of him, knowing he was admiring her shape under the sheets, had unsettled her. She'd just gotten back to sleep when the explosion jolted her. It had sent her scurrying from her bed. An instinct made her stuff her pillows under the covers, making it look like she was still sleeping.

Then she'd run down the hall to Sammy's room. He was wide awake, his eyes wide as saucers. He'd pushed back the covers on her approach and climbed out of bed, asking, "Mom, what was that?"

"Shh," she'd replied, reaching for his hand. "Time to play hide and seek."

He nodded, suddenly seeming old for his years, and quietly followed her.

They were slipping into the safe room when she'd heard a siren go off, followed by a bang. The echo and smell reminded her of Rupert's killing. She instantly guessed it was gunfire. She'd grabbed the broom off its hanger and quickly shut the door behind them. Pushing Sammy behind her, she stood guard, waiting for Mark to save them.

And he had. Serena looked at him now, seeing him in a new light. While he might be autocratic at times, the violence that went with his job had its purpose, to serve and protect. His jaw was set in a firm line, his grip tight on the steering wheel.

Then, she noticed a dark stain on his hand. Was it dirt? Squinting at it in the dashboard light, she realized with horror it was blood. She visually traced the hole in his white shirtsleeve to a red rivulet that traveled down his arm to the drying pool of blood on his hand. "Oh, my God, Mark. You were shot."

"It's just a scrape. I'll live." He looked out the rearview mirror and then apprehensively at her. "Aren't you going to yell at me?"

She was surprised by his question. Did he worry about her reaction? "You picked a fine time to worry about that, Agent Riley. Why don't we save the chewing out for later? First, we've got to get you patched up."

His mouth kicked up in a startled half-smile. "There's a flashlight and a first aid kit in the glove compartment."

From his astonished tone, she realized he'd been expecting her to give him hell. She wasn't going to. As far as she was concerned, he'd done a hero's work tonight.

She got out the kit and then helped roll up his sleeve. Aiming the flashlight at his arm, she got a graphic view of his gunshot wound. The bullet had made a raw groove in his forearm. It was deep and bloody. A trickle of fresh blood oozed out of it as she inspected. Her stomach clenched.

"It looks deep, Mark. You need stitches and antibiotics."

"We can't. Put some pressure on it with a gauze pad and patch it up as best you can. That'll have to do for now."

Was he out of his head? He needed more than a little first aid.

She frowned at him. "But we need to go to the ER."

"We can't. Do it."

Thoughts of blood loss and infection ran through her mind, but she had no other choice. He would sacrifice his arm, and maybe his life, for them. She grabbed several gauze squares and pressed them tight against the gaping wound.

His arm tightened, stiffening under the pressure she applied. It must hurt like hell, but he didn't make a sound.

She winced for him in sympathy. After a few minutes, she let up a bit, not wanting to cut off his circulation completely. Cautiously peeling back the gauze, she realized the bleeding had stopped.

"I think that helped. The bleeding is under control now."

He nodded. "Good job. Now slap some tape on it, and it'll do for now."

She put on fresh gauze and taped it. Sitting back, she let out a weary breath.

What a mess. Mark, her protector, was wounded, and she and Sammy were fleeing for their lives. She looked out at the lonely country road they were speeding down. All she knew was that they were heading north and out of danger, she hoped.

"Where are we going?"

"Someplace safe."

That's what they'd said about the safe house, and look at what had happened. Disaster. It was out of her control, and all she could do was go along for the ride. She leaned her head back on the headrest, closing her eyes. She trusted Mark's expertise despite the terror she'd just been through. After all, he'd gotten them out alive. He'd been the one alert to the possibility that their cover was blown. Not his superiors.

No, she'd stick with him. Still, she couldn't help wondering if a safe sanctuary was actually out there. "Is there any such place?"

"Stick with me, and we'll find it."

She recalled the gunshot she'd thought she heard inside the house. How close had she come to death? She couldn't help wondering. "Did they shoot at my room?"

"Sure did. Nailed your pillow good."

She guessed as much, but it hurt to acknowledge they were trying to kill her. "Then they think I'm dead."

"Maybe, but we can't take it for granted. Grayson doesn't hire dummies unless he's using them for bait. The assassin might have noticed you didn't cry out or move."

"Oh, I see." And here she thought she'd been so clever padding the bed with pillows.

"Not that I'm knocking your resourcefulness. You displayed quick thinking getting to the hole that quickly. I'm impressed."

"Thanks." At least she'd proved she could keep calm in a crisis. It was a small victory at best.

Hours later, Mark turned onto Rural Route 12, heading north toward the Riley Brothers fishing hole. His arm throbbed with each movement, and he felt a warm trickle as his wound reopened repeatedly. His head swam from the blood loss, but he couldn't stop. He was too close to the sanctuary.

The good thing was he was alive, and so were his charges. Now to make it to the cabin, he could heal and take care of them. He knew the safe house invasion was child's play next to the trouble they would likely meet on the way to court. They needed this quiet time so he could come up with Plan B.

He cast an intrigued glance at Serena as she slept. Looking angelic in her white nightgown, she touched him as no other woman ever had. She hadn't gone hysterical on him as most civilians would.

AIC Whittaker would have the crime scene secured by now. He'd be pissed Mark had stepped outside normal channels, taking his charges away. He didn't give a shit. Hopefully, Scott would sing his guts out. And why shouldn't he? He was undoubtedly some two-bit con, hired for last night's caper. He was meaningless to Grayson and just as expendable. There'd be no high-powered lawyer to bail him out. It would be another nail in Grayson's coffin. He slipped his turned-off cell phone out of his belt hook and tossed it in the glove compartment, preferring to remain incommunicado for the moment.

Turning off on a gravel road, he headed deep into the north woods of Wisconsin. Only a handful of people knew about his old family cabin. It was a derelict old shack he and his brothers coveted. Perfect for fishing, poker, and getting away from the women at his parents' luxurious summer home, just an hour away. He could get backup there if needed. Three of his brothers were in law enforcement, and his dad was a retired cop. The agency didn't know about the place, which made it a doubly secure location to hole up.

Rustling came from the backseat, and he turned to look at Sammy, who was waking up, rubbing his eyes. He stretched, his Spiderman pajamas hiking up, baring his tummy. Last night, the kid had been braver than some rookie agents he could name.

"Hey, pal."

"Hi, Mark. Mom, where are we going?"

"Shh, don't wake her." The woman needed her sleep. She'd been magnificent, as well. They were two of a kind. Mark only hoped he'd be able to make good on his promise to find her father. "We're heading up to a cabin to go fishing. Doesn't that sound like fun?"

"Fishing? For real?"

He shook off the exhaustion curling around him. It was from the blood loss, and he could control it. He looked back and smiled, tickled by the boy's excitement.

"For real."

"That's just wizard. My grandpa was going to take me some time, but we didn't go yet."

He nodded, his ears ringing a little. Only five miles to go, and he could make it. The cold realities of life wanted to intrude, but he pushed them back for the moment, concentrating on Sammy's gap-toothed grin. If he could show the kid a good time and make him forget about danger, why not.

"Well, now you'll get to practice, so you'll be terrific when you two go."

Serena stirred. She opened her eyes and blinked, looking out at the tall trees and thick forest. "Good grief, you've taken us to Paul Bunyan territory."

"Close," he murmured in agreement, gazing up at the sheltering pines. They never failed to restore his serenity.

"Mom," Sammy shouted from the backseat. "Mark's gonna take me fishing."

"He is?" She turned an inquisitive glance on Mark.

He nodded, pulling into the rutted drive of the old, dilapidated cabin. "Welcome to our new safe house and fishing hole."

She glanced at the sagging tarpaper shack and her jaw dropped.

He stifled a chuckle. She wasn't expecting La Casa Riley.

"Safe? I don't think so. It looks like it's about to collapse."

"Nah, it's sturdier than it looks." He grinned and turned off the engine.

Serena got out of the car and glanced at the cabin warily. "Come on, Sammy, let's go check it out." Holding his hand, she picked her way toward the place, lifting her long nightgown so it wouldn't drag the dusty ground.

Mark led the way, reaching above the door to retrieve the key. "Right where I left it."

She looked at the rusty key in his hand. "You've got to be kidding. A lawman that leaves his key in plain sight?"

He shrugged. "Who's going to try breaking into this?"

"You've got a point there." She smiled. "Any burglar worth his salt would pass this baby up."

The door opened with a creak. She peered into the dingy cabin.

Mark joined her in the doorway. "I know it's not exactly the Ritz."

Gazing at the sunlight trickling through the filthy windows, she had to admit, that was an understatement. But it was safe and that was all that counted.

"Now all I have to do is get the perimeter alarms set up, and I can rest. I'll be right back."

She glanced at him, her eyes widening with alarm when she saw his arm. She leaned forward to whisper. "You're bleeding again, Mark."

"I know. You can fix me up after you get Sammy settled."

"But..."

He put a finger on her lips, silencing her. "Little ears. You and Sammy can check the place out."

She gave him a baleful look. "Do you have a similarly well-stocked medicine chest here?"

"In the bathroom."

She went to the bathroom, finding a bottle of rubbing alcohol, band-aids, calamine lotion, and aspirin. Talk about a lack of provisions. The alcohol and aspirins would help. She carried them to the kitchen, but Mark was gone.

She glanced at Sammy. "Where's Mark?"

"He told me to tell you to sit tight. He had work to do."

She rolled her eyes. He was taking his protector role too far. The man was hurt, for Pete's sake. "In the meantime, you and I should clean up this place."

"Okay, Mom."

She glanced at the two of them in their pajamas, but there was no point in putting on clean clothes until they got this place clean. She handed Sammy an old feather duster, pointing him toward the living room.

"Try that in there." She picked up the broom and started to work, trying to keep her mind off Mark. Where did he go? What would she do if he collapsed out there? It wouldn't help to sit and worry. She and Sammy worked together to scrape off the top layer of grime, and then she scrubbed the place down with pine cleaner and an old string mop.

Serena sniffed the pine-scented air, gazing at the clean but threadbare surroundings. "At least it's livable now."

"Look what I found, Mom! Fishing stuff."

Sammy carried a bamboo pole, and was covered with dirt and cobwebs. The aroma of mothballs wafted her way.

She gasped. "Sammy, what on earth did you get into?"

The door opened, and Mark came in. He leaned against the wall and smiled, looking at the pole in Sammy's hands. "I see you found old Betsy."

"I didn't know it had a name," Sammy replied, intrigued. "Is she yours?"

Mark nodded. "I'll make a present of her to you."

"Wow. Can I practice with old Betsy, Mom?"

"Let's scrape some of that dirt off you first." She turned to Mark, who looked worse than before. His arm had to be hurting badly. She opened the aspirin bottle and gave him two with a glass of water. "Take these and sit tight. I'll tend to your wound next."

He nodded. "There's a tub in the bathroom and some clean towels in the bedroom closet."

Serena ushered Sammy into the small bathroom, put in the stopper, and ran bathwater into the old claw foot tub. Someone in the past had put little starfish grippers on the bottom. "Okay, Sammy, bath time."

"Aw, do I have to?"

She picked a cobweb off his hair. "Yes, you have to. Don't worry, you won't melt." She smiled, thinking of all the times they'd had the same argument. She reached for his pajama buttons.

"Mom, I'm five now. I can do it myself."

"Okay, yell if you need me." She shut the bathroom door and walked back to the kitchen to deal with Mark. She'd noticed earlier his wound had reopened, and she was dreading what she might find. If it was terrible, he had to go to an ER. He had to give up some control and let her help, especially now that he was hurt. The chair he'd been sitting in was vacant. She wasn't surprised.

Hearing a click behind her, she turned to find him typing on the laptop he'd brought. She walked toward him as he sent an email and closed the case.

"Who were you writing?"

He sagged in his chair and looked at her. "Bob, I let him know we arrived safe and sound."

At last, help was on its way. Mark could get the medical help he so sorely needed.

"When is he coming to join us?"

"He's not."

She gaped at his tight expression in disbelief. Did he mean they were on their own? "But, why?"

He shrugged. "We decided early on to split up if someone invaded the safe house. We each have a separate role to play. Bob knows we're okay, but he doesn't know our location. It's safer that way and our call, even if others don't see it that way."

She could see from his tight jaw that something was amiss. It was heavier than being stranded or ticking off his boss. "What's wrong?"

He smiled at her. "Perceptive as ever, I see."

"I already gathered that your boss was angry that you left, but there's something else, isn't there?"

"Angry is putting it mildly. But you're right. Something unforeseen has happened. Scott's dead."

"Who?"

"My prisoner from last night."

She recalled the man shackled to the stair rail. He'd been alive and swearing a blue streak before Mark had silenced him. "But how? That's impossible. He was alive when we left."

"That's what I intend to find out. Somebody put two in his brain. Whittaker blamed me until ballistics showed the slugs didn't come from my gun."

"That's horrible. Somebody must have been lurking nearby when we left. Why would they shoot him?"

"To keep him from talking. Scott and his accomplice were a couple of dupes they hired off the streets. They were only there to act as a diversion while Grayson's real thugs got at you through the window. He was supposed to die. I only wounded him, so they returned to finish the job."

It made sense. She gazed at him, surprised he'd told her that much. Maybe he was finally learning to trust her. There was one way to find out.

"Tell me more about what happened back at the safe house to make us run."

He hesitated.

"And don't tell me it's none of my business. I overheard you and Bob discussing back-up plans. Too bad I didn't know it pertained to this case. I might have been prepared."

He nodded. "You're right. A new agent was trying to get assigned to this case. We were on our guard, wondering if he was after more than my job."

"Your job?"

He shrugged. "It was either a brash new agent trying to sprint up the chain of command or trouble. I, being the cautious sort, decided it was trouble. Then, last night, as I was making my patrol, it happened."

"What about the agent who was trying to take your place? Why don't they haul him in and settle the matter?"

"According to Bob's email, he's vanished."

She wasn't surprised. Grayson was one step ahead of them. She hoped the clues she'd uncovered would lead them to her father in time. "Does this mean I won't be able to participate in the search for my dad?"

"I told you at the safe house it was a remote possibility. Now, it's impossible."

"But if they get the mole, and if the area is hopping with agents, it should be okay."

"That's a lot of ifs. Keep in mind, the mole could have an accomplice, and he also could have spread the word to Grayson we'd found the copies."

"This stinks, Mark."

He nodded. "I know. Bob will let us know if they find your father. It's the best I can do under the circumstances."

It made sense, even if she didn't like it. She was fresh out of options. "Let me look at your arm."

"No time," he replied, slipping into the chair. "I need to get this set up before—"

"You pass out." She filled in the blank.

"I'm not going to pass out, Serena. I'm just a little tired."

"Right. Did you at least take the aspirins?"

"Yes, I took them."

She shook her head. "Your computer can wait until later. Let me take a look at your arm now."

He gave her a considering look, then relented. "Fine." He pushed the laptop aside and laid his arm on the desk.

She stepped close, her white cotton nightgown brushing against him, and started to peel back the bandage gently. It was soaked with fresh and dried blood and stuck tight to the wound. As she gently loosened the edges, it started to bleed again. Pulling away the bandage, she looked at the terrible damage and shuddered. It looked angry, the flesh around the bloody groove red and swollen.

"It's still bleeding, and I think it's infected. You need to go to the hospital."

"I can't. Just get the first aid kit out of the car."

She gazed at his determined expression and knew he wouldn't give in. Sighing with frustration, she ran outside and fetched it from the car. She sprinted back into the cabin and laid it on the counter, opening it wide. It was double-hinged, and now that she saw it in the daylight, she was surprised at all it contained.

"Give me one of those blue capsules," Mark stated, indicating a bottle on the left. "They're antibiotics."

She handed him one, feeling a bit more at ease. At least they could cope with infection, but that didn't help the bleeding. He still needed stitches.

"Take the rubbing alcohol and clean the wound."

She wadded up some gauze and soaked it in rubbing alcohol as he ordered. Biting her lip, she cleaned away all the crusted blood to reveal the oozing gash as he stifled a curse.

"This looks bad, Mark."

"I've had worse," he bit out, "you're going to have to sew it up, Serena."

"What?" She gaped at him, horrified.

"There's a needle and medical sutures in that sealed bag."

"I can't." Her toes curled into the clean linoleum as she stepped back a pace, nervous.

"You've got to, beautiful. I'm counting on you."

She couldn't let him down. Decision made, she went to the sink, washed her hands, and then doused them with alcohol. Opening the sealed packet, she picked up the needle with a fine, clear thread. With her stomach clenching, she approached the wound.

Could she do it? She had no choice.

Mark rested his arm on the desktop, giving her excellent access. Thank heaven Sammy was occupied in the bath. She wouldn't want him to see this.

"Are you ready?"

"Yes. Go ahead. Pretend I'm one of those bags you decorate. Just don't sew any flamingos on me."

His attempt at humor touched her. She winced as she slipped the needle into his flesh. He didn't cry out, but sweat beaded his face. She tried to work quickly, doing a blanket stitch and bringing the raw edges of the wound together. The bleeding slowed. Finishing the last stitch, she tied it off and snipped the thread. Only a few droplets of blood oozed out now.

She glanced at him. He was pale, but he hadn't passed out. "You okay?"

"I'll live. Put a bandage on it, will you?"

She bandaged his arm and then went to the cabinet to get the bottle of scotch she'd seen earlier. She poured Mark a hefty drink and handed it to him. "I thought you might like this."

"Thanks, I needed that. Why don't you go check on Sammy?"

Her stomach still queasy, she turned and headed for the bathroom, grateful for the escape. She heard splashing as she opened the bathroom door. Despite her ordeal, she couldn't help grinning when she found Sammy covered with shaving cream.

"What on earth?"

"Mom, I found some nifty stuff," he crowed, rubbing it into his hair until it stood on end.

"I see." She let out a laugh. "It's time to rinse off."

"Aw, do I have to?"

First, she couldn't get him into the tub, and now she couldn't get him out. She stifled a smile. "If you're not hungry for breakfast..."

"I'm starving."

"Then you'd better finish up. I'll lay clean clothes out for you."

"Okay."

She walked away as he sang an off-key rendition of "Splish Splash," an oldie her dad had taught him. A great singer, her son was not, but she wouldn't change a thing about him.

She went to the back bedroom, laid out Sammy's clothes, and changed into a sundress and sandals. At least she'd look presentable.

Sammy came down the hall wrapped in a faded towel.

"Your clothes are on the bed. Need any help?"

"Aw, Mom, I'm five years old now."

"Oops, I forgot again." Sammy had taken great pride in turning five, thrilled he was graduating from preschool to kindergarten. "I'll go cook breakfast, then. See you later."

"See ya." Serena smiled. *See ya, nifty,* and *wizard* were three of his favorite sayings.

She went into the kitchen. Mark had drained the glass of scotch she'd given him. His color was better, but he still wasn't back to full strength. A little food would help build him back up.

"How about I fix us some breakfast? Sammy will be starving when he gets in here."

"Sounds like a good idea. I could eat."

She nodded. They were all hungry, she realized when her stomach rumbled. She went to the cupboard to see what she could scrape together for breakfast. She opened the kitchen cupboard and pulled out several foil packets. She turned to look at Mark, who was setting up equipment in the living room.

"What's this?"

"Freeze-dried dinners. They're not half bad."

She looked at the tall stack of packets and full canned goods shelf. "What were you expecting, a siege?"

He smiled. "Not exactly. My brothers and I don't like to cook. The shack is our hideaway from the women back at my parents' fancy summer cabin. We like them because they keep forever. I'll go into town tomorrow for fresh stuff."

She took out several packets of apple oats, a can of evaporated milk, and coffee. It would do. Rustling up a battered saucepan and stovetop coffee pot, she set to work. Dropping the oats into simmering water, she took an appreciative sniff. It smelled good. Then she mixed up the milk, adding a drop of vanilla extract to disguise the canned taste, then popped it into the fridge to chill. Next, she turned to the old-fashioned coffeepot. She wasn't quite sure how to work it, but Mark needed a bracing cup of coffee, and so did she. She scooped the grounds into the pot and set it on the back burner to boil.

Sammy came walking out of the bedroom. "Okay, Mom, I'm ready to eat."

She glanced at him. Everything was buttoned, zipped, and shoes were on the right feet. Check. He hadn't combed his hair, but she'd tackle that later.

"Okay, tiger, breakfast is about ready. Have a seat, and I'll serve it up."

Sammy climbed into a chair at the dinette. He looked at Mark. "Hey, aren't you going to eat with us?"

"Sure thing, pal." Mark hoisted himself erect.

She noted the effort it took him, and was touched. He understood her need to shield Sammy from the truth. She smiled, pulling out a chair to slide into so he wouldn't have to use his arm.

"Thanks."

"No problem." She went to the fridge, set pitchers of orange drinks and milk on the table, and put hot bowls of oats in front of Sammy and Mark.

Sammy took a big drink of juice and looked at the bowl. "What's this stuff?"

"Oatmeal, it's good."

Sammy looked at it doubtfully.

"It's apple oatmeal, pal," Mark commented, adding with a wink, "It's just the thing for fishermen."

Sammy's eyes lit up, and he took a mouthful. "It's good."

"Told ya," she teased, using his favorite word. At his lopsided grin, her heart melted.

She poured two cups of the boiled coffee, thinking it resembled chocolate syrup, and carried them to the table. When Mark looked at it and grinned, she said, "Yup, it's my first time making coffee that way. Can't tell, huh?"

She took a sip and choked. It was terrible.

"Try diluting it," Mark said, dousing his with milk.

She did, and found it made the coffee tolerable. She kept an eagle eye on him, noting his color was improving. While he moved his arm stiffly, it didn't seem to be bleeding. The bandage was still white.

"So, did you get your things set?"

"Fishing things?" Sammy put in excitedly.

"No, just boring old electric things, pal. How about if we get to the fishing things tomorrow?"

"All the way 'til tomorrow?" Sammy asked, disappointed.

"Mark needs to get some sleep," she cut in, "maybe you and I can spend today getting ready."

Mark nodded. "A closet full of fishing equipment needs cleaning and sorting. Okay, pal?"

Sammy huffed out a disappointed breath. "Okay."

She couldn't have been prouder of her son. Some kids would have thrown a fit over a disappointment like that.

Mark stood. "Serena, before I turn in, I need to show you something."

She got up and followed him into the hallway, out of Sammy's earshot. Was his arm bothering him? She glanced at the bandage. "Is it your arm?"

He flexed it. "No. Thanks to you, it's a bit sore, but usable."

She reached out to touch his forehead. "You feel a bit warm to me. I want you to keep taking those antibiotics."

"Yes, nurse," he teased.

"I made up the twin beds in the back room. Go get some sleep."

"Before I do, I have something to teach you."

"What?"

"Come with me."

He led her to a tall, funny looking safe she'd noticed in one of the bedrooms. Intrigued, she watched him use a combination to open it. Did it contain some sophisticated electronic equipment? She frowned when she saw him pull out a hunting rifle and shells.

"I don't know the first thing about guns, Mark."

"I know. Normally, I wouldn't ask you to do this, but we're in a jam. Come out in the yard, and I'll teach you the basics."

"I don't want Sammy to see it. Besides, you should be in bed."

"We'll go out the back door, so he won't notice."

She hung back, hating even the sight of the deadly-looking rifle.

He walked to the back door and turned to look at her. "You must learn this to protect Sammy if something happens to me."

She didn't like the sound of that, but she was determined to protect her son. She followed him out to the backyard.

"Let me check on Sammy first." She peeked into the kitchen to see him halfway through his oatmeal. "Mom has to run a short errand outside. Stay there, okay?"

"Okay."

She backtracked to Mark. "I can give you five minutes, tops."

"That'll suffice." He led the way out the back door to the edge of the property, where bales of hay were stacked on wooden sawhorses.

He held the rifle. "This is how you load it." He loaded the weapon and handed it to her.

She stood there feeling distinctly nervous with the thing in her hands. She gritted her teeth, determined to get it over with quickly. He stepped up behind her, holding his arms around her to handle the gun.

"Okay, here's the safety. You release it by sliding this catch." He coaxed her fingers to do it. "When the safety is on, it won't fire. If you need to fire, release the catch, got it?"

She let out a shaky breath. "Okay, I've got it."

"All right, now I want you to aim at the bales and squeeze the trigger."

She squinted and did as he said. She was unprepared for the kickback that bruised her shoulder. "Ouch."

"You hit it. Good job, beautiful."

"Thanks." She thrust the gun back at him. "I should get back in and check on Sammy."

He turned and walked with her. "I'll give you the combination of the gun safe."

"Okay." She watched him demonstrate how to open the safe.

He turned to her. "I have perimeter alarms set. If anyone comes around while I'm sleeping, wake me. And if attacked, shoot first and ask questions later."

She only hoped it wouldn't come to that. "Okay."

He pressed a kiss to her hair before he stepped away. "Wake me at noon."

She sent Sammy off to brush his teeth and then cleared the table. Hopefully, she'd never have to use the shooting lesson he'd taught her. The thought of running into Grayson's minions was chilling. She trembled, thinking of the unnerving events of last night.

Mark opened his eyes and stretched, wincing at the twinge in his arm. He felt much better.

He rolled out of bed, reached for his pants, and frowned when he spotted the long shadows cast on the floor. It was way past noon. Why had Serena let him sleep so long?

He stopped in the bathroom, splashed water on his face, and went to the living room.

Serena and Sammy weren't there. The front door stood ajar. Where the hell were they? Had security been breached?

A glance at his control panel showed nothing. He dashed out the door.

Serena was pushing Sammy in the old tire swing. She waved.

He stepped off the porch, his pulse returning to near normal. "Why didn't you wake me?" he grumbled.

"You needed to catch up on your sleep. Besides, nothing happened. Not even a deer passed by."

"You shouldn't be exposing yourself like this."

"Exposing myself? Agent Riley, you'll make me blush. Who's going to see me, Bambi?"

He frowned. "Very funny. You're supposed to be inside listening for the beep."

"I figured I could hear it from out here. I left the door open."

"I noticed."

"I defy you to keep a five-year-old occupied sitting around in a dusty old cabin with no toys and a few puzzles."

He had to give her that. There was very little chance of anyone seeing them in this remote location. He walked up to the swing. "I used to swing on this myself when I was a kid." He gave Sammy a push.

Serena stepped aside. "You did?"

"Having trouble picturing me as a kid?" He smiled.

"Kind of. It doesn't fit in with your oh-so-serious Agent Riley persona."

"Ask my mom, and she'd say I was all boy. Into things from morning to night."

"What kind of things?" Sammy asked.

She laughed. "Don't give Sammy ideas."

They went inside to eat dinner. Beef stew and biscuits. Serena gave Mark a double portion, seeing as he'd slept through lunch. She'd thought the recuperative power of sleep was more important.

She looked at Mark and Sammy. It was almost like they were a family. It was a nice feeling.

Mark took an appreciated sniff. "Smells great, Serena."

She liked the sound of her name on his lips, how he lingered over the sound. She gazed at him, enamored, then looked at her bowl.

She had fallen for him hard. But he didn't reciprocate. His FBI code wouldn't let him.

After supper, she started to put the dishes in the sink.

"Can I go back out and play, Mom?"

She glanced at Mark. "Can we?"

He smiled. "I suppose it's okay. I'll take him if you like."

"Thanks. I'll do the dishes."

"No problem." He and Sammy headed outside.

She washed the same plate twice, watching them through the window. Mark was so good with Sammy. She could picture him at her boy's age, getting into everything.

She looked away. It was stupid to be mooning over a man she couldn't have. Maybe when this was all over, she might have a chance with him, but until then, he was off limits.

Sammy's eyes were at half-mast as he followed Mark onto the porch. "Aw. Do I have to go to bed, Mom?"

"Yes. It's past your bedtime, kiddo."

Mark smiled at the kid who had wormed his way into his heart. "You and I have a fishing date in the morning, and you need to rest up for it."

"Fishing. You bet." Sammy ran into the house.

"I think you said the magic word." Serena smiled. "Come on. We've got a date with the sandman."

"I'll be chopping some firewood if you two need me. We might need to fire up the wood stove if the temperatures drop tonight."

"Okay." She doubted it would get that cold, but she was glad he'd thought of it. Ushering Sammy into the cabin, she steered him toward the back bedroom, where she'd already laid out his pajamas and toothbrush. After tucking him in, she sat down on the edge of the bed to hear his prayers. Despite his protests that he wasn't sleepy, she knew he had to be exhausted after last night. She was exhausted herself.

Lingering by his side, she watched him closely as his eyes drifted shut, and he seemed to fall instantly asleep. The poor kid had been through so much. Would he have bad dreams? She wanted to be there for him if he did. Gentle snoring came from the bed as he slept, oblivious to her worries. Sitting there fretting, she noted not even the sound of Mark chopping wood outside woke him up.

Satisfied, she got up and walked out of the bedroom, leaving the door wide open in case he should call out to her. It was good she was more affected by the danger than her child. She made her way out to the porch to the tune of Mark chopping wood. He had a log up on a stand, splitting it for kindling. She sat on the porch swing and watched him work, fascinated. He turned his back to her and stripped off his shirt. His gun was sitting within arm's reach.

Even the sight of his weapon couldn't tear her focus off his rippling muscles as he labored. She gulped. It was like a private Chippendale show all to herself. She could no longer deny her growing feelings for him, even if she didn't think they would lead anywhere.

Finishing the stack of wood, he went to the pump, working it to draw water. He splashed it over his face and shoulders, slicking his hands down his body to brush the droplets away. Sunlight glistened off the muscled planes of his tanned body. He was like a bronze statue of David, without the fig leaf. She couldn't help speculating about what his faded jeans concealed.

He turned toward her then. Their eyes locked as his attention focused on her, and her face heated. She'd practically been ogling the man. Did he know what she'd been thinking? Fantasizing? The knowing look in his eye told her yes. He walked toward her, his mouth curving in a warm smile.

She fanned her overly warm face. Was he feeling the same sensual pull? She was tongue-tied as he casually picked up his shirt and gun, then strolled up to the porch. He didn't bother to put on his shirt as he moved toward her. She couldn't tear her eyes away.

He stopped with his foot on the porch step. "Hot night, isn't it?"

Trying to focus on his twinkling eyes instead of his delectable body, she stammered. "Um, and yes. I guess it is."

He smiled and stepped up to the porch. "Nice night to sit out and catch the breeze."

"That's what I was doing."

"I see." He set his gun down on the railing and slipped his shirt on. "Mind if I join you?"

Watching him openly now, she was almost disappointed he'd covered up. That was, until the shirt stuck to his damp body, conforming to his muscular shape. Damn, that was almost more tantalizing.

"Why not? There's not much else to do for entertainment." Her face heated anew at the unintended double entendre.

He eased onto the swing beside her. It creaked, swinging back a bit. "Ah, that feels good."

"What?"

"Just to sit and relax."

Yeah, he had been through a lot. He'd had to spring into action last night and was wounded. That series of events had taken its toll, no doubt. "You must be exhausted. You haven't had much sleep lately."

He shrugged. "I'm used to going on light sleep, but I do admit, it's catching up with me." He rolled his neck.

"Sore?"

"Just a little kink, and my arm itches. It's healing nicely, thanks to you."

She reached out to rub his neck.

"Ah, Serena, that feels like heaven. You've got an angel's touch."

"Why thank you, sir." She turned and rubbed harder, kneading his tight muscles, feeling them loosen. "You should try yoga. It works for me."

"I'm not into all that mystical mumbo jumbo."

"Now, who's got a closed mind?" she teased.

"Guilty as charged. Okay, teacher, why don't you teach me some?"

"Right, let's try a little meditation."

"Okay."

"Close your eyes."

He peered at her through his eyelashes.

"That's cheating. All the way."

They swept shut.

"Okay, now visualize a tranquil setting. Your perfect Eden."

"What's yours?"

"Nosy, aren't you?"

"Teacher, don't be so judgmental. I learn best by example."

"Fine. Mine's a tropical sunset. I've been saving up to take Sammy to the Caribbean. Someday, we'll go."

"Pretty. Want to know what mine is?"

"No."

"This swing with you."

"What a sweet talker."

"Hey, my momma didn't raise any fools."

"We're veering off the subject. Picture your Eden and try to relax. Let everything go, and breathe deeply from the diaphragm." She put her hand on his middle, feeling it expand as he complied. His skin was so warm and pliant under her palm. She itched to run it down his hair-roughened chest to where it whorled around his navel and disappeared into his pants. Snapping back to reality, she murmured, "Very good."

"Umm," he rumbled.

She snatched back her hand. The tremor made her tingle. "Okay, now you need to pick a mantra."

"A what?"

"A mantra. A secret phrase that will help you relax, go deeper into the zone."

"Give me one."

"No. It doesn't work that way. You have to pick your own."

"What's yours?"

She wasn't going to reveal hers. Happily-ever-after might scare him because he was commitment-phobic, or he'd think it was sappy. "I'm not telling."

"Spoilsport."

"Tough rocks. Pick one."

"Alright."

"Got it? Okay, repeat it to yourself silently, three times."

She watched him go through the process. The sharp grooves in his face smoothed out, some fierceness left his features, and his shoulders relaxed. Good, she was glad she could help him this little bit.

A few minutes later, his eyes opened, and he turned her way.

"Feel better?"

"Yeah, I think I do. I'm amazed."

"I'm glad." She reached out to touch his arm.

He bent toward her.

They kissed. He pulled her to him, sliding her across his lap. The swing creaked in protest. She didn't care if it collapsed. She was hungry for this kiss.

His mouth was hot and demanding as it slanted across hers. She leaned into him, the muscles rippling in his chest. She purred, kneading her fingers into his hot flesh.

When they broke apart, she sagged against him, gasping for breath. His heart thundering below her ear was proof he'd been just as affected.

He tightened under her again, but for a different reason. He was aroused, but he wasn't acting on it. That, more than anything, opened her heart to him.

"Yummy."

"What?"

"You. I think you've got me under some spell."

"That's me, a master magician."

Chapter Eight

Serena rolled over in the twin bed. Mark's hushed voice drifting from the kitchen woke her.

"Shh, Sammy. Keep it down a little. Your mom needs her sleep."

"Whatcha makin'?"

"How about some more of that apple oatmeal?"

"Yum."

She smiled. They were making breakfast. How sweet. She rolled over and winced. She still felt the pangs from an exciting night on the swing. Magic, indeed. She and Mark had spent half of the night on the swing. Talking and kissing, then talking some more. She felt closer to him, opening up, telling him about her past and her disastrous first marriage.

He told her about his childhood growing up as the son of a cop. Mark had three brothers and two sisters, all of whom had gone into government service—an ATF agent, a police chief, a CIA analyst, a field agent, and a small-town mayor. They sounded like quite a family, and she would enjoy meeting them when this ordeal was over.

Much as they'd shared, they hadn't talked about the future. He hadn't made any promises, and she hadn't asked for them. She'd told herself to be satisfied with what she had. Though they hadn't consummated their relationship, she was confident they were moving towards it. If it happened, she wouldn't regret it, come what may.

At last, she felt like a complete woman. He had healed that little hole in her heart, it seemed. Who would have expected her robot-turned-Prince Charming to have such an effect on her?

She'd crawled into the twin bed next to Sammy's in the wee hours of the morning. Mark had gone to sleep in the loft.

A tap came on the bedroom door.

Mark opened the door. "Time to wake up, Sleeping Beauty. Sammy and I have breakfast ready."

He wore tan shorts instead of his usual suit and an army green T-shirt. He also had on a short-sleeved unbuttoned over-shirt, probably to keep his holster hidden in deference to her worries about Sammy seeing it.

"I'm awake." She sat up and pulled back the covers.

"No, stay put." He grinned. "Sammy's got a surprise for you." He opened the door wider.

Sammy walked in carrying a tray. "This is for you, Mom."

"For me?" She grinned.

Mark fluffed the pillows behind her and helped Sammy place the tray on her lap. "That's right, Sammy and I cooked it special. Didn't we, pal?"

"That's right. I even picked you some flowers."

She looked at the dandelions in a juice glass and smiled. "They're beautiful. Thank you both."

Sammy's grin was crooked, and Mark's carried secret passion.

She watched them leave, and tears of happiness misted her eyes. She was one lucky woman.

Eating all of her oats, she hoped to build up her strength. It was amazing she didn't feel more tired after her partly sleepless night. Maybe she could live on love.

The coffee was much better than the muck she'd made yesterday. Mark must have boiled coffee down to a science.

They were busy doing the dishes when she carried her tray to the kitchen ten minutes later. "I see you've taken over KP duty."

Mark turned to smile at her. "It's my turn. You did them yesterday."

"In that case, I'll shower and get dressed."

"Wear something light. It's going to be hot."

She hopped into the shower and helped herself to some bath gel with a jasmine scent. Must belong to one of his sisters, she hoped. She didn't like the thought he might bring other women here.

She dried off, changed into pink shorts and a white T-shirt, and slipped on some sandals. She brushed her hair, taming the ringlets with styling gel some female had left behind, then she spread on sunscreen and cherry lip-gloss.

Did she look much different from the love-starved woman she'd been before? There was something in her smile, a new awareness of her femininity, and a twinkle in her eye. She felt free. Her lips seemed even fuller than usual, maybe still swollen from their kisses.

Her breasts, always full, now seemed more sensitized, and that wasn't the only tender spot. From what she'd experienced, she had a lot to look forward to. She rolled her eyes at her imaginings and headed for the door.

She wasn't a teenager who should be mooning over her dream date. She was a mature woman with responsibilities. What would the school board say if they knew? Necking in public with a man was frowned upon. It was pretty scandalous, she thought with a grin.

She walked into the deserted kitchen. Where were they? She looked through the window and saw her guys digging in the yard.

She walked onto the porch. "What are you two looking for, gold?"

Mark overturned his shovel. "No, worms."

"Yeah, look, Mom." Sammy held up a wiggly pink worm.

"Yuck." She wrinkled her nose.

"They're good. We're gonna use 'em for bait, right Mark?"

"Right." Mark waited for Sammy to put the worm inside an old coffee can and put the cap on. He looked up at her, his appreciative gaze lingering. "You look very nice, Serena."

"Thanks."

He picked up the can. "I'll get the gear ready. How about fixing us a few cold drinks to take along? There's a cooler under the sink."

"Okay." She went back in and found the cooler. When she opened it, a fishy smell wafted. One of his brothers might have used it as a bait box. She put it in the sink and scrubbed it with plenty of soap and hot water. After it was dried, she filled it with ice, soft drinks, and several boxes of animal crackers. That should keep her set for fishing this morning.

"Ready, Mom?"

She turned to look at Sammy standing beside her and grabbed the bottle of sunscreen. "In a minute. First, we need to put some of this sunscreen on you."

"I can do it."

She let him put sunscreen on his arms, legs, and face. She then got his ears and the back of his neck. "That should do for now."

She tucked the sunscreen into the bag with her sunglasses and one of the paperbacks from the bookshelf. She'd read and sit by her fishermen. After the attack at the safe house, she didn't relish letting either of them out of her sight.

"Come on, then." Sammy tugged on her hand.

She picked up the cooler and tote bag, then followed him out. She stepped off the porch.

Mark stood on the walk, fishing gear in hand. He had several fishing poles tucked against his shoulder. "Ready?"

"We're ready," Sammy replied, letting go of Serena's hand and running down by Mark.

She walked down the steps. "I'm ready. I brought along sunscreen."

"Good thinking." He turned and started down the path. "Okay, troops, let's move out."

Sammy marched behind him.

Serena fell in line, grinning at Sammy's intent expression. She could see he was drinking in every detail. He was so excited, she half-expected his ears to start wiggling.

This pristine wilderness was so different from their home in the city. As they walked through a field of wildflowers toward the lake, she thought about how right it was here. Even though tragic circumstances had brought them here, she was glad they'd come.

She followed Sammy onto the large wooden dock with a long bench on one side. The lake was so beautiful, calm, and serene. The tension she'd carried melted away as she gazed at it.

Mark set his fishing gear down and reached for the cooler. "Let me help you with that."

"Thanks." She smiled at him, appreciating his attentive behavior. She set her tote on the bench.

"Okay, Mark, I'm ready," Sammy announced.

"Alright, let's get old Betsy." Mark reached for the cane pole and handed it to Sammy. "Got it."

"Okay, the first thing we have to do is put on the bait."

"Worms?"

"Right." Mark opened the coffee can and pulled out a worm. "Okay, this is how you put it on the hook."

"Gross," Sammy noted, intrigued.

Serena wrinkled her nose and looked away. "Yuck."

Mark chuckled. "Next comes the tricky part. Casting."

He walked behind Sammy and put his hands on the pole, too. "Okay, we'll flick it back and forth, then cast."

"Like this?" Sammy followed the motion Mark started.

"Perfect."

They cast Sammy's line. It whizzed out and plopped into the water. "Good job. Okay, now you can take it easy and wait for a bite. Your bobber will get tugged down if you get anything."

"Okay." Sammy sat on the edge of the dock, swinging his legs back and forth.

"Now, it's your turn," Mark stated, turning to her.

"Me?" She put down the western she'd started reading.

"Yes, you." He grinned.

"I thought I'd just read."

"That's no good. You need to learn to take Sammy if I'm not around."

"Yeah, Mom. We dug extra worms for you."

"Worms?"

"Don't worry, beautiful. I'll provide you with a genuine plastic one." Mark went to the tackle box and pulled out a plastic worm. He added it to the hook of a metal pole and handed it to her.

She took it, determined to be a good sport, even though she thought fishing was as exciting as watching paint dry.

Mark stepped behind her. "Okay, I'll teach you how to cast." He stepped up close, his arms around her, his hands touching hers on the pole.

She leaned into him. What had been educational with Sammy was now enticing to her. Her senses quickened.

"You smell great, beautiful," he whispered.

"Jasmine bath gel," she murmured.

"What are you guys waiting for?" Sammy looked at them.

Mark cleared his throat and backed away. He started to move the pole. "This is how you wind, then cast." They cast it several yards past Sammy's.

"Thanks." Serena took her pole to the far end of the bench to avoid temptation, noting the rueful look on Mark's face. It was no time to introduce Sammy to the new man in her life. When this was all over would be the proper time.

"No problem." Mark cast his line past Serena's and sat by Sammy on the edge of the dock. "Any nibbles?"

"Not yet."

Serena gazed warmly at the two of them. Anyone would think they were father and son. Mark would make a great dad someday. Despite his tension when he'd first met Sammy, he had a natural rapport with her son. They were both changing for the better.

Something tugged at her. She looked at her bobber going up and down, the pole jerking in her hand. She gasped, her eyes wide. "I think I've got something."

Mark jumped up. "Coming."

She started to reel in the line.

"Here, I've got it." Mark scooped it up in the net. "It's a beauty, a good-sized lake trout. Looks like fish for lunch."

"Good job, Mom."

"Thanks, Son." She smiled at Sammy's praise.

Mark put the fish in the creel. "How about something cold to drink, celebrating the first fish caught?"

"Yeah," Sammy replied.

"Sounds good. I'm thirsty." She took the cola he handed her and smiled. "I'm up one to nothing on you, Mark."

"Beginner's luck," he stated with a grin. He turned to hand Sammy his drink. "Here you go, pal."

"Thanks." Sammy guzzled down a thirsty swallow. "Whoa, I think I got something, too."

"I'm on it." Mark helped him reel it in, then netted it. "Wow, two for two. A nice perch."

"Wow!" Sammy stood and gave Mark a high five.

"Good work." She beamed, thrilled for him.

"Another lucky beginner," Mark joked. "I think that calls for some animal crackers." He looked at her.

She smiled and pulled two boxes out of the cooler. "Here you go."

"Hey, I think I've finally got a bite." Mark reeled in his line.

"You caught a stick." Sammy's eyes widened.

"Yup, a genuine piece of driftwood."

"Wow." Sammy laughed.

"I'll add it to my collection," he replied, chuckling, pointing to a pile on the bank.

"We could start a bonfire," she joked.

"I tend to catch the stuff."

An hour later, Mark looked over at Sammy. The kid was beginning to get fidgety. "I think you've caught your limit for today."

"Me, too." He handed Mark old Betsy and turned to Serena. "Can I go swimming, Mom?"

She looked at the beach a few yards away and then at Mark. "Is it safe?"

"Sure, he should be fine. We have a nice sandy beach without any drop-offs." He turned to Sammy. "Stay in the marked area, okay, pal?"

"Will do," Sammy replied, tugging off his shoes and socks. "Okay, Mom?"

"Fine, take off your T-shirt and cutoffs. You can swim in your briefs."

"My Spiderman swimsuit," Sammy stated, obviously a bit embarrassed.

"Right."

Sammy quickly stripped to his briefs and ran down to the beach. He waded out until he was knee-deep and turned to grin at them. "It's kind of cold."

Mark smiled at his reaction. "It's a northern spring-fed lake, son. It's supposed to be cold."

"Cool! I'm getting used to it," Sammy stated, dipping underwater.

"Come out if you get too cold," Serena cautioned.

Mark turned to look at her. She was a great mom, allowing her son the freedom to try things while setting clear boundaries. "Don't worry, I spent plenty of summer days there and never froze to death."

"Thanks for the reassurance. Sammy's had swimming lessons, so I know he'll be fine. He and I started baby swim classes when he was six months old."

"Sounds like fun."

"It was. Picture of a pool full of moms, dads, and fussy babies. Sammy took to it right away. He loves the water."

He conjured the images. She had counted all of Sammy's milestones solo. It couldn't have been easy for her to do the job alone. He'd never understand how Joey McLain could walk away from sweet Serena, but that fool's loss was his gain. She had wrapped her way around his heart. Serena's web of love had ensnared him. He didn't want to get away.

"I'm sorry you didn't catch anything," she commented.

"Don't worry. I caught my limit last night." He felt himself stir thinking about the passion they'd shared. For a woman that could blush at the drop of a hat, she had surprised him. She'd been as greedy as he'd been.

Flustered, she busied herself reeling in her line. "Yes, well, I think we both did."

Sammy came back toward them. "I'm done swimming."

Mark looked at the kid, covered with sand and seaweed. He stood and packed their gear. "Okay, let's go home and cook lunch."

"After we clean up," Serena stated, wrapping Sammy's shirt around his damp shoulders as they walked up the path.

"Not another bath," Sammy replied.

"Afraid so, tiger. I think you brought half the lake with you."

Mark smiled at their exchange. He could remember when his bedraggled mother had hosed them down outside to keep them from tracking in sand. "I'll clean our fish while you get washed up, Sammy."

"Okay." He perked up.

"Thanks for cleaning them. I'll go fix something to go with the fish."

Mark watched them go, amazed by how much he felt like one of the family. He'd never been a marriage-minded man, but Serena was beginning to change his mind. Not that they'd talked about anything permanent last night. Hell, she'd probably object to his profession. He knew her view on that already.

Driving negative thoughts from his head, he went to the shed to clean the fish. He'd done it so often that he was a pro. He soon had a neat stack of fillets.

He carried the catch into the house and sniffed appreciatively. Something savory was cooking. His stomach growled. A morning of fishing, to say nothing of a night of passion, made a guy hungry.

Serena was stirring something on the stove. She sure was cute in that short outfit.

"Whatever you're cooking smells good."

She turned to smile at him. "Au Gratin potatoes, peas and carrots, and lemon pudding."

"Sounds delicious. Almost as delicious as the woman who cooked it." He put the fillets on the counter and bent to kiss her. Her mouth opened under his, and he took full advantage, thoroughly reminding her of last night. He felt her hesitate and pulled back. "You taste like cherries."

"It's my lip gloss."

"It's nice." He gave her another quick kiss, then turned away. "I'd better go get cleaned up."

"Okay. I'll get these started." He left the room. Damn, he'd almost blown it by pushing too hard. He'd have to remember to keep it light and not spook her. He felt better than he had in years, more alive. It was as if someone had lifted a weight off him. It wasn't that he was hard up. He could get sex, the meaningless, mindless kind, anytime he wanted. But there was something different about Serena, sweet and honest, and he meant to keep her.

Still, he couldn't help looking for trouble, waiting for the other shoe to drop. He told himself to get a grip as he climbed to the loft.

He'd scrub and look as presentable as possible. And he had to change his shirt. He was sweating his ass off because of the two shirts he'd been wearing in the sun.

He peeled off the top one, tossed it on the bed, and then took off his shoulder holster. It was why he'd worn the extra shirt. Given her prickly reaction to a shooting lesson yesterday, he didn't want to risk her freaking out if he wore it out in the open. He peeled off his sweaty T-shirt and went to the sink to clean up.

As he put on a fresh T-shirt, the aroma of fish frying wafted up to him.

And she could cook, too. His mom would be pleased if she ever got to meet her.

He put on his holster and pulled on a fresh sleeveless shirt. He would have to do some wash later, or he'd run out.

After lunch, he'd check in with the home base for updates. Hopefully, this wilderness retreat would last a while longer. He was counting on it to cement their budding relationship.

"Lunch is ready," Sammy called from the table.

"Smells great," Mark replied, joining them. He sat between Serena and Sammy, holding their hands as Sammy led them in saying Grace.

"This fish is yummy," Sammy said through a mouthful.

"Especially the one you caught," Mark told him.

"Right."

Serena served the dessert and looked at Mark. "Is it okay if I use the wringer washer on the porch? We'll all need fresh clothes soon."

"Sure. Do you need me to teach you how to use it?"

"No. My grandmother had one. Bring down your clothes, and I'll do a full load after I do the dishes."

"I'll do the dishes. You do the laundry, deal?" He held out his hand. The old washer still worked.

She grinned and shook his hand. "Sounds good to me." She turned to Sammy. "Want to help me?"

"Yup."

Mark cleared the table and watched them take the basket to the back porch. He cleared the table, putting leftovers in the fridge. They'd make a tasty midnight snack later. Maybe after he and Serena had a repeat of last night, he thought with a grin.

Dragging his mind off the image which made him hard, he went to work on the dishes. He scrubbed them until they shined, working off his tension. He dried the last one and then hung the dishtowel up to dry.

He walked to the back porch to check on them. The chugging washing machine told him she had mastered it before he'd opened the door and looked out. She put a load through the wringer while Sammy swished the whites in the rinse bucket. "How's it going?"

She looked up and smiled. "Fine. It came right back to me once I started."

"It's more fun than our washer back home," Sammy replied, swirling the clothes around.

"Right," she sarcastically stated with a smile. "More hands-on, at any rate."

Mark smiled at her high spirits. "Need any help?"

"No. I think we've got it covered."

He went inside to check his email.

"Domino, they've moved up her deposition. Grayson's legal team is trying to dismiss the case, and AIC Whittaker wants to use her as a star witness."

Mark wasn't sure he liked the sound of that. He would prepare for all contingencies. He had a few cards up his sleeve he could play, but first, he had to broach a touchy subject. Sammy. He wanted Serena to keep her focus, which meant she had to know Sammy was okay. He walked out to find her. She was hanging the wash.

"They've moved your testimony date up. We'll have to head back to the city tomorrow."

She put down her clothespin. "Why so soon?"

"Grayson's lawyers are trying to get the case dismissed. The DA needs to speed up the process. Also, Detective Sinclair turned state's evidence. He's singing like a bird. And they want to get his statement down before he changes his mind."

Serena nodded, absorbing Mark's info. "I suppose it's better to get it over with. I'll have our bags ready to go."

"About that. There's something we need to discuss."

"What?"

"I have an alternate plan. We need to leave Sammy behind with a babysitter."

"That's impossible. How can you even suggest such a thing?"

"Hear me out. I want you focused on the job at hand. You can't do that with your son in tow. Besides, he'll be safer away from the action."

"Even if that is true, I don't know any babysitters around here. And if you're suggesting I temporarily place Sammy in the foster system, think again."

"That thought never crossed my mind, babe. My parents live an hour away from here. My mom is a total grandma, with nine grandkids running around. And my dad is great with children. I've already called, and they'd love to take care of Sammy for a few days. He'll will love them, and he couldn't be any better protected than at their compound. It's only a temporary arrangement, several days at most. I think you'll be able to function better knowing he's out of the line of fire."

She wanted to protest, but she knew he was right. She did want Sammy to be safe, much as she hated to leave him behind. Now that she thought of it, she recalled Mark mentioning his parents' luxurious summer home being an hour away. But was it the best place for Sammy? More importantly, he'd never spent the night away from her before. Was he even ready for that step?

"I agree it would free me to know Sammy was out of danger, but I'm not sure he's mature enough to spend the night with strangers. He's never even had a sleep-over with friends yet. He's been a trooper through all this. I don't want to stress him out any more than he already is. I don't want to cause separation anxiety in him."

"Why don't you ask him?" He looked at Sammy, swinging on the tire swing.

She stepped away from the clothesline and walked toward her son. He'd ridden through these turbulent changes so smoothly. Could she ask this of him?

Out of the corner of her eye, she noticed Mark following her. How did he see her son? As a bother, a tag along? No, they'd developed a genuine affection. He was doing this for the right reasons, even if it didn't sit well with her.

She reached out to still the swing. "Sammy, honey, I've got something to ask you."

"Push me, Mom." He peered up at her. "What is it, Mommy?"

She gave him a gentle push. "How would you like to go on a sleep-over?"

"A sleep-over. Where? At Jeremy's house?"

"No. Mark's mom and dad's house."

Mark stepped forward, reaching out to give Sammy a bigger push. "There'll be lots of kids there for you to play with. They have an even better lake and get lots of visitors this time of year. They're having a party this weekend."

"Oh boy, a party! Can I, Mom?"

She bit her lip. He was excited about the party, but how long would it last? "Sure. If that's what you want."

"Your mom can get your suitcase, and we'll all go. We're invited for supper. That way, Sammy can see if he likes it there."

She felt some of her tension ease, thankful he'd considered her concerns, making it easier on her. She was willing to bet other agents in this situation would be more autocratic. She appreciated him trying to ease the distress she felt.

So far, she was the only one with separation anxiety.

Half an hour later, she couldn't help feeling a bit melancholy carrying Sammy's bag to the car. He ran ahead, a big smile on his face. They'd never spent the night apart, and it was killing her. He wasn't taking it as hard as her. She needed to develop a life outside the nucleus she'd formed with her son. There'd be lots of firsts—high school, dating, and college. She couldn't keep him small forever.

She buckled Sammy in the backseat, giving him a smile of reassurance. She then got in front, buckling her belt.

Mark reached out to squeeze her hand before starting the car. He understood. It went a long way to soothe her ruffled feelings. He was a good man, a bit rough around the edges, maybe, but a good man. It helped that he'd taken them close to home, to the sanctuary, when the going got rough. It was a good sign. He came from a close-knit family. He was a man who appreciated family ties.

"Are you sure they'll be home?"

"Yes. They're expecting us. I called my dad before I came out to discuss our departure with you. They *are* having a party this weekend. Sammy will have plenty of kids to play with."

"What kind of party?" She sat back and admired the scenery as they drove off the gravel road and onto a scenic rural route. It snaked around the pristine countryside with wildflowers blooming on the banks. There was a lake in the distance, boats dotting the surface.

"It's a tenth-anniversary party for my brother Ross and his wife, Stacey. The place will be full of family and friends, most of them state troopers, like Ross."

A big party. She glanced at her challis print skirt and silk blouse, hoping they were fancy enough attire. She'd probably stick out like a sore thumb, and she didn't have a gift for them.

"I don't even have a gift for them."

They were coming to some homes dotting the shoreline. Big lots with large, well-kept homes and docks by the water. People were having fun splashing in the lake. She certainly didn't fit in.

"Me, neither. It'd sort of slipped my mind until I called home. Besides, I think you're the only gift they'll want. I don't bring women to these family affairs. So, don't take it too seriously if they give you some ribbing. They've been trying to marry me off for years."

"They sound nice."

"They are nice, just pesky at times, especially my brothers. My mom is thrilled to take care of Sammy. She loves kids. She and dad are dying to meet you."

"That's nice." She felt awkward suddenly, like a prospective bride being vetted by an extended family. She read between the lines. They'd been trying to marry him off for years, and he'd eluded their attempts. Being the commitment-phobic Peter Pan, he was.

Mark turned into a long tree-lined driveway leading to a gigantic modern log home. "This is it. Mom and Dad's Shangri-La."

She could see why the ladies preferred it to the tarpaper shack they were staying at. The colorful flowerbeds spoke volumes about the care Mark's mom lavished on them.

The car came to a halt. She got out, noting several kids playing tag in the yard. Music wafted from the back deck along with the savory aroma of a charcoal grill. Having lived in the city all her life, she wasn't accustomed to this kind of rural Eden. She could see why his folks referred to it as Shangri-La.

Before she could open his door, Sammy practically bounded from the car, catching sight of the kids playing.

"Sammy, those are my nieces and nephews," Mark explained. "Would you like to go play with them?"

"Yes." Sammy nodded.

Mark let out a whistle. "Hey, Jeffrey."

A gangly towheaded boy stopped running and looked their way. "Uncle Mark," he yelled, running toward them as the pack of kids followed.

Mark smiled and put his hand on Sammy's shoulder. "This is Sammy. He'd like to join in the game. Okay?"

"Sure," Jeffrey replied. "I'll look after him. We're just about to play kickball. You're on the red team, okay, kid?"

"Okay," Sammy eagerly stated, letting go of Serena's hand. "Is it okay, Mom?"

"Sure." She smiled, watching him scamper off, but there was a tear in her eye. So much for him having separation anxiety.

Mark slung his arm around her shoulders. "You okay?"

She leaned against him, absorbing his strength. "I think I'm the one with separation anxiety."

"Don't blame you. He's a great kid." He looked at the house. "Oops, looks like we've got company."

A tall older man was bearing down on them, followed by a lady with elegant white hair. "Your parents?"

"Yup."

She was acutely aware of their scrutiny of her in Mark's arms. Oh goodness, how embarrassing.

She separated from Mark, only to have him tug her back. A twinkle shone in Mark's mother's eyes and his father chuckled. They were obviously accustomed to his caveman tendencies.

"Let go," she whispered, and gave a firm tug. She was rewarded with separation, and almost fell on her face.

"Son." The father reached out to shake his son's hand, then hugged him.

"You must be Serena," the mother stated with a welcome smile. "This is Eldon, and I'm Maria. I've heard a lot about you. Welcome to the family." She opened her arms to hug Serena.

Hugging her back, enveloped in Chanel No. 5 and cinnamon, she wondered what Mark had said about her. *Welcome to the family*. It wasn't like they were a couple, or were they?

"Thank you. He told me about you, too. About how you hose them down to get rid of the beach sand. You must have had your hands full raising the six-pack."

She chuckled. "I remember it like it was yesterday. Mark tells me you're staying there. Mark, you should have brought them here, love. That place is only fit for poker playing and ice fishing."

Serena took pity on him. "It's okay, Mrs. Riley. We're enjoying roughing it."

Maria hugged her son. "She's a keeper," she replied with a chuckle.

He shook his head as they withdrew. "This is business, Mother."

"Sure."

Serena listened to their exchange. Hearing her status as business was unsettling. Before she could fret about it, Eldon reached out, enveloping her in a bear hug.

"Nice to meet you, Serena." Eldon patted her back.

"Same here," Serena stated, gasping for breath. The man didn't know his strength.

Maria made a clucking sound. "Let her go, you brute. You'll bruise the poor girl. First girl Mark's brought home in ages, and you almost scare her off."

Maria hooked her arm with Serena's and started walking toward the house. "Mark told us about your father. I'm ever so sorry for your loss."

"Thank you." Serena blinked back tears at the mention of her father. She hadn't accepted that he was gone, and never would until all hope was exhausted. "Mark has men out searching for him."

"Well, if anyone can find him, it's my Mark," Maria stated confidently.

The pride in her voice had her looking back at Mark, conversing with his father. "He's the best agent, huh," she teased.

"Pretty much. He was at the top of his class at the academy," Maria agreed with a smile.

Sammy kicked the ball and ran to first base. "Look at me, Mom, I got a hit."

"That's good, son. This is Mrs. Riley, Mark's mom. You'll meet her later."

"Okay, nice to meet ya," he yelled, taking off for second base.

Maria smiled. "Yes, nice to meet you, too." She turned to Serena. "That's a nice son you've got there. He's all boy, that's for sure. I raised four of them, so I should know. He's playing so well with the grandkids and doesn't even know them yet."

"Thanks." Serena swelled with pride, watching him laugh and play with the others. He *was* a great kid. "I've always tried to raise him to be independent and get on well with others. Thank you for agreeing to take care of him."

"Nonsense. Mark explained the circumstances very well. I'm happy to do it. I always wanted more grandkids. Sammy will make an even ten. Let's head up to the house." Maria ushered them forward. "You'll want to put Sammy's things away and see where he will stay. After you settle in, I'll introduce you to the family."

"I'm sorry for crashing your party."

"Nonsense, the more, the merrier."

Serena walked in the front door with Maria. She glanced back to find Mark and his father still deep in conversation. Maybe they were talking shop since Mark's father was a retired law enforcement officer. Were they strategizing about the logistics of their move tomorrow?

Maria tugged on her arm. "Don't worry about the men. Let them do their war session in private. It helps them to feel in control. In the meantime, you and I can put our feminine skills to work. I figured on Sammy bedding down in the boys' room. It's right this way, Serena, dear. That's a lovely name, by the way."

"Thanks. I was named after my great-grandmother, a very serene and regal lady. Although, I'm not sure I always live up to the title."

She followed her down to the boys' quarters. It was a massive room with four bunk beds. Big enough to house her five grandsons and their friends. "Wow, you've got enough room for an army."

"That's what I asked for when Eldon built our dream retreat. There's plenty of room for the extended family. I've got nine grandkids, ten with Sammy."

"Well, you sure got it. I think Sammy will like it here."

"You can put his bag on the bottom bunk to the left."

Serena laid out his pajamas and put Spiderman on his pillow.

"I'll leave you alone to settle in. Bathroom's down the hall. Come and join me out on the deck when you're ready."

Serena was grateful for the woman's sensitivity. "Thank you."

"Don't mention it. Don't worry. Mark will take good care of you both."

"I know he will."

"You're the first woman he's brought here, by the way."

So she'd said. "It's just business."

"That's what he said, but I think it's more than that. Mothers have an instinct for that kind of thing. I heard how you took care of my son. Thank you, from one mom to another. And welcome to the family."

"Right." Serena didn't know what to say. She sensed it was more, too. She couldn't hide her desire. "See you outside."

She finished putting Sammy's clothes away, smoothing out wrinkles, then walked into the bathroom to put out his toothbrush and hairbrush. Maria's presence made her feel better about leaving him here, but it still was a wrench. She looked in the mirror and smoothed back her hair, then splashed cool water on her wrists and face.

She hoped the rest of Mark's family liked her.

"You ready to face the throng, beautiful?" Mark stood in the bathroom doorway.

"As I'll ever be."

"Don't worry. We Riley's don't bite. Hard, that is."

"What were you and your dad talking about?"

"Fishing."

She gazed at him, knowing he was lying. He was very good at it, better than her, that was for sure. Maria was right. He was trying to protect her.

Letting it go, she nodded. "Okay, let's go." She linked her arm with his and let him escort her onto the large wooden deck. Glancing down the flagstone patio below, she thought it was paradise. "Is Sammy still playing out front?"

"No. I had the kids move the game around back where we can keep an eye on them." He pointed to the back lawn. "See, there he is."

She picked him out of the crowd of high-spirited grandkids. "Good," she replied, reassured.

He walked with her to the railing. "Let me give you the low-down. My brothers, Chip and Aaron, are supervising the game." He pointed to the two athletic men flanking the kids' game. "That's my brother Ross, flipping burgers on the grill. His wife, Stacey, is putting out the salad. It's their tenth wedding anniversary. My sisters, Meg and Mary Beth, are helping Mom set the table. Their spouses are around somewhere. Lots of Ross's police staff are here, too, so there's plenty of police protection. Most of the family is around somewhere."

"Nice family." She noticed Mark's family were polite, but shot curious looks their way. No doubt, there'd been some speculation going on. From Maria's casual retort about scaring her off, it seemed Mark wasn't in the habit of vetting his dates with his family.

"Thanks. Well, we'd better get down there and get it over with before they come up and get us."

Serena walked with him down the staircase to the flagstone patio. She felt all eyes on her, polite but curious.

"Ross, Stacey, this is Ms. McLain."

"Serena," she corrected, "it's nice to meet you. Happy anniversary."

Stacey reached out to shake her hand. "It's nice to meet you, too."

Mark nodded. "Can I talk to you for a minute, bro?"

"Sure, let's take a walk."

Mark turned to Serena. "Will you'll be okay here alone?"

"I'll be fine," she replied, not wanting to cramp his style.

Stacey nodded. "Sure, she will. It'll give us a chance to get better acquainted. I'll take good care of her."

Mark stood by the window in his father's den, keeping Serena in sight while he waited for Ross to join him. She sat at one of the tables, flanking the large flagstone patio where the party was in full swing. He'd wanted to keep this talk private.

Some guy had stopped to talk to her. Probably one of the other officers. Damn it, didn't she know the sight of her in the evening lantern light was like catnip to a tomcat?

"That's a pretty girl you brought with you, bro." Ross entered the room carrying two beers.

Mark took one and tried to ignore Ross's curious glance. He looked back at Serena and scowled. She was smiling at the guy. He'd have to ensure the single guys here knew she was taken, if only temporarily.

"Yeah, she is."

Ross watched Mark's irritated reaction. "Cute kid, too. Didn't know you went for the family type."

Mark looked away from the young stud chatting up his woman. His brother's amused expression didn't make him feel any better. "Maybe I'm maturing."

"Good God, not that," Ross mocked, "want to tell me again this is just business?"

So, Ross didn't believe his brief explanation outside. His brother could always read him like a book. No, it wasn't just business. He'd broken the cardinal rule of non-fraternization. And now she was under his skin, but good.

"It's true. They're my subjects, but it's a bit more complicated than that. We had trouble at the safe house and had to run. I took them to the cottage."

Mark heard a noise, and looked up to see his other brothers drift in, followed by their father. He'd figured on them wanting to be in on the action. Together, they were a formidable force. It was time for some tricky explanations.

"So, you taught the boy to fish. Did you catch anything this time?" Ross asked with a barely straight face.

"Probably another stick," Allen chimed in with a chuckle.

Mark accepted the jibe with good grace. "Yup. I added to the stack of driftwood."

Mitch grinned, singing off-key, "Throw another log on the fire."

"Right." Mark nodded.

"How'd the kiddo?" Nick asked.

"Caught a beautiful perch, and before you ask, his momma caught a trout. I couldn't believe it when I saw her reel that monster in."

"Okay, boys," Eldon stated gently. "Enough shenanigans. Time to get down to business. How can we help your lady friend?"

Mark cast a grateful glance at his father and brothers. Some things never change. They'd always been in each other's corner. "I could use your help, but I won't snow you. There could be trouble. First, Dad, you'll have to take special precautions while Sammy stays here. We got here undetected, but I'd rather be safe than sorry."

"Don't fret, son. We'll treat him like one of our own."

"Thanks, Dad."

"Who knows, maybe he will be someday," he murmured.

Mark cast him a troubled look. He might be falling for Serena, but that didn't mean she reciprocated. "It's just business, Dad."

Ross cut in. "I've assigned one of my patrol women to stay with Sammy for the duration. She's sharp-eyed and good with kids. So, rest easy, bro."

"Thanks."

Nick moved forward. "What other kinds of problems do you anticipate?"

"I'm expecting a blow-up at the courthouse. I want to circumvent a possible attack there. The invasion at the safe house confirmed my suspicion of a leak in the agency."

"How deep do you think it goes?"

"I'm not sure, but I think it runs deep. That's why I've taken things out of the usual channels. I've got inquiries out to try to catch the traitor."

Dad nodded. "Does it have any connection to your misfortune last year?"

Mark shrugged. "I'm not sure, but there have been a lot of coincidences making me suspicious of that fact. That's why I'm going outside of normal channels."

"We'll do what we can, bro." Allen handed him another drink. "I can pull some strings at City Hall and get a last-minute change of venue. Do you think that will solve your problems?"

"Maybe."

"There's one problem we don't have a cure for," Ross teased.

Mark frowned at him. What was he getting at? "What?"

"L-O-V-E, love."

Mark looked at each of his smirking brothers, willing them to knock it off. "Who said anything about love?"

Ross chuckled. "I can see from the fierce look you're giving Ronny Walters out there that more than fishing went on."

"Yeah, trouble. I broke code, and you know it."

Dad cleared his throat. "Maybe so, son, but I'd say there were extenuating circumstances. Your ma's pleased as punch about it, too."

Ross grinned. "And I'd say, judging from how she looked at you when you dropped her at that table, it wasn't all one way."

"Maybe, but that doesn't change the fact that things are complicated."

"Complicated, huh?"

"Yeah, I'm an FBI robot, according to her. Let's get back to the subject. I'll tell Serena about the change of plans."

"Bro, you ask, don't tell. That's the first lesson a marrying man has to learn."

"Yeah, but who says I'm a marrying man?"

"Mom, can I please watch videos with Aubrey?" Sammy begged from the edge of the patio.

Serena smiled at Mark's six-year-old redheaded niece doing cartwheels in the grass beside him. The kickball game had subsided, and the two kids had bonded. The moment Sammy had set eyes on her, he'd been happy as a calf in clover.

"They'll be fine." Stacey smiled and handed Serena a frosty glass of punch. "The television is in the great room, so they'll be in sight at all times. Ross has assigned one of his female patrol officers to keep an eye on him, too."

She'd noticed the tall girl, dressed in plain clothes, standing by the edge of the patio, and wondered if she was there to babysit. Serena smiled, feeling some of her tension abate. Mark was right when he'd said this was an armed camp.

"Go ahead, just make sure you keep in sight of an adult." She watched Sammy sprint away, the patrolwoman following close behind.

Coming from a law enforcement family, he'd known it was the perfect place to shelter Sammy while she did her civic duty. Mark's whole family had gone out of their way to make her feel welcome and safe. She was touched.

She couldn't help noticing a young patrolman from the bar closely watched her. Had she been assigned a watchdog, too, or was he planning on making advances? A few days ago, the notion would have flustered her. Now, thanks to dealing with a macho FBI agent, she felt confident in handling it.

"How's your drink?"

Serena sipped the frozen concoction. It was delicious, sweet, and tangy with a kick. "It's wonderful, and boy, do I need it."

The breeze lifted her challis print skirt around her legs. A drop of condensation dripped onto her white blouse. She smiled at Stacey Riley, a petite bubbly lady with strawberry blonde hair and a kind, open expression, wearing a green dress.

Stacey shook her head sympathetically. "I suppose you do, after all you've been through, you poor thing."

Serena was warmed by her concern. "Did Mark tell you about having to run from the safe house?" She crossed her legs, a sandal-shod foot swinging tensely.

"Just the barest details." Stacey shrugged. "I suppose it's classified. Part of the FBI code."

She sighed. That sounded about right. He probably had to keep that sort of information confidential. "Yeah, the danged code."

Stacey looked at her for a long moment. "The code bothers you?"

Appalled at what she'd said aloud, blusher cheeks grew hot.

What the heck? She needed to talk to someone, and Stacey seemed an excellent listener. "I suppose it shouldn't, but it does. It puts a straightjacket on his emotions." Stacey frowned, and Serena hurried to add, "Not that I'm complaining. Mark's done a marvelous job for us both. He's saved our lives, that's for sure."

Stacey leaned forward. "But you want more."

Serena gazed at her kind blue eyes. The woman was very wise. "Does it show?"

"To another woman, yes. I see the look in your eye when you look at him. Mark needs you." She reached across the table to pat Serena's hand. "Don't give up."

How could she say that? Hadn't she heard his brusque tone when he'd left her to sit at this table alone? He'd been all business, scanning the yard, even though there were at least half a dozen uniformed police officers. She'd sat there dutifully, listening to the music, watching the dancers whirl across the floor, glad that Sammy had the outing. She knew her obligation just as he knew his.

Serena shook her head. "No, he needs work, the code, not me. He's only doing his job."

"I think you're wrong. I've seen how he looks at you when you aren't paying attention. He's torn, maybe confused, but he feels a lot more for you than a need to do his duty. He's had girlfriends before, but I've never seen him like this, honest."

Serena considered the notion. Could she be right?

Mark walked out of the house, flanked by his brothers and dad. They made a formidable team, she decided while gazing at them.

"Here they come."

"Ah yes, the dream team," Stacey stated with a chuckle. "I've seen that look before. They've been plotting something."

Mark followed his brother Ross down the stairs to the bar. They stood talking while they waited for a drink. They seemed to be arguing a bit. They both had the same focused energy, Ross a bit taller and heavier.

Mark turned her way. Their gazes snagged. What was he thinking or feeling?

He said something to Ross, and they turned to glance at her.

"Happy anniversary again." Serena felt awkward as Mark's hot gaze locked onto her.

"Thanks. It's hard to believe ten years have gone by. That's what love will do to you. Make time stand still."

Mark and Ross started walking toward them.

"Looks like they're coming our way," Stacey murmured. "Now's the time to test out our theory."

Mark stopped next to Serena and smiled. "Having a good time, beautiful?"

The pet name seemed to slip off his tongue naturally, and it sounded nice. She made an effort to regain her equilibrium. "Yes, I'm having a great time. Everyone's been so kind. Sammy is having the time of his life." She turned to smile at Ross. "I have you to thank for assigning a patrolwoman to him. Thanks a lot."

"You're welcome. I think our daughter Aubrey is smitten."

Serena chuckled. "I'm afraid Sammy's the same way. Heaven help us when they reach their teens."

"I don't even want to think about it." Stacey grinned.

Ross grunted. "Maybe knowing I carry a gun will keep the teenage punks to a minimum."

"Dream on," Serena and Stacey echoed back.

"Well, I'm going to dance with my wife," Ross stated, taking Stacey's hand.

"I don't have to be asked twice." Stacey went into his arms. "Have fun, you two."

"Remember what I said, bro," Ross said as he waltzed her away.

"What did he say?" Serena asked, intrigued.

"He and I discussed a few game plans for the courthouse."

That brought her up sharp. How could he do that without consulting her? "What, weren't you even going to ask me?"

Mark sat next to her, frowning. "No, I wanted to have a handle on things before I approached you with them. We came up with a few options. I thought it might ease your mind while testifying to know Sammy's being looked after."

"Thanks, Mark, you're a good man."

"Good for some things, at least. My mother thinks I don't want to settle down."

She took a deep breath, then asked a question that had been playing on her mind. "So, is that why you never married and had kids?"

"It's part of it, and the other part was I hadn't found the right woman."

She gazed at him, drawn by the tender look in his eyes. "And now?"

"Dance with me." He rose and pulled her into his arms.

She stepped closer, nestling against him as they danced across the stone patio.

Had he asked her to dance to change the subject? Was she pushing too hard?

His arms drew her closer as his hand slid down her back. His cheek rubbed against the top of her head, and he sighed, whispering, "And now, I think maybe she's in my arms."

Her heart skipped a beat. Had she just heard what she thought she heard?

Stacey had been right. He did care.

He brushed against her, and her nipples beaded. Heat pooled in her nether regions. He could turn her into a quivering pile of jelly with a look, a touch, or a word. She drew in a deep breath as her sensitized nipples rubbed against him.

His hand on the small of her back drew her closer. "You're driving me crazy, beautiful."

Serena felt his growing manhood press against the juncture of her thighs, and gasped as a thrill surged through her. "Not half as crazy as you're making me, magician."

"So, you remember that?" he asked in a low rumble.

"I'll never forget, even if I live to be a hundred. I'll tell the old ladies in the retirement home about the magician who showed me a few spells."

"Oh, beautiful, you ain't seen nothin' yet."

She shivered against him. "Promises, promises."

"We'd better sit down before I embarrass the two of us." He ushered her to the table. "Sit a spell, and I'll get us some refills. What are you drinking?"

"Some of Stacey's concoction. How about you?"

"Ginger ale. I'm driving."

"Good man." She smiled at him, but his words reminded her that she'd soon leave her son behind. Was she ready to take that step?

Mark flashed her a grin and made a beeline for Ross, pulling him aside to talk.

Ross looked up at her and smiled.

She wondered what they were talking about.

Mark walked back toward her, a greedy gleam in his eye, and she forgot to breathe for a moment. Her pulse sped up.

He took her hand. "Let's go. I know you want to spend some time with Sammy before we leave."

She let him usher her inside, his arm around her waist. She didn't miss the approving looks from his family. They thought something permanent would come of this, and who knew? Maybe it would.

She couldn't worry about that. She had to concentrate on her son.

They walked into the great room to find Sammy and Aubrey sprawled on the floor watching Sponge Bob. Millie was sitting on the sofa and enjoying the video, too.

Sammy's eyes lit up when he saw her. "Hi, Mom."

She sank on the floor with him. "Hi. Are you having a good time?"

"Yes, lots."

"We're going to play video games later," Aubrey stated.

"And eat pizza and popcorn," Sammy added.

"That's good." Serena reached out to hug him, resisting the urge to pull him onto her lap like she did when he was a toddler.

"Do you have to go now?"

"Yes, Mark and I have to leave. Will you be okay?"

"I'll be okay as long as you are."

That adult sentiment rocked her a bit. Sammy was growing up fast after the stress of the past few days.

"I'll be fine, and I'll be back to get you in just a few days."

"Okay," Sammy stated slowly.

Mark crouched beside Sammy. "I'll take good care of your mom, sport." He handed him a business card. "Here's my card." He flipped it over to scrawl a number on the back. "This is my cell phone number. Call us if you get worried or need to talk to your mom. I'll keep the phone on day and night."

"Okay." Sammy took the card and put it in his jeans pocket.

Serena felt abandoned on the drive home. It hurt to leave her son behind, but she knew it was the best thing for him. She gazed out at the scenery flying by as Mark drove. She was grateful for his sensitivity in not pushing her to talk. The sun was going down, making beautiful colors in the sky.

They turned onto the gravel road to the cabin. "Feeling better?"

"Yes, thanks." She was sad about leaving her son, but also excited about being alone with Mark. Was he feeling the same thing? They drove the rest of the way in companionable silence.

Mark pulled into the driveway and killed the engine. "I'm going to go out and check the perimeter."

"Fine." She was grateful for the breathing room. "The clothes should be dry by now. I'll take them in and start packing."

She went to the clothesline and took down the wash while surreptitiously watching him walk away. He was perfect. He made her son feel secure. But how did he think of her outside of duty? She mulled it over as she took down the wash, folding, smoothing out the garments, and putting them in the laundry basket.

That done, she carried the basket into the cabin.

Trying to shake off her lonely sensation, she went to the pantry and got out a pouch of lemonade. She might as well make them something cool to drink. Shaking off the sadness, she reminded herself she'd left Sammy behind to protect him. She'd have to get over her separation anxiety for his good.

With time on her hands, she made them a cool pitcher of lemonade, more to keep her busy than anything else. She put it in the refrigerator to chill and then went to the bedroom, laying out her pajamas and a change of clothes for the morning. She packed everything else, wanting to be ready.

She was nervous about seeing Grayson in court and worried about her dad. She'd have to fight off the desire to pounce on him and demand he give back her father.

Tension built in her. She walked out to the kitchen and noticed Mark coming. She poured them lemonade and carried them out to the porch, fully aware of what might happen.

He looked up at her approach. "What's up?". It was time to get to know Mark Riley better.

"I thought you might enjoy a cold drink." She handed him a glass, their fingers brushing and lingering for a moment.

He took a seat on the swing, and she sat next to him, gazing out at the dusky woods. "Thanks."

He chugged it, his throat opening and closing gustily.

She looked away and took a sip from her glass, quenching her sudden thirst. She set the glass on an end table and smiled when the breeze stirred her wisps of hair.

He looked at her. "You must be tired."

"A little."

He casually wrapped his arm around the back of the swing. His fingers went to her nape, rubbing lightly.

She leaned into his touch. It felt like heaven. "I think we need to talk about us."

"Us?"

"Yes." She drew a deep breath and decided to lay her cards on the table. "In case you haven't noticed, I've developed a bit of a...crush on you, and I think you like me, too. So, I guess, where do we go from here?"

She gazed at him. He couldn't have looked more surprised if she'd pulled a gun on him. And then he smiled, a wicked heartbreaker kind of smile, and her mind went blank.

"Why don't we start here," he murmured, bending to kiss her.

Their tongues mated as his arms went around her.

She kissed him back, her arms around his neck. She was floating.

All of a sudden, she found herself sitting on his lap. She broke the kiss and blinked at him, bemused. "How did that happen?"

He grinned. "Magic." His hand cupped her breast tenderly. "Shall we try another spell?"

She knew he was asking her permission and was glad. She wanted him with every fiber of her being.

"Oh, yes," she replied breathlessly.

He kissed her again, fingering her nipple, slipping his hand inside her blouse. She moaned, feeling his body harden in response. She realized he wasn't holding back when she suddenly felt a chill. She broke the kiss long enough to notice her blouse open.

"What a spell."

He chuckled. "Beautiful, you ain't seen nothin' yet." He gazed at her breasts. "You are so perfect."

She gasped when he opened the front clasp to her bra and bent to take her nipple in his mouth, teasing it with his tongue, drawing on it hard. She squirmed against him and tugged open his shirt. She needed to touch him. Her hands went to his hair-roughened chest, his tight muscles, pinching his nipples.

He groaned. "Beautiful, you're driving me crazy."

She laughed, delighting in her power. "Big guy, you haven't seen nothin' yet," she teased, imitating him.

"In that case, I'll have to cast another spell." He chuckled, then groaned when she wriggled against his growing manhood.

"I dare ya." She laughed as he pulled up her skirt, then moaned when his hand cupped her mound over her pink lace panties. He pressed ever so slightly, and a shock wave of pleasure rushed through her. "Oh, my."

"Like that, do you?" He laughed, pulling her panties aside. "How about this?" He slipped a finger down the middle of her nest of curls, teasing her.

"It's okay." She unzipped his pants and wrapped her hand around his stiff shaft. "How's this for magic?"

"Not bad." He groaned, pushing into her hand. "Beautiful, you're killing me." He pulled a silver packet out of his pocket, ripped it open, and sheathed himself with the condom.

She whimpered when his hand left her, but then she was floating again.

He lifted and turned her so she straddled him and lowered her onto his erection. "Time for another spell."

She gasped as he entered her. "Nice spell."

"Thanks." He gripped her hips and drove into her. "It's just for you, beautiful. Only for you."

She moaned as she rode him, slipping up and down his stiff shaft. She'd never felt this much passion before. He *was* a magician.

His hand tightened on her hips, grinding her against him, and she exploded. Waves of orgasm rippled through her, drawing him deeper until he groaned, finding his release.

She leaned against him, her head on his shoulder and her lips curved in a smile as old as time. She'd found her true love. "Pure magic."

Chapter Nine

Serena rolled over in bed and nestled against Mark. There were benefits to sleeping with a naked man. They were so lovely to wake up next to. Her hand slid down his warm chest. They were both delightfully nude. It was such a sensual feeling to rub up against his hair-roughened body. She hadn't needed her pajamas, after all. She stretched, enjoying his warm, muscular body against hers. She was turning into a wonton woman, and she reveled in it.

She lifted the sheet and looked at the prominent part of his anatomy she'd loved last night. It was much less pronounced now, but as she watched it, it began to stir.

"Enjoying the show?" he asked, amused.

"Yes." Her face heated, despite her bold answer.

He chuckled. "That's what I like, a wild, sexy woman who can still blush."

"Oh yeah?"

"Yeah." He pulled her down for a sensual kiss.

She collapsed on him, brushing her breasts against his chest, thrilled at the electric sensation it caused the sensitized tips of her breasts. Her nipples hardened, and she spread her legs, rubbing her wet mound against his thigh. She smiled when he growled in reaction, and she reached down to take his burgeoning erection in her hand.

He let out a groan, sliding her up his body. "You're driving me crazy, beautiful."

She chuckled, reveling in her feminine power. Her laugh turned to a sigh of surrender when he took her nipple in his mouth. Holding her suspended over him, he sucked on one and then the other until she was writhing against him and his hot mouth.

"Oh, please."

"I will." He bent his knee, bringing his thigh between her legs, teasing her, rubbing against her.

He was taking over again, but she was determined to win this battle of the sexes. Shards of pleasure rocked through her as he teased her femininity.

"My turn." She squeezed his shaft, cupping his balls, making him halt his sensual torture so she could think straight. When he stopped, she took the opportunity to climb on him. Hovering over him, she slowly lowered herself onto his hot velvet shaft until she took him all.

He laid back and grinned. "Take me. I'm all yours."

She sat there for a second, just enjoying the overfull sensation of him inside her, and then she started to move. Up and down, slowly at first, then faster and faster. The lightning glimmers of pleasure shot through her at their joining. He grabbed her hips, held them trapped as she ground against him and came, exploding on top of him.

He slammed into her once, twice, and then held her tight.

She lay there on top of him, her head nestled on his chest, and she listened to his heart thundering under her ear. They were both spent.

His hands roamed up and down her back.

She arched, seeking his soothing touch as he petted her.

Getting her breath back, she sat up, smiling. "Good morning."

He smiled. "Feeling pretty cocky up there, are you?"

"Yup. I thought I'd see how the other half lives."

He grinned. "And did you like it?"

She kneaded her fingertips into his chest. "I could get used to it."

He laughed and turned over, taking her with him.

An hour later, Mark got up. "I'd better move before you do me permanent damage."

She yawned and rolled over. "Five more minutes. I think you wore me out."

He nodded and walked into the bathroom. Much as he hated to tear himself away from her, there was work to be done. After showering, he padded out to the bedroom with a towel slung low around his hips. She'd fallen back to sleep. The sight of her damned near tempted him to climb back in with her. He resisted the thought, knowing he had to get his head on straight for the ordeal to come.

"Time to get up, beautiful."

She sat up and yawned.

He put on pants. "I'll take care of my daily check-in while you get ready."

He didn't miss the troubled look on her face. It was almost time to return to reality, and it seemed both of them weren't looking forward to it.

He walked into the living room and went to the computer. He logged on using his remote connection and checked his e-mail. There was a note from Bob, so he opened it.

"Domino, my trip is going as well as I suspected. Saw some interesting sights today. Lots of sharks at the aquarium, but I didn't let them get too close. I gave Junkman the good news. I will check at the usual time. Eagle."

So, Bob had picked up a tail. It was gratifying to know their suspicions were confirmed. Maybe Whittaker would cut him a bit of slack now. He knew that Bob, a seasoned agent, could care for himself. He'd immersed himself in a tour group. Grayson hadn't discovered Serena and Sammy weren't among the crowd yet.

That was the good news. Now for the bad.

He logged out and picked up his satellite phone. It was a secure line he had confidence in. He punched in Whittaker's private number.

"Whittaker."

"Domino here. I just heard about Eagle's tail."

"Where the hell are you, Riley?"

Mark frowned. It was the reaction he'd expected. "Someplace safe. I'll be coming in on time. That's all I can tell you."

"Fine, play it your way. It's your job on the line."

He chose to ignore the barb. He was well aware of the chance he was taking with his career, but Serena was worth the fall. There were more important things to think about. "I heard about Scott."

"Ah, yes, Scott. Funny thing, him winding up dead."

"Don't bother hinting at it. I didn't shoot him, and you know it."

"Do I?"

"Yes. Ballistics has proved it."

"Ah, but who's to say you don't carry an extra piece?"

Mark didn't bother to respond.

Whittaker made a harrumphing sound. "Anyway. We've had some developments here."

"What?"

"Ms. McLain's father has been recovered."

"Dead?"

"Injured, it's critical. He got caught in the crossfire. He's undergone surgery for a bullet wound and is in the ICU. He's comatose."

"Damn."

"Yes, well, you might want to inform Ms. McLain her notes helped us find him."

"That might help soften the blow."

"One more thing. Don't forget Ms. McLain is scheduled for court on Monday morning. Check in with me the day before, and I'll set up her escort."

"I think it might be better if I handled that end of things."

"Damn it, Domino, don't give me more of your speculation about that alleged leak. Even if it was true, the guy is gone. It's over."

He hung up. Her father was critical. Mark hadn't expected they'd even find him alive. It was good news the guy was still breathing, but he knew it would be a blow. He also knew she'd want to run to her father, but that wouldn't be allowed.

He'd have to go back to being the FBI robot again, damn.

He firmed his resolve and went back to the bedroom. Serena was dressed, standing by the dresser, brushing her hair. Her beauty drew him. How could he break the news?

She turned and smiled as he approached. She looked at him, and her smile faltered. "What's wrong?"

"We need to talk." He took her by the elbow and propelled her to the bed, sitting her down on the edge. "Sit," he insisted.

She sagged, casting him a sad look. "What is it? Is something wrong with Sammy?"

"Sammy's fine. You've nothing to fear on that account." He looked into her haunted eyes, wavering, and then found his voice. "We found your father."

She bit her lip. "Alive?"

"Yes."

She smiled and looked heavenward. "Thank you, God."

"But..." He watched her wary gaze snap back to him. "He's been shot. There was a shootout, and he was caught in the crossfire. He made it through surgery, and the doctors hope for the best."

She cocked her head, looking at him, and then frowned. "Which means they don't think he's going to make it?"

He hesitated, searching for the right words to soothe her. "They didn't say that. He's got a fighting chance. That's what you need to hold on to."

She sighed. "I know, you're right."

She was taking it better than he had expected. Reassured, he continued, "One thing you might like to know. Your clues led us to him."

"Well, that's something, at least." She blinked and looked away, standing up. "I want to—"

"You can't go to him," Mark interrupted, forestalling her plea.

"I've got to." Her frustrated gaze snapped back to him.

"Sorry, no. It's too dangerous. Grayson's men will be watching the hospital." He gazed at her tear-stained face, willing her to understand. He wasn't being an insensitive jerk just for the hell of it. He had to stand firm, unyielding under her displeasure, for her good. "After you testify, I'll see about getting you in." He reached out to touch her shoulder.

She stepped away, eluding his touch. "That's not good enough, robot."
"I know, but it'll have to do, Ms. McLain."

Chapter Ten

Serena was silent on the ride back to civilization. She sighed, tired from a sleepless night spent in the throes of passion. Now it was in sharp contrast to her worry about her father. Her fears about going to court were insignificant in the face of this greater tragedy. But she was hanging onto the fact that her father had made it through surgery. He was a fighter. She couldn't worry about her fizzled love affair now. From the ice that had formed between them in the last hour, it was obvious it was over. They were back to the formality of last names.

She still couldn't quite believe it. As Mark had given her the bad news this morning, he'd undergone a metamorphosis right before her eyes, becoming stiff and professional in the face of her distress. She still wasn't quite sure how to deal with the 'all business' change in his demeanor. Gone was her tender lover, now replaced by his calm FBI persona. Logically, she knew he had made the right decision to keep her away from the hospital, but she couldn't stop herself from fighting against his restrictions.

The more she pushed, the farther he withdrew, until they were now polite strangers. She wasn't sure how to heal the breach between them or if she wanted to. Risking her heart twice might be too hard to do. She'd made all the moves, and he had never said he returned her affections.

Maybe he didn't.

She was glad Sammy was safe with Mark's family. She didn't want him to pick up on her fear for her father. She'd wait to tell him about his grandpa, holding the news until she knew the outcome. He didn't need another thing to worry about. After overhearing his conversation with Mark last week, she knew he thought of himself as her protector. It was touching, but he needed to be a kid and not worry about her.

"I never said it before, but thank you for finding a safe place for Sammy with your parents." She turned, catching sight of Mark's startled smile.

Did her gratitude mean that much to him? Maybe there was a way to penetrate the wall that had formed between them.

"You're welcome."

She'd worry about her relationship later. Right now, she had to concentrate on her father. She recalled Mark's kind but professional message this morning. Her father was still alive, but unconscious. He remained in the ICU, but was improving. She knew having made it through the night was an excellent sign. When she'd told Mark that, he'd nodded in agreement, but refrained from comment. He was back to following the FBI code of being impersonal.

She reached for the radio button. "How about a little music?"

"Fine," Mark replied, turning off the gravel road and onto a two-lane highway.

She tuned to an easy listening station, looking for the serenity she usually found in music. Mark was distancing himself from her even more. She could hear it in his voice.

She sighed and gazed at the north wood's scenery. Thick pine forests grew on either side of the road with bright wildflowers along the ditches. It was beautiful here, a perfect family vacation spot if one wasn't afraid for their father's life.

His shooting had jolted her into a new place emotionally. She felt more afraid now than she had the night Grayson's thugs invaded the safe house. Giving the deposition was going to be hard, but she would face it squarely.

She watched the trees whiz by as her eyes drifted shut.

Two hours later, Mark drove into a run-down area in the city and pulled into an apartment building's underground garage. Time to activate Plan B.

"Wake up, Serena, we're here."

She opened her eyes and looked around, her eyes widening. "Where's here?"

He gazed at the shadowy recesses and derelict cars, trying to see it through her eyes. "Our next stop. Don't worry, despite its appearance, it's someplace safe. We'll hole up at a friend's place while I make arrangements."

He gazed deep into her fearful sapphire eyes, hoping to reassure her undoubtedly shattered nerves. She was probably still furious with him for thwarting her desire to see her father. And she was frightened. He'd seen her metamorphosis from a relaxed lover to a frightened subject when he'd broken the news. She'd wanted to run to the hospital. He understood it was a natural reaction, but he couldn't allow it, not yet anyway.

He learned a hard lesson this morning when she'd turned on him. The Bureau had a non-fraternization rule for a reason. He shouldn't have touched her while on the job. It wasn't fair to either of them. Now he was backpedaling, returning to his duty, trying to forget how good it had been with her. He couldn't undo what he'd done, but he could protect her, despite herself. Frankly, he wouldn't blame her if she handed his head to Whittaker on a silver platter.

She nodded and opened her door.

He heaved a sigh of relief. At least she trusted him in this area.

He got out and walked around the car to join her. Thank God she wasn't fighting him on the small stuff. He didn't want to ruffle her feathers more than he had to.

"Okay, let's move out." He escorted her to the elevator, keeping a wary eye out for trouble. He noticed a couple of winos making a home out of an abandoned vehicle, but they were harmless. Once they were in the empty elevator, he relaxed a notch. It wasn't pleasant, but he knew it ran smoothly. He'd used his connections to see to it personally six months back.

They were going to a place he knew was beyond suspicion. Manny the Toad's was the last place Gerald Grayson would look for her. It wasn't the ritzy part of town he hung out in. Whittaker wouldn't expect him to take her here, either, which made it the perfect place to spend the day while he made some more permanent arrangements. Since her father was recovering, barely alive, it had caused him to alter his plans. He wouldn't seek a change of venue. They might be expecting that. He'd have to go at it from a different angle.

He hit the button for the fourth floor. "Now, don't let this associate of mine disturb you. He's just a bit unusual."

"Unusual? How so?" She gave him a suspicious look.

"His name is Manny Ortega. He's my best snitch. Corrupt, no doubt, but very trustworthy."

"Good grief." She followed him off the elevator. "What did he do?"

"Five to ten for dealing in stolen property."

"What?"

"He's reformed, sort of. He used to be a fence. Now, he only dabbles in crime to keep his hand in. I got him busted. I also got him off early. He and I have a relationship, of sorts. And he owes me."

Mark steered her down the corridor to 415. He gave three sharp knocks.

Serena shrank back, and he had no doubt she thought he was a low life.

The peephole opened. "Who is it?"

"A friend."

After a moment, the triple locks were being undone. The door opened a crack. "Who?"

"Riley," Mark said, sticking the toe of his shoe in the door.

The door opened a bit more, and a swarthy, heavyset man peered through his thick glasses. He looked closely at Mark, then gave Serena a thorough once over.

"Who's she?" he hissed.

"A friend of mine. I've come to collect a favor from you."

"Señor Riley, why didn't you say so in the first place? Any friend of yours is a friend of mine."

"She's not that kind of friend," Mark stated, blocking his view.

"Too bad, business is down lately. Come in, you two, and tell me what you require." He heaved his girth aside so they could enter. "Come in, come in," he gestured. "My casa is your casa."

Serena stuck close to Mark's side.

He glanced at the Mexican and tie-dyed décor. She probably felt like Alice in *'Through the Looking Glass.'* It might be a seedy place, but it was a safe one. The Toad never betrayed a customer. It was terrible for business.

He took Serena's hand and tugged her deeper into the apartment. The Toad slammed the door shut, then noisily shot the bolts, locking them in.

"What can I do for you, compadre?"

He looked at Serena. "Wouldn't you like to freshen up, honey?"

She frowned at him. "In other words, get lost?"

"Something like that," he replied apologetically.

The Toad smiled, showing yellow stained teeth. "Down the hall, first door to your left."

"Right." She turned on her heel and stomped off toward the bathroom.

Mark didn't miss the dirty look she threw him over her shoulder. She probably thought she'd fallen into a den of thieves. On the contrary, The Toad was a first-class fence and a part-time snitch. He didn't steal the stuff himself and only dealt with the best.

"I need a favor."

"Tell me more."

Serena splashed water on her face and looked at herself in the fish-shaped mirror over the avocado green bathroom sink. The scales were multicolored rhinestones. This stuff all looked like it had come straight out of the sixties. It almost reminded her of the stuff her mom had been fond of.

But The Toad wasn't warm and cuddly like her mom. He reminded her of a near-sighted gorilla with his bulk and yellow teeth. Imagine Mark being friends with such an unusual character. She supposed he mixed with all kinds in his line of work. Just what sort of business did The Toad think she was there for? Even more intriguing, what favor did Mark want from him? She resented being shuttled off to the lady's room so the men could talk business. Mark was taking his protective role a bit too far. He was probably lurking outside the bathroom door, just in case. She'd have to make a stand for equality.

Making up her mind, she opened the bathroom door, half expecting him to be waiting outside. She was surprised to find the hall empty. He must trust her to go to the powder room alone. It wasn't a big blow for independence.

She flicked off the bathroom light and started down the hall. It was time to set a more level playing field. She walked back to the living room, finding it vacant. She took a moment to gaze at her surroundings. She hadn't wanted to stare before, but now she got an eyeful.

Wow, who'd have thought Mexican serapes and tie-dye would go together? Obviously, The Toad did. She also noticed ashtrays on most of the tables, an unusual sight these days. He must have a big tobacco addiction.

Where were the men? "Mark?"

"I'm in the kitchen, lady," came the dulcet tones of The Toad.

She followed the sounds of chopping to the kitchen. Something savory was cooking. "Hello."

"Keep coming." A blender whirred.

Intrigued, she kept going. She walked into the kitchen to find The Toad bustling about the kitchen, wearing a frilly blue apron.

After she finished gaping at him, she noticed Mark wasn't in sight. She had a sinking feeling before she voiced the question.

"Where's Mark?"

"He had some business to take care of." The Toad gave her a stern glance. "He told me to tell you to sit tight, and also to feed you lunch."

She didn't like being ordered around like this, mainly secondhand. Why hadn't Mark told her before he'd left? "He did, huh? How about if I leave?"

"I wouldn't recommend it, lady. Besides, I'm under orders to stop you if you try. He figured you'd be angry." He flashed an apologetic smile. "Sorry."

What a jerk. He knew she'd be irate, so he'd ducked out the back. "Of all the high-hand-ed—"

"I hear you. He's left me hanging a few times, as well. But that doesn't mean I won't stand in your way. Don't try it."

She gazed at him, noting the strange dichotomy of the big man in a frilly apron, and wondered for a minute if she could take him. Sanity prevailed, and she fought the desire to walk out, knowing it would be suicidal. It was a typical tactic to ditch her like this without giving her a voice. She thought he was mellowing out of the tendency. She'd thought wrong.

She might as well make the best of a bad situation. "Can I help you make lunch?"

"The kettle's on the boil. Why don't you make us a nice pot of Earl Gray, and we can talk while my chili heats up."

She went to do his bidding. Maybe she could pump him for information. He might be able to tell her about Mark's past, as well.

She scooped loose-leaf tea out of its house-shaped caddy and dropped it into his purple and green swirled teapot. Pouring the boiling water over the leaves, she took a long sniff of the aroma of Earl Gray. It was just like having tea with Fern.

Almost, she amended, giving The Toad a sidelong glance. She hadn't reasonably categorized him yet, but she did find him likable.

He tasted his delicious-smelling soup and smiled. "Almost ready. Want a taste?" He took a spoon out of the drawer and handed it to her.

She took it, wanting to be a gracious captive—make that, guest. Besides, the simmering pot of chili smelled delightful. She spooned a taste from the bubbling pot, blew on it, and took a little sip. An ambrosia of flavors burst on her tongue.

She turned to smile at him. "That's the best chili I ever tasted."

He grinned. "Thanks. The secret is a pinch of cinnamon in the spices. Now, let's have tea, shall we?"

"Sounds good."

He picked up the tray and carried it into the living room. "Sit a spell. I'll pour."

She perched on a chaise lounge, amused despite the fix she was in. She watched him pour.

"One lump or two?" he asked, hovering over the sugar bowl.

"One, please, and a splash of milk." She accepted the cup from him and watched him fix his own.

Inhaling the aroma, she felt her crushed spirits start to restore themselves. She watched him sit in a big brown chair. It was his favorite chair, judging from the grooves warn in the chenille fabric.

"What shall we talk about?"

She cast him a level look. "Where's Mark?"

"Not sure, lady. I'm not privy to all his movements. He said he'd be back in about an hour. Don't worry, he hasn't abandoned you."

He looked her straight in the eye with no hesitation. He was telling the truth.

"I didn't think he had. Tell me, how did you two meet?"

He shrugged. "He saved my life."

"Really?" She gaped at him. It had sounded like he'd meant it.

"Uh-huh. He was part of a government sting. He was around when one of my prospective clients tried to turn the tables and rob me at gunpoint. Well, quick as you can blink an eye, Riley was kicking the gun out of the felon's hand. He arrested me, but he saved my life. I've tried to repay the favor by providing him with little bits of information I glean on the streets."

She was impressed despite being angry with Mark. "Wow." She grinned at him. "So, what kind of client did you think I was?"

"On occasion, people come to me who want to disappear. I can get them new identity papers."

She was surprised. Hot toasters she'd expected him to deal in, forged papers were a whole other thing. It made her uncomfortable. He wasn't the small-time hood she'd taken him for. Why did Mark tolerate his sideline? But then, Manny had thought she might be a client. Had Mark brought other women here?

"So, has Mark brought you clients before?"

He nodded. "Once, but that was long ago."

The disclosure intrigued her. "Who?"

"Sorry, I can't reveal the lady's name." He looked down, stirring his tea. "I must keep some secrets, you see."

She sipped her tea, disgruntled and intrigued. Another woman. Who? Why?

Manny cocked his head to the side and looked at her closely. "Tell me a bit about yourself."

She fought the urge to fidget under his study. What other women had he brought here? And more importantly, how did she stack up? She was plain and ordinary. "I'm a kindergarten teacher. I have a five-year-old son. Mark is assigned to look after me for a while."

He gazed at her, intrigued. "Those are just the surface things. What else?"

"Well, let's see. I'm into new-age healing. Crystals and the like, you know."

"Delightful. What else?"

"Hum. Well, I've been practicing yoga for years. And I recently took a self-defense class, so I think I could take you."

He chuckled. "Charming. Want to wrestle?"

"No, thanks."

"Right. Mark wouldn't thank me for mussing up his girl."

"I'm not his girl. He's my protector."

"And I'm the Queen of The May."

She smiled.

"Let's go dish up the chili. Your protector will be back soon."

Chapter Eleven

"Are you comfortable, beautiful?"

Serena got in the car. Mark had been warm and tender since he'd returned to The Toad's house, and she lapped it up like cream.

At his intense tone, she turned to look at him. Where was he taking her? Drinking in the sight of him, she decided it didn't matter. She wanted to savor this last evening like a miser hoarding gold.

When they drove back into town and toward the hospital, and he pulled into a rear parking lot, she couldn't have been more surprised.

"But you said it was too dangerous."

"I've got it covered, sweetheart. I called in a few favors. A trusted crew is standing watch. Best of all, your dad's doing well. They moved him out of ICU under an assumed name."

"Thank God." She waited for him to open her car door and then ran with him to the rear door marked 'Employees Only.'

The door swung open as they neared it. Bob stepped back so they could enter.

"About time you two got here," he commented, smiling.

"Bob, it's good to see you." She smiled at him.

"Everything going all right, partner?" Mark asked.

"So far, so good." Bob turned and glanced at Serena. "How have you been, ma'am?"

She was glad to see him after all this time. "Fine, and better now that I'm here."

"Let's move." Mark took her arm and ushered her down the corridor to a doorway.

She hurried to match his pace, glancing ahead at Bob. "How's my father, Bob?"

He stopped by a door marked 'Women's Locker Room' and turned a troubled look at her. "Better, but still unconscious, Ms. McLain. However, the doctors think he'll pull through."

Noting his qualified statement, she wondered what he wasn't saying. She could tell he was concerned about something. "What else aren't you telling me?"

Mark put his arm around her, squeezing her shoulder gently. "We can't hide a thing from you, can we?"

She leaned into his touch, feeling comforted by it. "No."

Bob sighed. "Okay, I won't sugarcoat it. The doctors can't tell if there will be long-term brain damage, Serena."

Her stomach tightened at the thought. Her father made his living with the pen. Would Gerald Grayson's violence silence his unique voice? What a horrifying thought.

Mark ran a soothing hand up and down her arm. "But they aren't saying it'll happen, either, Serena. Keep a positive thought, okay?"

"Okay," she agreed. She glanced at the locker room door. "So, what are we doing here?"

"Time to play dress up," Mark replied, smiling to lighten the mood. "My sister-in-law, Lori, is inside.

"Oh yes, the RN. She's Allen's wife."

He nodded. "Right. She works here part-time. She'll fix you up with a nurse's uniform. It's between shifts, so you should go unnoticed. That's important because the security's been tightened to the max lately."

She hadn't expected to go incognito. His mention of security got her thinking. This visit had to be against the rules. Could he and Bob get in trouble for it? She hadn't considered that in her desire to come here. And Lori, too, she didn't want to jeopardize any of their jobs.

"We don't have to do this. I can—"

"Yes, you do." He cut off her protests.

She looked from Mark to Bob, noting their resolute expressions. "But I don't want to get you into trouble."

"Let us worry about that," Bob replied.

She nodded, reassured. It might have been fun if she weren't so concerned about her father. "Wow, I guess I'm going undercover."

She pulled open the door and walked into the white-tiled room. It was empty, save for Lori in the far corner of the room. She recognized Allen's wife from the cottage.

Serena rushed over to her. "Lori, thank you for helping me do this."

"No problem, sweetie. I'm glad to do it," she stated, smiling. "Oh, by the way, Mom told me to tell you Sammy's fine."

Serena felt some of her tension abate. It had been playing on her mind. "Thanks for the update. I have been worried. So, what do we do now?"

"I have your uniform and shoes waiting in the cubicle." She opened the door to reveal a changing cubicle with a bench and mirror.

Serena rushed inside and quickly stripped off, anxious to see her father. She was confident her voice would help him wake up. She slipped into the nurse's uniform and put on the thick-soled, sensible shoes that went with it. She glanced at her image in the mirror and thought she looked the part. Hopefully, nobody would ask her to render first aid.

She took her can of mace and slipped it into her pocket, just in case. Then, she stepped out of the cubicle to see Lori dressed in a similar uniform. She had her nametag pinned to her top. She'd have a real nurse for backup. It was a comforting thought. Not that she was frightened, just a bit nervous. If Mark said it was safe, she believed him.

Lori looked her over. "You look fine. Here, pin this on." She handed her a nametag.

Serena looked at it. "Sara Holmes."

"She's a new nurse. She starts work here tomorrow. I stole it off the security guard's desk. Keep your distance from the Dirty Harry Wannabes, and you'll be fine."

Serena pinned it on and took the stethoscope Lori handed her, draping it around her neck in the same fashion. It sounded like they'd tightened security since her dad was admitted. She, for one, was happy about that. All she'd have to do was steer clear of them.

They walked out of the locker room to find Mark waiting outside the door. He was still dressed in his street clothes, she noticed. They turned, and she noted Bob was at the end of the corridor. He was wearing scrubs. He waved them forward, and she and Lori followed him, with Mark bringing up the rear.

As it was the middle of the night shift, they didn't encounter anyone.

They turned the corner and went into a staff elevator. Bob pushed the button for the third floor.

"They moved your father to a private room on four west," Mark stated. "Bob will go first to make sure the coast is clear. Then, Lori will walk with you. Going around the nurse's station is the only tricky part I anticipate. Don't make eye contact with anyone. Keep going to room 410. If anyone asks any questions, Lori will stop and distract them. I'll follow along behind you."

Before Serena could respond, the bell dinged, and the elevator doors opened.

Bob took off, and she didn't even have time to be nervous before Lori nudged her out of the elevator. The fact that Mark was right behind her was comforting. They waited until Bob was around the corner and then started. She and Lori walked purposefully down the hall.

As they rounded the corner, the nurse's station came into sight. It was a hub of activity, as nurses and doctors did their charting. Despite Mark's orders to the contrary, she looked over at them. Only one gave her a second look, an older nurse who looked her over thoughtfully. She pretended not to notice and kicked up her pace, hurrying toward her father's room. Bob stood outside, flipping through a chart, looking like he belonged.

She opened the door and went in. Her father looked so small lying in the hospital bed. He always seemed larger than life, and now he seemed to shrink overnight. A large bandage covered part of his head. She hurried forward and reached out to take his cool hand. It was flaccid, without response.

Her heart sank as visions of brain damage raced through her mind. "Dad, it's me, Serena. Wake up, Dad." She could hardly believe it when he stirred a little bit. From the corner of her eye, she noticed Mark standing slightly to her rear. She turned a shaky smile on him, touched by him for doing this for her. "I think he's starting to come around."

Mark stepped up, putting his arm around her. "The doctors said just about the same thing. He's been rousing a bit more each day. They're hopeful that, in due time, he'll regain consciousness."

"Thank heavens." She leaned into him, absorbing his strength. She'd need it to go up against Grayson in court tomorrow.

Bob came in. "Mark, can I talk to you?"

Mark nodded, stepping away from Serena. "I need to confer with you, too, but later."

Serena glanced at their intense expressions. They probably wanted to plan for tomorrow. "I'm fine, go have your conference. I'll stay right here."

Lori nodded. "She'll be fine, Mark. I'll stay with her. She probably wants some alone time with her father."

"Right," Serena replied, backing her up. She didn't want to be a burden. Besides, there was nothing dangerous stirring here. They hadn't even caught sight of the dreaded security squad.

Mark nodded. "Okay, wait here. I'll be right back. I'll give you some private time."

Serena watched him go, feeling almost like she'd pushed him away. She hadn't meant to do that.

Putting it out of her mind, she went back to her dad's bedside. She needed to concentrate on her father. If only she could get through to him.

"Dad." She touched his cheek, brushing it softly with her hand. He seemed to turn his head toward her hand, ever so slightly. Her breath caught. Had she imagined it? She brushed the other cheek, and he turned the other way. He was waking up. She turned to Lori. "Look."

Lori watched. "Oh goodness, sweetie, that's amazing. He's responding to you."

His eyelids fluttered.

"He's waking up. We've got to tell a doctor."

"I have a friend at the desk. I could go and quietly report it without mentioning your name." She hesitated. "But I told Mark I'd stay."

"I know, but it's important. It should only take a few minutes. Go. I'll be fine."

Lori hesitated momentarily.

Serena understood her dilemma, but this had to be done. "I'm fine here. Go."

Lori walked out the door and closed it behind her.

This was marvelous, an actual pick-me-up, to know her father was waking. She talked to him some more, watching him stir. Glancing up at the clock, she noticed five minutes had passed.

What was keeping Lori? Was there a problem?

She walked to the door and opened it, peeking out. A security guard was talking to Lori down the hall, and from the frown on his face, he wasn't happy.

Oh no, they were caught. Would Lori get in trouble?

A doctor came down the hall with a flock of interns in his wake. He glanced up at her, his brow wrinkling. Could she slip past him, brazen it out?

Slipping out of the room, she made a beeline for the elevator. If she could make it, all would not be lost.

"Nurse," he called sharply, blocking her path.

"You're not on the floor staff, Nurse Hughes. What were you doing in there?"

Serena bit her lip, hesitating for a second as she gazed at him. Good grief. Lori hadn't been kidding about tight security. She feinted to the side, slipping around him and rushing down the hall.

"Security, stop her!"

She kept going, rushing past Lori and the guard. Lori grabbed for his sleeve when he turned toward her.

He pulled away, yelling, "Hey, you. Stop!"

Serena kept going toward the elevator, his heavy footsteps behind her.

Damn it.

She slipped into the stairwell and stopped, gasping for breath as the door clicked shut behind her. Pressing back, out of sight, she watched the security guard run past her hiding place, heading for the elevator.

She let out a sigh of relief. She was in the clear as long as he didn't double back. She started down the stairs in search of Mark. He'd find a way to square things for Lori.

Halfway down the first flight, the stairwell door opened behind her. She froze, holding her breath. Had the security guard doubled back?

She glanced up and relaxed. It was only a doctor in a lab coat. They hadn't found her, after all.

She turned and continued down. The doctor had looked a bit familiar. She must have seen him in the hall.

She sped up, eager to get away. Although the security guard probably wouldn't chase an errant nurse this far, she hoped. The man behind her sped up, his footsteps echoing on the metal stairs. It gave her the willies. Was he chasing her? She shot a wary glance at him over her shoulder. He was looking at her with a focused glint in his eye.

Her breath caught. He *was* after her! She broke into a run, taking the stairs two at a time, wincing when her ankle twisted.

"What's your hurry, sweet thing?" he asked mockingly.

Oh God, it was the goon from the party. She stumbled, hitting the rail, and almost toppled over the railing. Catching herself, she noticed he was closing in on her.

Her mace! She pulled it out of her pocket as he reached for her. Glaring at him, she knew she only had one chance. She'd have to hit him dead on.

He grabbed her, snarling. "Mr. Grayson wants a word with you."

Jerking away, she raised her hand, spraying him square in the eyes.

"Argh," he screamed, falling back with his hands at his eyes. He wobbled on the step for a second and lost his balance. He fell, tumbling down the rest of the way, landing in a heap at the bottom of the stairs, and went still.

She gaped at him, not believing her luck. The mace worked.

She began hobbling down to the bottom when the basement door opened. Oh no, was it another goon? She held her spray at the ready.

Mark ran in, gun drawn. He looked at the felled goon and then up at her.

"I got him with my mace."

"Good God," he commented with a shake of his head. "Are you okay?"

"I'm fine. I twisted my ankle a bit, but otherwise, fine."

"Where's Lori?"

"She got waylaid by a security guard. She won't get in trouble, will she?"

"No. I'll see to it." He walked over and scooped her up in his arms, plucking her off the stairs.

She snuggled in his arms and then looked up at him. "I can walk, Mark. You don't have to carry me."

"Humor me." He shouldered her out of the stairwell just as Bob arrived.

"I'll take care of him," Bob said, looking at the fallen man. "And I'll help your sister-in-law out, too. You two get going."

"Right, we're out."

Chapter Twelve

"Are we going back to The Toad's place?" Serena asked as they drove along.

She wiggled her foot, testing her ankle. It was sore, sprained but not broken, she guessed.

"No. I figured the tie-dye and tassels might give me nightmares," he joked. "I figured you'd like to take this somewhere more private. And hopefully, a damned sight more secure. I'm sorry about what happened back there. It was inexcusable."

She gazed at his tight expression. She'd figured he'd be mad at her for not staying put. They might as well get it out in the open and over with. "I know. I'm sorry I gave us away."

He slanted a grim look her way. "I was talking about me, not you. I shouldn't have left you alone like that. Hell, I shouldn't have brought you there at all."

She looked at him. He was blaming himself. "You're wrong. You did the right thing by taking me to see my dad. It helped settle my mind for tomorrow's day at court. Besides, things would have been all right if I hadn't panicked, cut, and run."

He shook his head. "You're some kind of woman, Serena."

"What kind?" she teased, trying to lighten the mood.

"My kind."

"So where are we going?" Was he going to take her parking on lover's lane? The thought made her smile. When he turned into a motel, she chuckled.

"What?"

She grinned up at him. "I thought maybe we were going parking."

"Do a lot of parking, do you?" His brow shot up with displeasure.

"I'll never tell. This will do nicely instead."

He turned to look at her under the motel's exterior light. "You're calm."

She endeavored to sound sophisticated. "Why not? We're both consenting adults, and there's nothing new here."

He flashed a rapacious grin. "Aha, but you haven't seen my entire gamut of magic spells," he stated as he went to check-in.

She watched him go, feeling bemused. New spells were intriguing. He came back out, showing her the key, and she smiled.

He pulled the car around to the back, got out, and walked around the car to open her door.

She took his hand and let him help her out. She looked into his intense brown eyes and found tenderness, and her heart melted.

He put an arm around her waist and led her to the motel room. She leaned on him, letting him help take her weight off her sore ankle after he unlocked the door. He ushered her inside, and she stepped onto the green pile carpet. The room had a king-sized bed, television, and dresser. But they weren't there for the décor.

She turned to smile at him. He was watching her, suddenly hesitant.

She smiled to reassure him. "About those new spells…"

"Your ankle."

"It'll keep." She reached for him, loving the heat in his eyes. He was obviously burning for her, as well.

He pulled her into his arms and kissed her.

When he broke the kiss off after a moment, she was disappointed. She reached for him again, but he stepped back.

"Not so fast, beautiful. We're going to take our time."

"We are, huh?" She brushed up against him, frustrated. "Maybe I want to go fast."

He smiled. "Stop trying to influence me with your womanly wiles." He gently rocked her back on her heels and started to unbutton her blouse slowly. "One step at a time." He undid the last button and let her blouse fall open. "You're so lovely, Serena."

She shrugged it onto the floor, smiling. She'd never considered herself lovely. "Thank you."

She reached for his shirt, tugging it out of his pants. Her trembling fingers tried to undo his buttons. He sucked in a deep breath, his nostrils flaring as she fumbled with them. He was ready for her, she knew. Tired of fooling with the stubborn buttons, she tugged, listening to the pop. They flew through the air, landing all around them. She didn't care. She needed to touch him badly. It must have been the adrenalin rush from being chased, but she was suddenly swamped with desire. Dizzy with it.

"You ripped the buttons off my shirt."

"I'll sew them back on." Her hands went to his hot skin. She kneaded her fingers, feeling his strength. "You're magnificent."

"You say the sweetest things." He reached for the button on her skirt and undid it, pulling down the zipper. It was loud in the quiet room. He let go, and the skirt dropped to the floor, pooling around her feet. He gazed hungrily at her in her black lace bra and panties. Then, he lightly brushed the crests of her breasts, the nipples hardening, peeking at him. "Perfect ripe strawberries," he murmured, bending to lick them through the lace.

Trembling at his tongue's damp heat, she leaned forward, offering herself for his pleasure. He nipped at her, and she whimpered, her knees buckling. He seemed fiercer tonight, more demanding, as if almost losing her had pushed him over the edge.

"Time to get naked," he stated with a sexy growl as he reached behind her to unclasp her bra. The straps skittered off her shoulders, and it dropped to the floor.

He looked at her long and hard, gazing hungrily at her breasts. He reached out to touch her, his fingertips grazing over her full curves, touching them, pinching the nipples, and rolling them in his fingers.

She whimpered as a surge of pleasure tore through her causing heat to pool inside her. "Please."

"I will." He bent to take her nipple in his mouth, drawing on it hungrily.

She lost all thought, tugging on his pants. She wanted him naked now.

He moved to suckle her other nipple, which drove all rational thought from her mind until she was shaking, pressing against him, and letting him ravish her.

When he slowly pulled away, she noticed her panties were down around her feet. "How did that happen?"

"Magic." He flashed her a wicked grin and kicked off his loafers, slacks, and briefs.

He picked her up, carried her to the bed, laid her down, and eased on top of her.

His hot mouth went back to her nipple while his hand went between her legs, rubbing her clit, dipping inside her, and she was out of her mind again. She grabbed for him, overcome with need, drawing him to her. If he didn't take her soon, she thought she'd set the sheets afire.

But he didn't take her, instead bending to drop scorching kisses down the length of her body while she shivered. He stopped to dip his tongue in her navel. She gasped and writhed against him. He went farther down, kissing the insides of her thighs, touching his tongue to her womanhood, and pleasuring her as he lapped at her clitoris.

She went still, surprised for a second at the exquisite sensation. Her body tightened, and she thrashed on the bed.

"Oh dear, please, please." She tried to pull him back up, but he wouldn't stop. Pleasure consumed her as she flailed against him, pure magic. He took the button in his mouth, and she convulsed as the orgasm rushed through her body.

He moved up her body and surged into her, filling her. His thrusts were fierce as he drove into her time and again.

She rocked against him, her pleasure rebuilding at the delicious friction. She was moving against him, wrapping her legs around him, taking more of him in. Grinding against him, waves of sensation built. She cried out, nipping his shoulder, tasting the salty tang of his skin.

He growled, slamming into her, and she came, spasms of orgasm rippling through her. She muffled her cry on his shoulder, murmuring, "I love you."

He thrust deep into her again, his body tightening, and gave a hoarse shout of satisfaction.

Chapter Thirteen

Mark glanced out the motel room window for the third time that morning, and fought the tension that assailed him. The van pulled up and some of his tautness abated. Backup was here, and it was time to implement Plan B.

Serena was in the bathroom, dressing for her day in court, and he was determined it should go off without a hitch. Since the attack at the hospital yesterday, he wasn't prepared to take any chances. He was still kicking himself for letting down his guard. It wouldn't happen today. His contingency plan should keep him one step ahead of Gerald Grayson and the mole in his department.

The bathroom door opened, and he turned to smile at Serena, not wanting her to pick up on his concern. She needed to keep a clear head for the task ahead. She looked pretty as a picture in her tan linen suit, just the sort of thing to wear in court.

"You look lovely, beautiful." His heart melted as he watched her blush a bright pink. She *was* beautiful, and she was his. After she gave her testimony, they'd get on with the rest of their lives. Last night had given him hope she would be a part of his.

She stepped closer. "Thanks, I needed that. I'm jumpier than a long-tailed cat in a room full of rocking chairs."

He closed the distance, noting her limp was hardly noticeable today. Her ankle was better. He pulled her close for a hug, feeling the tension in her body soften. She sighed and leaned against him. He'd protect her with the last breath in his body.

"Don't worry, I'll stick with you every step of the way. You'll do fine."

"I know. I guess I'm just dreading the thought of facing Grayson and his, no doubt, sleazy lawyers. What if they twist things around? Maybe they're still claiming I shot my PI."

He nestled against her for a moment before dropping a kiss on the top of her head. "They don't have any proof. I talked with Bob, who said with what we've got on Sinclair, he's turned state's evidence. Just tell the truth, and you'll be fine." He picked up her bag. "Ready?"

She nodded. "As I'll ever be."

"Our escort is here."

"Escort?"

"Yes. I've made a few alterations to the morning's plans. Just think of it as me being overprotective."

She smiled at him and picked up her purse. "One of the things I like about you, Agent Riley."

"Only one?" He chuckled as he went to the door. "Later, I'll have to remind you of my other fine points. Hold tight while I check things out." He ducked out of the motel room.

Serena stood shuffling her feet on the green carpet while she waited for Mark's return. Seconds turned into minutes.

The door opened, and he popped back inside. "It's clear. Let's go."

She nodded and slipped out the door. She understood the need for secrecy, but he might be carrying it too far. Still, after her scare at the hospital, she was glad he was being overprotective.

As she stepped out of the door, she noticed their car was gone. "Our car."

"We're making a switch."

"With what?" She followed his glance toward a van two doors down. The door opened, and Bob got out, followed by a younger man. Her cheeks flamed. Did they know they'd spent the night together? Of course, they did. This was the new millennium, and it was time she altered her puritanical feelings.

"Bob, how nice to see you again."

He nodded, glancing at the two of them tentatively. "Same here. I'm glad to see you looking so well. You feeling okay after your scare last night?"

Her apprehension faded when he smiled. He was on their side. "I'm feeling strong, thanks. Mark took good care of me. What about the guy I attacked?"

"We patched him up, and he's in custody, ma'am." He turned to Mark. "The guy had a mile-long rap sheet and two outstanding warrants for his arrest. He's going away for a long time. He won't bother you again."

"Good." She hoped they threw the book at him.

"You still got your mace?" Bob asked with a grin.

She patted her tote bag. "I never leave home without it."

"That's fine."

Mark glanced at Serena. "The young man with Bob is a fellow agent, Alex."

The guy smiled. "Nice to meet you, ma'am."

Ma'am, was it? She must be showing her age today. No doubt, the idea of going to court was to blame. She wanted Gerald Grayson to get his comeuppance, but the idea of being in the same room with him made her edgy.

"Good morning, Alex."

Mark took her arm. "Let's get moving." He escorted her to the van and opened the rear sliding door. "Get in, Serena."

The van seemed very familiar. She climbed into the backseat, and he slipped in alongside her. Bob and Alex climbed into the front seats.

She suddenly remembered where she'd seen it before. "You had this parked outside my condo last week."

Bob flashed an apologetic smile. "Right you are. We were keeping an eye on you."

She gazed at the sophisticated listening equipment. "If only I'd known." She reached out to touch Mark's hand. "Thanks for saving my life."

Mark nodded. "You are most welcome."

The radio crackled. Bob reached for it. "Eagle here."

"Where's Domino?"

"Sorry, sir, I'm not sure."

"Right. I've got a squad ready to take the subject at the courthouse's front door. Tell him he'd damned well better be at court on time this morning, or his badge is mine. I'm fed up with his Rambo attitude."

"Right, sir." Bob hung up.

Mark's hand tightened on hers for a second. The man on the radio had to be his boss. Just how much trouble had he gotten into for her?

She slanted a curious glance his way. "Was that Whittaker?"

He scowled. "Yup. Old chicken hawk himself."

"In that case, maybe we should do what he said."

He sent her a searching gaze. "Having second thoughts?"

He thought she'd lost faith in him because of what happened at the hospital. Nothing could have been further from the truth. "No, nothing like that. I trust you with my life. I don't want you to jeopardize your career for me."

He squeezed her hand. "It's nothing for you to worry about, beautiful. He's always mouthing off, isn't he, Bob?"

Bob hesitated, then nodded.

They were selling her a bill of goods.

"He's right, Ms. McLain," Bob replied.

Their story sounded hollow to her ears, but she knew she couldn't sway them. They were an unstoppable force. It was probably far worse than Mark had let on. And Bob had lied to Whittaker, as well. It was professional suicide for them to defy Whittaker's authority, and they didn't seem to care. What could she do? Events were spinning out of her control. Maybe if they sped things up, they could get there in time to keep Whittaker from blowing his top.

"Well, step on it, Alex. I don't want you to risk your positions on my account."

"Negative," Mark countered, tightening his grip on her hand. "He already has his instructions. Stay on target, Alex."

She sat back with a huff. So much for trying to manipulate two FBI bulldozers.

Alex pulled out of the parking lot and took a left. She couldn't help fidgeting as he drove in a circuitous route in the general direction of the courthouse. At least, she hoped they were heading for the courthouse. There would be no rushing them.

"We *are* going to the courthouse, aren't we?"

"Eventually, but I want to check out the lay of the land first. Being the cautious sort, I decided on a slight change of venue. I'm not taking any chances."

"But we'll be late. I don't want you to—"

"Let me worry about that. We're going in the back way to avoid the press and any reception committee that might be waiting."

She knew he meant Grayson's shooters. A sneak attack in a stairwell was one thing, but would Grayson try something in such a public place? She gazed at Mark's focused attention. Even though she thought it was a remote chance, she was grateful for his overprotective tendencies. She didn't fancy meeting with the press, either.

"Okay, we'll do it your way."

Mark's cell rang. He let go of her hand and flipped it open. "Fine. Watch for us." He hung up and looked at Serena. "My contact on the inside is ready for us. Are you ready?"

"Yes." She sat still, holding tight to her tote bag as they pulled up to a back service door. In half an hour, this would be over, and she could walk out of court free from fear with Mark at her side.

She took Mark's hand and let him help her from the van. Bob and Alex stepped next to her, forming a human shield. She wanted to protest. Surely, Grayson wouldn't be stupid enough to try something at the courthouse. But what if he did? She reached into her tote bag and found her mace.

They entered the building by the service entrance, going down a back corridor to a janitor's storeroom. Mark pulled out a key and opened the storeroom's door.

She blinked up at him, puzzled. "What are we doing here?"

"It's as good a place to wait as any and safer than most. The janitorial crew is at a staff meeting right now, and from here, we'll have a direct route to the courtroom." He looked at the mace in her hand and cracked a smile. "I see you're ready to fight."

She nodded. "I'm ready for whatever Grayson throws my way." She would have preferred to head directly to the courtroom where there were dozens of witnesses if Grayson should try anything, but she trusted Mark's judgment. If he said this was better, she'd take his word for it. She walked inside, glancing at mop buckets and shelves of supplies near a work desk. "Are you sure this is necessary?"

Mark dusted off a desk chair for her and propelled her toward it with a determined glint in his eye. "You're precious cargo. Let me fuss a bit."

Just as she started to sit, a crashing thud reverberated through the walls making her plop into the chair.

She blinked at Mark. "What on earth was that?"

"I don't know." Mark's cell phone rang. He stepped away from her to answer it. "What happened? Is she okay? What about my car? Totaled? Crap. Okay, keep me posted. What's Whittaker doing? As bad as that, huh? Well, tell him for me, he can lump it. Demote me if he wants. I don't give a damn. You, too. Okay, we'll go in fifteen minutes. Thanks, bro. I owe you a big one."

"Was that Ross?" She glanced at his stern expression. "What's wrong? Is it Sammy?"

"No, nothing like that. Sammy's back at my folk's cabin, safe and sound. Ross was part of the crash you just heard. He and one of his female deputies acted as decoys out front. They were driving my car. Somebody rammed their vehicle, and the hit-and-run driver took a potshot at the deputy pretending to be you before speeding away."

Serena gasped. "Oh no, that poor girl. Is she...?"

"She's okay. She was wearing a vest."

"That could have been us. Oh, dear Lord. You were right to be suspicious, and here I thought you were going overboard."

Mark patted her shoulder, then turned to look at Bob. "Whittaker was standing there. The useless bastard didn't even get a shot off."

Bob scowled. "Figures. I guess that was Grayson's last grasp. The funny thing, though, is Whittaker standing there to witness the crime and not firing."

Mark nodded. "I was thinking the same thing, partner."

Alex's brow wrinkled. "You don't think..."

Mark shook his head. "I think now is not the time to worry about this." He turned to look at Serena. "Do you still want to go through with testifying? I can smuggle you out the back door if you want."

She glanced at his resolute expression. He was giving her an easy out if she wanted to take it. But Gerald Grayson had to pay, and if she could play a small part in convicting him, she had to do it. "No, I've got to do this. I'm ready to go."

"Good girl." Mark drew her to him for a hug and walked her to the door.

Bob stood with his hand on the knob. "You're doing the right thing, Ms. McLain. Don't worry, we'll look after you."

Serena nodded and let Mark escort her through the door. Bob and Alex drew up beside her, and she thought wryly she was the best-guarded woman in town. Now that the time was here, she was eager to get it over with. How dare Gerald Grayson try to intimidate her into not testifying?

They walked down the back corridor and into the main hallway. The courtroom had a few people milling around the open door and a scowling man standing by the door. Tall and gaunt, with sandy brown hair, he was dressed in what appeared to be an expensively tailored gray suit.

"Is that Whittaker?"

The man spotted them and started walking their way, frown lines bracketing his thin lips.

"That's him," Mark Confirmed.

Whittaker stopped in front of them. "Well, Riley, I see you finally showed up. Late as usual and not dressed for court." He raked a scornful glance over Mark's jeans and turned to scowl at Bob. "I don't even want to hear your excuse, Wilson." He eyed Serena. "Mrs. McLain, allow me to apologize for my underling's unprofessional conduct. It won't go unpunished. Thank heavens you're still with us, no thanks to Agent Riley."

She froze, shocked at the words coming out of his mouth. He was spinning the truth, turning Mark into a villain instead of the hero he was.

Mark's hand tightened on hers as he eyed Whittaker coolly.

She glanced up at his rigid stance and then turned to scowl at Whittaker. How dare he pull this stuff? He had no idea what they'd endured.

"I'm still alive thanks to him, as you know. Lucky for me, Mark used his head rather than follow questionable orders, or I'd have been the one shot at outside the courthouse this morning. If anyone asks me, that's what I will say."

Ice formed in Whittaker's gray eyes and his forced smile faded. He didn't like her insinuation, but that was too bad. She was through taking crap from bullies in any form.

He sniffed, looking pointedly at her hand in Mark's. "The district attorney is waiting for you inside, Ms. McLain."

Serena dropped Mark's hand, recalling Bob's concern he'd get in trouble. Whittaker raised his brow, and she knew it was too late. He'd already guessed their connection. And Mark, darn him, wasn't making it any easier as he stepped closer and took her arm. Didn't he care about his career?

"The district attorney is waiting for you, Ms. McLain," Whittaker said again.

She started toward the courtroom, deciding to ignore the man. She could see why his men didn't respect him. He seemed utterly unconcerned about the breach of security outside.

"Not you, Riley. I'm suspending you, pending an investigation. Bob and Alex can stay on the detail for now. Let this be a lesson to you all. When I give an order, I expect it to be obeyed."

Serena froze as Mark came to a halt. She slanted Whittaker an icy glare. How could he be so vindictive? She looked at Mark, and found resolve. This wasn't a surprise, and as far as he was concerned, it wasn't over. He'd suspected Whittaker of misconduct, but that wouldn't help them now. Whittaker seemed to delight in jabbing at him, probably hoping to provoke a response he could punish. She couldn't allow that to happen. She had to put on a brave face and go it alone.

When Mark let go of her hand and took an angry step forward, she reached for his sleeve to stop him.

He stopped in his tracks to look at her.

"I'm okay. Do what you have to do. I need to go this alone."

Mark nodded, his expression softening as he looked at her. "Right. Good luck, beautiful. I know you'll do fine. You're a strong woman. Bob and Alex will stick with you." He reached in his pocket and pulled out a business card. "It might be a while before I see you again, but this has my cell phone number. Call me if you need me."

Serena took the card he handed her, concentrating on him while shutting out those around her. She refused to let Whittaker intrude on their moment. Would she see Mark again? If he did battle with Whittaker, could he win? She couldn't let herself worry about those things now. She had this ordeal to get through.

"Thanks, Mark. I'll do my best." She walked into the courtroom, willing herself not to turn back. She feared she might break down and cry if she did. Calming herself for the task, she spared Gerald Grayson a defiant glance. He sat beside his high-priced lawyer, looking smug and unrepentant in his two thousand-dollar suit.

They called ex-detective Lyle Sinclair to the stand. She sat there looking at him in his orange county issued jumpsuit, recalling the night he'd cornered her on the beach. She couldn't help reliving it as she remembered Mark saving her from certain death. So much evil had happened because of Gerald Grayson. Kidnapping, assault, and murder because some mobster thought he was above the law. She was ready to do her part in putting him away.

When they called her name, she walked to the witness stand with her head held high. The DA prompted her to relay the events of that evening, and she answered calmly, looking Grayson in the eye. The defense attorney tried to shake her, insinuating she and the PI had broken in. She took a deep breath, reminding herself of all the damage Gerald Grayson had done and remained calm.

After she testified, she walked out of the courtroom, Bob and Alex at her side. She'd done her part. The rest was up to the judicial system.

Bob shut the door behind them. "Well, it's all over with now, Ms. McLain."

"Thank God." She looked around the hallway, feeling suddenly bereft.

Mark was nowhere in sight, but she hadn't expected him to be. Her legs felt a bit shaky.

Bob steered her to a nearby bench. "Are you okay?"

She sat and smiled at him, hoping to reassure him. "I'm fine. I guess it was just a delayed reaction. Thank you for everything."

"You're quite welcome." He sat next to her and patted her hand. "Even though my assignment is through, I want you to know, I'm here for you if you need me."

She glanced at his kind smile, feeling reassured. Life went on, and it was time she got on with hers. "Thanks, I appreciate that. But hopefully, the agency is right, and I'll be safe now."

He nodded. "I think at least they got that right. I know Mark would want to be here if he could."

She nodded, seeing Bob's troubled expression. He'd warned her before about getting involved with an agent. Maybe she should have listened. It would have been easier on her heart.

"I know he's got his career to think about."

A footstep sounded behind her, and she looked up hopefully, only to find Whittaker bearing down on her. If only it had been Mark. She at least wanted to say goodbye. No doubt, Whittaker had sent him far away.

She looked away, pulling some coins from her tote bag. She'd call a cab to come to get her. Then, she'd drive out to the lake to get Sammy. It was time to move on. Maybe a clean break was best.

Whittaker smiled, stuffing his hands in his pants pockets. "The agency owes you a debt of gratitude, Ms. McLain. Can I drop you somewhere?"

His smile didn't reach his eyes, she noted. It was false, like the rest of him. He seemed uncomfortable under her scrutiny, fidgeting, jingling the change in his pockets.

Still, she forced herself to be civil. "No, thank you. I've made other arrangements." She turned away, hoping he got the message.

Tears misted her eyes, but she refused to let them fall. It would give the creep too much satisfaction. She and Mark had split up because of him, and there wasn't a thing she could do about it.

Five days later, Serena sat quietly in her father's hospital room. She hadn't heard from Mark since they'd parted at the courthouse. She'd tried to move on with her life. Things were better on the home front. Sammy was happy to be home, and they were returning to their old routines. She hadn't brought him to the hospital yet. She didn't want to scare him with how her dad looked now, hooked up to all the tubes. So, she left Sammy home with Mrs. Monroe while she made her daily visit. Her father still hadn't regained consciousness, but he was improving daily. The doctors thought he might wake soon.

He groaned and turned his head.

"Hello, Dad." The nurses had told her to talk to him, and he did seem to recognize her voice. He'd been restless as of late, which the nurses said was a good sign. He turned his head her way, and then he opened his eyes.

"Dad!" She jumped up and stepped toward the bed. His eyes were unfocused, the lids at half-mast. "Dad, it's me, Serena. You're awake."

"Argh." He coughed and then licked his lips.

The specter of brain damage raced through her head. But then he cleared his throat, his eyes opening more and focusing on her.

"Serena?"

"Yes, Dad. It's me."

"Baby, it's so good to see you." He stretched and winced. "What's going on? Where am I?"

"You're in the hospital." She pushed the nurse call button. "Come quick! My dad, he's awake."

He tried to sit up, his brow wrinkling. "What happened?"

She pressed him back down. "Easy, Dad. You were shot. You were on your way to meet your agent when you disappeared."

He lay back against the pillows. "Ah, yes. I remember now. They snatched me off the street. Did you get the key I sent?"

She smiled. His mind was as sharp as ever. Too bad she'd been so slow to figure out his poem.

"Yes, but I must admit, it took me a while to figure it out. Your book is safe. The FBI has it."

"Good. I didn't want him to get it." He closed his eyes, relaxing against his pillows.

She smoothed back his hair. "Don't worry, it's safe, and so are you."

His eyes popped open. "Where's Sammy?"

Of course, his concern had always been for his family. Touched, she gave him a shaky smile, tears coming to her eyes. She cried too darned quickly these days. It was all Mark's fault. He'd turned her into a marshmallow.

"Sammy's back home with Mrs. Monroe. He'll be thrilled to find out you're awake. I'll bring him to see you later."

Serena hopped into her car and drove home. Back to the haven she'd made for them. She knew something was wrong when she saw Mrs. Monroe standing in her yard wringing her hands.

Serens jumped from her car, hurrying up to her. "What happened?"

Fern sniffed back a tear. "I was going to call you. Sammy's missing."

"Oh, my God." Grayson! Were his partners doing this for revenge? She reached into her tote bag for her new cell phone. She'd programmed Mark's number on speed dial, just in case. Now she needed it, and not for any silly romantic reasons.

She pushed in the code. It rang twice, and then he picked up.

"Riley here."

"Mark," her voice quivered.

"Serena, what's wrong?"

She brushed away the tears from her face. "Sammy's missing."

"That son of a bitch. Dry your tears, Serena. I'll get him back. Sit tight. I'll be right there with reinforcements."

Serena let Mrs. Monroe lead her into the house. How could the unthinkable have happened? The FBI had assured her she'd be safe.

Fern placed a cup of tea in front of her, but she couldn't drink it. She unconsciously ripped a paper napkin to shreds in her lap.

The bell rang, and her heart stopped for a moment before she rushed to the door. She tore it open to find Mark on her doorstep, surrounded by Bob, Alex, and two other steely-eyed agents.

She fell into Mark's arms, sobbing. "My God, Mark, they took my baby. Why, why? Whittaker said we'd be safe."

"You should have been. Still, he should have kept a detail on you to be sure. Come on, let's take this inside. We've got work to do." He put his arm around her and propelled her inside.

She watched the agents, frantic, as they set to work attaching devices to her phones. It seemed they were expecting a call. A ransom demand. What would Grayson want? Her to recant her testimony? She'd do it in a heartbeat if it meant getting Sammy back.

"Why haven't they called yet, Mark?"

"Give them time. Let's go into the kitchen." He urged her toward the kitchen and sat her in the breakfast nook. He looked at Mrs. Monroe. "Tell me what happened."

"I was here babysitting Sammy. About half an hour ago, the phone rang, and I went in to answer it. When I came back, Sammy was gone. I looked for him and couldn't find him, then Serena arrived."

"Who was on the phone?"

"A telemarketer."

Bob rushed into the room carrying a piece of paper. "I found this ransom demand in the mailbox. They want Serena to personally deliver ten thousand dollars to the lady's room in the bus station at five this afternoon."

Mark frowned. "That's all, just ten grand?"

Serena looked at him, puzzled. She supposed it wasn't much as ransoms went. And besides, she expected a demand to recant her testimony. "That doesn't sound right, does it?"

Mark shrugged. "It's certainly unexpected if Grayson is behind it."

"He might want me to recant my testimony, but not money."

"Right, and why so little?"

She shivered. It was almost worse to have some shadowy figure behind Sammy's kidnapping. "Which means someone else has him. But who?"

Mark cast a curious look at her. "You tell me. Is there anyone else that has it in for you? Anyone you can think of that's hard up for cash."

She racked her mind trying to think of enemies and couldn't come up with any except Joey. He had it in for her and mentioned her father's latest advance when he'd accosted her at school. "Joey."

Mark nodded, his eyes narrowing. Then his cell phone rang. He jerked it out of its holster to answer it. "Riley. Hello, pal, where are you?" He looked up and smiled at Serena.

Serena gasped. "Is it Sammy?" she whispered. He nodded. "Okay, okay, son, slow down. Sit tight, and don't say anything. I'll be right there to get you. Wait for me." Mark closed his phone and turned to Bob. "They're at a flophouse on State Street, the Belton Hotel. Send a team in, but tell them to proceed with caution."

She touched Mark's arm. "Tell me! What's going on?"

"Sammy still had the card I gave him. He called from the phone in the room. He said his dad was sick in the bathroom."

"Probably drugs," she said grimly. "Is Sammy okay?"

He nodded. "He sounded scared, but okay."

Her heart sank. It shouldn't have happened. "Why didn't I see this coming? Joey resurfaced at the school year's end and has been bugging me since then. He seemed weird, strung out, you know. But he never gave Sammy more than a passing glance."

"You did all you could, beautiful. You raised a strong, healthy son who will get through this. You couldn't have known your ex would do something like this." Mark cupped her cheek tenderly, then turned to Bob. "I need to go now."

"I'm coming." She reached for her bag.

"That's not possible," Mark replied.

She turned a determined look his way. "Try and stop me." She'd stand firm, no matter what he said.

He frowned, stepping back. "Okay. Have it your way, but you darned well better obey my orders."

She was edgy all the way there. She'd obey Mark's rules up to a point, but if she had to take some risks to save her son, she'd do it.

They walked up the stoop into the shabby hotel.

Mark stopped at the front desk. The clerk came out, munching on a doughnut, his threadbare shirt buttoned tightly over his big belly.

He brushed the powdered sugar off his shirt. "What can I do for you, bud? Do you and the broad need a room? Twenty bucks an hour."

Mark scowled and leaned across the counter. "Listen, stupid. This is a lady." He flipped open his badge. "And we're the FBI."

The clerk gulped, choking on a mouthful of doughnut. Coughing, he gaped at the badge and flicked a nervous glance at Mark. "FBI, what for? I didn't do anything."

"Save it." Mark pocketed his badge. "Joey McLain, is he upstairs?"

The desk clerk nodded. "Yeah, room 515. What'd he do?"

"Does he have a child with him?"

The clerk hesitated. "What's it to you?"

Mark leaned over the desk, grabbing a fistful of the guy's shirt. "Try again."

The clerk froze in his grasp, gulping. "Yeah, they're here. I ain't got nothing to do with it, man."

Mark let him go. "Wrong. You let dirtbags have kids upstairs and don't think anything of it? Aiding and abetting a kidnapping is a crime. Hand over the passkey. And you'd better not tip him off."

The clerk slid the passkey on the counter. "What does this look like, the Ritz?"

Mark turned and headed for the stairs, the other agents joining ranks. Serena took off behind them. They stopped at the fifth-floor landing, and Mark grabbed her wrist, tugging her behind him.

"Stay back," he whispered. He nodded at Bob, and the agents moved out, drawing their weapons. They wove their way down the hall in a flanking maneuver. "Stay here," Mark ordered, drawing his gun and moving out to join them.

As they approached Joey's door, Serena watched them, shaking in her shoes. Was Joey armed? She couldn't just stand there. Slinking down the hall, she tucked into a recessed doorway of a room two doors down, earning a scowl from Mark. She'd worry about that later. She held her breath and listened, hearing cartoons blaring through Joey's door.

Bob used a visual probe under the door. "Sammy's alone in the bedroom. Joey's not in sight. I can hear water running in the bathroom."

"Okay, we go." Mark tried the knob, finding it locked. He took the passkey and opened the door.

Sammy scrambled off the bed, his eyes widening. "Mark!"

"Shh, come here, sport. Your mom's waiting."

"Mommy." Sammy ran out into the hall.

Mark scooped Sammy up before he could get to her and handed him to Alex. "Get them out of here, quick."

"But you..." Serena had to run to keep up with Alex racing down the hall with Sammy in his arms.

Mark was being overprotective again, but she was thankful to get her son back. She'd accept his high-handed tactics with good grace, she decided, as she followed Alex down the stairs. Hopefully, Joey would realize he was outnumbered and give up. Mark, she knew, could take care of himself.

Mark heard the shower shut off and nodded to Bob.

They slipped into the room, flanking the bathroom door. Agent Collins took post outside the door.

The bathroom door opened.

"Hey, kid, how about keeping the sound down?" Joey took a step out, rubbing his eyes. He turned toward the bed and frowned. "Where are you hiding, brat?"

Mark rushed him, shoving him against the dresser. "This is the FBI. Make a move, and my partner will blow your head off."

"What the fuck?" Joey jerked away, pulling a gun out of his pants. He fired a wild shot, bouncing off the dresser and back at Mark before dropping the gun.

Stifling a groan at the searing pain in his side, Mark took him to the floor, sitting on his back to subdue his struggles. Damn, the druggie had shot him.

"You have the right to remain silent," he stated grimly, waving Bob off. He needed to make this collar no matter the cost. Wincing as he pulled Joey's hands to cuff him, he felt a warm gush of blood at his side. He jerked the dirtbag up beside him and shoved him toward Agent Collins.

"You're hit." Bob scowled. "I'll call EMS."

"No," Mark demanded, fighting to stay upright as Agent Collins took over, grabbing Joey's arm. He didn't want to scare Serena and Sammy. "Get Serena and Sammy out first."

Bob nodded grimly. "I'll call down to Alex." He stepped aside and made the call, then turned back to Mark. "Okay, they're out. I had him tell them that you were busy."

Mark sagged back against the wall. "Good."

Bob got out his cell phone. "Agent down. I need EMS to the Belton Hotel room 515, stat."

Joey struggled in Agent Collins's grip as he was hauled toward the door. "I didn't do nothing wrong," he protested while trying to pull out of his grip.

"You shot an FBI agent, fool," Collins replied, adding dryly, "and last time I checked, kidnapping was a crime."

"Kidnapping, that's bull. How dare that bitch involve the feds? He's my kid as well as hers."

Mark sunk onto a chair, putting his hand to his side to stem the flow. "You're no more a father than some anonymous sperm donor." He looked at Collins. "Get that dirtbag out of here."

"My pleasure." Collins hauled a swearing Joey out the door.

Serena paced the floor outside the child psychologist's office. In the three hours since Alex had driven them to the ER, Sammy was given a thorough but gentle physical, and was found to be physically refined—outside of being dirty and hungry. Now they were seeing to his emotional well-being. The child psychologist had asked to see Sammy alone, and she'd complied. Even after losing him, she was reluctant to let her son out of sight.

She still wondered why Mark hadn't come with them. Alex had said something about him being busy. It seemed like he'd left her for the second time after the danger had passed. Was he tied up with paperwork, trying to distance himself?

She didn't know, and she couldn't worry about it now. Sammy had to take precedence.

The door opened, and Dr. Morrison stepped out. "May I have a word with you, Ms. McLain?"

"Certainly." Serena looked into the cozy toy-strewn office. Sammy was playing with modeling clay, and she was reassured he had a smile on his face.

"I need to talk to your mom, Sammy. We'll be right outside," Dr. Morrison said.

Sammy looked up, frowned, and dropped the modeling clay.

Dr. Morrison smiled. "I know you're worried about your mom. I'll keep the door open so you can see her."

"Okay." He went back to playing, his frown erased.

"Worried about me?" Serena was startled by the doctor's statement.

"Yes, I'm afraid so." The doctor drew Serena over to a bank of chairs in the waiting room. "We can talk here undisturbed."

Serena sat down, waiting for the doctor to sit next to her. "Why is Sammy worried about me?"

The doctor crossed her legs, smoothing out her linen pantsuit. "Joey told him that you were hurt and had sent him to pick Sammy up."

"What? I drummed it into his head not to go with strangers."

"Ah, but he isn't a stranger. He's his father."

Serena sighed. "Biologically, yes."

"At any rate, Sammy recognized him and went with him."

Sammy would have remembered him from the unpleasant incident at school. "Joey showed up on the last day of school. He confronted me in front of Sammy."

The doctor nodded. "Yes, he told me. I'm sorry to say it, but kids always fall for predators. They can be very tricky. Will you help me find my lost puppy, give me directions, or your mom sent me, these are classic scams."

"That bastard. How could Joey have done such a horrible thing?"

"I don't know the answer to that."

She looked into the doctor's sympathetic eyes. "So, how is Sammy? Emotionally, I mean."

Dr. Morrison smiled. "Scared, but for the most part, all right. He experienced a trauma, but as far as I can determine, he wasn't physically or sexually abused."

"Thank God." She felt some of her fear abate. She'd been concerned about that.

"Yes. However, he was verbally abused and frightened. He also said something about some adventure you've been on." The doctor looked at her curiously.

Serena noted the speculative gaze and hurried to fill in the blanks. "Yes. My father was kidnapped, and we were in protective custody with the FBI. He was recovered a week ago. My dad is a patient on the third floor here."

"Ah. It all makes sense now. He talked about someone named Mark. He seems to look at him as a male role model."

"Yes. He's the FBI agent who was guarding us." They'd both gotten close to Mark. She wasn't surprised Sammy looked at him as a role model.

The doctor hesitated. "Was? Then he's out of the picture now?"

Serena hesitated, a denial on the tip of her tongue, but it might not be true. She couldn't take the chance. "I'm afraid so."

"Pity. Sammy's probably going to ask for him. You'll have to explain it to him gently. Hopefully, your dad will be able to fill in that gap for him."

She felt the pain of losing Mark, but her needs came second. Sammy was the important one now. The doctor was right, he needed a strong male role model. "My dad and Sammy are great pals. Is Sammy going to be okay?"

"Given time, stability, and reassurance, yes. Let him open up. Give him time to talk." She stood.

Serena rose and shook her hand. "Thank you so much. His grandfather is in the hospital here. Do you think it would be okay to take him to see him?"

"I think it might start you both off on a positive note." She smiled. "Call my receptionist next week to set up some follow-up appointments."

"Will do." Serena followed her toward her office. Sammy was making long snakes with the blue clay. "Are you ready to go, son?"

"Sure am, Mom." He put the modeling clay back in the canister. He ran toward her. "Are we going home?"

"Yes, but I've got a surprise for you first." She took his hand and walked down the hall.

"What?" He tilted a glance up at her.

She smiled at him. "That would spoil the surprise."

He tugged at her hand, drawing her attention. "Was that bad man really my dad?"

Wow, he was opening up already. She stopped in her tracks, noting the worried look on his face. She crouched to get to eye level. "Yes, but he's sick, Sammy. They're going to take him where he can get some help."

He bit his bottom lip. "I thought he was sick. He was in the bathroom a lot."

"Was he mean to you?" She held her breath, dreading his possible answer.

"Well, he yelled at me a lot, but then he let me watch cartoons. So, he was just kind of mean. He said you sent him, and I believed him at first. I remembered him from when he came to my school. He didn't take me to you. He took me to that place instead. Then, I remembered Mark's card and called him. I knew he'd save me. Where is he?"

She'd expected the question, but it still hurt. "He had some work to do."

"Okay. What about my dad? Do I have to see him anymore?"

"No, Sammy, he's going away now, and he won't bother you anymore." She'd see to it personally.

"Good. He's not much fun."

She stood, and led Sammy down the corridor and to the elevator. They went up to the fourth floor. She led him down to her father's room, who was in a chair when they went through the open door. He was looking better.

"Grandpa," Sammy shouted, running to him.

"Sammy boy." Dad hugged him back.

"You're looking better, Dad." Serena smiled, walking up to them. "I'm surprised they have you up already."

He grinned. "Tomorrow, they're going to have me walking, or so they say. Maybe Sammy and I can have races down the hall."

Chapter Fourteen

She drove to the hospital six days later to bring her dad home. He was recovering nicely from his wounds and ready to be released.

She hadn't heard from Mark in all that time, and she'd resigned herself to the fact he'd moved on. It was probably better this way. The psychologist said Sammy needed stability, and a dangerous FBI agent wasn't exactly stable.

She glanced in the backseat at Sammy. He hadn't left her sight since Joey had kidnapped him, but he was improving. His bad dreams had ended after another session with Dr. Morrison. She said he was doing so well that he only needed a follow-up visit.

She pulled into the parking structure. "Ready to go spring Grandpa?"

"Yes, I am," Sammy piped, undoing his seatbelt. "Hey, there's Aubrey."

"Where?" Serena looked around, but didn't see the little redheaded girl. Was he coming up with imaginary friends now? It could be his way of dealing with the stress.

"She was there a minute ago, Mom, honest. She went up in the elevator."

Maybe it was best to humor him.

"Okay." She got out and opened Sammy's door. It would be good to get her father home. More stability was what Sammy needed. Although, they wouldn't see that much of her dad for the next month. With his book coming out six months from now, he'd be bogged down with the editorial process.

It should be a happy day, but there were clouds on her horizon. She was worried about her son, and the painful thoughts of Mark kept intruding. She missed him badly. She tried to tell herself he'd walked away without a word, and meant goodbye. But part of her didn't believe it. He'd always be there, deep in her soul, even if he didn't feel the same about her. Maybe she should join a singles group and find a mate that would stick around when the going got dull.

They walked into the hospital and toward the elevator. "Push four, Sammy." She knew he liked to work the controls. They got off the elevator and walked down the surgical wing to her father's room. He was dressed and sitting in a wheelchair.

"Grandpa, we're here to get you," Sammy said.

"I see." He smiled at Sammy and looked at Serena. "The nurse should be back with my paperwork soon."

"I'll hurry her up." She grinned at Sammy sitting on her dad's lap. This was more like it. Lovely stability.

She turned and went out of the room, going down to the nurse's station. Waiting patiently for the nurse to look up, she casually glanced at the charts on the shelves, looking for her father's.

Morris, Callahan, Riley, Johnson.

What? Was that Riley?

Her gaze snapped back to the file. *Riley, Mark M.* "Oh, my God," she gasped, staring at the file in disbelief. It couldn't be. She blinked, but it was still there. Was it her Mark? It couldn't be.

"Nurse." She eyed the nametag. "Laurie."

The nurse looked up from her charting. "Can I help you?"

"Well, I wanted to tell you my dad is ready to go, but I noticed that other chart. I think it might belong to a friend of mine. Could you tell me about Mark Riley?"

The nurse hesitated, looking at her quizzically. "Are you family, ma'am?"

Serena bit her lip, hesitating. "No."

"Then I can't tell you anything about it, ma'am. Sorry." The nurse shook her head.

Serena stepped back. She should have known. What now? Search the halls for his room? But did she want to appear that desperate?

A familiar face walked past. Ross's wife, Stacey.

"Stacey?"

She stopped in her tracks. She looked at Serena, shocked. "Serena! Is that you?"

Serena rushed up to her, noting the new disapproving look on her face. Something was wrong here, and it had something to do with Mark.

"What's wrong with Mark?"

"You mean, you don't know?" She cocked her head, looking at her closely.

There was an undercurrent of suspicion in Stacey's voice. Mark was sick, and he hadn't told her.

"No."

Stacey bit her lip, looking down the hall cautiously. "He hasn't wanted to talk about it, and we all just assumed you knew. I told him I would call you, and he ordered me not to."

So, he was back to being Mr. Controlling again? She wasn't surprised. What was so bad that he'd kept it from her? "Spill it. What's wrong with him?"

"Okay, but this is just between you and me."

Serena nodded. She would have promised anything at that point. What was so hush-hush? Was it another operation gone awry? "I promise."

Stacey nodded, pulling her aside. "He was hurt during an operation. It was touch and go there for a while, but he's supposed to recover fully."

"Injured? How? What happened?"

Stacey bit her lip. "He was shot, honey. He underwent surgery last Saturday evening. They had to remove his spleen."

"Oh, my God." Saturday? That was the day Sammy had been kidnapped. Joey must have shot Mark. A weight of guilt pressed down upon her.

Stacey looked at her, and steered her toward some seats in the lounge. "You'd better sit down before you fall, girl. You look kind of green around the gills. I'm sorry to be the bearer of distressing news."

Serena slumped in the chair. "Why didn't he tell me?"

Stacey shook her head. "I'm not sure. As I said, we assumed you knew. I figured you'd had a falling out. He made us promise not to call you. He said it was better that way. He said he didn't want to put you through any more. Since he came around after surgery, he's been tight-lipped about the whole thing."

"Where is he?"

"He's down in radiology right now. Would you like to wait to see him?"

Nurse Laurie walked up. "Excuse me, ma'am. Your father is ready to go."

"Okay, I'll be right there." Serena gazed at the nurse as reality intruded. She couldn't get lost in the past. She had to do her duty to her son. She turned back to Stacey, touched by the concerned look she saw in her eyes. "I can't wait for him. He knows my number if he wants to talk to me."

"Are you sure you want to leave it at that, honey?"

"No. I'm not sure about anything anymore, but I have to do right by my son. What he needs most in his life right now is stability, and if that means walking away from a man who doesn't want me, that's what I'll have to do."

Stacey nodded, then reached out to hug her. "Take care of yourself. I'll call you later. We can have a long talk."

Serena got up and walked away. She collected her father and son, and wheeled them out to the car.

Walking away was the hardest thing she ever had to do. Luckily, she didn't run into Mark on her way out. She had a feeling her strength would leave her if she had.

Four days later, Serena unloaded the dishwasher while watching Sammy play in the yard. She still had difficulty letting him out of her sight, but they were both working on that.

The phone rang, and she reached for it. "Hello."

"Hi, honey, this is Stacey."

"Oh, hi, it's nice to hear from you." Was there something wrong with Mark? There was a nervous edge to Stacey's voice.

"It's nice to talk to you, too. I need you to come out to the folks' cottage."

There was something wrong. "Why, what's wrong?"

"It's Mark. He needs to see you right away."

Mark? He hadn't bothered to call her. Why was he having Stacey do his dirty work? She frowned into the phone. "Why didn't he call me himself?"

"He can't."

Her knees buckled. He couldn't use the phone. He was hurt worse than she'd thought. Guilt weighed down on her. She should have swallowed her pride and called him.

"I'll be out later today."

"We're having a barbeque. Bring Sammy."

A barbecue? "I don't know..."

"Bye."

Serena hung up the phone, wondering if Stacey was stringing her along. Would they have a barbeque when Mark was so ill? Maybe they would raise his spirits? She had to go.

She was nervous on her way to Mark's parents' house. How badly hurt was he? It had to be serious from the sound of his summons.

She looked at Sammy in the backseat. Maybe she shouldn't have brought him, but he'd overheard her mention the lake house and begged to go. He'd been asking about Mark, so he needed closure, too. Hopefully, there'd be some grandkids to act as a buffer. She didn't want Mark's parents to be disappointed by their fizzled love affair.

"Mom, will Mark be there?"

"I think so, but he might be lying down. He's been sick, Sammy."

"Oh, too bad."

She shared his disappointment, but she couldn't voice it. She might break down and cry. The good news she could bring Mark was that Gerald Grayson had been convicted. He was doing twenty years in prison. Positive things had come out of this. Would Mark be happy to see her? He'd banned Stacey from calling her.

She pulled into the lake house's long driveway.

"Hey, I see Aubrey," Sammy shouted with excitement.

Serena noticed the little redhead running in the backyard. Good, there'd be a playmate to distract him so he wouldn't see how affected she was. She got out of the car and went around to hold Sammy's hand when he burst from the backseat. He needed a bit of wrangling, and she drew strength from his little hand in hers.

"C'mon, Mom." He tugged at her hand.

"Okay, let's go." She walked with him up the walkway.

The cottage's front door opened, and Mark stepped out.

Her heart skipped a beat. He was walking, and he looked healthy enough to her. She'd been had.

Mark smiled. "Hello, Serena, Sammy."

"Hi, Mark," Sammy shouted, letting go of her hand and running ahead.

"Hello," she replied, tongue-tied when his intense gaze focused on her. He'd always had this power over her.

He held open the cottage door. "Come on inside, you two. I've been watching for you."

What was he up to? There was a nervous edge to his voice she hadn't heard before, but his eyes were twinkling.

"Okay," she said hesitantly. She followed Sammy up to the porch, hesitating on the threshold as Mark stepped back to let them in. She couldn't help feeling an instant jolt of awareness at his nearness.

Why had he lured her here?

He smiled. "Come on in. I won't bite. Hard, that is."

Sammy chuckled, and Serena felt her cheeks flame. Thank goodness the double entendre went over her son's head.

She walked inside the foyer and turned to look at Mark as he followed her inside, shutting the door behind him. He was moving slowly, painfully, his wounds obviously hurting him.

She felt the pain, as well. "Are you okay?"

"I'm fine. Never been better, thank you."

She didn't believe a word of that. "Whittaker. Did he...?"

"I don't want to talk about that turkey here. He's been charged with corruption and removed. We've nothing to fear from him anymore."

"Good."

He slowly dropped on one knee, and her jaw dropped. Was he proposing? He reached into his pocket, but he pulled out an envelope, not a ring.

She gazed at him, puzzled.

He broke into a grin. "Will you two go on a honeymoon with me to Barbados?"

Sammy bobbed his head up and down. "I say yes, but what do you think, Mom?"

She gulped, swallowing the lump in her throat. How romantic. He'd fulfilled her fantasy for her tropical sunset. "I say yes, too."

And then it occurred to her, a honeymoon came after a wedding. "Did you say honeymoon?"

"I sure did. So, what do you say to happily-ever-after?"

"Yes!"

His family applauded as Mark pulled her into his arms.

"I'm glad I fell into your web, sweet Serena."

She smiled. "And I'm glad I've come to happily ever after."

IT HAD TO BE YOU

Julie Castle

Chapter One

"Look, Greg, that biker chick is here. Remember how she tore through the football field on her Harley, half-naked, during graduation? I guess they must have mailed her diploma. That's right. You were at military school then."

Greg Morris smiled as he pictured Candy speeding by the ceremony wearing only a smile and a string bikini as she shook up the crowd. Greg had been cooling his heels at St Sebastian's Military Academy at the time, thanks to his father's interference. By the time he'd graduated from that prison, Candy was long gone.

Greg stepped away from his booze-soaked former classmate while he made a mental note to see about getting him into Morris Papers' treatment program. One hour into their ten-year high school reunion, Chad Daly, one of his key employees at his subsidiary company, Pinnacle Publishing, was already soused.

Greg's gaze snapped over to the registration table. Candace Blake was sticking a nametag onto her silver evening gown. Sweet Candy with butterscotch hair and soft, pink lips. Greg had often wondered if she'd taste like butterscotch. Tonight, he hoped to find out. The sight of her made him groan.

After spending the past three months studying her business proposal and photographs, he already knew her good looks were all he remembered. Her long, *long* legs inflamed his imagination. She had the body of a Botticelli nude, the face of an angel, and most of all, and attitude in spades.

He knew she wouldn't recognize him and was counting on one magical night to make her see him in a new light. The Candy-Wear account would bolster Pinnacle Publishing's bottom line. Pinnacle Publishing was his baby, but Greg didn't just want her business. He wanted her.

The proud tilt of her head said *don't touch me* to any male who might take her sultry appearance as an open invitation. Her feisty attitude didn't deter him. On the contrary, he was intrigued by it. This summer, he intended to correct old wrongs, make a new life for himself, and discover what made Sweet Candy tick.

He moved to a secluded corner and pulled out his cell phone, ready to set his plan in motion.

Candace Blake took note of the surprised expressions of the couple at the registration table as she gave them her name. She recognized Ted Adams and Sandra Burns without looking at their nametags. A glance at Sandra's told her the two had married. They were former class officers who'd never given her the time of day back in high school.

Not that she cared.

Ted's gaze homed in on her cleavage as she bent to sign in. Winking as she straightened, she asked, "Did you enjoy the view, Ted?"

Candace enjoyed the dirty look Sandra threw at him as she turned away. She heard him yelp as she walked toward the ballroom. It served him right, the lecherous jerk.

She supposed she had to expect that kind of reception. Growing up a dirt-poor foster kid, she'd never fitted in with this crowd. To compensate, she'd become a hell-raiser in high school. The fact she was now a successful lingerie model and designer probably did little to improve her reputation in   this morally rigid little town.

Successful might be putting too good a spin on her designer status. But if everything went well with her negotiations with Pinnacle Publishing, she hoped to expand her fledgling catalog operation into a nationwide firm.

Why had she let Ma pester her into attending this reunion as a birthday treat? Some treat! She would have been thrilled never to see any of these snobs again.

Little did her curious former classmates know how far removed she was from her wild child teens. After long photo shoots, she returned to her lonely apartment to sketch designs late into the night. All work and no play made Candace a dull girl.

Well, if she'd been pushed into coming to this shindig, she might as well try to have fun. Yes, sir, it was time for Candace Blake to kick up her heels. And set this small town on its ear again. The thought made her grin.

She fidgeted with the silver bracelet on her wrist, then took a glass of champagne from a passing waiter. Taking a fortifying sip, she scanned the crowd, looking for any familiar faces. All her former classmates were paired off. She was the only one love had passed by.

Her eyes met those of a tall, dark, devastatingly handsome man standing near the bar. He watched her, and his interest was palpable. He winked at her, and a mischievous smile played across his sensual mouth as he raised his glass in a salute.

Who in the heck was he? She certainly would have remembered a hunk like this if he'd been in her class. He began to walk her way.

Butterflies fluttered in her stomach as he drew near. She bit her lip and stepped back at a pace. He stopped before her, topping her five-foot, ten by a good six inches.

Who could he be? She scanned the front of his tailored black tuxedo, but couldn't find a nametag.

"Hello, Candy."

He remembered her, but his smooth, baritone voice didn't ring any bells in her memory bank. "You're not wearing a nametag."

"I don't like nametags."

"So, I see. But you have me at a disadvantage. You know my name, but I don't know yours. Are you here with someone?"

His deep blue eyes glittered with devilish amusement. The crowd seemed to disappear as his magnetic presence filled her senses. Her pulse sped up in response. What was he up to?

"No, I'm here all alone. How about you?"

"Same here. It looks like we may be the only two singles."

"We aren't singles anymore."

His confident statement intrigued her. He wanted to remain a mystery man, and the thought appealed to her sense of adventure. It would be nice to have an exciting partner this evening. He fit the bill. Suddenly, her birthday was looking up.

He smiled a heartbreaker's smile, and the cleft in his chin deepened. He clinked his champagne glass against hers, and she drew a steadying breath, inhaling his crisp, woodsy scent.

"What are we toasting?"

"Us." He gazed into her eyes as he took a sip.

She followed suit. "I didn't know there was an us."

"There is tonight. Dance with me."

She frowned at what was more a command than an invitation. He was used to issuing orders, but she didn't take them.

"I don't think so." She started to turn away.

"Please."

She turned back, captivated by his tender plea. As she did, she noticed they were the center of attention and narrowed her eyes at him. "Will you cool it? People are staring at us, and while I could give a rip what they think of me, I'm sure you wouldn't like to be the subject of gossip."

"What's the matter? Chicken?"

She gaped at him, startled by the playful taunt. "What did you say?"

"You heard me. Chicken!"

A slight grin kicked up the corners of his sensual mouth.

Enraged, she spat out, "Nobody calls me chicken."

"*Braak...*"

"Shut up." She cast a glance around. People were stopping to stare.

"Make me."

She rolled her eyes. "Of all the stupid, juvenile ways to act." She wavered when he continued to gaze at her hopefully. Relenting, she started to smile. She *had* vowed to kick up her heels.

He held his hand out. "Please, dance with me."

"One dance."

As his hand took hers, she instinctively took a step back, alarmed by the sensuality of the gesture. His smile was soft, tender, and sexy as hell. Entranced, she allowed him to lead her onto the dance floor.

His warm palm slid along her spine, molding her body to his as the band started a slow number. They fit perfectly. Her breasts nestled against his muscular chest. Her belly pressed against his hard torso, and their thighs brushed together. She clung to him for a moment and pushed away, embarrassed by her instinctive reaction.

"Give me a little space to breathe."

"Why? Tonight, we can fulfill all our youthful fantasies, Candy Baby. And I've got to tell you, this is one of my favorites." He waited a moment, then continued, "Cat got your tongue?"

The hungry look in his blue eyes startled her. She had no idea she might have had a secret admirer back then. And the fact that he still apparently carried a flame was unsettling. Ten years was a long time to hold a crush.

"Are you joking?"

"I'm dead serious, sugar."

"But I don't even know you."

"That's what makes it perfect. We start with a clean slate." He bent to brush a brief, burning kiss across her lips.

She melted in response, then, returning to her senses, pulled away. "What about your reputation? Aren't you afraid associating with me will get you into trouble?"

"I don't give a damn about my reputation." He spun her around in a dizzying circle.

She laughed, startled by the intensity of his statement, and her heart leaped in response. Her instincts for self-preservation told her to slow things down, but it would be such a liberating experience to laugh and dance with this man. She wanted to play near the flames for one glorious night and then walk away. As he said, tonight was just a fantasy, and she did have a wild reputation to uphold.

"Okay, I agree. Tonight, is for us."

"And our fantasies."

His words were so like an excited little boy's, she grinned. "And our fantasies."

When the song ended, he drew her off the dance floor. He snagged two glasses of champagne from a passing waiter and handed her one. "Here's to a night to remember."

She licked the bubbling foam from her top lip, savoring the intoxicating flavor. Watching his hot eyes eat up the action, her blood sizzled as a shaky breath left her body.

"To tonight." She lightly clinked her glass against the one he held out.

"Why don't you introduce me, Greg?"

Greg, was it? Candace recalled four Greg's in her class. Greg March, a foreign exchange student. Greg Allen, who'd transferred in from out of state. Greg James, who wound up in juvenile incarceration. And Gregory Morris, the Toad. One glance told her the handsome man beside her could not possibly be the Toad. Relieved he was eliminated, she decided that her mystery date wasn't the French foreign exchange student. He didn't have an accent.

Shorting the list of possibilities, Candace looked at the intruder and sighed. Ten years later, Magi Bains was still easy to recognize even though harsh frown lines now bracketed her mouth. She'd been one of the biggest snobs in school. How would Greg react? She glanced at his handsome face. He was scowling at Magi, but noting Candace's gaze on him, he relaxed.

"Magi, you remember Candy Blake. She was a classmate of ours."

"I didn't recognize you, Candy." Magi's haughty voice was saccharine sweet. "It's quite a surprise to see you looking so well after all these years."

Candace smiled back through gritted teeth. "You probably figured I'd wind up in the slammer like my old man, huh, Margaret?"

Magi gasped, turning pale.

Greg put an arm around Candace's shoulder, drawing her close to his side. "Candy and I would like to be alone, if you get my drift."

Magi stared angrily at their embrace. "The two of you could at least show a little decorum. Neither of you belongs here."

The list narrowed to Greg James, who'd done a stint in juvie for shoplifting. She glanced at Greg, impeccably dressed and every inch the gentleman, and smiled. He'd come a long way, and the two of them fit together, both having been outcasts.

"Decorum, schmorum," Candace replied with a chuckle. "Like Greg said, why don't you blow?"

Magi glared at the two and turned away, saying, "Low rent gutter trash like you ought to stay where you belong."

Stiffening at the insult, Candace was about to respond when Greg interrupted.

"Oh, Magi, one more thing," Greg stated.

She stopped and turned around, glowering at him. "What is it?"

Candace took a sip of her drink and gazed at Greg, surprised by his suddenly serious expression. His fingers caressed her arm.

"You might want to spread the word. Candy and I are together. Anyone that insults her will have to deal with me."

She choked on her drink.

Magi's jaw dropped. Candy thought she looked like one of the carp swimming in the river outside.

She regained her poise and smiled sourly. "You bet I will."

Candace frowned as Magi trotted off with the news. So much for keeping a low profile during her stay here. "Why did you tell her that? Magi Burns is the biggest gossip in the world."

He smiled at her, looking so dashing, she found it hard to focus on her protest. She should thank Sir Galahad for saving her from the awful Magi Dragon.

"Now you won't have to worry about my reputation anymore. Look, you can watch the news spread around the room."

She looked at the crowd. It was like watching the game Telephone. One group told another until it ran around the room, and everyone was abuzz. Candace wanted to fade into the woodwork when people turned their way one by one.

"Now I know you're crazy."

"Yeah, about you."

She gazed at him. He'd been in more trouble than she had back in high school, and wound up being arrested. She'd never gotten to know him back then, but now she looked forward to making up for lost time.

"Cheer up, Candy Baby. The damage has already happened." He smiled and led her back onto the dance floor. "Let's dance."

She stepped into his arms as the song began. The sensual rhythm of the salsa music strummed through her. Other dancers stepped aside and let them have the floor. They made a striking couple. Greg was dark and dashing in his tuxedo. She was the light to his dark with her shimmering designer gown and blonde hair. They moved together in tandem, enjoying each other's sensuality unabashedly.

He dipped her to the floor as the music ended. She hung suspended, her breathing rapid, her eyes locked on his. He raised her slowly, and then his lips touched hers, hot and sweet.

Electricity sizzled between them. She was truly alive for the first time in years. Time stopped, and blood pounded in her ears. No, that was applause.

They broke apart to find the crowd clapping. She smiled at him as he twirled her around and took a bow.

He grasped her hand and led her off the floor toward the exit.

Startled by the applause, she struggled to catch her breath. Since when had this crowd ever approved of her?

"Where are we going?"

He turned to look at her, boyish charm enhancing his masculine assurance. "Trust me. We're going someplace special."

"I don't know." She stopped in her tracks. Seeing the disappointment on his face, she reconsidered. "Okay, this is our fantasy night."

He ushered her out of the building into the starlit night. "Don't worry. I'll take care of everything." He opened the door to a low-slung black sports car. "Your chariot, my lady."

She grinned at his playfulness, sliding onto the leather upholstery, and inhaling the new car scent.

He got in and started the car, gunning the engine. "Sit back and relax. We'll be there in ten minutes."

Her mind whirled in anticipation. Just what did he have planned? If anything went wrong with this magical night, she'd die. Tonight was her ultimate teenage dream come true, and she'd enjoy it to the hilt. She supposed most people would think the life of a lingerie model was glamorous. In fact, the demanding work of trying to compete with fresh-faced eighteen-year-olds left her with a nonexistent social life.

He pulled into the parking lot at Silver Lake, and she looked at him in surprise.

"It's kind of dark for a swim, Greg."

"Not for a skinny dip, it's not."

She thought he might be joking, but it was too dark to see his expression.

He got out of the car and opened her door. He held her hand as he led her down toward the beach. The full moon turned the beach into a fairyland, creating frosted silver ripples on the dark water. A soft breeze billowed her skirt around her legs. Near the water's edge was a patch of light.

As they walked toward it, she spotted two empty champagne glasses and a bottle of champagne chilling in an ice bucket on a blanket spread across the sand. Lantern light turned the scene into a romantic candlelit nook. Soft music from a radio drifted toward them, enhancing the spell.

Astonished by the elaborate scene, Candace turned to him. "You were quite sure of me, weren't you? Or could it have been anyone?"

He was watching her, his face a shadowed visage concealing his thoughts. "No, it had to be you." There was sincerity in his voice.

He stepped into the light, and his soft, intimate smile melted her heart. Tears moistened her eyes, but she fought them back. Tough girls didn't cry. But then, he'd already guessed she was a marshmallow inside.

He started singing along with the song, *It Had To Be You*. His voice was a smooth baritone. He swung her into his arms and waltzed her across the sand.

She smiled, tucking her head against his shoulder, his white linen shirt crisp and the ebony studs cool against her cheek. The song resonated through his warm chest as he serenaded her.

It was like something from an old Fred Astaire and Ginger Roger's movie, and she was a sucker for them. He stopped singing and looked down at her hungrily before claiming her with a kiss.

She sighed into his mouth as it brushed hotly against hers.

He broke the kiss and grinned at her. "Yum, butterscotch and jasmine."

"What?"

"That's what you taste like." He bent his head for another quick kiss and then led her toward the blanket. He poured them a glass of champagne and handed one to her. Then he trailed his finger along her bare arm and shoulder, causing a delicious tremor inside her and making her heart race.

Tomorrow was time enough for regrets. Tonight was for her memory scrapbook.

She sipped the champagne and studied him. Lantern light highlighted the classic curves and planes of his face. His forehead was long, his nose straight, and the look of blatant desire in his eyes took her breath away. She reached out to run a finger across his smooth cheek.

He inhaled, his nostrils flaring.

She drew back her finger and smiled. "This is perfect, Greg."

"You're the one who's perfect, Candy Baby." He put down his glass and reached for her. "Come here. We've got, ten years to make up for."

She fell into his arms with a hunger that surprised her. Nothing else mattered. They kissed, and then he nuzzled her earlobe. He nipped it, and she gasped as heat raced through her. Her hands snaked their way underneath his jacket, and she pulled his shirt up in the back, aching to touch his skin.

"Hold on, baby, and I'll help you."

He leaned back, peeled off his jacket, and then yanked on the end of his tie, loosening it. His hands shook when he started to unbutton his shirt. Frustrated, she grabbed the edges of his shirt and yanked, trying to help. Ebony studs popped off, flying, but she didn't care.

Her hands were on him immediately, pushing the shirt off his shoulders and combing through the rough, dark hair on his chest. He groaned and leaned into her caress. His reaction caused a fission of heat deep inside her.

"My turn," he said, running his hands through her hair. His grasp tightened as he held her tethered while he claimed her mouth in a deep kiss. He licked her upper lip, smiling. "Definitely butterscotch."

"What?"

He smiled. "That's what you taste like."

She laughed. "You're crazy."

"Only about you." He looked deep into her eyes while he slowly reached behind her and pulled down her zipper. The silky fabric pulled away from her firm, rounded breasts.

He groaned at the sight as moonlight bathed their peaks in honey light. He ran a tentative finger along the curved slopes. "Your skin is softer than the finest silk."

She gasped as he cupped her and pushed more firmly into his magical touch. She was so sensitive, and his large hands were warm and strong. Her strawberry-peaked nipples beaded against his palms, and she moaned. All sensations seemed centered on the aching peaks of her breasts. His touch felt so good.

She rubbed against him, pleading for more. "Please, more."

"Oh, baby. You don't have to ask." He lifted her hand to his lips. Then he met her eyes as he slowly drew her index finger into his mouth and sucked on it.

She couldn't look away from the passion in his eyes. She moaned as his mouth tugged on her finger. It caused a tugging deep inside her. He pulled her wet finger from his mouth and brought it to her breast to circle her nipple. She gasped at the naughty caress, wondering what he was up to. Then he bent down and blew on her damp nipple. Pleasure rocked through her.

He tasted the tight, rosy bud, and she was lost. She arched off the blanket restlessly as he gave her pleasure and caused an aching tightness in her abdomen. He pushed her dress down, and she was covered only by a high cut pair of silver panties. His eyes darkened as he moved lower to lovingly cup the damp heat covered by her panties. His talented hand pressed against her mound, rubbing that sensitive area, and she cried out, coming apart in his arms.

Above the thundering beat of her heart, she heard tires crunch in the gravel parking lot. A spotlight suddenly bathed them in its chilling glow.

She squinted.

Greg spun around to see who it was.

"Okay, you kids, break it up. This is the police," crackled a voice through a bullhorn, "it's after curfew so get dressed and get out your IDs."

She sagged behind him, mortified.

Greg sat up. "It's okay, officer. It's just me."

"Sorry, Mr. Morris. I didn't know it was you. I thought it was those darned kids partying again."

The Toad?

Oh, good grief!

She gasped, and Greg stiffened in response.

That wasn't the only thing that was stiff. She hoped the officer wouldn't shine the spotlight on that part of Greg's prominent anatomy. How had a creep like The Toad managed to transform himself into this handsome hunk of masculinity? Greg Morris had been a head shorter than her, skinny as a beanpole, wore thick glasses, and had a case of the hots for her back then in high school.

He moved to the side to further shelter her from the spotlight. "No harm done, Gus. We'll leave in few minutes."

The police car drove away, and she shivered. She'd almost made love with The Toad. What a disaster!

The Morris's were her sworn enemies. Her father had died of a heart attack in prison when she was eleven. Greg's father had put him there, accusing him of embezzlement at Morris Papers.

Despite the animosity she had for the Morris clan, The Toad had worn her down during their senior year. She'd agreed to go out with him, fully intending to make it such a miserable experience that he'd leave her alone thereafter. But the guy hadn't shown up.

The next day, she'd learned her foster brother, Mike, had beaten the snot out of Greg. A week later, Greg had left town for boarding school. The buzz was that his parents had sent him away to keep him from mingling with undesirables.

As if she'd have him.

Oh, good grief, she almost had. They'd been as close to making love as a couple could be without doing the deed.

Rushing to her feet, she pulled the last vestiges of dignity around her. She tugged her gown up to cover her breasts. He still sat on the sand, gazing up at her, a calculating gleam in his eyes.

She refused to look at him. "Take me back to get my car."

"First, we need to talk about this."

"No."

"Our evening is ruined, but that doesn't mean we can't put things right. Please give me a chance to explain. I wanted you to see the real me before the past muddied the waters."

"I want to go back to my car right now. You can explain tomorrow." She did not intend to see him again, but he didn't need to know that if it would help put some breathing space between them.

He shot her a humorless smile. "I'm not ready to go."

"Why not?" She glanced at his rock-hard anatomy, and gulped. "Oh, I see."

"Maybe you'd better turn your back." He stripped off the remainder of his clothes and walked toward the lake.

She gave in to the urge to peek just in time to see Greg wade into the water. Moonlight highlighted his flanks, giving her a spectacular view of his tight buns.

She sighed with regret. The first man she'd been attracted to in years would have to turn out to be The Toad. There was no way in the world she could ever have a relationship with him. He was a Morris. And he'd conned her into this cozy little trap, damn it.

She was dressed by the time he walked out of the lake.

This was a fantasy evening never to be repeated, and now it was blown to smithereens.

He tried to take her arm, but she pulled away.

"Trust me, Candy, this is just a minor setback. We can work it out."

She reached down to help him gather up the picnic things, not wanting to meet his hope-filled eyes. "Let's just leave."

They drove back to the ballroom in silence. He smoothly shifted the powerful sports car, and she felt a twinge of regret. Too bad he was a Morris. In a different time, a different place, they might have been made for each other.

But they were who they were and that was that.

The Toad may have turned into a prince, but he wasn't *her* prince. As a Blake, she had a vendetta to uphold and no scheming, handsome Morris was going to dim her resolve.

They pulled into the parking lot at the ballroom, and Greg switched off the engine. She could feel his gaze on her, but she wouldn't look at him. There was nothing more to say. It was over.

She reached for the door handle, but he held her hand, stopping her flight as her irritation went up a notch.

"Please, Candy, let me explain."

"Go to hell, Toad. I have all the explanation I need. You're a lying, stinking Morris."

She caught a flash of anger in his eyes before his pillaging mouth came down to claim hers in a deep kiss. She could feel his leashed frustration as he tried to coax a response.

Despite her best intentions, her hungry body remembered his tantalizing touch all too well. Desire was quickly rekindled as his arms encircled her. She clung to him, touching his hair, his face, the sexy cleft in his chin, desperately trying to memorize his features. She trembled from the force of wanting him so badly. The need wasn't only sexual, and it scared her.

If an abortive attempt at lovemaking rocked her this deeply, how would she feel if they got involved and he walked away? Just like everyone else she'd ever loved. Panicked, she pulled away, and reached for the door handle. He kept a restraining hand on her arm, halting her escape.

There was power in his touch. He wasn't hurting her, but he wasn't letting her run away, either. She sat motionless, staring out the car window at the dark parking lot, not daring to look at him. She was too near the fire and about to get burned.

"I have to go."

"I'll call you in the morning."

"Don't bother."

"I don't give up that easily."

The resolve in his voice had her daring a glance. The strength of purpose in his gaze held her spellbound for a moment.

"Don't say that. Tonight was just a fantasy, remember?"

"I lied."

She pulled away and climbed out of the car, slamming the door behind her.

Chapter Two

Candace placed a small porcelain teapot filled with herbal tea on the breakfast tray. She glanced over at Joan Babcock, her friend and former foster sister.

Joan sat sideways at the dining room table to accommodate her advanced state of pregnancy as she scanned the morning newspaper, searching for a review of her band's performance at a coffee house the evening before.

Candace tried to soften the blow of a possible critical review. "You know, Joan, I'm not sure Morris Point, Wisconsin is ready for a pregnant punk rocker."

Joan's purple shadowed eyelids fluttered as she frowned and flipped over another page. "I've told you a thousand times, Candy, it's not punk rock, it's alternative rock. There's a difference."

Candace smiled at her exasperation. "If you say so. To me, it's all about the same."

Joan's smile was enhanced by gold lip gloss. "Especially to somebody whose musical taste is stuck in a fifties time warp."

Candace recalled Greg's romantic rendition of *'It Had To Be You'*, and felt a pang of disappointment. What had appeared magical last night, now in the cold light of day, seemed idiotic.

Joan gasped, regaining Candace's attention, as she pointed to an article. "Candy, you'd better look at this."

She added a starched napkin to the tray and stepped toward Joan. "Good review?"

Joan shook her head, making her spiky dark hair jiggle and her silver drop earrings clank. "Actually, they said we stunk."

Candace raised an eyebrow at the impish grin spreading across Joan's expressive face. "Well then, what are you so happy about? What's going on?"

"That's what I'd like to know." Joan eyed Candace inquisitively. "Just what went on last night? I thought you didn't even like Greg Morris. It says here you're engaged to marry him! You sure work fast, girl."

Candace gripped the back of a chair, as her world tilted off axis. "Oh, good grief, we're not engaged! Greg told Magi we were a couple to get her to back off. He was just kidding around. It was all a joke."

Joan's long carmine fingernail pointed to the headline.

'GREGORY MORRIS TO WED LINGERIE MODEL.'

"Some joke. It's plastered all over the society page, for heaven's sake. There's even a picture of you from your latest catalogue in that blue nightgown I liked so much."

Candace felt herself blush, knowing Joan's perceptive gaze wouldn't miss the dark circles under her eyes. They were caused by a restless night spent having sweet dreams about Greg. Joan could read her like a book.

She snatched the paper out of her hands. Last night, she'd vowed to put her lapse of common sense behind her. But one way or another, Gregory Morris kept intruding into her life. She ran a horrified gaze over their wedding announcement. Mr. & Mrs. Gregory Morris, Senior, announce the engagement of their son, Gregory Morris, Junior, to Miss Candace Blake. The accompanying photo showed Candace clad in an aqua satin peignoir set and draped across a chaise lounge in a sultry pose. Sleepy little Morris Point would be in a bigger uproar than they had been when she'd streaked through her graduation ceremony.

She sank into a chair. "How could they reprint this photo without my release?"

"Maybe your agent thought he was doing you a favor."

"Some favor. After I serve Ma breakfast, I'll give Mark a call and find out. He might have provided the picture, but a local has to be behind this bogus announcement. Whoever is responsible for this travesty is dead meat. Greg and I spent part of the evening together, but that does not constitute an engagement."

"Spent the evening, huh?"

She recalled Officer Gray interrupting their make-out session and frowned. "Not the entire evening."

"My, my, you and The Toad." Joan let out a surprised chuckle. "Will wonders never cease? Want me to get our old foster brother, Mike, to beat him up like he did after prom?"

"This is no laughing matter. I just hope Ma doesn't catch wind of this. It might drive her into a relapse."

"Speaking of Ma, weren't you about to carry her breakfast up to her?"

Candace swatted Joan's hand as she reached for a wedge of toast. "Yes, if you don't eat it all first."

Joan withdrew her hand with a pout. "Ouch, I'm eating for two, you know."

She gazed at her eight-month-pregnant friend and smiled. "You big baby. If you're eating for two, one of you must be a bull moose."

Joan struggled to get up. "Just for that crack, I'm leaving. I don't have to stay here and be insulted. I can go home and be insulted."

Candace hurried around the table to help her up. "I take it back. You're gorgeous and you know it. Get insulted at home, my Aunt Fanny. Jerry is crazy about you and thrilled about being a new dad."

Joan smiled and rubbed her expanded tummy. "I know. It's nice to have a man think you're terrific. You should try it sometime."

Candace and frowned. She remembered how Joan had goaded her into accepting The Toad's invitation to the prom back in high school.

"You've got to go to the prom, sis," Joan had said. "Mas got the dress all picked out for you. So, what if your only invitation came from The Toad. You can ditch him after you get there."

She'd caved to the pressure and her secret desire to fit in with the popular crowd. She wouldn't ditch him. Instead, she'd make the date a dud so, in the future, he'd leave her alone. On prom night, she'd sat on the porch all decked out in the pink net gown Ma had bought her, waiting for Greg to pick her up. And to her utter mortification, he'd stood her up.

Oh no, Greg Morris was not the man for her. Intending to nip any future attempts at matchmaking in the bud, she hastened to add, "Greg was wrong for me back in high school, and he still is. We travel in different worlds, and I intend to keep it that way."

Joan smiled ruefully. "You can't blame a girl for trying. Just remember, you're just as good as the haughty Morris clan, Candy. Don't let anyone, including yourself, tell you differently."

She picked up the breakfast tray and walked with Joan into the foyer. "Thanks for the pep talk, sis. Last night was just a fantasy. It would never work."

Joan tilted her head. "A fantasy, huh? That sounds intriguing."

She looked away, unable to talk about last night's disaster without falling apart. It would take a long time before she would recover her objectivity where Greg Morris was concerned. "I can't talk about it right now, okay?"

Joan placed a comforting hand on Candace's shoulder and sighed. "Okay, I'll stop pushing. It's just that I want you to be happy."

Candace noted the glint of concern in Joan's eyes, and smiled softly to reassure her. "I know you do, and believe me, I appreciate it, but I'll be fine."

Joan turned toward the door. "That's okay. Ma's kids must stick together. Even if Greg isn't the man of your dreams, I know there's someone out there who's right for you." She looked back and grinned. "Speaking of fantasies, maybe after I have the baby, you can design some lingerie to help me fulfill a few of my own."

Relieved to move onto a safer subject, Candace's tension subsided. "I'm ahead of you, little sister. I've already started a few sketches. Although, from what I've seen, the fire between you and Jerry doesn't need much fanning."

"Gee, thanks for noticing." Joan laughed. The doorbell rang, and she glanced down at her watch. "Who could be here at quarter to eight in the morning?"

Candace headed toward the stairs. "Who knows? You answer it. I'm not dressed."

A moment later, Joan called to her. "Candy, you have company."

Candace stopped part way up the stairs and turned to look at the door, as two well-dressed women stepped inside the foyer. "Yes, may I help you?"

The older lady moved forward, looking as if she'd stepped out of a fashion magazine in her tailored ecru-colored suit. Her dark hair was swept up into an elegant twist. Her smile was cool, her expression reserved as she slowly looked Candace up and down.

"Perhaps. I'm Gregory's mother, and this is my daughter, Kathleen."

Kathleen was a carbon copy of her mother, right down to the strand of pearls around her neck. Mrs. Morris's eyes were the same shade as Greg's.

Candace had spent a restless night conjuring up sweet dreams of those midnight blue eyes, and every other part of his anatomy, too. They were dreams she knew would never come true.

Mrs. Morris's disdainful gaze incensed Candace. She must have been out of her mind to dream of a future in Greg's arms. She tamped down her outrage, not wanting to make a scene.

"Joan, I know you have an appointment to keep. Why don't you run along? I'll take care of this."

Her friend pinned her with an anxious gaze. "Are you sure?"

"Positive."

Joan wrinkled her brow as she walked out the door. Candace would make a point of calling her later to reassure her after she got through this ghastly showdown.

Focusing her attention on the intruders, she met Mrs. Morris's intense gaze with a steady one of her own.

Mrs. Morris nodded, acknowledging the gauntlet was thrown. "We're here to discuss my son's alleged engagement to you."

Candace smiled ruefully. Greg was too chicken to do his own dirty work. He thought that she'd changed her mind and decided to go after him for his money.

"This is between Greg and me. It's really none of your business."

"Nonsense," Mrs. Morris replied. "Gregory's home in bed, and I'm not going to let him be bothered by this."

So, he hadn't sent the disdainful duo. Candace had known the shit would hit the fan, but she hadn't counted on it happening so soon.

"Well as you can see, ladies, I'm not prepared to receive you. If you'd care to make an appointment for this afternoon..."

Mrs. Morris frowned at her. "Young woman, this is important. I'll wait."

"Suit yourself." Candace turned away from the dragon lady and her cub, and continued up the stairs. She tapped on Ma's door when she got to the top.

Her foster mother's weak voice called out. "Come in."

She entered the bedroom.

Ma Brown, a petite lady with iron-gray hair and a will to match, sat up in bed, her merry gray eyes twinkling.

Candace smiled, recalling how she used to tell herself the similar eye color made them look more like a real mother and daughter. Her biological mother had run off with another man when she was a baby. Father and daughter had lived a nomadic but happy life while he flitted from job to job, until he'd been unjustly arrested for embezzlement while working in the accounting department of Morris Papers. Candace had been eleven years old. He'd died of a heart attack in jail while awaiting trial, never getting the opportunity to prove his innocence. She spent her teens being shuttled from one foster home to another, finally ending up with Ma when she was sixteen.

Ma usually ended up with the challenging cases that were on the borderline of entering the juvenile justice system. Her strict but loving home had turned Candace's life around. She'd straightened out, finished school, and left on graduation day to seek her fortune.

Over the years, she had stayed connected with the woman she considered her real mother, but she'd resisted coming back to Morris Point. Instead, she'd take Ma on vacation every summer.

But this summer was different. A few months ago, her bookings had suddenly dried up. Pinnacle Publishing, a company with headquarters in a nearby town, had offered a sweet deal to launch her Candy-Wear catalog. Ma'd had heart surgery and needed help at home while she went through rehab.

Candace knew it was time to return and face her demons. The summer off would give her time to complete the designs for the fall launch of her catalog. Pinnacle Publishing was only an hour's drive from here, which would give her a chance to oversee its production.

Getting back home to Small Town America should be restful, too. But the memory of Greg's scintillating touch had haunted her dreams.

Squelching the memory, she set the tray down on the dresser and fluffed Ma's pillows.

Ma smiled and patted her hand. "Honey, you shouldn't go to this trouble for me."

She smiled at her. "I'm happy to finally be back here to help you out."

"So, did you have a good time at your reunion last night?" Ma leaned against freshly plumped pillows as Candace placed the tray over her lap.

Ma would keep on pumping her for information unless she nipped the inquisition in the bud. She meant well, but now her good intentions rubbed against Candace's bruised emotions like sandpaper.

She avoided Ma's curious gaze as she poured her a cup of herbal tea. "It was fine. It was nice to see the old faces."

Ma lifted the napkin off the tray and spread it over her chest. She looked at Candy patiently as if waiting for more.

When Candace remained silent, she asked, "Did you see anyone special?"

She refused to rise to the bait. "I had a nice time."

Ma let out a frustrated harrumph as she stirred her tea.

"I'll come back for the tray. Be sure you eat it all. We want to make you strong again."

"I thought I heard the doorbell. Do we have company?"

Candace sighed, thinking of the upcoming skirmish. "It's just a little unfinished business I must take care of. I'll see you later, Ma."

Ma waved her out of the room. "I'm sure you're tired from your big night. Don't worry about me. I have everything I need. So, relax and enjoy your day off."

Candace closed the door. It was a good thing Ma didn't know the source of her exhaustion. Fevered dreams of Greg hadn't left much time for slumber. Now she had to face the aftermath alone.

Like a knight preparing for battle, she slipped into the armor of well-worn sweats and running shoes, and swept her hair back in a ponytail. She frowned as she glimpsed her fatigued reflection in the vanity mirror. She looked like hell. It wasn't fair, but then she, of all people, ought to know life wasn't fair.

She jogged down the stairs. The twin dragons had to be dealt with before she could go for her morning run. Running cleared her mind and focused her thoughts, and boy, did they ever need focusing this morning. She strode into the living room, prepared to get this over with quickly.

Kathleen was seated, stiff backed, on the sofa. Mrs. Morris was prowling the confines of the room. She looked ill at ease. No, she was just annoyed at being made to wait.

Candace could just picture a mental calculator whirring in Mrs. Morris's mind, assessing the value of Ma's homey possessions. She gazed at the cut glass fruit bowl and then moved on to scrutinize the senior photos of Ma's kids perched atop the spinet piano. She stopped to frown at the one that featured Candace astride the battered old Harley she used to ride.

That bike had been her pride and joy. She'd bought it with money she'd earned doing alterations in the back of Ma's dress shop every day after school, and had worked on it until it had hummed. Feeling the powerful machine vibrating between her legs gave her a feeling of control and freedom. It was her first step toward independence.

Unfortunately, she'd had to sell it for money to live on after she got to New York. She still missed it. She could only think of one thing more stimulating, and that was Greg between her thighs last night. Her face heated at the errant thought, and cleared her throat.

The twin dragons turned her way.

"Well, ladies, I don't want to keep you long. I'm sure we can clear this matter up quickly."

Mrs. Morris flicked an appalled glance over Candace's grungy running shoes and baggy sweats. "I hope so. I have a schedule to keep." She walked to the sofa and sat beside her daughter.

Candace perched on the arm of an easy chair across from them and returned Mrs. Morris's thorough appraisal. Kathleen's glare was mean enough to kill, but when Candace resolutely met her gaze, she looked away. Mrs. Morris let a reserved half smile curve her lips, but the smile didn't reach her eyes, which remained cool and watchful.

Well, why didn't the woman say something? Candace would be more comfortable with a shouting match than this cool, detached manner. Greg's mother continued to quietly assess her, as if she were trying to make up her mind about something.

Candace suppressed the urge to squirm. She felt like a specimen under a microscope, as if every flaw were being zeroed in on and exposed.

She sat back and crossed her legs. "You said you had some business you wanted to discuss."

Mrs. Morris nodded. "Yes, I came here to talk about the engagement. To be frank, you're not the kind of woman I pictured my son marrying."

Kathleen scowled and leaned forward, her voice mocking, "It was rather sudden, wasn't it?"

Candace grinned, feeling the sting of battle. This was more like it. Open antagonism was something she knew how to deal with. "Yeah, it surprised the heck out of me, too."

"Sure, it did," Kathleen snapped.

"Ladies, this is getting us nowhere," Mrs. Morris commented. She snapped open her purse and pulled out her checkbook. "How much?"

Candace merely raised an eyebrow. The witch was trying to buy her off. It was an astounding move now. Fine, she could play hardball, too. Just how far would the dragon lady go?

"How much what?"

Mrs. Morris fixed Candace with an impatient glare. She tapped her expensive gold pen on the check pad. "How much do you want?"

Steam rose inside her head. She flashed a ready smile to hide her irritation, an old habit from her years of modeling. "For what?"

It was obvious from the lady's assessing glance that she now thought Candace was stupid, as well as a gold-digger.

Mrs. Morris began to write. "Why, to call this ridiculous farce off, of course. How does fifty thousand sound to you?"

"But if I married him, I could get have half of his wealth."

Kathleen gasped, but Candace ignored her, focusing all her attention on Greg's mother.

Mrs. Morris stopped writing and glanced up at her shrewdly. "Very well, how does one hundred thousand sound?"

Candace curved her lips into a frigid smile. "It's an interesting number." Her stomach twisted as she watched her fill in the amount. It was a classic Morris tactic—quick, concise, and ruthless.

"Fine." Mrs. Morris nodded solemnly. "I'm glad we understand each other." She tore the check from the book and thrust it at Candace.

Candace managed to keep her hand steady as she took it. She gazed at it, appalled, noting its art deco border and Mrs. Morris's elegant script. Everything about Greg's mother was picture perfect, right down to her neat penmanship. Looking up, she met her eyes just as her outrage boiled over.

"I understand you perfectly, Mrs. Morris. You're a snobbish, narrow-minded prig."

Mrs. Morris raised a startled eyebrow.

Kathleen gasped and stood up. "Well, I never."

Candace fixed her irate gaze on Greg's sister. "The same goes for you, little dragon."

Kathleen scowled. "Listen to me, money-grubbing little witch. If you think I'm going to stand still and let you marry my brother, you are sadly mistaken."

"Quite right," Mrs. Morris replied as she stood. "Gregory has had enough heartache in his life without you adding to it."

Candace remained seated, wondering what kind of heartache Mrs. Morris was referring to. It had been ten years. He was bound to have a past. For all she knew, he could have a dozen ex-wives and sweethearts. He had the looks, charm, and money to be a babe magnet.

Shaking off the speculation, she stood and tore the check into confetti. "This is what I think of your son and this phony marriage announcement. I can assure you, it didn't come from me. I wouldn't marry him on a bet."

Mrs. Morris frowned at her. "Do you really expect me to believe that? Magi Bain already filled me in on the scandalous way you behaved last night, tricking him into making some rash statements. You always were a bad influence on him."

Meddling Magi was working overtime. She must have called Greg's mother at sunrise. No wonder she and Kathleen were so riled up. But that was no excuse for their high-handed behavior.

"It's the truth." She ushered them to the door. "You'll have to excuse me. I have other business to take care of."

Mrs. Morris lingered in the doorway and gazed at Candace with a speculative look in her eye. "Just see to it that you don't break my boy's heart."

She was shocked by the unexpected statement. "I plan to keep well away from him for the rest of the summer." At the lady's continued look of doubt she continued. "Honest, there is absolutely nothing going on between us."

Chapter Three

Candy shut the front door behind her and walked onto the grass to do a few stretches. Good Lord, she felt as if she was held together with baling wire.

As she worked out the kinks, her body relaxed. The battle with Greg's mother had disturbed her. She wasn't as adept at rebuffing attacks as she used to be.

She started at a slow jog down the front walk, and then turned left at the sidewalk, gradually picking up speed.

The first step to squelch this sham engagement announcement would be a retraction in the newspaper. After that, she would avoid Greg and keep an extremely low profile while Ma finished rehab. At the end of the summer, she would quietly slip out of town. It was the only solution she could envision.

It would have to work.

Based on Mrs. Morris's statement, Greg had been equally surprised to see their names in print. One of their overeager newshound classmates must have thought he was printing the scoop of the year.

Greg would just have to tolerate the local rumor mill. On the bright side, this experience would undoubtedly kill his interest in her. Fate, in the form of a meddling classmate, had taken control of the risky situation, pulling her onto safe ground.

There weren't many people stirring on this Saturday morning. Most of her former classmates were home sleeping off their celebration. She ran past Daley's Drug Store, Haley's Hardware, and the front door of the Morris Point Daily Journal.

Screeching to a halt, she hesitated a moment, catching her breath. She hadn't intended to end up here, but subconsciously her footsteps must have taken her here.

Glancing at her sweaty, rumpled attire, she debated the wisdom of going in. She wasn't properly dressed for a business call, but there was no time like the present. They could run the retraction in tomorrow morning's paper. She pushed open the door and entered the building.

A young dark-haired girl perched on a stool behind the front counter looked up. She popped her chewing gum and smiled. "What can I do for you, ma'am?"

Candy frowned. Ma'am, was it? She must really be showing her age today. "I'd like to speak to the society editor."

The girl arched a perfectly penciled eyebrow as she looked Candy up and down. "I'm sorry, ma'am. She's not in right now."

Candy stifled her growing exasperation. At that age, she would have reacted the same way with a sweaty, bedraggled woman who asked to see the society editor. "Well, who can I speak to about a retraction?"

The girl shrugged and went back to the crossword puzzle she'd been working on. "How about Mike? He's the reporter in charge around here on the weekends."

"That would be fine." Candy waited, but the girl seemed to have forgotten her. Irked, she leaned forward over the counter. "Could you point me in the right direction?"

The girl gestured toward the stairway. "Up the stairs, first door on your right."

Candace sighed. So much for friendly service. Turning on her heel, she jogged up the stairs. If she had any luck, the reporter would be more professional.

She stopped at the open door the receptionist had indicated. A redheaded teenage boy with a prominent Adam's apple sat at a desk typing on a computer keyboard. As he glanced up, his eyes, shielded by thick glasses, held a distracted look.

"May I help you?" he asked in a squeaky voice.

"I hope so." She entered the room, surprised to see a boy this young working as a reporter. Was the whole place run by teenagers on the weekend? "I need to get a retraction printed in tomorrow morning's paper."

He sighed and glanced back at the screen dejectedly. "What section?"

"The society section." His shoulders slumped. Obviously, he didn't consider the society section to be big news. "The Morris Blake engagement announcement."

He clicked a few keys and glanced up at her. "What's the problem?"

Irritation flared at his bored expression. It might be deadly dull to him, but it was of paramount importance to her.

"It's not true. We're not engaged."

His eyes widened and he did a double-take from the screen to her. "Wow, this is you?"

She rolled her eyes, realizing he was looking at the cheesecake photo. He leaned around the screen to stare at her, obviously trying to make out her form under the baggy sweats. She fumed. Her toe tapped impatiently while she waited for him to stop gawking at her.

He reached for a notepad and thrust it at her. "Can I get your autograph, Miss Blake?"

Instead of taking the pad, she glanced pointedly at the screen. "Later. Let's get my business done first."

He gave her a final lingering once-over. "Okay, what were you saying?"

She leaned over the desk to get a better view of the screen. "This engagement announcement needs to be retracted. We're not engaged."

He kept his gaze focused on her breasts as he said, "I'm sorry, Miss Blake. I'm not authorized to print retractions."

She straightened, annoyed by his negative answer. She was darned if she'd be thwarted by a pubescent cub reporter. "Then who is authorized?"

"The society editor, Margaret Bain. I can give you her number."

"No thanks, I've already got it." So, Magi Bain was the society editor. Meddling Magi had struck again. She'd undoubtedly done it all for spite. Finding out she was the troublemaker didn't make this predicament any easier to take. From bitter experience, she knew Magi could be dangerous. One could never be quite sure when she would strike. The likelihood of getting her to print a retraction was about zero. Candace would be forced to rely on Greg's help. "But it was just a joke."

The boy clicked his mouse and brought up a different screen. "It says here the story was called in by Gregory Morris himself. So, he ought to know whether he's engaged or not. Congratulations, Miss Blake, you're engaged." He grinned, picked up the pad, and thrust it at her. "Now can I have my autograph?"

Her jaw dropped in disbelief. She'd planned to seek Greg's help, and he was the source of all her trouble? "That Toad! How could he humiliate me like this? Just wait till I get my hands on him. He'll be sorry."

She jogged down the stairs and sprinted out of the building. She was going to have a showdown with The Toad. Why did he do it? What motive could he have? Revenge? It didn't make sense. He'd be just as tainted by the scandal.

Her muscles were screaming for relief when she crested the top of the hill and caught sight of the Morris Mansion. That was what the locals called it in reverent tones. The house was huge and perched on the top of a hill, giving it beautiful vistas.

It was a favorite trick-or-treat stop among the local kids because the Morris servants always gave out caramel apples and big candy bars.

Candy stifled the pleasant memory. This was no social call. It was going to be down and dirty. She was going to knock him down a few pegs and bruise his handsome face before she left.

She marched up the cobblestone front drive, past the wrought iron gate, and beyond the fragrant rose bushes surrounding the front porch.

She tensed at the thought of the upcoming battle. She'd long ago made a practice of not giving in to her fears, developing a cool facade that most people never got beyond. But Greg had touched the soft, vulnerable side of her last night. It was going to make dealing with his betrayal even more difficult.

She felt dwarfed standing in front of the imposing double doors. She reached for the brass lion's head knocker and pounded it against the mahogany panel. The deep sound resonated through the wood, making her hand tingle.

The door opened silently on well-oiled hinges. A tall gray-haired lady, dressed in a black maid's uniform, stood behind it. Her light blue eyes were cautious, her mouth held in a dignified line.

"May I help you?"

Candace recognized Mildred, the Morris's maid, right off. She was a longtime customer at Ma's dress shop and extremely hard to please. She always viewed the world with a critical eye. Candace cringed as the maid gave her sweaty running attire a sniff of blatant disapproval.

She should have cleaned up and changed before coming. It would have given her a more confident edge, but it was too late now. She had to see this skirmish through before she lost her nerve.

She held her head high and straightened her spine. "I'm here to see Greg."

Mildred frowned, stepping forward, blocking the entrance. "Do you have an appointment?"

Her cool voice told Candace she didn't think it likely. This forbidding gatekeeper wasn't going to keep her from giving her employer a piece of her mind. "No, I don't."

Mildred frowned. "Young Mr. Morris is resting now. Why don't you come back later?" She started to close the door.

Candace wedged one foot inside the door, stopping it from closing.

Mildred stepped back a pace with a startled look on her face.

"I'll wait for him to wake up. My business is important." Nothing short of being bodily thrown out was going to keep her from doing what she came for.

Mildred's annoyed gaze lingered on Candace's face for a moment. Finally, she gave a stiff nod and stepped out of the way. "Very well, follow me."

Chalking up the small victory of gaining admittance to the inner sanctum, Candace grinned and followed the maid through the foyer and into the sitting room. She glanced around the dark paneled walls and vaulted ceiling. Despite its size, it was an amazingly comfortable room, and the furnishings were done in cool creamy colors.

Mildred watched Candace with narrowed eyes as she looked around the room. "Whom shall I say is calling?"

Refusing to be intimidated, she flashed the maid a cocky grin. "Tell Greg his fiancée is here. That should get him down here in a hurry."

Mildred squinted and glanced from Candace to the copy of the Daily Journal lying on the table.

She realized the woman was unfavorably comparing her sweaty appearance to the alluring photo in this morning's paper. Candace didn't look that bad, did she? She caught a glimpse of herself in a wall mirror, and grimaced. She looked like a wild woman. Her hair was falling out of the ponytail and rivulets of perspiration ran down her flushed face. She brushed away the dampness with her sweatshirt sleeve.

Mildred cleared her throat. "I'll tell Mr. Morris you're here." Her tone was still cool, but her expression was now intrigued.

"Thank you." She glanced away from Mildred's speculative gaze, uncomfortable with the attention. Damn Magi Bain for being an interfering fool. She never could keep her mouth shut, even in high school, running to the cops every time Candace even so much as jaywalked.

"There's a powder room through that door, if you'd like to freshen up." Mildred pointed to the door at the far end of the room.

Candace took the hint, feeling Mildred's curious gaze follow her all the way. She probably didn't want her dripping sweat onto the oriental carpet or the Chippendale settees.

She shut the powder room door behind her and walked over to the white pedestal sink. She ran cool water on her wrists to calm her racing pulse. This little episode was nothing compared to what was to come. She had to get her emotions under control.

She noticed a wicker basket containing a rainbow of rolled up plush washcloths and decorative soap on the counter. She helped herself, washing her hands and using a washcloth to scrub her face clean. Then she pulled off the ponytail holder and finger combed her hair, putting it in some semblance of order.

She glanced at herself in the mirror. Now, instead of looking like a wild woman she looked like a fresh-faced kid. A light sprinkling of freckles ran across the bridge of her nose, and her eyes were wide with a nervous gleam.

She practiced a stern look, and realized it made her look as bad tempered as Mildred. She stuck out her tongue at the reflection. If she could remember to keep her distance from Greg's captivating presence, she'd be okay. With that thought in mind, she opened the door.

Greg stood nearby wearing only a tight pair of jeans and a smile. He looked like he'd just tumbled out of bed. His jaw was shadowed with stubble, and his eyes carried a sleepy sexiness that made her catch her breath. His mouth slowly curved into a dangerous grin as he straightened away from the wall and sauntered her way.

He put a hand on the door jam and leaned toward her, his voice a husky bedroom rumble. "Hello there, beautiful. I didn't expect to see you so soon."

The predatory gleam in his midnight blue eyes transported her back to the beach. Last night's encounter was imprinted on her senses, never to be erased. She was close enough to reach out and touch his bare chest. Her intrigued gaze focused on the soft thatch of hair on his chest and followed it down to where it curved around his navel and disappeared into the waistband of his jeans.

She remembered all too well what those jeans concealed, but this wasn't the time for fantasizing. She had important business to take care of, if only she could recall what it was.

Stepping back to put some breathing room between them, she regained her equilibrium. He continued to smile as if he didn't have a care in the world. She put her hands on her hips as her irritation returned.

"How could you do this to me?"

He reached out to cup her cheek with his hand. "Do what?"

She pulled away, devastated by the gentle touch. Why did he have such power over her? It wasn't fair, not when she now knew him to be a master at playing games. This face-to-face confrontation wasn't such a good idea.

"I didn't come here to be manhandled." She stepped past him and into the parlor, seeking some breathing space, but his footsteps were close behind.

He took hold of her arm, stopping her flight. "What's wrong?"

She was aggravated by his puzzled tone. His warm hand rubbed her arm, creating chaos to her senses. She kept her back turned, not daring to look at him. "You know damned well what's wrong."

"No, I don't."

She bristled at the patent falsehood. "Bull. I know a setup when I see it. I also know a come-on when I feel it." She jerked her arm away. "There isn't going to be any more of that kind of activity between us."

He leaned into her space. "What kind of activity?" His voice was a suggestive rumble.

She knew he was talking about their rendezvous, but she couldn't risk being drawn in by his sensual tricks again. Determined to keep this impersonal she said, "You know precisely what kind of activity I'm talking about."

His grip tightened on her shoulder, holding her fast. "We almost made love, Candy Baby. I'm not ashamed to say it." His voice lowered to a sensual rumble. "You came all over my hand."

She froze, humiliated by the reminder of her needy response to his touch. "I did not."

"Yes, you did. I've experienced enough of the fake ones to know a genuine orgasm when I feel it. It was the most mind-blowing experience of my life, and I'm ready to finish what we started any time. That is, after you tell me what's wrong." He spun her around.

She dug in her heels, even though it was hopeless. He was much stronger. Her running shoes squeaked on the parquet floor. She looked in his eyes, and the genuine concern she found there shook her to the core. Could he be innocent?

"I'm not here to discuss last night."

He studied her face. "Tell me what's wrong. Has Magi been bothering you again?"

She bit her lip at his sympathetic tone. Did she owe him an apology? There was only one way to find out. "Did you put our engagement announcement in today's paper?"

"What?" He straightened, paling slightly.

"It's right here in black and white." She picked up the paper off the table and thrust it at him. "I tried to get them to print a retraction, but they told me *you* called in the story."

His jaw tightened as he read the story. "Shit."

His short, muttered curse startled her. His shoulders sagged.

"I didn't call this in."

His denial sounded sincere. In fact, he appeared to be totally off balance for the moment. Then, after a moment of studying her photo, he smiled, looking like a beefcake pinup with his bare chest and unsnapped jeans. All it would take was a zipper pulled down and he'd be naked.

"You don't have to look so happy. This is a total disaster. Meddling Magi has struck again, and it's going to take a concerted effort for us fix this mess."

He studied her heated reaction. "I was hoping to take things slowly this summer. I wanted you to get to know me and see me as something other than The Toad. But Magi seems to have forced my hand."

She chose to ignore the part about getting to know each other better. "You should never have told Magi we were a couple. I could have handled her just fine on my own. You didn't need to come to my rescue."

He shrugged. "The damage is done, but it may turn out to be to our advantage."

His practical tone made her uneasy. He sounded far too confident.

"To our advantage? Exactly what do you mean by that?"

"I own Pinnacle Publishing."

Her jaw dropped. "What? That's impossible. I've been negotiating with Chad Daley."

"He works for me." He folded his arms across his chest. "You signed a contract with my firm for the Candy-Wear Catalogs."

She gazed at his resolute expression, appalled. If she'd had any inkling that a Morris owned Pinnacle, she never would have signed with them. Damn it all, she'd jumped at the offer he'd dangled like a hungry trout.

"You lied to me."

"You didn't ask, and I didn't tell. It'll be a good deal for both our companies. I know a good deal when I see it, and I go for it." A nerve pulsed in his jaw. "I knew you'd go to the ends of the earth to avoid doing business with The Toad."

blusher cheeks heated as he so easily read her feelings. "I want out."

He shook his head. "No."

She was shaken by his sharp refusal and the thought that followed. Was last night just business? "So, last night was just a little fringe benefit of doing business together?"

He scowled. "You should know better than that. What we have goes beyond business."

The flare of masculine outrage on his face gave her satisfaction in confirming last night had been based on passion.

"Not anymore. You can go to hell, Morris. I'm tearing up my fraudulent contract."

"You can't. A community will be affected if this blows up or my stockholders get wind of it. I don't want to be forced to lay people off. I'll have to sue you for breach of contract."

"I see." Candace gazed at him, stunned, wondering if this was what a hostile takeover felt like, feeling a rush of sympathy for the people whose jobs could be in jeopardy. "I may have to do business with you, but we still need to hush this false engagement announcement. It certainly isn't advantageous."

He shrugged. "Magi sent this story national. It's likely to come out alongside the promos for Candy-Wear. People will be intrigued by the sweetheart deal. If you publicly dump me, the negative press will hurt you."

"So what. I can handle it." She frowned at his harsh expression.

"No, you can't. Your fledgling company will crash and burn, and Pinnacle's stock will nosedive. For both our sakes, we need to play this through."

She was well and truly trapped. He had left her with very few options other than to go along with him. "If I agree to play along, what's to stop Magi from making more trouble?"

He scowled. "I can handle Magi. She must have thought the story and picture would have you heading for the hills. Instead, you're going to stay here, hold your head high, and pretend to be in love with me. We have to make the engagement look real."

She blinked at him. His intense gaze seemed to will her to go along with the deception and more. "That's all it's going to be—just a pretense. When I leave town at the end of the summer, we'll break up." She held out her hand. "Agreed?"

He shook on it. "Agreed, but let's seal the agreement properly." He pulled her off balance and into his arms.

She tumbled against him. Her lashes swept shut as his mouth came down to claim hers. His bare chest was hot against her hands as she braced against him. For the briefest second, she let her fingers curl into his resilient strength.

His lips brushed hotly against hers, once, twice, and then they were gone. She gazed up into his handsome face, her head swimming with conflicting emotions. This steamy kiss did not bode well for the rest of the summer.

Chapter Four

Greg pulled his Lexus in front of Ma Brown's house and let the motor idle. He turned to glance at Candy. She sat stiffly by his side, not daring to glance his way. She was quiet, stunned by the rapid change of events. Good. It suited him to keep her off balance. He'd take any advantage he could get to keep her by his side.

"I'll pick you up at seven."

She slanted a resentful glance his way. "If you insist, but I still think this is a mistake." She reached for the door handle.

He placed a hand on her arm. He could feel her strained tension under his palm. "Dinner with my parents at the country club will prove that our engagement is real."

She pulled away, scowling at him. "You may have the power to get me there, but I very much doubt your family will come. After the showdown with your mother this morning, I know your family would rather face a firing squad than have dinner with me."

He understood her apprehension, but after he talked things over with his mother, he knew she'd come around. She wanted him to be happy, and Candy made him happy. He felt a vitality he hadn't known for years.

"Cheer up, Candy Baby. Being engaged to me isn't a fate worse than death."

"We're not really engaged, Gregory Morris." Her eyes narrowed. "Make sure you keep that in mind."

He tensed at her icy response. He remembered the way she'd exploded in his arms last night, coming apart at his touch. He could still feel the ripples of her passion. Hell, he ought to. He'd done nothing but dream about it all night long. She wanted the mystery lover from last night, not The Toad from this morning.

He skimmed a finger down her arm. She leaned into his touch. "We could have a lot of fun together this summer."

She jerked her arm away and got out of the car. "I'm not interested in that kind of fun with you. Mind your manners, Greg Morris, and I'll go through with my part of this farce. Remember, you have just as much to lose this summer as I do."

He watched her stride up her front walk, head held high. She had claws, he had to give her that. What she didn't know was his future was in danger, too. The Candy-Wear account was the last link in his five-year independence plan. He'd leave Pinnacle in the competent hands of a board of directors after his father retired, with only a token group of the Morris family involved. The way he saw it, it was a no-brainer, to have people with a passion for papermaking at the helm.

Greg slipped the Lexus into gear and drove away. He needed to confront Magi Bain about the bogus engagement announcement in this morning's paper. The revealing photograph of Candy had Magi's spiteful tone. And she had the means to pull it off, being an editor.

A few minutes later, he strode up the walk to Magi's townhouse. He glanced down the empty street as he leaned on the doorbell. It wouldn't do to have any speculation about his early morning visit. He and Magi were once an item, but that was long ago. He was an engaged man now, and he didn't want to risk fouling that up.

"Alright, alright, I'm coming," Magi, muttered as she jerked the door open. "Well, well, well, if it isn't the soon-to-be-married Greg Morris."

He frowned at her smirk as she stepped back into the foyer and waved him in. She was dressed in a pink chenille bathrobe.

He held fast, irritated by her triumphant expression. "Why did you do the hatchet job on Candy?"

She chuckled and turned away. "The picture added a bit of spice to the story, don't you think?"

"No." He held his outrage in check as he stepped into the foyer.

"I'm going to get some coffee. You can have some, too, if you want."

He shut the door and followed her. He intended to make sure Candy wouldn't feel Magi's sting again. He stopped in the doorway to the kitchen and watched Magi pour herself a cup of coffee.

She leaned against the counter and flashed an icy smile his way. "If the slut can't take the heat, she shouldn't pose for those explicit pictures. As soon as you made that announcement at the party last night, she became fair game, lover boy."

He frowned at the derisive endearment. "Don't call me that. You and I are ancient history."

She smirked. "Why not? I've got more right than her to call you that. Or did you get what you wanted last night?"

He bristled at her mocking tone, but refused to be baited. He and Magi had gone on three dates four years ago. They'd both been on the rebound. His fiancée had dumped him, and her marriage was over. They'd both needed the comfort of their brief intimate relationship and, in the end, had gone their own ways. He'd thought their breakup was amicable. Obviously, he'd thought wrong.

"We decided our liaison was a mistake and went our separate ways."

She thumped her coffee mug on the counter. "I didn't decide jack shit. You were the one that dumped me. Well, now you'll know how it feels to be rejected. I hope she stomps all over your heart, you rat."

He was stunned by her outburst. What could he say? He'd never given Magi any idea that they were more than casual friends since their breakup. Anything else had been cooked up in her scheming little mind.

They'd turned to each other when they were at low points in their lives. But it was over. Whatever attraction he might have felt for her faded long ago.

He studied her disgruntled expression, doubting she still had romantic feelings for him. She was dating Tim Marshall, owner of the Daily Herald, for Pete's sake. Why did she begrudge him a little happiness? Did her animosity stem from feeling that she was losing out to a woman whom she considered a lower class than her?

At the risk of escalating her ire, he resolved to set Magi straight. He refused to let Candy be hurt by her venom. "Just for your information, Magi, she didn't dump me. We're still engaged."

"What?" Her jaw dropped.

"Candy didn't dump me. We're engaged, so I guess, in a way, you did me a favor." He was satisfied by the stunned look on her face.

After a moment of dismayed silence, she spat out, "Get the hell out of my house."

He stayed put. Knowing her, she wouldn't stay down for long. "Not until we get this settled. If Candy gets any worse press, I'm going to have your hide."

She glared at him. "I'm not the only reporter on the Daily Herald. Your trashy little fiancée is sure to generate plenty of bad press without my assistance."

He was prepared for this flanking tactic. No doubt, she'd instigate a campaign of scandal just to get back at him. "I'll know you're behind it, even if it carries another reporter's byline. I don't take libel lightly, and the Herald won't take a lawsuit well. You'll lose your job, even if you are cozy with Tim Marshall." He softened his tone. "Be reasonable, Magi. I thought we were friends."

Her lips thinned as she crossed her arms over her chest. "And I thought we were more than friends. I guess we both were wrong. As for that tramp, Candy Blake, I hope she takes the next broom out of town. If there's anything I can do to speed her along, I'm going to do it."

He was rapidly losing his patience. "What's behind this? You can drop the lovelorn act because I know you never loved me."

She pursed her lips and looked away. Her nose was raised high in the air. "She doesn't deserve the Morris name, and she's not going to get it. I split you two up back in high school, and I'm going to do it again."

He froze. He remembered the prom night from hell all too well. His car wouldn't start that night, and as he'd been tinkering with it, some friends had driven up and offered him a beer. Nervous about the date, Greg had downed it in one pull. The next morning, he'd woken up slumped in the backseat of his car, his tux as messed up as his head. Candy's foster brother, Mike, added a few lumps and bruises to his misery a day later. And his father had hustled him out of town the next week.

His jaw tightened as it all became clear. "You had me drugged."

Her grin was brittle. "Got it in one, lover boy. You ought to thank us. We did it to keep you from being tainted by the tramp. Your family's reputation was at risk. If you think with your head instead of your dick, you'll realize I'm right. She's not in our class."

"You bet she's not. She's ten times better." Magi hadn't acted alone. He had a vague memory of his sister tending to him through the night. Come to think of it, her formal gown had been just as messed up as his tux the next morning.

Magi's sputtered curse words bounced off him as he mulled things over. He ignored her. It would be a cold day in hell before he let her affect his life again.

"Just stay out of our way. You've been warned."

He turned and headed toward the door. At least now he knew what had Magi's back up. His dear sister. There was going to be hell to pay.

Greg knew right where to find his sister. She was hosting a luncheon at her house for the Junior League. And Kathleen, being a control freak, would be there now overseeing the smallest details. He pulled up in front of his sister's estate, walked past her carefully trimmed juniper bushes, and made his way to the back door. He gave a brief knock, then let himself in.

Joe Barnes, his brother-in-law, looked up from the morning paper he was reading at the breakfast nook and smiled. "Hey bro, I guess congratulations are in order. Or, on second thought, looking at your frowning face, condolences. Maybe giving up the single life won't suit you."

Greg schooled his savage expression into a civilized smile. He looked over Joe's shoulder and glanced at the copy of the Daily Herald spread out on the table.

Their engagement announcement took center stage. He thought Candy looked like an angel in the picture, but he knew most of Morris Point would condemn her for posing for it. He reached down to run his finger over her image. He wanted her and he was going to fight for her.

Looking up, he noted Joe's sympathetic gaze. His sister was damned lucky to have found the love of her life. Why couldn't he have the same opportunity himself?

"What'd she do, run you out of the dining room?"

"You know how your sister likes to take care of every little detail. I figured it would be safer to stay out of her way. So, what are you doing here?"

Greg frowned as he thought of Kathleen's interference. He could understand his mother's worries, but this was none of his sister's business. "I've got a little bone to pick with your wife."

Joe leaned back in the chair, rocking on the back legs, and sighed. "What's she done now?"

He gritted his teeth as he gave Joe a savage smile. "She and Mother made a surprise visit on my bride-to-be this morning."

Joe's chair crashed back down. "Uh oh."

He nodded. "Kathleen and I are going to have a knockdown, drag out fight. Any objections?"

Joe shook his head. "Not as long you keep it polite. I don't blame you for being ticked off. I know she can be abrasive, but keep in mind, she was trying to help. Kathy cares about you."

He rolled his eyes at Joe's patience. That's why they got along so well. Kathleen was aggressive and Joe was laid back. "I don't know how you can stand being married to that she-devil."

Joe frowned and gave an expansive sigh. "The trouble is, most people don't understand her. Kathy isn't mean. She's just frustrated."

Greg snorted and walked toward the kitchen door. "Frustrated? The woman runs every charity in town. She and my mother, to a lesser extent, rule the Morris Point female society with an iron glove."

"Did you ever stop to think maybe the reason she gets so involved is that she doesn't have any direction in life?"

He thought about Joe's statement as he walked into the dining room where his sister was laying out the place settings.

She frowned when she saw him coming, then turned back to what she was doing, placing the elaborately folded napkins at the proper angle. "Don't you have people to do that for you?"

"I prefer to do it myself. That way I know it's done right."

He noticed the way she avoided his gaze. Maybe she was actually feeling some remorse for her sneak attack this morning, but he doubted it. "We need to talk."

"She ran right to you, didn't she?" she snapped. "That lying, conniving little tramp. She claimed it was all a misunderstanding and that you weren't stupid enough to propose to her. I didn't believe her, and it turns out I was right."

He tightened his jaw, reigning in his temper. "Why'd you, do it?"

Kathleen glared at him. "Mother and I were only trying to avoid a scandal. I told her that gold-digger, Candy Blake, had tricked you. It was just a bizarre coincidence, you run into each other last night. A chance encounter is nothing to build your future on, Greg."

He studied her defiant, but guilty, expression. Maybe she did feel remorse. "It wasn't a chance encounter. It was a carefully planned, logical campaign, and you damn near ruined it. I'm not going to give you a second warning, Kathy. Back off."

She plopped into a chair, her eyes widening. "What do you mean by a well-planned campaign? You're talking crazy."

He slipped his hands in his pockets and shrugged. "I knew damned well Candy would be there. I arranged it. Pinnacle Publishing just signed a five-year contract to publish her Candy-Wear catalog. I arranged for her to have a summer off, and I conspired with her foster mother to have her needed at home. I finally managed to get her back in my arms, but you and Magi came along to try to ruin everything again."

Her mouth hung agape. "Me and Magi? Oh God, she ratted me out, too, didn't she? I had no idea you were still interested in Candy. We figured you just wanted to get her into bed back then. Magi had sympathized with my embarrassment at your foolish behavior and produced a solution."

"Some solution. You two idiots could have killed me. I understand your motivation, but what about Magi's?"

"She's my friend. She was only doing it to help me out."

He shook his head. "Wake up, little sister. She wasn't your friend then, and she certainly isn't now. Candy and I didn't place that announcement in this morning's paper. If we had, it wouldn't have contained the photograph. She did it to humiliate Candy."

She gasped. "If what you say is true, she didn't care who her graphic announcement hurt. How are you two going to handle it?"

"Candy has agreed to play along for the summer for the sake of our businesses." He watched his sister's startled re action.

"Then Candy didn't lie to Mother when she said it wasn't true."

He shook his head. "No. It took a bit of coercion to persuade her to keep up the illusion. Pinnacle Publishing needs her account to grow to the next level. But more importantly, this bogus engagement will give me some time to win her over. Like I said, I won't allow you or Magi to interfere."

She looked away. "I did it for your own good."

"Bull. I cared for her, and you knew it."

She turned to glare at him. "Alright, fine. I couldn't stand the talk. You had no business going out with such trash. For God's sake, her father embezzled money from our family business. You should have avoided her, not take her to the prom."

He gritted his teeth, aggravated by her snobbish attitude, but not really surprised by it. "You always were overly proud of our social standing."

She glared back at him. "Overly proud. That's nice, coming from you. This social standing is what I've built my life on. I couldn't just step into Dad's shoes like you did. I had to carve out a niche for myself."

He stepped back a pace, stunned by her vehemence. "I had no idea you felt like this, but try to understand, I haven't had it so easy, either. There are a lot of responsibilities to running a mill, with a lot of people counting on me."

She looked away and replied quietly, "I wouldn't know about that now, would I?"

He had to get through to her somehow. Frustrated, he blurted out, "I still want Candy. That much hasn't changed. I need to give us a chance."

She turned to look at him, frowning. "But you were just kids back then. You've dated lots of women since. Heck, you were even married. Jill was a much more appropriate mate."

The memory didn't crush him anymore. Candy had made him want to live again.

"I can't live in the past, Kathy. Can't you see that Candy's good for me? Furthermore, she doesn't give two figs about my wealth or social position, unlike every other woman I've dated. When her business proposal hit my desk six months ago, it rekindled my interest."

She sniffed. "This isn't going to go over too well with Mom and Dad."

"That's not your problem. I'll smooth things over with them today." He gazed at his sister, hoping she'd gotten the message. She seemed cooperative now, but what about later? He needed to reinforce the idea that Candy was in his life to stay. "Have dinner with us tonight at the club. We're going to celebrate our engagement."

She shook her head. "I don't think I can ever accept her as your fiancée, even if it is just a pretense."

He stood firm. "All I'm asking is you don't interfere."

She sighed. "Okay. Joe and I will be there. We'd better make the best of a bad situation."

Candy knocked on Ma's door. She was hoping she would still be asleep so she could put this off a little longer. How would Ma take to the fact that their engagement announcement was splashed all over the morning paper?

"Come in," Ma called.

Candy poked her head around the door. "I don't want to disturb you if you're taking a nap."

"Nonsense. I'm wide awake."

Candy walked into the room and helped Ma sit up in bed. What should she tell her? She didn't want to cause any shocks. Ma had seemed so delicate since she'd been home.

Much more fragile than she'd remembered her being. So much so, Candy had agreed to stay for the summer to give Ma plenty of time to recuperate from surgery. She'd have to break it to her gently.

"Ma, there's something I've got to tell you."

Ma put her hand up to her chest. "It's not bad news, is it?"

Candy bit her lip. This mock engagement was a total disaster, but she couldn't say that. *Yes, but it means a sensual summer spent with the man of your dreams,* an errant part of her mind shouted.

"Not exactly."

Ma pursed her lips. "What does that mean?"

Candy shrugged, then held the morning paper out. "My engagement to Greg Morris was announced in this morning's paper, but..."

Ma shrieked, then grabbed Candy with a bear hug. "Oh honey, I'm so happy for you."

Candy gasped for air in the tight embrace. Ma suddenly seemed to have gained a lot of strength.

She pulled away and looked into her twinkling eyes. "Yes, but, as I was saying..."

Ma beamed. "This has made me feel better than I have in ages."

This wasn't going as planned, but she couldn't bear to burst Ma's happy bubble. "Yes, well, we're going out tonight to celebrate. I get to meet the whole family, including Greg's father."

"Don't worry, honey, they're going to love you."

"That's not what I'm worried about. I don't give a rip what they think about me. I don't think I can stand to spend time with the man who killed my father."

Ma shook her head. "Now, honey, Mr. Morris did no such thing."

Candy looked away. "He might as well have. My father died in jail after Greg's dad sent him there, didn't he?"

"But you can't blame the man for that. Your dad was arrested for embezzlement. It was his fault, I'm sorry to say. His heart attack could have happened at any time."

Candy sniffed. "He told me he didn't do it, before they sent him away, and I believe him."

"Now, now, I know you have strong feelings about this, but it doesn't mean that your dad couldn't have told you a lie to spare your feelings."

She looked away. She could vividly recall the moments before the police had arrested her father. They'd both known it was coming. He'd proclaimed his innocence, and she'd believed him then. She still did, didn't she?

Of course, she did. It would be disloyal to think otherwise.

Ma sighed. "It's all water under the bridge, honey. Your father is dead and gone. You've got to look to the future now. And I couldn't be happier."

Candy wasn't so sure. The past and the future were all inextricably woven together. There could be no future with Greg Morris, she was sure of it.

Chapter Five

Fastening the clasp on her silver ankle bracelet, Candy gazed at her reflection in the mirror. She'd dressed to kill, and it showed. The red satin party dress she wore clung to her figure, held up by gossamer thin spaghetti straps. Twirling, the multi-layered skirt fluttered around her legs.

She fastened matching silver hoop earrings on her lobes and reached for the perfume bottle on her dresser to apply scent to her pulse points.

If Greg was determined to show her off, she was going to make him pay for the privilege. Hopefully, this sexy dress would help her to assert her independence, and at the same time, keep future family get-togethers down to a minimum.

When Greg's father got a look at her, she hoped he'd run in the other direction. His mother and sister she could handle, but the thought of meeting his father again shook her to the core.

She swallowed the lump in her throat. Years had passed since she'd been that frightened girl, alone in the police station. The prospect of seeing him again made her feel almost as insecure. She fastened her evening wrap around her. There was no need to give Greg a preview of her sexy dress.

Grabbing her red beaded evening bag off the dresser, she turned and headed out of her bedroom.

She stopped at Ma's room to say goodnight, but the bed was empty. Had she gone downstairs? If so, it would be the first time since her heart surgery. Candy hoped she hadn't overdone it.

Candy ran down the stairs to the sound of the television in the living room. She poked her head in the room to find Ma comfortably ensconced in her favorite chair, watching Wheel of Fortune.

She looked up and smiled. "You look nice, dear."

"Thanks." Candy hugged her wrap close around her, thankful Ma didn't have the full view. Would she approve of her tactics if she knew the truth? "I'm surprised to see you out of your room."

"I was feeling stronger, dear. Must be the good news about your engagement bucking me up."

Candy bit her lip as she took in the fresh rosy glow on Ma's cheeks. She did look better. So much for denying her fake engagement here at home. She couldn't risk throwing Ma into a relapse. And besides, it might be nice to keep her dream lover for the summer. If Greg could use her for business reasons, she could use him for personal ones.

She'd been toying with the idea since he'd dropped her off this morning. The thought had hit her after her initial shock had subsided. There'd be no friends trying to set her up with blind dates, so she'd be safe from Joyce and Joan's matchmaking attempts. And she'd finally get to see what she'd missed out on all those years ago. It was an irresistible prospect.

"I'll be leaving soon. Greg should be here any minute. You've got my cell phone number if you need me."

"Don't you worry about me, dear. I've got a friend coming over to play a few rounds of Canasta. You and Greg have a good time."

Candy flashed Ma a bright and hopefully reassuring smile as she heard a car drive up. "That must be him now."

"Well. Off with you then."

"Right. Call if you need me." She turned and hurried toward the door, her tension building. Maybe she'd get lucky, and Greg's father wouldn't show up. She brightened at the thought.

Opening the door, she almost tripped over Greg on the doorstep.

He smiled at the sight of her. "You look lovely, Candy."

She warmed at the compliment. "Thanks. That's pretty much what Ma said."

"Ready?"

"Sure am. Let's go." She tried to slip out the door.

"Let me say hello first." He stepped around her and headed into the foyer.

She chased after him. "That's not needed." She skidded to a halt beside him.

"Hello, Mrs. Brown."

"Well, hello there, Gregory. It's good to see you. I couldn't be happier about your and Candy's engagement."

He reached out to take Candy's hand, drawing her close. "We appreciate it. Don't we, Candy?"

"Um, yeah. Of course, we do. Well, we're off to the country club."

"I'm sorry you can't join us."

"Me, too. But the doctor wants me to take it easy. Give my regards to your parents."

"We will." Greg escorted Candy out the door.

She looked at the old red pickup truck parked in the driveway. It was a far cry from the Lexus this morning.

***

Greg noted Candy glancing at the tattered upholstery in his old pickup and grinned. He'd chosen it because of the bench seat. It was much more conducive for making out. That was, if he ever got the chance again. She sat as far away from him as she could get, hugging the door.

He knew the prospect of dining with his family had her on edge, but was there something else? Was she trying to find a way to break their agreement?

He cast an assessing glance her way. "Why didn't you ask Ma Brown to come with us?"

She hesitated. "She's not strong enough to go out. Besides, I don't want her to get hurt. She's going to be crushed when she finds out this is all a sham."

So, it was just nerves. He felt his stress level back off. "You're the one who's going to make people doubt us with your prickly ways. Engaged couples don't normally have three feet of space between them in the car. Slide over, Candy Baby."

She frowned and inched over a tad. "Stop calling me that."

He grinned. "Pet names go with the territory. You can call me honey."

She let out a sigh and slouched in her seat. "Honey. You don't look like a honey to me."

He shrugged, pleased the hated nickname at least took her mind off his family. "I'm easy. Dear, sweetheart, honey. Pick one you like."

She gasped as he turned into the parking lot of Silver Lake.

She slanted a wary glance his way. "What are we doing here?"

"We've got some unfinished business to take care of. I thought this place would give us some privacy."

She inched away from him. "And I told you we aren't going to do any more of that. At least, not until I decide the time is right."

He smiled at the softening of her tone. She was so beautiful. The sight of her, bathed in the sunset's glow, made his mouth dry. He ran a finger down her arm.

She leaned into his touch, her gaze locked with his. Heat sizzled between them as the air became charged with unfulfilled desire. He leaned forward to brush a whisper soft kiss across her sweet lips.

Her eyes swept shut as she kissed him back, running her hand up his arm while her other arm wrapped around his neck.

He unclasped her seatbelt, drawing her to him as he deepened the kiss.

Her arms tightened around him as she melted into his embrace.

He groaned deep in his throat as her hands found their way under his suit jacket. He palmed her breast, fanning his fingers over her nipple until it peaked.

She moaned, pressing against him, then pulled away as if burned. "I'm sorry, I shouldn't have done that. I'm not trying to be a tease, but I'm not ready for this yet."

He knew she had mixed emotions. Hell, he had them, too. Instead of being able to romance her properly, he had to do it the hard way.

"I know."

Damn Magi all to hell. She'd laughed in his face when he'd confronted her this morning. Then, he'd informed her that the engagement was true, and she'd been speechless.

Without a word, he pulled a jeweler's box out of the glove compartment, flipped it open to reveal a ring, and reached for Candy's hand.

She tried to tug away. "Why?"

"Engaged people wear rings." He slipped it on her finger. It was a beautiful round solitaire diamond, encircled with deep blue sapphires. "Now, it's official. You're mine."

"Temporarily," she murmured, gazing at the ring on her finger. "What did you tell your family?"

"Kathleen knows the truth."

"Why?"

"Sorry, she badgered it out of me."

Candy walked into the Morris Point Country Club feeling edgy. Greg's ring was heavy on her finger, making her feel like he'd staked a claim on her. She unclasped her cape, handed it to the coat check girl, and turned an expectant glance his way. What would he think of her dress?

He let out a low whistle. "You look good enough to eat, Candy Baby."

"Gee, thanks, I think." She frowned at him. He was supposed to be outraged, not turned on.

He smiled. "You're hoping to have my family heading for the hills, I see."

"Got it in one, *honey*."

He winked. "It won't work. We Morris's don't scare that easily. Besides, I'd take you in there naked if I had to."

She scowled. "Shut up."

He took her arm and steered her toward the dining room. "Or, better yet, I'll borrow one of the tablecloths and swath you in it, toga-style."

She slanted an annoyed glance his way. "Try it, Toad, and you'll draw back a bloody stump."

She noticed a hush fall over the dining room as they entered. The engagement had probably been the chief item of gossip around town today. She slanted a wary glance Greg's way to see how he was taking it, and was startled by his sympathetic smile in return. He folded her hand in his, and she clung to him like a lifeline.

They approached the table, and she was shocked to find Greg's family sitting there as promised. He must have done some fast talking to get them here. Mrs. Morris's smile was a bit too bright, and Mr. Morris looked stiff and grouchy as they caught sight of her. Kathleen, on the other hand, just sat and scowled. Of course, she knew it was all a sham.

Joe stood up as Candy approached, and Kathleen tugged him down. He slanted an apologetic glance their way.

They drew to a halt, and Greg pulled out her chair. She slid into it, staring at Mr. Morris as she would a cobra. Just being at the same table with him had her tied up in knots.

Greg sat in the chair next to her. "I hope we didn't keep you waiting too long." He reached for Candy's hand. "We had some unfinished business to take care of, didn't we, Candy Baby?"

"Candy Baby?" Kathleen asked dryly, her voice slightly slurred.

"That's right," Greg said as she downed her cocktail. He flashed his sister a tight smile. "And she calls me honey."

"Isn't that nice," Mrs. Morris said, a bit too brightly.

"Right," his father said, grimly.

"That's some dress you're almost wearing," Kathleen snipped.

Candy flashed her an icy smile. "One of my designs. I can get you one wholesale if you like."

"No, thanks. I don't think it's up to my standards."

Greg's father cleared his throat, drawing everyone's attention. He picked up his champagne glass. "The occasion calls for a toast. To Gregory and Candy."

Greg smiled and raised his glass.

Candy clinked her glass with his, feeling like a total fraud.

Mrs. Morris sipped her champagne and smiled. "I thought you were going to bring Mrs. Brown. It would be nice to include your family in the celebration."

Candy shook her head. "She's still recovering from surgery and too weak to go out."

"Well, then. You must have some other family to include, dear. Do you have any relatives I should consult on our pre-wedding planning with?"

Slanting a stricken look Mrs. Morris's way, she tried to come up with an excuse. Family? She had none, other than her foster family. Her mother had left, and her father had died in prison for embezzlement. Not much of a family pedigree. "My mother died shortly after I was born." She hoped to leave it at that.

Mrs. Morris nodded. "There must be someone else."

Couldn't the lady take a hint? Her patience at an end, she stated flatly, "My only family was my daddy, and he died in jail, if you'll recall. It was in all the papers."

"Oh dear," Mrs. Morris replied plaintively, casting a panicked look at her husband.

"Young woman, I'll thank you to lower your voice," Mr. Morris grumbled.

"You can take my manners and—"

Greg pulled her up before she could finish the statement. "Dance with me."

As they started to dance, she stood stiffly in his arms, still stinging from Mr. Morris's rebuke. She trembled in Greg's arms.

"Calm down, honey." Greg slid a gentle caress down her back. "You're safe with me."

Settling into his arms with a sigh, she murmured, "I'm sorry, but I had to say it or burst. If you want to rethink this summer engagement, go right ahead. I don't think it's going to work. Your father and I can't be in the same room for ten minutes before we're at war."

Gazing down at her, he gave her a little smile. "It'll all work out."

"Easy for you to say." Her chin raised a defiant notch.

His jaw tightened. "Just remember, I'm on your side."

"Are you really?" She gazed at him, uncertain.

"For the long haul," he stated, smoothing a gentling hand down her bared back.

"Thanks. It's just that mention of my dad reminds me of that time. He'd said he was innocent, and I believed him. And then he died of a massive heart attack in jail while awaiting trial. It was horrible."

"I could do some digging and see what I can find out about your father's case."

Candy sighed and leaned her head against his shoulder. "What's the point? It happened. My father's gone. It's over, but thanks for the offer."

"You're welcome. Just remember, if anyone else bothers you this summer, I've got your back."

His thoughtful tone soothed her hurt feelings as much as his words. She smiled at him, finding promise in his eyes. He really was on her side.

"I'm starting to see you in a whole new light, honey."

Leading her off the dance floor, he flashed her a warm smile. "Honey, is it? Hallelujah, The Toad is dead." As they walked back to the table, he bent to whisper, "Remember, I'm here for you in all sorts of ways this summer, Candy Baby."

Feeling herself blush as they reached the table, she snatched up her evening bag. "I'm going to go powder my nose."

As Candy stood in front of the vanity mirror reapplying her lipstick, the ladies' room door opened. Glancing at Kathleen's somber reflection in the mirror, she felt her tension renew. Had she deliberately followed her here?

Brow wrinkling, Kathleen glided over and slid into a vanity chair. "I thought we should talk."

Braced for an attack, Candy turned to smile wryly. "They send you in here to beat me up?" She couldn't help recalling being the victim of pranks and dirty tricks in high school. She'd been the butt of lots of them, but she'd dished out a few of her own, too. Of course, she and Joan were usually the ones who got in trouble for them. The preppie crowd could do no wrong according to the local authorities.

Kathleen shrugged. "I think we've grown beyond those days, don't you?"

"Sometimes I wonder."

"I came in here for one reason, to tell you to behave with a little decorum. I'm putting you on notice now. All I have in this town is my family and my social position, and I'm not about to let you ruin either of them."

The woman had been born with a silver spoon in her mouth, for heaven's sake. How could she think little old Candy Blake could upset her life? "For starters, I have no intention of ruining anything for you. The world doesn't revolve around you, and believe it or not, this town doesn't, either. You've got a lot more than I started out with. You've got the mill."

"No, I don't." Kathleen looked away, her frown deepening. "Daddy doesn't approve of women from our family getting involved in the business."

Stunned, Candy's jaw dropped. How old fashioned could the man get? Why hadn't Kathleen stood up for herself? Maybe she needed a shove in the right direction.

"And do you always do what Daddy says?"

"Don't you?" Kathleen sneered. "You've spent your life as an outcast just like your father. The apple doesn't fall far from the tree from what I've seen."

Taken aback by the accusation, Candy went quiet. She had spent her life as an outsider fighting against an unjust system. She supposed she did have a chip on her shoulder.

Rising to her feet, Kathleen walked to the door.

Finding her voice, Candy stepped forward, determined to regain control of the situation. "I'll make a deal with you. I promise not to make trouble for you this summer if you'll do the same for me."

Kathleen cast an assessing glance her way. "I agree. But there is one important condition. Take it easy on my big brother. Break his heart, and I'll make you sorry."

It was a ridiculous request. She and Greg shared a slow burning attraction, but he didn't love her. It was purely business. Kathleen knew that, but it didn't seem to mollify her.

"You don't have to worry about that, Kathy."

Kathleen glanced at the ring on Candy's finger. "That's quite a sparkler. If you were just a gold-digger, it would be reason enough for you to play him for a fool. I've noticed the soft way he looks at you. He's head over heels. He hasn't looked at a woman that way since Jill. You've got him good and hooked, and you know it."

Who was Jill? Greg had history she didn't know about. Maybe a string of broken romances lurked in his past. The thought bothered her, even though she reminded herself this was just business.

The door closed behind Kathleen.

Break his heart, indeed. As if that were possible. She caught sight of the ring on her finger, and her breath caught.

Shaking off the sensation of being claimed once more, she took a deep breath.

When she walked back to the table, Kathleen sat alone, surrounded by several empty glasses.

Kathleen's grin was crooked. "It seems they've all got other fish to fry."

"So, I see." Candy's brow wrinkled as she looked around for Greg. He'd better get back before Kathleen drank herself under the table.

"Don't worry. I'll keep you entertained." Kathleen refilled both their champagne glasses. "The karaoke DJ is here in the back room now. How about we take a stroll up there?" Rising to her feet, she started walking away.

Picking up her glass, Candy hurried to follow. Maybe some time with Kathleen would give her a chance to find out about Jill.

"Right behind you."

Kathleen laughed and reached back to tug her along. "Come on, slow poke."

Skittering behind her on high heels, Candy's champagne sloshed over the side of her glass, spilling on the floor. When they reached the bar, she dug in her heels, bringing Kathleen to an abrupt halt.

"I'm pooped, let's take a seat."

Kathleen sat with a snort. "You sure don't have much stamina for a big-time New York model party girl."

"I'm not the party girl you think I am. I'm a plain old hardworking nine-to-five catalog model."

Tilting her head to the side, Kathleen eyed her quizzically. "Maybe I was wrong about you. Come on, let's sing," Kathleen requested with a giggle. "Nothing like a good singsong to bring a family together."

"No, thanks."

"Aw, come on." She pouted. "How come no one ever wants to sing with me?" Then she grinned, slurring, "What's the matter? Are you a chicken?"

"Jeez, it must run in the family." Candy rolled her eyes.

Kathleen frowned. "Are you bad-mouthing us Morrises again? I thought we settled all that in the bathroom."

Decorum was flying right out the window as Candy realized the champagne was starting to relax her. She stifled a giggle, saying, "Alright, fine. Just shut up."

She reluctantly followed a wobbly Kathleen onto the stage. Greg couldn't blame her for this one.

"What'll it be, ladies?" the DJ asked.

Candy held onto Kathleen so she wouldn't fall over, and they started singing along to an off-key rendition of 'We Are Family'. She gazed out at the sparse crowd to find Greg's parents watching from the doorway with horrified expressions.

At that moment, she wished a hole would open up in the floor she could hide in.

Greg and Joe wandered in from the bar and stopped in their tracks.

Oh, great! Now the whole family had a ringside seat to her and Kathleen's awful duet. She cringed as Kathleen screeched out a high note.

Greg grinned at her, and then said something to Joe. Joe hurried up to the stage, scooped up a sputtering Kathleen, and headed for the door.

Sauntering toward the stage, Greg held out his hand to Candy. "Time to go, Candy."

Grateful for the timely, if embarrassing, intervention, she ran off the stage and linked her arm with his.

As they roared out of the parking lot, she slanted a glance Greg's way. Was he angry about the evening's end? No, he was actually smiling. Good!

Sighing, she leaned back in the seat and rolled down the window to let the wind whip at her hair. The cool breeze blew away the remnants of champagne as she gazed up at the stars. It really was a special night, and here she was with her dream lover.

It was then she noticed they were driving in the opposite direction of Ma Brown's house. Where was he taking her? She glanced expectantly at the sharp planes of his face in the moonlight. When he turned into the Silver Lake driveway, her hopes were confirmed.

Leaning back against the car door to smile at him, she asked, "What are we doing here?"

He unbuckled his seatbelt and smiled at her. "Guess."

Gazing at his heartbreaker's smile, she wondered once again about his past. She needed some answers before this went any farther. "Who is Jill?"

The flash of pain that crossed his face was unmistakable. "I see Kathleen's been gossiping." His hand clamped tight on the steering wheel for a moment.

Trying to read his emotions, she studied the tight set of his mouth. Jill had been important to him, that much was obvious. But did that leave any space in his heart for her?

"Not really. She just warned me not to break your heart like Jill. Who is she?"

Letting go of the steering wheel with a sigh, Greg murmured, "Jill was my wife."

"Wife?" She could barely form the word. An ex-girlfriend, she'd expected. An ex-wife, she hadn't.

Turning to face her, he looked her square in the eyes, unflinching. "We met in college. We were only married six months when she was killed by a hit and run driver seven years ago."

She traced the line of a tear down his rugged face. "Oh my God, Greg. I'm so sorry." Her hand moved down to rub his shoulder tenderly. "Tell me about her."

"Like I said, we met in college. You've met her cousin, Chad. He's the man you've been negotiating with at Pinnacle. He and I attended UW Madison's School of Business together, and he introduced us. Jill was sweet and loving, with a zest for life. I think you two would have been friends. It still doesn't seem real that she's gone sometimes. She helped me build Pinnacle Publishing from nothing, even going so far as to work in the accounting department for free."

Candy was touched that he felt safe enough with her to open up in this way. His heart had been shattered by the loss of his wife. She could see it in his unguarded expression, the glimmer of unshed tears in his eyes. It helped put his aggressive business style in proper perspective. He was determined to make Pinnacle a success, maybe for Jill as much as for himself.

When she digested his words, his statement about leaving his father's firm penetrated. "You're leaving Morris Papers," she realized out loud.

"I'm almost out the door. After I leave, there'll still be a token group of Morris family members on the board."

She thought about Kathleen's statement about being shut out of the family firm. This just might give his sister the opportunity she wanted. "What about Kathleen?"

"What about her?"

Hoping he wouldn't be as close-minded as his father, she said, "It would give her a chance to get involved in the business."

"I've been thinking about that." He shrugged. "Quite honestly, she's never shown any interest in the business before this morning."

Candy could understand his confusion. After all these years, his sister was chafing under the confines of her conservative family role. "Maybe she was afraid to make waves. Ask her. She might surprise you."

"I'll do that."

His reasonable attitude pleased her. She was definitely seeing a new side of him tonight. The sudden need to get close to him had more to do with that than to comfort him because of his losses.

"So, what are we doing here?" She unfastened her seatbelt and inched toward him.

"I thought our place would be a good spot to talk." He reached out to trail a finger down her arm.

"About what?" She watched his finger on her arm, enjoying the little explosions of fire his touch ignited in her. Talk, indeed. His actions could say so much more than words. All her willpower dissolving, she decided that they were destined to have this summer of love.

"About us." He moved forward, pulling her across the bench seat and into his arms. "About this." His mouth came down to claim hers.

"Umm…" She groaned, returning his kiss. His lips were so warm, coaxing a response from her. She sighed, melting into his arms.

He tugged her onto his lap. Her hands snaked under his jacket, seeking the muscled planes of his back. Her fingers kneaded his hot flesh.

"My little vixen." He growled, nuzzling her neck.

She smiled. "I've always wanted to neck in a car."

"Well, I don't want to disappoint you, then." He cupped her breast, slightly squeezing it in his grasp.

She gasped, pressing against his palm at the delicious sensation. He smiled and pinched her nipple through the cloth of her dress. Plucking at the hardening nub, he rolled it between his fingers until she squirmed. Then he moved to the other breast which ached for the same tender torture.

"Oh, yes," she sighed.

When his hands fell away, she blinked at him, bereft. Why did he stop? His sultry smile took her breath away.

He reached out and flicked first one, and then the other spaghetti strap holding up her dress. They skittered off her shoulders. He reached back and loosened her zipper.

As her bodice fell, she shook it loose, baring her breasts for his sweet attention. He bent to take her nipple into his hot mouth, and she cried out with delight. He licked and sucked until little mewling noises poured from her throat.

Two could play the teasing game. Tugging his shirt out of his pants, she scratched her nails up his back, so great was her need. Smiling, she reached for his zipper. Finding him, she stroked his hard shaft with her trembling fingers, tickling its velvety head. He was magnificent.

Groaning, his mouth left her breast as he pressed her back against her seat. Lifting her skirts, he rubbed her bare legs until he reached her satin panties. He tugged her thong aside and reached for her hot, creamy center.

She cried out when he touched her clit, pressing it, rubbing it. His fingers teased her, moving in and out of her until she was all but humping his hand.

"You're so wet. Are you ready for me, Candy Baby?"

"Yes." She shrieked and writhed against him. She needed him inside her now.

Sitting back, he picked her up, holding her so she hovered over him.

Straddling him, she spread her legs wide. Tantalized, she burned when he butted against her, teasing the very edges of her femininity with his erect manhood. Why didn't he take her?

"Please," she pleaded.

"Open your eyes, Candy," he demanded.

Her eyes popped open at his command. The heat she found almost made her swoon.

"That's right," he husked. "I want you to be a willing participant. Every inch of the way, together."

"I am." She gasped as she slowly lowered herself onto his rigid manhood. He filled her to tightness until she was sitting on his lap, struggling for breath. Gazing into his deep blue eyes, she murmured, "I think you're too big, Greg."

Beads of sweat sprung on his brow as he leaned forward to kiss her. "No, honey, just give us a moment to adjust." He reached down to rub her clitoris again.

All her senses seemed to be tied into their joining. She ground against him, gasping at the sweet, aching sensation.

"Easy, baby." He cupped her bottom, squeezing it as he slowly urged her to ride his shaft.

She didn't want to take it easy. Leaning forward, her mouth found his neck, sucking it as he sped up the pace. She pinched his nipples, and he thrust into her in reaction, growling. He buried himself to the hilt inside her, as she cried out her delight.

"Little witch."

He tightened his grip on her bottom. Holding her still, he thrust into her harder, time and again. Spasms started deep inside her as she ground her clit against him.

"Yes, yes, yes," she screamed. Her orgasm took her and her spasms tugged him deeper. Holding her tight, he surged hard into her, groaning as he came.

Sagging against his warm chest, she sighed. Come what may, she'd have her dream lover for the summer. She wouldn't let herself think beyond that.

"We need to talk." He slid a hand up and down her bare back.

She froze. She wasn't ready to discuss the details of their summer fling.

"We'd better get dressed before the police make their patrol. I should hurry home. Ma will be waiting up."

Chapter Six

Candy hung a dress on the display stand and winced as the quick motion made her head throb. It was the morning after, and she had a king-sized hangover. She'd have to remember not to indulge in six glasses of champagne ever again.

Last night had been a roller coaster of an evening. The lowest low was facing Greg's father, the highest high finding bliss in Greg's arms when they'd made love. The cliffhanger? The sober feeling she had later when Greg had wanted to discuss their love affair.

Now, she was facing the aftermath alone as she did her morning stint behind the counter at The Golden Peacock. She gave the dress one final adjustment. Walking back behind the counter, she picked up her sketchpad once more.

Working helped take her mind off her headache. She added the final touches to the sketch of a teddy she was designing for Joan. It would be satin and lace with a low sweetheart neckline.

The bell rang, indicating a customer had come in.

She looked up and dropped her pencil as Greg's sister came inside. Kathleen was the last person she expected to see today.

Moving swiftly, Kathleen slipped behind a rack of dresses and peered out of the plate glass window.

Was the woman trying to be incognito? Eyeing her dark glasses and floppy wide-brimmed hat, Candy decided the woman must have flipped her lid. Or maybe she was ashamed to be seen with her. The notion got Candy's back up.

After a moment, Kathleen turned and headed her way.

"Are you wearing a disguise or something?"

"Not so loud," Kathleen said with a groan, then slipped off the glasses and sank on one of the counter stools.

Gazing at the woman's bloodshot eyes, Candy winced in sympathy, all thoughts of possible insults fading. "You poor kid. You look worse than I feel. How about a cup of coffee to pick you up?"

"Thanks. I think you'd better pour yourself one, too." She slapped the morning's paper on the counter. "You're going to need it after you see this."

A picture of Joe carrying Kathleen off and an accompanying photo of Candy and Kathleen on stage held Candy's appalled attention. Snatching the paper, she read the caption.

Candy Blake—notorious lingerie model—causes riot at country club. Will her sweetheart deal with Pinnacle Publishing go bust?

"Oh, my God. Meddling Magi has struck again."

"Got it in one. She's managed to turn our local paper into a hotbed of tabloid-style journalism. But we're not going to take this lying down. We're going to fight fire with fire. Dad's gone to the editor-in-chief to get a retraction and try to get Magi fired. And you and I are going to present a united front."

As she gazed at Kathleen's outraged expression, she wondered where Greg was in all this. Why were his father and sister taking charge?

And then a horrific thought flashed through her mind. Was Greg putting space between them, trying to cut his losses business-wise?

"What about Greg?"

"He doesn't know about it yet. He's back in Landis Hills attending to business at Pinnacle, and we thought it better to keep him out of it for now." Kathleen winced. "Dad was afraid Greg might stir things up more. You see, Magi is kind of hung up on him, and it just grinds her jaw that you're the one he picked over her."

She sighed, relieved Greg wasn't backing away from her.

"Oh," she replied as Magi's motivation suddenly became clear. There'd been bad blood between them for years. Had her jealousy over Greg been behind Magi's spite back in high school? "How long has this been going on?"

"A long, long time. I have a confession to make," Kathleen said softly.

"What?"

"Remember the mix-up on prom night when Greg stood you up?"

"Very well." Remember it? It had been a humiliating experience, a turning point in her youth that had sent her packing after graduation.

Kathleen looked down at her hands. "Well, Magi and I were to blame. We drugged Greg so he slept the night away."

"What?" It was the last thing Candy had expected to hear. She gazed at the other woman's shamed expression in amazement. "How could you do that?"

Kathleen met Candy's gaze directly. "I know. It was a stupid thing to do, even by teenage standards, and I'm genuinely sorry. I finally owned up to it with Greg the other day."

Candy nodded as sincerity came through her shock. "Let me guess—Magi instigated the whole thing."

"Most of the blame goes to me." Kathleen shook her head. "I know how stupid it was now, but back then, I was embarrassed Greg wanted to go out with you. Magi provided the means and opportunity to prevent it. I regretted it the minute I did it, but it was too late. He'd already drunk the doctored beer Magi brought with her. So, I stayed home, sat up all night with him, and threw up all over both of us. Do you think you can ever forgive me?"

What good would anger do now? "Of course, I do. We've both grown up and can look at the past through different eyes now." She poured two cups of coffee for them and placed them on the counter. Then it hit her. "Oh, my God. Mike beat up Greg because he stood me up. Greg must have hated me for that."

"I don't think so. Things happened so fast that Greg didn't have time to react. I do know he tried to see you after he came home from military school, but by then, you were gone."

"Thanks for telling me the truth." Even as she said it, Candy felt like a fraud for keeping the secret of her and Greg's false engagement. But she couldn't spill the beans without jeopardizing both their businesses. "It puts a new spin on that episode of my life."

"Thank you for being so understanding. It's a big load off my conscience, believe me." Kathleen picked up the sketchpad. "What's this?"

"I was working on some designs for my foster sister, Joan. She and her husband are about to have their first baby, and she wanted something to rekindle their passion afterwards." Candy smiled. "Between you and me, it doesn't need much of a fire to rekindle it, but every woman wants to look sexy for her man."

Kathleen nodded, flipping through the pages slowly. "These are really good, Candy."

"Thanks. I just hope they sell after Greg publishes my catalog. If Magi doesn't sabotage the launch, that is. It was kind of a big step to go out on my own."

"If they're like this, they can't miss." Kathleen smiled. "With Greg's promotional expertise and your designs, it's a match made in heaven. And besides, you and I are going to see that Magi goes down. She won't have a chance to hurt you again."

Candy felt some of her stress subside. "Thanks. I appreciate the vote of confidence and the help."

"You're welcome." Kathleen set the pad down and looked at Candy with a twinkle in her eyes. "Do you think you could design some things for me? I wouldn't mind lighting a little fire under my love life, either."

Seeing the other woman's excitement, Candy smiled. She'd been wrong about her being a conservative prig, after all. "Of course. Just as soon as I finish these, I'll get started on yours."

"Good." Kathleen nodded, adding, "In the meantime, about that united front. I would like you to go out for lunch with me at the club."

"Back to the scene of the crime." Candy winced as she glanced at the paper.

Kathleen grinned. "That's right."

"I'm not sure that's such a good idea."

"Sure, it is. And we're going to hold our heads high and spit in Magi's face."

Candy gazed at her determined expression. She had as much grit as her brother, and clearly was just as single-minded. "What time?"

"You only work half a day, right?"

"How did you know that?"

"I called Ma Brown and asked. So, how about if I meet you there at twelve-thirty?"

"Fine. I'll be there."

After Kathleen left, Candy phoned Joan.

"Hey there, sis."

"What's up?" Joan asked.

Candy gazed at the picture in the paper. "Did you see the paper?"

"I really don't have time to talk now, Candy. Call back later, okay?"

Candy hung up with a frown and went back to the designs.

Riding up to the country club entrance in the passenger seat of Kathleen's Caddy, Candy steeled herself for the stares she'd probably receive. She was coming back to the scene of the crime, indeed.

Getting out of the car, she looked around, expecting Magi to leap out of the rose bushes with a camera. Seeing that the coast was clear, she walked into the entrance. From the corner of her eye, she noticed some openmouthed gapes. She and Kathleen passed by groups of golfers and well-dressed ladies lunching with their heads held high. No doubt, they were wondering what kind of ruckus she might cause today. She could cheerfully wring Magi's scrawny neck for all she'd cost her—her home with Ma when she'd been in her late teens, her romance with Greg back in high school, and now her privacy.

If their prom date had happened, who knows? Maybe it would have blossomed into a friendship or more. Now that she'd gotten close to him, she could see he was far from The Toad she'd thought him.

She came to a halt at the hostess's podium.

"May I help you ladies?" the hostess asked with a smile.

Kathleen nodded. "We have reservations, under Kathleen Morris."

"Oh yes, the Morris party." The hostess turned, saying, "Follow me, please."

Candy trooped along behind Kathleen to the end of the room, hearing conversations stop as they passed by towards the dimly lit back end of the room.

Good grief, were they putting them back in no man's land to avoid another scene? She cast a sidelong glance at Kathleen, who seemed to be taking the slight in stride. There was a pleasant smile on Greg's sister's face.

Well, then, who was she to complain? She dutifully followed her through the doorway and into an even darker back room. This was going too far. It would spoil Kathleen's plan to present a united front if they sat back here. Just as she was about object, the lights came on.

"Surprise!"

Candy's jaw dropped, her gaze sweeping over the balloons, streamers, and noisy gaggle of women. And then she spotted the banner.

'Best wishes Candy and Greg.'

Oh no. She realized, belatedly, that Kathleen was throwing her a surprise bridal shower.

Joan stepped forward with a big smile on her face. "Now you know why I was too busy to talk to you earlier, sis. Kathleen and I had our work cut out for us arranging this last-minute shindig."

The crowd laughed.

She gazed at Joan's and Kathleen's happy faces. "You guys shouldn't have gone to all this trouble." She could understand Joan going to these lengths, but Kathleen knew this was a bogus engagement. Had she gone along with it simply to present a united front?

Joan grinned. "Of course, we should, and look who we brought along to help us celebrate." The crowd parted to reveal Ma seated in an armchair.

"Ma, what are you doing here?" Candy asked, startled. She hadn't set foot from the house since her surgery two weeks ago. "You're supposed to be home recuperating."

"You ought to know I wouldn't miss an occasion like this for all the tea in China." Ma sat up straighter. "Don't worry. I didn't try to drive, so you can stop fussing over me like a mother hen. Mrs. Morris sent a driver to collect me, and he'll drive me home, too."

The crowd chuckled.

"I guess that's okay then," Candy replied and smiled. She walked over, giving Ma a hug. "Just see that you don't overdo it, or Dr. Wang will have my head."

"Yes, my darling daughter."

Mrs. Morris stepped up and smiled. "Come along, Candace, and let me introduce you to the rest of Gregory's family."

Candy was swept along, feeling awkward as she was introduced to throngs of Morris family and friends. In the back of her mind, she kept thinking about all the gifts she would have to return.

As they made their way around the room, she glanced at Greg's mother. She seemed genuinely pleased about the whole thing. Was the lady really warming up to her?

"Thank you for the introductions. I was feeling a bit tense about entering the throng."

Mrs. Morris smiled, her eyes twinkling. "It's no trouble at all. I felt the same way before I married Greg's father. Meeting the group en-masse can be a bit overwhelming. Forgive me for being so nosy and upsetting you last night when we discussed wedding plans. I meant no offense, dear, I just thought you'd want to share your joy with all your friends and family, both old and new."

Recalling her angry reply to Mrs. Morris's probing her about family last night, she couldn't help but feel chagrined. She'd overreacted, big time. "I realize that now. I'm sorry for overreacting the way I did. Thank you for being kind enough to introduce me to your family."

"It's been my pleasure, my dear. Some time when we have privacy, we'll discuss the past and your father, and get everything out into the open."

"I'd like that," Candy agreed, responding to the genuine warmth in Greg's mother's tone. She took her place next to the gift table and started opening the beautifully wrapped presents.

She tore open Ma's first, gasped, and held it up for the girls to see. "A set of hand-embroidered linen."

There were 'oohs' and 'aahs' at the sight.

She gazed at the exquisite work in awe. When did Ma have time to complete this? Maybe she had her part all done and was waiting for Candy to snag a man? It was the sort of thing she would do.

"Thanks, Ma. I love it."

"You're welcome, Candy. I hope you'll use them for many years of wedded bliss."

Candy felt a pang deep inside as she put the gift aside and reached for another. The sheets would always be a reminder of what might have been.

Mrs. Morris's gift was next. She unwrapped a square, gold velvet jeweler's box. She looked at Greg's mother, who had an expectant look on her face. What could it be? She opened the case to find a lovely pearl necklace.

"It's beautiful, Mrs. Morris, but far too expensive."

"Call me Madeline or Mom if you like. The pearls have been passed down the Morris line for generations. I wore them once, and now I'm giving them to you. I know Gregory will be happy to see you wearing them." She stood, took the necklace, and clasped it around Candy's neck.

Gazing out at the smiling crowd, Candy felt well and truly trapped. Joan's smile was huge, and Ma had tears in her eyes. Even Kathleen looked a little misty. Candy wondered again why she'd gone to all this trouble knowing the truth about the false engagement. It could be all for show, but it didn't feel like it. Maybe she was a born romantic just like her mother. It wasn't real, but somehow it felt genuine. She couldn't help feeling like a blushing bride-to-be. A little voice in her head said that maybe their love affair would lead to more.

Shaking off the tender feeling, she reached Kathleen's gift. She ripped open the box and pulled out a silky garment. A red teddy! "It's one of my designs, but how did you get it this soon?"

"I had to get it air expressed. If you look in the card, you'll find a gift certificate for a sweet little bed and breakfast upstate. I thought you two might want to do some rekindling of your own."

Candy blushed, thinking of her and Greg's parking session the night before. "Thanks. I think."

The ladies laughed.

She quickly reached for Joan's gift. She tore open the gift to find peach scented massage oils and some rather scandalous accessories. "Oh, my."

"What is it, Candy?" Kathleen piped up.

"To be delicate, I'll call them marital aids. And I don't think I'll pass them around." Candy threw Joan a wry grin as she held up the massage oils. "Thanks, sis. Only you would give me these."

"You're welcome." Joan grinned and winked.

Twenty minutes later, Candy was surrounded by a sea of gifts, including can openers, cookbooks, and lingerie. Obviously, the ladies thought she might need help in the kitchen and bedroom. They were right about the kitchen part, she thought with a grin. She was the first to admit, she wasn't much of a cook.

"You're far too generous. I don't know how to thank you."

"Just be happy," Kathleen and Joan said at the same time.

"Amen," Ma chorused, much to everyone's amusement.

"Now for the entertainment," Joan said, getting to her feet and toward the stage. "Direct from the Windy City! Mr. Wonderful and The Power Tools Revue."

The lights dimmed and music started to play. Three handsome hunks came strutting out of the wings. They were dressed in flannel shirts, cut-off jeans, and tool belts slung low around their swiveling hips. They started doing a sexy bump-and-grind to 'It's Raining Men' while playfully stripping off their shirts.

Grinning, Candy concluded this had to be Joan's idea. How had she talked Kathleen into it? Oh no, how would Greg's mother and aunts react?

She turned to survey the crowd. There were a few dropped jaws, but Greg's mother was clapping along to the music. Go Madeline! Candy glanced over at Ma. Even she was tapping her toe along to the beat. Mildred, who sat next to her, was fishing dollar bills out of her purse.

"Oh, good grief," Candy snapped her gaze back to the stage in time to see the tool belts come off. Next, went the shorts, and then they were down to their G-strings.

Mr. Wonderful, a tall, dark, Latino, strutted up to the front of the stage, grinned, and held out his hand to her. "It's time for the blushing bride to get in on the act."

Candy sat back, stunned. She firmly stuck to the chair. She'd already had one bad experience on that stage.

"Go on." Joan gave her a nudge.

"Yeah," Kathleen echoed. "You aren't chicken, are you?"

Candy reluctantly walked up on stage and was instantly flanked by the men.

"Go, Candy, go!" Kathleen shouted.

The dark Adonis sat Candy down on a chair. The two other dancers joined in, forming a wall of muscular, dancing beefcake, around her.

Just then, the door burst open.

"This is a raid," a police officer shouted from the back of the room.

He marched up to the stage, shouting, "You're all under arrest."

For what?

"Oh no." Candy groaned, shooting to her feet. She was destined to be humiliated twice on the same stage.

"Freeze, lady," he snapped, quickly cuffing her while other policemen rounded up the strippers.

Shivering as the cold metal circled her wrist, she shot a mournful look at Mrs. Morris. It'd been nice while it lasted, but the lady was, no doubt, sorry she'd ever gotten involved with her now. Greg's mom looked angry alright, but she was glaring at the cop as he jerked Candy's other arm behind her to fasten the other end of the cuffs.

Mrs. Morris stood up. "Don't worry, dear, I'll handle this." She turned to the officer. "What do you mean by this, young man?"

The crowd started to grumble their agreement.

"Mrs. Morris, what are you doing here?" The young patrolman froze, turning to survey the group of angry women. "I'm here celebrating my son's engagement to Miss Blake—the woman you're arresting."

He gulped. "I'd better call Chief Miller."

"Yes, you'd better. But what about my guests?" She waved a hand to include all the ladies present.

"They'll have to wait a moment. I'm sorry, ma'am. It's regulations."

Candy breathed a sigh of relief when he released one arm and sat her back down in the folding chair, cuffing her to it instead.

"Sorry, miss." He walked to the back of the room to make his call. He came back looking shamefaced as he strode to the stage, looking at Candy, then Mrs. Morris. "I'm afraid the chief can't be reached. Except for the main parties involved, the rest of you can go."

He turned to look at the dancers. "Go with Officer Gray and get dressed. We don't want to cause a stir. The chief can decide on the charges."

"If you ladies will come with me, we'll see if we can get this cleared up."

"Are you running us in, young man?" Mrs. Morris asked with a frown.

"I'm afraid so. The chief will want to take charge of this matter."

Candy really wanted to know what manner he was talking about.

Kathleen stepped up. "I'm going, too."

"Me, too," Joan piped in. "After all, we arranged this shower entertainment. And I want to remind you, there's no law on the books against male strippers."

"You can't come, lady," the cop stated. "You're just about to pop."

"That's discrimination against pregnant people."

"I'm going to have to put you all in the paddy wagon then."

"Fine," they all chorused.

"What about me? I demand to go, too."

"No, Ma," Candy cried out. "You're not going to the police station."

"Quite right," Mrs. Morris echoed. "Mildred will take you home. Don't worry. I won't let any harm come to Candy."

Mildred stood. "Don't worry about the two of us. I'll see that she gets home safe and sound. We'll take the gifts with us, so they don't go astray." As Candy bounced along in the back of the paddy wagon, she swept an apologetic glance over the motley group of her accomplices. This fiasco had all the earmarks of a meddling Magi attack. If Magi had her way, her engagement would be over. Greg's father would be furious at having his wife and daughter tainted by scandal. He'd probably try to have her run out of town, pronto.

Chapter Seven

Candy paced the confines of the police chief's office while they waited for him to arrive. There had to be some easy painless way out of this mess, but right now, she couldn't envision it. Thank heavens Officer Lewis had shooed them in here rather than book them. It gave her a little more time to think. She could call Greg for assistance, but after the way they'd parted last night, the thought rankled.

She frowned at Joan and Kathleen, who stood in a far corner of the room talking to each other in hushed tones. What were those two loose cannons plotting now? If she'd been asked, she would have vetoed the bridal shower. She felt like a bit of dandelion fluff being blown wherever the winds chose to send her.

She slanted a worried glance at Greg's mother, who was seated behind the chief's desk, casually using his telephone. Clout did have its perks.

Madeline hung up the phone with a smile. "Don't worry, ladies. My husband is coming down here to straighten this mess out."

Candy groaned. She wasn't in the mood to face his disapproval. "I'm sure that wasn't necessary."

"Trust me, Candy." Madeline stood. "The Morris name still has a little influence down here at City Hall."

Candy bit her lip, thinking of that agonizing day so long ago. She had a very clear memory of Mr. Morris's influence when she'd remained in jail while Greg was hustled out of town ten years ago. She'd always suspected Mr. Morris of pulling strings to keep her incarcerated for shoplifting.

There was a tap on the door as it opened. Chief Malone stood in the doorway. He cast a nervous look over the group of irate women, gulped, and ventured into the room.

He walked to Madeline's side. "I'm so very sorry for keeping you waiting, Mrs. Morris. I was busy in a city council meeting and only found out a moment ago that you were here." He escorted her to a chair facing his desk. "I can assure you, I'll do my utmost to work this out so there won't be any charges against you."

Madeline frowned as she sat down. "Do you mean to tell me we were hauled down here, embarrassed in front of our friends, only to find out there would be no charges?"

The chief blanched, hesitating for a second before scurrying behind his desk to take a seat. "I'm sorry for the inconvenience, ma'am. Officer Lewis acted hastily, but there were laws broken and someone must be held accountable. So, it actually is a good thing you're here, so we can get this cleared up without undue scandal."

"Laws were broken! Such as what?" Madeline frowned. "He said we were disturbing the peace, and we were doing no such thing."

Chief Malone's apprehensive gaze flitted over Joan for a moment, then homed in on Candy. His face furrowed into deep wrinkles. "Morals, for one. Look on this as a caution, Mrs. Morris, not to get mixed up with the wrong element."

Candy sat straighter, burning under his harsh inspection. She'd had plenty of nasty encounters with him during her youth, and had never liked the man. "You're referring to me, I suppose."

Mrs. Morris held up a hand. "I'm sure he wasn't talking about you."

The chief's eyes narrowed as he continued to study her. "Actually, I was. She and I are no strangers to each other. I ran her in six times for shoplifting before she turned thirteen. Take it from me. She's a bad egg."

Candy stiffened, lifting her chin a little higher in the face of his disapproval. She was damned if she'd let herself be cowed by his obvious distaste for her. That was ancient history. If he couldn't see that, she felt sorry for him.

She turned to Greg's mother, expecting to see the same damnation in her eyes. Instead, she met a sympathetic smile.

Madeline turned back to him. "Chief Malone, I'll thank you to speak to my future daughter-in-law with more respect in the future."

He went silent. After a moment, he gulped and looked down, nervously shuffling the papers on his desk. "Of course. I didn't mean to offend. I just wanted to make sure you knew the facts."

Madeline stiffened. "I know what I know, and you can—"

"What about those charges?" Candy interrupted. She had to take control of the situation before the chief and Greg's mother came to blows.

Chief Malone blinked at her. "Oh, yes. The charges."

Candy noted he almost looked relieved at the interruption and suppressed a smile. At this rate, she and him might become pals.

"*Yes*, the charges."

He picked up a scrap of paper from his desk. "We got a call saying a group of women were raising hell at the country club. They also claimed there was a drug deal about to go down. That's why my men charged in there like gangbusters."

"Preposterous."

Chief Malone darted an alarmed glance her way. "Of course. I realize you women weren't involved. We searched your bags, and they're clean. However, I can't say the same for one of the dancers. We found some controlled substances in his duffle bag. He claims to have a prescription for them, and we're checking that out now."

"What's the meaning of this, Chief Malone?" came an outraged male voice from the doorway.

Candy turned a reluctant gaze in that direction, and groaned. Mr. Morris cast an apprehensive glance around the room of angry women, stopping to frown at Candy.

She froze, transported to an earlier time. He'd worn the same troubled frown when she'd begged him not to take her daddy away.

"Come in, Mr. Morris." Chief Malone leaned back in his chair. "We're in the process of clearing up a few charges."

Mr. Morris closed the door behind him and walked toward Candy. "What happened?"

Her eyes narrowed. Of course, he'd try to pin it all on her. "Don't you mean, what did I do? You're ready to act as judge, jury, and executioner again, I see."

The flash of hurt in his eyes made her wish she could call back her hasty words. She knew they weren't true. He wasn't the monster she'd always believed him to be. He'd been a victim of circumstance, just like her.

"Don't you dare put words in my mouth, missy." He heaved a heavy sigh and turned to face the chief. "Please explain what's going on, Frank."

The chief picked up another piece of paper. "Well, Leon, we brought them in on charges of lewd and lascivious behavior, disturbing the peace, and possession of a controlled substance."

"What? I don't believe it." His jaw tightened.

Madeline stood and walked over to him. "Hush now, dear. They hauled us all into the pokey because of an anonymous tip, an overzealous detective, and... Oh yes, Mr. Wonderful's G-string was too skimpy. Apparently, it was two inches too small for the local regulations."

Mr. Morris's eyes widened in shock, and Candy wished a hole would open up that she could drop into. Now he definitely would think she was a sex-crazed nut.

Chief Malone cleared his throat. "As Mrs. Morris was saying, there is a matter of disturbing the peace. The country club doesn't have the proper permit for that kind of entertainment. As for the lewd and lascivious, Mr. Wonderful's costume was too small by our local regulations. And we found the drugs when we searched his bags. Mr. Wonderful claims he takes them for a bad back."

Mr. Morris groaned. "Mr. Wonderful and the Power Tools."

"The entertainment at the shower, dear," Madeline replied with a smile.

"Shower?"

"Yes, we had a little impromptu bridal shower at the club. I wanted Candy to meet the family, and we thought it would help establish our approval of the match."

Candy all but cringed when Greg's father turned a quizzical glance her way. Of course, he knew the truth behind the fake engagement, and he probably wondered at her involvement. He frowned deeper when his gaze focused on the Morris pearls around her neck.

"So, what now?" He asked the chief.

"I can see my way clear to drop the charges against the ladies, but it'll come down to cash or time in jail for the entertainers. If you want to avoid any publicity, I'd advise you to pay up, because the entertainers say they're strapped for cash."

He sighed. "I'll pay the fine for them. I'll do whatever it takes to keep this quiet."

Mr. Morris took Candy by the elbow, walking her out of the office. She high tailed it to the door.

"Stop a minute so we can talk."

"About what?" Candy hesitated, turning to gaze at him. What was wrong now? They'd seemed to reach some kind of pact earlier, but had it been all for show on his part? Was he going to lay into her about the shower now? He probably thought she'd grown to like the idea of being Greg's wife and was doing her best to make it a permanent role. "Listen, if this is about the shower, it wasn't my idea."

He drew her into an alcove with Joan, Kathleen, and Madeline in hot pursuit. "No, it's not that. Given the way things have been going lately, I think it's best to keep you out of sight until the launch party next week."

Candy felt some of her tension slip away, gazing at his earnest expression to the nodding heads of the ladies. Obviously, they agreed with him. She had to admit, she couldn't seem to put a foot right lately. The last thing she and Greg needed was to have bad press casting a shadow over the launch gala.

"I can hole up at Ma's until then."

Leon shook his head. "I don't think that will do the trick. Not until we make sure Magi's friends at the paper have been mollified."

"He's right, Candy," Kathleen chimed. "Remember, I know how vindictive Magi can be. If she catches wind of this incident, we're all in trouble."

Candy looked at their expectant faces. This meant a lot to all of them, but she couldn't just walk out on Ma. "I can't leave Ma alone for a whole week. She's just recovering from surgery and needs help."

"I'll look in on her, Candy," Joan volunteered.

Madeline smiled. "And I'll send Mildred to stay with her. They're old pals, and they'll have a great time."

Feeling totally outnumbered, Candy mumbled, "Well, where do you suggest I go?"

"She can go down to Greg's place in Landis Falls, Dad," Kathleen injected.

"No." Candy shook her head. There was no way she could go there. Not after the way they'd parted last night. She got anxious just thinking about it.

"Why can't you go?" Joan asked with a frown.

Candy hesitated. She couldn't tell them the truth. Greg's mother would probably have a case of the vapors. "I can't barge in on him like that. It would be too rude."

"Nonsense. Gregory will be glad to have you," Madeline replied.

"Right," Candy stated wryly, thinking that Greg's mother didn't know how right she was. He'd be glad to have her in his bed. "I still don't think it's a good idea."

She patted Candy's shoulder. "Don't worry about a thing, Candace. He'll take very good care of you."

"But..."

"It's settled then," Leon proclaimed.

Candy packed only one suitcase, deliberately leaving most of her things behind. She wasn't going to give Greg the idea she was moving in with him. This was only a temporary arrangement until the gala. If it weren't for Magi and her venom, she wouldn't have to run away. It stuck in her craw to be chased out of town like this, but she knew Greg's dad was right. Not all publicity was good publicity.

She glanced around her childhood room, still decorated with posters and art she and Joan had hung during their teens. It touched her that Ma had left it. She'd just gotten settled in, and now she was being uprooted, but that wasn't what worried her. Would Greg be happy to see her?

There was only one way to find out.

Pulling out her cell phone, she punched in his number. It rang busy, again. Who could he be talking to all this time? Pocketing the phone, she reached for her bag. She'd stalled long enough. It was time to get moving. Greg would just have to put up with an unexpected houseguest.

She ran down the stairs, eager to get it over with. The sound of the television drew her to the parlor. Ma and Mildred sat at the card table playing Rummy. They looked up and smiled at her.

"All ready?" Ma asked.

"I sure am." Candy pasted on a smile to hide a sudden attack of nerves. It wouldn't do to worry Ma, and she wasn't sure she could trust Mildred not to gossip if she relayed her fears. It wasn't as if Greg was a stranger, for goodness sake. They knew each other in the most intimate way possible.

That was what was worrying her. Would he take her arrival as an open invitation to carry on as they had before? Her resolve to keep her independence was wavering.

Ma looked her up and down, skeptical. "Hmm. You look a bit on edge, my girl."

"Who, me?"

Mildred nodded. "Pre-wedding jitters. That's what it is. Take it from me, young lady. You've got nothing to worry about. Gregory is a perfect gentleman."

"Right." That was what worried her. Greg was perfect in all sorts of ways, but that didn't mean she fit into his life. She smiled at them both and kissed Ma's cheek. "Are you still sure you want me to take your car, Ma?"

"Of course. You heard my doctor. I won't be doing any driving for the time being. It will get you there in style."

Candy grinned. Ma loved her Ford Fairlane. She'd babied the classic car over the years. It was a reflection of their close relationship she'd even allow Candy to drive it.

"Don't worry. I'll take good care of your baby. I hate to leave you in the lurch like this."

Ma shook her head. "Nonsense. Mildred's going to stay with me, and Joan will check in from time to time."

Candy nodded, but couldn't help feeling guilty about abandoning Ma. She glanced at the neat room, wavering. "Is there anything I can do for you before I leave?"

"Not a thing."

Her gaze hit on the pile of library books on the hall table. "Would you like me to return your library books on my way out of town?"

"Wonderful idea."

Mildred nodded. "It'll save me a trip later."

"Good. I'll get going then." She scooped up the books and headed for the door.

"Call me later," Ma called.

Candy carefully placed her suitcase and the books in the car's backseat. She slid behind the steering wheel and started it, enjoying the roar of the engine. With its V-8 and stylish chrome work, she could see why Ma loved it.

Cruising toward the library, her spirits started to lift. It was a lovely day, and she rolled down the window to get the breeze. This getaway might be a good thing. It was an opportunity to put her relationship with Greg on a different footing. Slowing things down would help them delve deeper, see if there was anything they could hang onto after the summer was over.

She parked in the lot and got out. Scooping up the books, she sprinted inside. Maybe she'd check out a few books to read. A few juicy mystery novels would keep her occupied.

She nodded at the librarian as she walked past the checkout desk, stopping to drop Ma's books in the return slot.

There were a few patrons in the library, but she didn't see a familiar face. She headed to the adult fiction section. She was walking backwards, perusing the aisle from J to S when she bumped into someone.

"Oh, excuse me," she murmured and turned, then froze.

Magi stood there scowling as she blocked the aisle. She clutched a book to her chest. "So, we meet again, Candy."

Trembling, Candy took a steadying breath. Was it possible she was being stalked? No matter where she went, Magi always showed up in one way or another. "Have you been following me?"

Sniffing, Magi looked away. "Don't flatter yourself."

"Oh, grow up, Magi." Her irritation ratcheted. "I'm tired of playing these childish games with you. I'm warning you. Stay away from me."

Magi's eyes glittered with anger as she smirked. "Read any good stories lately?"

"No. They were pure trash."

"Takes one to know one," Magi yelled.

"*Shh*," whispered a man passing by.

Candy stifled a groan. "Listen, this is spinning out of control—"

"Yeah, and it's your fault," Magi interrupted, hissing. "You made it impossible for me to stay at my job, slut. I'll get even if it's the last thing I do."

"I'm genuinely sorry that it had to come to that, Magi, but you left us with no other choice. Maybe if we—"

"Don't do me any favors, bitch." Magi spun on her heel and stomped away.

Candy stood there stunned, the desire for a juicy mystery gone. She shivered, recalling Magi's vindictive words. She'd have to watch her back. Magi seemed completely unhinged. Turning, she headed out of the library. It was time to get going. And she was eager to get out of the line of fire.

She got back into Ma's car, feeling depressed. The sun still shone, but there was a shadow over her formerly high spirits.

Magi, fired. She deserved it after the stunts she'd pulled, but Candy didn't like to see anyone crushed like that. She'd lost enough jobs to know how devastating it could be. Maybe she could get Mr. Morris to smooth things over.

Chapter Eight

Candy drove east out of town, pointing the car towards Landis Falls. She'd let herself be badgered into this move, but she was determined to keep things on a businesslike footing for her stay. It wouldn't do to let proximity goad her into making a big mistake.

Even so, it would be interesting to see Greg on his home turf, away from Morris Point. Had he and Jill lived there? Strangely enough, she didn't feel like an invader. Greg had said she and Jill would have liked each other. And they sure enough cared for the same man.

But how did he really feel about her? She was falling for him, but she wasn't sure hers were reciprocated. What would he think of her showing up unannounced? That she was there to collect her White Knight, as he'd said last night.

She shook off the thought and snapped on the radio to drown out her worries. He'd have to help her. Together, they would survive this summer.

As she continued down the county highway with cornfields whizzing by on either side of the car, tension began to build in her spine. It was ridiculous, but she couldn't hold back a sensation of impending doom. Greg would just have to lump it if he didn't like her decision to slow things down.

Squinting into the dazzling setting sun, she kept going. A moment later, a dark SUV zoomed up on her tail, its big headlights flashing bright. What an ass, she thought, shielding her eyes with her hand. She looked down to grab her sunglasses.

Wham.

The SUV slammed into her, sending her car hurtling forward. Clamping onto the steering wheel with a death grip, her nails digging into the vinyl, she fought for control of her fishtailing car.

Oh, my God.

She gasped, trying to pull to the side of the road. As she started to regain control, the SUV shot past her, but it crunched against her front fender with a glancing blow.

She screamed, her car spinning in a dizzying circle. Skidding sideways into the ditch and cornfield beyond, she squeezed her eyes shut.

Coming to a shuddering halt, she heard the tinkle of broken glass. The shards rained on her like little shards of popcorn. She winced as they stung her arm. Opening her eyes, she saw a tangle of broken cornstalks on the hood of her car, as she gulped air.

She was still in one piece. Her seatbelt had saved her.

Who the hell had just tried to kill her?

One name sprung to mind. Magi Bains. She'd acted unhinged at the library, but would she really do something this violent? That answer would have to come later.

She turned off the engine and, on shaking legs, got out of the car. Cringing, she surveyed the damage. Ma's poor old Ford Fairlane was a goner. Its front bumper was bent and torn off at a horrible angle, plus its side door and the powder blue fender were dented. The broken glass from the driver's side window crunched underfoot as she walked around to survey the damage.

Rounding the back to look at the crumpled trunk, she realized it was in total shambles. Some road rage asshole was in big trouble. The jerk, of course, was nowhere in sight, and neither was anyone else. She looked up and down the empty highway with dismay.

If she were going to get out of this, she'd have to do it herself. She shivered. The sun was going down, and she felt very vulnerable all of a sudden. She sniffed, but didn't detect any spilled gas. Maybe the car was still drivable. She had to try. It was either that, or walk the rest of the way to Landis Falls.

Sliding back behind the wheel, she buckled her seatbelt, and turned the key. The motor sputtered to life.

Halleluiah!

She shifted into reverse and slowly started extricating the car from the corn maze. That done, she cautiously started driving toward Greg's place. She needed sanctuary. She needed him.

"Okay, Ben, give me a call the minute you get a lead on his whereabouts."

Greg hung up the phone and frowned. Chad Daley was still nowhere to be found. He glanced at the stack of unanswered messages he'd brought home with him, and sighed. He'd have his work cut out for him fixing this mess.

Only a disaster the size of the Titanic could have torn him away from Morris Point and sweet Candy this morning. Hopefully, when he'd had a chance to talk to her, she'd understand his desertion. Maybe if he got lucky, he'd be able to convince her to come here. They still had some finishing touches to put on the launch bash. That would give him the excuse he needed.

Damn Chad Daley, wherever he was. Probably out on the bender to end all benders. He'd taken two weeks off, ostensibly to seek treatment for his drinking problem. Instead of going to the treatment facility, he'd vanished. Nobody had informed Greg he was missing until he'd been gone a week.

Greg had rushed down here early this morning to assess the situation. In short order, he'd found the sales department in shambles. He had a stack of complaint calls from buyers two inches thick. Orders were either missing, late, or wrong. It was going to take a concerted effort on his part to smooth things over. He could only hope the audit he'd just ordered wouldn't reveal anything worse.

The doorbell rang, and he went to answer it. With the way his luck was going today, it was probably more bad news.

He opened the door, and was startled to find Candy on his doorstep. She looked pale and a bit teary-eyed. "What's wrong?"

She fell into his arms with a sob. "I'm so glad you're home."

She was chilled to the bone, despite the warm temperatures outside. He closed his arms around her while she trembled. What had her so shaken?

He scooped her up in his arms and carried her inside, kicking the door shut behind him. "Tell me what's wrong."

She nestled her head against his shoulder, clinging to him. "I was in an accident."

"What?" His gut tightened. Stopping in his tracks, he looked down at her. There were scratches on her arm, caked with trickles of dried blood. Her fingernails were broken. Embers of fear haunted her troubled gray eyes.

"Some nut ran me off the road." She blinked back tears.

"My God, are you okay?"

"I'm a little knicked up, but I'm all in one piece. Too bad I can't say the same for Ma's car. I think it's a lost cause, but maybe Jerry's garage can patch it up."

"Let's take care of you first, okay? You're more important than any old car." He carried her into the den, stopping to switch on the gas fireplace. Then, he sank down on the brown leather sofa with her on his lap. "First, we need to warm you up." He pulled a soft throw off the arm of the sofa and draped it over her. "Better?"

She snuggled under the throw, clinging to him. "Yes."

"Okay. Now tell me what happened." He stifled a groan as she innocently rubbed her bottom against his crotch.

"I was driving along and some road rage idiot in a big SUV forced me off the road. Thank heaven the cornfield cushioned the blow. Of course, the jerk took off. I thought at first it was Magi, but the driver seemed bigger than her. He probably doesn't have any insurance."

He ran a hand down her body, looking for other injuries. "Are you okay?"

"I'm fine. I guess I overreacted." Looking around her, she blinked, and started to move off his lap.

He groaned aloud when she ground her bottom against him again. Clamping an arm around her waist to hold her fast, he murmured, "Easy, baby."

"Sorry."

He had to smile at her embarrassed fluster. It gave him hope to know she was just as powerfully aware of him. "Sit tight while I go put on a pot of coffee to warm you. Then I'll call and report this to the police."

"Okay." She pulled the throw tighter around her.

Five minutes later, he came back carrying a tray with two mugs of aromatic coffee and some chocolate chip cookies made by Mrs. Olsen, his motherly neighbor from two doors down. The sugar buzz would probably help keep her going.

She was curled up on the sofa, fast asleep. He set down the tray and stopped to gaze at her. Her long lashes looked like angel's wings against her pale cheeks. No doubt, the aftermath of her adrenaline rush had wiped her out. He tucked another throw around her.

He'd let her sleep while he called the police. He walked to the desk and pulled out his phone. After the police, he made another call, this time to the P.I. he had on retainer.

"Yeah, Ben. This is Greg Morris again."

"More on Chad?"

"No, this isn't about Chad Daly. Something more important has cropped up. My fiancée was just a victim of a hit-and-run. I want you to do a little deeper nosing around than the cops will. I want the bastard who did this caught. First name on your list should be Magi Bains and her associates."

Hanging up, he heard Candy stirring.

He walked over to the sofa, touching her shoulder to fully wake her. "Wake up, sweet cakes. The police are on their way here."

Sitting up with a sigh, she murmured, "I'm not too thrilled about talking to the police twice in one day."

"Twice?" He raised an eyebrow at her wry expression.

What other surprises did she have up her sleeve?

"Oh, that's right. You don't know. Kathleen and Joan threw me a surprise shower. We're going to have lots of presents to return, by the way." She bit her lip, hesitating. "And we were all arrested."

"Arrested?" He grinned, picturing his sister terrorizing the cops.

"The police would have been satisfied just to haul me in, but Kathleen and Joan insisted on tagging along, and so did your mother."

He started to chuckle. His mother being arrested was mind-boggling. "I can just picture it."

"It's not funny," Candy muttered. "Your father didn't find it amusing, I can tell you that."

"I'll bet." He laughed harder.

"He had to pay fines for Mr. Wonderful and the Power Tools."

"Mr. Wonderful and the Power Tools?"

She smiled. "The entertainment. Male strippers."

The surge of jealousy was stupid, but he felt it just the same. "Strippers?"

"Joan does not throw your ordinary everyday shower. You should see some of the presents they gave me." She grinned. "Quite scandalous, I can tell you."

He grinned at her words and raised his eyebrow. "Did you bring any samples?"

"Behave yourself. That's why I'm here. Your father banished me from town until the party. He says we need to start acting with more decorum. He figured I'd keep out of trouble that way."

The doorbell rang.

"I guess I showed him. Trouble seems to have followed me." She sighed. "You'd better go let them in so I can get this over."

"Sit tight, and have a sip of this." He handed her a mug. "I'll bring them in here to interview you. There are some cookies, too. Try them. My neighbor lady is always baking, and I get the overflow."

The warmth from the coffee mug seeped into her cold hands as she watched him go. She inhaled the coffee's tantalizing aroma and braced herself for the upcoming interview. Hopefully, this officer wouldn't be as cranky as Chief Malone had been. There probably wasn't much chance of catching the guy who'd hit her. He was long gone.

A minute later, a middle-aged man in a dark suit entered the den and approached her. "I'm Detective Ronald March, Miss Blake. I'm sorry we're meeting under such bad circumstances. I'm here to take your statement."

"Okay." She smiled when Greg entered the room. It felt good to have someone she could count on.

Detective March sat on a wing chair facing her, and pulled a pen and paper out of his pocket. Loosening his tie, he glanced at the roaring fire. "Isn't it a little warm to run the fireplace?"

"Candy was cold," Greg replied. Looking at her, he asked, "How about it? Are you still cold?"

Buoyed by Greg's thoughtfulness, she smiled. "I'm all warmed up now, thank you. You can switch it off."

The detective nodded. "Shock can make you cold. Okay, tell me what happened, ma'am."

She took a deep breath. "I was driving here from Morris Point around six p.m. I was kind of daydreaming, and the sun was in my eyes. I didn't notice the car drive up behind me. All of a sudden, some bright lights—combined with the setting sun—blinded me. And then, *thump*. The jerk bumped right into me. I hardly had time to react as I skidded forward and to the right."

"You didn't just run off the road and hit some mailboxes?" He studied her carefully. "After all, you did say you were daydreaming."

"I'm positive that someone hit me," she said, her despair returning.

"Have you looked at her car, Ron?" Greg walked up to stand next to her. "Surely you can see the impact of another vehicle."

"Our people are taking samples now, Greg. We'll run some tests to see if we can match it up with a make and model. In the meantime, I have to get as clear a picture as possible." He turned to Candy. "Don't take it personally, ma'am. I have to ask these kinds of questions. It's just an effort to gather all the facts. Please, go on."

She sighed. "Sorry. I guess I'm a little sensitive. Like I was saying, he slammed into the back of me, then roared past me and caught my front fender. I spun off the road and wound up facing the opposite direction. Thank God the cornfield slowed me down and cushioned the blow."

"You keep saying he. Did you see who did it?"

"Not really. It all happened so fast. I thought at first it was a woman, but the driver was too big to be a woman. And he was wearing a baseball cap pulled low on his head."

"Unless, she was wearing a disguise," Greg commented.

She bit her lip, considering that possibility. "She wouldn't do something that stupid."

He shook his head. "We can't assume that."

The detective cleared his throat. "Who?"

She trembled at the memory of their encounter at the library.

"Magi Bains. She's been harassing Candy."

"Were there any witnesses?"

"I was all alone on the road, and nobody passed by."

Greg gently squeezed her shoulder.

She raised her chin a notch and slanted a grateful smile his way.

"One more thing, ma'am. I see you've got a few scratches. Do you need medical treatment?"

"No. I have everything I need here." She smiled up at Greg, knowing in her heart she meant it. Right now, he was all she needed.

"Okay, Miss Blake. I'll file this report, and we'll go try to locate the crime scene and interview the Bains woman. We'll also be checking the local garages for a dark SUV with body damage."

While Greg showed the detective out, Candy finally took a deep, relaxing breath and glanced around the den. It looked very masculine with a sense of fun—just like him. The leather sofa was soft and smooth under her hand, and the pillows and throw were a riot of primary colors.

He walked back into the room. "Let's take care of those scratches."

"Okay." She followed him into the bathroom. Wincing as she sat on the vanity bench he drew out for her, she realized she was starting to stiffen up. No doubt, by morning, she'd be hard as a statue.

He glanced at her. "Feeling kind of sore?"

She rolled her shoulders. "I think I tensed and strained every muscle in my body."

"These pain relievers should help." He handed her two tablets. "But if it gets any worse, let me know."

"Will do," she agreed.

He turned on the whirlpool tub's tap and sprinkled some bath salts into the water. "I think a soak will help."

"Sounds like heaven," she stated with a smile as the scent of jasmine filled the air. "It smells real pretty, too."

"It isn't mine," he replied with a wry grin. "Kathleen left them here last time she stayed overnight." He pulled first aid and manicure kits out of the medicine cabinet. After putting some antibacterial wash on a gauze pad, he reached for her arm. "Let's take care of those cuts."

She wasn't used to being taken care of by a man. A girl could get used to this kind of thing if she wasn't careful.

"Ouch." She yelped, the antiseptic's sting penetrating her musings.

"Don't be such a baby." He bent to blow on the stinging area.

Her heart did a flip-flop, recalling him doing something similar that first night on the beach. She pulled her arm away. "Thanks."

"You're welcome."

He was recalling that evening, too. She could see it in the darkening of his eyes.

"I'm not here to collect my White Knight," she said firmly, hoping to disabuse him of any such notion.

"Are you sure?" he asked in an intimate rumble, leaning forward to kiss her.

She kissed him back and, just as she started to reach for him, he pulled away.

She opened her eyes, feeling bereft as he stepped away from her. Oh, so persuaded to give in to temptation, she instead firmed her resolve. She needed time to think. This steamy, jasmine-scented space was no place to make a rash decision.

"Positive."

"I'll wait. I'll go bring in your bags and you can hang your things in my closet later."

Watching him walk to the door, she snapped back into focus. "Make sure you put my bags in the guest room," she insisted.

"You can't blame a guy for trying." He shut the door behind him.

Opening the manicure kit, she pared back her broken nails. Gazing at her reflection in the mirror, she decided she looked like a lovesick kid. Mooning over a man wouldn't make him permanently hers.

Shaking off the thought, she quickly stripped off her clothes and stepped into the tub. *Ah, bliss,* she thought as the fragrant water swirled around her. Bless Katherine for leaving the bath salts here.

She soaked until her toes got pruney and the water started to cool, loosening the kinks in her body. Getting out and toweling off, she faced the dilemma of not having any clean clothes to put on. Then she spied Greg's robe hanging on the back of the bathroom door. It would do until she got to her suitcase.

Cinching the big robe's belt, she detected the aroma of his woodsy cologne. She sighed, inhaling a lungful of the stuff and told herself to stop mooning. She was worse than Gidget on the beach pining after Moondoggy.

Renewing her resolve, she walked out of the bathroom with her head held high and padded down the hall. She stopped by the first open door. It had to be the guest room because her bag was laying on the double bed. She gazed at the stenciled walls and sleigh frame, and was taken by an overwhelming urge to snoop.

It wouldn't hurt to peek into Greg's room just to see what she was missing. She softly trekked the rest of the way down the hall and poked her head in the open door. This had to be the master bedroom. A king-sized four-poster bed, covered in what looked like a red velvet throw, stood front and center.

She tiptoed inside to get a closer look, stopping by the side of the bed. Running her palms over the soft surface. The feeling of this under her back would drive her to distraction, just like Greg did. Her cheeks flamed at the wanton thought, but she sat on the bed.

The sound of a throat being cleared caused her to turn her head toward the doorway.

Greg stood there watching her, and she couldn't help noting the wicked twinkle in his eye. She popped up so fast, she stumbled and had to catch herself on a bedpost.

"I got lost and decided to sit down for a minute." The excuse sounded lame even to her ears, but she was determined to braze it out.

"Right," he commented with a small chuckle.

She marched past him and into the hall, feeling her blush intensify.

"I was coming to tell you dinner will be ready in half an hour," he rumbled from behind her.

"Okay." She hurried to the guest room and firmly shut the door behind her, then sagged against it. This was not a good way to start their all-business two weeks together.

Thirty minutes later, she made her way down the hall toward the kitchen. She'd taken pains to dress with more decorum, wearing some tan slacks and a matching striped silk blouse buttoned all the way.

Greg, wearing oven mitts, pulled a cookie sheet with two TV dinners out of the oven.

"You're just in time. Dinner is ready." He turned to smile at her. "Sorry for the limited selection. I'm not much of a cook. I usually subsist on these things."

"They smell great." She took an appreciative sniff, and her stomach gave a hungry rumble in anticipation.

"Thanks. We're having Salisbury steak, one of my favorites." He picked up the dinners with hot pads and turned. "I've got us set up in the dining room, if you'd care to lead the way."

She walked into the dining room and smiled. He'd made quite an effort to set a beautiful table. There were matching place mats, cloth napkins in silver rings, and wine in two crystal goblets. A haphazard bunch of pansies, petunias, and marigolds stuffed in another goblet were the centerpiece.

"The table looks lovely, Greg."

"Thanks." He put the dinners on the table, and then walked forward to pull out her chair. "Milady."

She slid into the chair. "Thank you, kind sir." She leaned forward to sniff the centerpiece. "What pretty flowers. Did you pick them from your flowerbed?"

He looked sheepish. "Nope, I sneaked them out of Mrs. Olsen's flowerbed."

"You didn't."

He shrugged. "I did. When I put the dinners in the oven, I glanced over at her lawn and thought of you." He grinned, adding wryly, "It'll be your fault if she stops baking me cookies, but I think you're worth the risk."

Later that evening, Candy climbed into the guest room bed all alone and pulled up the covers. She'd emerged from this evening's battle of the sexes unscathed. *And alone*, she added to herself morosely. But it was for her own good, she reaffirmed, tugging up the covers.

She fell into a restless slumber, tossing and turning, and then she began to dream.

She was in a dark and misty place full of shadows that were deep and daunting. The beast pursuing her was relentless. She wove her way in and out of the shadows, but she couldn't shake him. And then he pounced, going for her throat. She screamed, trying to fight him off.

Arms reached out to grab at her anew as she came awake.

Oh, my God, it was real, she realized. Shrieking, she pushed him away.

"Hush, Candy Baby. It's only me."

Greg's voice gradually penetrated her fog.

"Greg?" She blinked at his moon-washed shape.

"Yes, it's me. You were dreaming, sweet cakes."

"It was horrible." Curling her arms around him, she pulled him down next to her, shuddering in his arms.

He settled next to her and cuddled. "It was just a dream. It's only to be expected since your accident."

Snuggling her head on his chest, she was comforted by the reassuring beat of his heart. "I'm sorry if I woke you."

"I was already up going over some paperwork."

Lying against him, she was suddenly struck by the realization this was meant to be. She ran her hand up his chest, petting and feeling his pulse speed up. There was another connection between them. A primordial connection that couldn't be denied any longer. Even if he was using her for business purposes, it didn't matter. Come what may, she would claim her White Knight.

She wriggled up to kiss him. He went still for a moment, and then kissed her back.

Wrapping his arms around her, he drew her closer, totally claiming her mouth.

When they broke apart, he murmured, "Don't play with me, Candy. You know where this will lead."

"I know exactly where it will lead." She grinned, noting his startled expression. "I'm ready to claim my White Knight."

Bending to kiss her, his hand moved to cup her breast.

She squiggled out from under him and was pleased by the startled, uneasy look on his face. Good, let him be the one on edge tonight. "Not here. Let's go to your room."

"Next time," he murmured, reaching for her.

"No. Now." Hopping out of bed, she took off toward the door with a giggle. She sprinted toward the master bedroom, hearing his feet thunder down the hall behind her.

So, this was what it felt like to have the power. She kind of liked it.

Greg raced into the room and skidded to a halt beside her. "Okay, we're here. Let's get going."

"Not yet." Taking a half step back, she grinned at his glowering expression. He didn't look like a man in the throes of bliss. "You did say I could set the pace, and I quote. *'Any time, anyway, anywhere.'*"

"Get on with it then," he stated with a repressive frown.

Laughing, she reached for the top button on his shirt. "First, you're wearing too many clothes." She slowly unbuttoned the shirt and tugged it out of his pants. Brushing against him as she slowly peeled it off him, her nipples beaded. She let out a little gasp.

He groaned and reached for her.

"Not so fast, buster." She eluded his grasp. "Next come the pants."

His hand balled into fists at his side as he flashed her a dangerous smile. "Didn't anyone ever tell you it's not nice to tease the beast?"

"Ooh, Mr. Tough Guy," she teased, unbuckling his belt and unsnapping his pants.

"You'll find out."

"Promises, promises." She tugged down his pants and briefs, sinking to her knees before him. "You're magnificent," she murmured, touching the rock-hard length of him, then flicked her tongue out to taste him.

"Enough." He tugged her up to her feet. Scooping her into his arms, he flung her onto the bed, as she let out a startled squeak. He stepped out of his pants and shoes, coming down on top of her with a growl.

She pulled him close, her mouth opening under his, hot enough to melt into the velvet spread. Squirming, she realized she'd been right. The material was incredibly sensual under her back.

His big hands cupped her breasts, rubbing his palms against her pebbled nipples.

Sighing, she leaned into his exquisite touch, moving restlessly against him. She needed more.

"Please."

He continued to tease her. "Please, what?"

"Please, take me." She gasped when his fingers went to her wet, slick flesh.

"Not yet." He grinned, probing her gently.

She writhed against him, only to have her legs trapped by his. "Now who's teasing?"

He settled between her thighs, his pulsing manhood touching, but not taking. "I'm not playing, Candy. I'm serious."

She went still hearing his tone. Her body was trembling, craving him, and needing him badly.

"Ask me, Candy." He moved against her. "I want no more subterfuge between us."

She blinked at him, overcome by sensation, and knew he wasn't playing games. A bead of sweat trickled down his brow as he held himself in check.

"I want you. Please take me."

"You're mine." His gaze locked with hers as he entered her.

She moaned as he drove into her, setting a steady pace.

This obviously meant a lot more to him than a brief affair, even if he didn't say it. She met his demanding thrusts, rocking against him as he drove her out of her mind.

Suddenly, an earth shattering orgasm rippled through her as she convulsed in his arms.

Chapter Nine

Candy walked, picnic basket in hand, down the hall of Pinnacle Publishing toward Greg's office. He'd left for work early this morning, mumbling something about long hours and problems at work. Even her offer to take him out for lunch had been turned down. So, consequently, lunch was coming to him. If he was bogged down like he'd claimed, he could probably use the break.

Turning right, she entered the door to his office suite. She stopped in the outer office at his secretary's desk. A nameplate read Mrs. Mavis Floyd.

Mrs. Floyd looked up from her file cabinet. "May I help you?"

Candy smiled at the friendly, middle-aged lady. "Hi. I'm here to see Greg."

Pushing her glasses back on her nose, the secretary glanced at her calendar. "I'm afraid he's rather busy today. Do you have an appointment?"

"Not exactly. I brought him sustenance." She held up the picnic basket.

"And your name would be?" The secretary looked at her curiously.

"Candy Blake."

"Well, hello, Miss Blake. He told me to put you right through if you called, so I'm sure he wouldn't mind an interruption from you."

"That's nice to hear." She grinned at the curious glint in the secretary's eye.

"No problem. He hasn't had lunch yet and he sure could use a break." She smiled. "Go ahead. I'll hold his calls to give him time to eat."

"Thanks." Candy tapped on his door and entered.

"What is it, Mavis?" Greg asked without looking up.

"It isn't Mavis," she commented, making him look up. "I brought you some lunch." She carried the basket to his desk.

"You didn't need to do that. I'm sorry I couldn't take you out some place fancy."

"Don't give it a second thought. From what you said this morning, I knew you'd be too busy to go out. So, I came in." She opened the basket and took out the sandwiches and salad she'd made, then pulled up a chair for herself. "Mavis is going to hold your calls while you eat."

He took the sandwich she handed him and took a bite. "This is great. You take such good care of me, Candy."

"It works both ways." She grinned, watching him wolf down the sandwich and reach for the second one she'd made him. The poor guy was starving. "I'm glad you approve."

She opened the veggies and dip. "So, what's been keeping you so busy?"

He sighed and put down his sandwich. "I need to level with you, Candy. Chad Daley ran out on me and left things in a bit of a mess."

No wonder he was working overtime. "Why didn't you say so?"

He shrugged. "I didn't want to bother you. After all, you've had enough problems of your own lately. So, as much as I'd like to squire you around town, I've got my work cut out for me here."

She glanced at the stack of receipts on his desk. "How can I help?"

He reached out to take her hand. "Thanks for the offer, but you don't need to help. I'll take care of everything."

She entwined her fingers with his. He was determined to be the big, strong, protective man. It was probably a throwback to being raised by his sexist, old-fashioned father. What he needed to learn if they were going to build any kind of future together, was she was equally determined to demonstrate just how able she was.

"I've got all this free time since I came here. I'd like to have something to do. And anyway, I'm involved in the business because you're handling my launch party and fashion show next week."

A reluctant grin curved his mouth. "You win. For starters, you could place a call to your modeling agency and make sure things are square there. I was going to do that this afternoon."

"Good. I'd intended to touch base with my agent, Mark, anyway."

He stood. "Go ahead and use my phone. I've got a few details to check over in the plant. I'll be back soon."

He walked out, and then she went around his desk to slip into the chair. She punched in Mark's cell phone number and waited for him to pick up. He'd volunteered to assist her with the opening a few months back. He was her booking agent and longtime friend.

"Hello, Mark. Candy Blake here."

"Hi, Candy, how are things in the wilds of Wisconsin?"

"Fine. I'm just calling to make sure everything is set for the opening show Saturday night."

"Next Saturday?"

"Yes." She was alarmed by his hesitation. She knew her show was small potatoes in comparison to his usual projects, but Mark had been so encouraging about her branching off on her own. Had he changed his mind for some reason?

"I'm not ready. I didn't know we'd firmed the date."

"What!" She gasped.

"Your publisher had talked about some tentative dates, but we hadn't set one."

"Oh no." It was a total disaster. She couldn't put on a fashion show without models. Hanging garments on static hangers just wouldn't be the same. The critics would cut her business to shreds before she even got started. She'd been counting on positive buzz to get it launched properly. And what about Pinnacle? Greg's business would suffer, too. Her shoulders sagged.

"I'm sorry, Candy. Chad told me you were having a few problems there. I figured you must have run into extra snags there and were temporarily putting the show on hold. I was going to call you if I hadn't heard from you pretty soon."

Chad? It figured. He was an affable guy, a real charmer when she'd signed her contract with him, but he'd ruined her future with his carelessness. From what Greg had said, she knew he had a drinking problem.

"Can you still send the models?"

"Only a few. The rest are booked, just like those at every agency worth its salt in the country."

She took a deep breath as her planned fashion show started to vaporize before her eyes. She'd have to come up with a Plan B. "Go ahead and send as many girls as you can. We'll have to make do."

"I should be able to scrounge up three. I'm sorry it can't be more, Candy."

"Me, too, but as the saying goes, if you get lemons, make lemonade. The three models will be fine. I'll come up with something else to fill in the gaps."

"I bet you will. You've always been the creative one."

She laughed, hearing his nickname for her and felt some of her tension slip away. If she walked the runway and she recruited a few willing amateurs, things might still work. "So, will you be here?"

"I wouldn't miss it for the world."

As she hung up the phone, Greg came back into the room. She turned to glance at him. "Chad Daley has struck again."

He stopped in his tracks. "How?"

"Chad never booked the models for my fashion show. Mark will come with a skeleton crew, and we'll have to make do."

"Will you be able to pull it off?"

"I think so. I've come up with a few ideas. If I come out of retirement, recruit a few local ladies, and put some other items on display, it just might work."

"I don't know how I ever got along without you, Candy."

Two nights later, Candy added her homemade creamy salad dressing and tossed the salad for dinner. She and Greg had fallen into a comfy routine in the past week. Kind of like an old married couple, she thought warmly. Greg was enjoying her cooking, and she was tingling from his prowess in bed. The thought made her smile.

He wandered in from the den and came up behind her. He snaked an arm around her waist and pulled her to him. "Hey there, sweet cakes. What's for dinner?"

"Chicken parmesan." She nestled against him for a moment. "Set the table, please. It'll be ready in a minute."

"Later, then," he promised with a kiss to her nape.

As she pulled the garlic bread out of the oven, she acknowledged that she was looking forward to later. Smiling, she mused that he was turning her into a wanton woman.

She carried the salad and bread into the dining room and placed them on the table. Then she slipped into the chair Greg pulled out for her. "So how are the launch plans going?"

"So far so good, thanks to your help. The modeling agency, caterer, hall, and promo calendars are ready." He leaned over to kiss her. "We make a good team, Candy. Thanks for everything."

Warmed by the compliment, her cheeks heated. "You're welcome. Thank goodness you came back before Chad Daley could ruin things. I wonder where he got to?"

He gave a mirthless chuckle. "I'm of two minds on that subject. Either he's on a helluva long bender, or he's defected to one of my competitors. I still can't believe it. He, Jill, and I started Pinnacle from nothing. How could he torpedo it like this? I want to thank you again for being so understanding about the launch foul-up."

"I didn't do all that much."

"Yes, you did. Your smooth touch with the vendors and your modeling connections made all the difference." He reached out to take her hand. "Like I said, we make a good team." Looking deep into her eyes, he murmured, "Maybe we should think about..."

The doorbell rang.

"I wonder who that can be? Maybe it's my secretary with those missing invoices." He reluctantly let go of her hand, and got to his feet. "We'll talk about this later."

Candy took a sip of her iced tea while he went to the door. It had been a hectic three days, but she and Greg were finally on top of the situation.

"Dad. I'm surprised to see you here."

She put down her glass. Mr. Morris, here?

Ma, she thought suddenly. There might be something wrong with Ma. She stood up just as Greg walked back into the dining room with his father behind him.

"Good evening, Miss Blake." Mr. Morris eyed her apprehensively.

His gentle tone alarmed her even more. Why was he being so polite all of a sudden? "What are you doing here?"

Mr. Morris frowned and looked at his shoes. "No special reason. I felt like taking a ride."

"I'm sorry, I didn't mean to sound so rude." Candy bit her lip. "I thought maybe something was wrong back home. With Ma, you know."

Looking at her with a slight smile, he replied. "She's fine. Beating the pants off Mildred in Gin Rummy, from what I understand."

Greg stepped forward. "Won't you sit down, Dad?"

She cast Greg a grateful smile for taking the focus off her for a moment so she could regain her composure. "Yes, as a matter of fact, why don't you join us for dinner? Greg can set another place while I bring in the entrée. I'll be right back." She fled the room before he could object.

She pulled the chicken parmesan out of the oven and sprinkled it with freshly grated cheese and parsley. It wasn't exactly company food, but it would do. All of a sudden, she felt like a bride giving her first dinner party. She put the casserole in a serving basket and carried it to the table where Mr. Morris was already wolfing down his salad, she noted with a smile.

He put down his fork. "I didn't want to be any trouble."

"It's no trouble, at all. I always cook enough for an army. Greg will tell you that. It's an old habit from my modeling days. That way I only had to cook on the weekends and had leftovers to warm up all week long."

Greg took an appreciative sniff of the casserole. "It smells great, Candy."

"I agree," Mr. Morris echoed. "Confidentially, I've been fading away since Mildred moved over to Ma Brown's house. Madeline isn't much in the kitchen."

Candy grinned at the revelation. It seemed he was opening up to her. "I'm glad you like my cooking. So, have there been any more scandal stories in the paper since I left town?"

He scooped up a large serving of chicken parmesan.

"Well?"

Why the hesitation? She gazed directly at him. "Tell me."

"There was a big splash about the raid at the country club, then nothing."

"I was afraid of that."

"Magi Barnes seems to have gone to ground."

She let out a sigh of relief. "I'm glad to hear it."

Greg shook his head. "The police are looking for her."

"What?" She looked at him, surprised.

"I didn't want to shake you up. They want to talk to her concerning your hit-and-run."

"I know she's angry, but I don't think she's crazy enough to try to kill me. I'm hoping she'll let things lie."

Mr. Morris stopped mid-bite. "She's left town since leaving the paper."

Candy still felt bad about that. Even though Magi deserved it, she didn't want to ruin the woman's career. In fact, she kind of felt sorry for her. "I only hope she finds peace of mind."

"Hopefully, she will. I heard she went off to write that novel she's been talking about. So, don't feel bad. Anyway, her kind of yellow journalism had no place in our town. If she wanted to do that, she should go get a job with a tabloid."

"I had a long talk with Tom, and he was plenty steamed. It seems he'd given her an ultimatum, and she'd pushed her luck too far this time."

"Well, maybe it's stupid of me, but I wish her well. I hope she finds happiness and stops living in the past."

Greg lifted his glass. "Amen to that."

Mr. Morris put down his fork. "Greg told me about your accident. Are you feeling, okay?"

Candy rolled her neck. "I'm still a little sore, but I'm fine."

He watched her movement, then looked at Greg. "Did they find the guy that hit her?"

Greg's jaw tightened. "No, they've been checking with local garages for a dark SUV with body damage, but so far, they've come up empty. I put my P.I. firm on the job, and they haven't had much success, either."

She went still. What P.I. firm? It was the first she'd heard about it. After Mr. Morris left, she'd ask Greg about it. She passed the breadbasket to Mr. Morris. "Jerry came to tow the car, and he's trying to put it back together."

Mr. Morris helped himself to a roll and passed the basket on to Greg. "So, is everything set for the opening next Saturday, son?"

"We think we've got all the bases covered."

She knew Greg hadn't let his father in on the mess they were clearing up. He didn't need pressure from his father now. "Greg's been working overtime to put it across. He's doing the best that he can."

Mr. Morris's eyes widened. "Of course, he is. I didn't mean to sound like I doubted him."

"Sweet cakes, I can defend myself."

"I know."

"It's nice to see you kids present a united front. It gives an old man hope for the future."

Chapter Ten

Candy pressed the pleats on the cotton lace dressing gown and handed it to Kathleen. Luckily, with the help of her friends, this show would go off without a hitch.

Switching off the iron, she turned to smile at Greg's sister. "Thanks again for all your help."

Kathleen added the garment to the long rolling rack that already held a rainbow of Candy-Wear Lingerie. "I'm glad to help. It adds a little excitement to my humdrum day."

"Humdrum? From what I hear, you're turning that dusty old mill on its ear. A female in the executive suite! I'm sure the old boys are buzzing."

"Actually, I was meaning to thank you for stirring things up a bit. Thanks to your influence. Dad has really loosened up. He's starting to see those business classes I took in college weren't a waste of time."

"I'm glad to hear it, but I really didn't do that much. I just told Greg I thought his father should drag himself out of the dark ages. I didn't realize he'd actually agree with me."

Kathleen nodded. "You've got a lot more influence over Greg than you realize. We were all stuck in a rut before you came home. I know I haven't said it before, but my opinion of you has totally changed. I heartily approve of my brother's choice of a wife."

Candy's face heated at the unexpected vote of approval. It touched her that Kathleen had come to accept her as one of the family. But she knew it was all an act. Or was it? Since Greg had slipped this ring on her finger, neither of them had broached the subject of the end of the summer. It was as if they didn't want to spoil their magic interlude.

She knew she'd changed just as much as Greg had. She realized now that she'd been in the same kind of rut, living life with blinders on. Greg had freed her from the past and opened up a limitless future. She hoped she added a new dimension to his life, as well. It gave her hope this temporary alliance might morph into something more.

Jerry walked in carrying a mannequin under his arm. He plunked it down in front of her. "Where do you want this?"

"Take it out front and be careful. They're rented. Mark will show you where to set them up. We're going to have them flanking the sides of the runway to make up for the lack of models."

"Will do," he replied, picking the mannequin up again, and gently holding it, headed toward the front. He stopped by the table where Joan was folding programs and dropped a kiss on her head. He turned to grin at Candy. "By the way, don't let Joan overdo it, will ya?"

"Don't worry. I gave her a sit-down job. I think between the two of us, we can make her behave."

"You two don't need to talk about me like I'm fragile China," Joan chimed in with a scowl. "I told Candy I could do more than this, but she's being bossy, as usual. And as for you, husband of mine, you're being way too overprotective."

"Tough." Jerry hoisted the mannequin once more and headed for the stage.

Candy grinned at their affectionate exchange. "I don't want my future niece or nephew to be distressed, so humor me."

Joan huffed out a frustrated breath. "Okay. At least I can get in on the act tonight."

"That's right. You're the perfect model for my maternity line. Now I won't have to have a model wear a pillow on her middle."

Greg walked in carrying a box and set it on the table. "Catalogs, hot off the presses."

"Ooh, let's see." Kathleen rushed over to rip open the box. She lifted out a stack and spread them out on the table. "Nice work, big brother."

Candy picked one up and gazed at it almost disbelievingly. Years of blood, sweat, and tears had brought her to this point. She owed a great deal to Greg. In honesty, she knew he'd given her company a better deal than anyone else would. And this catalog was first class.

She reached out to take his hand. "She's right. It's beautiful, Greg. Thank you."

He leaned over to kiss her. "You're welcome. This is only the start of our dreams coming true."

Candy paced the backstage area, clipboard in hand, checking off models as they lined up. Ann, Sue, and Molly— three friends from her agency—were in red, white, and blue teddies. Kathleen stepped up behind them, looking regal in a jewel-toned caftan. And Joan looked like an angelic punk rocker in her white lace, maternity peignoir set.

Candy turned to check the rack one more time, then handed the clipboard to Madeline. She'd been shocked but pleased when Greg's mother had agreed to act as stage manager. With her experience in local dramatic societies, Candy had eagerly taken her up on the offer.

"Thank you, Mrs. Morris."

"Break a leg," she replied with a smile. "And you might as well get used to calling me Mom."

She felt a pang of longing deep inside, but kept a smile on her face. "Thanks, Mom."

Candy took her place at the end of the line, feeling like her head was swimming. The idea that Greg's family was pulling for her took some getting used to. She gazed down at her baby pink satin pant and bra set she was wearing, and felt a bit weak in the knees. Was it good enough? Would the critics like her designs? So much was riding on this fashion show.

The music started, and the emcee began his patter.

She turned to her models. "Okay, ladies. Here's to a good show. Follow the planned routine, and we can't go wrong. And thanks for everything."

"I just hope I do the turn right." Kathleen said.

"You practiced for two hours, and you looked great," Candy rushed to reassure her. "I'm sure you'll do fine."

"Thanks for the pep talk. I'm a little bit nervous." Kathleen smoothed a fold in the caftan.

Candy watched her fidgeting, and then glanced at Joan, who was nibbling at her lower lip. It was probably too much for them. "For you two civilians, I know this is outside your comfort zone. If you don't want to go through with it, I'll understand."

"No way." Joan grinned. "How often do I get to parade around in my undies in public?"

"I'm with her." Kathleen's lips curved up in a reluctant grin.

Nodding, Candy let out a sigh of relief. "I owe you both big time. I want you to know how much appreciate your help. I couldn't have pulled the show off without your help."

"For family, it's worth it." Joan stated.

"Right," Kathleen agreed. "And besides, how often do I get to turn Morris Point on its ear?"

The curtains parted, and the first model started out to the strains of *'She's A Lady.'*

A smattering of applause and flash bulbs popped as Molly started out.

Candy blushed with pride. Her own fashion shows! It was her dream come true.

Greg poured two glasses of champagne and carried them out to the hot tub on the terrace. He stopped when he caught sight of Candy. God, she was beautiful, and she was his. Moonlight highlighted her blonde hair and caressed the sweet curve of her face.

She turned and spotted him. "I wondered where you'd gone."

"I thought we needed something to celebrate the start of a beautiful collaboration." He walked up to her and handed her a flute of champagne. "Here you go, sweetheart."

"Thanks." She reached up to take the glass. Her breasts lifted in the swirling water.

His hungry gaze ate up the action, knowing she was naked in the water. Even after two weeks of sharing a bed, he was just as insatiable as he'd been that first night on the beach. The good thing was that he thought she felt the same way. She'd had him every which way, just as she'd vowed the first night. He'd taught her the ways of love and she'd taught him a thing of two along the way, as well.

He put his glass of champagne down on the table and untied his robe, letting it drop to the floor. He saw her eyeing his semi-erect hard-on and stifled a smile. He was horny as a teenager these days, and she was to blame.

"See anything you like?"

She smiled and leaned back in the water. "One or two things." She took a sip of bubbly, licked the foam off her lip, and looked pointedly at his manhood. "From the state you're in, I can see you got started without me."

He flashed her a wry grin. "Are you kidding? A look at you wet and naked in the moonlight is all it takes. And seeing you model that lingerie earlier gave me plenty of things to fantasize about, too."

"So, you liked my designs?" Her eyes twinkled.

"I sure did. That black garter belt get-up has definite possibilities. But the clothes weren't all I liked. Confidentially, I've got the hots for one of the models."

"Which one?"

"Guess." He slid into the tub, took the glass from her hand, and set it on the table. Then he reached for her, pulling her to him, her wet, slick body sliding against him. "Let me see if I can convince you of my devotion."

He slanted a kiss across her lips. Her mouth opened under his, and he tasted her honeyed sweetness. His hand sought her breast under the water. Cupping it, he reveled in the sweet, sexy weight as he held it his palm. He pinched the nipple, and she whimpered into his mouth. Her nipple puckered into a tight bud.

Her breathing quickened, and she sucked on his tongue. She reached for his growing erection in the water, capturing him in a confident grip.

She knew just the right touch to drive him wild, the little minx. He groaned, pushing himself harder into her hand and reached for the hot, creamy flesh between her thighs. He pressed against her clitoris, and she moaned, gripping him even tighter.

He knew what she was doing—trying to control the pace. But this time, he wouldn't be rushed. He wanted to savor their intimacy like the fine champagne they'd been sipping. He slid one, then two fingers into her, teasing her, testing her readiness. His digits moved in and out of her as she clenched around him, then he withdrew his fingers.

She shuddered, crying out her protest, clinging to him.

He picked her up, leaned back, and swung her around to face him. Lifting her high so her breasts dangled like ripe fruit for his tasting, he suckled one and then the other nipple until they were wet and hard. He drew hungrily at the sweet, strawberry-peaked globes.

Squirming against him as she hovered over him, brushing tantalizingly against his manhood, she cried out.

Slowly lowering her onto his rock-hard erection, he restrained his own violent need. Burying his aching member inside her hot velvet sheath, he felt beads of sweat break out on his forehead.

She ground against him. He wrapped an arm around her back, restraining her movements. She stilled for a second, but her internal ripples tugged at him, making him jerk inside her when he wanted to savor the moment.

Her breathing was quick as she bent nibble at his ear. "What are you waiting for, Morris? An engraved invitation?" She nipped at his shoulder, wriggling.

"Be patient." He cupped her shapely bottom, laughing as he surged up to meet her, pulling her down onto him. He set a slow deliberate pace that gradually grew faster and faster.

Bouncing up and down on him, Candy clung to him. Sucking on his neck, she shrieked his name as she came, her rippling spasms tugged him deeper inside her.

He erupted, pounding into her two more times, holding her to him as he buried himself to the hilt.

Sagging against him, she laid her head on his shoulder.

Smoothing a hand down her back, he caressed her.

And then it hit him. This was the first time they'd done it without protection. He'd been in such a fever for her, he hadn't even thought about it.

Chapter Eleven

Candy turned over in bed, her hand coming down on an empty, cold pillow. She opened her eyes, blinking at the bright sunshine streaming through the bedroom window. Then it dawned on her. Greg must have gone to the office.

He'd mentioned last night pressing duties might keep him busy all day. Maybe she'd surprise him with another picnic lunch. They'd be all alone in his big office. Maybe she'd wear the black garter belt set.

Grinning at the thought of his response, she stretched, feeling a few twinges from their fierce lovemaking the night before. It had been a night to remember in more ways than one. She loved him, plain and simple, and she had reason to believe he cared for her.

The phone rang.

She leaned over, reaching for the receiver on Greg's nightstand. "Hello."

"Hello, beautiful," Greg replied. "Did I wake you?"

She nestled into the soft pillow, his deep baritone sending a heat wave up her spine. "No, I just woke up." Her voice dropped to a sensual tone. "I miss you. Wish you were here beside me right now so I could demonstrate how much."

He groaned. "You'll be the death of me yet, Candy Baby. All I need is a little phone sex to keep me off my game." He chuckled, adding, "I'm going to have to pop some Viagra if you keep it up."

She laughed. "You don't need Viagra to keep it up. Have you forgotten last night?"

"Don't get me started, or I'll never get any work done. The reason I called was to tell you there was a review of your fashion show in this morning's paper. It was glowing, by the way. You're on your way, Candy."

She smiled. "Thanks. What a wonderful way to wake up. Work fast so you can come home and help me celebrate."

"Will do," he promised, adding in a sexy rumble, "I'll make up for lost time when I see you later. Wear the black garter belt." She brought in the paper from the front steps and took it into Greg's den. She sat at his desk and read the rave review twice, breaking into a huge grin.

'The Candy-Wear line is new and innovative—A sure winner in the growing lingerie market.'

Greg had been right. If this was anything to go by, she was on her way. She glanced at the smooth mahogany desktop, hunting for scissors to clip the article. His caddy contained pens, pencils, post-its, but no scissors.

Undeterred, she pulled open a drawer and spotted scissors wedged beside a stack of files. When she reached for them, she noticed a file poking out from under some papers. The first two letters on the cover were BL.

She went still. It could be Blake.

Greg wouldn't have her investigated, would he? No, he wasn't capable of such deceit. On the other hand, it might be her father's file. But why would Greg have it? Telling herself all this speculation was stupid, she stared at the file as if it was a snake. Plenty of names started with BL.

There was only one way to find out. Shaking off her feeling of unease, she reached for the file and laid it on the desk. Tears sprang to her eyes as she looked at the name Harry L. Blake—her father.

Why would Greg have this? It didn't make any sense, unless... Had Greg had the case reopened? He'd once offered to do it, and she'd turned him down for personal reasons. Dredging up past wounds wouldn't make them any better. Did her feelings mean so little to him?

The file's cover was faded and old, which told her it was probably her father's original employment record. Greg shouldn't even have access to this. And then a stinging thought hit. If she looked hard enough, would she find a corresponding file on her? Greg could have had his P.I. do a little background check on her, as well. He'd said that he kept a P.I. firm on retainer.

Horrified by the direction of her thoughts, she got a grip on her emotions. It did no good jumping to conclusions. Emotions had gotten her into trouble. It was time to start using her head. First, she'd read her father's file.

She opened the folder. Clipped to the inside was a letter from the P.I. dated two weeks ago. Greg had this for two weeks and hadn't said anything. Why? She read the letter, her stomach clenching.

"My recent investigation of the facts in this case has turned up nothing new. Harry Blake was responsible for the thefts. He was a compulsive gambler and needed the cash to pay his bookie. Do you want me to break the news to your lady, old buddy?"

Her father was guilty. Why hadn't Greg told her?

Candy brushed tears away as years of uncertainty and denial washed away. Denial and anger that had colored every part of her life that she now knew was based on a lie. She read through the aged documents inside. The proof was irrefutable—forged documents, in her father's handwriting. But why had her dad lied? Anger surged through her as she hung her head. What good would anger do now? He'd probably done it to spare her feelings at the time. No doubt, he'd thought he'd have time to make it up to her. But fate had stepped in the way.

She had to forgive her father if she was going to move on.

This summer with Greg had taught her the futility of carrying around old grudges. Her father had probably let her think he was innocent to protect her.

Why had Greg reopened the case? Did he want to investigate her background before making a commitment to her? No, he'd never said one word about her staying after the summer was over. Or was it to be a goodbye gift? The summer was almost over. If only she'd told him how she felt. But it was too late.

She couldn't stand to say a calm and civil goodbye. She needed to go home.

Tears did flow then, tears of chances lost, and sweet remembrance. She slowly got to her feet, the urge to run overtaking her. No way could she face Greg and not break down. She was going home. It would be up to him to make the next move.

She called for a taxi, swallowing the lump in her throat. Then, getting to her feet, she turned and fled to the master bedroom to pack.

If Greg had more to say to her, he could find her at Ma's. Retrieving her suitcase from the closet, she laid it on the bed and gazed at the bed, grief stricken. They'd shared such sweet nights here, as well as their hearts. Or, at least, she'd shared her heart with him.

She couldn't let herself waver. She'd walk away on her terms.

Pulling her clothes from the dresser, she tossed them in the bag in a heap. There wasn't time to worry about being neat. She had to get out before Greg came back because she didn't think she could face him.

She closed her bag, and then glanced at the engagement ring on her finger. Tugging it off, she laid it on his pillow. There could be no false ties to bind him to her. The catalog was launched, he'd done his part, and now she'd do hers and walk away. There was no reason to linger. It would only make the parting harder.

Crying, she picked up the bag and walked out the bedroom door. Turning to take one last lingering look at their love-nest, she blinked away tears of regret. Renewing her determination, she turned and headed down the hall. Tears blurring her eyes, she ran directly into a hard body.

Oh God, not Greg. She couldn't face him right now. Not like this.

She blinked at him, her vision clearing. She gasped as Chad Daley came into focus, scowling at her.

Shocked, she blurted out, "You scared the hell out of me. Greg's been looking everywhere for you. What are you doing here?"

"Damn," he muttered, "just my rotten luck."

She took in the beads of sweat on his brow and noted his disheveled appearance.

His scowl deepened as he cast a frantic look around. "So, Greg isn't here?"

"No, he's out attending to business." Then it hit her—all the doors were locked. He must have broken in. But how had he done it? More importantly, why was he here? The burglar alarm hadn't gone off.

Growing nervous, she backed away. "How did you get in here?"

"Jill gave me a key. I used to come and water the plants when they were traveling," he replied distractedly, pulling a gun out of the waistband of his jeans. He aimed it straight at her heart.

"You've got to be kidding."

"I'm dead serious. So, shut the hell up." He nudged her forward. "Get moving toward the den, and I won't shoot you."

She stood frozen, staring at the gun he held in his trembling hand.

Chad screeched, "I said move."

"Okay." It wouldn't take much to set him off. Gone was the genial guy she'd dealt with in the past and a nervous wreck stood in his place.

She led the way into the den and stepped aside as he rushed past her to the desk. Seeing an opportunity to escape, she stepped back.

He whirled, leveling the gun on her. "Don't even think about it. Sit on the sofa where I can see you."

She reluctantly complied, feeling his eyes on her every step of the way. What the hell was he doing here? She sank on the sofa, setting her bag beside her, and watched him.

He pulled a key out of his pocket and opened Greg's bottom drawer.

She frowned. "Where'd you get the key?"

He grinned. "I stole it. What else?"

He rifled through the files, sweat dripping off his face.

"What are you looking for?"

"Proof," he stated with a cold smile. "Aha," he yelled, lifting out a thick file. He got to his feet, cradling it in his arm like it was a baby. He picked up the gun and pointed it at her again. "Come on."

She scowled at him, thinking about balking, but he was just crazy enough to shoot her. She slowly rose to her feet.

"Bring them." He pointed at her bags.

She frowned and picked them up. He didn't want to leave any evidence, she thought sickly. She walked past him with her head held high, making up her mind to get out of this some way. Her cell phone was in her purse. Of course, that was her ace in the hole. She had to play it cool until she could use it. Keeping a firm grip on her purse, she walked out the front door.

A black SUV was parked in the driveway. She got chills looking at its dented front fender. "You're the one who hit me."

"Yup. That's two for two for old Betsy. Although, to keep the score even, you shouldn't still be walking around."

He killed another person. Two for two—*Jill*. Had he been responsible for Greg's wife's death? It seemed unthinkable.

She gasped at the casual admission. "You killed Jill?"

"I had to. She would have ruined everything with the audit she was going to do. I needed more time. I don't mind telling you. I did it neatly. She didn't have time to feel a thing. You, on the other hand, have really put me through a lot of trouble. Too bad you didn't take the hint and leave. Pinnacle would have gone down the drain, Greg would have gone back to the paper mill, and I'd be in the clear. But we're going to rectify the situation, now." He nudged her toward the back of the SUV. "Get in the cargo bay. Fast."

Three houses down, Candy noticed Mrs. Olson weeding her flowerbed. Should she yell?

She glanced at Chad. His nervous twitch made her hesitate.

"Don't try it," he muttered.

She frowned. He'd probably pull the trigger if she startled him. No, she'd have to bide her time.

"Move," he hissed, yanking her bag out of her hand, and tossing it into the open cargo bay. He reached for her next.

She eluded his grasp and clambered in after her bag, keeping her purse tight in her hand. She moved as far away from him as she could and pulled her knees up, making as small a target as possible of herself.

He slammed the hatch shut and sprinted around the vehicle. He got in, gunned the engine, and drove away.

Candy crouched, shivering in the back. They drove down the block, and she looked at Mrs. Olsen.

Mrs. Olsen noticed her and waved.

Candy mouthed the words "help me" and watched the woman's puzzled expression. If only the message got through. But Candy couldn't count on it.

She quietly opened her purse.

They turned onto the highway, and she noticed Greg's car driving toward home. She surreptitiously fished around the purse for her cell phone.

"What are you up to back there?" Chad snapped.

She froze. "Nothing."

Greg pulled into his driveway and smiled at the thought of a little afternoon delight with Candy. He'd wrapped up his business early to hurry home to her.

He got out of the car and walked up to the house. The front door was ajar. That was odd. Candy probably failed to latch it when she went out to retrieve the paper. No doubt, she was glowing over the good review.

He smiled and entered the house, shutting the door behind him. "Candy Baby, I'm home."

There was no reply.

He frowned, unsettled by the silence. Maybe she was napping. He walked by the den and skidded to a halt. The Harry Blake file lay on top of his desk.

"Shit." He should have told her about it right away. He'd sat on the bad report, not wanting to dim her excitement for the opening. She was probably madder than hell. After all, he was a lying, stinking no good Morris. He went toward the bedroom with a sinking feeling in the pit of his gut.

The bedroom was empty. He stalked over to the dresser and jerked open the drawer. Damn, her clothes were gone. She'd left him. Then, he noticed her engagement ring lying on his pillow, and his whole world imploded. The business, his life, meant nothing without her to share it with.

Damn, why hadn't he told her he loved her? *Because you didn't want to scare her off, schmuck.* Well, he'd sure as shooting fucked this one up.

He sagged on the bed, groaning. She was gone, and he'd never dared to ask her to stay. He'd been too scared of spooking her by talking about forever, and now she was gone.

He gritted his teeth and stood, slipping the ring into his shirt pocket. He wouldn't give her up without a fight.

A car horn honked.

He hurried toward the door. What now?

A taxi idled in the driveway.

The driver rolled down his window. "You the fare I'm supposed to pick up?"

His jaw tightened. So, she was running away by taxi.

But where was she? "No. She's not here."

The cabbie frowned.

He walked up to him, pulling a hundred dollar bill out of his wallet. "I'll make up for your lost fare if you give me some information."

"Yeah, what do you want to know?" The cabbie eyed the bill.

"What time did she call? And where was she going?"

"Let's see." He looked down at a clipboard on the passenger seat. "She called half an hour ago, and it says here she was going to the bus station."

Greg handed him the money. So where was she?

He went back in the house to look for a note. Her father's file was still sitting on his desk, but there was no note from Candy. Then he noticed something odd. His locked file cabinet was ajar. Had she broken into it?

He shook his head. That wasn't her style. Which meant someone else had. Had she encountered a burglar?

The doorbell rang. Maybe she was back. He sprinted through the house, tore open the door, and scowled at Mrs. Olsen on his doorstep.

She stepped back a pace, her eyes going wide. "Whatever's wrong, Gregory? You look like you've seen a ghost."

"Sorry, Mrs. Olson. I don't have time to chat."

"You're going after Miss Blake, aren't you?"

His jaw dropped. "How did you know that?"

"Well, the look on your face for one thing, and the fact that I saw her leave a while back. It struck me as odd she was sitting in the back of that big black monstrosity. That's why I came over."

He shuddered. It sounded like the hit-and-run vehicle. "Was she riding in a black SUV?"

"I guess that's what they call them. It took me a while to figure out what she was trying to tell me. It looked like she was mouthing the words *help me* on the sly."

"Was a man or woman driving?"

"It was a young man about your age."

He rubbed his face. That left out Magi, but it put Candy in the clutches of some guy.

"He was thin and sandy-haired, as a matter of fact. I think I saw him at your barbeque last year."

"Chad Daley," Greg muttered as the list of suspects narrowed. What in the hell was Daley after? "Thanks, Mrs. Olson. I owe you a big favor."

She smiled. "Go get her."

He went into the house to call the police. He was talking to the officer when he felt his cell vibrate. "Hold on, Steve. I've got a call on my cell."

He answered cautiously, "Hello."

There was dead air on the other end. He listened hard.

"So, where are you taking me?" Candy yelled. "Is it the same place where you killed Jill?"

His knees buckled. He slid down the wall onto the bench.

Chad had killed Jill?

And now Candy was in his clutches.

"I told you to shut up," Chad snapped.

"How could you do something like that to your own cousin?"

"Like I said, it was quick. She didn't have time to feel a thing. Besides, they deserved it. Always lording their wealth around me. I deserved more, and I'm going to get it."

Greg felt sick, listening to Chad brag. The man he'd considered his close friend, who'd been his best man at his wedding, had betrayed him.

A cold resolution filled him, driving out his grief. Chad would not kill Candy. The police could follow the signal.

He hurried inside to pick up the phone in the study where the police were on hold. "Steve, I've got Candy on my cell phone. She has hers with her and managed to sneak a call to me."

"Did she say where she is?"

"No. She's not saying anything directly to me, but I'm able to hear their conversation. She's left the line open. It's Chad Daley. I recognized his voice. And what's more, she got him to admit he killed Jill."

"That bastard. Keep listening. We'll get the cell company to break in on the conversation and track the signal."

Greg put the cell phone back to his ear.

"I just thought you might like to tell me why," Candy prompted.

"What does it matter?" Chad asked.

"It matters to you."

"For money. What else?"

"Is that all?"

"Maybe I liked putting one over on the high and mighty Gregory Morris." Chad chuckled. "You of all people should understand that."

"Me?"

"Yeah, you." He grew agitated. "Hell, your old man found himself in the same position."

"Don't you dare compare yourself with my father!" She snapped. "He might have been a thief, but he never tried to hurt anyone."

"Shut up, bitch," Chad bit out.

"No." She added in a gentler tone, "Will you at least tell me where we're going?"

"Sure. Why not? We're going to the farm."

Greg scowled. It was an old, abandoned farm where he and his friends had held their beer parties during high school. It was an isolated place where Daley could do heaven knows what to Candy.

He told the police where they were heading and sped off. He had to save his woman.

Greg pulled off the lonely country road and parked a few drives down. There was no need to tip Daley off to his presence. He ran toward the farm. Parked by the barn was the black SUV with a dented right fender. Greg rushed toward it. It was empty, but Candy's suitcase lay in the back. The police hadn't gotten there yet, but Greg couldn't wait for them.

He inched toward the barn, hearing Chad's angry voice.

"You should have kept your nose out of it, Candy. I tried to scare you off, but you couldn't take the hint."

Candy stood frozen, watching Daley with horror. "Please, you don't have to do this, Chad."

"It's too late to turn back now. I can't afford to leave any loose ends. The Morrises play hardball. You should have learned that by the way Greg tricked you into doing business with him."

She frowned, hoping Greg was listening in. It might be her only chance to tell him how she felt. "He's changed. Heck, times have changed a lot since my dad was arrested."

"I'm sorry, but I'm not going to jail. I'll dispose of you, get rid of the files, and disappear. Greg will be so nuts about you running out on him, he won't even know what happened."

"You don't have to do this. I won't say anything. I was leaving him, as a matter of fact."

He sneered. "Like you'd walk away from the Morris money." He raised the gun in his shaky hand and stepped forward menacingly.

Greg jumped out of the shadows, bringing Daley down with a flying tackle.

Chad let out a screech, and the gun went off.

Candy screamed.

Greg grunted, feeling a sting on his arm. Outraged, he knocked the gun out of Daley's hand and landed a solid punch to his jaw.

Chad groaned, his head snapping back, and fell unconscious.

Greg bit his lip against the searing pain in his arm and rolled to his feet. He had to make sure Candy was okay.

Sirens wailed outside the barn as the police arrived.

He looked at her, noting the stricken expression on her pale face. "Are you okay?"

She glanced at his bleeding arm and winced, tears pooling in her eye. "I'm fine. It's you who's been hurt." She choked on a sob.

Lieutenant Sinclair charged into the barn, gun drawn. He frowned, taking in the whole scene. "You kill him?" He gestured toward Chad.

"God, I hope so," Greg bit out.

"Is she okay?" Sinclair nodded at Candy.

"I'm fine." She sagged on a bale of hay. "You'd better get an ambulance here for Greg. He's hit."

Sinclair nodded. "They should be here in a second. That was smart thinking, young lady, using your cell phone. We tracked the signal all the way."

Daley moaned, slowly waking up.

The police swarmed the area, handcuffing Chad and placing him in the back of a squad car.

"Damn you, Morris," he shouted.

The ambulance arrived and the paramedics immediately began treating Greg.

He tried to shrug them off and step toward Candy, but she retreated and blinked at him, tears shimmering in her eyes.

He bit out a curse, telling himself he should give her some space, and waited for Sinclair to wander over. "Would you mind giving Candy a ride home? I think this has all been too much for her."

Sinclair glanced at her pale face. "Sure, no problem. She does look all done in."

Greg let the paramedics load him into the ambulance. "Go back to the house, Candy," he called. "We'll talk when I get home." "I just want to go home. Would you mind taking me all the way back to Morris Point?"

Chapter Twelve

Candy paced the parlor at Ma's house the next day. Her packed suitcases waited by the door. She glanced at Ma's downfallen expression and winced. She didn't mean to distress her, but she had to leave. She didn't want to be a painful reminder to Greg.

Ma looked up at her sadly. "Are you sure you can't stay a bit longer?"

Candy shook her head and smiled at her, willing her to understand. "No, it's time I got back to the real world. It's been a nice summer, but it's time to move on."

Ma sighed. "But Joan is going to have her baby any day now. You'll miss all the excitement."

"I'm sure she'll send me lots of pictures. They'll have to do."

"Why can't you and Greg work things out? Isn't it worth one more try? You look so sad, baby."

Candy flashed her a small smile. "Sadder, but wiser. That's what I get for getting mixed up with a Morris."

"You love him, girl. Why don't you just admit it?"

"You're right. I love him, but he doesn't love me. The engagement is over." She patted Ma's arm. "It's better this way. Trust me."

The roar of a motorcycle pulling into the driveway distracted her.

She looked out the window, and her jaw dropped. Greg was astride the battered old Harley. It was identical to the one she used to ride as a teenager.

"Here he is. Right on time," Ma chirped.

"It can't be," Candy muttered. "Greg, a biker. No way." She walked outside to get a closer look.

It *was* Greg. She watched him dismount. Reluctantly, her steps took her to the bike. She ran her hand over the sleek black Harley Davidson, complete with the silver pinstripe she'd added her senior year. It wasn't a replica. This was *her* old bike.

She gaped up at him. "How?"

He took a step toward her. "Yeah, it's your old bike. I tracked it down the day we got engaged and had it restored. I was planning to give it to you as a wedding present."

His words penetrated, and she blinked at him. "Wedding present. But our engagement was fake."

His eyes narrowed. "Not to me. It was very real to me. Why did you run off? Was it because of your father's file?"

She bit her lip. "That started it. I jumped to the conclusion it was a goodbye gift, but mostly, I left because you never asked me to stay. I was upholding my part of the bargain. And then, on my way out, I bumped into Chad. He'd broken into your house. And you know the rest. You deserve a woman who can fit into your life, not a flaky lingerie designer."

He shook his head. "What a pair we are. I never asked you to stay because I was afraid of scaring you off. Well, I've got news for you. I'm not scared any more. I love you with all my heart and soul, and I don't want you to go. As a matter of fact, if you run away this time, I'm going with you."

She heard the sincerity in his voice. She'd been a fool to run away.

She glanced at his bedroll tied to the back of the bike and grinned. "You'd really run off with me?"

Greg nodded and pulled the engagement ring out of his pocket. He reached out and took her hand. Slipping the ring on her finger he vowed, "I'd follow you wherever you run. Life isn't worth living without you."

Candy smiled up at him. "You're crazy."

He grinned and picked her up. "I know. Crazy about you, Candy Baby."

Julie Castle is a natural-born romantic with a modicum of artistic talent inherited from her mom and a love for telling tall tales she got from her dad. That set her up for being a starving artist, the biggest fibber in the world, or a romance author. She's so glad she chose the latter. She's always had a love affair with the written word. As a child growing up in a small town, she loved visiting the local library, a converted gilded age mansion, and getting lost between the pages of a book. The drafty old mansion could be a spooky place, but she still loved it. She enjoyed poking into behind the scenes areas she wasn't supposed to venture into. She's still the same way, which is why she loves writing romance with an edge, paranormal, suspenseful, super sexy, or just laugh your pants off funny. She resides in Wisconsin with her family.